D0793893

The True Confessions of an Albino Terrorist

by the same author

MOUROIR

Mirrornotes of a Novel

The True Confessions of an Albino Terrorist

BREYTEN
BREYTENBACH

faber and faber
LONDON · BOSTON

First published in 1984
by Faber and Faber Limited
3 Queen Square London WC1N 3AU

Filmset by Goodfellow and Egan Cambridge
Printed in Great Britain by
The Thetford Press
Thetford Norfolk

British Library Cataloguing in Publication Data

Breytenbach, Breyten
The true confessions of an albino terrorist
1. Political prisoners – South Africa
I. Title
365'.45'0924 HV9850.5
ISBN 0-571-13393-2

SONG OF THE ORIGIN OF THE FOUR NATURES

Others do not know my nature.
As I know not the nature of others,
The nature of things as that of men,
Just like universal nature.
This universal nature is like my partial one.
If I were to know my nature well,
I should be knowing universal nature.

Quoted in *Tai-ji Quan* by Jean Gortais

Contents

Part One

THE MOUTH OF VOICES AND OF EARTH

being the veritable account in words and in breaks of how a foolish fellow got caught in the antechamber of No Man's Land; describing the interesting events, including a first trial where various actors and clowns perform, flowing from the arrest; continuing by sketching the story which took our protagonist to the land of sadness and of spiritual mirages in the first place; in which the reader is introduced to Skapie Huntingdon and his henchmen, to a judge and lawyers and informers and heroes; containing reflections provoked by guilt; as also a flowering sunset; consisting of fourteen sections of which five are inserts;

The name you will see under this document is Breyten Breytenbach. That is my name. It's not the only one; after all, what is a name? I used to be called Dick; sometimes I was called Antoine; some knew me as Hervé; others as Jan Blom; at one point I was called Christian Jean-Marc Galaska; then I was the Professor; later I was Mr Bird: all these different names with different meanings being the labels attached to different people. Because, Mr Investigator, if there is one thing that has become amply clear to me over the years, it is exactly that there is no one person that can be named and in the process of naming be fixed for all eternity.

What did your face look like before you were born? What did *you* look like before you or your father or your mother were born? Where were you then? In fact, where do you come from? And will it be possible one day to know where you come from, and therefore where you are, and therefore where you're heading, and therefore what you are, in which case you should be able to attach a name to it? Isn't that the whole process of our being, this looking for a name?

And then, this same process is an open-ended one; I can hear the echoes. As it continues – this jumbletalk, this trial – I can go on searching, and I can hear the reverberation of my own voice. I'm sitting here – I have this little instrument in my hand; I have the earphones on my head and I speak to you and I listen to the voice coming back. And I learn from these words the reality as it is being presented at the moment of emitting the sounds. That is perhaps as close as I can come to what the identity is considered to be. That is as close as I come to the truth. Here I am. Here the truth is also.

I hope, Mr Investigator, that that is what you expect of me. Because, you know, you could force me to deny whatever I say immediately after having said it; and you could probably force me to start all over again. I can tell you in advance that if I were to do that it would come out differently; it would be different; I'd no longer be there; I'd be somebody else – as sincere, as keen to help, as obsessed by the necessity to confess.

But let us push him back into the darkness of non-existence and let us go forward with what we have in hand at the moment. May I be your humble servant, Mr Investigator? Listen to me. I shall confess.

1
Here I Was

It's dark outside. Against the slanted window set into the roof there is this very soft rustling of rain coming down. I can look at it and I can see the wet tracks on the dusty surface. Across a dark space beyond the building there are windows alight and if one looks long enough you can see people moving behind the curtains, intent upon their nightly tasks and fancies, each living in his own little cocoon of fantasy and desire and ritual and habit.

When they finally identified me that other night, more than seven years ago now, it was dark too, though it was not winter then, at least it was not winter in Europe and it's never really winter in Africa, not on the Highveld. It was in August 1975. I had arrived earlier that evening at Jan Smuts Airport on my way back to France. I had known even as I arrived that I was blown, that they knew about me and rather in the fashion of a small child closing its eyes hoping that in so doing the hideousness will go away, I'd hoped against hope that I'd be able to slip through the net which had been closing around me for some time.

As I booked in at the departure counter I noticed a man, young, rather well dressed, looking at me. He then turned around, walked to the telephone, picked it up, talked to someone. You know how it is when you get that tingling feeling down your back. In later years I'd get to recognize that sensation and respect it far more clearly, in the same way as one develops in due time a heightened sense of smell: being able to sniff out these policemen from quite a long way away.

I booked in. I reserved a seat by the window. I spoke to the counter girl in Italian, which I was rather proud of, and then I moved through customs and the customs official looked at my passport, stared at me for a few seconds, did something else with his hands below the counter where I couldn't see, flipped my passport back at me, and I continued. In the departure hall I became intensely aware of several men sitting there, moving around, watching me. One is never so obvious as when you're trying to integrate with your surroundings. In fact, I became so paranoid that I went downstairs to the gents' toilets with one of them dogging my footsteps, and there, unzipping my pants, hunching my shoulders, I managed to swallow a few lines of paper with names on it. Not everything, unfortunately, could be disposed of in that way. If only I had been more rational I might have been able to get rid of more incriminating evidence. I then went back upstairs and suddenly over the intercom system an announcement came asking for Monsieur Galaska to present himself at counter so and so. I didn't budge. The soothing voice with the airport accent called again. I realized that there was no way out: I couldn't go back the way I'd come in – that would have meant going through customs again – and there was no other exit. I therefore went up to the counter where a girl from South African Airways was talking to various passengers and before I could even address her a gentleman at my elbow put his hand on my shoulder and said, 'Are you Mr Galaska?' I said, 'Yes.' He said, 'Would you mind following me please?' and he led me off into a little office giving on to this departure hall. He then asked me for my passport, my ticket – which I gave to him – and with these he disappeared, leaving me in the care of a young man loitering behind a big table.

Just so one is delivered into the hands of one's enemies . . . Well, it was obvious that the game was up. My plane hadn't departed yet. I enquired after the reason for my hold up and was told by the young man that he didn't know any more than I did, but surely it was just a matter of checking my identity and that everything should be all right in a few minutes when I would be allowed to proceed. In any event, he said, I needn't worry about my luggage or anything like that – they'll take care of those little mundane matters. At one stage during this interval a young Black girl came in, very distraught: she was due to have left on the same flight and she now suddenly found that she had lost her passport somewhere in the departure hall and was therefore prevented from going. A big search was started and the passport wasn't found. Time passed. The young man asked me if I'd like to smoke. I said I'd rather have one of my own cigarettes and took out a packet of Gauloises and my body was cold. The door then opened and in walked the man who had originally asked me to follow him, now accompanied by two others, one of whom was very familiar to me indeed. Colonel, I believe he had the rank of colonel, Jan Snaaks. With him a man younger than he was, medium height, very athletically built, very sharp blue eyes, the obligatory civil service moustache; and in a very friendly, even quite polite way, they started asking me questions. They meticulously searched my hand luggage which I had with me. They then asked me to strip and went through all my clothing and came up among other things with a strip of paper which I had unfortunately not destroyed, upon which was marked, 'La révolution est un art d'exécution' – which, I think, one can translate as 'Revolution is a practice.' As in a hallucination I saw on the table the small personal belongings, inconsequential as these things always are, being an element or an indication of the stranger's identity, of the foreigner, the I.

I was subsequently asked to write briefly my *curriculum vitae*. One did so. I remember that it was with a feeling somewhat akin to having a high. It came right off the top of my head. I had to invent on the spur of the moment thirty years of life, starting with where I was born, which I knew from the passport; going on to primary school, to secondary school, to my studies after school, to the work I did; including references to friends, to the area in which I lived, to the bank where I was supposed to work; and I remember that I had parading in front of my mind's eye the faces of my mates and I included them in this picture that I was asked to draw up. In fact, I borrowed heavily from what I remembered, knew or surmised of their young years in France. One stole from life in a derisory attempt to stave off death. I think that my interrogator was quite impressed by my effort. Much later he would tell me that he remained convinced that I'd been given this cover and that I'd memorized it carefully. He did not deem it possible to invent a life at the drop of a hat. But you would understand that, Mr Investigator. *You* know that we're always inventing our lives. *You* know that what I'm confessing now is also the instantaneous invention of what might have happened.

'You are a Russian agent!' Snaaks snarled, his eyes close to his nose. He has the strawberry nose of a toper. What could I answer? The man was so desperately and bravely living for the *big* catch.

It became obvious that they weren't going to let me go. I asked for permission to make contact with my Ambassador and this was refused. Sarcastically. As the night wore on it more and more happened that the various officers – I cannot call them gentlemen – spoke to one another in Afrikaans within my hearing, watching for the reaction that it might have on me. I remember Blue Eyes saying to Snaaks, 'Look, his knees are trembling, he must be scared shitless'; and I tried to control my knees. At a later stage Snaaks would look very keenly at me several times. Again he left this holding area. Apparently went to phone. Came back. Asked me to take hold of the pipe which he'd found in my luggage. And then pointed to the little wart smack between my eyes and said in Afrikaans, 'Come on, Breyten, the game's up, we know who you are. Do you want us to go and fetch one of your brothers and confront you with him?' And knowing that he could do so I said in Afrikaans too, 'No, it won't be necessary.' I learned later that I had had rather bad luck – as I was preparing to leave from Jan Smuts Airport the plane bearing John Vorster, then Prime Minister of South Africa, and his entourage, on return from a visit to South America, landed. One of my brothers happened to be in the party accompanying Big Chief Sitting Bull and of course there was a large number of security officials both arriving with him and awaiting him at the airport, so that the place was literally crawling with lice. (And flushed with excitement they were, having just cemented ties with staunch fellow democrats like Stroessner and Pinochet.)

Snaaks and Blue Eyes were BOSS agents.* Not only did Snaaks insist, foaming at the mouth, that I'm a KGB man, but that I'm one of an ultra-secret section of killers led by a certain Colonel Unpronounceable. In the following days, as the interrogation unfolded, 'Uncle Jan' Snaaks would drop away – Blue Eyes would be BOSS's man with the Security Police proper – and I, after having been successively (unsuccessfully) a French, British

*BOSS – the Bureau for State Security; after the so-called 'Information Scandal', the demise of General van den Berg, and the coming to national power of P. W. Botha (by means of a camouflaged *coup d'état* in fact), BOSS became the DNS – Department of National Security.

and Israeli agent, would end up being accused of working for the CIA. How Blue Eyes stumbled over my glorious career in the CIA I shall describe later . . .

After this undramatic revelation of my true identity I was allowed to take hold of my hand luggage, pocket my half-empty packet of Gauloises, and told to follow a young man who had turned up in the meantime. This young man escorted me to a car, one of the very typical broad, comfortable security vehicles, parked in an underground parking lot. Another man came up out of the dark dressed incongruously in a battle jacket, and took the wheel. I was told to sit in the back next to the young man in his little navy-blue blazer. He was tough, with a modish haircut. He sat in his corner and never let me stray from his eyesight. The he-man in front drove at a comfortable pace from Johannesburg, at least from the airport, to Pretoria, all the while shooting questions at me, wanting to know why, why, why do you people *do* this? *What* is it that motivates you? He said, 'I'm not interested in the small facts, the petty crimes, the little political actions. I want to know what *causes* you to do something like this? *What* is the ideology line behind it? I want you to tell me all about socialism, I want you to tell me about Marxism, I want you to get to the gist of the matter.' He sounded very much like the university professor he probably was in real life, which he probably still is. Because, Mr Investigator, I don't know if I need tell you this; surely you must know that so many of the agents working for BOSS are very respectable, well-to-do bourgeois professionals holding down positions at university, or at law firms, or as insurance agents or whatever. Some of them are even, quite improbably, disguised as policemen. BOSS/DNS constitute a *political* force *in* the country, both as a decision-making organ and a controlling agent. They are in fact deeply involved in internal mind-control. The demarcation of territories isn't very clear, and there's much strife and jealousy among the various intelligence groups. The SP (Security Police or Special Branch) have their own agents abroad – witness the Williamson incident.*

*Craig Williamson, an officer in the Special Branch (as opposed to BOSS) infiltrated opposition forces – starting with the National Union of South African Students when he was still a student, and eventually the International University Exchange Fund based in Geneva, from where he reported on the Liberation

Koos Bruin, smooth and rather likable BOSS operator, once told me of how he was involved, as a student representative, in organizing a staff/student protest meeting on the campus of Witwatersrand University. The lady professor chairing the meeting expressed to him, her confidant, concern because she knew for a fact that there must be three 'government spies' present. He had to laugh in his sleeve, he told me, as he was one of the *seven* undercover agents in the hall that day.

Maybe it was all a farce. Maybe the spooks and the controllers only feigned surprise at coming across a mask called Breytenbach under a mask named Galaska. Their being at the airport had nothing to do with the arrival of Sitting Bull. And they were loath to turn me over to the SP. Blue Eyes later explained to me that they would have preferred to whisk me off to 'The Farm' without anyone (ever) knowing. ('The Farm', as far as I could make out, is indeed a farm where the BOSS/DNS people prepare their 'dirty tricks' in all impunity, and where they can work over their suspects in absolute secrecy – without the intervention of the Prisons Department or the Department of Justice.) Had it not been for crossed lines and inter-agency rivalry I might never have been here to whisper to you, dear Investigator. Blue Eyes – he's still there – fancies himself as a psychologist, an experimenter, a washer of brains.

It was unreal: going for a quiet spin to Pretoria in a big limousine with a phosphorescent-green dashboard – being chauffeured by a ranting political scientist who believes himself to be in the Bush, facing clever ideologues.

We arrived in Pretoria. My two accompaniers, if that's the right word, handed me over into the care of two gentlemen from the Security Police proper. I was introduced into the masher. I was delivered at the Compol Buildings which served as the head-quarters of the political police in that area. It's an old building, claimed to have been built during the time of Paul Kruger. The walls are very thick. In the daytime, because over the next month I got to know the building rather well, in daytime there will be

---

Movement and Anti-Apartheid groups. When finally unmasked in the late 1970s, General Johan Coetzee (his 'handler' later to be head of the SP) went to Switzerland to retrieve his agent.

quite a lot of people moving through the corridors, mumbling away behind doors. At the back they had a cell where I was to spend a lot of time; it had a barred window giving onto the street level outside. Upstairs they had a police museum. In due time I believe my passport, my beautifully crafted false passport, would figure there amongst the exhibits honouring the grand exploits of the South African Police, probably tucked in between a bloodied axe and a few sticks of dynamite.

But that night the place was quiet; not even the blind lift attendant whom I would get to know later on and who knew his way around the building so well – what a horrible thing it must be to spend one's blindness in a place like that – not even he was there then. As far as I could hear and see we were the only ones present in the caverns of the night. They took me into an office, cold, giving off the smell and the presence and the colour of brownness: the kind of chocolate station waiting room brownness; and stale, dusty, impersonal walls having witnessed many break-downs. Walls which in the way of all walls will never say anything about it. On one such wall behind one of the tables there hung a framed picture of C. R. Swarts who had been, a long time before, the Minister of Justice. I don't know whether this was out of particular loyalty to whatever he stood for or whether time hadn't moved since the period of his tenure as minister.

My hosts weren't violent in any way. Why should they be? I was dead. All they had to do was to process the dead, to pick over the bones. They weren't particularly interested. Again I had to go through the procedure of stripping and then I was counted: that is, all my possessions were itemized and these were then carefully noted in red ink on a large sheet of paper. Night was ticking away like an unsatiable beast.

Mr Investigator, as we arrive at the end of this first talk, permit me to give you a brief extract of what I consisted of as written down on this sheet of paper. I have it here in my hand. The paper's called P21: i.e., it is a lined single sheet of folio paper. I translate:

1 bed ticket
1 SAA ticket No. 710902 dated 6/8/75

1 red handbag with the following items therein:
  3 ballpoint pens: 2 green, 1 silver
  3 keys
  Scissors and keyholder
  1 book *A Universal History of Infamy*
  1 blue notebook
  14 envelopes and Hotel Elizabeth writing paper
  1 Hotel Elizabeth receipt No. 39110 for R41.25
  1 500 lire note, Italian
  1 silver coin, 100 lire
  3 glass bangles
  1 necklace of beads, yellow, black and white
  1 French matchbox
  1 blue toothbrush
  1 tube of toothpaste
  Receipt No. 3570, some sum (I can't make out the writing there), Berg resort
  1 Banco Nazionale di Lavore statement
  1 Alitalia boarding pass
  1 Alitalia passenger ticket and baggage check
  1 piece of paper with *'L'art de la révolution'* etc. written on it
  1 strip of paper with Bergville code 03647/1801 written on it
  1 Johannesburg street map
  1 shorthand notebook
  1 piece of paper with 433236 written on it
1 bottle of brandy Oudemeester
1 paper bag with the following therein:
  A packet of protea seeds
  1 gramophone record
  1 small clay flute
1 light brown envelope marked 'Dollars $370', with the following notes in it:
  five $10 = $50
  eleven $20 = $220
  one $100 = $100
  seventeen notes altogether $370
(On the back is written, according to the writing of the police scribe):
  'W 430730' (scratched out)

'W 930430/km 877314'
1 tie black with blue dots
1 pair of glasses
1 glass bangle
1 match folder 'Berg Holiday Resort Bergville' written on it
1 box of matches, Lion matches
1 brown portfolio with the following contents:
R15 (fifteen Rands) in notes equalling R15
R4.70 (four Rands seventy cents in silver equalling R4.70)
15½ (fifteen and a half cents copper equalling 15½ cents)
the total being R19.85½ cents
7 silver French coins
1 $50 note equalling $50
4 dix francs notes equalling F10
3 cent francs notes (F100)
(I can't imagine how they got those totals.)
4 Banca d'Italia Lire Mille
1 Banca d'Italia Lire Cinque Mille
2 Volkskas cash receipts for R69.93 (a little bit further on
they've written $100)
1 Barclays Bank receipt for R70.14 (again it's written $100)*
And 6 *metro-autobus* tickets
1 pipe
1 tobacco pouch
And finally one inoculation certificate in the name of
C. Galaska, 672774.

There you see me, Mr Investigator, in all my naked glory, with all my possessions around me, as I stand that first evening. *Ecce homo.*

I was quite rich, wasn't I? There was something for them to work on, something to keep them busy. What a beautiful collection of clues! But of course, that was not what they were interested in. Maybe that's not even what would interest *you*. (Am I reading the signals correctly?) They would much rather want to know the

*The Japanese tourist, complaining on the third day about the jumping exchange rate, is told by the cashier it is due to 'fluctuations'. 'Fluctuations?' the Japanese splutters, 'Well, fluck the Eulopeans too!'

whole history and all the schemes and all the dreams that I was carrying around with me. You see, I was a travelling salesman in dreams and illusions.

And even more than that – they must have been dying to use me to get hold of all manner of other people, to sniff out the dark secrets threatening the State, to bring to light all the evil conspiracies; particularly to prove that this was only one more manifestation of the worldwide onslaught against this small, embattled nation of pure and upright, Godfearing, chosen ones.

So, perhaps, once and for all, I should tell you about those dreams, about where I came from and where I thought I was heading.

INSERT

Where did I know Colonel Jan Snaaks from and where does the pipe and the tobacco pouch fit into the story? You remember, Mr Investigator, I am sure, that I tried to describe how, when we visited No Man's Land in 1973 and spent one season in that paradise, I was followed all over the country by certain security agents, and how towards the end of our stay, one night in Paarl, thanks to the intervention of one of my brothers who is certainly a close friend and colleague of these people, I was confronted by two grey eminences chomping at the bit, and this was exactly then Jan Snaaks and another big, bulky fellow called 'Kleintjie' (the little one) Heiden, I believe, with the head of a dog and a long history as hunter of political dissidents. (In a totalitarian state the political police operate quite openly, *à visage découvert*, although they always have their underground activities also of course. The point is: to fulfil their function of intimidating and terrorizing the population they also have to be visible to some extent. They can be affable people to meet, real Afrikaner gentlemen, good drinking companions, opening doors for ladies. What distinguishes them will be the way they look at one, something around the eyes, and the brutal power they exude.) During the ensuing evening they tried to impress upon me the extent of their knowledge of my activities and contacts, and tried frightening me into giving them information. That was my first mask to mask confrontation with the Greyshit, the BOSS people, and as my luck would have it, it had to be the same Jan Snaaks at the airport that specific night. Was it coincidence? Wasn't he on my tracks the whole time of my passage in South Africa? Since I was known to be a pipe smoker I deliberately took no pipe or tobacco with me into the country, but started smoking cigarettes – hence the packet of Gauloises. Then, whilst passing through Cape Town, I remember going to Greenmarket Square where, years before, many, many years ago when I lived and dreamed around the corner, in Long Street, I used to buy my supply of tobacco. One could have it mixed on the spot to one's taste and I couldn't resist the temptation of walking in there again, into old times' youth, sniffing the beautiful aroma of freshly prepared tobacco. (I was on the run then: perhaps I was looking for some form of innocence.) Having bought some tobacco I obviously also had to acquire a pipe. I thought I'd be clever, I thought I'd leave it in my suitcase to smoke it only in the secret of my hotel room. And of course they dug it up at the airport and they had me hold it and they recognized my way of fondling the pipe as someone else might have recognized my way of handling a pen or my way of stuttering into a tape recorder. These are the indelible finger prints of the fugacious identity. There is no 'I', there is no name, there is no identity. But there are unchanging manifestations, habits, a hulk, a carcass, recognizable. There is a sore thumb. The cause has disappeared, the symptoms remain.

What fastidious workers they are, how obsessed they must be! Look how they dig into one's past, how they project one's future, how they alter one's present. I have no private lives: it's all in their hands; they know the I better than I do, they are far more interested in it than I am. They have the files, they have the computer. Or they know all about my ways, my preferences, my accretions, my little secrets – my gardens – be they political or sexual. And they are fascinated by it. They smell it like freshly mixed tobacco. They knead it. They manipulate it, they slobber over it. It justifies their lives . . .

INSERT

Home. Home, James, and don't spare the horses. Screaming down the tunnels of darkness, careening down the passages, going deeper ever deeper into the labyrinth; but I'm home now, maimed, diminished, splayed, with my vision impaired, my horizon narrowed, my reference points vague, obscure; and yet there is this total clarity even if it's only at the level of language, which is the surface, which is the superficial, which, by the definition of language must disappear to be allowed to exist.

When first I came out of prison I was thrown into emptiness and I found all space around me cluttered. For so long had I been conditioned to the simplification of four walls, the square of a barred window, a double square door, a square bed, emptiness, nowhere to hide the smallest illegal object, nowhere to hide the crust of bread to which you were not entitled, nowhere to efface yourself, or tuck away the soul or to protect your three dreams from prying eyes and acquisitive fingers, nowhere to hide your anguish: all these had been erased by being made apparent. It just became language. So that when I found myself ejected into what *you* would consider to be the normal world, I found it terribly confusing. Why are there so many people moving through the theatre décor of streets? How come the air is so bloated with useless words? Why on earth do people have so many objects in their houses? Why do they have to hang things on the wall, or have to have more than one set of clothes? Why do they collect possessions? You should know by now that one can never possess anything, and when The Law strikes you will lose everything anyway. And I remember, because now it is passing, that whenever I entered a new space I lifted my feet very high and I pulled my head down between my shoulders from fear of the unexpected step or beam.

What else must I describe? Do you really want to know what it's like to be free?

Freedom is not knowing where to stop. It is a gargantuan appetite; it is a need to burn clean, with whatever is spicy and hot, the taste of dullness which has encrusted your memory and your appetite; it is the unquenchable thirst; it's the need to absorb, to take, to grasp, to experience, to renew and to drink, because it is simultaneously the necessity to deaden the nerve ends. I have not the slightest measure of what ought and ought not to be done and when and how. I should eat whatever you put before me. I read on the wall 'Mangez-vous les uns les autres', and I discover all kinds of lusts: a yearning for seafood; I must have mustards; I must have pickles. I must exercise the regrets and the shame and the guilt.

Ah, Mr Investigator, don't you think I'm guilty? Yes, I have the guilt of the survivor. All my friends are dead because they are still alive, locked in the cleanliness of asexual and dehumanized space. And I, I'm outside alive in the deadness of my surroundings.

I'm the Lazarus. I came back from that paradoxical paradise and have no life left. I have lived it. What remains is gratuitous, free, no attachments, no importance. I have no affairs. I have no interests. These too have been scorched clean.

Now I must get rid of the unreality. I must vomit. I must eject this darkness. I must plead with you, Mr Investigator, to not stop asking me questions. Do not desist, do not turn away from me.

The people? What about the people? Yes, I know, I'm the man who went down to the corner to buy cigarettes and who came back eight years later. Of course my return was a shock to my friends. I'm the 'happening' in the slur of their daily existence which gives it a different colouring. I'm the horse in the soup. And then very quickly I'm the invisible ghost, because their lives must continue as their lives had continued for seven years and had changed and had grown finally around the absence or the arsehole which I must have been for them, the way a tree grows around a knot in its fibres.

Which is why I turn back to you, Mr Investigator, Mr I, and I talk because you must give me sounds. You must allow me to regurgitate all the words, like the arabesques of a blind mind. I am the man on the corner, with dark glasses, waiting for your coin. I am the lift attendant in Security Headquarters. Don't ask me any questions. You don't have to. You will not be able to stop the answers in any event. The black vomit must be spewed out. See here, I hold it in my hands. I have the black gloves. Feel it. Feel the gloves. Look at the glasses. I know. I know what it is like to be black in a white country.

Freedom is the minotaur outside the walls.

2

About Where I Came From

No, you won't catch me, Mr Investigator. I know how it is done. They let you sit down, they do not ask you any questions; they simply say, 'Write'; and I've written volumes, volumes. My life is eaten up by words. Words have replaced my life.

It is all surface. Nothing can be hidden there. My life has been devoured by these insidious ants. But don't you believe those documents. Do me the honour, extend only one measure of grace to all prisoners: you must admit that whatever the detainee does or doesn't do whilst in prison is done under pressure. Never forget that the purpose of detaining and grilling and convicting and then holding people, is to disorientate them, to destroy their sense of themselves and the whole field of unquestioned awareness of the surrounding world, the whole cloth of relationships with other people, all the tentacles of grasping and understanding ideas, and finally to burgle and to burn down the storehouse of dreams and fantasies and hopes.

This is what they do. This is their destiny. The prisoner must be kept in a permanent state of unbalance. And the prisoner in a game of trying to outwit the 'other', the human being in front of him, the Man, the *boer*, the Gat,* isn't he only pulling the strings tighter and tighter around himself?

'Write', they say, and you write. Two sheets. 'What must I write about, sir?' '*You* know: just write.' And they come and they read the two pages, and they smile and they tear it up. 'Write',

**boer*, pl. *boere* – meaning 'farmer' or 'peasant' originally, but when written with a capital (*Boere*) it is also the way the Afrikaners sometimes refer to themselves – has become a generic name for policemen and prison warders and, by extension, for Whites; derogatory.

Gat, pl. *Gatte* or *Gatta*, collectively *the Gat* – meaning 'hole', 'backside'. Used in reference to policemen; derogatory.

they say, and you write. You write the same two pages. You want to please them: you don't want to annoy them. They outnumber you. And inside you have the wildness of completely irrational hope: a miracle will happen, they will find out that they'd been mistaken. Daylight come an' I wanna go home. They'll let you go. Or they'll say, 'Oh, we know it's not really all that serious, you're just a prankster; we'll let you go.' They will say, 'So we've been naughty, haven't we? What's all this romantic nonsense then? Deathwish of the ineffectual intellectual? Trying to join in the dirty game? Well, Lord Byron, we will let you go home . . . Go, and sin no more.' One will be punished lightly but finally even the punishment will be a measure of reassurance, as it used to be when very small and one's father felt the need to correct one.

But this wild beast of expectation is entirely caged in. Perhaps that's why he's so agitated. They know about him: they use it, they exploit the fact of their knowing. They stroke this beast through the bars of your ego. They pretend to feed it with promises of letting it go. So why not write? And so you write, again. What's your alternative? They will only keep you until you start writing. You yourself become the master of your time; it is *you* who will decide the length of your incarceration. There's nothing, there's nobody, no power anywhere in the world that has any say over them. They can keep you for ever. They can put heavy hands on you. They can break you down. They may even go red in the face and really let rip. They may have to use 'the telephone' on you, or 'the parrot', or 'the submarine'; they may have you leave through 'the Bantu exit'.* Do you remember about that Black employee of the Christian Institute whom they picked up on the street and took to the top floor of a building and how two men in tracksuits just kept on thudding into him all the way across the room, and how they dropped him on the street again, unconscious but unmarked, still without a word of explanation? Do you remember how the *boer* called 'Red Russian' broke down Wally Serote over a period of months? Shouldn't you cooperate? Besides, if you're innocent, what do you have to hide? Don't forget that you're innocent. It is all a matter of relativity. So why not write . . . and so you scribble. This time

*Reference to torture methods. See note on torture, p. 349.

four pages. And they come, and they take it, and they read it, and they tear it up. And perhaps by now they stop smiling.

Or they start asking you small questions about one or two little facts you may have mentioned in passing in your first efforts at writing. (You have to show your open-heartedness and your innocence by admitting to facts you *know* they know about. But how much do they really know? How did they break into you? For how long have they had you on a line?) How about telling us a little more about that, or about him, or about her? And you write. Hoping that you are still repeating the same story which you had invented and knowing that you are now deviating from it gradually, but not knowing how much. Because time, which for you has become the heavy encroachment of total obscurity, to them has no sense: they are not in a hurry. They can wait for you to start contradicting yourself, and they can relay themselves; you, you have to stay awake because you have to write, scribbling, filling page after page, repeating, altering, having it torn up, starting anew. *They* leave, they are replaced by two fresh interrogators and you sit there. 'May I go to the toilet, sir?' They do not answer, they wait. You write. You have become desperate. 'May I go to the toilet, please?' And you're accompanied to the toilet where you are stripped of the last vestiges of privacy or the dignity you may have thought you had, because you are not allowed to close the door of the closet and you have to do whatever nature calls you to do in full view of the cynical man standing there, observing you, picking his teeth. Not even sneering at your testicles.

You go back to that brown room giving off the stale odour of policemen and again you're given more paper and you are asked to write.

So it went on continuously for forty-eight hours – a day and a night, another day, plus the first night, always the night, more and more the night; and then when it is dark again they put you in a car and they drive you through the deserted streets up to the portals of a building. Nobody knows my name. You were supposed to be in Rome by now. Your wife would have been waiting at the place of rendezvous. August. Balmy nights on the piazzas. The oleander and the laurel in bloom.

The Transvaal winter nights are bitter. Above, the crystalline stars. Comes morning the crystals will be deposited as white rime over the veld. The crust of time. You get out with them. They knock on a very big door. A small judas-eye is opened. You hear bolts being drawn. A door is unlocked from inside and you are let in to the entrance of Maximum Security Prison.

That first night I was too tired to count the number of gates through which I was led until I finally arrived at the cell where I was due to spend the next two years. I was handed over to a young prison sergeant. Later I learned that his name is Nit Arselow. A thin fellow, bristling little moustache, sharp very pale green eyes, wild look, tight jaws, ears sticking away from his head. A complete marionette, fierce and violent. He opened my door with a brusque gesture, pointed to my bed which was a bunk built into the wall, and said, *'Ek is die baas van die plaas* (I am the master of this farm). *I* shall make you crawl here; you will still get to know me.'

Yes, I did get to know him.

They locked the door and without taking off even a shoe I crawled onto the bunk, onto the thin mattress there, pulled the blankets over me; and then I couldn't sleep. Not at all. Everything came tumbling back. I couldn't control my body. I was shivering, my legs were shaking; I couldn't even quieten my lips. And in the background, all around me in this weird place, I heard male voices; it sounded like scores of voices singing in unison very rhythmically, very strongly, what sounded like tribal music and sometimes like religious hymns.

'Beverly Hills' the place is called in prison parlance. It's a prison for Blacks essentially though a few Whites are kept there too. I sensed that first night, and it was confirmed later on, that this was the place of death; this is the shameful place to which people are brought to be killed legally and in cold blood by the representatives of the State. I saw so much. With the ears only, since the eyes are confined by bars and walls and steel partitions never more than seven yards away. The whole place is impregnated by this one overriding function: this is the reality of Maximum Security. Terminus. Death house.

I lay there in the unreal tumbling condition between sleep and wakefulness, with the broken film slapping in my head; not even daring to think further than what was in my head at that moment, not even allowing myself to imagine the pain and the shock that my arrest must have meant to my wife and to my parents. I couldn't even know – I had no way of knowing – whether they had been informed. For all the world I might have been wiped from the face of the earth; I might have died in some mysterious accident. Nobody would have been the wiser ever. And nobody would have dared suggest that I had been done away with by the police because that would have been tantamount to admitting that I was involved in illegal or subversive political activities.

The night must have passed. The door was unlocked in the morning. Arselow, who later on I got to call 'Red Shoes' because his shoes were of a specific red shade and always shining brilliantly – he spent nearly all his hours on duty boning them – Arselow called me out of my cell, took me down a short passage to a bathroom, told me to clean up. He handed me a bar of green prison soap. I undressed and got into the bath and he never left the bathroom. I had to wash my body and my hair with the same bar of quite strong-smelling soap; dried myself; dressed; was handed a razor by Arselow, with which I was told to shave. There was no mirror; just a metal sheet screwed into the wall. In this surface one could see a vague reflection of yourself. Just enough to shave by. Like looking at a memory of yourself through an opaque sheet of glass. I dressed in the same clothes I had on the night before. Neither hand luggage nor my suitcase had been returned to me.

And then very early the police turned up. They took me back to Compol Building.

The second day I started identifying the people interrogating me. I realized that this was a team specially assembled for this inquest. In the end they became quite familiar. We can say that we'd covered a fair amount of ground together. It would seem that political police from various centres in the country had been ordered to Pretoria to work on my case. There were two from Cape Town: a certain Hakkebak, and the infamous Nails van Byleveld.

Mr Investigator, if you are really whom I think you are, Mr Eye: how you would have loved to have Nails van Byleveld before you. What novels that man must have in the coffin of his memory! What a paradox, what joy it must be to unravel the skein of the apparel within which he goes clothed. Later more about him.

There was a tall young man from Port Elizabeth, a lieutenant; there were in the beginning two people from Durban; one from Kimberley; and then of course there were the locals: Colonel Huntingdon, the chief investigator, your colleague, your example, perhaps your master; with him Hendrik Goy, Derrick Smith, Koekemoer, the one with the brown skin and the black and white shoes.

I shall tell you more about them as I go on. I think I must stop now for a little while. Because it's a new day, a new loop of time, darkness, the night, streaming down the corridors of night, falling into limitless space, dying to be reborn so as to die to be reborn. . . .

3

From Room to Room

From room to room. Dying so as to be reborn. To die. To be reborn from room to room. From womb to space. From space to room. From room to coffin. From coffin to the density of space. From space to nothingness. From nothingness to seed. From seed to womb. From womb to pain. From pain to roomwomb. To wombroom. To another tomb. Other worms. To another room. Into the car. Up the street. Screaming down the corridors of darkness. Through the door. Beyond the grills. Careening down the passages. Feeling the cement. Touching the steel. Hearing the doors closing. Tasting the salt. Experiencing the shivering. Listening to the chants. Lifting the darkness. Mumbling. Writing. Writing with eyes closed. Writing with black gloves holding the black pen through which the blackness flows where there is no light. Waking not knowing whether you're awake or whether you're still a dream feeling the ache of the mind. From room to passage, to bathroom, to corridor, through the grills, through the gate, by car careening down the narrow lanes of darkness past the blind man. From room. To room. To room. To room . . . .

It was the second day or perhaps it was the third, no, it was the first day. Then it was the fourth day, I mean it was the second day, it must have been the morning of the second day. On that morning, the morning of the third day, they took me back to Compol Building and the questioning continued. Nails van Byleveld came into the room. He has very big hands, he has very big ears, he has two very small brown eyes rather like those of a hedgehog the better to pin you down with. The skin of his face is very rough and porous. His skull runs to a narrow point at the top. Perched on his head he has, parted in the middle, a small neat oily patch of hair shorn close to the scalp above the ears and behind. Under his nose he has the faintest little reference to his master, Herr Hitler. He has a very big body (what a waste of meat!) which he props up against the wall or drapes over the table, casually. He thereupon produced and read to me the Terrorism Act in terms of which I was now formally arrested. This was just a small interlude.

The questioning continued. From time to time I was taken to the toilet. I made use of these occasions to splash some water on my face. Then back to the interrogation room. Here there was only one table and a chair and a second chair in which I had to sit. There was a window in one wall just slightly below street level outside. How weird it was to see the shoes and the ankles of people passing by in front of the window – so close, my God, so close – and completely oblivious to what was happening behind this very thick wall separating us. People on their way to work or on their way to some happy rendezvous with a friend or a lover, for a quick cup of tea.

The questioning continued. At one stage – it must have been the second day – on that morning of the fourth day, no, I remember now, it was the third day, I was taken into a second room, slightly bigger. At one end of this room, behind a table, three or four officers sat rather like judges having an imaginary meal. Very involved in what they were whispering in each other's ears. Nodding sagely at the wise advice. Never looking at me. Getting up. Leaving. Coming back with urgent messages, shaking their heads, tapping the table. And while this was going on I was put in a chair and a photographer came to take the official mug shots – from the front, in profile, with glasses, without glasses. Some of these pictures later on appeared in the press. I'm sure you must have seen them, Mr Investigator, but you didn't know they were of me, did you? Well, neither did I. And then, maybe they weren't of me. Those were the pictures taken of the hulk that they were excavating at that point, or of that man who was alive in that web at that time – and he has nothing to do with me. That is another room.

On my way being accompanied into this room of the fixing of images, I saw lying folded on a chair a fresh newspaper, and in passing my eye caught a headline and the first fat introductory paragraph which announced that some people had been arrested in Cape Town, that these included a university lecturer and several student leaders, and immediately I knew that the net had closed not only around me but also around the people with whom I had been in contact in Cape Town. I couldn't tell you, were you to ask me, whether this newspaper was left there by accident or whether it was done so on purpose to fuck around with my mind, because you must understand, you, being of the *métier*, that planting the doubt in a detainee's mind makes him that much more amenable to disorientation and to pressure. If others had been arrested, weren't they also writing away, each in his own little room? And if they were writing, what was it? Were we all building our own labyrinths, our own little palaces of ice, hoping that these would dissolve with the first rays of the sun? Or were they perhaps already beyond hope, telling what they thought would be the truth? The fools – don't they know that truth is a convention? Or could it be that this bit of information was left lying there as a warning, a friendly tip-off by one of the policemen, one of the Blacks perhaps? I'd noticed on my second day, or perhaps somewhere during the dark period between the first and the second day, that there were some Black security policemen working there also.

How stupid I was, Mr Investigator! I thought these blokes at least must have some sympathy left in them somewhere. Aren't they *black* after all, members of the oppressed majority? Surely they can't be complete sell-outs. Somewhere they must have retained some link to their own people and to their aspirations and their longings. And of course then they must know that I identify myself with these ideals, and then, *for sure*, they must want to help me. . .

It was perhaps that same day, or maybe the next, that one of the people on duty, Goy or van Byleveld, called in very ostentatiously two of the Black security policemen and said, 'Come, *you* tell him. You tell him what you think of Oliver Tambo and Johnny Makathini.' First one and then the other started laughing and said, 'What a monkey, what a monkey he must be to have believed that they would support him now that he's in trouble, to ever have thought that he could collaborate with them. They were only using you, white boy, they couldn't care a damn for you. We know them, they . . . are . . . our . . . own people!'

Yes, Mr Investigator, simple tricks, tools of the trade, I know, I know; but remember – at that point you are swinging over the abyss holding on to a very slender thread of sanity. It doesn't take much to split the last fibre and to have you plunging down screaming into the opening-up of completely empty space, a space which is at the same time crowded by voices singing their death, intermingled with voices whispering, 'Write.' Because to write is to celebrate death. 'Write why, who, where, when, with what . . . .'

Many more people had been arrested. Not just those with whom I had been in contact in Cape Town, but also all those whom I might eventually have wished to contact in Johannesburg and elsewhere, and even some people whom I had no intention of meeting, whom I didn't know, whose very names were unknown to me. This I couldn't know at that time yet. But it became obvious as we went along that the political police disposed of enough information to make the necessary cross-references, to plot all the actual and the potential courses. I remember that they tried to get me to help trap Schuitema who had entered the country with me and who had slipped through their fingers. They were aware of the liaison that we used, a person living in Pretoria whom we could phone and where we could leave messages. What they didn't know, of course, was that we had also established a danger signal so that when one called and was told a certain word he would know that the game was up. Thus I had to pretend to cooperate and a meeting was fixed with Schuitema in Joubert Park in Johannesburg, but naturally the message included the detonator so that there was no chance whatsoever of Schuitema going anywhere near the appointed place.

It was interesting though to conclude from these manoeuvres that they had not yet arrested our contact in Pretoria – for obvious reasons – and, more importantly, that my own arrest had not yet been made public. But it was also stupid at the same time, since the arrest of the people whom Schuitema must have known that I would have seen or met, had been announced. Even so it would seem that news of my arrest – exactly eight days after the fact – was made public inadvertently, in a 'gaffe', by the then Minister of Justice (known for his propensity to put his foot in his mouth), probably for short-sighted political goals: the Transvaal Nationalist Party was having its annual congress.

At night, every night, I was driven back and turned over to the gentle care of Nit Arselow, and my nights were populated and punctuated by the terrible outpouring in song of the so-called 'condemns' or 'ropes'. I wrote one day a desperate plea addressed to Snaaks, going in my words down on my knees, asking to be removed elsewhere because I couldn't stand this stench of death. But it was probably of the same effect as of praying to a god.

At this stage some of the other detainees were kept in the same prison where I was. I deduced this one night from hearing Karel Tip trying to converse with Glen Moss. I don't know whether they were in adjacent cells. Evidently they didn't know that I was somewhere close by. Poor chaps – they were completely bewildered. 'What did they want to hear from you?' one was anxiously asking the other. 'Oh God,' the other answered, 'they keep on accusing me of having been recruited to go to terrorist training camps in Algeria.' 'What? You too? They're onto me for the same thing, but we don't know anything about that.' That's how it went on. Indeed, it's clear that the political police were making me out to be a terrorist in the minds of those with whom I had been in contact.

You feel like laughing, Mr Investigator? You splatter. What? Am I not a terrorist then? No, no, no, don't get me wrong, I'm not denying that. I've accepted it. *Mea culpa.* (I am guilty in any event. All that's still lacking is the crime to fit the guilt. I'm sure you can help me there, Mr Eye.) I was accused of being a terrorist, I was brought before the courts in terms of the Terrorism Act, I was convicted of being one, I was sentenced as a terrorist, on my jail ticket where it asked 'sentence or crime' it was written, carefully, 'terrorism'; therefore, because this is the way we do things in No Man's Land, therefore I am indeed a terrorist. But at the time when these interrogations were going on it was still a secret to the minds of my young friends.

I shall not bore you with all the details. It must be like trying to teach the old grandmother how to suck eggs. Let us conclude with the reality that the written pages were piling up. It was a senseless exercise really, because it was so clear after some time that these gentlemen knew far more about me and my life and my lies than I could ever hope to do. They knew exactly when I was last home (because I had in fact left home several days before departing for Rome, and thence for Johnny's), what I did the last days hour by hour, whom I was frequenting.

It is a principle in underground work never to go directly to your destination, but to rendezvous or complete the preparations in a neutral area or in a sanctuary. In my case the Greys had obviously penetrated the sanctuary. I later learned that the South African embassies abroad had been alerted, several days *before* I even applied for a visa, to facilitate 'Galaska's' request. Although this may be part of the confusing game of disinformation, of sowing confusion and suspicion. You see, my story isn't finished yet.

What it all adds up to is that, at least as far as France is concerned, the Greys were either allowed to operate quite freely on French territory,* or that they benefited from collusion with – at least – certain 'elements' in the French secret services.

They had well-thumbed manuals with photos and *curriculum vitae* of the South African 'terrorists' and 'trainee terrorists' abroad – these they prized and brought up to date the way other perverts would care for their girly magazines. And their knowledge of the 'enemy' was quite astounding. They have files on senior ANC militants going way back in history and, quite apart from the mixing of fact and interpretation and imagination, containing enough incriminating information to have these act as time bombs within the exile movements. If I were Tambo or Makathini, I'd not sleep easily.

They also had girly magazines, of course.

They confronted me with printed documents, in English, containing a breakdown and an analysis of the various organizations with which I had been in contact, including, for instance, Solidarité, which I had been led to believe was ultrasecret and safe. They had at their disposal lists of names, the *noms de guerre* – with next to these the real names – of people I had never met, people I didn't even know the existence of. They knew all about Henri Curiel. They wanted me so badly to admit to the name of Henri Curiel and I refused right up to the end, stupidly, as if by not admitting to knowing that the mysterious 'Raymond' or 'Jacques' or whatever was in fact Curiel I could deny my links to him.

*After my arrest South African agents brazenly visited, and attempted to intimidate, several of my Parisian acquaintances. The letter-box at my studio was forcibly opened. In some instances the dirty collaboration would have drastic consequences: cf., my next section.

Naturally they tried to make out that this Curiel was a KGB agent. In fact, the line of questioning during the first few days, it must have been on the second day or perhaps the fifth that it became very clear, was that I too am a member of a highly specialized group working within the KGB, charged with the specific and dangerous task of eliminating certain people. We were supposed to have as our commander a certain colonel. The name was mentioned. I don't remember it, Mr Investigator, no.

Ah yes, these spies – I'm talking now of the people who have questioned me – they have such wonderfully fertile thumbs. I've always felt that they read too many, far too many spy thrillers. Take Blue Eyes for instance, rolling his shoulders, narrowing his eyelids, combing his moustache, swaggering when walking, muscular: the brute. How he thought himself to be James Bond! I called him Jiems Kont in my mind. Excuse me for taking refuge in my own language: there's always another language behind the present one; there's always another world living in the shadow of the one we share; there's for ever another room behind this one and in this other room there's another man sitting with a little tape recorder whispering in his own ears, saying, 'There is another world living parallel to this one, there is another language on the other side of the wall being spoken by another man holding a little instrument, etc., etc.'

Anyway, if you have the lack of respect or common decency of not wanting to call a Black man by his own name you call him by the generic name of Jiems, our Afrikaans version of 'James'; and 'Kont', well, it is just the untranslatable Cunt.

He was so sure that he'd brilliantly stumbled across the master spy of the century that he could hardly contain his own excitement. (He saw promotion winking on the horizon. . . . I have a suspicion that the handling of my case got Huntingdon his promotion.) And when this didn't work, because even amongst them there are some cooler heads, they changed direction diametrically.

What was interesting to notice was that parts of the volumes of evidence which were piling up were analysed supposedly in an expert fashion by specialist groups presumably either within BOSS or working on a contract basis for BOSS. One of these groups produced a working paper which showed by analysis that

I'm a CIA agent. Let me quickly explain to you, Mr Investigator, how they arrived at this beautifully self-evident conclusion.

There used to be an old man, Black, from the southern States of America, living in Paris. A painter. Beauford Delaney was his name. I believe he is dead now. He died sitting upright in his hospital bed, oblivious to the world. I'm told that when one went to visit him towards the end, taking flowers, he was apt to munch away at the bouquet. That's beside the point. He was a beautiful artist. I was asked by a friend, Lewis Nkosi, who worked for a publication in London called the *New African*, to do an article for them on an exhibition of Beauford's paintings here in Paris, which I did, and in fact round about the same time James Baldwin also wrote an article on Beauford – Beauford having been a friend of Baldwin's for many years. And this article – the one that Baldwin wrote – was reproduced by the *Classic* in South Africa: another magazine. Don't get confused, listen carefully to my argument. We are in the presence of superior minds. The *New African* was partially funded by an organization called The Congress for Cultural Freedom, with headquarters in Paris. This organization also to some extent funded the *Classic*, being printed and distributed in South Africa. It came to light that The Congress for Cultural Freedom was in its turn partially financed by the Central Intelligence Agency. It was a slush fund for them, a cover, or at least an organization which they could use in the way spies use whatever organizations they can. Like lice feeding on whatever body they can get hold of. Such is the filth that our societies have secreted, Mr Investigator, be they from the West or from the East. This is the real vermin living amongst us, the secret services, the spying brotherhoods.

As I said (or as they claimed), since the CIA was pushing money through The Congress for Cultural Freedom which was funnelling money to various publications with the people working for these publications quite innocently benefiting from the lolly, and since I in my ignorance had written about Beauford Delaney whom Baldwin had also written of, it was therefore evident, surely *you* must understand that, Mr Investigator, that *ipso facto* I had to be a CIA agent.

I'm sorry, excuse me for the cheek of attempting to breathe, but it's true: that is the level of their deductions and arguments.

Such is the house of suspicion which they inhabit. It is in terms of this type of reasoning that a nation's policies are being fashioned. It is with this grasp of reality and with this knack for clarity that they've walled in a people doomed to destruction. In this way they can prove that the whole world is against them and that they're the only ones who are right and brave and pure. God talks to them on Sundays. God spoke to them through Calvin, who said, according to them, 'Since we have the power we are *right*!'

Not all of them were of the same brilliant calibre of Jiems Kont. The two with whom I had to spend a lot of time, it may amuse you to know, were different. Jiems Kont always pretended, enigmatically, to know far more than he actually did, hoping that he would in this way lure you into giving yourself away. Huntingdon, on the other hand, is a slyer fellow, always trying to make out that he knew far less than he really knew, playing the role of the stupid one, saying, 'I'm just a simple Boer, I don't have the facility of you chaps playing with words.' He dripped sarcasm.

Certainly he was also hiding a personal complex. He was a touchy man, given to attacks of white anger. Vain – natty suits, dyed hair, carefully repaired teeth; and pretentious – living in a 'better' suburb, insisting that his children go to university, frequenting *hogene mense* (higher-ups) like professors of Afrikaans; and fatalistic – 'I know we shall die here, but there is *no* other way, and I shall be among the last with my pistol up in the hills'; complexed about his youth as the son of a poor mineworker; sexually obsessed; sensitive enough to get a kick of pain from the exercise of breaking people down; in awe of authority in a submissive way – 'The Big Man' up above was God whose ways are by definition unknowable, but 'The Big Man' was also the judge; anti-Semitic – a hundred times he bitterly told me the story of the Jew who sold eggs from door to door in their neighbourhood when he was young, and who went on to become a millionaire; realistic – scoffing at the then Minister of Justice as 'that ridiculous little man'; and above all power hungry – 'Don't forget it is *I* who will decide whether your wife obtains a visa to visit you. *We* have the real power.' Crawling when in the presence of superiors, tight-throated when talking to journalists, cold to his subordinates. A man of the church. Pious. Jiems Kont went down on his knees to him. Nails van Byleveld hated his guts.

Derrick Smith – ah, what a dilemma he must be in! English-speaking, not entirely rotten, working with this crew, having to listen – in my presence – to remarks made about the bloody 'Red Necks', meaning The English-speaking White South Africans. It was a measure of the insensitivity of his own colleagues. I can still see him blushing, and yet he continued the filthy work. I wonder why? In his way he tried to be nice to me. Maybe also trying to impress me – telling me about his youth among the Pondos,* showing off his knowledge of Pondo. Apparently he specialized in 'treating the ladies'. He became quite a friend of one of my co-detainees, the lady telephonist from Pretoria; even after the trial, during which she testified so abjectly, coached by him, he used to go and help her with her gardening problems. He was also the one who had to handle Moumbaris's wife when, very pregnant, she was arrested with him. (Alexander Moumbaris, a French national, was accused of smuggling ANC fighters from Swaziland into South Africa; he was sentenced to twelve years' imprisonment.) He claims to have become quite fond of her – and once showed me a rather brave statement made by her. Yet, I have respect for Derrick Smith, trying so hard to be 'one of the boys', a *real* South African.

There was Willem Koekemoer whom I think was truly lost; not a man of violence at all, a religious man, and I do not think he liked the work that he was doing. You must remember that some people become policemen, perhaps originally for fairly honourable reasons (really wanting to help society, and pushed into it also for economic considerations), however hard it is to understand, and it can happen that someone like Koekemoer gets posted to the Security Police without his asking for it. He was a sensitive, intelligent man. I remember the scorn with which he referred to Jiems Kont as a 'Christmas detective', seeing a communist behind every bush.

There was Hendrik Goy, tortured, chain-smoking, again ambivalent; capable of fierce hatred, a chip on his shoulder, aware somehow of being a pariah in society, but being allowed to cover this knowledge with the veneer of the power of being able to terrorize others. I still hear him in his crude way trying to bring

*A South African tribe, related to the Xhosas, many of whom live in the Transkei.

me to other insights, trying to argue into the silence that what they're doing is right. 'I don't mind them (meaning Blacks),' he said, 'I grant them the same privileges as I have; but how would you like to sit next to them in a bus, with their stinking bodies? Could you allow your wife having to live next to one of them seeing him standing on his lawn taking out his fat blue prick and pissing?' His favourite aphorism was that one of taking the *kaffir* out of the bush but never being able to take the bush out of the *kaffir*. The poor man.

There were the others, the more mysterious ones pulling the strings, the higher-ups whom I saw or rather who came to gawk at me the way one would look at a rare capture. Brummel, he of the one brown eye and the other green one, Mr Vanity himself with his three-piece suit and his moustache and his treatise on Trotskyism. Pulled himself up by his own bootstraps, he did, to the position of probably the third most powerful man in No Man's Land. Amoral. Living on cold hatred. Perfectly dishonest. A kingmaker. Embodying the Afrikaner suicide urge.

And Withart, the Commissioner, with his ticks, pulling up his trousers which he tried to secure with a very broad belt, his facial muscles stretching, his thin moustache twitching; a man who sleeps badly.

Others. Always others. A political detainee is in a private zoo for the *boere* to come and tease or touch. As during the trials, when there are trainee *boere* present, they come to get the 'feel' of a political. Also to recognize him later? People come to talk shit to me. To talk to me about trade unions or labour relations. Even (once, a rumpled, thick-glassed, 'intellectual' Grey) to ask if I would do a confession on 'the role played by English-speaking South African writers'!

Then, the Blacks. The sad traitors having to live in armed compounds among their own, trotted out for the dirty work, being humiliated by the White *baas* – perhaps in the way a necrophile is made to fornicate with corpses in public – and, as I saw in the offices, serving as tea-boys! Such a one was 'Snow White' who had to uncover himself during the Moumbaris affair. Gladstone his real name is – truculent, living in fear from his own people.

But what does it matter, Mr Investigator, what does it matter? I can go on forever evoking these caricatures of mankind.

But, listen: they are *killers* down to the last man! They torture and they kill, again and again. Sometimes you see them in daylight, caught in the glare of another inquest after a 'death in detention'. See their dark glasses, their ill-fitting suits, the faintly laughable haircuts. Do you feel the menace? Do you get the message? Watch it – they kill!

Let's get beyond that, let's move, let's get it over and done with, let's get to the point. What about the case, let's make the case, come now, give me the charge sheet! Because once I'm given the charge sheet I am supposed to be allowed to contact lawyers, I'm supposed to be admitted to be alive to the outside world again.

We shall come to the charge sheet. Two short little things before the end of this tape. Today, it must have been the first day, maybe it was the sixth, no, no, no, it was the fourth one after I was arrested, Huntingdon comes in with a little paper bag containing chocolates and a few packets of Gauloises. Somebody had sent in a parcel, knowing who I was – why else would it be Gauloises? I never found out who this mysterious donor was. Secondly, my one brother is allowed in to come and see me briefly and in so doing there's this terrible destruction of the love that I had for him as a brother, him, on such close terms with them, him taking exactly the same line they did, doing their talking for them.

Who is my real brother then? In what room sitting with what machine listening to what conversation? Ha, Mr Investigator, come closer now – don't make me laugh.

4

I Found Myself Confronted by

I think one of my most pervasive and naïve drawbacks must be that I always assume people to be reasonable. Maybe this is an elitest approach, or perhaps it is conditioned by the need to be accepted by others. Somehow I seem to think that if only people could sit down and give themselves the time to really think, or to see the situation objectively for what it is, they will come to reason. The implication is that seeing reason would be seeing it my way, and that would bring about ultimately that people would understand I do not really intend them any harm. This is a dangerous delusion on my part.

In Pretoria, what was perhaps the most disconcerting experience was that I now found myself confronted by, to my mind, entirely unreasonable people. They were and they are fanatically committed to their view of reality, to the justness of their analysis of the situation, and finally to their way of life. So, although we could smile at one another and joke, and although, after an interrogation session, I would be offered a cup of tea brought in by one of the Black Greyshits, deep down underneath there was the rock-bottom realization that we are irreconcilable enemies.

At times the atmosphere was quite relaxed, but at best it was the kind of relaxation of a cat playing with a mouse which is entirely in its power. Not for a single moment was I ever left alone; never was there a crack in their vigilance. And if by chance I had the impression of momentarily having established a privileged relationship with one of them, never could I be sure that this too wasn't just part of their intricate game of manipulation and disorientation. If for some reason the officer interrogating me had to leave the room, he would call one of his colleagues and ask him in an off-hand, affable way to *hou vas* for a moment, meaning to hold on to me until such time as he could return.

They are fanatic in the same way that the Israeli security

agencies are, or so they claim; that is, not only do they believe their cause to be just, but so convinced are they that the whole world is ranged against them, that any and all methods used in breaking and destroying those they finger as the enemy are justified. But the Israeli society is not monolithic – looked at from the outside it would seem that it benefits from a vigorous democratic life, with at least 50 per cent of the people clearly anti-expansionist and probably also against some of the 'values' embodied or promulgated by their security experts and their militarists. (What a strange identification the Afrikaners have with Israel. There has always been a strong current of anti-Semitism in the land, after all – the present rulers are the result and the direct descendants of pro-Nazi ideologues. And yet they have the greatest admiration for Israel, which has become – let it be said to the eternal shame of some Israel politicians – White South Africa's political and military partner in 'the alliance of pariah states.' They identify themselves with Israel – as the Biblical chosen people of God, and as a modern embattled state surrounded by a sea of enemies. Which, they believe, justify aggressive foreign military adventures. . . Jiems Kont, alias Blue Eyes, proudly displayed a star of David ring on his finger, given to him – he insisted – by David Ben-Gurion himself, after a South African Israeli 'dirty tricks' operation presumably somewhere in Africa.)

The interrogating officers are also very conscious of their own image. Some of the worst moments were when they regurgitated phrases that I had used describing them in a poem or in a work of prose. For instance: they never forgave me for having referred to them as people with chewing-gum minds. And where in *A Season in Paradise* I described one of them as a lap dog – and in fact I was not even referring to a security policeman, but to a hanger-on accompanying them to the airport that night in 1973 when we left – that adjective or description kept on surfacing and being thrown back at me. Heine once advised that when you refer to an easel you'd better identify him by name – else too many people will recognize themselves in the allusion. In the same way Snaaks, with his tight little purse of a mouth, wanted to know from me how I dared call him a lap dog.

They were keen to know what the outside world thinks of

them. 'We are the best, aren't we!' Huntingdon used to say. Perhaps the general disgust with which the people of South Africa regard them does get through to them. Even though they move around quite openly on their missions of terror, they still seem to feel that they live in the shadows, even that they are not appreciated as they ought to be. Therefore, when they get their hands on the sworn enemy, they tend to really let go to make up for all the pent-up recriminations.

They're dangerous. One always had the feeling that one had to placate them. Later on, with prison warders, I had similar experiences. One was not so much afraid of the harm they might do you on purpose, but that they may lose control of themselves and maim or exterminate you, as it were, by accident. (This risk was compounded with prison warders since they were also nervous from a lack of experience or training.) One was always trying to calm them down, not making any untoward gestures, not saying anything that would infuriate them. I'm often reminded of the story of the *tokolosh*, one of the enduring myths of our country. The *tokolosh* is said to be very small and very puckered and very unattractive, but also to be extremely sensitive about his appearance. He it is who will break and enter the house of a political prisoner to rape the wife. It is claimed that he sneaks up on one; but be careful if you are suddenly confronted by him – do not show any surprise, and if he asks you whether you were expecting him, be sure to answer in the affirmative and to make him believe that you had really seen him coming from a long, long way off.

They are dangerous furthermore because they live in a world of make-believe where fact and fancy mix, and their reactions to any stimulation become unforeseeable. For example, they are completely convinced of the conspiracy of the whole world led by the communists or orchestrated by them, to attack and destroy the citadel which they defend. They seem to think that the subversion of their republic is a number one priority of the masters of the Kremlin. They are sure also that what the communists really are after are the gold and the diamonds and the strategic materials in the subsoil of the country. They are not open to the simple, and one would have thought natural, process of altering their views according to their experience of reality.

This, of course, makes them ultimately dangerous to those who created them. I cannot see how the security of the country could ever be built on the analyses of professional security experts who have no means of separating simple facts from emotionalism and conditioning. They are certainly also a mortal threat to the politicians who suppose themselves to be their masters (this is a feature common to totalitarian states) – as their power is unchecked. They create the enemy and in the name of combating him they have usurped the powers of judge and executioner. They have learned to fabricate and manipulate information. They have learned the value of spying and collecting information on everybody, their puppet masters included. After all, in the State of Abject Fear and Taboos we are all guilty – we are just, sometimes, clever or lucky enough not to be caught.

They do not even seem to be able to recognize fiction when they come across it. Many years ago I had written a short prose work called *Om Te Vlieg* (In Order to Fly). It was basically the sad story of a perfectly absurd character called Panus who tried by any means, fair or foul, to acquire the art of flying. This meant sleeping in trees, dissecting locusts. Towards the end of that story he died in three or four different ways. But, when writing *A Season in Paradise,* I decided to resuscitate him and I imagined a meeting between Panus and myself in Cape Town. I then described how this man (more properly – this fictitious character) turned up at the place where I was staying; how old he'd become; how pathetic and bare his wings were. In this weird world of ours many things are possible, Mr Investigator, but it still came as a surprise to me to be interrogated by Jiems Kont about Panus. 'Who is he really?' he wanted to know. And especially, 'What is his political orientation?' No way could I convince him that this personage 'twixt prick and bunghole was simply an outgrowth of my imagination.

You'll understand why, under such conditions, the line between reality and illusion is effaced. For, to the extent that they believe something to be real and act accordingly, that thing does become real.

They are dangerous also because, despite the fact that they are conditioned to their work and believe blindly that they are justified in doing their thing, and questioning authority or the validity of an order has never been part of the Calvinist tradition, they are nevertheless very human with the same brittleness and the same doubts that you or I may have. The danger then comes from the internal conflicts they have to struggle with. The dichotomy is between doing what they have been conditioned to do unquestioningly and the leftover feelings of humane compassion, and – as they are not mentally or culturally equipped to resolve these contradictions or even to recognize them – they tend to become very violent in an unconscious effort to blot out and perhaps to surpass the uneasiness. However strange it may sound, Mr Eye, I am convinced that some of the people they have killed in detention probably died when the interrogator was in a paroxysm of unresolved frustrations, even that the interrogator killed in an awkward expression of love and sympathy for a fellow human being.

They may be experts in riot control; when in their hands one must learn to become an expert in killer control. Don't upset them, don't talk down to them, don't play with them, try to foresee what they may want, try to forestall the anger they would experience when they make fools of themselves or are led up a cul-de-sac. Talk to them about the weather, get them talking about rugby, or motorcars, or *braaivleis* (barbecue), or sex.

But they can be much more dangerous than that. I learned, a few years after this, that Curiel had been assassinated brutally on his own doorstep in Paris. At that time I was already in Cape Town and a senior prison official on visit from Pretoria brought me a laconic message from Huntingdon to the effect that 'We got Curiel, you're the next'; intending it perhaps as a joke. But I remembered then, and still do now, their all-obliterating fascination with, and the hatred they had for, Curiel. As if by eliminating one man they could destroy what they considered to be a menacing network of conspiracy against them.

Much later, about two years before my release, I asked my lawyers to start proceedings against a Johannesburg Afrikaans daily that had abusively headlined my name in a transparent attempt to link it to that of Curiel and his supposed terrorist organization.* The tone of the article sounded very familiar

*The matter was settled out of court to our satisfaction.

indeed. Let us say it was an 'inspired' piece of writing. It was exactly the line of argument that I'd heard the political police use whilst interrogating me. In the course of our preparation for the legal proceedings I finally learned the essential elements of the killing of Curiel, or rather of the plot preparing the event. Some time after my arrest an anonymous article appeared in a French magazine which had connections with a South African publication of the same title – and I know that the South African magazine is used by the South African spying services. Not long afterwards, then, a cowardly French journalist became the mouthpiece of the South African masters and smeared Curiel. During the resulting polemics Curiel was isolated, consigned to house arrest by the French authorities, only to be released when the accusations were found to be groundless. But this was only part of the diabolical plan to put him up for marksmen. It was never their intention to have the French immobilize Curiel, but only to create a climate which would permit his extermination. Which it did.

There again one day the truth will have to become known. As for now, it would seem that the actual killing could have been carried out by elements within the French intelligence establishment, rightist groupings which are still there and which, naturally, collaborate with the South African fascists.

Mr Investigator, there are a few last little incidents and impressions that I wish to describe and which may help you to understand how it becomes possible for one ultimately to be like the rabbit assisting open-eyed and without kicking at one's own eating. (It is against the law to struggle when you are throttled.)

I've mentioned how these persons move in a make-believe and a twilight world. An illustration of this would be the photos with which they decorate their offices. These are functional places with working tables, safes, filing cabinets, many filing cabinets, telephones – one assumes everything wired for sound, because they certainly don't trust one another. But I recollect being struck by the photos of themselves taken somewhere on the border. Like parties of big-game hunters. Yes, in their capacity as security policemen they also spend periods of service at the border. One wonders how their particular talents are employed.

The border, this mythical concept in modern-day White South African awareness. . . Not so modern after all. The history of the Afrikaner has been one of borders, of the enemy lurking just over the horizon, of buffer states used against the world wanting to take over the lands their ancestors conquered. They were proud of their periods on the border, of the hunts they participated in. But I think they conceive of their activities inside the country as just an extension of the same hunt and patrolling the same border.

Later, when in Cape Town, I often had a likewise impression from the prison warders: that looking after me was their way of combating and fighting communism on the frontier.

A similar myth, even more pervasive, more sick, is their obsession with sex; the sex lives of their victims, maybe even those of their colleagues and superiors. Like repressed puritans all over the world, the sexual dimension becomes a primary source of wonder and titillation and envy. So many of their questions turned around that aspect. When they talked to me about previous victims like Bram Fischer, or about fellow detainees such as Jim Polley, it was always the sex lives that fascinated them. Huntingdon described to me how he'd spent time hidden in a flat opposite that frequented by Fischer at the time when he was under surveillance, and what stuck (and festered) in his mind were the couplings, the love affairs, what he called 'the orgies'. I think, given his attitude of a voyeur, he probably would have spent even his off-duty hours behind his peep-hole.

Similarly they thought it very funny to have lured Polley into the situation where he believed that they would carry love letters to his girlfriend, Meagan, who had been arrested and was kept in a female prison. These letters were of course the source of endless amusement to them. Meagan, though, was released not long afterwards. It must have been impossible even for them to make out a case against someone who so obviously had had nothing to do at all with Okhela. But they made sure that her telephone was tapped, and Huntingdon was furious, livid, had to be restrained from using his formidable powers for the sake of immediate revenge, when in one of the first intercepted calls Meagan was overheard to give her frank opinion of Huntingdon to a friend, explaining how he, Huntingdon, had made sexual propositions to her, which she rejected, not because he was a pig, to call the police by their American name, but because he was to her such a detestable and ludicrous male.

At one point during this period, I was taken to Compol as usual one day, and inadvertently shown into Huntingdon's office while he was still busy with Garfield Thurston, another of the arrested ones. Garfield turned round, had his back to Huntingdon, saw me at the door, winked broadly, and was quickly shunted off. And for the rest of the afternoon Huntingdon tried to regale me with tales of young Thurston's illicit homosexual love affairs. Again by quoting in length from intercepted letters.

Repression, power madness – two faces of the same coin. You cannot imagine how strange it is to live in that perverse world, superimposed upon the normal one but worlds away from it. And yet, how they love to flaunt their power to underline the inaccessibility of their charges, to brazenly parade them practically in public – knowing that they have the power of death and life over them. More, that they have managed not only to make lepers out of their victims, but to render them invisible. What greater kick can there be than to decide for the world, the people in the street, what they see and what they don't see?

I was summoned once from my cell and taken out of the front door of Beverly Hills. Huntingdon particularly was proud of the facility with which he could come and go in the prison, and he had nothing but disdain for the prison staff. Outside the front door, still within the enclosure of the wall with the electronically controlled gates, his car was parked, and in this car there was a young girl, perhaps seventeen years old. He introduced her to me as his niece, studying to be a teacher in Johannesburg. He then left her alone with me. She claimed to be a fan of my poetry and so emotional did she become at the thought of my plight that she ended up weeping. He was standing a little way off, hands in his pockets. When he'd enjoyed himself enough he came and had me escorted back to my cell.

On another occasion, one morning, having perhaps other fish to fry, he instructed van Byleveld and Hakkebak to put me in their car and to go show me the Voortrekker Monument. Imagine, Mr Investigator: here you have the terrorist held incommunicado, this danger to South Africa, and the newspapers were full of it –

in fact the detention and the trials were run also as exercises in media communication by the security police, even to the extent of them inviting readers to try and crack the so-called Cuban code which Okhela had made use of in their correspondence. In any event, here, on a beautiful spring morning, I was driven to the holy place of Afrikaner nationalism just outside the capital. It was a normal visiting day; there were other people moving around. Van Byleveld and Hakkebak allowed me to stroll through this horribly depressing edifice to the warped history of the Afrikaner. Of course I was never out of their sight, but they weren't next to me either. Imagine passing by normal human beings in the marble hall, or as normal as anybody who visits the Voortrekker Monument could be. Truly, one was hiding in the light.

I had to lift my hat to them. It was perhaps the same principle that I was working on when I entered the country clandestinely: that it was so unexpected, so far-fetched for one to be there that one could walk by one's mother in the street without her recognizing one.

They were inevitably and duly moved. Their souls were touched by the barbaric altar in the crypt upon which it is said a single shaft of light is calculated to fall on a certain day of the year to light up the chiselled words: *Ons vir jou, Suid-Afrika* (We for you, South Africa). After that we went next door to the little museum and looked at a replica of an ox wagon, the dresses and utensils and firearms they used at the time.*

Van Byleveld had unexpected sides to him. He proudly showed me a photo of his little daughter in her ballet tutu standing on the kitchen table of their suburban house in Parow, and he told me of his great joy in driving back to the Cape from Pretoria, picnicking by the side of the road even when transporting a political prisoner, and going for a stroll – because his passion was to collect rare indigenous bulbs and plants in the Karoo. Recounting this, talking of the beauty of the sunset over the bare hills, would bring tears to his eyes. Killing a political suspect with his bare hands obviously did not.

*The first and only other time I'd seen the Voortrekker Monument was at the age of eighteen when, on my first visit to the Transvaal, I hitched a lift from Johannesburg to Pretoria from two Blacks in a little Ford Prefect. As we passed by the sandcastle the chauffeur asked, 'Have you ever visited *that*? No? Well, I've seen it. I used to be in a prison span [team] taken there to clean up the pigeon shit.'

But perhaps the most telling example of this cynical display of power must be the one Saturday morning when Huntingdon, accompanied only by his son, came to fetch me from prison and took me to his house. On the way there we stopped at the rugby stadium, Loftus Versveld, which was then being enlarged, and he showed it to me with great provincialist pride. I could see no other escort, but perhaps they were there – invisible to me. When we arrived at his house, he introduced me to his wife, his two daughters, and in a very relaxed fashion conducted me around his garden, talking about the difficulty of establishing his proteas, the way any normal gardener would.

And my mind, Mr Investigator, my mind was in turmoil. . . . Their house is on the edge of town from where you can see the first hills and the empty space, and apparently there was nothing preventing me from running. What was this? Trap? Was that what he wanted me to do? To shoot me while I was trying to escape? Or, in his convoluted way, offering me the possibility?

We went indoors. He showed me his study with his hunting trophies on the walls: pictures of him and Ludi on either side of Bram Fischer going to court. In due time my picture would be there too. It is probably there now. . . . His two daughters came and asked me to write something in their little visitors' book; you know, the way kids, girls particularly, up to a certain age, have these books of mementoes. And I did. For the little one I even wrote something in French. Then his wife called us to table and I sat down, completely bewildered after these several months of not having used a knife and fork or even eating from a plate – since one got one's food in a plastic dog bowl in Maximum, scooping it up with a spoon.

I don't remember what we had for lunch – salads most likely. Weird, schizophrenic to carry on conversation with people, everybody pretending to be normal. And then, before the end of the meal, there was a phone call for him which I couldn't overhear, but he came back to the table smugly, told me that I could make use of the bathroom facilities, even use his toothbrush if I wanted to, clean myself up a little bit, excused himself that they now had to take me back. So we returned still with only his son riding shotgun.

And when we arrived at Maximum, instead of being taken

through the clanging steel doors and grills, he took me to the left, down the wing where the officers were. And, without saying anything, ushered me into an office where Yolande was.

Mr Investigator – imagine, try, close your eyes the way I do now, and imagine what the effect must be on one. What a psychological shock! The completely cynical manoeuvring of the morning – because the intention, apart from showing his absolute power, must have been to try and create to my family, to my wife, the illusion that I was treated humanely; why, I'm even invited to his home! But further, to walk back into the house of death with that man accompanying me, and then to see, without any preparation, the person who is the dearest to me on earth. And not to break down. Not to break down. Not to make it more difficult for her. To try and comfort her. To reassure her. To pretend that it is less serious than it would seem. That there is still hope. To invent hope for her where there is none. And just to hold her hand. But feeling the gaze of this monster, avid for a strong emotional charge, hungry to partake of the plunging emotion of the pain so as to feel alive, and justified. He had to have that. He needs to abase himself even more, to rub the raw nerves so as to forget about the dead hole in his centre.

(RECAPITULATION)

I must know (he says). I must sniff out. I must uncover. I must gut. I must reconstitute. I must comprehend. I must *prove*. That is, I must allow it to reveal itself. The secret secrets. Therefore I must ask. Do you mind that I ask, I ask, I ask? Don't you know it's necessary? That it can *never* be any different? That it has been like this from the beginning of time – you and I entwined and related, parasite and prey? Image and mirror-image? You are my frame and my field and my discipline. I bring for you cookies in a tin – my wife made them with her own two hands. In you I live. Do I see all the evil concretized. Do I try to cherish the little good. You must come to other insights. You must realize the implications. You were used. You are the pawn. Don't you know it yet? You are the sly one. You are the sheep that strayed, you are the rejected one, the excretion, the bosom-adder. You don't want to know about me. I'm beneath you, am I not? I am the rock, the flatfoot. I am stupid, not so? But you *know* of me. Here we are, today, still today, still this interminable dark day, days and days for ever. I am with you. I never let go of you again. You are programmed. I cleanse you. I break you in. I break you down to the pure outcome of spontaneous confession and give-away and self-oblivion. Since I love you so. Something that's barren in me goes out to you. You are the dew in the chalice of my soul. Ah, what a grand game this is.

I am the controller. I despatch you. I drive you on. I manipulate you. You are my lifeboat. You must open up, go open. You must just say. Say that which I must hear. Tell that which I know. I know you so intimately. In such a profound way you will never know yourself. I nose around in your psyche. You are my excursions to wanton cellars. You are my book. I create your past. Your future is in my hands. I leaf through all the painfully constituted files on your comings and your goings, the records of your thinking and the organigramme of your associations. We are never free of one another again. I am your control. I am your handler. I squint up your arse. Relate your deepest fears to me, your best hidden desires. Forget about yesterday and tomorrow. The world knows only ending, ending. Pain is *now*. You are mine. You are the human. You are the bad. I am your present time, forty-two hours per day, from now on until all eternity. Come, I'll show you who you are. Look in this mirror, look. I bring you the image. Look how naïve you are.

I know already. I always know. But I must *prove*. You are the confirmation. You prove. You are of my making. I am the controller. I slit open, and then I sculpt. You make sense of my anxieties. You flesh out my dreams. You are, and therefore my life is not in vain. You flower. You are the true-coming of my prophecies. You are the product of my education, the crystallization of my heritage, the grail of my sacred task. Ah, what a grand game we play.

Talk to me! Write for me your cacography. We have time. Nobody will disturb us. There is no world outside. Night is pumping through the panes. You don't wish to walk in the night. We have come so far together. I know you. I know your private life so much better than you will ever know. Why do you resist?

Why do you argue? You know that right is on my side now and this endless day and forever more. Our path has been traced for us. Accept what I give you. Be rich! Occupy the references I create for you! Are you surprised by my ability to induct? I know. I know all deduction and the creation of proof and all suscitation or alteration and all precipitation and all delay and all irritation and all stimulation and all the impulses and all transferring and all input and all feedback. I am the practitioner. I am your companion. I walk in your tracks. I am your tracks. I know of the eye before the keyhole, of the lens by the window, of the ear in the telephone or the ceiling or the floor or the tree, of the dagger in the back, of the explosive in the manuscript. I know of the stool pigeon and the provocateur. I know of the boot in the face when you're down. I love you so. I need you so. Don't you see? You permit me relevance, you give me my outline. You give me status. You make me accept myself. You make me feel that I know I *am*! Come, I'm your father confessor. Together we are the embodiment of the reality of my thoughts, my wishes, my anguishes, my existence. In me you are as safe as death. I have the two faces. Because you are, life is infamous. Because you are, there is sin. You make me humble. Through you I touch eternity. Through you I see that the looking-glass is true. You bring me to my knees. Because you are you and I am I, I am saved. There is relief for me in the holy hills before the shiny portals. Ah, how grand.

Do I go too far? Do I delve too deep? Are you ashamed of not having any shame left? Does it bother you to soil your pants? If you could only know how strongly it links us! Look, I am your safe harbour. You searched for me, you found me. I am your forever today still, and this day which will never stop screaming, which will never fade or lose its circles. I am your *reality*. Even of the most hidden things you need never be afraid again. Isn't it wonderful that you may share everything with me? Let go – I lead you to new dimensions. You don't think I'm just being curious? Do you not see the implications? Ah, what a grand game. I shall reveal all discourses to you and take them to logical conclusions, I shall point out every orientation. Surely you know that you are the old human nature. Come, I am the conductor. Trust me. Open up! I shall put together your prognosis. I am your proctoscope. You are my wondrous thousand and one nights. Describe your relationships to me. Tell me about what is veiled. Admit even to that which you don't know. Be glorious! I must test your credibility. I know everything. How lovely your confidence is. Don't struggle so!

I touch you. Why are you so withdrawn, so crumpled? Be dependent. *Talk* to me. But don't leave me! I am the controller. Don't you know me? Help me! Don't slide away like that from under my fingers. Resist! Be rich! Be! Don't leave me alone! I am the Afrikaner. Why dost thou not love me?

5

Then I am Presented in the Death Hole

Then I am presented with the indictment and the dance of the law starts. In the offices of the political police I am introduced to my legal team: Sam Norval, attorney; Pieter Henning, barrister. They were appointed, they said, by my family. Both of them were visibly very nervous, anxious even. It was only much later that I learned that it took great courage on their behalf to agree to represent me at all, that enormous pressure had been brought to bear on Sam Norval's firm, for instance, to try to get him to withdraw from the case. The firm of attorneys of which he was a partner also represented, amongst others, a major newspaper publishing concern (the chairman was a personal friend of Sitting Bull) which threatened economic blackmail, saying they would withdraw all future business from this legal firm unless Norval desisted from aiding me. It required the backstage intervention of some just-minded jurists to allow me to have any legal representation at all.

Huntingdon used to say to me, 'Why bother to have legal representation; why don't you leave it in my hands – I shall defend you.'

The charge sheet was a very hefty document indeed. It accused me, amongst other heinous crimes, of having smuggled weapons across the border, of having plotted violent acts of sabotage, of being involved in spying activities in the ports. And conspiracy! Conspiracy is a heavily punished crime in No Man's Land. The court is not so much interested in what you've actually done, but in what you *intend* doing, and especially the *implications* of what you were conspiring to do. (The Bible says that the end of time is near!) To be convicted of this the State only needs to show that you *associated* with known subversives. You should have seen the list of absent co-accused! So, on the advice of the legal team who so obviously operated within very strict parameters, bargaining with my tormentors was started. I had refused to give evidence against any of the other detainees. Things looked very sombre. If we allowed this indictment to go through unchallenged there was a very good chance that the prosecution may demand the highest penalty and the court may well grant it its wish. I myself was no party to whatever negotiating that took place, but I was aware of the intense insistence by Huntingdon and his cohorts, as also by the prosecuting team, that this case should not be allowed to become a political show trial – from *my* side that is.

You must remember that the trial took place during the 'secret' invasion of Angola by South African troops. What a heaven-sent gift, propaganda-wise at least, my capture must have been to the government! No wonder such a big fuss was made of it in the papers. (Poor editors – prevented by law from writing about the real war being waged.) If, as a bonus, I could be prevented from using the court as a political platform – well, then the good little Nationalists could really wag their tails. (And, come to think of it, when one now remembers how much back-stabbing there was going on between the CIA and the Greys concerning Angola, it becomes clear why BOSS was so uptight and anti-CIA.)

Gradually, also aided now by being able to look back on the events, gradually a line emerged. In return for my pleading guilty, and in return for my not insisting on making political statements from the dock, and in return for the freedom of the other arrested ones, the State graciously agreed to alter the charge sheet so as to delete any reference to violence, to not attempt to have me convicted under the Suppression of Communism Act, and it was agreed that the prosecutor would ask for the imposition of the minimum sentence, which was five years.*

*None of this could have been agreed to except, on their side, by the highest authorities – meaning Krüger, then Minister of Justice, and the Sitting Bull himself. After I'd done five years my legal representatives of the time petitioned the Minister for a remission of sentence, with arguments based in part on the pre-trial agreement arrived at in 1975. Dr Yutar, the prosecutor, by now retired and back in private practice, went to see his ex-boss, the Minister, on my behalf. I was told that an extremely hostile Krüger warned Yutar that their conversation was being taped from the moment he entered the office, and then proceeded to deny any knowledge of the agreement (despite written confirmation from his Department). Yutar was shocked and humiliated; felt he'd never been treated in such a cavalier fashion in his life. In Afrikaans we call this *stank vir dank*, meaning 'stench for thanks'.

My family was obviously and understandably trying to limit the damages. Sam Norval and Pieter Henning are certainly very capable jurists in the fields of their respective specialities – Civil Law and Corporate Law – but neither of them had any experience as a political lawyer. I don't think they could have designed the strategy for a political defence even if they wanted to, because they were far too closely integrated into the Afrikaner establishment. (By this I mean that the political police – the State for that matter – were not natural enemies for them.) I believe that they tried, mistakenly but with such solicitude, to do what they thought best for my interests at the time, and the atmosphere of terror created by the powerful political police was such that they felt we ought to tread very lightly indeed. During consultations Sam Norval used to be wet with perspiration and say, 'God, my God, we must be *so* careful!' I was aware that they were also having talks with the police and with the prosecuting team, but, strangely, all of this was quite beyond me. I was not aware – I don't remember now – of a formal agreement being reached, or how it would affect my future. I was numbed. To my mind the whole world was hostile (expressions of support were carefully kept from me, and the offices where I could consult the lawyers were bugged) – legal gown and policeman's uniform blended. All I wanted was to please. And in my cell I was alone in the house of dying.

One wanted to have it over and done with. I felt quite passive. I can understand how the mouse is paralysed although still alive whilst being eaten by the snake – celebrating with open eyes its own death.

But, Mr Investigator, let me not create the impression that I repudiate my lawyers. Had I instructed them differently, had I been strong enough to call the bluff of the interrogators, had I felt that I was entitled and justified to defend myself *politically* (which I did not: I was no ANC member, and Okhela was formed in support of a *faction* within the ANC so that a political defence would also have been an embarrassment to people I then still considered my friends), or had I been willing to make a martyr of myself – they would probably have outlined a different type of defence. I could not have been an easy client – that is the story of my life, Mr Investigator: not to be an easy client. As it was they advised particular caution – perhaps seeing the real dangers more clearly than I then did. And I went along.

I was asked to prepare a short statement. Without being political it was an attempt to explain how I got to be standing where I was, without rejecting my convictions. Read it – you will also hear the insidious voice of the controller in it. This was in the hands of Huntingdon a week before the trial commenced, and Vorster himself had it on his desk before it was read in court.

Mr Investigator, the public play is not really the part of the story which interests you most, is it? Do you want to dance? I think you'd rather like to know about what was happening behind the walls. (Are you also one of those who believe that the unsaid must be more truthful?)

The trial itself was a strangely muted affair. It took place in one of the courts of the Pretoria Supreme Court building – wood-panelled with carved motifs, very morbid, very depressing. I believe the building served at one time as a synagogue.

The prosecutor was the attorney-general of the Transvaal at the time, Dr Percy Yutar, a small bald man with glasses and one withered hand. Worth his weight in gold to the Nationalist government he was, because he allowed them the pretence of justice and objectivity they so sorely needed. After all, a Jew – that is, a non-Afrikaner – in their service, being their henchman: surely, they argued, it must prove to the outside world that our justice is not a partisan one. (This coming from a party which supported Hitler during the war and which is still marked by anti-Semitism!) They used him only for the major show trials such as the Rivonia case or the trial of Bram Fischer. He served them well, Percy Yutar, he sold his soul over and over again and in the end I don't believe that he was paid in kind. His senior assistant was a tall supercilious man called Dennis Rothwell. (Long after the trial Rothwell came to visit me in my cell with Huntingdon. He then admitted to being a Satanist – seriously! – and felt we might have something in common there as he sensed, he said, an admiration for the Devil in me too!)

The judge was an old flunky going by the name of Silly, son of a minister of the Church of the Free State. It is curious how these fanatic Afrikaners, entirely biased, with tribal loyalties only, and therefore completely disqualified for the elevated duty of administering justice, succeed in hiding their rottenness behind a robe of respectability. Silly must have been an important functionary of the Broederbond.* He also most surely received instructions from Sitting Bull defining the line to take during the court proceedings and the type of sentence to be imposed. And yet he put in his daily appearance as if he were really an objective and stately elderly judge. He did once warn against people attempting to influence the decisions of the court – but I learned, much later, that he was referring to individuals from abroad who had sent telegrams in my support.

Despite the muted proceedings there was quite a lot of interest in the case. In the body of the hall I could see every day the senior security police officers sitting there. They are fascinated by the mechanism of a trial. They love to assist at the conclusion and the accomplishment of their handiwork. It gives them, in their own eyes, the appearance of legality. It is nearly as if, in this way, they feel that they are justifying in public, by their own appearance, the dark deeds committed in the sad cells and interrogation offices. But they are there also to observe, to advise, to control, to make sure that the noose fits snugly. The other State officials will not be allowed to forget that they are there. The investigating officer, of course, is part of the prosecuting team. There are other, younger political police present, to allow them to become acquainted with the accused and the witnesses and inevitably with the politicized spectators who turn up in solidarity with the accused.

It became clear fairly rapidly that even though I had been tricked into renouncing any attempt to politicize the trial, the State, by mouth of Dr Percy Yutar and his assistants, was going to go all out to smear a few organizations which, up to that time, they had not yet succeeded in eliminating. I'm referring to NUSAS, the National Union of South African Students; to some

*The Broederbond (League of Brothers) – an Afrikaner secret organization, started in the early years of revived Afrikaner nationalism, into which only 'right-thinking', influential, White Afrikaner males can be ritually initiated. Pretending to be a 'cultural organization' – most Dutch Reformed ministers are members – it in fact, through its occult presence and because you have no future in Afrikaner public life unless you are a member, directs Afrikaner political ideology and practice, as well as its economy and its cultural life. And, by extension, the country's.

of the more Christian elements in the churches, such as those then grouped around the Christian Institute; and even to dissident Afrikaner thinking as expressed to some extent in the writing of a few colleagues. I should add that I had been until that time an honorary vice-president of NUSAS, that several of the other detainees were involved in trade union activities sponsored by NUSAS, and one at least was a Christian Institute worker.

They did not bother to call too many witnesses. (Nails van Byleveld was asked to tell how he searched a house in Cape Town. He arrived at the front door, accompanied by a detainee.

Prosecutor: 'What did you do then?'

Van Byleveld: 'I entered the house.'

Prosecutor: 'And then?'

Van Byleveld: 'I went deeper into the house.'

Eventually he found a document hidden away in a book on the bookshelf.)

Of those they did call there were three kinds: one such as Mrs Röhmer, or Lewis, who went out of their way to wag their tails and ingratiate themselves with the prosecution to the extent that they would invent and ascribe intentions to me which did not even exist, with allusions to spying, to violent terroristic activities. (Mrs Röhmer, her head covered by a mantilla veil as if going to church for confession – yes! – when asked how she felt about her role, said, 'I think I ought to be taken outside and shot.' Lewis, I learned, was suffering from uncontrolled bowel movements, and appeared in an ill-smelling, rumpled suit. On his way back from the witness box, passing by the dock where I sat, I couldn't refrain from advising him to have his suit cleaned.) There was a second kind of witness who answered strictly and only the questions put to him. And then there was the third kind, such as Karel Tip for instance, who quite obviously was most uncomfortable in giving evidence and managed to convey that he regretted having to do so and that his loyalty to our cause had not changed. ('Could you describe the accused to the court?' 'He is of medium height.' 'Colour hair?' 'Medium.' 'Colour eyes?' 'Medium.')

I'd like to think that there were some people in detention who refused to give any evidence at all, but I bear no grudges against those who did. Why drown just because another madman did?

We on our side, when I say 'we' it means essentially the legal team, influenced and pressurized by the political police, decided not to call any witnesses. I myself was prevailed upon to enter the box to allow myself to be cross-examined, and during this passage the smearing tactics of Yutar came to fruition. Two witnesses were summoned for mitigation of sentence. To my everlasting shame Huntingdon went up to testify to my cooperation. No 'uncontaminated' literary expert (that is, no literary figure of any standing) was willing to appear for me. So a young lady was called upon to talk about my poetic abilities and she read some verses in an embarrassingly dramatic fashion. And then we rested our case.

On the days of court proceedings I was fetched every morning at the prison by the political police. I'd managed to recover two of my own suits and borrowed a few ties from one of my brothers, and the security police would flutter around me, helping tie the knot around my neck, pretending to be concerned about my appearance. We would then drive down to the Compol Building which was obviously heavily guarded by armed policemen and there I would sit around waiting for them to take me to court.

One morning I noticed Huntingdon taking exceptional precautions about his own appearance, combing and recombing his hair, and patting one of his flashiest broad ties into place. He then nonchalantly announced that since it was such a beautiful morning we were going to stroll to court.

I was preceded and flanked and followed by a phalanx of Greys through the streets of Pretoria, with Huntingdon and his dark glasses to my right, and sure enough, as we approached the Supreme Court building the photographers stormed at us and started clicking away. The whole operation was stage-managed by Huntingdon to get his mug in the newspaper. He is a very vain man, but probably he also tried to convey the impression that the security police had the situation entirely in hand.

During the sessions, when I wasn't actually in the dock, I was kept down in the court cells behind a locked door. The court cells are watched over by an aged, idiotic functionary. Upon arrival one is handed over to him, but one's escort must have a 'body receipt'. If the police or prison officials don't provide food for lunch, this bald shuffler will do so: a slice of bread ('but the bread is white') and a mug of coffee. These court cells are atrocious places. The walls are painted black, they're filthy inside, the toilets are broken, and all over you see on the walls the scratched graffiti of desperate detainees leaving their messages of hope or their exculpations or just a curse or a threat. Never was I alone in any of these cells. Always there were two or three of the Greys with me. (It wouldn't do to be found hanging with Judge Silly waiting upstairs; the show must go on!) To them the proceedings were like a circus. One of them would leave the cell, go for a stroll around the building, and come back reporting that he'd seen Helen Joseph or Winnie Mandela. One was not aware, whilst in the court cells, of what was happening upstairs or even what the weather was like.

The trial of the SASO student leaders (South African Student Organization) was going forward at the same time as mine, in an adjoining courtroom. Sometimes, during recesses, I passed by them in the stairwell or the corridor. They were all dressed in complementary African shirts – very flashy. I envied them their warm and rumbustious camaraderie. Once, on my way in, I caught a glimpse of Rick Turner's red beard, sitting alone in the SASO court. He was to be assassinated not long afterwards. I shall have the chance to tell you about the echoes of his death as I heard them in prison.*

Upstairs then one sat on a very narrow wooden bench slightly higher than the rest of the spectators in such a position as to see the people in the hall. My father used to be among the audience, day after day, sitting half way towards the back, very straight, with his face entirely closed. How he must have suffered. His life was coming to a close, but his years of deepening shadows were not going to be easy. He had lived through the feuds pitting Afrikaner against Afrikaner. His father – my tough old grandfather – had been a labourer on other people's farms. He himself had worked with his hands: building canals, ploughing and planting, mining. His first son, my eldest brother, was (is) the commander

*Rick Turner was an academic at the University of Natal. He was also active as an adviser to the nascent Black trade unions. He had written an important book (banned in South Africa) on the economic impracticabilities of the Bantustan policy, called *Through the Eye of the Needle*. At the time of his assassination he was living under a banning order.

of his country's crack anti-guerrilla special unit, a brigadier-general, a trained (and enthusiastic) killer, be it with knife or gun, a 'dirty tricks' expert for Military Intelligence; his second son was (is) a reporter, fellow traveller of the Greys, with decidedly fascist sympathies; and now there was me, a terrorist, vilified by many (but that didn't bother him, he was used to it, except that some neighbours stopped talking to him – although others, ordinary folk, would be heart-stopping in their continued support). Plus, he hated being in the Transvaal. My sister, who stood by him day after day, used to remark that Oubaas (as we call him in the family) would get physically sick the moment he crossed the Vaal. My mother didn't come. It would have been too much of a strain for her. And we'd agreed that Yolande shouldn't be there either. Why increase the pain? She wasn't even living in Paris anymore. Never, until the end, did the *boere* stop attempting to implicate her – people like my brother and the writer, Chris Barnard,* concurred in this plot: they continued trying to use my marriage to her as a pressure point; and some of the fine and loyal people who offered her friendship and hospitality on her periodic visits to the land were confronted with photographic and other evidence of their association with Yolande in an attempt to blackmail them into working with the *boere*. But, being under the protection of the French embassy – representatives of a 'friendly' power – they left her alone apart from the obligatory shadowing and tapping of the phones where she sojourned.

From time to time I spotted the presence of other friends; so close they were and yet out of touch – moving in another world altogether. Although there were no barriers between us we were already irrevocably separated from one another and I might as well have been dead. Once, during a break, a few fellow writers were allowed to come up and say hello to me. It was an awkward

*Their attitude seems to have been: she's Vietnamese, therefore she must be communist; she's considered racially inferior here and if we were in that situation we would have been embittered – she must be also, so she must be plotting against the State; she is intelligent and cultivated and we can't catch her, so obviously she is very dangerous. Barnard, the author, in a series of opportunistic articles in a popular Afrikaans weekly, *Die Huisgenoot* (which I saw later), suggested – or had it suggested to him – that if it had not been for Yolande I'd never have gotten involved in politics; that she instigated and probably master-minded my acts. Well, hen-pecked I am . . . but not to that point!

moment, for what does one have to say at a time like that? There was also an observer coming from Switzerland on behalf of an international organization of jurists. I tried to communicate with him rapidly in French whilst being taken past him, but that did not succeed. I saw neither hide nor hair of any of the more prominent literary figures. Fear was at their throat. Fear and *Schadenfreude*. They had rejected me entirely by then; they were not going to be identified in any way with a terrorist.

The State summed up its case and asked for the imposition of the minimum sentence of five years. Dr Yutar even allowed himself the luxury of advancing a certain number of grounds for leniency, in other words, justifying his asking for the minimum sentence only. My defence then made their final statements and on the same day, with hardly a break, the judge who had sat there nodding away in his sleep, pronounced my conviction and his sentence.* 'Mumble, mumble, mumble . . .' he said; 'You are a very dangerous man . . . mumble, mumble, mumble. . . If we let you continue the results are unforeseeable, blood and death . . . mumble, mumble, mumble. . .' And then nine years. Perhaps I should write – And: then nine years. Or – And then nine: years.

When someone says to you 'Nine years' like that (like saying 'the white cow'), it's like dropping a mantle of steel on your chest, and yet, at the same time, the sense of it does not penetrate. You cannot come to grips with it.

I was allowed to say goodbye to my father. I felt the need to console him. I didn't want the avid crowd of vultures hanging around outside – those sick ones who'd come to stare at the misery of other people – I didn't want them to see my father weeping. After that there was the indignity of having souvenir photos taken by my brother – of me, my father and a team of hunters all around us. Thus we have the beast, mated, tamed.

And then back down to the cells with the sad explanations deeply gouged into the walls. *To USSR with love*, or *A hippy was held here for no reason*, or *David Makwana was here for kak*, and *Kilroy is here for terrorism*, or *Make love to Jesus*, or the warning *All you murderers look out for justice Theron, he's got ropes on his brain*,

*But he did ask my age first, and then remarked that I was in the 'flower' of my years. I never worked out whether he considered this an aggravating factor when considering sentence.

Good luck, or, very succinctly, just *The palace of injustice*. And further *You Nats, today you have the say, but just wait till the Chinks get here, then I will laugh*. And sadly *Time is but the thought of getting closer to hell*.

I was escorted from the court cells to Compol, made to sit in a corner of Huntingdon's office. The door giving onto the corridor hid my presence. Huntingdon, like a hyena, had pretended to be aggrieved and surprised by the severity of my sentence, but now, as he sat there behind his desk, two of his colleagues suddenly came in, not seeing me, to congratulate him warmly on the success that he had obtained. They knew all along that he'd get me, as he said he would. There was some discomfort all round when they became aware that I was there. People came and went. Fellow-detainees were released and welcoming parties were gathering on the sidewalk. Released people had to be booked out, had to sign for the pawed-over, desecrated possessions returned to them. It took time. Interrupted lives could be resumed. A youngish BOSS agent who happened to be in the offices was asked to *hou vas* me for a while. He told me how one hunts jack rabbits by jeep and agile Bushman tracker in the Kalahari. Then he took me past the blind liftman to the toilet and conspiratorily poured me a large paper cup of white wine, a last one for a long time 'for old time's sake'. He handed me back into the care of Huntingdon and I was worried that he might smell the alcohol on my breath and punish me!

My interrogator then allowed a journalist by the name of Jack Viviers to come right into the heart of the fortress. It was time for the loyal collaborator to get his morsel of recognition and Huntingdon needed to preen some more. Jack Viviers was later to write a book on my two trials, so obviously inspired and dictated by the political police. He was their man doing the fetching and carrying and smearing for them. In return he would get his scoops and build up a reputation as a security expert. Mr Jack Viviers probably forgot about the possibility that the day could come when I may be out again.*

In this shocked state in which I found myself he came with the

*At the time of dictating this (August 1983), Viviers actually works in London with the traditional cover of the flatfoot abroad: foreign correspondent. He had the cheek, some time after my release, to try and contact me in Paris!

characteristic Afrikaans hypocrisy of softness and sympathy for one's dilemma. 'Please,' he said, 'won't you just write a few lines for me, personally, in memory of today?' And stupidly I did so. Of course, the next day this was splashed over the front page of his newspaper.

I'm then driven back to Maximum Security by Huntingdon. No longer can I look, hopefully, on Beverly Hills as a way-station; it would have to be home for as long as I could see into the future. No more excursions down to the court, no more winking at friends or acquaintances in the audience, no more private suits or soft shirts, all that was finished now. . . . He takes me all the way in.

In my cell the implications finally hit me and I have what one could only describe as a nervous breakdown – with this monstrous man sitting there in a chair, hidden behind his dark glasses, watching me, finally reaching the apotheosis of his own search for satisfaction. He goes all white in the face. To him it must have been like an orgasm.

Then he starts talking to me, telling of how he'd not always been like that, of how naïve he'd also been when young, of his hard life as a constable, of coming home on his motorcycle to a small flat and a young wife, of hitting the bottle too hard (and bottling up emotions), about being posted to the Illegal Diamond Buying Branch (which was an education in treachery and play-acting and greed), and then becoming the State President's bodyguard (so overwhelmed to still get the occasional postcard from him), but how this type of life, the life of an interrogator, Mr Investigator, how it has changed him over the years.

It was a miserable experience: this man with his stunted psyche needing the satisfaction of destroying his opponent and at the same time lucid enough to perhaps perceive the extent of moral decrepitude and corruption such an attitude implies.

INSERT

Somewhere in Sri Lanka, the ancient Ceylon, the even more ancient Serendip, where at present Tamil prisoners are being massacred by their non-Tamil jailmates and where buses of Tamil passengers are stopped, the doors locked, gasoline poured over the vehicle with its trapped, gesticulating passengers, before fire is brought to devour everything (see how they dance, take a whiff of the stench, dear Mr I – that the compassionate ways of life of the Far East could not prevent such bestiality!) – somewhere in the highlands there's a temple with a mural showing Hare in the mouth of Lion. The lion does not close its jaws except, perhaps, gently, to save the little one from falling. It is said to be a picture of the goodness of Buddha. There is another one showing Crow flying along flip-a-flop with Fish in its beak, and a little further along the wall a whole area of skeleton fish. I have been told the interpretation of this one, but it has flown out of my mind. Man is a mythical beast.

On the door of the room where I work (the door is open to the breeze off the sea from Africa, it has no lock) the owner of the house has pinned a sheet of paper with an Italian text. It is called *da Una Certa Enciclopedia Cinese,** and translates: 'The animals are divided into (a) those belonging to the Emperor, (b) embalmed ones, (c) domesticated ones, (d) suckling pigs, (e) sirens, (f)fabled ones (or fabulous ones?), (g) dogs running loose, (h) included in the present classification, (i) which are madly agitated, (j) innumerable ones, (k) indicated by a pelt finer than the skin of the camel, (l) et cetera, (m) which make love, (n) which from a distance look like flies.'

*A note to my translators: my corrupt translation, I learned later, was from a corrupt Italian text, which was a translation from Jorge Luis Borges' *Otras inquisiciónes,* which he had translated in part from the Chinese.

6

Which from a Distance Looks like Flies

I understand, Mr Investigator, that you want me to go back in time a little bit to try to explain to you rapidly what this is all about, what Okhela was all about, and how I got myself into this mess in the first place. Well, I cannot give you the whole history, but I must indicate that what ended up in court started with an appreciation of the political situation which, forgive me for saying so, Mr Investigator, I still subscribe to. It further reflected, personally, the need of a person coming from a specific background, from a certain country, to become involved and to live out the convictions he had, based on a complex situation, on that appreciation, and naturally also on the dreams which he shared and still shares with the vast majority of the people in that country. I remain convinced, now more than ever, of the sickness down there, because I had the dubious honour of seeing it in effect very closely. I believe, more than ever, that the system existing in South Africa is against the grain of everything that is beautiful and hopeful and dignified in human history; that it is a denial of humanity, not only of the majority being oppressed but of the minority associated with that oppression; that it is profoundly unjust; that it is totally corrupted and corrupting; that it is a system with which nobody ought to be allowed to live. It is to the honour of large parts of the world that they reject Apartheid, even if only half-heartedly so, even if for self-serving reasons, even if it is instructed by a false sense of being culturally superior to the 'Boers', even if the outrage is intended to divert attention from the dirt on their own doorsteps.

But what does one do if you are White, if in fact you are part of the privileged minority in power? When you come in revolt against such a system, how do you oppose it effectively? One of the effects – and perhaps it was intended to be so – of Apartheid has been that it has splintered the opposition to the system. The gulf between Black and White, or between Whites and all the others, is so enormous that in fact we are strangers to one another. The only common ground we share is Apartheid. But we interpret that ground differently. We are conditioned, each in his own way, by the privileges and the iniquities of the system. To pretend differently would be taking and mistaking one's desires for reality.

How could I, as a White man, express my opposition to the system, which means to the exploitation and the degradation, effectively whilst identifying myself with the cause of the Black majority? How could I relate to them? I could do so on the plane of ideas, concerning the absolutes of justice and dignity and freedom, even of socialism.

I repeat: my revulsion to Apartheid could not only be because of what it is doing to all the 'un-Whites', could not be really resilient if motivated by a 'do-good' approach, but because of how it was affecting *me*. The corruption of the élite is the corruption of privilege and ease and power and paternalism. The panacea found by Whites who have twinges of doubt and bad conscience is often Liberalism: disdain with a patronizing mask.

Man suffers because of his separation from the boundless, Anaximander said. If there is a life force, Apartheid goes against it. Surely what we live towards is a greater, even metaphysical, integration, however hazardous and dangerous. And just as surely we are inspired to do so by a profound sense of brotherhood. Apartheid is a mutation of *power* and *greed*. No religion can justify it, except that warped doctrine the Afrikaners have fashioned from their desert faith. Their god is a cruel, White interrogator.

I could relate particularly on the grounds of socialism. The commitment of a whitish citizen of No Man's Land can, to my mind, only be an ideological one. To the so-called Black it is dictated by the daily necessity of the struggle for survival.

Mr Investigator, I think you will realize that I am trying to describe to you a situation whereby I felt it necessary to become involved in the freedom struggle. But I cannot, could not, do so within the framework of the existing political organizations. I have since many years given my allegiance and support to the African National Congress which is the political formation representing the majority of South Africans. It is an African nationalist organization, forbidden in the country; its leaders are either in prison or exile or fighting underground. But it is also an organization working in alliance with several others, and in fact the pacesetter of these organizations is the South African Communist Party. The SACP actually has the nerve centres of the liberation movement in its control.

I shall be more specific, Mr Investigator. The SACP has in its hands the secretariat of the ANC, the financial structure of the ANC, the control over the armed wing of the ANC which is called Umkhonto we Sizwe. It constitutes the major link between the ANC and its foreign supporters, both on a government level, that is, support coming from the socialist countries, and on the level of anti-Apartheid organizations scattered all over Western Europe. The SACP evidently also controls, through its intervention and by dint of being the intermediary, the facilities offered to the ANC for the military training of its future soldiers. Above all the SACP has outlined and enforces the ideology by which the ANC is guided.

All of this I do not trot out as criticism or as 'red-baiting' or to pour oil on the fires of the South African strategists and warlords. I believe that a communist party is by its very nature and by definition a power machine. It is shaped and intended with that one goal in mind: to obtain and to exercise power. In South Africa the SACP for a long time was not exactly popular among the African masses, because of its flirting in earlier years with the White labour movement which, as you know, Mr Investigator, is profoundly reactionary and pro-Nationalist Party. The SACP represents numerically a very restricted number of people. It is therefore necessary and inevitable if it wants to guide the revolutionary struggle, that it should work within the framework of the liberation movement. The interests and the goals of these two organizations married in the Revolutionary Council which is, to my knowledge, practically exclusively in the hands of members of the SACP, even if they sit there as representatives of the ANC. The goals and the intentions of these two organizations overlap but whereas the ANC is open to ideological influence from the West, according to the speeches from the dock of Nelson Mandela at the time of his sentencing, and whereas the ANC is concerned primarily with liberation and the coming to power of the Black majority of the country, and whereas the ANC sees its task in attempting to accomplish this as being free from the dictates of class analysis – the SACP, on the other hand, and again to my mind quite correctly, sees the liberation, the throwing off of the yoke of Apartheid, as only the first step in allowing the process of a profound transformation of the South African society into one which will be characterized by a socialist economy and by pervasive State control of the kind that we see in the Eastern European countries.

The SACP, your Honour, is in principle and in practice a multiracial, non-racist organization. It has among its members people from all the various cultural and linguistic and ethnic groupings in the country. And this was exactly where I and my friends felt that we differed from them – not that we weren't yearning for the day when race or sex or language would no longer be a consideration when forming a political party, but because we thought that the SACP was papering over the real problems of cultural awareness (after all, we've had Black Consciousness in the meantime!). We thought that by grouping Black and White – in this way, at this level – in the same organization, one was diminishing the effectiveness of the militants by confusing the feedback and making it difficult for people (with their daily experience of harsh Apartheid, of differences between experiences) to identify with the Party. (What a long sentence!) We furthermore, perhaps due to diverse leftist experiences during the sixties, felt a strong opposition to Stalinism – because it needs also to be pointed out that the SACP, being the oldest communist party on the African continent, and perhaps because of its numerical weakness, could probably be considered as the most rigidly loyal supporter of Moscow's foreign policy.* To my shame as a South African I have to admit that it was among the first organizations lauding the Soviet Union for its invasion of Hungary and again later of Czechoslovakia. It is not a party which admits much internal questioning. It is finally, and that was another of our

*Stalinism, or Stalinist, in this sense, means to be doctrinaire; to always follow 'Mother's' line, however often it may be revised or changed; and to be bureaucratic in the extreme. Also to be non-democratic by means of the astute formula of 'centralized democracy'.

criticisms, not a very effective communist party, just as, in my opinion, the African National Congress is not a very effective liberation movement. (For the sake of power the party breaks the revolution. It occupies terrain which could be far more vigorously used by other formations. What happened in Zimbabwe must be a dire warning to the SACP. If ever there were to be an uprising, the party would in all likelihood be engulfed and lose its grip on the course of events.)

We were proud of the ANC's record as the oldest, most respectable, political organization in South Africa and of its kind on the African continent. Well, it is also by now the greyest, the most ancient, and perhaps eventually one ought to point out that it has squandered its assets and was only lukewarm in the struggle when more thorough opposition might have swung things the other way. But that is only a very superficial criticism because at the same time it must be admitted that after all these years of being illegal in the country – being in exile since 1960 – it is at this stage of its history more powerful and has wider support among the African population, among the so-called Coloureds too, than ever before. Is that not a victory? (These personal remarks about the ANC are made in passing: even if I were that capable I should not pretend to be analysing the ANC or its history here.)

Be that as it may. I repeat, our criticism of the SACP was coming from the left, and it was informed by the way in which we saw the profile of the Party *then,* clearly or obscurely. And the above are some of the objective causes for the coming into being of Okhela.

In practical terms: I was recruited during the early 1970s for the specific purpose of creating forms of aid to militant White opposition to the Apartheid regime in the country, of establishing these points of aid abroad, of helping the White militants in obtaining a basic training when abroad, permitting them to carry on the struggle clandestinely upon their return to the country. The people forming these organizations of assistance abroad, on behalf of the ANC, were grouped in an organization called 'Solidarité', with as its responsible executive a man called Henri Curiel. (I'm jumping in history: at that point of course I didn't know what his name was.)

I was told about the activities of Solidarité glance by glance, a little in the way one is taught to look in the mirror. Over the years I built up a fairly good working knowledge of how they operated. I may mention, Mr Investigator, for your footnotes, that Solidarité essentially grew out of a spirit of resistance during the Second World War. These people are imbued with the same thirst for independence and freedom, and tried to answer to the practical need of maintaining and propagating and continuing the methods which years of occupation had forced upon them. By the nature of their commitments they were in contact with liberation movements from all over the world and also with organizations representing political or social minorities in various countries, such as the Kurds or the Basques, in their struggle for independence from oppression.

I'm going to have to take short cuts. Everything I'm telling you now is known to the agents of No Man's Land. It turned out later on that they had infiltrated over the years both the ANC and the SACP, and Solidarité, and who knows, perhaps even Okhela. So I'm not giving away any secrets, but it's tedious to have to repeat this type of story (an interesting little turn-off from the path of our story is the fact that the court records of both trials, the first, and the second one we are coming to, disappeared from the Pretoria Supreme Court archives; I don't know who has them, I don't know for what purpose they are not available; mysteriously nobody seems to know where these records are if they still exist). But we won't worry, will we, Mr I, since I'm giving you these confessions. The blood of my heart.

During 1973, earlier, in '72, I created with a few fellow White South Africans in exile the kernel of a political formation which we called 'Okhela'. Very rapidly we organized some clandestine visits to South Africa and we were able to extend our support in the country in the same way as we were able abroad to extend the scope of our activities. When I was caught later in 1975 we were, however, still only in the beginning processes of establishing this organization and of defining, in consultation with those active on the ground in the country, the aims and the forms of our activities.

Nevertheless, for what it's worth, let me admit that during the few years of our existence we managed, *inter alia*, to penetrate the South African embassy in West Germany and to lay our hands on enough secret material to prove that the two governments – Bonn and Pretoria – were flaunting the international decisions of withholding nuclear research knowledge from the South Africans. In fact, we were able to show conclusively that there was collaboration with the Germans enabling the South Africans to start their own programme manufacturing, ultimately, nuclear arms. Similarly we were able to lay bare the machinations of several international oil companies in Rhodesia, how they circumvented the then officially applied oil boycott policy, and naturally the type of aid they were receiving from South Africa in particular. These are not negligible accomplishments. I am not so sure that we, at our level, in our context, were not at least as effective as the officially established anti-Apartheid groups and the representatives of the liberation movement abroad.

We had also succeeded in obtaining the promise of substantial sums of money directed to the nascent Black trade unions in South Africa and we were going to have our contacts in the country – who were instrumental in the formation of the Black unions, although not necessarily part of them – channel this money to the intended recipients. To be able to do that, though, we needed to establish a trade union office abroad, in Europe, manned by a Black and a White trade unionist from inside.

So, Mr Investigator, briefly, the purpose of my illegal trip into South Africa was, first of all, to recruit two such people and to make it possible for them to leave the country, most probably illegally, because it was expected that at least one of them would be a banned person and therefore not allowed to travel freely. Thus – to move these people across the border, to receive them in Europe, to install them, and to make it possible for them to function. And further than that my task was to go and see for myself what exactly the scope for Okhela-type activities was inside the country; to talk to our underground people there; to submit to them the proposed platform; to debate with them the basic issues: our stance, our attitude towards the liberation movements, our attitude to violence, how we see or saw our role in the White community, whether our intention of working in the

White community only was correct, the need to stimulate and mobilize creative *alternative* thinking breaking the mould of Apartheid *thinking* and abetting the coming about of future structures by *conceiving* them), the function of culture, the link-up with outside, the strategy to be followed and the tactics we could allow ourselves – all the million little things which go into knitting a tight, loyal, effective organization.

Well, that is the nice Walter Mitty (or Robin Hood) side of the story; the darker side is that I was betrayed even before I arrived there. You can push me, Mr Investigator, you can tear this up and ask me to write again, you can fish for my tongue with a tuning fork, and still I shall not be able to tell you who exactly betrayed me. Yes, of course, I have my doubts and I have my guesses, and I know objectively in whose interests it might have been to do so. (Don Espejuelo taught me to *think* through the haze of self-deception and the smokescreen of grey disinformation by always asking: *cui bono*?) I can also divine the motivation of some people, perhaps even very close to me, who thought that in doing so, in exposing me, they could provoke a certain situation – a catharsis which would benefit the struggle. All I know is first: very few people, very few indeed, were in the know. Secondly: it was not my idea to go down there but I had to submit myself to the majority decision to do so. Stupidly vain, when told there were certain things which only I could do, it touched me, and I fell for it. And, of course, thirdly, I felt a moral commitment, a necessity to go. How could I pretend to want to lead an organization of which some of the members would have to do dangerous things if I was not willing to do so myself? (Yes, you see how inept, how inexperienced, how vulnerable to blackmail – or whitemail – I was!) I went, and I'm going back to the beginning of my story.

And I add to that beginning of my story this little subsidiary thought, seeing as how there are a few more loops of the spool left for this particular chapter, and that is: that my dear, ineffective, fat, institutionalized friends in the liberation movement who got me involved in the first place, those professional diplomats, those living off the fat of the suffering of our people back home and who've done so for years and will do so until they die, not really worried about ever going back, the suave politicians – they then dropped me as an embarrassingly hot potato the moment I was caught, and they avoid me now like the plague; because I am that of course: I am the plague. . . .

INSERT

Very fascinating reflections may flow from an appraisal of clandestine political activity or from the evaluation of any one underground political organization. Underground organizations, secret societies, seem to be a phenomenon of our time but they have quite a long history of course. Suffice it to say that nearly always the decision to go underground is imposed by conditions in the country where the political struggle takes place. Underground struggle is one expression among many of the continuing fight against fascism, totalitarianism, sometimes colonialism, even imperialism. As one of the characteristics identifying a totalitarian state is precisely that it prohibits any form of effective opposition to the party or class in power, one may say that therefore, the rulers of such a country make clandestine opposition to them ineluctable. They are the ones who make the rules, they create the conditions. But this is only partially true. There is and there has always been a line of thinking or *fascio* of theories that values underground action for its own sake. It is true that it is, as near as possible, a clean form of political activity divested of the more mundane horse-trading and compromising of everyday politics. There is a certain purity of thinking. There is often a heightened political consciousness because the awareness must be applicable to direct and nearly always immediate translation into action. There is therefore not the gap between theory and practice which so often is a debilitating aspect of political life. Clandestine activity imposes a rigorous discipline on those participating in it. It satisfies the Spartan urges we all seem to have. It brings about a greater confidence in oneself; you quickly become more aware of the value of confidence – where it is justified and where not – since people have confidence in you and entrust you with work which by definition is perilous, and you yourself have to continually test the canons of confidence, the extent to which you can use confidence in your relations with others. One finds great generosity among people involved in clandestine activity. Danger and fear tend to weave a more solid cloth of interdependence and mutual support among the various members. You may meet somebody passing through on a discreet mission – you have confidence in the contact who referred him to you, you abide by the rules of not asking him what his work is about or where exactly he comes from and where he's headed – and although you may not see him again, or perhaps *because* you'll never see him again, you are willing to do just about anything for him. Underground work generates loyalty. Sure, the training for it and the circumstances under which it takes place form a measure of conditioning. Unquestioned loyalty, discipline – these are some of the ways in which the conditioning makes itself felt. Since information cannot circulate freely you are willing provisionally to put the best face on even incomprehensible actions of a comrade. Pending an eventual explanation you withhold criticism; you trust him, you have to trust him because discipline, confidence, generosity, loyalty and trust are the basic components without which there can be no clandestine political work. It is true too that in such a milieu you may get to know a comrade whom you perhaps only meet briefly once a week far better than you would know lifelong friends. You may never find out the real name of this comrade, you have no idea of his situation in life – whether he is a priest or a doctor or an electrician or a soldier – but since your dealings with him will be direct and guided by the characteristics I have indicated, it will be as if the useless accretions normally clogging up and covering your relationships with people can now be jettisoned. When you are a mole or a shadow you cannot afford to lie to a comrade, and you know that neither can he try to pull the wool over your eyes. Your relations are based on rock-bottom mutual needs. Clandestine action teaches you to check and to counter-check every move you make: this is what it ought to do at least. You learn to think coherently, to the point, but not to trust your own thinking; to make up a mental checklist to go through again and again. You acquire, like a second nature, the instinct of being aware of your surroundings. When you book into a hotel you automatically look for the alternative exits, and you do not relax before you've checked out the quarter in which it is located, to get a feel of the topography, of the structure of your environment – where the danger points such as police stations are, how possible escape routes can be recognized. The same attitude of checking and counter-checking is applied in your communications and dealings with comrades: they know that you do this, they do the same, and the knowledge serves again to strip excess and unnecessary sentiments from the sinews of your relationships with others. Ah, what a grand game. . .

Some believe that underground work is of itself a transforming agent, that it slots in with, say, the theory of a *fuoco* as expressed by Guevara – that is, that the underground work of a small, dedicated group using effective means can, as it were, liberate specific areas of thinking and of appreciation, which may lead to them being exemplary and encouraging the establishing of other, similar zones of freedom. It – this work, or this type of action – is supposed also to form strong cadres for the future. True, to the extent that it inserts itself in a long and glorious line of historical struggle and similarly to the extent that it brings one into direct contact with all the implications of political action. It may well forge dedicated revolutionaries. It also favours convinced internationalism. You'll find, Mr Investigator, a tendency among clandestine action groups of various countries to help one another, even when they are not in total ideological agreement. I think it comes from a sentiment of fraternity, of being outlaws together, of being among the few just. Practically by definition underground organizations are small groups inclined to identify with other small groups elsewhere; and then too, the techniques made use of by clandestine militants are quite specialized so that one may find a situation, for instance, in which several groups tap the same specialist forger. But even beyond that, the very fact of having opted for such action usually implies that one has established a certain distance between yourself and the traditional, overt political groupings in your country. You are thus less bound by the nationalist symptoms that these groups may manifest. In choosing to go underground one moves out of the family constituted by legal or aboveground political parties. Frontiers become less important; one sees the struggle going beyond borders, growing from similar conditions in many points of the world. Also, you must not forget that clandestine work, as we know it now, is a distant descendant of the work and the theories embodied in various Internationals – the Comintern, for example, which was consciously internationalist. And then, as this type of action nearly always grows from a class analysis, it is understandable that it cannot be bound by the historical accidents which constitute different states. If we say 'class analysis' we are referring to conditions and objective agents creating similar classes and relationships between classes all over the world. We tend to call clandestine work a form of political expression proper to the working class. It has a history, as I've said, as old as the world itself though: from ancient secret sects through the Chinese *tongs* to the *illuminati* and the Italian carbon burners and the Bolsheviks. (Always there was the fascination of being a member of an exclusive group – the mystery of initiation – but too, the lure of concentrated power.) But do modern versions like the Tupamaros, like the Weathermen, like the *brigatisti*, have much to do with the working class? It is interesting when one looks at the continuous upheavals, revolutions, *coups d'état*, plots and counterplots, insurrections and uprisings in Latin America, to reflect that this may very well be the legacy that Italian exiles round about the time of Garibaldi took to that part of the world. I think we see it in its most baroque and sometimes absurd form there – *à la* García Márquez. In a certain way the relationship between clandestine activity and more open political action resembles the type of relationship between an avant-garde party and other mass expressions of political striving such as trade unions. Many of the theorists of clandestinity secretly hope to play the same type of leading role as a Leninist party is supposed to play *vis-à-vis* other fronts and political groupings.

But, and a very big *but*, must be: that all the above is a very romantic view of underground work. Is it really always necessary? Has it ever been successful, apart from, in some instances, making it possible for the clandestine activist to come to power? Does the need for such a type of action always correspond to a truly rigorous dissection of the conditions in the area you choose to operate in? Have all the other alternatives been exhausted? In South Africa, for example, we have a very poor tradition of underground work. We don't even have, as you'd find in Europe or Latin America, a generally shared code of conduct to be adhered to when confronted by the police. Our clandestine operators are amateurs; very often they have not been prepared for the dangers that face them when trapped. I was once told that, until quite recently anyway, the average time of survival for an underground militant in South Africa was barely eight days. But to come back to my argument: true, all effective political opposition to the Nationalist government has been outlawed, and in answer to that the underground organizations have opted for armed struggle. (To be generous to them one must hope that the armed struggle will make them, also individually, stronger.) But again – have we finally found it impossible to bring about change in any other way? Have we veritably thought *through* all the negative connotations and results of armed struggle, and the dangers to the political ideas, which we cherish, of underground work itself? Isn't it very often just a Boy Scout game? Adults carrying forward the excitement the child has when teasing fire or running round the garden for a game of hide-and-seek? Because it must be underlined that we have seen over the years the aberrations that clandestine activity gave rise to. We've seen, as in the case of the *brigatisti* or of the Red Army factions in Germany and Japan, how the means corrupt the men, how such groups become a law unto themselves, so infatuated with their own analysis, so turned in upon themselves and so cornered when these analyses prove to be incorrect that the only way out seem to be even more vigorous forms of terrorism. Maybe one day there will be a new analytical science called structurology, close to but not the same as structuralism. It would concern itself more with the study of the using of structure for its own end, the satisfaction derived from that. This – the need for structuring when involved in underground activity, because the matrix is a unit made up of cells, with information strictly channelled, with walls separating sector from sector, with a hierarchy which cannot be questioned – all this makes of underground work a very undemocratic process and it constitutes a structure which can be a very manoeuvrable vehicle for whoever happens to occupy the central nerve point. Cells, colonies of grave dwellers, are so easily exploitable. The hand demands no accounting of the glove. It is rather as if such a unit, to survive, must remain in quarantine. So we see the biological result that, as with other isolated cells, it loses some of its normal reactions against attacks from without. It becomes less immune to the sicknesses that every structure, every political party is subject to. It therefore easily becomes sectarian. And in a last analysis – what is it that makes an underground cell of militants any different from a spy cell, an intelligence network of the masters? Don't we here see the mirror and its own mirror image?

We should put our sights much lower. Maybe we ought to settle for the slower processes; maybe we must, very paradoxically, extend our confidence to the people and whatever mass organizations the people may throw up. Ah, but that means that we have to accommodate the very notion that our way, and particularly our goals, may be diluted or changed completely . . . since we shall be losing control over the evolution that we become part of. Isn't that what 'power to the people' implies? It is more important, I think, to know how to get from Long Street to Shortmarket Street than to go and write in the dust on the moon. The difficulty, Mr I, is not to learn to fly but how to walk on earth. So, if I may sum up: the struggle itself is a means of political awareness, of cultural awakening, ultimately of social and economic transformation. But to cling to the idea that we can make pure and honest militants is under-estimating human nature. It is subscribing to the fallacy of a theory which postulates that human character can be transformed, and that there is a measurable progress in the quality of human intercourse. The liberating concept is exactly to give over to the people the way a fish gives itself over to the sea; and also, despite, or because of the watery taste of failure in the mouth, to continue struggling. *To do* without necessarily believing that there ever was any sense in the doing. I agree, Mr Investigator, here you also have the formula for your most pure fascist who will kill or extort without there being any reason for it or any sense to it. But that is not quite what I'm turning over in my words. I mean that a struggle for freedom and justice is such a natural instinct that one fights for it, again in the words of a Chinese writer, as the fish struggles for water. I am intrigued though, by my interest for structures. What I've just uttered with a twitch of originality about 'doing without believing that it's worth doing', or that there could be an outcome, seems to show me that therefore I am enthused by the form for its own sake. By the word for its spine. By emptiness for its falling. By the tree for its quality as an enclosure of light and by the mind as an enclave of dark mindlessness. Why do I bother to confess, to transcribe the confessions, to package and parcel it in a book for you, Mr Investigator, if I believe that it has no use, that it would not change a single gleam on a hair of a fly held in the mind as the talisman of an image, that it would not come up to the standards of aesthetics – beauty and all that jazz – and that it will not even be a particularly searing human document, bringing nothing extraordinary, nothing we didn't know or is not a banal description of what has become commonplace in so many countries? It does not unlock the passes to a secret Tibet and does not have the flavour of one of Sheherazade's reports to her lover late at night. Why then? What is this obsession for feeling structures, for flowing with the rhythm? Is it to escape objectivity? Is it to get away from the strictures of treachery? Is it to loosen the grip that time may have on us? If I have no end I can have no beginning and therefore there can be no ageing. Yes, if there is nothing beyond the organic reality of pattern and repetition and illusion and rhyme and rhythm, then the idea of breaking a structure becomes exciting. The concept of the fuck-up is a liberating idea. Freedom is accepting unfreedom, denying that they are opposites, reading one in the other, and going beyond.

Today I am not sorry that I went through the experience, be it marginal, of deepening the consciousness of structures which underground activity implied. As a matter of principle I am not sorry about having been through any experience. What one has gone through becomes a new corridor outlining the innards of the labyrinth; it is a continuation of the looking for the Minotaur, that dark centre which is the I (eye), that Mister I: which is a myth, of course. The thing is to kill the devourer of virgins and not to forget to take down the black sails of the soul when rounding the cape of the home port.

Now, Mr Investigator, if talking shit was grass, I would have been through the donkey's arse a long time ago. Or if it were a sin, I would have been any old priest's lifelong joy.

I don't think I need to continue this exhibition of myself by weaving more tales about Okhela or about Solidarité and what they stood for. I'm abbreviating, but I must just briefly talk about three people I got to know in this way.

Some time after I'd been recruited for clandestine activity, I wrote, with a comrade called Yves, a paper on the aims and the methods of recruitment. Maybe I'll show it to you one day if I can find the hiding place where I've tucked it away. Still, I was recruited and the very concept of what I was to do was implanted subtly and gradually in my mind by my recruiters. The man directly responsible for me in the beginning, the 'elder brother' (in Intelligence slang he would be known as the 'handler'), was a young American whom I knew as 'Richard'. Was that perhaps why my name became Dick? It is a privilege, when recruiting someone, for the father or the elder brother to name the new member. He was about the same age as I was. He had been in the American Air Force in Vietnam, probably received specialist training while there, deserted and was one of those who found his way via Japan to a sanctuary in Paris. He had been taken up by Solidarité. He was bright, dedicated, thin but wiry, energetic and strangely effaced – or, more precisely, with the kind of face that would fit in and pass unnoticed anywhere. I saw him in different transformations. Not much was altered and yet he was a completely different nonentity every time. He left Paname quite some time before my débâcle, but before doing so it was he who conceived, at least in writing, of the Atlas groups for which I took responsibility and which were to be the underpinning of Okhela. What shook me to my socks was, when during my interrogation in Pirax, I was suddenly shown a photo of Richard. Well, two photos – front and profile – taken by the FBI in California somewhere. According to the date underneath, it was taken even before I'd known him, and chalked, you know, on that kind of false blackboard one must hold under the chin, was his real name. It makes me think that finally nothing is unknown. Perhaps somewhere everything is known about everyone and it is only plucked out and made to surface when the need is there to do so. So that underground activity becomes just an elaborate form of self-delusion.

The second person I wish to salute in passing, now for the last time, is Henri Curiel. Seldom have I met someone so single-minded and so warped by his single-mindedness. In my own vernacular I called him 'Spider', sometimes shortened to 'Spi'; because, yes, this theory advanced by the Greyshits and their colleagues elsewhere that Curiel was a KGB operative had crossed my mind too. It's not really so far-fetched. (He himself laughed when relating how he'd been accused, at different times, of spying for any and all conceivable foreign powers. But it is true also that some of his oldest friends quit Solidarité because, they say, he was using it as a vehicle to serve the Soviets.) He never made any bones about his total commitment to orthodox Soviet communism, call it Stalinism, and I often felt that he was a Secretary-General in search of a Party. Too, he did have his hands uncontestedly on an organization which, at its own level, was a perfect information-gathering machine, perched at the crossroads where many leftist organizations, particularly from the Third World, met. Not only was he in a position to know all about these organizations and to give them real aid – although I am convinced that Solidarité was never involved in violence, either for themselves or on behalf of others (Where does it start? What is the first step in the process ending in unavoidable violence? And was its non-commitment to violence why it was 'tolerated' by the French services?) – but it was also well situated to influence. Given Curiel's ideals it is only reasonable to assume that he would have used Solidarité to achieve his goals, and I can't blame him for it. I would have done the same. I don't think he was trying to dupe anybody, though there were levels of confidence and there was manipulation: hence the 'Spider'. He was a fine and a subtle thinker, a master in the concrete ways to bring a mind to bear on political problems. He was an inspiring man: a limpid ideologue, and a man who remained committed to the better instincts in mankind. Never did he lose sight of the ongoing eternal struggle for justice and a slightly larger measure of freedom. Never did he waver in his belief that it is possible, if the right forces are mobilized, structurally to transform society for the betterment of humanity.

And the third, a man close to my heart, a Latin American romantic, the archetypal 'colonel'. Pierre was his name. Not his real name. Mr Investigator, when you write up your notes one day, take the pains to transcribe Pierre's story of how, as a dedicated communist even before the war, he joined the Republican forces in Spain and from there passed straight into the Résistance in France, which is when he attained the rank of colonel. He it was who organized the freeing of a number of resistance fighters, captured by the German occupying troops, from a prison in Perpignan. After the war he returned to his native Brazil and after some sojourns in Moscow, which were enough to disillusion him with traditional communism or the lack of it, and after disagreeing with the strategy of the Brazilian communist party, he, like Marighela, left and formed his own party called the Revolutionary Communist Party of Brazil. Captured by Brazilian police, he was very severely tortured. Together with nineteen of his comrades he was exchanged against an abducted Swiss ambassador in Latin America. It was one of the first incidents of its kind. They were flown out to Algeria, a country then still committed enough to revolution to want to accept them, and after living there for a few years he returned to France where he carried on his underground work. I met him there late in his life: a tall man, distinguished, beautiful grey hair, blue eyes, regal bearing, relaxed, full of wisdom and humour. He was still trying to enunciate what he called 'the laws of social transformation', but with humility, and a generosity and kindness and enthusiasm and a youthful spirit that I shall never forget. To Richard, in whatever deep cover, with whatever wild beard he has grown to survive, to Henri whose blood was splashed over the grey cement of Paris, and to Pierre,* who has lost his memory but not his peaceful enjoyment of life – I wish to pay homage. I embrace them.

*Pierre's son, who took over the reins from his father – not that the old man has ever retired – has adopted a little boy. Day by day the boy's genes are imposing themselves and he is visibly growing blacker. 'My grandson is looking healthier every time I see him,' Pierre laughs, 'and more and more like me!'

7

I am the Plague

My going, my being there, was contrary to all the principles of underground organization.

After receiving my false passport from Solidarité – Curiel was under the impression that I was going to use it for visiting Swaziland where I would be meeting White militants coming from South Africa – and after having arranged with him means of retaining contact during my absence, I flew off to Rome. I had also agreed with Schuitema, who had spent the period preparing for the trip in Paris and was going to fly to South Africa via London, also on a false passport, on the ways of coordinating our activities.

Before leaving I had a last meeting with Curiel who dramatically decided to tell me his real name. Like removing the last barrier between us. In one of those faceless apartments where we used to rendezvous he wrote his name on a slip of paper, showed it to me, and then destroyed it. (He did not swallow it!) Why am I now reminded of the kiss of death? We talked for a while. He had the knack of talking out of the side of his mouth without moving his lips – to frustrate lipreaders in public places. Over the phone he had a grey voice. He knew that he was being watched, of course. From time to time he changed the *centrale*, by means of which we kept contact, because it had become unsafe. Several people who had worked with Solidarité over the preceding years had tried to warn me off. They considered the group to be thoroughly penetrated. Watch, they told me, how they are 'allowed' to carry on their minor activities, but whenever they attempt a major operation it is always blown wide open. I was convinced that Curiel knew, or suspected, my true destination. At times, I thought, his hearing aid wasn't functioning very well. I shook his hand and found the stairs.

I arrived in Rome, where I stayed with one of our Atlas people.

There I altered my appearance slightly, shaving off my beard, retaining my moustache, combing my hair differently and donning a pair of heavy-rimmed glasses. I went through my outfit carefully to remove any traces of my previous personality. Armed with my new, or rather used but altered, passport in the name of Galaska, I went to the South African embassy there and applied for a visa, which was granted to me without a hitch. I'd never met the Galaska who is the original owner of the passport – but a few days after my arrest Huntingdon, pleased as a cat who has been at the cream, showed me an extract of a communication they had received from Paris with the full particulars and the photo of the real Christian Galaska – an open-faced young man who never dreamed that he had a shadow who would end up doing time for terrorism. I booked my flight with South African Airways.

It was late July. The grapes were starting to ripen. My friend in Rome accompanied me to the airport. I was quite intrigued by the security check at the point of departure and watched the X-raying of my luggage, particularly since I had hidden in my luggage some very incriminating items. In the false cover of one book there was a copy of the proposed Okhela manifesto, and in another several newly printed blank passports of the kind used by Blacks only when crossing the South African border to neighbouring territories. We had thought that these might come in handy later, and in any event, they would have constituted a gift for our militants in the country, reinforcing their usefulness for Blacks who may have to leave the country surreptitiously. We had to win a place on the market. A very big, red summer sun was bleeding to death over the ancient city of Rome when we boarded our flight at Fiumicino airport. It made me think of Africa, as dust always does.

There was one stop-over in Portugal. What was noteworthy was that, after having been allowed to disembark and to wander around the airport, before being allowed back on board we were body-searched and our luggage was checked not by Portuguese security officials but by two South African security policemen travelling on the same flight.

It was a long, tedious journey. Some time towards the end, before arriving at Jan Smuts, while we were still flying over the withered Northern Transvaal, one of the air hostesses on board started a conversation with me, asking me where I was going and what I intended doing there. White South Africans are always keen to sell their country. I was acutely aware of the security man sitting not much further down in the back of the plane and pretended to be just a normal tourist not knowing much about my destination. Her name was Anna van Niekerk, and before landing she gave me her address and telephone number with the invitation to call her if I felt the need for anybody to show me around Johannesburg.

We arrived and I passed through immigration and customs smoothly enough, although my heart was in my throat like a monkey in its cage. Now I suddenly found myself outside the airport building, standing in the shade of a pillar, trying to work out how I was going to get into town. But I was light-headed. What a sense of relief, of freedom nearly, after the long night, after the tension of not knowing what was waiting for me. One could smell the thin, dry air. White men in shorts and socks up to their knees and moustaches were striding purposefully through the halls. Black men in loose-fitting, sloppy overalls dog-trotted over the same floors, trying hard to pretend that they were on an errand to somewhere specific. No Man's Land. Another world. A world of genteel manners and old-fashioned picnics. And a vicious world. A land of harsh, dream-like beauty. Where you can feel your skin crawling. Ever on that last lip of annihilation. You had to shade your eyes against the glare of the sun. It was with a sensation of incredulity that I found myself there on a very bright, clear but slightly cold winter's day. The three occasions on which I'd been back in the country of my birth over the previous fifteen years had always been dramatic. It had been a shock every time to find one's feet back on that soil and to recognize so distinctly the sounds and the movements of the people. I changed some money, took a bus into town and found lodgings in the Victoria Hotel.

Then my foraging started. I went for a walk and, feeling that there was still too much of the old Breytenbach in me, I bought some dye to lighten the colour of my hair. Incidentally – that is how I later realized that the *boere* must have been on to me from the very first moment I set foot in No Man's Land – Huntingdon, after my arrest, told me of having found the very same bottle in the hotel room where I stayed. They must have been even quicker than the cleaning lady. I now had to find a way of alerting the person in Cape Town (who was the 'essential' link) to my imminent arrival. I did not dare to do so directly, so I had to set about finding a neutral person in Johannesburg who could effect the necessary communication for me. I also called Mrs Röhmer in Pretoria, who had been warned of my coming, since she had to confirm to someone in Europe that I had arrived safely. We agreed that I should take the train to Pretoria to meet her. It was wonderful to travel by train, jostled by the other commuters, an everyday face in the crowd; to flow with the movement, to stamp your feet the same way they do and to dip your hands in your pockets; to buy a local newspaper and to read the small ads page or the punter's tips for the afternoon races. Even, like a regular White, to find it perfectly normal that trains and station platforms and ticket offices should be racially segregated. I was home and nobody knew it.

This was the life! Yet, simultaneously, it was a disconcerting experience: I was the faceless face in the crowd, I was the invisible man. Around me there was the space of death. I was a zombie only, a visitor from another planet – painfully aware of pretending to be regular and accepting as normal the ways of an unruffled bigot. If someone had attempted to start a conversation with me, he or she would have found just emptiness behind the name and the how-are-you? What if I got involved in a street fight? The girl sitting in the same carriage as I (was it coincidence? Was she really innocently going to the same destination?) was a million miles away. My smile was dry and my chest made of paper. I was home and nobody knew it! It is perhaps just as well that I did not know, then, that I was shadowed everywhere I went, that I was never alone. Jiems Kont, ole Blue Eyes, told me later how he tailed Ashoop who had accompanied us to South Africa in 1973, how he loved to come as close as possible to him 'just to smell the fear'.

Röhmer fetched me at the station, we went for a drive, and I finalized with her the procedure for maintaining my link with Schuitema.

Days passed. I was at a loose end in Johannesburg. My part of the work was more to be in Cape Town, and then to follow up whatever developments might come from my meetings there. I phoned an old friend who was not related to my political work but whom I knew well enough to trust, conveyed to him the necessity of not saying anything to anybody about my being there, and made an appointment to meet him in the airport terminal near the main station. We met and got into his car. It was evening, with neon signs reflected on the pavement outside. We went to have a beer in a working-class pub, and it must have been as strange for him as it was for me to be standing there with the smell of stale alcohol and sawdust, men chucking darts in the background with grunts and whistling sighs, and to pretend that everything was just normal. He laughed and couldn't believe his eyes. (How much of my trip was to impress people like him? How much of it was an attempt to force a break in the contradictions in which I was caught up: the dreamer ensnared by political work – neglecting his art – and suffering from it; the exile who had never accepted the finality of his exile, whose roots were still in South Africa; the man, becoming a European, writing in an African language, with the world evoked by it, which no one around him understood? How much of it was suicidal? Or repentant homecoming?) He agreed to make contact with Paul in Cape Town and to arrange a meeting and a meeting place for me.

This was to take a few more days. In the hotel I received a call from Anna van Niekerk inviting me to go to the theatre with her. I acccepted and had to play the role of someone being shown around Hillbrow, learning a bit about South African cultural activities and nightlife. She proposed introducing me to some friends of hers the following evening, to experience the typical South African *braaivleis*. She duly took me along to the house of two young homosexuals. It was a revealing and amusing evening. My story was that I worked for a publishing firm in France – I had to justify my interest in South African literature after all! – and they fed me snippets of gossip and conjecture about South African authors. (They also, to make me feel at home, played records of Edith Piaf and Georges Moustakis.) They were all three of Afrikaner descent and it was highly entertaining to hear them discussing (and disagreeing about) Etienne Leroux and André Brink and Breytenbach who, they said, was not living in South Africa but in China, being married to a Chinese girl. Every once in a while, as South Africans tend to do, they would leave off speaking English and converse among themselves in Afrikaans – with me looking the blank dummy since I was not supposed to understand a living word. I did learn in this way, though, that Anna van Niekerk was having a very difficult love life, since it would seem her husband had left her for another man. Perhaps the two youngsters were friends of her husband.

A day or so later – it was a Sunday – while I was still waiting for my Cape Town connection to be made, she took me in her Peugeot 404 for a drive to see some sights of interest in the vicinity of Johannesburg. Again I had this double-visioned experience of being driven through a landscape seared by winter, the grass all white but the sky so blue it could crack at any moment, and yet to have to mouth the oohs and the ahs of someone seeing this for the first time. So that I sat there watching the land running through my eyes and at the same time watching myself watching myself. (In what room, Mr I? Which brother? Listening to what spool of the tape? Which closed circuit? What empty mirror? What semiotic structure? Which or what movement?) For the last couple of days I moved into Anna van Niekerk's flat as she was away on one of her periodic flights.

The Cape Town meeting was arranged. I was to find Paul at a certain time on the steps leading up to Jamison Hall on the campus of the University of Cape Town. But first my Johannesburg friend invited me to have lunch at his home with two other friends, writers both, and for a few hours we all sat around the kitchen table laughing and joking, with them being amused by my naked yellow face, and not forgetting to talk seriously also. Like self-respecting South Africans, they were wine connoisseurs and we smacked our lips; they stroked their beards and I my absence of one, singing the praises of this vintage or that one. We discussed books, your Honour. My friend is a fine cook and his wife is very shy. (One of them said, 'Perhaps we Afrikaners need a civil war again, with real shooting like during the Rebellion.') I was never going to make any attempt to recruit or even to inform them of the real nature of my visit: that would be abusing their friendship, but I knew instinctively and without even asking that they were going to respect my desire for anonymity. When later I was arrested and brought to trial they remained loyal to me and gave support to my wife, as they continued to do through all the years following. Whatever private doubts they may have had about my sanity or wisdom of the course of action that I chose, never did this interfere with the warm support and friendship that I got from them. I would step out of court with my hands in bangles and find them there, smiling and with their thumbs up. They are the Three Musketeers.

I flew down to Cape Town and booked into the Hotel Elizabeth in Sea Point. (The taxi which took me there was transporting another passenger, a middle-aged American on his way to some posh visitors' club. His presence irked me. But surely if he was what, in my paranoia, I thought he was, he wouldn't be getting into the same taxi with me?) From there, the next evening, I made my way first to town and thence by bus to Rondebosch and to the University of Cape Town, where I found Paul waiting for me, sitting in the dark on the steps.

It was a joyful reunion. We went for a walk through the quiet lanes of that area (with dons dreaming in cool rooms of quantum and Darwin and Freud and de Saussure) as the *katjiepierings* – little cat's saucers, as we say in Afrikaans, meaning gardenias softly spread their sweet-though-sad odour. I briefly sketched the outline of my mission. My young friend is by nature a very thorough and cautious person. He asked for time to think things over. I left the Okhela manifesto with him and it was agreed that he would facilitate my meeting several other White militants, some of whom we'd been in contact with before. I also asked him to be the intermediary between me and Thurston, which was no problem for him. Things were going well. (Those whom the gods wish to destroy . . .) Paul drove me back to the hotel on the back of his motorcycle and the wind touching our faces as we came over De Waal Drive was balmy. One could imagine, because it was dark, just out of sight in the bay, the lurking island where Nelson Mandela and Walter Sisulu and the other Black political prisoners were kept. I have a nostalgia for the smell of the windswept Parade late at night, perhaps with some oily papers in the gutter. I have Cape Town in my bones. Long Street runs down my spine.

Between meetings for discussions with Paul and other militants I found that I had quite a bit of time on my hands. It was early

August, the vineyards were blind, but the weather so beautiful that I could actually go down to Graaff's Pool and sunbathe and have a dip and watch the old naked sun lovers who sit there leathering themselves like seals the whole year round, wondering whether the ocean liner whose white breath they espy on the horizon may be making its way to New York, and idly speculating about stock market prices. I did notice one young man watching me rather intently but ascribed his attention to other less pure and certainly not security motives. And once I went down to a protected cove. I was going to miss my regular European summer, but this was even better, brighter. And no one else was around apart from the whirling seagulls, a few municipal workers raking together and carting off a rich harvest of seaweed and a bored office worker in black glasses stealing the day.

Here the ocean could get very turbulent, a green-and-white rage making furious rushes at the coast and the grey clouds scudding along, whipped by a keening wind. But today, that day, both water and land were as calm as the stretch and the glitter of a smile. White sand. Waves gurgling at the jokes whispered in their ears by the rocks. A tape of laughter. I lay back, rubbing warm sand over my belly, losing my eyes to the impenetrable sky. Looking for shells I found nine perfect examples. I gave them names. The number nine has magical connotations for me. It denotes Buddhistic infinity. It is also the number of the years that Boddhidharma spent facing the wall of a cave after his notorious interview with the anxious Chinese Emperor whom he told, in effect, 'You big-shit-no-sound; you mistake merit for bread. Who I? No-know.' I made a few scratches on my mind, reminding myself that I must try to reinterpret the resulting scars in(to) a poem. I thought that, as one sees in shells, emptiness is the rich heritage from the sea. I thought of my father.

I also phoned, and subsequently met in town, another old friend, the Swami, and spent an agreeable evening at his house in that part of town which borders on the old District Six before White greed bulldozed that into oblivion, into dust-devils, and real estate developers started building 'quaint Cape cottages' on the slopes. With him I discussed a topic we had explored earlier during one of his trips to Paris, the possibility of starting a literary magazine which would group the work of South Africans both in the country and in exile or banned. I met his girlfriend briefly. Wind screeched down from the mountain. The weather was sickening for a change. (It is said that, during the Second World War, White soldiers passing through here on their way to the front sometimes had their sex protuberances sliced off with knives wielded by dusky whores in the dark alleys.) On another night I had an appointment with them on the terrace overlooking the winter-closed Sea Point swimming pool, eerily deserted in the moonlight.

There would be, it seemed, no problem to complete that part of the mission which consisted of finding two militants who would be willing to come abroad to take care of the trade union office we intended to open. I very much wanted Paul to be the White one, although he was also becoming more and more a very important figure for us in the country due to his abilities and his clear insight and his extensive network of contacts with the live young political forces. But he was seriously considering our offer. The Black person whom he had in mind to win over was none other than Steve Biko, and we were to travel to the Port Elizabeth area to meet him. I sometimes wonder if, had we succeeded in our plan and had Biko left the country with our help, the course of political developments in the country would not have been slightly different from the way it turned out after the murder of the leader. History is seldom changed by a single man. Biko was a powerful figure though, a natural rallying point for Black Consciousness and non-ANC forces.

But at the same time that things were apparently moving smoothly, with very interesting reactions coming from the chosen few who had a look at the Okhela manifesto, at the same time I started feeling that I was perhaps pushing my luck. Maybe it was the opening of the fourth eye. If it was, it came a bit late. I decided to change hotels and moved to another one, in Three Anchors' Bay, ideally situated in that it was less public but with a good way out the back.

One day – it must have been about ten days after my arrival in the country – I was due to meet Paul together with one of the NUSAS leaders he wanted to introduce to me. We were to rendezvous along the main street running through Sea Point and, as I'd done several times before, I went for a walk, roaming the streets, passing the time.

There was a little coffee bar that I had visited once or twice. As I walked in there that morning I overheard part of a conversation between the girl who might have been the manager or the owner and a client: they were talking about being harassed by the cops and it sounded to me as if she'd been approached by the police quite recently and was very reluctant to collaborate with them. When one lives like that, the way I did, one's ears become keenly attuned to any anomaly, but one has to keep a tight grip on oneself all the time so as not to go around the bend utterly.

One says to oneself: after all, not every policeman in town is on the look-out for you particularly, and there must be many coincidences. I was close to the corner, near to the crow. I remembered how, the night before, whilst wandering through the streets, I came across a Coloured man doing the same thing, that is, nothing, and how we both watched from a distance a party going on in a hotel 'for Whites only'. We rested our chins on the wall surrounding the hotel and exchanged a few bitter remarks about the poor looking in upon the well off, how it's the same the whole world over seeing as how it's the rich that get the gravy. (And the geese.)* Then we turned and looked out across the bay at Robben Island, which is like a ship of ghosts patrolling just offshore along the Cape coast, like a knife thrust of conscience, like a warning. With him, that anonymous Brown man, I could speak like a native without a name, not having to pretend that I'm a foreigner with this slight French accent. But there too, afterwards, I asked myself: how did he find himself in my way, as if by accident? Wasn't he planted there? And earlier still that same evening, when I was taking a stroll along the promenade running down the seafront, a car stopped just as I was about to sit down for a drink in one of the beer gardens open to clouds and stars, and two men got out. The older one of the two (looking like a seedy Jean Gabin) turned to me, gestured at the glorious sunset which was turning the sky into a mother-of-pearl shell from which the moon would grow anon, nacreous and globe-shaped, and said in French, 'How beautiful! What a pity that it will all be

*In the Boland area there was the case of a labourer one night stealing and eating a certain farmer's very rare, imported black swan. Before being given a tough sentence for 'theft and wilful destruction of valuable property' the magistrate enquired after his reasons for taking the bird. 'I was hungry, *baas,*' he said.

covered in blood.' And my first reaction was: how on the bloody earth did he know that I would understand French? What was this – a warning? Or simply a slip of the tongue? And what about that girl, the barefoot art student, I started talking to one night while queueing to get into the cinema? (The place was booked out: I never did get in.) I had been there earlier the same evening, killing time, idly taking some photos of myself in the Self Photo booth in the cinema's foyer. Perhaps I wanted a record of this fugitive person with the moustache like a black grin, staring back enquiringly at me from the eye-level mirror facing the stool. How come Snaaks, later, knew all about the girl and the photos (which I'd torn up two days later)?

In any event, I'm trying to describe to you. Mr Interrogator – sorry, Mr Investigator – that I was in a constant state of jitters, suspicious of any and everyone, expecting my good luck to come to a disastrous end at any moment and now, after ten days, intensely aware of my isolation and my helplessness if something untoward were to happen. Suddenly I could measure inch by inch the enormous distance between the southernmost point of the African continent and far off Europe which had become a haven of security.

Walking along Main Street, waiting for the hour of my appointment, a young and scruffy White man accompanied by an equally sloppy Brown girl came to me asking for money, pretending to be Portuguese – 'You know how it is, these people here don't consider us Portuguese as Whites' – and I gave him some. The funny thing was that later, after the fall, during the interrogation, Hendrik Goy wanted very badly to know who that contact of mine in the street in Sea Point was, the man they had on the photo with me. And what was it I gave him, perhaps a roll of microfilm, a capsule containing the secrets of life and death? But again – was he just trying to twist my mind? Wasn't he in reality one of their staked-out agents? Or was there competition?*

*Schuitema claims that months after his first clandestine visit to South Africa (eighteen months earlier) the CIA tipped off the Greyshits that he had been there. From that time on the *boere* would have been keeping Paul, whom Schuitema had seen when there, under surveillance (did the CIA give their South African counterparts a complete breakdown of Schuitema's contacts then?), and so they were inevitably right on top of me – still according to S. – the moment I met Paul. Seductive explanation, but it doesn't quite fit.

Sea Point is in some ways like a foreshortened illustration of the South African folly. The rich live there in retirement with their little scented dogs (there's a shithouse, exclusively for dogs, built on the esplanade), the hippies or the bohemians populate some of the less well-appointed flats, and in the backyards you find a myriad of Blacks and Browns working there, particularly servant girls who often fill their spare time by being prostitutes, and very boldy so I may tell you, since they seem to be quite accustomed to the fact that every White man prowling that area is on the look-out for easy nooky. I heard, after leaving the Brown man the night of our brief encounter, how he tried to pick up one of these girls. But she knew the colour of the hand in which money came to her. Very tartly she laughed at him, saying in a sing-song voice that she didn't 'fok ghoffels' (meaning Browns). The Whites living there mostly belong to a party which supports the idea of a decent minimum wage for servants; at the same time they form residents' associations to pressure the authorities to remove the Blacks, to 'clean up the beaches' (meaning to have zoning and segregation enforced) in the name of 'combating crime' and preserving Sea Point's good standing.

My two friends turned up. I got in the car. We were going to talk while driving, and immediately upon leaving Sea Point we realized that they were there. Paul saw them first in the rearview mirror and alerted us coolly. They were making no attempt to camouflage themselves. There was this big white Ford sitting on our tail. We tried shaking them, accelerating down around Clifton and tearing through Camp's Bay, up one side street and down another. Patiently they waited for us to re-emerge on the main road, and whenever we did, there they were again. We took the road hugging the coast towards Cape Point and crossed over to the Indian Ocean side of the Peninsula by Chapman's Peak. Let me assure you that we were quite panicked, our NUSAS acquaintance especially so. Paul claimed that this little game was nothing out of the ordinary, that it happened often enough. I wanted to believe that it was not for me that they were there, that since both Paul and Glen Moss – a person I was meeting for the first time – were known activists intercepted by the police from time to time, the tail was just a routine check or silly harassment or curiosity on their part about who the third fellow (looking like a lost spy) with the two students might be. On the other side of Constantia we decided to return to town, to suspend our intended discussion, and that I should by all means try to escape from our pursuers. We went back via De Waal Drive at a terrific speed with them never very far behind, and upon arriving in Cape Town I made use of a red light to jump out of the car and run into one of the big stores in the centre of the city. I had in my pocket a little red knitted woollen cap. Rushing down to the basement I put this on, took my raincoat off, and went out a different exit; and then, on foot, tried to get as far away as possible from the place of ill luck where my friends had dropped me off.

Late that afternoon I made my way back to the hotel on the edge of Sea Point, changing buses, going uphill and downhill, like one of those mental cases one sees sweeping up his own tracks, and of course my mind was now seething with doubts and questions. We, that is Paul and myself, were at a point of concluding our preliminary discussions with the other comrades in Cape Town, and we had made an appointment with Schuitema, who was operating in the northern provinces, to meet him in Durban. We were due then to take the Garden Route for Port Elizabeth and ultimately for Durban. It was important that we should do so if possible, lest all of these plans be abandoned or postponed for too long. I was to confirm the next morning whether we were to go ahead or not. Back in my hotel I paced the room, nervously glancing out the window at the sea, which was grey and stormy. Cape winters can change rather abruptly from one day to the next, and obviously now a storm was in the offing. How many boats had come to grief here? What treasures the waves must be turning over, and what skeletons! How the voices must have been choked! The foam there, can it be the residue of confessions? And when it's dark – what ghost ships, islands and whales bump into each other there?

It became dark and then, luckily, before I thought of putting on my light I peered out the window again. I noticed a car parked a short distance away from the front entrance of the hotel. There was the glowing tip of a cigarette. The white Ford was back!

I watched them from behind the curtains, two gorillas sitting there patiently and obviously not being able to withstand the temptation of sending up a little time in smoke. (Their doctor should tell them about the dangers of nicotine.) Which was a dead giveaway. Who would be spending a stormy night in the dark in a car along the sea front, not even fondling another's sex? But it meant that matters were far worse than I allowed myself to imagine. Our afternoon escapade was not a coincidence. It wasn't Paul or Glen Moss they were after, but Galaska, the albatross. Or Breytenbach. (But surely not *me*!) Did they know that I was in the hotel? And if so, what were they waiting for? Was the idea to give me more rope or to see what other contacts I may have? Much later in Pretoria I was to learn that the two ghosts in the car were severely hauled over the coals for their blunders.

I was supposed to have dinner again at the Swami's that night and when I didn't turn up a call came for me to my hotel room. I could give him nothing except a lame excuse that wouldn't raise suspicions with those listening in. Remember, I was Galaska. Your men out front there are making a big mistake! I can't remember what I said. Rain lashed the windows, the wind was blowing in force outside and the sea was rising behind the black wall of night to come thundering against the cement ramparts protecting the street running along the sea front. Would that it could rise up and swallow my enemies!

I spent my night destroying as much as I could of whatever notes I had. I had to lighten my luggage. Above all I had to get going. Come on now, do something! What are you waiting for? But I was strangely apathetic. First my stomach had to get used to the new situation. My mind was flowing with the storm. Does destruction exercise a fatal attraction? What was the best way again of getting rid of compromising documents? The hotel manager was not going to like these repeated flushings. Reluctantly I decided to leave my nine perfect shells, my beautiful nine lives, behind. It wouldn't do to be suspected of receiving messages from the deep. Did Skapie Huntingdon ever find them? And in what laboratories were they analysed to dust? I tried to work out how I was going to get out of the trap. There is a saying that someone is so weak he can't even fight his way out of a damp Kleenex. They never budged. They were burning up their salaries. Once, to test them, and without my dunce's cap, I risked it a few yards outside the front gate: the car immediately growled. I didn't leave the hotel in the dark for fear of attracting undue attention from the night staff (what, leave without paying?), but with first light I went down with my bags. It was a Sunday morning. No, I won't wait for breakfast, thank you. I precipitately settled my bill and then went out the back without being seen. But Sundays, dammit, the back gate is locked, so there I was scaling the wall and throwing my bags over to the other side. What an undignified way for a gentleman to leave, like a guilty lover! From there a very steep road was going up the hill, crossing several side streets before it ran, near the top, into the road used as a bus route from and to Cape Town City.

Grey was the morning, mournful and empty. Rain still came down incessantly, like it was going out of fashion. I had had no sleep but it wasn't only the cold that made me shiver. Water in the stomach. Was the intention to trap me with my cheeks bulging with marmaladed toast? Or weren't they sure that I was there still (my windows dark) and were they waiting like decent Protestants for first light before bothering the landlord? (Afrikaners aren't popular in those quarters.) Did they not know about the possible back exit? Or were they satisfied that no one but a servant would use it?

They must have found quite soon after my departure that the bird had flown the coop because suddenly, in these deserted early Sunday streets, I could hear their car going from one side street to the other. I managed to hide behind a hedge as they came round the corner and when they were out of sight I made my way to the upper road and to the first bus stop I could find. Trying to make myself small behind the bus stop, with hunched shoulders. Misery. A bus, luckily for me, turned up not much later and I got in with my cap pulled as low as possible over my eyes. And found to my discomfort that I was in a bus reserved for non-Whites only. There were a surprising number of early morning workers aboard, probably domestic servants going into town to prepare breakfast for their masters. How they move and watch while the Whites still sleep. Since none of them seemed to mind I just slouched down in my seat, hoping not to be thrown off by the conductor for being in contravention of one of our Apartheid laws. That would have been too funny. ('I'm just a stupid, colour-blind tourist, finding my way back to respectability after a night's whoring in Sea Point, sir.')

The bus terminus was near the Parade in the centre of town. I got off, and hardly had I started walking, my bags slung over my back, when the white Ford emerged screaming with fury from one of the side streets on to the Parade. I ran. They spotted me and as I was dodging between the rickety fruit stalls, empty now, they started weaving in and out, trying to corner me. Take this down nevertheless, Mr Investigator. It was like something out of a very corny third-rate movie. Rain swept the plaza, the deserted stalls, the squashed fruit and vegetables underfoot. There the false Coloured who is a false Frenchman who is a false South African goes running hell for leather with his possessions in a bag of which the strap broke soon enough, and here comes this powerful automobile like a blind beast howling around the corners, slashing through the mush, and actually pushing over some of the stalls. Smoking slows down the reactions. I managed to get away from the Parade. That part of town with its many one-way streets has a lot of arcades joining one street to the other. It turned out that I succeeded in losing them quite close to Caledon Square, which is the police headquarters.*

But now, what was my next move going to be? I found a public phone booth and tried calling the one person I considered safe and on whose aid I could count – I had him up my sleeve like a last card – but all I got was an empty ringing tone on the other side. I could not even think of reaching Paul. If they were so furiously trying to get me they probably already had him or otherwise would be waiting there for me. Sunday morning in Cape Town. No one around. The masters are having their breakfast. One sticks out like a sore thumb with a red cap on. Staying close to the walls, flitting from entrance to entrance, I worked my way uphill past the last mosque left standing in the naked District Six and on to the Swami's house. I rang the bell. Had to ring again. Hard. Had to insist. Thought: my God, what if he too should not be home? But eventually aroused him and was allowed in. They were still in bed in a darkened room but in his

*And manage to lose them I surprisingly did. Years on in my sentence I met a fellow-prisoner with a natty appearance, shoes a-shine, etc.: an ex-cop. He told me how he begrudged me having to get up one cold winter's night in the East London area, to help man a road-block when they were looking for me. They were searching for me all over the country. I was lost – like Mr Eliot's cat Macavity.

honour I must say that he evaluated the situation immediately and never for a moment vacillated in his warm acceptance of my being there and in his willingness to help.

I was given a bed, a glass of brandy and a cup of coffee, but of course I couldn't sleep. The same shivers ran down my back. It was a feeling of utter lassitude prefiguring the situation of a few weeks later when in another bed I would be lying, shivering with all my clothes on. I used the bathroom for removing my moustache which, strangely, took more time and was more difficult to shave off than the beard. Regretting it rather. I thought I was quite the dandy with my Latin American macho emblem under my nose. The question was: where to now, and how? Not long after my arrival the Swami's phone rang, but when he took the receiver there was no one on the line, or at least no one willing to say good morning and discuss the weather. He informed me that he had had several of these anonymous calls over the preceding days, so it was clear now that a check was kept on him too.

There aren't, when you think of it, that many ways of getting out of Cape Town. Imagine yourself, Mr Investigator, in a similar situation at any time, and suddenly you realize how tough it must be for the camel to get through the eye of the needle. You're a marked man. Anybody can take a pot shot at you. And what normally seems such amiable disorganization suddenly becomes strictly controlled entrances and exits.

The Swami went to the airport to find out about the possibility of a flight out. We'd agreed that we couldn't try doing this by phone since a glum controller was obviously listening in, and he came back saying that the place was crawling with Greyshits. The port? Perhaps. But what boats were there? None was due to leave, and anyway, you have to go through police control again before getting into the port area. So the train then. But if they are at the airport and the harbour, surely they'll have the station covered also? The Swami had the brilliant idea of smuggling me out of town in his car to the first mainline station outside Cape town. He was quite willing to drive me all the way to the border. Had I but taken up that offer! But there were good reasons not to. If he was being watched, as seemed to be the case, his absence would only confirm their suspicions and get him into really deep trouble. Also, how was he to explain his sudden absence to his employers, and how could he leave his family on such a foolhardy mission? I felt it incumbent upon me to refuse with my hand on my heart, bowing slightly. (In my mind, Mr Investigator, in my mind, much later, when I could afford to be polite.)

The Swami left the house and returned with, for the first time that day, some encouraging news. He'd been down to the station and he'd bought and booked a seat for me, a ticket in the name of E. Christie. I have since often asked myself why he chose that name. Was it an obscure reference to his past as a Methodist minister? The astute idea he had was that I would not be getting on the train in Cape Town but at the first stop along the line to the north, which would be Wellington, my old hometown.

We waited until fairly late that afternoon. I felt cornered. Although I hadn't slept the night before, I was in no condition to sleep then: my nerves wouldn't allow me to. As it started getting dark, the Swami brought his car as close as he possibly could to the house, scouted up and down the street, and when we saw nobody I scurried out and hid myself between the back and the front seats. I think we were all very wound up. There had been several more of the mute phone calls during the day. But I was finally on the move. We drove out of town and tried as rapidly as possible to lose ourselves in the flow of traffic. In Paarl we stopped, waiting for time to pass, because we were too early, and after walking around for a while on the outskirts of the town we even dared to stop at a Portuguese greengrocer's to buy some fruit for my trip. We continued on to Wellington. The Swami had the consideration to drive past the house of my parents. They were no longer living there – they had retired to Onrus – but the big old boarding-house, 'Grevilleas', was still intact and lights were on in the windows which used to be mine and those of my father and mother. We drove by slowly. I stared, feeling the tug of memory at my heart and not knowing when I'd be seeing that house again, if ever.

At the station we had to wait some more. We were parked off to one side of the deserted lot in front of the Railway Hotel where some local dignitaries entertained my wife and me in a welcoming reception during our 1973 trip. A dog came to bark his heart out. This was certainly, as far as I could judge, the last time that I was going to be in the Boland for many years to come. One feels inexplicably safe and at ease there. Maybe the looming walls formed by the mountains have something to do with this feeling. But even that the people in power managed to desecrate. A very prominent and very ugly monument to the Afrikaans language (to Afrikaner power, in fact) had been erected on Paarl Mountain not very long before. The original movement for the recognition of Afrikaans had spread from the Paarl area. I never saw this *Taalmonument* but one of the fancies of the security police which I found very difficult to contradict was that I had attended the inauguration of this monument several weeks earlier, disguised as a woman. God only knows how that denunciation or observation got into the omnipotent files of the Greyshits. I assume that I was supposed to have been wearing one of those Voortrekker dresses reaching down to the ground and a *kappie* on my head – as these deep, sinister sun bonnets are called. How else could I have disguised my hairy legs and my moustache?

It was time for the train to arrive. I took leave of the Swami and the girl who'd assisted me so bravely, negating all personal danger in doing so. I must underline, Mr Investigator, that their aid was inspired strictly by humanitarian instincts. Truly, they are the kind of people of whom it might be said in biblical language, 'I was hungry and you fed me, I was ill and you dressed my wounds, I was in prison and you visited me.' It was an emotional farewell.

I didn't want to appear on the platform: I wasn't so sure that the station master or one of the railway workers on duty would not recognize me. Didn't I grow up with some of them?*

I got on and there was the whistle that I'd heard so often when I was a boy sleeping on the verandah during the hot summer months. That mournful whistle would evoke then all sorts of memories and vague desires. It is as if the whistle of the train opened an inner eye, or a little window inside the mind, on a wide expanse, but an empty one. The conductor came by, studied and nicked my ticket, and I settled down to sleep for the night. The Swami had made sure that I had a *couchette*. There was one

*My one uncle worked as an 'assistant electrician' for the railways. His job it was to take the lightbulb from the Black helper and to pass it up to the man standing on the ladder to replace the dead light. I also had a cousin, Kowie, working as a train driver.

other passenger in the compartment that I was booked in; I never saw him until the next morning. Perhaps I must have dozed a little, or perhaps I just drifted off to that in-between state when one is neither awake nor asleep.

When we woke the train had already entered the Karoo, that huge, central area of semi-desert that you come upon when you cross the Hex River Mountains from the Boland: as if going through a little window opening the mind to a naked land. But the Karoo is not naked.

Now there started for me a dream time, maybe corresponding to what the Aborigines in Australia would call the 'walkabout'. The land is magical. It was winter. The colours so subtly blended into one another that one believed everything to be washed and grey. Far on the horizon there sometimes showed a mountain range, discernible but unreal, and nearer one had the prehistoric figurations of hillocks and then the veld, as far as you could see the veld, with here and there mysteriously, seemingly without there being any cause or origin, a fire burning unattended: little red flames licking at the crystal-clear air. There weren't all that many animals to see. Even fewer people. Very occasionally, if the railroad stretched for some distance along a farmroad, one might pass a little Brown boy ostensibly on his way back from school, skipping along, lifting his bare feet very high so that one saw how nippy it must be outside. The train would stop at even the most insignificant little siding – a quaint name evoking some hunting feat, some flowers, a few dusty shrubs, a water-tower, the office of the foreman or the station master, an outhouse with a painted door, waiting rooms for White and non-White. The farm labourers one saw had the slight physique and the physiognomy of a vanished race: pale yellowish skin, prominent cheekbones, slanted eyes set deep in folds and wrinkles.

But people got on, stayed with us for maybe a hundred miles before they got off again. One such itinerant entered our compartment. He had no luggage, he was dressed in khaki pants and shirt, and the face with the ruddy skin of an outdoorsman was drawn and pale. He had red hair. It soon became evident that he was in pain. He would groan and clasp a hand to his waist. Eventually, to our horror, we saw a reddish stain spreading over his shirt. He opened it, removed a soaked plug, and showed us what I could only describe as a hole in his stomach. It was probably the result of a very recent operation. As he spoke only Afrikaans and I was not supposed to speak any I could only deduce that the old man had discharged himself from some hospital, desperate to get away from the theatre of pain, or perhaps only to get back home. Or was he on the run from some prison? It became so bad that I went to look for the conductor who helped him off the train and presumably handed him over to the local station master at De Aar. Maybe the conductor had phoned ahead from some small halt because the De Aar people were waiting when we pulled in. Another old wanderer joined us for a while. In broken English he engaged me in conversation. Suddenly he took from his pocket and showed me a box of South African matches, grumbling about how the boxes contained fewer and fewer matchsticks all the time and how – 'Look, see how easy they break?' – the quality was deteriorating. He gave me his address in case I ever needed any assistance: he was from Pretoria! (There are many drifters, wandering over the face of South Africa – burnt out cases with defective matches.) I had to think of another old one I came across in Pretoria a week or so earlier. (A week only? So much had happened since then!) I had stopped off on a bench there to greet the sun. There was nobody around except for this old body, sitting in the shade of the statue of President Pretorius. He watched me for a while, and then produced some soiled items of underwear from a voluminous coat pocket (he had no luggage), trying to flog them! I was not in the buying market that day.

I did not converse with my fellow pilgrim, and time stood still. Nothing happening in this vast land on the other side of the windows. One was edging all along the rim of the world and one could see in that limitless sky all the graduations of blue, from a very dark, nearly black canopy right down to the white haziness above the distant horizon. Night came. Maybe because the land is so flat it seems to spread very slowly and nature was exhibiting itself in a peacock tail of colours as the sun came to rest behind the earth. There were bands of blue and then green interspersed with vivid orange. We were crossing the Orange River into the Orange Free State and the sky looked to me very much like the flag of that old republic. Under the high bridge dusk was gathering among the pillars over the water. One couldn't see much anymore. Bloemfontein. I've never been to Bloemfontein. I don't think I will ever get to Bloemfontein. Not that I regret it particularly. There must always be places on earth that one never visits so that they may remain embalmed in history books and discoloured chronicles.

And the next day we arrived in Johannesburg. The station is huge and cavernous. The Swami had had the foresight to lend me a coat and a pair of shoes in Cape Town, partially as protection against the cold of the northern provinces, but also because I felt the need to attempt to alter my profile and a shabby, longish South African overcoat of the kind that one takes to rugby games on a Saturday afternoon was about the best I could do. These I now put on; the shoes were too big. (I returned a few mornings later to deposit the Swami's possessions in one of the luggage lockers – maybe they're still there?) At least I wasn't reduced yet to selling my underpants and my socks. Skulking, but trying not to look as if I was skulking, I made my way out of the station, convinced that at least some of the beady-eyed gentlemen in the arrival hall, frozen in their watchfulness, must have been from the security police. Johannesburg station is a sad place with a few desperate prostitutes plying their trade, some down-and-outers trying to bum a drink and white-faced gentlemen trying to take a look (as long as possible) at your penis when you're having a pee. Security police complete the picture nicely.

In town, in Hillbrow, I booked into a cheap hotel still using the name of E. Christie, holding thumbs that I would not have to show any identity papers when registering, but it wasn't necessary and I made it safely to a temporary haven. What was I to do now? I could not even begin to evaluate the extent of the disasters that had overtaken me. I'd left Cape Town in such a hurry that there had been no chance to make contact with either Pretoria or anybody elsewhere. (I did succeed, thanks to an intermediary, in leaving a message of warning for Schuitema, cancelling our plans, but I didn't even know whether he was still free.) I didn't know whether or not Paul and the others in Cape Town had been captured. We had agreed, you will remember, Mr Investigator, we were on the point of travelling via Port Elizabeth to Durban and in fact we already had an appointment in Durban with Jan –

which is the pseudonym Schuitema used – and together we were to finalize the Okhela manifesto in the light of reflections and objections made by the people I had been seeing over the previous weeks. All that was blown out of the water now. I didn't dare try to reach my friends in Johannesburg. If they knew so much about me in Cape Town, didn't it go back further and didn't they also know about my friends in the north? But to get to any border I would need help. Also, I was running out of money; my ticket was one of those excursion ones, which meant that I had to wait until a certain date before using it. You can imagine how isolated I felt, Mr Investigator. How I now longed to be the invisible man I had imagined myself to be in the beginning. Now I felt myself only too obviously standing out like a fool with a red cap over his ears. I even felt uncomfortable going into the street. It is one thing to be invisible – it is quite another to be a bat outside in daylight.

One night I did go for a walk through Hillbrow, though, browsed through a bookshop and, becoming convinced that I was being tailed when seeing the same man with twitching ears hovering near me for too long, started going uphill and downhill again, retracing my steps, using one-way streets, and eventually slipping into a cinema.* The film showing was one of those kung-fu pot-boilers starring Bruce Lee. Never in my life had I seen a kung-fu movie before, but one is never too old to learn to fly or to win the lissom heroine's hand by stopping bullets in mid-air and chop-chop eliminating three hundred and ten adversaries. (The Swami's shoes on my feet would have made my high kicking too clumsy though, too much like the final shiver a dying person may shake out of his trouser leg.) Before the main picture, as is customary down there, they showed a few newsreels and some documentary or other. The documentary turned out to be on the so-called Recces, that is, the reconnaissance units, the first of which was commanded by my eldest brother John Wayne himself. So I found myself in the utterly incongruous situation of hiding away in a dark cinema hall watching my brother and his men on the screen jumping from aeroplanes with their parachutes

*No Man's Land with its sexual taboos and political paranoia (everyone being either a *boer* or a terrorist) can be confusing for the isolated, for those on the run. You don't know whether you are being picked up by a pervert or a policeman: the dividing line is so often non-existent anyway.

blossoming in the sky like cherry trees in a Japanese chain verse, blowing up gullies and skewering blackened dummies with the audience applauding patriotically. We were ready for the Ruskies, the Chinks, the Yankees too, and all the *kaffirs* of Africa.

I remembered being told by Anna van Niekerk before going to Cape Town that she and her two friends intended spending a few days in a holiday resort in the Drakensberg Mountains. Not knowing where to turn, not knowing what was burnt and what not, I now went to her place, found her there in the presence of one of her colleagues, a steward working for South African Airways (and again the question crossed my mind whether such an unexpected presence was coincidental or whether I should read anything more in it). But I decided to push ahead and joined the party that was leaving later that same day for Natal. I could not broach the real reason for my wanting to go there. To them I still had to keep up the façade of the slightly cynical Frenchman who'd been down south and who'd come back minus the moustache this time – but still in his very own underwear – and who was keen to see where the White Voortrekker heroes had crossed the perpendicular mountain walls from Natal into the safety of the Transvaal (obstacles strengthen xenophobes) and maybe even where the Zulus carved out their kingdom.

It was quite some trip. Night overtook us. We were travelling in two cars. Van Niekerk's developed some engine trouble. I took over the driving and after leaving the high road we started climbing up the mountain, going along very badly kept earth tracks in the fear that the car might stall at any moment. We once passed some Africans along the road who tried to motion to us to stop when the headlights of the car fell on them. I was on the verge of doing so because it looked to me as if they only wanted a lift – perhaps their car had broken down – but I was surprised by the absolute panic the very idea of stopping seemed to provoke in Anna van Niekerk. The Whites live next to the Blacks and as long as the sun shines and the cars don't give any trouble and the roads are well frequented they feel no fear, but when night hides the face of light and the conditions worsen and one seems to be lost, the White seems to be convinced that the slightest contact with a Black would inevitably mean rape, if not mutilation, murder and mayhem. Brother, do we know one another!

When you go up into the high regions during this time of the year, you can very often see mountain fires. One whole valley seemed to be burning. (*'And the mountain a haze of flames. . . .'*) It was like looking down, from very far up, upon some mythical city, some prehistoric necropolis perhaps, a place where the spirits of the ancestors gather for an *indaba* and where they make little fires to warm their cold bones against the frosty breath of a winter's night. The next day you will see only windblown ashes.

The place we arrived at is just a hotel high up in the mountains above Bergville. There was nothing special about it. A big dining room overlooked the flanks of the purple mountain. But one could rent horses there and go for a ride up the canyons, accompanied by a guide. The Lesotho border is not very far away. This was what was at the back of my mind. (I have a mind crisscrossed by borders, the knife edges between safety and death.)

So we went riding, climbing higher along narrow trails. Still I could not take anybody into my confidence. Could I be sure that there weren't any super-*boere* around? How much room was I to leave for the little animal of suspicion fouling up the lines of my mind? Anna van Niekerk had told me of how she and her colleagues had been pressured by 'security people' to act as spies on exiles when abroad, even on in-flight passengers. They had been, she said, dismayed by the very idea. But surely such an overture meant contact, and the South African system is one of back-stabbing and blackmail. Was she really as naïve and as ingenuous as she seemed to be?* And besides, for once I had no confidence in my own evaluation of how people might react if I asked them to help me get across the border. They were good, loyal Afrikaners – never really doubting the wisdom of their masters, never openly questioning any of their decisions, conditioned to apathy and despair. I forgot myself one night over a meal and argued with them, telling them that they didn't know the Black at all, that they were driving around in the dark with

*Gordon Winter, ex(?)–BOSS operative, in his book, *Inside BOSS*, claims that van Niekerk was simply one of their agents. Her then later marrying my second brother bears out the point, he seems to think. Birds of a feather . . . But Winter's book is a sagacious and judicious mixture of real fact and true fact and false fact and non-fact and fancy and . . . disinformation?

defective vehicles, that, after all, the accumulation of injustices perpetrated against the Blacks must make any hope for a future of the White man inconceivable. There was no way, I said, that the ultimate conflict could be avoided. Remembering only from time to time who I was supposed to be, I would spice my arguments with references to French colonialist experiences in North Africa and in the Far East. The march of history is inevitable. Maybe it is not as mechanical as the phrase seems to imply, perhaps it also takes far longer than the human mind can sometimes conceive of, but I must continue to believe – if I want to retain any sanity – that such obvious and blatant iniquities as the South African masters impose on the majority, make their system anti-historical. Natural forces will eventually wipe it away. It was sickening to see my companions sitting there like beaten dogs thinking only of going to die in a desert.

An old man with a quizzical expression sat not very far off in the nearly empty dining room, listening to this, and eventually in a quiet way he just had to intervene. He was not at all of my opinion, although he could take a slightly more objective view than his South African cousins, who were stupidly squandering their future (maybe, he was implying, because they are *boere* and we all know what *they* are like). He was from Rhodesia, he said. He had come down to Natal in fact to prepare his retreat from Rhodesia. There was no more hope for the White man up north – the good sense came too late and because they weren't fighting the war the right way. They were now giving away too much, or not in the right way. They'd gone soft on the *munt*. (The gist of his remarks was, I think, that the Blacks had – because of the Whites' shortsightedness – started calling the tune; they should only be taught to whistle psalms really.) He seemed quite a civilized sort of chap, perhaps equitable and humane in his personal relationships with his servants, but nothing could remove from his mind the etched conviction that the White man was entitled to rule because White equals civilization which equals progress which equals uplifting which equals doing God's work which equals being recompensed for it which equals wealth and power over others for ever and ever for their own good which they would accept if it hadn't been for the communist snake in the garden of Eden. ('Africa for the Africans? Not in our time,' snorted good old

Smithy.) I had to be careful not to unmask myself in a fit of demagogic enthusiasm.

But these were futile splutterings. Everything was coming to a close; the various pieces of the jigsaw puzzle were being fitted together and, perhaps fatalistically, I felt that it was no longer possible to fit the odd-shaped blank piece that I am into any other hole than the one that seemed to be preordained for it. Choices were being made, held up to the light, and discarded. I was not going to reach the Lesotho border on horseback, not alone in these unknown mountains, nor with the help of these conservative young Afrikaners. I couldn't ask them to take me to the Swazi border either, for the same reasons. And if I wanted to use my last exit line, which was my return ticket, I would have to do so soon. So, maybe with death already in the soul, I decided to go, booked a seat on a flight leaving on 19 August, and then spent the last day sitting in the sun on the side of the mountain above a little swimming pool they'd built there, lying back, dozing, absorbing myself in the blue sky, stretching my arms up as high as they would go: it is surprising how long you can hold your hands in the air when lying flat on your back, seemingly forever – they just do not tire.

We drove back to Johannesburg the next day. There was no trouble with the car now. I recollect passing a road sign that said 13 kilometres to Jan Smuts Airport and the wave of superstitious fear that flooded me. Why the hell 13? Why now? Nevertheless – in the same way as, they say, the body knows about a pending heart attack quite a long time before it actually takes place, and in the same way that one senses an oncoming cold several days before it manifests itself, by the mental depression which foreshadows it – in a similar fashion, I think, I was already entering the loop of time which would carry me forward and deposit me at the feet of the interrogators. To play with for some time before feeding it into the grinding prison system.

I do not subscribe in any way to the theological concept of predestination. I do not think that man is a blind maggot with no choice except that of digesting more or less putrid matter, no; but I know I'm experiencing the law of Karma and in prison I learn about that of Reti but this comes later in our story, Mr I. Karma is not just a simple matter of cause and effect; it is an ongoing process without beginning or end, or rather, the beginning is the end of what went before, as the end is the beginning of what comes afterwards; and within this intricate and interdependent network of history and free will and sheer accident which together form a structure we call life, flowing always, flowing forward, the obscure stream penetrating the dark land, creating it by depositing its reflections and gnawing away at its crumbling banks, invaded by emptiness – part of all of this, I'm sure, is the fact that you can and do prefigure to some extent your own future: you cast a spell over yourself, you can confess things into happening, and I had been moving to the pulpit of Judge Silly and Colonel Huntingdon's subterranean cavities of morbid fascination for quite some time.

I asked Anna van Niekerk to mail for me some material containing notes of my travels through No Man's Land; I had already left with James Polley in Cape Town the first outlines of a series of poems called 'The Journey of a Guilty Fool'; and now I was quite divested of most of my baggage. I was ready. It was August 1975. I had arrived earlier that evening at Jan Smuts Airport, on my way back to France. I had known even as I arrived that I was blown, that they knew about me, and rather in the fashion of a small child closing its eyes hoping that in so doing the hideousness will go away, I'd hoped against hope that I'd be able to slip through the net which had been closing around me for some time. As I booked in at the departure counter, Mr Investigator, you took shape in me –

INSERT

The other night I dreamed that I had to return to prison for the outstanding two years I still owe them. What a calamity! My pluck was gone, my heart sank like a fish going down to the bottom to die: night was not deep enough to hide my defeat.

But what was it that mortified me so? The idea of losing my freedom? No – I have learnt that a wall is a point (and a joint) of relativity. There is no more freedom outside than inside. Mine is total. The sadness of being separated from a loved one? No – seven years had taught me to be like an ox before the plough with each hoofplod like a lightburst of the heart they can never destroy. And I was a fatalist: I knew they have the might to lead me away again. I was not afraid of prison.

What then? My spirit waned at the thought of having to start all over the process of creating a liveable world for myself behind bars. Everything was gone. Like a philanthropist drunk with largesse, I'd liquidated all my assets upon release. My tobacco I'd given away to Doug, Mossie inherited my precious flask, to Piet I entrusted the task of distributing my carefully hoarded muesli, and the few books I had struggled so long to be allowed to obtain I now left to the 'public domain', our common library. *Nulla bona!*

I had to start all over from scratch and what a tedious process that was going to be! How long before I'd make A-Group again? With what was I going to buy a broom from the storeman, or a 'suit of clothes' that would fit? Naked as a shorn lamb, I was going back.

Except . . . All I had left was an inkwell that Yolande had given me, old-fashioned and beautiful even though the bottom was uneven so that it sat before me at an angle. But it was empty! Inside it there was only an evaporated reflection of blue. Like a memory of sky . . .

Part Two

A MEMORY OF SKY

which shows us the first person learning about the fact that Death is structured; passing through a second trial, wherein a writer emerges with raised finger; how the reader learns with pained surprise of the extent some people will go to to deprive others of their lives, but also how strong the urge to survive can be; bringing more news about security policemen and other monsters; in which said reader enters by the way of understanding the mazes of boop; showing that there is always action in non-action (wu wei) *and that one has to penetrate to the non-heart of movement to be still, for to be decay is to deny the law of decay; consisting of fourteen sections of which six are inserts:*

1

The Maze

Have no fear: Death is here.

(THE ENTRY)

Nature has turned its face away from me.

It is 25 November 1975 when I am sentenced. I shall not be seeing the stars again for many years. In the beginning I don't realize this; I don't miss them; and then suddenly it becomes very important, like chafing sores in the mind – something you've taken for granted for so long you now miss the way you'd miss a burial site if you died in space. It is not natural never to see stars, or the moon for that matter – it is as cruel as depriving people of sound. I see the moon again for the first time on 19 April 1976 when, at about twenty-three minutes to four in the afternoon, I am in the largest of the three exercise yards, which has towering walls, making it rather like a well. I looked up and to my astonishment saw in a patch of sky above a shrivelled white shape. Could it be a pearl in my eye? Was it the afterbirth of a spaceship? No, it could only be the moon. And they told me that she'd been hanged, that she was dead!

The sun and its absence become the pivot of your daily existence. You wait. You build your day around the half an hour when you'll be allowed out in the courtyard to say good morning to the sun. You follow its course through the universe behind your eyelids. You become its disciple. The sun knows not of the justice of man. You know exactly where it touches at what time – winter, autumn or summer – and if you are lucky, as I was for some time, to be kept in a cell just off the main corridor with windows giving on to the catwalk which was not closed to the outside, you would have a glimmer, a suspicion, a hair-crack of sunshine coming in during certain seasons, but never reaching far enough down for you to feel it. I used to climb on my bed, stand on my toes on the bedstead, and then, sometimes, for something like two minutes a day, a yellow wand would brush the top of my hair. Of course, you develop an intense awareness, like a hitherto unexplored sense in yourself, for knowing exactly when the sun rises and when it sets without ever seeing it. With the first shivers of the very early morning, even before the call for waking up sounded, I used to get out of bed and try to position myself in that one spot of the cell where the warder could not see me directly and then for half an hour sit in *zazen*, and I could always feel in me a very profound source of light inexorably un-nighting the outside; with eyes half closed I could feel it first tipping rose the roof made of glassfibre, giving shape to the trees one knew must be growing not far off because the birds talked about these trees, and then jumping over the walls which were made of red brick, and generally investing the day. It was the quiet moment then: the *boere* for the morning shift hadn't arrived yet to come and stamp their feet, and those who'd been on for the second watch from twelve at night were nearing the end of their turn of duty and so they were sleepy, perhaps dozing with the FNs in their hands hanging limply.* On summer days when you were cleaning your corridor you could see through the grill clouds passing along the blue highway above the yard wall facing you: boats on their way to a dream, bit actors always dressed in white being taken to an empty space where Fellini would be filming a saturnalia, a wedding feast. There was wind which you never felt on your face but which you got to know through its aftermath – the red Transvaal dust you had to sweep up. There were the most impressive summer thunderstorms tearing and rolling for miles through the ether, slashing and slaying before big-rain came to lash the roof with a million whips. It was like living underneath a gigantic billiard table. Behind the walls with no apertures to the outside, behind the screen of your closed eyes where you hid from the *boere* – you still saw the stabs and the snakes of lightning. There was also the defiance of those singing their death.

Excuse me, Mr Investigator, these are discordant thoughts, but

*FN stands for 'Fabrication Nationale'; it is a Belgian rifle produced under licence in South Africa.

I need to start with what is the most striking in prison. When your sentence starts you are first of all aware of being buried; that you entertain the fancy of still being alive is of no consequence. There is no death. You are buried to what you know as normal life outside: the rhythms of day and night, of the seasons of the year, the rhythms of intercourse and communication between people with hands, between butterflies and *croissants* and dolphins, the million little things which weave the cloth your life consists of. This death world is filled with sounds you never imagined, steel on steel, fear and rage; with the pervasive smells of not very clean men (with no joy) cooped up in a restricted area, of evacuation and badly cooked food, of clothes worn for too long by too many different bodies; with the sights of nearness – grey, brown, grey-green, brown-green.

So let me try to be more organized. When you are sentenced your city clothes, your private clothes, are taken away from you. If your stretch is less than two years these are stuffed in a property bag and kept somewhere up front for the day you are released; if longer, your people have to fetch them or else they are destroyed on the premises. That is, of course, the theory. In practice over the years I very often saw private clothes either being claimed by the warders or smuggled back into circulation inside – in fact used as means of exchange among the prisoners.

(Maybe this is the moment to regale you with the way in which my friend Jerry got a bit of his own back. At the time of his arrest the *boere* stole nearly all his possessions. During his trial he wore a flashy jacket to court every day, with a blocked pattern, and this he handed in upon being sentenced. Very rapidly though, being an old ape, as we say, he managed to sell the jacket for a few packets of snout to the Coloured prisoner working in the reception office. Came his release after a few years and he wanted to reclaim the jacket, which of course was no longer there. Now, since it had been entered on the books, countersigned by Sergeant Prins, and as he was doing less than two years, he insisted that he should be paid an amount equivalent to the price of the 'bootiful' garment. Naturally he also claimed then that this was a very unique, hand-tailored, made-to-measure piece of clothing imported from France. After many months and threats of laying a charge for theft, the poor old sergeant just had to fork out the sum of money that my friend insisted on. I must add that the jacket had been bought off a hanger in the OK Bazaars.)

You are then given your prison outfit with a printed form on which your kit is marked. In Beverly Hills it was:

Jacket, moleskin	1
Trousers, long green	1
Shirt, green	1
Shirt, safari	1
Shorts	1
Jersey, brown	1
Socks, pair	2
Shoes, pair	1
Raincoat	1
Blankets, grey	3
Pillow	1
Spoon, stainless steel	1
Mug, plastic	1

I never saw the raincoat and in the beginning I was allowed to keep my own underpants. No dixie was provided because in Maximum Security one eats out of a plastic bowl. You could keep your mug to drink water from during the day.

Your hair is cut to regulation shortness. Since I was kept in isolation, mine could not be cut by a fellow prisoner and one of the *boere*, more often than not Nit Arselow, had to take this task upon himself.

You are issued now with your prison identity. In normal circumstances your booking in takes place in the reception office but in my case I was privileged enough (or exclusive enough, or enough of a sight for sore eyes) to have a warrant officer displace himself especially to come and enrol me in the ranks of the people of the dark. The initiation consists of one being fingerprinted and one's complete physical description being entered in a really gigantic book looking like the ledger one imagines St Peter – or whoever keeps the records in Heaven – has ready for all us sinners on earth. Literally every birthmark or scar must be written down. The beautiful side of this – administration getting ensnared in its own regulations – is when one sees them or hears of them having to spend days describing laboriously and with tight tongues all the various tatoos on an average Brown gangster being admitted. Depending on the gang and the length of time you have been a member, you can be covered virtually from the hairline right down to every single last toe and the balls of the feet by an uncountable number and an unimaginable variety of designs.

Reception offices are segregated, of course. From the moment of arriving there the process of 'breaking you' starts. White warders take their own sweet time. The prisoners are screamed at. Don't think you arrive in prison to be processed just like *that*. (The tall German who did time for murder with us in the Cape came with his lawyer to see the Officer Commanding a week before booking into the prison to ask what he should bring with him. The officer smiled, 'Of course Mr Humferding, by all means bring your sports gear and your electric shaver.' When he did arrive the reception *boere* laughed until the tears came as they kicked his tennis racket, his running shoes, his shaver and his radio around before locking them in a vault.) If you are transferred from one prison to another you may very well spend a day and a night and the major part of the next day in the reception cell, or the court cell as it is also known, waiting for the *boere* to finish all the necessary procedures.

Sometimes there is confusion, particularly in the Cape, over whether a prisoner should be considered as White or Brown. I've known people who've done time both as Brown prisoners and as Whites, and the majority of them prefer to be Coloured. The Coloured prisoners are 'stauncher', they say, more loyal to one another. One, Skippie (of Portuguese descent), went on a hunger strike of protest when he was dragged out of the Coloured prison (called 'Medium') and put in with the Whites (called 'White Males'). It happened in the Cape that a prisoner was 'demoted' to a Coloured prison. Ghana, as we knew him, maybe because of his dark colour, had organized a written petition to complain about the dictatorial ways of Tattie Swart, the section sergeant, and was promptly isolated and moved across the street. There was also the case of one man being booked and nobody being able to make out where he should be shunted off to. Until the sergeant in charge shouted in his frustration, 'Now tell us what the hell you are – Black or White?' And the man answered, 'But of course I'm White, my *baas*.'

These books then – because there also has to be one for your private possessions – were dragged up to the office in C-Section, and I was born. As prisoner 436/75. A card is made out with your number. In South Africa it is numerical, every institution (with its name on the card) starting the new year with No. 1. They later introduced a letter after the number which would make it clear that you are White or Coloured or Black. When I was moved to the Cape I became No. 573/77/W. On this card, which you must have with you at all times – it is your birth certificate and your calendar – is marked your name, your alias, the Church you belong to, if any, the nature of your crime, the length of your sentence, previous convictions; and convictions you may further receive or be subjected to while in prison will be inscribed there too. It also has – the one date you watch – your day of release. The poor 'indeterminate sentences' have no dates. Their whole struggle in prison is the attempt to obtain one. I had at least that. But my card stated ominously: Sentence: *9 yrs no remission of sentence*.

You are now a member of the clan. No longer are you Mr Breytenbach, if you ever were; you are now the fucking dog, the *bandiet*, the *mugu*, the mother's cunt. A prisoner awaiting trial is theoretically treated a little more leniently than a convicted person. You may receive food parcels from outside, you don't wear the outfit, and the warders are less strict when it comes to scrubbing floors and walls. But that, of course, changes dramatically once you have become a permanent resident, a 'hard labour'.

As a political prisoner you are supposed to spend about three months in Maximum Security in Pretoria, during which time you are visited by various prison officials specializing in what is called 'observation'. They may be psychologists or officials responsible for studying privileges, also the warders whose duty it is to make you fill in all kinds of stupid forms, after which, without any reference to the forms, it will be decided what kind of labour you will be allotted to. This decision, as also the decision about the prison to which you will be sent, is made by the Prison Board, consisting of senior officers – in previous years the nominal chairman was a senior retired prison officer or even somebody from another State Department, offered this sinecure for his declining years – the psychiatrist, your social worker and the spiritual worker or chaplain. That is the set-up for normal prisoners. For a political there can be no choice: he can only be sent, if White and male, to Local, and the work in Local is very restricted in kind. And again, a political normally has no truck with the chaplain. And they don't trust politicals to consort with social workers either (who are perhaps not security conscious enough?). I once accidentally met a social worker in a front office of Pollsmoor and jokingly asked her when I'd be getting to see 'my' social – after all, was I not human too? Was I to go through all these years with my soul in perdition and my family life in tatters without any aid? She blanched and said, no, they had strict instructions not to see me, and if ever I asked, they were to inform Pretoria, who would then fly down a brigadier to come and feel my troubled heart. But this comes later.

Your three-month 'observation' period is the occasion for teaching you the ways of prison life. South African prisons have the pretensions of being organized along military lines: you fall in for various 'parades': the 'sick parade', the 'work parade', the 'roll-call parade', the 'food parade', the Saturday 'cinema parade', the 'sport parade'; and in the criteria they impose for your personal appearance and the apearance of your cell they try to follow the military tradition too. The initial period is, then, what corresponds to boot camp for the marines when, quite consciously, your personality is broken down, to be reassembled in the right way, the 'reel Sot Efrican' way. The *boere* would say that you learn to keep your place, which is at the bottom; you learn about your privileges – which are few and will have to be worked and compromised for very hard, since you have to acquire the knack of wagging the tail – and about your rights, which are none.

For me it was going to be different. My 'observation period' was to stretch into nearly two years. I was also in complete isolation. Isolation meant never seeing another prisoner except when I happened to be taken down the main corridor and passed by the flunky employed there as a cleaner. It meant, naturally, never being able to talk to another prisoner. It also involved the warders not being allowed to converse with me, so that the talk was restricted to orders on their side and requests on mine.

Up above my cell, on the catwalk where I couldn't see it, there was a notice threatening the warders with prosecution under the Security Laws if they were to communicate with me. A sympathetic youngster on night shift once read it down to me, in a whisper. When I subsequently complained about the restriction to Brigadier Dupe, the sarcastic and uncertain man in charge of everything pertaining to politicals, he climbed the stairs with great show and feigned surprise at finding the notice. And when later, during the second trial, General Bliksem – small, slicked-down hair – was questioned by my advocate about the reasons for keeping me isolated, he was most indignant: no, no, no, he exclaimed, the prisoner was never put in isolation; he was just 'segregated'.

There have been enough studies made of the effects on people of long-term isolation. For my part I think I should like to divide it into two kinds. One is the obvious kind – parts of you are destroyed and these parts will never again be revived. You are altered in your most intimate ways exactly because all objectivity is taken away from you. You watch yourself changing, giving in to certain things, becoming paranoiac, staring at the wall, living with an ear at the door and yet cringing at the slightest noise, talking to the ants, starting to have hallucinations – without ever being able to ascertain the extent of these deviations or this damage precisely because you have nothing against which to measure it. And this damage is permanent even though you learn to live with it, however well camouflaged. You have seen them, Mr Investigator, those who have been through camps and salt mines and 'breakwater-building' (as we refer to No Man's Land's jails), and you marvel at their serenity and their conviviality. But just make them jump and you'll see how brittle their eyes are. You don't really know what they do behind closed doors, do you, Mr Investigator? You don't know of the bitterness under their tongues. Of how they watch the doors. Isolation has made me sick of myself, and sick of others.

Then there is the second kind: by being forced to turn in upon yourself you discover, paradoxically, openings to the outside in yourself which you have not been aware of before. You grow rich with the richness of the very poor; the smallest sign of life from outside becomes a gift from heaven, to be cherished. You really see things for what they are, stripped of your own overbearing presence. A blanket really is a blanket, and though it is grey, it has a million colours in it. A bird, when it comes to nest at night in the gutter running round the outside of the roof, really does make a very wide range of comments and it has a rich relationship with its partner. You roll and smoke a cigarette and its aroma is worth all the valleys of Turkey. You find a brown chrysalis in the small courtyard, like a finger of gold – already it is wriggling. You take it inside and you watch the fascinating birth of a death's head moth; how it waits, still tame to the touch of the world, for its wings to dry, and when it takes off a whitish spot the size of a one cent coin is left. No king was ever as blessed as you are. The days aren't long enough! You learn how things, appearances, fit together. About illusion. About stopping and space and you yourself just one vibrating pretence among many. That you outline absence by placing and fixing anything. You look at the wall and you see the battles between Saracens and Christians for Jerusalem and you see a beached whale and how it is burned down for oil and you realize your eyesight is weakening. At night you lie looking at the weak bulb very high against the ceiling (you get to know the placing of that bulb very well) and someone comes into your cell. It is Fyodor Dostoevsky, scruffy and unshaven, with black dirt under his fingernails, wrapped in a coat so sloppy that he must have filched it from some locker in a station, and he never says a word. You describe your cell and all your little utensils to him (how crowded your life is!) and it becomes too much because you must then also enumerate everything which isn't there: isn't thereness relativity? You tell him minutely about what has happened to the world since his departure. He utters not a word. Night passes like a whispering. You promise to finish for him that poem in *The Brothers Karamazov* which he never got around to writing, that one about the return of Christ. You learn about rhythm and about balance. How nothing is sacred or personal because *boere* come to *skud* you (shake you down: cell search and body search) three times a day, turning everything inside out. You learn that all is sacred, since everything regains the value of having been touched, despite the repeated desecrations. You lose interest. You sleep and you dream that Kasyapa sends for you to reveal to you the Teaching of the Sky, a dynasty of patriarchs passing nothing from generation to generation – taking care not to lose it. You dream that the mattress is emptiness.

You wake and in the dark you write a poem to the man who held up a flower by way of transmitting the it, the only-all. You enter the temple to help him by holding down his head when he goes for the final somersault. You wake. It is quiet. Everyone is awake. Not a sound in the night but for the lone voice singing. You remember that this week only one is due for hanging. What a shame to choke off such a beautiful voice. 'Lord, I'm coming home. Coming home, coming home, never more to go . . .'

'You're taking liberties, hey?' the thick *boer* in charge of the night shouts. 'You're bloody lucky you're hanging this week, *kaffir*. Else I'd have charged you and seen to it that you got spare diet!'

(THE LOCALITY)

Maximum Security, or Beverly Hills, is a building all by itself. It often goes hidden under the name of Pretoria Central, but Central is a whole complex of buildings within the perimeter of the prison compound, which contains, furthermore, the houses of the staff, their club buildings and their sports fields. Until a few years ago the grounds were freely accessible; now prisons are more and more becoming armed camps, not so much as a security precaution against the inmates wanting to go for a spin, but as forts in a sea of uprising around. During the 'riots' in Cape Town it was a common sight to see carloads of warders, armed with shotguns, go tearing off. And when I left the workshops in Pollsmoor were producing rotating machine-gun nests, the first of which was to be installed on the roof of Maximum there. Pretoria Central is now closed off by huge, manned gates, and strategically positioned television cameras sweep the terrain so that 'control' can at all times watch the staff and the visitors moving about their business.

There are four prisons in the compound. First the original 'Central', dating from the last years of the nineteenth century, parts of which have been renovated. It has an imposing entrance: the gates of perdition. Some wings still have no toilet facilities apart from the ubiquitous slop buckets. There must be quite a few nooks and crannies because people sometimes manage to get on to the roofs to be shot down from there. That building is called 'Big House'. All male White prisoners who pick up more than two years in South Africa have to spend a few months in Big House first, for their observation period, before being redirected to various other prisons elsewhere. Short-timers and some long-timers do their whole stretch there.

Then there's the female prison where both Black and White women are kept together. Then Pretoria Local (over-)populated by the people awaiting trial – the so-called *stokkies*, meaning 'sticks', perhaps referring to their being 'behind sticks' – which also had, and has again now, a special section for political prisoners. That part has recently been rebuilt, after the break-out of Moumbaris and Jenkins and Lee, into a super-special high-security sector. The new place, I believe, has (for instance) artificial light only.

And there is Beverly Hills, sitting on a slight incline behind the others. The cherry on top of the cake. If one had windows giving on to the outside, one would have had a lovely view over the city of malediction, Pretoria. But there are no windows to the outside and there's also a very high wall encircling the building completely. In this wall is an entrance gate which is electronically controlled by a *boer* sitting, in fact, in the wall itself. You drive in, gates slide open before you, you are in a space between two gates, those behind you close before those in front of you open. Sure, there are also watch-towers on the wall. Congratulations: you are now in the space between the wall and the prison building – immaculately kept with lawns and shrubs and a few wild deer they allow to roam there. So peaceful. The approaches to the prison and the grounds around it are constantly observed by rotating television eyes. When I left they were to proceed with the installation of television eyes in the corridors and in the ceiling of every cell. Mount the few steps to the entrance. Don't be shy – knock! Use that big brass knocker. A little judas eye will slide open and an eye and ear will inquire after the nature of your death wish. Now a small door in the portal is unlocked and you are among the chosen few allowed inside to tread the sacred soil. Look at how clean everything is, listen to the quiet: like being at the undertaker's. Oh, you're not very far inside yet, only in the space separated from the foyer of the building by a grille. Once your identity has been ascertained by a man sitting behind a table, keeping his big ledgers, balancing his columns of death and life ('You have an appointment?'), with death winning hands down because surely not even one percent of all those admitted ever leave the same way again, the grille will be unlocked – not by him but by a warder whose sole duty it is to unlock grilles from morning to night. Keep a stout heart. You are at present in a corridor-like space with grilles blocking off either end. If you're just a visitor to the slaughterhouse, a spectator from another prison – warders from elsewhere can, by special permission, assist at hangings (once all the members of the Prison Orchestra were entertained in this way: some puked and others fainted – what fun!) – or one of the hangers-on of death (a lawyer or some such), you can turn left and move into the wing where the offices of the personnel taking care of the administrative functions are. Down there too is the room for legal consultations. Or you can turn right to where the officer commanding the prison has his office full of carpet and pass other rooms where warders on duty or off duty spend their time. You are welcome.

But you, as a prisoner, have to go straight on through a gate in the grille which has to be unlocked by the key carrier. Up a few more steps and now you can turn either left or right depending on whether God (which is the Nationalist Government) made you Black or Brown or Asiatic or White: left to C-Section for the Whites, right to A- and B-Sections for the others. Another grille. Sounds vary from gate to gate. (You could, lying in your cell, follow the progress of an officer through the building just by the foot-stamping of his underlings.) One of the clowns who passes for a warder has attached to the top of this grille a small *pawp-pawp* hooter of the kind you sometimes fix to your bicycle and this is then squeezed to obtain the attention of the *poisan*, that is, the Black warder whose task in life it is to look after that particular gate – 'He won't get away from me, *baas*.'

You are home. C-Section. Of course, you will be taken even deeper into the labyrinth to your *own* room. Another steel-plated door will have to be opened to let you into your small corridor and from there your door has to be unlocked so that you can finally find yourself in your cell. There is a corridor, similar to the long one making up C-Section, running down the other side of the building, from which A- and B-Sections lead. On that side there are many more cells, big ones too, for all the Black prisoners condemned to die are kept there.

Both these corridors have at the other extremity doors locking off the access to the stairs leading up to the gallows. Sometimes I was employed in cleaning that end of the corridor (travelling to China in my mind) and I'd go right to the fatal gate. It was a sombre area. People believed that it was haunted. 'I'm not afraid of any ghost,' a young *boer* on night duty once said to me, seriously, bravely. 'If I see him, I'll shoot the shit out of him with my gun here.' The steps lead to a room called the 'preparation room', where the final little touches are put to those being prepared for departure – pulling a shirt straight, making sure that a hood fits snugly (neatness counts, you know: it forms character), and from here, this antechamber, this terminus, the door opens in to the execution place itself. Back of that again, but at ground level, is the area with big washbasins and tables with little furrows allowing blood to run off them. This is the space, then, where the bodies are sluiced down and dissected if necessary. In any event, the doctor assisting has to make a little cut in the neck to verify the cause of death. Here too are the big ice boxes in which the bodies can eventually be kept. Beyond that there is the workshop where the bodies are put in coffins. From entrance to 'over-and-out' not more than, say, 200 yards. Functional, Mr Investigator, what?

For your unpublishable information I add that a catwalk frames this whole area. The catwalk covers the corridors (it is a grid) and from there the alligators (as the *boere* are also called) look down into every cell. Down a part of C-Section the catwalk is open to the big yard, and if you are in that part, the winter wind will fill the cells at night with its bitter cold. Windows, set high in the walls, giving on to the catwalk, have to remain open. The catwalk *boere* are armed with FNs. (Black and Brown *boere* are issued with ·303s, from warrant officer up, the staff are entitled to pistols – all of these apart from the shotguns, riot guns and light machine guns locked away in the arsenal.) They used to have walkie-talkies too – and kept one awake the whole night with their obscene chattering – but the whole place has since been equipped with a two-way intercom system.

Let me give you an example of why their inexperience made me nervous. One winter night a poor sod up there complained of the cold, and to illustrate his point he passed his firearm down through the narrow window, barrel first, just holding on to the butt. 'See, if you touch the metal, your hands will stick to it, frozen stiff!'. . . All it needed was a good tug. (And then: I'd shoot my way through the door shoot my way through the grille shoot the *poisan* shoot my way through the grille shoot the *poisan* shoot my way through the grille shoot my way through the grille shoot the nightshift-member-in-command shoot my way through the door shoot right through the television the wall the night go shoot Big Chief Sitting Bull himself so that the blubber and the sighs leaking from him can blot his miserable volumes of repressive decrees. . . . But they are given only six bullets at a time, I believe.) Set in the floor of that part of the catwalk, about 50 cm. wide, overhanging the cells, were small, oblong, bullet-proof windows through which the *boere* could observe the 'blind angle' area underneath.

Finally, to give you an idea of the Hills' accommodation – it holds probably up to about two hundred and thirty people at a time, nearly all of whom are Black – that is Black and Brown and Asiatic – and a few Whites. I don't think there are ever more than four or five White 'condemns' at any one time. Plus the politicals in observation, again never more than one or perhaps two. Stefaans is also kept there – Tsafendas, who's been there since the beginning of the sixties without ever having been tried, and who has not a dog's hope of getting out as long as the present regime lasts. Apart from the warders manning the watch-towers, the television room, the entrances, the catwalk, there is also permanently at least one warder locked up in every sub-section (C2 for the Whites) where the 'condemns' are held, to keep them under twenty-four-hour surveillance. The particularity of Beverly Hills, if you are a White prisoner, is that, for the average of five *mugus* they had there during my time, they had a day staff of fifteen *boere* looking after us. Bored stiff they were. Polishing their shoes, telling dirty jokes, chucking a ball about the yard, just getting up every now and again (in force) to go and take a prisoner and his cell apart.

On two occasions during my stay other White prisoners were

brought up there. (There is always one White cleaner, a short-timer from Central 'lent' to the Hills.) These were the so-called 'Springboks', escape artists who had 'taken the hole' more than once from other institutions and were considered to be either very dangerous or else were sent to Maximum for more severe forms of punishment. A rough lot of chancers they were. It was amusing to listen to their stories – since they were each in his own single cell they had to shout to be heard, and one profited by this; you were, in a manner of speaking, sitting in the circle. (But like hawks the *boere* watched me to prevent me from participating.) They would moralize, 'We should have been beaten with sticks when we stole our first bicycle, then we wouldn't be here now!' Or reminisce about films they'd seen (nearly always in prison), depicting the Second World War, for instance. And patriotic! One informed his mates that he knew for a fact that South African fighter pilots are the best in the world. 'Did you see in that war flick the way they drive their planes sitting *outside* the cockpit, just like that? They fly them bareback, I say.' Or brag about their achievements in sport. One claimed to *skommel* ('shake', meaning to masturbate) for Western Transvaal's second team! And in this way too I heard about how one of them stood out one morning during the 'requests and complaints' parade and handed in a written request asking to be released for two weeks only (and to be issued with a rifle) 'to go and kill Idi Amin'. Since these fellows were deprived of cigarettes, we worked out by sign language – right under the nose of the *boer* accompanying me to the bathroom which was down their corridor (C3) – a way for me to leave them some *entjies* (little ends: cigarettes) and *scratch* (matches). Their dirty clothes were thrown in a corner of the bathroom. I'd have the necessary articles in my pockets, undress (with the *boer* watching me glassy-eyed), put my pants on the same pile, and after washing just put on another pair of shorts.

There were always empty cells enough to take in detainees falling under the control of the security police, but who were in fact also having to submit to the prison regime and the prison staff, as happened during the detention of the people involved in my trial. Once, and once only during my stay there, five or six Black political detainees were lodged in C-section. A *poisan* was then stationed in the corridor, basically to eavesdrop as they were talking to one another from cell to cell in Sotho or Zulu. I believe they were from an outfit called the Azanian People's Organization, and I don't think very much came of their trial: their detention was probably already the intended punishment. They kept up good spirits while there, exercising in unison under the leadership of one of them, engaging the *boere* in talk quite often. They were all students, way above the intellectual level of their keepers, and it was funny to hear them manoeuvring the *boere* until they had them talking about their motorcars or about their girlfriends.

It was a period when I lodged in the 'suite' on the main corridor – someone else was occupying C1 – so that for my ablutions I had to be taken past the cells where the Blacks were kept to the bathroom of C3. It was quite a palaver. Their windows (that part of the door which was barred only, and the small window each cell had looking onto the corridor – because there were no windows to the outside) had to be blocked out with newspapers every morning before I could pass. This was to obviate any possibility of our communicating or even seeing one another.

I was kept in two different cells during my stay in Beverly Hills. C-Section consists of a long main corridor running down the length of one of the wings of the building, with three side corridors, called C1, C2, and C3, leading off this main corridor to the left. To the right were the offices used by the warders, the store room, the visiting rooms and two other rooms which in fact were used as cells also. In earlier years these served as dormitories for Black warders going on duty or coming off duty at midnight. I was kept either in C1 or in one of the cells giving directly onto the main corridor. The side corridors are separated from the main corridor by a steel plate reaching about 13 feet high, with just enough space at the bottom to allow one to slide one's spoon or one's mug through.

Upon entering C1 there was a bathroom immediately on the right which also had a toilet used by the warders, and then two small single cells. On the left were two single cells and a third door which gave onto a slightly bigger space converted, incongruously enough, into a little chapel: two wooden benches, one wooden pulpit. At the other end this short corridor was barred by a steel door plus a steel grille which, when open, gave access to the small walled courtyard which was exactly 6 yards wide by 9 yards long. It had running round the four sides cement paving, and the centre consisted of what could only pass for a little handkerchief of soil: a minute lawn and four flower beds. In one corner there was a white rose bush and in the other a red. Despite the most scientifically dosed mixtures of tobacco and water I never quite managed to rid the roses of plant lice. In between these two I had some carnations, flourishing in the shallow sandy soil. They never stopped flowering. Religiously every night Arselow picked one flower which he carefully fitted *inside* his cap before putting it back on again. I assumed that he wanted his hair to smell nice, but in fact he was smuggling out the flowers to offer one every day to his (illicit) sweetheart. I also had a tomato bush bearing small sweet fruit. I remember eating a tomato the morning Engelbrecht and Fourie were hanged, how fresh it tasted, and my being very aware that they would never eat tomatoes again. But after I'd mentioned the existence of the tomato bush in a letter to my mother, the brigadier had it removed immediately.

I was the gardener there. One learns quickly to try and make your time outside stretch by any possible means. When I had to water my little kingdom it had to be done by bucket, which I had to fill up in the bathroom, so naturally I took as long over this as I possibly could. In the same way when it was the season for planting, because it was never the season for harvesting, one would spend as much time as one could wheedle out of them turning over with a stick the soil which was only about a foot deep – underneath there was cement again – making your little holes, planting your seeds, doing all you can to dissect time with your fingers the way one would eat a fish off its bones.

The brick walls around the courtyard reached as high as the catwalk, and they were closed over the top by a very heavy wire grid resting on steel beams and crossbeams, so that you never saw the sky unimpeded, but always blocked off in small squares. These apertures were just big enough to allow a bird as big as a dove to be able to enter, looking for seeds, but it could not go out again once it was inside. In this way we caught several birds which had hurt themselves attempting to get out. One of these I was allowed to keep for a short while as a pet. For a few days it lived under my bed, sharing my food, watching me with a smooth eye. The wagtails though had no problem in getting in and out. Cheeky chaps in their grey morning suits, like ushers for a high-class wedding. Or slightly navicular lamps for burning oil in ancient shrines. In reality they were quite tame and flew right into the prison, emitting the most eery and beautiful tones which I learned to imitate. They are very inquisitive little beasts. When you lure them by making the same sounds they come as close as they can, tilting their heads, trying to find their mysterious Mr Bird. They never tired of the game. I wondered sometimes whether in some obscure part of their imagination they actually saw me as just a very obscene, bloated bird without wings. Maybe one of them was even trying to woo me!

On the C-Section side there were three courtyards: the small one which I described to you, belonging to C1, also had a small balcony protruding above the wire grid. On this a *boer* would take position with his firearm when I was in there with another *boer*, doing my exercises. A second, slightly larger courtyard, was for the use of C2, that is the 'condemns'. And then a fairly large one for C3. That one, perhaps because it was so big, was not wired over. The courtyards had not always been covered. That only happened after the one and only escape ever from Maximum Security – by an ex-policeman, due to be hanged, called Franz von Staden, who made his way from the C1 courtyard on to the wall, and from there he got away. At that time the wall around the building didn't exist either. Even so it was believed that he had been given a help-me-up by one or more warders. His freedom did not take him very far since he went straight to the station where an off-duty policeman recognized him and re-arrested him promptly. He also was among the many who tried to commit suicide before his execution by diving head first from his bunk into the cement floor. Not successfully so. This is one of the reasons the death candidates are watched continuously while waiting to be killed: so that they do not deprive the State of its rightful vengeance.

The cell itself, because I want to invite you right inside, Mr I, could not have been much larger than 6 feet: I could just barely brush the walls with my arms outstretched. In length it must have been about 9 feet. But for what it lacked in floor space it made up in depth: it was a good 16 feet high, with just open space for the last 6 feet, blocked off from the catwalk by a wiremesh. It had a steel door with again, from chest height, meshed openings between bars. The cell had one bunk set into the wall itself, with on the bunk a thin mattress. At the head of the bunk there was another small wooden plaque bolted into the wall, on which you were supposed to fold your clothes neatly. Next to that, hollowed out in the wall, was a small water fountain. You pressed the knob in the wall above it and water squirted into the receptacle. Next to that there was the toilet bowl, without any lid, activated by a wire loop just protruding from the wall. You hooked a finger through and you pulled. (On Sundays, immediately after lunch, the Black prisoner cleaners used to gather on the other side of that wall for a religious sermon, led by a visiting preacher – probably telling them to accept their fate, that the White man's ways are mysterious because they are the ways of God – and they sang the saddest dirges. One of them could wriggle the wire leading to my throne. I would bend and squint down the wire through the conduit and just barely perceive, pressed to the other end, a friendly black eye. I would jiggle it and he would respond likewise. It was like touching a finger. We communicated. It was also like a monkey groping behind a mirror after its own image.) The floor cement. The walls painted an off-white.

The whole prison was sagging slightly: it had been built not all that many years previous to my arriving there on a site which apparently had been used as a rubbish dump, so the foundations were not very solid. There were already cracks in the walls.

The other cell, the one on the main corridor, was much larger – consisting in fact of two rooms communicating. In one room there was a bed, a small table with a chair, and a little wooden cupboard. The other room was entirely bare except for a wash basin and a contraption they had built specially for toilet purposes. They'd given me a bucket which was inserted in some kind of a box that one could cover. In the mornings then, I had to take the bucket and, accompanied down the corridor, I had to go and empty it in the toilet of C1 bathroom. I don't think they particularly appreciated my referring to this morning ritual as 'bringing the Brigadier's breakfast'.

Those were my two living spaces. The floors of the two-roomed apartment, if I may call it that, were covered with plastic tiles of the same kind as those in the main corridor, and these had to be polished and kept shiny. But so also had the cement floors in C1. You had to be able to mirror your face in it. That was my Sisyphus task: making of my floor a mirror which could capture and return my real face –which would immediately be walked over and sink back into greyness: washing it, taking off the old polish, putting on some new, using the brush first with swaying shoulders, and then moving over it again and again on your 'taxis', which are little squares of folded blanket. We used old blankets or old mats for that purpose. I've travelled many miles, Mr Investigator.

(THE WAY)

Your whole life in prison is regulated by rhythms, and the breaks in rhythm, the exceptions to these. You adapt yourself to the rhythm. (You have no choice but to.) Adaptation becomes a factor of security: it is part of the process we describe as 'institutionalization' – meaning that the ups and downs and the reference points of every day become your territory and you hate any intrusion, anything out of the ordinary happening, even if under other circumstances this happening would have been felt as something pleasant, like an unexpected visit. The routine existence becomes a shell and you withdraw into it. The *boere* know this attitude and they know how to play with it. By making you skip one meal they in fact destroy your peace of mind for many days. When you are used to being unlocked at a certain time and suddenly you're not, everything is upside down. You go grovelling for the most insignificant thing – in fact for security – for your hand-holds on reality. You lose face. You become weaker *vis-à-vis* the warders. I've heard a 'condemn', Skollie, due to be destroyed in two weeks' time – and the inevitability of death apparently did not disturb him – go into a screaming and weeping fit, banging his head against the door, because he didn't get, that Wednesday, the Louis Lamour westerns he'd requested, but some other junk like Tolstoy. He read only westerns.

Rhythms – understanding them, to some extent using them – these also are your means of survival in prison. It is the way you chop up time in manageable entities. There is the rhythm of every day, that of the weeks, that of the months, and then the years. Living from pulsebeat to pulsebeat, recognizing the salients particular to the unit, be it a month or a year, is a way of putting these behind you, allowing the possibility to say to yourself: so many down so many more to go. And you live for these recognizable points; you look forward to them.

But one's conception of time is not an immutable faculty. Some periods are far longer than others. The first days, for instance, as you lie there 'eating head', are interminable. You never expect to survive the first month. The first year, once you've been given your go, rears up in front of you like an unclimbable mountain – and you say to yourself: if one year is as bad as this, how in the name of King Kong and I am I going to survive the other eight? (Prisoners are obsessed by time. One 'does time', or you push it. You are a 'timer'. The best wish you can emit is: *roll on time!* We used to say that magistrates and judges are most spendthrift with other people's time: they are time stealers. We also described prison officials attempting rehabilitation as baboons trying to repair broken watches.)

Still, the same events coming around again, the rhythms being repeated, the familiarity of your situation – these deaden you to the passing of time. You look down from the bridge and you don't remember any water having passed under it. The past has the taste of water and you can't imagine now why it was so traumatic then. You haven't aged: the years were empty. People come and go, the equations remain the same. You forget perhaps that you were then a different person, that you have become that entity which inhabits this time which consists of clearly defined patterns, repetitions, the same again and again and again. You yourself are purified or reduced to some other personality.

This, the texture of life in prison, the absence of texture, or at least the way you experience it, will be different from one jail to another. It will depend on the stage you have reached in your time. There will also be regional differences between, say, the Transvaal and the Cape. What remains the same is the diet, the clothes you wear, and inevitably the type of relationship you have with authority.

In Pretoria Maximum the day started off at 6 o'clock when

someone would be coming around to switch on your light and take a peep at you through the bars on the door. You get up, make your bed the regulation way, dress, and maybe half an hour later two people would be doing the rounds again – this time to count you. The door between C1 and the main corridor is opened with a bang, a voice shouts at you to 'stand to!' and you show your face behind the bars. You also say, 'Good morning, sir.' Once this ritual is completed, provided the figures check with those of lock up time of the night before, the *boer* on duty would return and unlock you. You now proceed to the bathroom with your toothbrush, your soap and your towel. You have recovered your shoes which had to be left outside your cell door for the night. (When I was rooming off the main corridor and had to be taken to C1 for a bath, I always used to see – during a certain period – a shoe and next to it a *leg* and shoe parked in front of one of the cells. The temporary resident there at that time, obviously minus a leg, would remain locked up until I'd finished my ablutions and had disposed of the Brigadier's breakfast. This *bandiet* one day casually told the *boere* to have a look inside his artificial leg, where he had squirrelled away R25.)

The warder hands you the razor which was kept in his office, and under his supervision you wash, shave the reflection in the dim metal plate, brush your teeth, and are taken back to your cell to be locked in.

Another half hour would pass and again there's the whole rigmarole of unlocking you. This time the cleaner confined to the main corridor would deposit your morning graze just outside the main door. You could see his pimply prison feet in the gap between steel partition and floor. On the one foot was tattooed *lets run* and on the other *to hell*. The door is now unlocked, you take in your breakfast (stealing a quick look up the corridor to try and see another inmate going through the same motions), take it to your cell and eat. Personal rule No. 1: always eat everything you're given. You never know when the world is going to explode. You would have taken your spoon which overnight is wedged in the wire mesh covering the bars on your door. Your food will consist of a plastic bowl of 'pap', a porridge made of maize, and some milk already poured over it. There will be a second bowl with an exact measure of brown sugar, an exact measure of jam (the same mixed-fruit jam year in and year out), an exact measure of margarine and two slices of brown bread. Also a mug of coffee. You lick your bowls clean, break wind and go through the fetch-and-carry process in reverse. I soon learn to hide away some of my precious brown sugar, to dampen it at night and eat it on my evening bread which would be served without anything.

Now the warder normally leaves you unlocked (if he doesn't, you're in for a troublesome morning) as you have to clean your small kingdom: your cell, the bathroom, your corridor. Cleaning means sweeping up whatever dust there may be; dusting the window sills, the ledges, the bars of the grills; scouring the toilet bowl and the wash basin and the bath; polishing with Brasso all the copper appurtenances such as door handles and light fixtures. When needed, which was about three times a week, you would scrub the floor with water and ordinary soap, dry it, apply fresh polish with a little rag, go over this first with your brush, and then commenced the ever on-going process of shining the surfaces with your 'taxis'. It is a good time of the day. The morning is fresh, and with your ears you try to steal the news from the magical world beyond the partition. Working close to this partition you could, through the crack of the door joins, catch a glimpse of the office across the corridor. Often Stefaans would be taken there, haggard and grey, to complain of his worms and to plead for a special diet. They – the *boere* – would laugh and play around with him. Sometimes they would pretend to be solicitous and accommodate him. For a time his lunch consisted of only one whole carrot and nothing more. Once I even hit the jackpot: the cleaner came to rub away just on the other side of the door and whispered his dream to me. He was going to profit from his time inside (he was innocent, as all prisoners are; it was a frame-up that got him there) and have all the necessary operations – get his back straightened, have all his (perfectly sound) teeth pulled and replaced by smart dentures, get glasses (for his perfectly sound eyes) – and then, upon release, he was going to buy and put on an electric blue suit, buy a real electric guitar (which he couldn't play) and nonchalantly strut into a swanky restaurant, dragging the guitar after him. Man!

At any time after 9.30 and before lunch, which on a normal day is at about 11.30, you will be allowed out into the small courtyard for your half an hour of exercise. Prison regulations prescribe that you ought to have half an hour in the monring and half an hour in the afternoon but very often the afternoon session was skipped with the excuse that the warders were too busy doing something else or that there were not enough of them: one of the perks for the staff was that they could practise sport during service hours. The grille leading to your little courtyard is unlocked, then the outside steel door; you are let out with a warder accompanying you and the grille behind you is locked. There's a second warder standing on the balcony looking down on you. They time it very exactly. Now you do your Tai-Ji or whatever you can to profit from the fresh air, and if you're lucky, if it's the right season and the right time of the day, also from the rays of the sun entering the courtyard. You get to recognize every pebble and lost twig there: they are your friends. After exercise you are taken back in and locked up.

Lunch time: same ritual as the one you went through in the morning. You knew in advance what food you were having, on what days.

To save space, Mr Investigator, let me finish the food (story) once and for all. Prisoners' diets, it is claimed, are worked out scientifically by dietitians. You can survive on it. It is boring and bland and you often are hungry. The time between your last meal of the day and your first one the next morning is very long. Supper is handed out at 4 o'clock – Sundays often at 2.30! It is my experience that if you have to live from that only for any length of time, you end up with a vitamin deficiency. I started having trouble with my hair and my skin and my eyes. Suddenly I developed boils and cold sores. (In Pollsmoor I employed a fellow convict – since I couldn't circulate in the prison – to buy for cigarettes as many pieces of fruit as people were willing to sell after the weekly issue.) Regulations prescribe the exact amount of food a birdie should receive. A White prisoner, all in all, receives 210 grams of bread per day, 120 grams of meat on meat days, five eggs per week – three of which disappear in the dough of Friday's fried fish. (But then, while I was in Pollsmoor, it happened several times that one F-Group warder or another, kitchen *boere*, got caught stealing eggs by the dozen and selling them to their colleagues. Not that anything much ever happened to them: they'd be transferred elsewhere for a while before returning to the kitchens.) These diets are not the same for White, Black and Brown prisoners. For example, White prisoners are entitled to one fruit per week, which the Blacks or the Browns never get. White prisoners also receive a small portion, 60 grams, of peanut butter a week, on Wednesdays, and similarly 30 grams of cheese on Sundays. Again Blacks and Browns don't qualify for these. Blacks and Browns will get more 'pap' than Whites do, and boiled-down fat in the place of the Whites' margarine. The Blacks are also given *puzlamansa*, or *magou*, which is some kind of fortified soy-based powder that can be made into a paste or, when more liquid, into a drink. They do not get much bread. The Coloureds on the contrary get more bread. Blacks and Browns get less meat than Whites do: the bread and the *puzlamansa* are supposed to replace it.*

The only time Blacks or Browns are entitled to the same food as Whites will be once they have been condemned to death when, immediately, they qualify for the so-called 'White diet'. This holds true until the ultimate meal when again a White will be getting a full chicken for his last meal on earth – cooked in the warders' mess – whereas the Black will receive half a chicken only.

These different diets provoke a continuous smuggling of food. Whites try to obtain *puzlamansa* because it is reputed, if prepared in a certain way, to have a slightly intoxicating effect. The Blacks and the Browns of course, particularly those working in the kitchens, steal and sell and trade items like peanut butter, which they cannot lay their hands on otherwise.

For breakfast you have, five times a week, your *mieliepap*, and twice, on Wednesdays and Sundays, it will be oats. I've already mentioned the rest, and that every Sunday is Christmas because

*It is, I believe, the Prison Department's policy gradually to eliminate the discrepancies in diet among various prisoner groups, as also the differences in clothing. Some Brown prisoners in the Cape even sleep on beds now – no mattresses yet: 'Let them first for a year or two get used to not falling off the beds,' the Store Master sneered. And, just as I left, it was decreed, despite the tenacious opposition of the storemen, that Browns and Blacks can wear underclothes too. Only certain categories to start with: those employed as waiters, the cooks, those working as 'monitors' in White warders' houses, and the sick in hospital.

of your finger of Cheddar. Your lunch on Mondays will consist of two boiled eggs, your vegetables, either *samp* (which is mealies) or broken rice, also called 'mealie-rice', and a mug of tea. For the other days of the week that the good Creator made, the same, except that the eggs are replaced by meat – either pork or chicken – and on Fridays you will always get fish. We, the prisoners, at least in the Cape, say the year has two seasons: one season is cabbage and one is carrots. Many a time people used to 'stand fast', dixie in hand, disgust or incredulity written large on the features, to complain: mostly about the meat. At one stage our pork (which we'd get uninterruptedly for weeks, and then chicken for weeks) used to consist of whole pigs' heads slung into the pots, boiled, and then crushed. Some *mugus* found within a week or two enough pigs' teeth in their plates to make necklaces. As for the chicken – it came in either one of two ways: 'smashed chicken' or 'chicken *à la* fuck-up'. We knew the officer's reply by rote, 'You think this is a five star hotel, hey? You should have worried about this before coming to prison. And what do you have outside anyway? Fuck all! You come here and eat up the State's food. Lot of fat *skelms* (crooks)! Who pays for it all? *I* do. And *I* don't eat as well.' And then, as often as not, the complainers found themselves charged for being 'agitators'.

Your evening meal will consist of a *kattie* of bread. (*Kattie* is short for *katkoppie*, cat's head, which traditionally was the size and the shape of the measures of bread baked in the ovens of Pretoria Central Prison when they still functioned; this custom was stopped to prevent the prisoners stealing the yeast which is an indispensable ingredient for fabricating any alcohol.) So at night you get your *kattie* – four slices of bread it is, and a mug of soup.

After lunch: in your hole. If you are let out, it will be for a short period just before lock-up. If not, you may score a short end of time to give the floor a final going over. Lock-up on weekdays just before 4 o'clock. The lights are switched on, the process of counting takes place all over again, you 'stand to', you are checked off on a list, and now you have a whole lot of nothing to do until lights out at 8 o'clock. You hear the warders patrolling on the catwalk, and every once in a while one of them may stoop to look down on you and, if he is bored enough, to exchange a few words.

The interruptions in your day's rhythm will be when the warders come to ramp your cell, or when you are called out because some officer wants to blind you with the 'irons' on his shoulders or the 'doveshit' on his cap's peak, or because you have to have your hair cut.

Your weeks are marked by three days: Monday, when you get your clean clothes and fresh sheets; Wednesday, which is when you get your two permitted library books (joy! bells peal in heaven!); and Sunday, when for lunch the cooks make a little effort and still using the same basic components, try to provide a salad or attempt at least not to mash up the meat too badly. Sunday was furthermore distinguished by the fact that we had our meagre supper much earlier and often found ourselves locked up for the night by 2.30 in the afternoon. Weeks were also marked by the weekly inspection, on Sunday mornings, by the head of the prison or sometimes the officer commanding the Pretoria Prison Command, and during the week on a Wednesday or a Thursday by the visit of the chaplain, an old gentleman called van Jaarsveld. The week's rhythm could be destroyed by a hanging. This normally meant that I would see the very short doctor, who had to assist at the execution and made use of the occasion to visit his other charges also. Or the lulling routine could be interrupted by one's not receiving one's library books (this was catastrophic!) Or, again, by being unexpectedly called out for a visit by some psychiatrist or higher-up, passing through on his way. (They also had to show that they actually *earned* their salaries.)

The months were marked by three major events – important because they constituted one's contact with the outside world. Once a month I was allowed to receive a letter and to write one. Once a month too, I was entitled to a visit lasting half an hour. And at the end of every month the prisoner could – from his 'private cash', that is the money he has on his name up front, and for a limited amount fixed by the authorities – buy a certain number of items from the local 'tuck shop' or canteen. Until such time as he becomes A-Group, these will consist of toilet articles and tobacco and writing material only.

The letter, both that going out and that coming in, could only be 500 words long and naturally had to be very bland – not referring to any specific conditions or events behind the walls. These were censored by the section sergeant first, then the officer responsible for security and, in the case of politicals, certainly also by the security police. (Anybody else handling it along the way also perused it as a matter of course. When I knew a letter had arrived for me, and tried desperately to obtain it before the end-of-month deadline, I often felt like asking, 'May I read it *also*?') The visit took place in one of the tiny visiting rooms leading off the main corridor. You were separated from your visitor by a thick glass and you spoke through a trumpet-like contraption inserted in the table before you. There was at all times at least one warder present on your side, breathing his stale hamburger breath down your neck, and one present on the other side. These visits, although the Prison Department always strenuously denied it, were taped, and I assumed that these tapes or their transcriptions were vetted again by the security police. Actually I have objective proof that my visits were taped.

One's month could be ruined by the alteration of any of these salient features: a letter not arriving on time or a visit being interrupted because one spoke about forbidden things.

There are other rhythms, Mr Investigator. There are the movements of light and darkness down the walls. There was the coming back of the swallows once every year, rebuilding their nest in the same place under the eaves. Seasons change and one morning one is issued with a heavier jacket and with long pants. You know that winter must be burning up the veld. It gets warmer, the sun grows a beard, thunderstorms: summer. You start to capture also the rhythms of your own body – the depressions succeeded by lighter periods, the recurring dreams, the touch of rheumatism you have in the right wing when it's damp. And in this way, bit by bit, you go through the year, and then another, and you learn that the years have a routine of their own also. There is at least Christmas to use as a benchmark, although it is a very sad occasion for prisoners. Christmas: the time of the year when there are the largest number of attempted suicides and escapes.

Rhythms, routines, elements of your understanding and experiencing the self and the environment; fetters which make you weaker: but, as always, within the weakness the strength already lies – and so they become the ways in which you destroy time.

INSERT

In this room the corpses are taken to the fathers for embalming. (One goes to visit the deads from time to time, talking to them, telling them about how Aunt Agatha lost her favourite speckled hen. It entertains the dream of immortality.) The visceral parts, the heart and the lungs, will have been removed and kept separately in a container on the mantelpiece: 'For the best mum in the world – your loving son.'

The naked corpse of the deceased remains for several hours in a bath of arsenic – quicklime is cheaper but it removes the body's natural colouring and thus plays havoc with the system of having everyone in his rightful place. Thereafter it is locked away for eight months in a stagnant cell behind a closed door. Just to give it the right patina of ageing. Food is pushed through under the door. Only now will it be taken out on the roof or a terrace, to dry out in air and in sun.

Look, there they are – dressed in their best greens. See, there a bullet nicked a scalp or here a knife creased the stomach. The weal? Oh, that's the bite of the rope. Have mercy on them. They are in heaven. Their angels incessantly look upon the face of our Mister Father who is in heaven too. Prison is just another heaven.

Mr Investigator, I hope you realize that it's not easy for me to talk to you like this, with an open heart. I'm trying to stick to a simple principle: to tell everything, hode-podge, be it a clapper-clawing or a whining, whichever way it comes. Naturally I have forgotten a lot – I wouldn't be human otherwise. That is why I try to structure my mind – the one incident carries the echoes of others – like death. There is no composition like decomposition: not just a rearranging or a falling apart, but verily rotting to the bone to bring to light the essential structure. The further you go the more you realize that there are no finites; just movements of the mind, only processes.

But it is not easy and neither is it pleasant. The only comfort I allow myself is the thought (or the hope?) that recollecting all the events will also allow me to put them out of mind forever. I am hoping for a purge. (That is why it is so important to dredge up *everything*: what one leaves behind will, like the bloodsucking head of the louse you remove from your skin, start festering.) So one must burn! The mind – this *mélange* of mindlessness and memory and metempsychosis (which is only a metathesis?) – is ever groping for the meridian where it can moulder in motionless meditation.

Maybe there are strong forces which object to my talking to you, Mr Investalligator. Force has no moral dimension. The fact that they're evil doesn't make them less potent!

My skin is packing up on me. It is peeling over the shoulders. In my moustache and between my eyes there are rough patches, like winter blisters. In the folds of my thighs I have a stubborn rash: I talk to you and I perspire and the sweat makes me burn all over. (I waddle along with legs wide apart like some old goose in heat.) So one must burn! Is the need to vomit the surfacing past a rash on the brain?

Madame la Générale washes up after supper and inexplicably lets fall eight plates to smithereens in one go. (She who has such sure hands!) My watch no longer works; when I shake it, it sets off again, sweeping a cat's paw over its face, but it watches and when I'm not looking it loses time as if I have nine years of it to spare. The mosquitoes keep us awake at night. Sluggish flies circle in the kitchen: I go after them blindly, but there are always others to take their places. Three kinds of ants invade the house like water seeping through cracks. I pour boiling water down the cracks in the walls. The acrylics I've made of masks and of men being hanged in heaven's gate as a warning to the angels – these fall off the wall. So now I shall have to make a painting of falling paintings. When I talk to you the tape is ruined by quarrelling neighbours, each reciting *Finnegans Wake* at the top of his voice.

On Sunday four young urchins try to steal the car we've been lent. I see them from the balcony just as they are moving away with it from under the trees on the Square of Pawnbrokers: I point a stiff arm, lift a trembling white beard, and bellow, hoping to give an imitation of a wrathful priest. (Imitation, all imitation.) They scamper off into the Street of Flying Chairs. We recover the car, but they (or their elders) have already succeeded in stealing the battery, so we are left with the carcass. I have to buy a new one and have no way of knowing whether the natives are taking me for a ride. No one saw the culprits. I shall not recognize them: they all look alike. Eyes slide away from your face. Don't know, don't know. It is life. Even at this level *omerta* works, efficiently.

(What have *I* learned about the law of silence?) And then I say to myself: if they were caught, what then? A first step on the way to prison? Is that what you want? Of course not! You've just come from there – what is it that you're thinking of?

There are portents and omens which I hesitate to read, but I dread them. (Ignorance is no protection.) The thuds and the febrile light of fireworks outside the city over the mountain where the resident guardian saint lies on her side in the cave she occupied during her life, now coated in gold. On two occasions lately I've crossed muttering nuns in the street. It is said that one should never travel on a boat with nuns on board – the waves will become wild because the nuns resemble them too much. A bird flies upside down. A fat beggar curses me when I refuse to give him alms. There must be a warship in the bay: suddenly there are scores of Egyptian sailors in the *sukh*. Over the television screen flit grey images of inscrutable Japanese divers bringing from the deep speared living things (coral?) called 'crowns of thorn'.

We drive down to Little World and the only available parking space I can find is in front of a house numbered 13. On the beach I see a pair of twins with silver reflections where their eyes ought to be. I also see a hunchback, who leers at me. And a poor child who is so ugly you instinctively make all the ancient signs to ward off calamity. At least I haven't come across any midgets. Another judge is gunned down on the steps of the court. Fantastic wreaths cover the blood. A mother holds the head of her nine-year-old daughter under the water of a bathtub in a *pension* until the girl has stopped quivering, and then wraps her in a shroud fashioned from a sheet: she had to 'wash the child's soul'.

Back in town I decide to break the silence. We're supposed to be incommunicado – to get this over and done with – but we contact the *centrale* twice a week for any messages. He tells me that he's just had the unexpected visit of a midget! So that too is done.

But we must go on, mustn't we, Mr Investigator? See, now that I've told you about all of this, I can forget it. One must burn! Maybe, once I'm finished, there will finally be neither you nor I left . . .

And, as one of the *boere* used to say grimly when whatever mishap befell him, be it the death of his first-born or the roof caving in, 'It is still better than being in prison.'

2

The Writer Destroys Time

I am the writer. I scribble. I have, stuffed in my pockets, old envelopes, small folded pieces of paper, the torn-off edges of newssheets. These I fill with cryptic notes. I scratch them out. I write over them. I ride them down. I fill in every blank space. I lose them. I find them and I'm incapable of deciphering a thing. At night, after the lights are turned out, I can't sleep. I used to be a night bird. Now I'm just a jail bird. It's too early for me. Winters, when it gets quite cold in the Transvaal, I lie on my bed with just my hands outside the blankets. Cement and steel concentrate the cold. In bed I keep my socks on. I have a chess-board with pieces, given to me during the time of my detention, and I have been allowed to keep it. But I have nobody opposite me to crack a game with. You are not there. In the dark I put the squares next to my bed on the floor, set up the men, and start a game. I put my soldiers in the dark. It is a schizophrenic experience, playing white against black, I facing I, me against Mr Investigator. I cannot lose. I cannot win. I am free.*

In the dark I am not in the way. There is nobody to look over my shoulder. I am relieved! Then, like an irrepressible urge, there would be the need to write. In the dark I can just perceive the faintly pale outline of a sheet of paper. And I would start writing. Like launching a black ship on a dark sea. I write: I am the writer. I am doing my black writing with my no-colour gloves and my dark glasses on, stopping every once in a while, passing my sheathed hand over the page to feel the outlines and the imprints of letters which have no profile. It makes for a very specific kind of wording, perhaps akin to the experiments that the surrealists

*Jerry tells me later of a chess game he watched, while imprisoned in Czechoslovakia, between a fellow inmate and one of the guardians. Whenever, during the course of the game, the guardian was called away elsewhere, the inmate would swallow one of his opponent's pieces. It is a hard struggle to survive.

used to make in earlier years. There is the splashing of darkness, the twirled sense. Since one cannot re-read what you've written a certain continuity is imposed on you. You have to let go. You must follow. You allow yourself to be carried forward by the pulsation of the words as they surface in the paper. You are the paper. Punctuation goes by the board. Repetitions, rhythms, structures, these will be nearly biological. Not intellectually conceived. Ponder for two beats and you're lost. It is very much, Mr Investigator, like me talking to you now with my eyes closed, seeing behind my eyelids the words moving by as if on a screen. Sighs looking for an orgasm. You write on in an attempt to erase.

In this way one plunges directly into a dream. I remember now that I am in the Hills – rowing down the main corridor in a little boat. In this boat there are my father and my mother and my wife. All the doors leading off to the side corridors are closed and the water is rising slowly but steadily to the point where I no longer need to use an oar. I can push the boat forward by using my hands against the ceiling. We need to escape. We need somehow to fit through the small space at the top between the steel doors and the ceiling itself. But we are heading deeper into the labyrinth. The Minotaur has drowned. His bloated body must be tumbling along somewhere, bumping the floor. My mother's hands clench the edges of the boat. Already she is as grey and as sad as the very water.

Writing becomes for me a means, a way of survival. I have to cut up my environment in digestible chunks. Writing is an extension of my senses. It is itself a sense which permits me to grasp, to understand, and to some extent to integrate that which is happening to me. I need it the same way the blind man behind his black glasses needs to see. But at the same time I soon realize that it becomes the exteriorization of my imprisonment. My writing bounces off the walls. The maze of words which become alleys, like sentences, the loops which are closed circuits and present no exit, these themselves constitute the walls of my confinement. I write my own castle and it becomes a frightening discovery: it is unbalancing something very deeply embedded in yourself when you in reality construct, through your scribblings, your own mirror. Because in this mirror you write hair by hair and pore by pore your own face, and you don't like what you see.

You don't even recognize it. It won't let you out again. . . . Who am I? Where and who was I before this time?

I have no common mirror during the first period of Maximum Security. It is only something like a year and a half later that Arselow, for some reason only he would know of, one day brings a mirror to my cell – a real one. I look at this naked-faced yellow monkey looking back at me. In an adjacent corridor the young Jewish security guard who attempted to take over the Israeli embassy in Pretoria, shooting a diplomat in the process, and who is now kept here under permanent surveillance, one late afternoon breaks a mirror and starts slashing his own wrists and stomach. I hear the warder with him screaming hysterically, banging against the steel partition to be let out. They save him. They save the prisoner too.

Even during the period of detention I had been allowed to write. It was something I could not ignore. A voice said, 'Write', and I wrote. And the more I had to enter the slithering area of confessing to and for the Greyshits, trying to pin down and imagine life, and becoming aware in the process of the ridiculous aspects of my illusions and my pretensions, the more I experienced the need to write what was 'true' – to communicate with someone else, not always with the enemy; to create, even if only precariously so, in the towers of verse the other world, the one where I could withdraw with my wife. And so I was allowed to write poems. These all originated over a period of hardly six weeks and were published not long afterwards under the title of *Voetskrif*, meaning 'Footscript'. The very existence of this volume was exploited by Huntingdon. He saw herein one more way to manipulate me and simultaneously improve his image and, he hoped, his acceptability to the literary community among the Afrikaners. He did not want to be known as a cultural barbarian, and in any event he was intuitive enough to understand that the real threat to the Afrikaner would come from within their own ranks – so, far-sighted, he already had to lay the first lines of infiltration into the ranks of the Afrikaner writers from whom he suspected subversive ideas or rebellious noises in due time to come. He insisted quite brazenly that the volume of verse should be dedicated to him. It was a naked instance of horse trading: you dedicate this to me and I allow you to have it published. But it had to be censored by him of course. One complete poem bit the dust. Let me quote it to you, Mr Investigator. The title was 'Help', and the body of the text consisted of 'Help!'

It is absurd, thinking back on that period, that my nemesis, the man who was – however insidiously – trying to have my guts and to flip me inside out, at the same time acted as my literary agent – in fact creating or giving me the possibility of survival. By means of their men in Cape Town I recovered the poems left with the Swami. I still have the envelope in which these were forwarded to Huntingdon in Pretoria with, written on the outside, 'These are the poems he left with so-and-so in exactly the condition we found them in.'

During this period also, at the beginning of my time in Pretoria, *A Season in Paradise* was published.* The Greyshits knew all about it long before publication. They are very keen connoisseurs of literature. In their impatience they will intercept a manuscript between author and publisher. They may even read a book before it is written! I mentioned that I was interrogated partially about material contained in that book. I felt, as every prisoner does very strongly, the need to be able to contribute something to life outside. There remained the urge to communicate, to shout, to get on to the roof and wave your arms and say: 'I love you,' or just 'I'm here; I'm dead but I'm here – be sure not to forget it!' But also there was, knowing how difficult life must have become for Yolande outside (or suspecting it – she was too discreet and considerate to refer to troubles) the strong desire to be able to help her in whichever way I could. Therefore, in order not to have my voice cut off entirely, I urged her to arrange for the publication of the manuscript which had never really been finalized to my satisfaction, and I agreed to certain cuts being made in the book on condition that these were supervised by people whom I trusted entirely and also that the integral version be used for any translations and publications abroad

There is an important principle to underline: in a repressive State inimical to the writer you will never find the perfect conditions for freedom of expression, but it is essential to continue,

*The first edition, a censored version, was published in Afrikaans by Perskov, during 1976.

even if only with the minimal demands of integrity that you impose on yourself and on your umbilical cord with the outside world. It is possible to falsify for some time the thrust of one's words by inserting them in an environment controlled by the enemy, but eventually – if what you write is 'true' to yourself at that moment – it will become evident and be rectified. (Even if it is true only in its absence of truth and its fumbling for checkpoints and references.)

Over the years, while I was in prison, several works were translated. There were volumes of poetry in quite a few European languages and there was *A Season in Paradise* in English and in Dutch. For a long time I was not allowed to receive any of these publications and never could I participate in any way in the preparation thereof. For instance, I was not allowed to go over previously unpublished work - that is, pre-prison time texts - to alter anything in them. (All I could do was, by means of my contact with Yolande, to try to advise her, and through her the publishers, about what material to use and to some extent in what order.) The ostensible reason for this was that any such participation while in prison is considered by the Prison Department, very narrowly, as continuing economic activity, which is forbidden by law. (Although you very often will find instances where businessmen, in some camouflaged way, are allowed to keep running their affairs. Prison lore will tell you about C, murderer millionaire, who continued directing his multiple business concerns from inside; also about how generously he paid for prison sports facilities, etc.; and that he was released after doing only five years of his twelve-year sentence, for 'exemplary conduct'. In Cape Town I knew a fellow convict who was regularly and often visited by his business partner – an Indian – for consultations. But he had to grease the palm of an officer to obtain the privilege.) In P'town, then, I never was permitted to read my own published work. The one occasion when I did see some of my books was when I was called in to the Commanding Officer's office and told that as the result of a petition to the minister I was allowed to take cognizance of the existence of some books. I was thereupon sent back to my cell and told to sit on a chair before it, and with a warder sitting facing me I could take in my hands and leaf through a copy of *A Season in Paradise*, a copy of the French verse, and my collected peoms united in two volumes printed in Holland, on condition that I did not attempt to *read* these.

But I am the writer . . . I need to write. . . . Soon after my sentencing I applied in writing, as always in prison, in duplicate, to the authorities for the permission to paint and to write. Without my knowing about it similar requests were being made from outside, emanating from the South African milieu of writers and academics. People who absolutely rejected me and my ideas and what my life stood for but who, perhaps from an obscure sense of uncomfortableness, if not guilt, and also, surely, because of a true concern for my work, applied to the minister to allow me to continue writing. 'For the sake of Afrikaans literature.' Was it a way for some of them to establish in their own minds their evenhandedness?

The request to paint was turned down with the excuse that too often painting or drawings are used as means to barter with in prison. (Perhaps also because someone, somewhere, had realized that to paint is truly to escape: it is a healing of the hands and the eye.) The officer telling me this had hanging on the wall behind him several paintings made by prisoners. Writing, he informed me, I would be allowed to do, with the following conditions attached to the permission: that I would not show it to any other prisoner or warder (that went without saying since I had no contact with anyone); that I would not attempt to smuggle it out of prison; that I would hand it in directly upon completing anything or any part of any work; that I would not hoard or keep notes for the work and would destroy these immediately after finishing the work. In return I was assured that the work would be kept in safe-keeping for me.

A bizarre situation, Mr Investigator, when you write knowing that the enemy is reading over your shoulder; when you have to write as deeply down in yourself as you can because you need this to survive; writing in a desperate attempt at communication with the outside, with the world, with the people closest to you, knowing beforehand that it cannot reach them and knowing also that you are laying bare the most intimate and the most personal nerves and pulsebeats in yourself to the barbarians, to the cynical ones who will gloat over this. Bizarre situation also when you cannot remember what you have written before and you have no means of recovering the previous jottings so that you do not know whether you are writing in circles, raking over cleaned soil, coming back to sniff again and again at the same old sour vomit. You wanted to write a metropolis of anthills and now find yourself lost among the ants. You collected seashells hoping to find the sea. Thus you start erecting elaborate structures in your mind and filling in the blank pages one by one, building a tenth floor before you do the second or the basement – and since you write your dreams and write in your dreams and dream that you are writing, you do not know what you have actually written and what you have only imagined. You write your mind. That is perhaps, Mr Investigator, why or how I have become so sensitive to living structure. Also to the objective existence of that which has been exteriorized. (I'm not saying exorcised!) That you are not only writing your past but also your future: you are cutting open new lanes to the heart of nothingness but you are also papering over cracks and blocking off routes. Much later, for instance, I realized that I had foreseen in my writing the experiences that my father was still to go through. There was the recurring image, surfacing through the words of that time, of an old man all alone with his head exploding in a thousand tears. It became only too true when my mother died and he remained utterly isolated – to later suffer a stroke and become paralysed and mute. I also recognized only afterwards that long before there was any question of my going south, there already appeared in my writing the mountain, the magical mountain, the manifestation and mirror of life which the mountain would become to me later on in Pollsmoor.

We were in 1976. It was – naturally I could not know this at the time – the time of Soweto. But I sensed that something was afoot outside, that there was mayhem abroad. (In No Man's Land one always lives with the expectation, the foretaste, of Apocalypse.) The *boere* were uncommonly tense. There were out-of-the-ordinary goings-on at night. Hooters blared. Shifts were doubled. I heard rumours of other prisons being over-crowded. I heard one *boer* say to another, 'Let's play Putco-Putco (the name of the bus company serving the townships), you be the bus and I'll burn you!' I overheard stones being referred to as 'Soweto confetti'. And once a young warder threatened that he was so fed up at being underpaid that he had a good mind to go and park a lorryload of stones by the roadside to sell. I thought I could smell acrid smoke in the dark. My mind was filled with images of fire. I heard voices crying over the desolate veld. My poems became vehicles of apprehension and destruction and bitterness. There was a singing death.

During this time I wrote what later would become *Mouroir*. I also wrote the feeling of a mirror looking at itself, a kind of essay (ecstasy) on what writing means to me, called 'Driftpoint'. This essay called for a continuation which I started on in Pollsmoor, giving it the title of 'On the Noble Art of Walking in No Man's Land', and quite naturally these enclaves grew into a third, which is 'Pi-K'uan', or 'Zen in the Way of Being a Prisoner'. It is a reference to the nine years Boddhidharma spent in his cave.

Was I ever going to get these texts back? Was it even important that I should? Writing took on its pure shape, since it had no echo, no feedback, no evaluation, and perhaps ultimately no existence. I had to try and get some recognition from someone, somewhere, admitting that these things did in fact exist. I kept note of whatever I handed in to them and informed Yolande accordingly. We soon tried to get them to recognize the fact that they had these by asking my lawyers to approach the authorities with the request of obtaining copies of the work, using the pretext that we were worried about what would happen if, say, the prison burned down. Sure, we knew there was no chance of their granting the request, but in the process we at least had a confirmation in writing from them that they were indeed in possession of so many pages. It was then too, that they formally undertook to return all of the material to me on the day of my release. This promise was kept.

But over all these years I never trusted them. It happened too many times that solemn promises were ignored; too often had one been duped and fooled. I've seen far too closely the basic falseness and hypocrisy and duplicity of the civil servant or the man in power ever to have confidence in them in any way. Don't ever trust a *boer*. His two faces are the result of a tragically flawed culture. Don't put your faith in any other category of South African either – the system of the *boer*, the elemental presence of discrimination and oppression, have tainted and corrupted one and all. Truly, South African culture is the picture of painted putrefaction! Don't believe, don't trust – navigate! Survive! (And tenaciously recommence and continue the struggle for social and economic justice.)

So, naturally, all along I continued trying to find alternative means of saving the material – smuggling it out of prison. A part of the story became known during the second trial. Other channels, Mr Investigator, that I am sure you will allow me not to talk about. Why embarrass the people who were kind enough to help me? They may be needed again. The struggle between prisoner and guard is always that of the captive trying to dig or find holes (to breathe through), and the keeper trying to fill them up. Why expose the furtive means? The attempts did not always work. One has to take many risks in prison and you have no way of making sure that your connection is a safe one, or that the person into whose hands you have given the work will not steal it for his own benefit or to impress his girlfriend. You cannot trust anybody: that is the first law; and the second one equally strong: you cannot survive at all without trusting some people to some extent. It is not a luxury. Conditional and limited trust is a precondition for any life at all.

Material smuggled out in the early days was used as evidence during the second trial to validate the charge of my having used illegal means of communication with the outside world. After the trial I was called one morning to the office of the commander and found there a general, lolling in a chair with his tunic unbuttoned. With the crossed sabres on his epaulettes and the carefully coiffed grey locks, he looked the spitting image of the idea one has of Custer. This was his only stand. He told me that it had been their intention to cancel my permission to write in the light of the abuses that came out in court, but that they had been put under persistent pressure by the literary establishment to allow me to continue doing so. If ever he thundered, if ever I misuse this privilege again, well, then Afrikaans lit-tera-ture can go to stink-ing hell!

'Culture' is in any event considered a threat, or at best an obscure pastime, by the Afrikaners. A luxury. Something indigestible. The people (and who are the 'people' if not the police, the warders and the prisoners? Certainly they are more 'people' than the intellectually long-haired writers!) are aware of the divorce. Often warders or prisoners would say to me, 'Of course, we don't speak proper Afrikaans.' And be half-proud of the fact that they read only the popular detective stories or Konsalik or Wilbur Smith. 'Why not?' Why indeed not? Poetry is a closed book. 'Do you actually mean to say you write it just like that, without copying it out of a book?' What to do when you have been subverted by other tastes? For years, in the various prisons I frequented, I tried – with limited success – to obtain 'alternative' books (Hemingway, Faulkner, Turgenev, etc.) through the library. Religious or educational books, yes; literature, no. 'You don't need them – you can write your own books, can't you?' an officer once asked me sarcastically. Even later, when politicals were permitted to subscribe to magazines, I never could get a literary magazine, not even the most conservative Afrikaans one!

I was the writer, but I was also the scribe. In prison everybody eventually finds his own function in terms of his usefulness to the inmate community. You may be the one 'sticking' the others, meaning that you decorate them with tattoos (you should have seen the infections!); you may be only a cleaner of cells and a washer of clothes; you may perfectly illegally be making cakes, or 'boop puddings' as they are called, and selling these for a measure of tobacco; you may be a 'grocery rabbit', that is, flogging your dubious sexual charms in return for some tinned food; you may be a 'boop lawyer' (often after having been a real one outside, to counsel the law-obsessed); you may be an interior decorator, if I can call it that – meaning that you go round offering to decorate people's artificial teeth by drilling small holes in them and inserting bits of coloured glass filed down smooth – you should see, Mr Investigator, how flashy some smiles behind the walls are; you may paint and sell pictures, using coloured toothpaste as pigment, or you may carve little objects from the prison soap and then stain them with prison polish (what a patina!); you may do needlework, embroidery, patiently building boats and houses from matchsticks (all of the above will periodically be confiscated and/or destroyed by the *boere*); or you could be the bookmaker, or be running a gambling school.

But I was the scribe. At the outset it was strange that people should approach me and ask me to answer their letters for them – it impinged upon my sense of privacy. I soon learned that a letter in prison is public property. Those who do not get any mail, even the poor 'social cases', can thus also vicariously have an outside dimension to their lives. No major decisions concerning love or family problems are made without being discussed widely among the prisoners. (One could also be a love consultant.) Often this brings about an amount of degradation. I have heard with my own ears how Dampies, lying in the 'bomb' (the punishment section), sold his fiancée for three packets of tobacco to Dexter lying in the next-door cell.

Nothing in prison is free. (If a fellow strolls by your cell giving you a broad smile, he is sure to be back within the hour to ask you a favour in return.) You cannot render a service for free either; you must enter into the customs or else become very suspect. So I had to submit – don't think I objected strenuously! – to being given fruit maybe in return for the writing that I did for my fellow prisoners. Once I even scored a dictionary from the deal. It was left as payment by an old man whom I had helped, composing his appeal for mercy when his case came up for review. Can you not understand that a man wants to go home and die in peace, Mr Investigator? (This was my line of attack.) He was one of my most successful clients. He left for court. It was just before Christmas that year and the judge, perhaps in a benevolent Father Christmas mood or subject to a faint recurrence of compassion-weakness, released him immediately. He came back to prison to pick up his thin suit, absolutely elated with the outcome and, true to his nature, begged to borrow a tie off a fellow prisoner – the tie being down in the reception office – so as to present a decent appearance upon coming out of the catacombs (barflies don't wear ties, and barflies may be refused admission to drink-holes), and of course he never returned it. I came across the same old gentleman again. My success was not to be crowned with permanence: he was back inside not very many months later, looking quite the worse for wear. He obviously had made up for his years behind the walls by hitting the bottle with gusto. (And he reminded me about the valuable dictionary – which had been confiscated immediately on orders from crazy Colonel Witnerf – and wondered if I, as an educated man(!), could perhaps help him in . . . but I moved away sharply.)

Among my more noteworthy successes I must cite two instances when writing bore visible fruit. The one was when an old lag going under the name of Pirate came to ask if I could refer him to anyone outside. He was due for release and he was in need of some money to, he said, buy tools. Tradesmen must have their own equipment. I knew for a fact though that, inveterate punter that he was, he was convinced that he had worked out the foolproof betting combination. Be that as it may. I wrote a poem, requesting the addressee (in rhyme!) to help the bearer out with R50. This he 'bottled' (you must know, Mr Investerrogator, that 'arse' in Cockney slang becomes 'bottle and glass'). He was duly discharged and after giving birth to the poem in freedom, presented himself to the consignee and did collect the immediate royalties.

The other instance was more problematical. Bames approached me with the request of giving him a hand with a translation. He was starting a new gang (a difficult undertaking) and he wanted them to have tattooed on their backs the Praying Hands of Dürer – an evergreen favourite with the pious time-pushers – and the Latin version of 'live and let live'. But no, man! I protested – I know not of Latin. But yes, Professor Bird, he insisted. Was I to lose face? I warned him that the best I could come up with would be an approximation in corrupt Italian (not even the vulgar form). Good enough for Bames. And before I left I could see his acolytes circling the exercise yard, like sandwich-men, with the respectfully folded hands on their bare backs, and written large and indelibly underneath: *vivere e lascare vivere.*

Dampies, however, had worked out his own motto. With a fine disdain for the niceties of grammar he commissioned the tattoo artist to write above the dotted line around his neck: 'my last words is a rope around my neck.'

People came and asked for love letters; for poems – particularly poems; or they wanted me to write requests to the *boere* for this or for that, or to help them apply for jobs outside when the time for release became imminent and parole depended on their having a job. So I was continuously inventing their lives too, Mr Investigator. Imagine – here I am, so-and-so, applying for the reasonable position, entirely rehabilitated, you see, having understood the errors of my ways, a trustworthy and honest man willing to break my balls and give my all for my prospective employer, who would be missing the chance of his life if he passed me up, and I have in front of me while I'm writing this a poor bugger who has no intention of working and no capacity for it either . . . I wrote requests for parole, for release, for transfer, for interviews. You name it. I am the writer. I wrote the personal histories of chaps, that they had to submit to their social workers. A prisoner would come and say: well, *you* know, just write that I'm OK, you know what to put in, I'm sure you know better. In fact, they were quite convinced that whatever life I could invent for them would be far better than the one they had. Some, the saddest cases, came wanting me to write a letter of contrition to a loved one. There were always references to having broken a mother's heart and seeing now, when it was too late, the ways of evil that their feet had been on. But Your Honour, my love, it was really all the fault of my friends. And some came and wanted me to write their life stories. One small-statured *robaan* (slang for robber) said to me, laughing with a big toothless purple mouth like the fig's overripe burst, 'If only I had the time to tell you my life, what a novel it would make!' And I'm sure it would have been true too. There are as many novels in there as there are human beings going to hell.

One tall distinguished multiple murderer (but he had the pasty mien and the stilted movements of Frankenstein's fix-me-up) with the name of Jakes, claimed that he'd gone through every possible trick to try to get to the same prison I was in. He had been in Paarl, in Victor Verster Prison, he said, and had even feigned a heart attack in the hope that they would be sending him to Cape Town, to Pollsmoor, for medical care. Because, he said, he had this unfinished manuscript which I must help him to complete. After more than ten years in prison he had come to the conclusion that the only real job for him outside would be that of a successful writer, and as he had had these incredible experiences as a mercenary in the Congo, surely all it needed was for me to help him divide the material in paragraphs and, you know, pop in the commas, and we would have a masterpiece on our hands. It was all there, ready to be poured out. All it needed was my say-so. He ultimately showed me the manuscript too. It was clear at that stage, judging only from the handwritings, it had already been written by five different people – all giving free run to their diverse fantasies.*

*I have managed – don't ask me how – to conserve a number of poems written by prisoners, and given to me over the years. Some are quite revealing. I intend to publish them in 'Pi-K'uan'.

It's not such a bad idea, Mr Investigator. Like a *cadavre exquis*, but in writing. Why not have several people all letting themselves go in one work? (Did I hear you say something? No?) The problem is that with prisoners these fancies and fantasies are extremely predictable and second-hand, and all of the same kind – the hackneyed prison images.

What people wanted were the same things. What they believed of themselves and of others were along the same lines. If I had to typify the genus 'prisoner', I'd say that it is someone who is socially weak, who has no control over his own desires and impulses, who has really no means of making a separation between the real world and the imaginary ones. (This predicament the prisoner solved by taking everything as real whereas the Vedantist would see all these words as *maya*, illusion. As a Zennist I would say, 'Oh, officer!') He is also of course someone without the slightest sense of responsibility to anybody else, and no feeling for originality, or 'property'. 'Look here,' one of them said to me seriously, 'I've decided to be a writer too. I'm going to take all those old books people no longer read and rewrite them, just changing the names.' And in Pretoria (I hope I'm not confusing you by this jumping from the Hills to Pollsmoor and back) I was most impressed when Skollie sent me a poem, just before being topped, of quite outstanding originality. It was addressed to God – a simple conversation in which he announced that he was looking forward to making His acquaintance soon. The poem, hidden and re-hidden, survived for years with me. I was going to do something for the defunct killer's literary reputation. I was going to rehabilitate the gallows bait. So much worse then my disappointment when some time after my release I came across the identical verse written by an American soldier in Vietnam.

Why do we have this obsession with 'originality' though? Why do we accord such value to what is 'unique' – as if anything could ever be that? Admittedly, our senses are jaded and we appreciate someone throwing fresh light on old questions – we like, through the medium of the artist, to 'look' at something and to 'feel' it anew: in fact we want to experience the unexpected or to unexpect the already experienced. Isn't it more a matter of wishing to make the experience of the object really *mine*, exclusively so? Isn't that why such disproportionate value is accorded to the 'new'? Is 'originality' not just a bourgeois vice?

Sometimes there were funny letters. One man came to me asking if I could please convince the authorities to let him have a three-hour visit with his wife. When I asked why (wanting to fulfil my task conscientiously), he said he'd had a letter from the Army asking him to return his rifle, and he needed three hours to explain to his wife where in the house the rifle was kept and how she was to go about returning it. Another wanted me to put in a request for him to have his religion changed. He said he wanted to become a Buddhist because it sounded like quite a nice religion, far-off and unknown enough for no one to give him a hard time about it, and he was sure that he should be getting better food as a Buddhist. But please could I write it out for him because he didn't quite know how 'Buddhist' was spelt, and also one had to give at least the impression of knowing something about it. When I asked him for his real reasons for wanting to change, it turned out that a friend had sent the *Kama Sutra* to him but that it was blocked 'up front' (by the censors) and that the only way he could obtain permission to receive it would be to prove that it was a religious work used by the faith he subscribes to.

I was the scribe not only for my fellow inmates but also for the *boere*. It started in Pretoria. Brigadier Dupe, very soon after I started doing my time, came to ask me if I would translate a certain number of French texts into Afrikaans. I was only too glad to do so, basically because in this way I could obtain paper which I would hide away for my own writing needs. And reading French, any French, was like being 'back home'. These texts turned out to be reproductions of articles published during the Boer War in the International Red Cross reviews of the time: reports written by their envoys in the Transvaal and the Orange Free State. Fascinating material in that it described not only the nature of the wounds among the warriors and their rudimentary medical care, highlighting the fact that far more people died of dysentery than ever did of wounds, but also because it contained reflections and criticisms on the conduct of the forces in the field. It pointed out the anarchistic way in which the Boer forces went to war and their lack of discipline – the bravery very often but also the abject cowardice of people inflicting wounds upon themselves in an attempt to opt out. It underlined the marksmanship of the *burgers* of the time: the majority of casualties among the English apparently had head wounds between the eyes. (Most of the fatal wounds inflicted upon the Boers were in the back!) I learned that the material was a subject of dispute between the South African authorities and the Red Cross. Brigadier Dupe and his colleagues were hurt by demands made on them by the International Red Cross Committee on behalf of political prisoners, and true to their own nature accused the Swiss delegation of being biased, of being anti-Afrikaner, and saying, I assume, that never would the Swiss do or have done anything for the Afrikaner in the way they were doing now for the enemy of the Afrikaner. ('The whole world is against us. The world is sick.') At which point it would seem the Swiss submitted the proofs of their previous aid and commitment to the Afrikaners. To the disgust of Dupe my translations bore out the Swiss position.*

I had to write love letters for the *boere* too, or applications for promotion. Another one of my successful cases, Mr Investigator, was when I managed to have a *boer* in Pollsmoor transferred from the sections (looking after us in the building) to the workshops where at least he could be taught a trade. Sometimes I was asked to write essays for their kids. Once, I remember, it was on the history of the Karoo. I absolutely lapped it up, sir; I loved it because I could use their need to obtain, illegitimately, material on the subject they wanted me to write about. Sometimes I would be asked to do their homework for them. Quite a few were attempting to finish matric or to obtain their junior certificates by correspondence courses, and I would complete their tasks. I became involved to the point of holding thumbs when it eventually came round to examination time, and analysing afterwards why 'we' did not succeed; agreeing very much that it was entirely unfair, that if one could only find the right person to send a bottle of brandy or a leg of springbok meat the decision to fail us might perhaps be reversed.

But there are two instances in my profession as scribe of which I'm not very proud, Mr Investigator. They remain etched in my

*I was told that some senior Afrikaners – not the top boys: these would have run away to Argentina or Taiwan before the crunch – are indeed worried whether, 'one day', the IRCC will be as solicitous of *their* fate, when *they* will be on Robben Island, as they are now about the Black prisoners. *Deus misereatur!*

mind. Both of them took place in Pretoria. The first was one night when a *boer* brought me over the catwalk a request from Johan, one of the 'condemns' due to be hanged not very long afterwards. He was asking me to respond, please, to a letter from his girlfriend. How does one refuse somebody who's going to be dead soon? So I sat down and I composed a letter, trying to put myself in his position. I must buck up the girl. Encourage her. Invent a future for us together – which all the time I knew there was no possibility of. A second letter came. Johan sent it along to me, and gradually it was as if he fell away. I grew into his skin. The contact between me – the Johan on the page – and the girl, living in poverty with her parents on some small farm back of beyond, became direct. And then came the time to die. Then the moment to take leave. How far, Mr Investigator, can one push duplicity? I was doing something filthy, surely, and yet at the same time I was extending a last hand of human solidarity to Johan, the shadow, who called me 'the Professor'. Don't think that the possibility of playing a mirror-game of chess with death never crossed my mind. What if I should continue writing to her, still pretending to be Johan? Communicating from beyond the grave? Or would it have destroyed the rosy memories glowing in her, that one major event in her life perhaps, when a man, with the black taste of daybreak already on his lips, poured out his last thoughts and sentiments, his last protestations of innocence and his deep commitment to a pure life ahead?

The other instance was even stranger. I was approached quite early on during my stretch in Pretoria, by the then head of the prison, asking if I would help him write a letter, in English: he did not trust his own. The letter had to answer an imperious demand Pretoria had received from the Clerk of the Transkei Supreme Court (the Transkei had acceded to 'independence' not very long before) to produce, before a certain date, two accused and convicted persons before the said bench. The hitch, Mr Investigator, the damn nuisance fly in the ointment, the slight technical fuck-up, was that these two gentlemen were no longer with us in the land of honey and milk and sunshine and mind movements. They had arrived condemned to death in Pretoria a month or so before Christmas. Things go rather rapidly immediately before the season of love to man and peace on earth. The hanging services are closed down over the festive period; the High Courts too. In this way, according to the letter I was asked to transcribe, as these two natives refrained from informing the prison authorities of the names of their legal representatives, and since they were quite illiterate and did not leave the addresses of their next of kin (we all know what complicated and unusual family ties these people entertain), nobody knew whom to inform when their demise became imminent. It is with much regret, the letter was to continue, that we now learn that an appeal had been lodged against their convictions and that said appeal is to be heard by Your Honour, the Judge President of the Transkei Supreme Court. But it wasn't really our fault, Your Honour, (*we err in a no man's land of ant-empires*), you must understand that there are language barriers and the warrant officer on duty the day they were booked into the foyer of Heaven perhaps forgot to do the necessary checking, so, inasmuch and herewith notwithstanding, with all our respect, sir, we the undersigned, etc., always your willing servant.

Mr Investigator, I often lay there thinking that these two men who had jerked their heels could still have been alive. I dared not show the depth of my revulsion to the head of the prison and the warders. I don't remember that they themselves were particularly affected. When you process humans by paper, a wee slip 'twixt last breath and noose is, alas, always possible. To err is human. And I think that the multiple hangings would have blunted them already. I could not then make any notes of the event, but for a long time I remembered the two names. Then one slipped away and now I have only one left: Sizwe Bethani he was called. I repeated to myself: this you mustn't forget – *Sizwe*. Just think of Athol Fugard's play. And *Bethani* – wasn't Jesus also reputed to have been to a certain Bethany? Ah, Mr Investigator, with all due respect we regret that writing can be used as topsoil for burying mistakes. Notwithstanding, I'm sorry if I sometimes forget that it is at the same time the maggots which lay bare the structure. . . .

The mind produces its own blackness from the dark. Light comes at first from other sources. There would be the monthly letter. Before my conviction Yolande had to write to me via Colonel Huntingdon (yes, he controlled that too). Now, processed and stamped, I looked forward to my 500 words. The martinet responsible for 'security prisoners' in Pretoria (I think the authorities even now still refuse to talk of 'political prisoners'), a relic of the Habsburg empire, a boop-bellied little grey monster with an enormous handle bar moustache growing into side whiskers, the veins in his neck permanently swollen, shorts down to his dimpled knees – used to wheeze up the hill to see me every once in a while. (His base was Local, where the politicals are kept.) *He* now handled my mail. A letter I'd written to my mother was refused because in it I referred to *tronk* instead of *gevangenis* – the familiar 'jail' instead of the fancier 'prison'. Exceptionally I'd be allowed to rewrite the letter, omitting the offending word. 'But watch it. Don't you try and be a *mister* with me. Here you're just a fucking *bandiet!*' Another time he came, proudly fluttering his handiwork: my mother, not quite used to having a son inside, and loquacious by nature, had tried ducking under the 500-word barrier by writing ever smaller towards the end of her page (like whispering), but Major Schnorff had cut her off in mid-air with a pair of scissors, exactly at the 500-word mark. (Do you see my power? And do you tremble?) (In Yolande's letters words were blacked over or simply snipped out.) And once he came to play cat and mouse with me. Called me into the office. I sat down. 'Get up!' he screamed. 'Who the hell gave you permission to sit down like a . . . like a *mister!*' Then took his time. I watched his hogshead of angry purple blood. Waited for the ire to subside. He, harrumphing and fiddling around with a few sheets of paper, 'Sit down.' A letter he had there for me, from a concerned lady in Johannesburg, Suzy Lang Tak. Chinese, would it be? (Squinting at me from behind his fierce glasses.) Very Christian, very worried about my soul. 'Do you want it?' I was keen for contact, novelty, yes. Kind sir. Then came the slow leer tasting its way through the white hairs of the whiskers. 'Of course it would have to take the place of your wife's letter.' (As if to say: what's the difference between one Chinese and another anyway?)

Never mind about Schnorff, Mr Investigator. I only knew him for a short while, I only knew his moustache. (When younger he had a beard because he'd made a vow never to shave until the advent of the Afrikaner Republic. And he looked religiously after the bullet-pocked wall in Local where Jopie Fourie had been executed as a rebel during the First World War: to him it was a shrine.) To him we, the politicals, were all just communists, scum and vermin that ought to be exterminated to a man. I, of course, was furthermore a traitor. (He refused my Afrikaans. Spoke his quaint English to me.) Others can testify to how he made life a misery for them. He was kept on way beyond retirement age by the Prison Department, exactly for that reason. Now he's gone. Dead perhaps. In the eternal *laer* of white-tented wagons. Having lived long enough to see Afrikaner *baasskap* (mastership). No retribution. Why should there have been, since there is no God (except his kind), and man's justice is much slower, much more tentative?

Never mind about oom-pah-pah. We prisoners always say: there's one thing they can't do and that is to stop time! And however many hands pawed and drooled over my monthly letter – however much they taunted me, holding it back for weeks sometimes (it was a constant complaint of mine to the Red Cross and once it needed a written request in duplicate from me, announcing that I wished to lay a charge for theft, for them to 'find' my letter – minus the date – where it 'had fallen out of the post bag, under the counter in the post office') – eventually I would get it. Not to read it immediately, no sir! (One learns to space one's joys; one learns how to spoil oneself.) Just to carry it around in your pocket at first. To decontaminate it. Then, eventually – after lock-up tonight – you would unfold it, sniff the faint traces of perfume, and the walls would recede. Blue sky. A million words between her lines. Her voice – laughing . . . scolding too! My hunger would come and sit on my chest. Too soon the end. Maybe a P.S., a snippet of news. To carry me into the night and forward for days and days. Back into the envelope. Careful now – don't open it too often lest the sweet breath be dissipated. One or two stamps – those reproducing the paintings I keep for myself, for my own miniature art museum – will go to the friendly rapist in Cell 3, the obsessive collector, who pays me a jar of peanut butter every month. (The next day – I'm in the Cape now, you understand? – Shorty or Mother Hubbard or Oldface or one of the other trusties and office cleaners – 'stinking of Boer' we'd sometimes say, unkindly – would sidle up to me in the food line. 'See you had a letter from the wife. Everything OK still? Shame. . . ' Or, 'Sorry to hear that.' Or, 'Jeez, prices have gone *up* in Paris, hey?' The ant hill.)

INSERT

I walk downhill. It's cold. The streets are empty. Once every now and then there's a dog trying to lift its paws as high as they would go possibly because of the cold paving stones. The bridges over the river have a thin white layer of frost. The river itself is of a brownish green colour, flowing fast; it is swollen, nearly washing over the banks. Down in the kernel of the city there's the old City Hall – the light-blue slate roofs, the green statues cut out of the skyline, green with combustion, and above that a very pale blue sky. I look up and like a memory another vision superimposes itself. Already now I know that there will be this blotting nostalgia, other scenes darkening under what the eye sees at the moment. The slight blue, the sniff of wind in the air, and the green figures having the shapes of movement make me remember that wild and desolate coast along the Atlantic Ocean with the primeval wind sailing over the dunes bending the grass to prayer, and that same light blue allied to white. I can taste it on my tongue. When later I walk up the hill again there is a folding into evening and outlines fading fast. Winter. But the light grows daily: already it stays luminous until nearly half past six. Unbelievable still every night to be taking another route. Walk up the straight streets so well remembered and yet so completely new. Everywhere, all over town, there has been a renewal, a take-over of little shops, small restaurants. And as you stroll by in the dusk you can see people sitting behind the glass panes quietly waiting for the first customers of the night. There's life behind the façades. It is an ant hill of the living. You suspect the space of courtyards behind the buildings, the spiralling shells of staircases winding up to rooms all askew under the roof, you know that there are rooms behind these rooms, someone is putting on the light, the floors are tiled, a fly buzzes around the bathroom bulb, on the settee (or an armchair), the evening paper open at page three, gathering dust on the floor behind the settee (or the armchair) the leg of a broken doll, one cough flew through the room. People are living there. It is the very . . . crust of life. And below that more life pulsating. Contrast it with that other place in No Man's Land having the attributes and the gestures of life but in fact being a labyrinth of death. In the thin alleys leading off these streets the lampposts start revealing the first yellow globes of darkness. Unseasonal fruit. Sky clear but smoky. And when you get to the highest promontory near the cathedral you can see the horizon falling away in the distance all smudged and stained like a receding battlefield. That's quite a nice image: the gunsmoke of struggle fading away. I look up and lo and behold above the spires the shiver moon on its back, curled because it's cold, and very slight again because it's so cold. This cold leads you by the nose. The buildings are dipped darker in darkness. In some rooms, breathing into the streets, there's still some mysterious activities going on. In some rooms the blind don't see that night has fallen; they listen for the moths. In some rooms vegetarians with pale thighs are wrestling in the dark, goosing the furniture. Suddenly I imagine hearing a rattling noise and again falls open in that inner man which never forgets a memory of an image of dusk-coloured grey with a verdigris glow over the mountains and he listens to the whirring sound of the gallinaceous birds with slate-blued white-spotted plumage that lived around the prison. We tried in many ways to capture these guinea-fowl. Fellows used to get hold of a length of string which meant unravelling one of the government blankets and tie to one end a few maize pips and these they would lower through the narrow slits of the window hoping that one of the birds would swallow its stupidity and then perhaps the string would be strong enough to hoist the meat up to the window and twist its neck. And then who knows. Maybe one could prepare hidden-hidden a meal. Please to eat my blanket and come into me. But it never worked. And one's nights were marked by the repeated chattering of the birds. A convention of spinsters. Other flying animals too. Bats. Plovers perhaps with their stretched plaintive cries as they whip over the prison, or (but that was earlier, in Pretoria) the wild doves coming to nest in the gutters along the roof, humming and cooing at the dying sun. At other times, very late when everything was quiet, one could sometimes hear an owl thataway and one crossed one's mental fingers because superstitiously one thought that the hoooot announced even more sadness. And regularly once a week the *piet-my-vrou* (*Notococcyx solitarius*) would return for a few weeks, shy to the eye but you could occasionally see him jotting against the skyline, delineating with repeated cries like beautifully crafted droppings the territory within which he hoped to charm a mate. Or during the long days one used to walk with one's ear along the busy lives of the little wagtails. They would enter the prison itself, flutter around the catwalk, perch on the windowsill and project the mirror of an eye down at one. I used to sing to them. *Wagtail bag snail how come no mail?* I also placed bets with myself, reconstituting the image of my wife while sitting back against the wall in a corner, feeling nightfall fall, fall around the grey fortress, layers of darkness silting up, and saying – if that bird, that little grey one, makes again that fluting noise it will be a sign, for sure, that she is also thinking of me at this moment. Come, little feathered friend – puke thy whistle! Your days are made of crystal. You become very attached to any form of life around you under those circumstances. One day, in the big yard, the one where we tried so hard to cultivate a lawn (how many times I broke my back carrying buckets of fertilizer, carting in wheelbarrows of sand to level the surface, watering, weeding, digging up the lot and starting all over – in vain: death had left its blight on that grey-walled enclosure), I watched a dove struggling to save its young. The young bird had just started flying and had landed in this courtyard not being strong enough yet to fly up and over the walls. Now its parent was trying to get it to flutter to freedom, and actually took position below the young one attempting physically to lift it, with awkward wings, higher against the vertical wall, again and again. There was the other one, the beautiful one, wood-pigeon or stockdove, with its red-rimmed eye and its coloured neck resembling some object of Egyptian mythology, which had entered the smaller courtyard outside my cell, the one covered with the steel crossword, and, in its fright when I walked out into the yard, it damaged a wing trying to get out. I caught it and was tacitly allowed to keep it in my cell. Where it became quite tame. Living under the bunk. Sharing my food. Venturing forth to watch me with a little black eye when it thought I wasn't noticing, extremely curious as to what I was doing. But unfortunately it didn't survive very long. There were too many shadows. One day, when I was called to the visitor's cubicle to see my wife (like a beautiful bird behind the reinforced glass partition), I must have left the door of my cell ajar and Lukas, the horrible cat belonging to the head of the prison (called Lukas too), must have entered and found the flip-flopping prey under my bed. There were only blood smears and feathers when I returned. . . . Droplets of blood. Images. Images are not confined to a place or to a time, they are now, thousands of them, even as I talk to you here. Images like birds, always present everywhere. We intrude upon their world. In the Cape, for instance, there were always seagulls riding the wind, being blown about, tattered and torn, uttering the most awful imprecations, swooping down on us when we were in the courtyard, probably hoping for a gizzard of food (craziness! what *bandiet* would ever leave a morsel?) and screeching at us, cursing the day. In the north, sometimes, very high, when one looked up from within the sunken well of the courtyard where you were allowed to walk the distance of half an hour a day, you could see floating vultures, nearly invisible to the eye, moving over the city. There were words flying about too. Although I was not allowed to participate in the talking, I could hear the thrumming and the rustling in the corridors behind my wall. And it struck me that these words were visible. And how senseless they were – some form of pollution dirtying the air, clogging up space. In a way I was quite happy to be deprived of words. I could be the monk chewing my silences. I realized how many unnecessary words one produces in the course of a day. Not even counting those scurrying around inside, unuttered, like ants, being the mind. Birds and words and other forms of life may be striking one so forcefully because they are seen separately, in isolation, and therefore imbued with far more penetrating importance. Later, down in the Cape again – on clear, early spring days – we often saw people practising hang gliding, jumping off the crest of the mountain behind the prison, feeling around in the air for the warm up-currents which will carry them higher, describing a wide arc over the valley, go whistling over the fortress, and land in a field not more than two hundred yards away. A beautiful sight indeed – the strong-coloured wings with the minute human being cradled below it. We tried to attract the attention of these flying humans. I wonder whether they ever saw us. I wonder if anyone outside ever sees a prison. Perhaps I could give you an example, Mr Investigator, of the evolution of prison language. You know how *dagga*, or marijuana as you know it, comes in various quantities – the smallest being a 'blade' and then a 'finger' and then a 'hand' and then an 'arm' and the jackpot being a 'bale'. As we were there on a Saturday afternoon all bundled up against one wall of the courtyard, to glimpse their parabolas and to try to see over the wall where these hang gliders would land, some of the *bandiete* started shouting: *'Kak 'n baal! Kak 'n baal!'* ('Shit a bale! Shit a bale!'), meaning, 'Why don't you throw us down a bale of *dagga*?' And this went on for quite some time, every weekend, until in due time the word for hang gliders in prison jargon became *kakkebale*, 'bale shitters'.

What is *my* name? *You* choose it. Take your word. A name is exactly the absence of definition. I've told you that I'm called Bird, *Mister* Bird if you don't mind, which means the jail bait. I've also explained to you how I involuntarily took a vow of not using words, because the words cluttering up the spaces on the other side of the walls of my cell were like birds without wings. Can you imagine anything more obscene than a bird with no wings? And yet it is exactly what I'm giving you here. I'm stuffing this confession of mine with all the other wingless birds. Perhaps it is the stuffing coming undone which brings with it unasked for visions of wings and sand and sea, and others of tame guinea-fowl mocking us from beyond the walls, moving through the evening becoming more opaque in their ever-repeated mating dance. Sounds, images, birds, insects, wirds and borms and names – the multiplication and manifestation of nothing.

3

A Separate Section

Mr Investigator, I'd like to open a separate section, a veritable visitors' book, for the various tourists one meets in prison. We prisoners have a very simple way of dividing them. A visitor is either a friend, at least potentially so, or an outright enemy. The friends are few and far between, and there are many false ones, but that falseness stems more from the hope which springs eternal in the anxious breast of every jail bird. When a senior general, for instance, visits the institution, there will always be some demented souls who cling, starry-eyed, to the conviction that by bringing their complaints to his attention things will change radically.

Seven years is a long time, and now when I try to greet again clearly in my mind all the trotters who passed through those citadels of misery during the seasons that I spent there, I realize that they add up to quite a crowd. So, to simplify my discourse, I shall try to categorize them for you. (All along, of course, there were the Greyshits who never stopped coming to see me regularly until May 1977, when I was formally charged again and the proceedings for the second trial started; and even afterwards, much later in Cape Town, there recurred a few odd visits.)

(1) All those who actually work within the prison system: the doctors, the psychologists, the chaplains and the preachers.

(2) Those who are part of the system but whom we do not see very often: the ministers, senior officers of the Department, judges, magistrates.

(3) Those favoured by the system and allowed special privileges when they want to visit someone inside: the 'personalities'.

(4) Those who in a larger sense are still part of the system but as a loyal opposition to it from within, or even as critics of the set-up: they inspect the prisons to help the authorities foster the impression of a democratic administration.

(5) The outsiders who have objective reasons for visiting the prison, resented by the authorities – but they're obliged to tolerate them: here I'm thinking of the International Red Cross Committee, the French ambassadors who came to see me, and naturally, also, my lawyers.

I have already said that Huntingdon never stopped coming. In fact, Mr Investigator, the interrogation never ceased and the first trial with its conviction was just one step in the ongoing process of dissecting and undoing the psyche and washing the brain. More often than not he would be accompanied by Jiems Kont. There was no urgency. It could not be that they wanted any information. What was there to be had from me, locked away from the world for months already? Although they kept on testing, prying and prodding. No, I think it was more out of a morbid and sadistic fascination with agony, a preoccupation also with their own mirror-problems. We seemed to be locked in an embrace of hate and mutual dependence. But one should not underestimate the ritualistic aspects either. The Calvinists have a strong belief in sin and preordained doom, and equally strongly do they believe that one must be brought to an acceptance of one's fate. The notion of the acquiescent victim is an important one. And the victim must be humiliated to the ultimate grovelling cry of recognition: to save all our souls, Mr Investigator. . . . I am reminded of that Company of Whites which came into being in 1541 in Palermo, during the Inquisition, consisting of 'gentlemen and honourable persons', who had the noble task of preparing the victim for the Great Step, convincing him by subtle or not so subtle (but infinitely absorbing) means of persuasion (or perversion) to willingly and liberatingly participate in the 'spectacle of justice'. For the just man to use base methods is an act of abnegation and purification, of becoming a blind tool in the hands of God. To preserve our security, Mr Investigator. . . .

In a way their visits were more relaxed. Yes, I even looked forward to these breaks in my dull daily routine. Huntingdon would have a few sweets in his pocket and these I appreciated. In that weird way he had, he would convey to me that we were conspiring together against the Prison Department. Prison officials were just a lot of stupid cabbages, he said. But we have to play the game, since I'm in their hands now. He would make me understand that we should be careful about the electronic bugs in the office where he used to meet me. Simple games destined to create a bogus sense of complicity.

It was also through him that I had confirmation that my monthly visits were being taped. He knew the process and one day actually asked me to say, during my next visit, a few kind or admiring words about him, knowing full well that the transcript would end up in the hands of his superiors.

Sometimes he would bring a senior member of the Security Police along, I suppose in an attempt to impress this visitor with his tamed political pet. In this fashion Withart, the Commissioner of Police, came. As also Zietsman, the second-in-command. He brought along Percy Yutar who became sentimental, wept, and told me that the day I'm released and reunited with Yolande he will don his best hat to go and give thanks in the synagogue.

But then there were also his colleagues and the others of BOSS who came, hoping to learn something useful in the conversations with me. Jiems Kont one day informed me that Colonel Jan Snaaks was now to retire to a smallholding he had acquired somewhere in the Northern Transvaal and that the service was throwing a big farewell dinner for him. He had the cheek to ask if I didn't feel like writing a small poem which could be read at that occasion. He thought it would be really funny, a nice joke. The two of them, Huntingdon and Kont, once even brought along my eldest brother. In they strolled with their hands in their pockets jingling cents and balls, and visited my little courtyard and my cell. Although my brother is a hail-fellow-well-met type, the hearty soldier, I think even he was somewhat embarrassed that day. For me it was quite an experience to see him and Huntingdon together, obviously with much mutual admiration. Real equals. At that point they had the same rank. (It must also, subtly, have been the chance for the flatfoot working as a flunky from an office in the capital to humble the soldier – engaged in 'dirty tricks' behind the lines – whom he was so jealous of.)

Huntingdon probably considered his finest achievement during that period the letter that he got me to write to Withart, offering my services to the Security Police, and motivating this offer in the name of the preservation of Afrikaner culture. I thought I was clever, Mr Investigator; I thought I could still manoeuvre and try to catch them at their own game. But those were the desperate delusions of the trapped animal as, without my knowing it yet, the pieces for the second trial were being assembled.

The visits of the Greyshits became rarer. I never saw Huntingdon during the second trial: I am still not sure of his role in the affair but it could well be that he was not the instigator of that episode and that the inquiry and prosecution was led by rival elements within the Security Police. But he still kept a grip on my case – after the trial, when it became too much of an embarrassment for the authorities to hold me in Pretoria, it was he who came late one night to the prison, pretending now to be even more wary of bugs than before, to inform me sarcastically that it had been decided to send me to a place where I can see the 'mountain' I keep on crying for.

In later years, as I said, I had some further visits from these people. Once Nails van Byleveld turned up: the same pig's eyes glaring from deep sockets, the same quivering little worm passing for a moustache (he probably thought himself to be the replica of some movie hero of the 1940s), the fingertips as hard and as square as ever. With him he had three admiring colleagues. They were ostensibly investigating an attempted escape. It was not long after the exposure of Williamson as a South African spy in Switzerland, and he literally crowed with pride. 'Did you see how we got you all? You must admit that we are fuckin' strong!' I answered by reminding him about the 'Info Scandal' – when so much of their overseas subversion was uncovered – and the brutal murder of Steve Biko. He went red in the face. What you lose on the roundabout you win on the horses. . . .

At a later time the pale and scheming Huntingdon himself came down from Pretoria. Schuitema had in the meantime returned to South Africa and had given himself up to them and they now made believe that they were going to try him. Huntingdon's visit was supposed to be with the purpose of asking me whether I was willing to give evidence in a possible case against Schuitema. When I asked to be allowed to consult my lawyers first, he left in disgust, muttering, 'Just as I thought.' Hendrik Goy then followed, again accompanied by several cold-eyed Greyshits. He'd forged ahead in the meantime, was now a colonel himself. He talked to me quite a bit about Schuitema in prison, and eventually admitted that they were not going to prosecute him. Seeing Goy after all those years had, strangely enough, the effect on me of meeting an old acquaintance to whom I had become indifferent. There might even have been a touch of gladness at seeing him again. (He brought me some chocolates 'for old time's sake'.)

Let me dispose of the Schuitema case immediately. Many of my friends are convinced that it was he, Schuitema, 'Jan' as we called him, who had shopped me. Even while I was still in prison I learned of an inquiry launched by people close to me, and the envoy sent to Europe to investigate returned with the verdict that Schuitema was the man. The facts I *can* vouch for are the following: After my arrest he managed to skip the country and return to Europe. Remember – according to his own words – that he had been tracked by the CIA during a previous clandestine visit to the country and, one must presume, under surveillance ever since (see my footnote to p. 101). So, again presumably, the police must have been aware of his every move in the country. Back in Holland he was pushed from his position as Secretary of the Dutch Anti-Apartheid Movement. A Communist coup, he could claim later. The existence of Okhela had exploded in the Liberation Movement;* the Party was tightening its control and purging non-Communists from the supporting organizations. Plausible. With the help of Curiel, Schuitema then tried to refloat his reputation and credibility, working from Brussels. (Already he had been branded as the infiltrator, the man who had fingered me.) Failure and fiasco. He was with Curiel up to shortly before the latter's death. In Scandinavia – and later in Holland too – he still managed to raise quite a bit of money. Okhela split in two factions – ostensibly on pro-Breyten and anti-Breyten lines. (Both factions have been in contact with me since, both claiming to have remained true.) He had to leave Europe and first went to Britain where he became involved, he claims, with the Irish Nationalists. Expelled from there, he went to America. By now he feared for his life, and asked for protection. Times must have

*'Liberation Movement' in this context refers to the alliance of Congresses – that is, the ANC, the Coloured Peoples' Congress, the Indian Peoples' Congress, the South African Congress of Trade Unions (SATCU) and the now defunct Congress of Democrats.

been tumultuous. From New York he arranged for his repentant return to the Republic of No Man's Land. He said, afterwards, that he'd returned to offer himself in exchange for my liberation. Huntingdon received him at the airport. The Greys held him for a hundred days. A veil descended. And then they released him. Because, they – the *Gatte* – said, the international oil companies whose sanctions-busting operations Schuitema had helped expose from Holland during the 1960s, when there was supposed to be an embargo on oil to the then Rhodesia, now preferred not to be involved in a case against him! Let it be. Some time after his release, he left for Zimbabwe, with a girlfriend. They were arrested there and handed back, in murky circumstances, into the care of the South African intelligence agents. Who promptly let him go. In interviews during this period Schuitema admitted to having given information to Craig Williamson, one of the South African spies abroad but, he asserted, only from 1978 on, and then only to counteract the communist domination of the Liberation Movement. And yes, Mr Investigator, he's been to see me since. Twice. Right here in Paris. Admitting to regular contact with, and/or control by, various South African security services. Particularly with Huntingdon. Playing Peter against Paul. And he sends me the weirdest epistles, written in a jargon of his own, consisting of a jumble sale of analyses and theories. It is British Intelligence, he now declares, which is at the root of his personal persecution and which is using the Black Liberation Movement as a stalking horse to abort the revolution and extend its imperialist influence in Africa. The only solution, he postulates, is to resist as Afrikaner nationalists, particularly in conjunction with the extreme Rightist neo-Nazis. Spy? Tragic fool? Tool? What is true is that the man is a broken pawn in this sordid game. But dangerous – because he must end by either trying to destroy me (which could have been his mission all along) or, in a paroxysm of frustration and self-hate because of the tangle of contradictions, by blowing himself up. . . . I leave the judgement to you. . . .

As my story continues unfolding, Mr Investigator, even when we leave the prison, there will be a few more shady characters whom we will come to in due time. The only other one I want to mention for now is an elderly English-speaking gent who rolled up one morning to Pollsmoor and had me summoned. Dressed in his immaculate blue striped suit, looking like a prosperous travelling salesman, he tried to hide behind an affable exterior in the office and in the presence of Colonel Witnerf. He proceeded to show me two albums filled with photos. Some were close-ups, others were obviously taken in the streets of maybe Johannesburg, when the subject photographed was not aware of it. It was not exactly an Asterix comic strip. He wanted to know if I recognized any of these people. I most certainly did not. He remained convinced that I most definitely should. Another dialogue of the dead. Obviously they were on some false track again. I believe the photos were largely of FLQ militants. (And how the Quebec Liberation Front – does it still exist? – fits into this story, I'll be damned if I know. You might as well have my eyes sucked by wild ducks!)

The Greyshits are the masters of No Man's Land's system. Together nowadays with some military people, they can come and go as they bloody well wish in any penal institution, and they can materially affect the conditions of your detention. I'm not sure that over and above the continued 'normal' control they kept on me by visiting me and by means of reports from their agents among the staff and by monitoring my letters and analysing the transcription of tapes, that they didn't have also undercover agents among the prisoners. It was clear that my slightest moves and gestures were known to them. I worked out with a fellow prisoner doing time for fraud, about to be discharged from boop, a very simple method by which he could let me know whether he'd been approached by them after his release. He had been – in Pollsmoor – in a big communal cell down my corridor for about a year, and during that time I saw quite a bit of him. To outsiders it might well have looked as if I had confided in him or that we'd become close friends, and sure enough, the day he was released and taken to the airport to be deported from the country was also the day that the Security Police confronted him with our association.

But let me tell you about the other 'foreigners' breaking the dull routine of our existence. There were the doctors, a group of individuals, it needs to be said, whose professional consciences, when working for the State the way they do, do not seem to suffer too many qualms. In reality they have become rubber stamps for the penal system.

Immediately after being sentenced, I was visited in my cell by one old fellow whose duty it was to give me a check-up. The results were presumably to be entered on my files and made available to the Red Cross when they asked for them. These files also served to protect the State in the event of one complaining later on about a bruise here or a break there. He had me lie on the bed and started prodding me in the ribs. All I remember about him was that he trembled, that his fingernails were long and dirty, and that the shirt cuffs protruding from the sleeves of his jacket were frayed and filthy on the inside. I felt quite soiled after this inspection, but I didn't see him again. The doctor normally responsible for the prisoners in Beverly Hills was a very stocky young man called Burns. He was of a friendly disposition with a penchant for minor operations. No surgeon, but he loved cutting and he didn't rest until he had me on a makeshift operating table in one of the offices, to get rid of some warts and other excrescences I had. As a doctor he was quite competent, but he also fancied himself to be an amateur moralist. One morning he tried to convince me that our prison set-up is the best, particularly when it comes to executions, at which he assisted. (And where he could allow himself the joy of innumerable small surgical interventions: it was his task to slit open the necks of the warm deads to visually establish the cause of demise.) I would never credit, he said, the contentment with which people go up to the gallows to be hanged. Convicting them to death and leaving them about a year – it was the average delay – in which to repent and give their hearts to Christ, was, according to him, a very humane procedure. How they were converted! How happy they were! How they sang! How touchingly they said goodbye in that last chamber before the inner sanctum and how they proffered a 'Thank you, *baas*'! I could not help but remark then that in that case you were hanging not the person you'd convicted but in fact a transformed and repentant sinner.

In Cape Town I had to do with two doctors. These apart from the several dentists I had the occasion to consult over the years and the eye specialist who once came to check me out. In normal circumstances any prisoner needing specialist care is taken to the hospital under guard, or even to the rooms of the specialist, but for me the poor man had to transport whatever instruments he could carry to the prison itself, the mountain coming to Muhammad, and he excused himself for having therefore to use very outdated equipment. The dentist one could theoretically have access to once a week. Sometimes there were long gaps: the regular appointee from the Department of Health and Public Welfare had many other mouths to peer into (those of reform school kids, inhabitants of old-age homes, etc.), and had to be replaced by a young man shakily doing his military service, or the dentist's chair would break down for a few weeks, or there wouldn't be transport available to truck the patients to the main prison in the same compound, or there wouldn't be enough warders to serve as escorts. And then, in Pollsmoor, the *boere* started making it more and more difficult for one to get there, since, quite correctly, they understood that people 'put their names down' for doctor or 'head-doctor' or dentist with the flimsiest of pretexts, really wanting only to be let off work for the morning, or to visit the other prison building – which opened up possibilities of smuggling! So they announced that the dentist would be there for 'pulling' only, not for 'drilling and filling'. Thus I saw some chaps, bored or desperate enough, with a perfectly good mouth of teeth, stand out for the dentist, to return round about lunchtime spitting blood and without a tooth left in their heads.

The two regular physicians, with one of them coming in nearly every morning for an hour or so, were Barnum and Pagel. Barnum picked up a bit of trouble with the Department after once prescribing the wrong cure to one of the members of the staff who nearly died from the medicine. He was suspended awaiting the result of an inquiry. He it was who gave me aspirins for a skin rash. Of Dr Pagel I became quite fond. He had been thoroughly impressed by the contact he was obliged to have with the International Red Cross. One member of the Red Cross delegation is always a medic and the collegial discussions between Pagel and his Swiss homologue sharpened his awareness of the important task he had been entrusted with – taking care of a 'political'. From time to time he would have me sent for and he was always very keen to let me have pills or syrups or antibiotics even – which he once prescribed for a cold. Anything, it doesn't matter what, as long as it could be written down on the big yellow medical card so that he could show the year thereafter to his honourable overseas confrère visiting the prison how conscientious he'd been concerning my health. When it became evident that periodically I was going through valleys of depression, he gave me a long talk, the gist of which was that there is nothing quite as good for a depression as trying to transform certain Bible stories into plays.

But for being talked to we had psychologists, the parasites living off our twisted souls. I had the occasion to meet some of them from the very outset. The big boss of the prison shrinks himself deigned to come and visit me immediately after my first trial ended. Master Basie, that is his name. At that time he was a short, fat, bald fanatic wearing glasses, but quite young still – younger than I am. He has travelled a long way since then and is now doing just fine, thank you. He sported the rank of brigadier-general and was soon after to rise to that of full general. He was made Assistant Commissioner. At that young age it was clear that he had been earmarked for the highest position in the Prison Department. It was not to be consummated however, since it wasn't commensurate with his burning ambitions. After a short flirtation when there was talk of his entering representative politics, he switched departments and went to Interior Affairs, and from there was promoted to the Prime Minister's advisory council. I believe he now occupies what could be considered the dominant place on that body. He is a dangerous man because he is a clever diehard and endlessly power hungry. Do not underestimate his intelligence; after all, even in the Prison Department it took a measure of grey matter to reach the rank he had at his age.

He was the instigator of what we in prison lingo call 'psycho city', which is a special wing for psychopathic prisoners in Zonderwater Prison. I talked to people who'd been through there. They had no privileges at all – no letters or visits, for instance. These had to be earned again and again on a points system based on Pavlovian principles, it would seem to me: if you are good you are rewarded; if you are bad you are punished. One of my informants was aghast at the fact that the 'psycho city' boys, when playing soccer against other prisoners, had to stand up and applaud vigorously when the opposing team scored a goal. Very unnatural behaviour for any prisoner, let alone the psychopaths.

When he first visited me together with Colonel van Holbaard, the resident psychologist of Pretoria Central Prison, Master Basie had with him a recently published article from a newspaper which claimed that one of my poems was prophetic in that I had foreseen my own arrest and imprisonment way back in the 1960s. Master Basie, I think, was intrigued by me. He came back several times and I could sense that he wanted to communicate. Perhaps he really wanted to find out what or who lived behind the name. Like Huntingdon, he was very publicity conscious; he loved showing journalists around some of the Prison Department's strong places or exhibiting his few words of French when showing the IRCC into my cell on one of their visits to Pollsmoor.

The last time I saw him was in Pollsmoor when – late one night at about ten o'clock – he had me brought from my cell to where he was sitting in an office with only his bodyguard present. Both of them kept their coats on: they must have been on their way North, perhaps after visiting Robben Island. The bodyguard chomped away furiously at his wad of chewing gum and kept on caressing the bump in his trouser pocket while Master Basie gave me a spine-chilling but quite coherent exposition of his own political beliefs. (The eyes of the chewing watchdog flicking with uncomprehension from Master to me.) I should not say beliefs – maybe these were more in the way of reactions. He was curiously needing to justify and defend his position, although I hadn't said a word. It came down to the old line: we are living in a dramatic period of exceptional importance, having to face and combat extraordinary challenges; we cannot afford to be manacled by concepts such as 'democracy' or even 'decency'; we – meaning *them* – need to be strong to go all out in a total answer to the total onslaught concept; our fate is fatal; rather suicide in the desert than . . . than anarchy; and Apocalypse, of course. (What else do the Afrikaners live for after all?) I think it must have been the first time that I came across this 'total onslaught' idea (meaning that the whole world is united in a communist coordinated conspiracy against South Africa) which has since become a favourite stalking horse of the Prime Minister. At that time Master Basie's conduct was inexplicable to me. It was only later, when I learned that his name had appeared on a list of 'enemies of humanity' published by the United Nations, that I understood partially his need for self justification.

I saw van Holbaard more often. Sometimes he would turn up in his colonel's uniform and at other times in civilian clothes. He was very young still and very inexperienced, the cap on his head unfamiliar and his mind still creaking with greenness, so everything he did had to be by the book. He had me go through the gamut of outdated tests, the Rorschach blots and blobs, squiggles and various IQ examinations. Naturally I was never informed about any of his deductions. I was the guinea pig. These perverted practitioners of the spurious science of psychology do not have as their first priority to help the prisoner who may be in need of it. They are the lackeys of the system. Their task, very clearly, is to be the psychological component of the general strategy of unbalancing and disorientating the political prisoner. Their learning is at the disposal of the investigators and the interrogators. I quite liked pointing out these contradictions to van Holbaard. Perhaps it was not nice of me to be amused at his discomfort – he was so young still and I could sometimes literally hear the clicks in his mind when he recognized in my behaviour the answers corresponding to bits of knowledge he'd underlined in a manual during his studies. I once told him that it would be impossible for any officer in the Prison Department ever to be an effective psychologist or a psychiatrist (spychologist maybe, yes) because in the mind of the prisoner he will always be identified with the oppressive authority, particularly when he has on that ridiculous uniform with the pumpkin peel on the peak of the hat.

Once he attempted to lead me through the free-association process. A dream that I recounted to him now surfaces in my mind again. . . . I was in this enormous building. Something, something of moment and of import, was happening outside and I just had to get to a vantage point so as to find out what it was. Maybe fire in the land. Maybe a mountain. Mount Maybe. The building had no windows – just an interior staircase – and there was no one else around. There would never be light again. I climbed the stairs and could hear the ring-neighing echoes of my boots on the metal runs. One floor, two floors, three floors. Going up. And up. I lost count of the number of storeys. Until I eventually emerged on the flat roof and walked to the parapet. I raised my eyes and I looked out, and as far as I could see there was an absolutely dead-flat landscape with not a shadow moving on it. Utter and complete desolation. And then I looked down at my limbs and saw that I was dressed in grey, in colourless clothing. I had become grey, as grey as grey. The upsetting part of the dream was that I was entirely indifferent to what I saw, both out there and inside me.

In Cape Town there were a few more of these odd fellows with studies on prison conditions – done, by others, in English – hidden in their briefcases. They needed to talk, they needed to be comforted. It must be hard for them: their field of study, however limited, must bring them into contact with alternative visions, even with the spectre of freedom, but their job and the society within which they evolve always force them back to the straight and narrow. No deviations could be condoned. The *norm* was all-important and had to be applied, and it was Calvinist, authoritarian, repressive. Some of them would spend a few years in the Service (which was a sinecure after all), but I think the reality of their incompetence and the absence of any grip on the hard matter of prison life eventually forced them out.

I made the acquaintance of a clinical psychologist called Zorro towards the end of my time in jail. He was not of the Prison Department, but in his capacity as director of a psychiatric institute he was used very often by the State for examining certain prisoners and reporting to the courts afterwards. It was as a result of a request by the Red Cross that I be given access to a psychologist that I started seeing him. I liked him. At least he was not one of 'them', although he could never be one of 'us' either. Not being one of them reduced his effectiveness within the framework. If, as happened, he insisted on one of his patients remaining in the Cape Town area for continued observation by him, the Prison Department showed no reluctance whatsoever in removing this person. In fact they needed to impose their authority: the longer a prisoner remained in the (occasional) care of someone like Zorro, the more he tended to become a *mister*. (A 'mister' is when the prisoner forgets his condition and starts having illusions about being human. Prison rejects this violently.) With him I felt more at ease and freer to talk about the true conditions of confinement and isolation, and I found in him a man with a firm measure of common sense and not too many pretensions.

Chaplains – our next category – chaplains and pastors and dominees and preachers and bible-thumpers and lay converters pollute the South African prisons. Again they are only functionaries of the penal system – the chaplains, I mean – proud as punch of their uniforms, their purple headbands and their purple epaulettes, and insisting on being addressed as 'Major' or 'Colonel' or whatever and to be saluted by their inferiors. Not exactly, one would think, the best persons to look after the well-being of one's soul – provided, of course, one has such a luxury item. In Pretoria it was old man van Jaarsveld, an old Afrikaner, true to type, fascinated by any illness or physical deficiency, by medicines and by operations. Out of curiosity, I think, he came to look me up regularly, only to launch into long and detailed descriptions of his bodily functions or malfunctions, opening his shirt to point out a scar or a weal. He was an old-school racist, regretting only that he was too decrepit now to be sent to the border with a machine-gun to kill *kaffirs*. As an afterthought he remembered that he was a minister of the Church and hastily embarked upon a prayer, cajoling and scolding his God. An old busybody, but a friendly one.

The one in Cape Town, Colonel Flêbê, was altogether a sadder case: a dry little man, a bigot who refused to live near the prison because the surrounding neighbourhood was English-speaking and he wouldn't want to have his children grow up in such an environment. He also refused to let his children take karate lessons because, as he said, when they finished their sessions with a moment of silence, *that* is when Satan entered their souls. I remember how he came one day into the General Stores where I worked, to whine about not yet having received his service pistol. We were very busy just then. The police and officials of the Department of Cooperation* had rounded up several hundred Black squatters on the Cape Flats – people forced by hunger to come and squat around the city – and we were issuing blankets and spoons etc., since they were to spend time in jail before being repatriated to their 'homeland'. Clergymen of various denominations were trying to save these poor people, protesting, paying

*Department of Cooperation and Development, previously known as the Bantu Affairs Department.

their fines, acting like Christians. The Reverend Col. Flêbê cracked a feeble joke about *kaffirs* coming to prison with babies and with dogs. All *he* wanted was to obtain his free firearm. One felt sorry for him. After hearing him preaching to the inmates once or twice, repeating the same words, which consisted fundamentally of: You are sinners, you have sinned, that is why you are here. Repent! Repent! Repent! – I felt that if I had any religious feeling I ought to be praying for him to find some juice, some joy, some faith.

Yes, there were others too. A Salvation Army colonel used to come in every second Sunday, as thin as a dried fish, jolly in his dark-blue uniform, hoping very much to find a few people willing to come and listen to his ranting. Not much success there, but at least the people he did lure were entertained by his lustful singing. I woke up one morning in my cell in Pretoria to the very forceful braying of Afrikaans hymns. My first thought was that perhaps the government had finally arrested some of the extreme rightists around Hertzog* for political subversion. There were several men singing and they were obviously defiant of some authority. But later that morning I learned that someone who'd been in death row for quite some time, so quiet that I was not even aware of his existence, was hanged at daybreak, and, being a member of some fundamentalist sect, he had obtained permission for his lay preacher, accompanied by a few elders of the church, to walk the ultimate steps to death's door with him. This then was the singing I heard. Van Jaarsveld, I imagine, must have been most upset at these intruders. He loved executions. He enjoyed the stab at the heart when walking the last fatal steps arm in arm with the candidate of darkness. It must give one a feeling of spiritual cleanliness and immortality.

(Sad to reflect that a White prisoner had to import singers from outside, whereas a Black prisoner will always be carried to death's gate by the supporting voices of the other Blacks.) Even the Reverend General in command of all prison chaplains came to see me. I thought that it might have been out of concern for my soul, but unluckily it was only because he was on his way to West Germany for some conference or other where, if asked

*An ex-Cabinet minister who had broken away from the Nationalist Party to form a new grouping on its right.

about me, he wanted to be in a position to say, 'I've seen the man myself. He is doing just fine, don't you worry. We are taking care of his soul.' His ignorance of prison regulations, however, was staggering. He told me of how a German pastor, locked up in isolation during the war years, had retained his faith and his sanity by scratching verses from the Bible on the walls of his cell. Was I doing the same? he wanted to know. In what fanciful world he lived! Did he expect one to get away with wall-writing in a South African cell, inspected daily?

Soon afterwards an English-speaking Methodist major, purple cap and epaulettes well in view, asked to see me. In the privacy of my cell he invited me to call him by his Christian name, Hartford, but please (he said), I shouldn't forget to address him as Major Keen in the presence of the prison staff. He wanted to make himself acceptable by claiming to have known two friends of mine, ex-Methodist ministers both – Jim Polley, and Don Morton who was a founding member of the germinal Okhela.

In Cape Town I met two holy men – Father Murphy and Mr Smith. Father Murphy was the Catholic priest allowed in every second weekend to attend to the needs of his flock. I listened to a few of his masses, nearly accidentally so: since there weren't enough chapels in the prison, the Catholic service sometimes had to be held in my cell. At that stage I occupied a very big cell all by myself. I managed to remain there when he came. This was something else. First, the Catholic prisoners are of a slightly different background from the others. Most 'birds' come from very diminished economic and social backgrounds, but the Catholic ones are even poorer than the others. They are more often than not English-speaking, from depressed 'mixed' areas, and something of the Catholic Church's condemnation of racism must have rubbed off on them. Father Murphy, one sensed immediately, was that rare outsider who was on 'our' side and not on 'theirs'; he never had to specify this, since it was so clearly implied in every phrase he uttered. I asked officially to be allowed to attend his services, not for any religious reasons but because the ritual attracted me and because of the kind presence emanating from Murphy himself. Ritual is a social necessity. One needs some form of it, even if only to evacuate one's fears. And he had a way of bringing Jesus into my cell and having him take up a position just behind my little table (used as an altar) where the slanted shaft of sunlight touched and ignited the drabness.

He (Murphy), on his side, similarly applied for permission to come to see me during the week as he was wont to do with the other prisoners, preparing them for the fortnightly mass. Both our requests were summarily turned down. I was furthermore expressly forbidden to continue attending Murphy's services, and not long afterwards these were suspended altogether in any event. It could be that 'they' were on to some of the favours he was rendering to his flock – the messages he carried out or the times he'd arranged for a fine to be paid.

Mr Smith was no Catholic but a Methodist lay preacher. I remember him for stopping off at the barred window of my cell whenever he came in on a Sunday, to shake my hand and to ask after my health and that of my wife, and to tell me about his small problems: how age was catching up with his legs and how his car wasn't running nearly as smoothly as it ought to, but he was going to put the purr back in a jiffy, just as he'd done with the lawnmower, and life was a great joy anyway, yes, it was a real pleasure to be alive especially since he was going to Heaven. All of this he conveyed with true human warmth.

I have said, dear Mr Investigator, that there is also the category of visitor who may be an eminent personality (a noble ass), part of the system but not necessarily of the good Prison Department. Had you come to find me down there, you probably would have been in that group. One is never told in advance who the VIP coming around will be, but you soon learn to recognize the symptoms of a pending visit. It is absolutely panic stations for the personnel; they run around like chickens with their heads in the dust, ordering prisoners back and forth, trying to get the place as spotless as possible – even those areas through which it is most unlikely that any visitor will pass. A whole new face is put on for the sake of the Man who provokes trembling, a false face, for sure, because all the defaults are hidden away for the duration of the visit. The misery is white-washed. Even some inmates are tucked away. Prisoners will get carefully prepared food that day,*

*'False' food is not always meant for consumption. Pat M., a *langana* (a long-term prisoner), relates the story of how he was chosen to play the role of a prisoner in an eating scene of a documentary film on prison life, made for local television.

perhaps with a sweet to follow, and everybody will be on stand-by. (And sometimes the visit is postponed at the last moment, to the next day, and then maybe to the next again: for days hysterical *boere* will be squinting at mirror-floors while we prisoners stand grumbling in our uncomfortable moleskin jackets behind the bars.)

The first time I experienced this type of visit was not long after being sentenced, when 'that ridiculous little man', as Huntingdon described him, the then Minister of Justice, Jack-in-the-box Krüger, was due to inspect the Hills. Prison warders anxiously asked me what form of address they should use when saying, 'Ja *baas*' to a minister. As it turned out I never saw him. All I heard from behind my closed door were rapid steps going tip-a-tapping down the corridor.

My next experience of a similar kind was when the then Commissioner of Prisons, General Du Preez, came sightseeing at the Hills. But thereby hangs a tale. I'd started having trouble with my scalp. One gentle morning I asked Arselow for permission to cut my hair short so as to be able to apply the ointment which the medical orderly had provided me with. He lent me his pair of scissors and, profiting from a moment of inattention, I started cutting off my hair entirely. When he returned and saw what was up (or off) he was horrified and immediately stopped the operation. The head of the prison was sent for. I was to be charged, but after a long argument it was decreed that the rest of my locks would have to come off too. I couldn't very well be allowed to walk around like some Cherokee warrior with a half-naked skull. (Punk was not yet the fashion.) Arselow completed the operation with curses and threats, and late that same afternoon, with a head as shiny as a lovingly polished egg, I had to stand to attention in front of my cell when Du Preez with his entourage came through on their rounds. The man was quite taken aback.

Let me tell you, Mr Investigator, that it is not an unpleasant experience at all not to have any hair. One forgets what a joy it is to pass your hand caressingly over a deliciously sensitive area which is normally hidden to hand and eye. And with one fell

---

Beautiful steaming *graze* (food). Take and retake. And when they said, 'Pretend to eat,' Pat did eat. Only to be charged afterwards for having eaten illicit food.

swoop you have become another person. Gone was Breytenbach, gone was Galaska, gone was the Professor or Bangai Bird – there we had the birth of the Billiard Ball himself! But having one's hair off is also an act of penitence and of submission. Years before, when I was accepted in Sensei Deshimaru's *dojo* in Paris, and after I had made the vows of a *boddhisattva*, a lock of hair was ceremoniously snipped off too. It's a cleaning process, a casting off of dead matter, a mental undressing, a way of taking leave of the world and becoming strong by making yourself vulnerable.

Another visit which caused me a bit of discomfort was when I was told one day by Arselow, without any explanation why, that I was to enter my cell and lie on the bed. Lie there and don't move! This happened during the afternoon. My cell was then locked and so of course also the steel door giving on to the main corridor. I heard, perhaps half an hour later, some steps going up the corridor (I couldn't see anything and nobody could see me) and when I was tired of lying down I got up and started moving around my cell. The *boer* on the catwalk however, probably did see me because that evening, before lock-up, Arselow came and shat all over me for disobeying his strict instructions. It was only much later that I understood that a journalist had actually entered the Holy of Holies escorted by the public relations officer of the Prison Department, to take a peek at Stefaans Tsafendas. Rumours had apparently been circulating for some time already that Stefaans was ill-treated and in bad health, and the visit was arranged as an exercise in lie control. Or truth-masking. Stefaans was as happy as a child with a Christmas toy when they showed him the subsequent article in the newspaper, illustrated by a photo of him sitting there with his smile like a yellow carrot, sipping tea with these visitors.

All the visits have the same purpose, Mr Investigator – to put up a façade by which the Prison Department may cover the ugly face of everyday reality; to comfort the Important Man by showing him what he expects to find, making it possible for him to stand up in Parliament or wherever and claim that South African prisons are beautiful, clean, humanely run institutions of rehabilitation. Unlike similar places in Egypt or Turkey or France, or Russia particularly. As he himself could swear to – having been there (the prison obviously – not the world.)

The only minister I actually met in this way was Le Grange. That was later, in Cape Town, when I was already working in the General Stores of Pollsmoor prison, which is where he found me. He was brought there by Du Preez, the Commissioner – chain-smoking as always, an elegant man but with the nervously shivering hands and the scented breath of the alcoholic, and he was showing the swellings of skin cancer – and the local yokel, or rather the brigadier commanding the compound with its four penitentiaries and the land around and some further outposts (like a warlord), whose name was Swart Piet Vangat. Le Grange, I believe, has the nickname of 'Clark Gable' among his colleagues, a name he is probably inordinately proud of – although I consider it to be an insult to the intelligence of the regretted real Clark Gable. The man is obviously satisfied with himself, with his neatly combed moustache and his stylish silvered and parted hair (he has the upper-lip growth of a minister – carpets also vary in size depending on the level of the civil servant), though perhaps less so with his low forehead. His is a cold, bone-imprisoned, police-directed, sinner-and-saved mind with strong prejudices taking the place of any thinking. Scheming not excluded – even *de rigueur*. (Thinking is an obsolete luxury, seditious by nature, a communist technique.) The purpose of this visit was to make it possible for him to answer his detractors in Parliament by saying that he'd actually seen me personally, that I was living all by myself in a large cell (at my own request) and that by implication any criticism of the government's treatment of political prisoners was unfounded and evil-intentioned. (He did actually declare this at a later date in the House, without ever having been to my cell, of course.) The few questions he put to me were intercepted and answered by either Du Preez or Swart Piet. In this way I learned to my stupefaction that, after work and during weekends, I went back to the White Male Prison, where I benefited from the extensive sports facilities. When asked what kind of sport I practised I did manage to be faster on the draw than the two intermediaries by replying, 'Chess.' The fact of the matter is that there were then no sports facilities of any kind whatsoever for White prisoners at Pollsmoor.

Other senior and cynical officers of the Prison Department would pass through on a rapid tour whenever the moon was blue, and once a year there was a general going-over by the Inspectorate, led by a senior officer. When this circus arrived the inmates were called together in the dining hall and, standing there, drawn up in ranks, we would be addressed by the hoity-toity visitor. Always beforehand there would be so-hear-me-God threats and mutterings among the prisoners in the warrens and overflowing into the corridors. This time, kiss-my-thumb, they were going to stand out, they were going to bring to the attention of the visitor the bad food, or the cruel behaviour of our keepers, or the lack of fresh air, or the fact that there was no music, or whatever, and particularly the fact that – by individual reckoning borne out by patient and endless cross-checking – the original sentence was unjust and, taking into account parole and remission, we should have been released long since ('I am being sequestered by the *boere* and the world has wiped its arse on me!'). But then, when the crucial moment at last arrived and the general or the brigaboer asked if there were any requests or complaints, a dull and sullen silence would go humming through the hall. The few misguided sods who did stand out would be marked people forever afterwards, they would be *misters* or *slimmetjies* (clever little ones),* and long after the visit they would find themselves punished without understanding what caused the sudden harsh treatment. In any event the requests which did go forward would more often than not be entirely ridiculous ones.

Periodically there would be a delegation of judges or magistrates and prosecutors coming to play the reality game – still part of the bigger one of self-delusion. I suppose the people who actually sentence one to such a place must feel the need to come and have the wool pulled over their eyes and to pass inane remarks, or to stroll down the alleys of sadness, whinnying with their hands in their pockets. It is striking that no senior visitor ever attempted to find out what was really going on inside any of the prisons that I was in, whereas the International Red Cross people would very

*There are basically three kinds of prisoners (in the classification system of the *boere*, but prisoners have adopted the order): the *slimmetjies*, i.e. those who pretend to be clever or who are cheeky, and are heading for a fall ('they will run *knop*,' meaning 'knob'); the *dommetjies*, i.e. the little stupid ones, the half-wits, or those pretending to be thick; the *malletjies*, i.e. the little mad ones, but truly so – because quite a few mental cases do walk behind the same walls as the criminals do.

systematically and very objectively try to form a coherent picture of the situation and the circumstances.

I must mention one judge who did impress me by her reaction – Judge van der Heever of the Cape Bench. She at least was aware that she was being lied to by those accompanying her. As he introduced me to her Swart Piet Vangat stroked his authoritative girth and bared his gums in a mockery of smiling to remark how well fed I looked, how fat I was getting, and she sharply intervened by saying, 'Well, then he must have been a spaghetti when he entered prison because he is certainly not looking very well fed now.'

I mentioned that magistrates and prosecutors didn't even bother to pretend to be interested in what they were shown. They would stand around for a few brief minutes, licking their pocket-smiles, and one would maybe ask you superciliously, 'Well, everything fine then?' and turn off his mind and look at you down his law-and-order nose through vitreous eyes so that you could answer seventy-bags-of-potatoes-and-one-dead-rat and it would make not the slightest impression on him. But that had been my experience of magistrates all along. After the numerous deaths in detention, Mr Investigator, the political police eventually conceded to detainees the privilege of being visited by a magistrate once every so many weeks. This government employee, scared to a standstill even at the very thought of hearing something bad about the security police, would come with a writing pad and a frown and pretend to take down whatever complaints or requests you may have the temerity or the stupidity to present. The one coming to see me in Pretoria for some inexplicable reason was always shadowed by an interpreter, who from long experience in court, had lost all respect for the man of the law: he would hop about, sniggering and pulling faces – literally a court jester. Or he would try out his few words of French on me. The magistrate never looked me in the eye. Whatever pain I gave voice to would be swept aside with a muttered, 'This is not of my concern,' or 'I'm not entitled to say anything about that matter.' No, don't talk to me about magistrates, Mr Eye – they are there only to give the illusion of legality to the system of oppression. The chapter is getting long, I know, but I must still talk to you about those people who are benevolent to the system without, normally, working within it, at least not in a narrow sense – the 'personalities': those for whom the doors would be opened wide and the red carpet rolled out. In this way I met Christ Barnard, the heart-plumber. I was summoned to the VIP visiting room in Cape Town one afternoon and, to my astonishment, left quite alone without any supervision in the presence of this doctor. He was very friendly, with a smile like a slice of bleached watermelon which he could neither swallow nor spit out but kept flashing like an advertisement for watermelons. The purpose of this visit was to convince me to allow myself to be interviewed for a film about South Africa that he was in the process of making for French television. Everything had already been arranged with the Prison Department, he said. And smiled a mile.

Again then the iniquitous choice one is faced with: the possibility, however faint, of communicating with the outside world (and remember that the filming would in any event be a break in the rotting away of everyday life in prison), but at the same time it could be a trick to use one for propaganda purposes. I therefore asked for permission to consult my lawyers before making any decision, and this was granted. I wrote a letter asking them whether they knew anything about the project, who was it made by, for whom was it intended, and how come – if it was, as Barnard claimed, really on the level, that is, that I'd be free to say whatever I felt necessary – the Prison Department allowed him such easy access to me. A few weeks passed and one afternoon Swart Piet Vangat had me fetched from the General Stores in a great rush. In his office he told me that I was to prepare myself immediately for the filming because the professor (before whom he literally grovelled) and the French crew were already on their way. But I hadn't heard anything from my lawyers, I objected. 'Very strange,' he clucked in sympathy. 'They can't be very serious about their work, can they now, because we have forwarded your letter. But *I* can assure you there's nothing underhand about this proposed film and besides, just think, these people are coming specially all this way for you. It's too late to stop them *now*; I can't even reach them. Think of all the expense!'

I should have known better, or been stronger, but I allowed myself to be bamboozled into the farce. Swart Piet himself, striding with legs wide apart, took me to the section store where our clothes were kept and had one of his underlings, a lieutenant who was literally standing there on shaking knees, run over to the Female Prison at the double with a brand-new outfit over his arm, to have it pressed.

The television crew turned up. Barnard saw me alone first and told me that I would not be allowed to speak to the Frenchmen in any circumstances, and that anyway I was not to speak French in their presence. The sequences they wanted were filmed with me receiving Barnard in my cell. Tattie Swart, the section sergeant, had arranged for a bedspread to be thrown over my bed and wanted to bring in a carpet too, but I objected to these foolish attempts at masking the bareness. Barnard, preening as usual, then proceeded to interview me with very hostile and very slanted questions. Whenever there was a break in the filming he would switch off the little portable tape recorder he carried – he was evidently taping our talk for his own private purposes too – and say to me softly, 'You know, I agree entirely with your views. I don't like this government either. I support you wholeheartedly.' And when the cameraman was ready for the next take he would go back to his mouthings of pro-South African government drivel. Swart Piet and his entourage of senior officers were lurking just outside the cell door. When it was over they bowed and scraped and invited the professor for 'a drink and a bite' which, miraculously, had been laid out in the officers' club. (Knowing how these things are arranged, I'm sure that the prisoner-cooks must have been sweating for hours to get everything ready.) Barnard disdainfully declined. You should have seen their faces fall, Mr Investigator!

So upset was I after this charade that I wrote to my wife asking her to intervene with the lawyers in an attempt to have the broadcasting of the film stopped, and at the very next visit I had from my father I told him all that had happened. He went to see Barnard with the result that the professor returned, trying to reassure me that the film was not anything like what I thought it might be. Many months later I learned that efforts to stop the broadcasting of the film in France were only partially successful. By court order it was to be preceded by a statement by the lawyer who represented Yolande and the Breytenbach Support Committee putting the film in context. Only then did I learn that the film was in fact made for the Department of Information – part of one of its very aggressive schemes to sell the South African anti-communist line abroad. (And the letter to my lawyers was quite simply never forwarded.)

Barnard came to visit me twice more. I must grant that these were pleasant occasions – except that I could never get a word in edgeways and he seemed to have a desperate need to impress with his possessions, with his successes, with his talent as an author (we were colleagues, he said) and even with his wife's knowledge of French. (Except also that his visits were 'contact' – not behind glass – and that they were in fact of the 'red-carpet' type, whereas I couldn't obtain the same privilege for my wife or my father.) Still, in his own tortured way he did sincerely attempt to put in a good word for me, whether by means of his weekly newspaper articles or (I imagine) in the course of his direct contacts with senior members of the government. I understood clearly enough that it was a two-way process in that Barnard's concern for me and my fate gave him a good image abroad, particularly in France, where he had been approached by French writers concerned about my situation.

We are coming at last to those visitors who are critics of the system or people who can be depicted as the loyal opposition from within, notably members of the Opposition political party in Parliament and first among them, of course, Helen Suzman. On two occasions during my years inside she visited the complex I was in, but I never met her. Maybe she was refused permission to see me, or maybe she didn't know that I was there, or perhaps she didn't consider it of any importance. I'm not sure.

I don't think it would be excessive to say that the prisoners, both political and common-law, regard her as Our Lady of the Prisoners. She is indeed a living myth among the people inhabiting the world of shadows. The quality of the food suddenly improves? Out of the blue a movie is shown on a Saturday afternoon? People have been sleeping for years on mats on the floor – 'sleeping camel', as we said, because the skin of the hips eventually becomes callous – and now beds are made available? Prisoners would look at one another and nod their heads wisely and say, 'You see, Aunty Helen did it after all.'

At the same time she was, or is, considered the final recourse for any prisoner, the ultimate threat of retribution or redress one would brandish when trying to get something done. I once heard old Johnny Blik in an exercise yard in Cape Town shout, beside himself with fury, at one of the warders that he was not going to take things like this any longer, he was finished with this eating-shit business, he was going to go to the head of the prison and, if that didn't work, to the brigadier ('I'm not afraid of anybody!') and beyond that he would insist in seeing the Commissioner himself, just let him come down here. And if he didn't get satisfaction by Jesus he was going to write directly to Helen Suzman. The remarkable thing is that it had the desired effect on the warder. It happened many a time that an old lag would sidle up to me to ask, out of the side of the mouth, if I had Helen's address, please.

During my spell in Cape Town one prisoner actually slashed his wrists while in the court cell below the courtroom one day, in an effort to force the authorities to allow him to see Helen Suzman. He was guilty of rape but he expected her to work a miracle and change his guilt into innocence. If I remember right, she did see him and advised him to accept his fate.

They, the *boere*, to put it mildly, didn't like her overmuch. They detested her sharp eye and her sharp tongue and her fearless criticism of whatever wrongs she saw. A fellow inmate who had spent time in Kroonstad Prison (or Crown Town, as we knew it) once recounted to me how Helen Suzman came through there once. Since, however, the institution was at that time somewhat over-populated – not an uncommon occurrence – a good quarter of the prisoners, among whom he found himself squeezed, were actually hidden away so that she would not notice the lack of living space. Ernie Wentzel, one of my lawyers, similarly tells with great glee of how he himself was visited in prison during the early 1960s when he'd been arrested as one of the young Turks of the Liberal Party. He had had a finger wagged at him beforehand, and been duly warned that he was not to talk about the conditions of detention in any circumstances. When introduced to Helen Suzman in the presence of the commanding officer, he turned to the poor victim and inquired loudly and clearly in his most humble way whether he had indeed understood it right when told that he was not allowed to mention that the food is of very bad quality. And the officer, going red in the face, 'Yes, you are not allowed to talk about that.' And Ernie would say, 'And I'm not supposed to mention anything about the dirty bathroom, am I, sir?' 'No, you are not allowed to talk about that.' 'Or about the fact that we have no visiting facilities?' 'No, certainly not!' 'Or about the cold floors and the moth-eaten blankets?' And the officer, apoplectic, five furious frogs in his throat, 'No, I told you, *no* talk of *any* prison conditions!' Ernie with deference, 'Thank you, sir, I just wanted to make sure. . . .'

The only time I actually saw her was from the back as she walked briskly over an empty courtyard behind the workshops. The stores I worked in then gave onto the same courtyard. She was surrounded by a cohort of nervous and angry prison officials, grinding their teeth in impotent rage and hoping to shoo her off as rapidly as possible. The sergeant looking after me, Hansie Cripple, hobbled to the window to look at her retreating back and hissed, 'The bloody bitch!'

Near the end of my time in the president's palace I was visited by Van Zyl Slabbert, the Leader of the Opposition, but I shall have something more to say about him by and by, Mr Investigator. For now I just want to enter the remark that if, as happened supposedly when God wanted to destroy Sodom and Gomorrah, if it ever were to become necessary to find three just and good men among the Afrikaners to save the tribe from extinction, I would have no qualms in proposing Van Zyl Slabbert and Johan Kriegler and – this may surprise you – Charles de Fortier as candidates. (Of course I know a few more just people who happen incidentally also to be Afrikaners. Very few.)

Finally there were the outsiders, the foreigners, those who had nothing to do with the Prison Department except that they needed in some way to fight it. I was once told by a sergeant who had spent many years working in the notorious farm-prisons of the Boland* of how, when years ago the first international delegation of investigators came to visit South African penal settlements, all the Coloured prisoners there were suddenly given

*These are rural prisons in the south-western part of the Cape Province – there are similar outposts in other agricultural areas of the country. The inmates are rented out by the Department as farm labourers, under the armed supervision of the farmers and their foremen, and a warder or two.

brand-new guitars (whether they could play them or not). Needless to say, they were overjoyed; needless to say too, the warders were most perplexed by this unprecedented largesse, spoiling the *bandiete* right into the ground. The visitors must have been bemused by the widespread musicality of the locals. But then the whole idea could only have been to create the impression in the minds of the visitors that our farm labourer-prisoners are a happy, singing, music-making lot.

The years have passed and the members of the International Red Cross Committee who came to see me were certainly never going to be fooled by such a ridiculous attempt at eye-blinding. One cannot but have the greatest respect for their dedication and their competence. Besides, what a joy it was once a year to meet a group of people who did not attempt to manipulate you, who took and treated you as a normal human being, and to whom you could speak French for a few hours! They would measure your exercise yard, test your light bulbs, listen to your heartbeat, taste your food, talk to your medic and go with you down their check-list of questions and observations – and the year after there would be the follow-up, when they'd inform you about their requests and the results achieved.

They were thorough; they knew what they were doing; they knew what they wanted to obtain; they were realistic about their chances of success; they never wavered in their commitment to justice and in their patiently pursued efforts to obtain more humane conditions for those prisoners they were allowed to see. So objective were they in their approach, sir, and so careful in their work, that even the South African Prisons authorities could not entice them away from the facts. Whatever privileges we South African political prisoners had or have are nearly exclusively due to the work of the IRCC.

Of course, they very often did not succeed. Quite early on during my sojourn in boop they tried to let me have an electronic chess player to alleviate my solitary confinement, my moves against an absent I. Years of fruitless negotiating ensued – the Department throwing up as excuses the supposed fragility of the apparatus, the absence of an electric plug in my cell, the risk that one may be able to fabricate a bomb from the thing's innards (that's why I was never allowed a record player or a tape recorder either) – and then endless trouble again to retrieve the gift from the office of a senior official who'd probably hoped to 'inherit' it. Years it took too finally to obtain a flask. A-Group prisoners are entitled to a thermos flask for the coffee or tea they are permitted to purchase once a month. In my case, despite efforts by the IRCC, it was considered too dangerous an object. I could secrete missives in the isolating space between the glass of the inner bottle and the outside cask, Colonel Witnerf argued. Or smash the thing and use the shards either to break out or to kill myself (which would mean damaging State property). So, Witnerf claimed, the flask would have to be dismantled daily by his men for security verification and in the course of their work they might well accidentally break it, in which case I'd go complaining again to the Red Cross with all the resultant embarrassment for the Department and the sacred cause of South African survival. . . . Serious attention was paid the matter by the pompous Witnerf and by Smoel, his red-headed security henchman (because the IRCC kept on coming back at them): alternatives were considered – maybe a flask made of Tupperware and thus without the glass casing, maybe one with a mouth so wide you could ram your paw down it to finger the interior, or, it was suggested, maybe a regular flask after all, but locked away in the section sergeant's office, and once or twice a day I could be let out of my cell to go and have a sip there, under supervision. . . . It took a change in commanding officer and, I suspect, palavers at the highest ministerial level for the matter to be settled about a year before my release.

The plant, the bit of greenery, the small locus of life, of *other* breathing matter, that I so repeatedly begged for (a request forwarded and supported by the Swiss delegation) – there we failed. Most long-term prisoners have some plant or other in their cells at Pollsmoor. The plants are naturally bought and sold, stolen, fought for and looked after by several inmates when in a big cell. (They sometimes, illegally, also have small pets: a derisory attempt at imitating 'normal life'. More about that anon.) Once I thought I was on the brink of success (I could already divine the play of light on leaf, in my mind I was going through the ritual of watering, the incalculable freedom of caring for someone or something *else*!) – the soft-bodied head of the prison foolishly said yes after I tried to talk reason into his eyes for the umpteenth time, and Yolande had my sister deliver a beautiful bonsai at the place of steel girders and concrete. But no, Witnerf screamed – how could we risk security in such a fashion? Again he patiently explained that his men would have been obliged to unearth the creature daily to check that I hadn't hidden anything among the roots, a pistol perhaps, a grenade, a vial of arsenic, a sword, a guided missile or a poem; and in any event, he considered, the bonsai was out because the pebbles used decoratively to secure the roots can be (he seriously did say this) dangerous weapons. And Smoel solemnly nodded his complete agreement. We were living by our wits. Total onslaught. God knows what the Japanese may think of next.

The mouth organ my mother sent me I did eventually get. I knew it had been sent but that it was kept in some office somewhere (although my mother was told that I'd received it). You see, I had my spies working in their offices. So the Red Cross came and I brought up the matter. The officer locally responsible for me at that time, in our section, that is, was Captain Sodom. Small, compact, clear blue eyes. The Red Cross, after the visit, had a first talk with Swart Piet Vangat, officer commanding Pollsmoor Prison Command and adjacent territories, etc. Swart Piet (knowing it was going to get to the Minister's ears) called in Witnerf and copiously covered his underling with verbal excretion spiced with threats of death, destruction, damnation – who knows, maybe even prison! Witnerf, with his head-wobbling red-haired sidekick Smoel in tow, went to locate Sodom and buried him under the type of shit that can only be provoked by gut-twisting panic. And so Sodom came into my cell. He was speechless. European with rage. Not knowing what to do with his cap. The thing kept sliding around on his trembling head. So that he eventually threw it down on the cement. (Smoel similarly once destroyed his recently acquired green-banded hat by jumping on it in a fit of anger.) I did all of this on purpose, Sodom swore, his blue eyes practically crepitating. I did it because I'm a *mister* and because I wanted to trap him so as to destroy his career! But he's no fool, he assured me. He knows what goes for what. He's no doll and he wasn't born under a turkey either. He had the little mouth organ fetched (it used to belong to my toothless old deceased Uncle Koot), and made me sign a paper admitting to my having received the said object. He went back to the office and banged his fists against the walls and returned and had me unlocked and stormed and raved some more. He would have killed me on the spot if he could do so without complicating the ownership of the false musical instrument. (In later years, late at night, fellows in the next door cell would request me to play them a favourite tune: more often than not it would be 'Blue Eyes Cryin' in the Rain' or 'Somewhere Between Your Heart and Mine' – the latter was very popular because of its line: *there's a wall so high it reaches the sky.* . . .)

The same Captain Sodom not long after had me charged for being in the possession of a dangerous weapon. I was still a pipe smoker then, Mr Investigator, and Jerry – my crooked Czechoslovakian friend who worked in the metal-working shop – made and offered me a pipe scraper made of lead. The material could not be sharpened. I could not even cut a slice of bread with it!

Sodom left for Medium (Coloured) Prison, was badly bludgeoned over the head with a brick swung by a prisoner in the sick bay, and returned to us with a scar and the star of a major. We were apprehensive about his cell inspections every second weekend when he was on duty. In prison one is issued with chunks of green soap ('soap, green opaline', in the storeman's parlance). You wash everything with it – floors, your armpits, walls – and in the corridors you always encounter its pervasive odour. It is good carving material. Out of boredom one Christmas I cut a little Buddha from it, seated in the cross-legged posture of *mokusho* or *zazen*. It lived on my bedside locker. In walked Sodom on his Saturday rounds. Picked it up. 'And what the f-f-f- hell is this? Don't think you can make a – f-f-f- *fool* of the State. Soap is issued for you to wash yourself with, not for making d-d-d- *dolls*!' And turning to the section sergeant, 'See that he's charged for damaging State property.' I destroyed the I-doll by washing it away gradually. Which was a good lesson: thus ought one to erase one's attachments, the same way that the mind must – like a blade – be sharpened down to nothingness. What a clean cut!

Many international agencies try to be of succour to political detainees. And often they destroy their credibility, and impair their effectiveness, by going off at half-cock or acting on half-baked information. (Deeper causes for their lack of success may be their ideological intransigence and the fact that they are often more concerned about the peace of their own consciences than about the conditions of those whom they are ostensibly trying to help.) They can learn a lot from the IRCC, which is precise in its approach, discreet, persistent and objective, and which individualizes its methods and its goals.

The other objective, non-system visitors I had were, towards the end of my time, the French ambassador to South Africa, Bernard Dorin, and – when Mitterrand came to power in France – his successor, François Plaisant. The French government (I learned later) had been attempting for some time to obtain my release. It also managed to alleviate my situation by getting permission for its representative to visit me once every six months. During one of Bernard Dorin's first visits Captain Smoel, who had to be present to take notes and to work the taping system, went even redder than usual in the face because we had exchanged a few words in French. (The *boere* hated the French visits and were always on the very point of being frankly discourteous to the visitors.) That was the occasion when Dorin gave me a short review of world events. I felt as if I was emerging from a profound cave. My mind was sitting there with its mouth all slack. In fact, I realized then how blunt and dull I had become. He told me about Poland and Afghanistan. And, in passing, Benin. Benin? I did not dare ask where it was but assumed that it must be a new African state. Were they reshaping the world while I had my back turned? Where was my time?

During his very next visit we were informed that it was forbidden to talk politics. It was likewise forbidden for me to talk about prison conditions. So we exchanged our mutually shared passion for literature. And I told Monsieur Dorin about *Mouroir*. (I grabbed every chance I could to tell visitors about my writing: to establish its existence objectively, which, so I hoped, would ensure the Prison authorities' returning it to me eventually.) I must also have told him that my biggest need was to keep the mind breathing.

The embassy, negotiating with the Minister of Justice, tried to help me by having French books sent to me. The Minister and the Commissioner of Prisons would diplomatically accede to the request, but the people lower down would systematically block the granted favour. Eventually I did receive some French classics translated into English – Balzac, Zola, Gide. . . . But the one Malraux among them *(The Fate of Man)* was eaten up by thin air. When I complained ('stood fast' or 'pressed up', as we say in boop slang) I was told by Smoel, staring at me from his small red orbits, that I couldn't have it because it contained too much . . . sex!

And I felt reassured when I was told by one of the cleaner-prisoners working up front that it happened, when Yolande came on a visit, that she was chauffeured to the compound in an official black car flying the tricolour from its bonnet. Whoever protected and helped her would be my friend for ever afterwards.

Because, Mr Investigator, there remains the last category of visitors – the most important – which cannot be categorized: my wife and my parents. Whenever Yolande came to see me or, during her long absences in Europe, when first my parents came and then – after the death of my mother – my old man, all alone, straight as a pine tree, hat on the head, then time would stop . . . only to flow away with a painful rush. You look at them through the glass panel and you see the contained sorrow. In Pretoria you had to bend forward as if with heartache and speak through a kind of funnel. You were one huge deaf ear. In Cape Town it was at first by telephone, over a crackling or buzzing line, taped, staring at one another from a distance of 4 inches. Like being in the mirror! And later, in the White Male Prison, again we had to talk through a temperamental squawkbox made of steel. These visits – once a month at first, more often when we obtained permission to group them during Yolande's stay in the country – were so deeply upsetting that I understood why some prisoners refuse to have their loved ones come to the prison at all. Why disturb the dead? Why come and prod the pain? It is better to forget that outside, unimaginably, another world and other life exist. And yet, if it hadn't been for these visits I could never have survived.

You know more or less when a visit is due. (Mine always took place either on a Friday or a Wednesday – the other weekdays were for visitors to those detainees awaiting trial, and weekends were for the 'hard labours', and the authorities went to great lengths to prevent an occasional outside visitor from accidentally catching sight of me. I always had my visit alone – apart from the obligatory guardians on both sides – whereas the other prisoners saw their people in lots of several at a time.) You live forward towards it. Then the day dawns and you smell its freshness and you put on the clean, pressed greens you have kept aside for exactly this; you polish your shoes and you try to keep the shine by rubbing the toecaps against your socks, and you shave carefully; you even use some of the deodorant you bought for tobacco off a fellow bird. All vanity! The visitor can neither touch nor smell you and will see you only dimly through the scratched and much talked at partition.

The agony starts too because life goes on as if this were not a big day. You can't talk it over with anyone. Morning passes and nothing happens. Anything wrong? An accident perhaps? Or maybe your lady or your parents have called the prison to postpone the visit or to explain about the hold-up – and of course 'they' will never bother to relieve you of your anxiety. They tell you to go and work. You can't refuse but you panic because you know how complicated it is and how long it takes to bring you back in when summoned from work. (Because you must be double-guarded and transported in a closed van.) And they don't care, obviously. Why should they? In fact, you are convinced that they would purposefully have the visit ruined by accident. You hate the idea of your visitor(s) having to wait, not knowing the cause for the delay. The warders know that you are on tenter-hooks. They sneer at you. They think they're funny. An old sergeant once expressed his conviction that 'She won't be coming any more – she's sailed away on a ship with a big black *kaffir*' – certainly expecting me to be insulted by the racist slur. Or they try to get intimate information. Who? What for? How does it feel? 'Rough, hey, when she's so near and you can't touch her!'

At last a call comes to your place of work. You can't hear what's being said but your sixth sense knows that this is it! Your eyes are glued to the lips. You are to be brought back. Visit! You stand around like a sick crow, waiting for your escort. They torture you. There's no van available. The warder riding shotgun cannot absent himself from work just now (always there must be an armed warder present when you are transported, even for the 150 yards from building to building within the same walled-in complex) or he doesn't want to. It's not his turn, he says. In any event, they will not be rushed – else you may end up forgetting that you're just a *bandiet*.

Or, if you stayed in, Smoel would come to your cell and wordlessly indicate that your wife is there by making the rude sign by which a woman is indicated among prisoners: imitating the tits by the thumb of a closed fist.

You go with the knot in your belly and the sea in your knees. You take your best hidden smile with you. You also have a little 'shopping list' of matters that must be discussed. Into the visitors' room. Wait. Warder with you. (You try to forget him.) Steps in that corridor leading to freedom beyond the grille, audible through the glass. Familiar, so familiar. A previous life. In she walks (with a warder – you try to forget him), the colour of the sun on her skin and the breath of mountain and wind in her eyes and a handbag I know and a new dress, no? and a ribbon in her hair and and and and another and. And in one hundred and twenty miserably minute seconds the accorded forty-five minutes are finished, over, done, *klaar, pelielie, flêbê, oppela*. . . .

Sometimes it happened that they would interrupt her visit just to be bastards. In Cape Town, during the reign of Witnerf, she wasn't allowed to bring her handbag into the cubicle. Once an officer came in to take away her watch because, I assume, it might have contained, what? A camera? A recording device? Another time they took away her pen. Same pretext.

You fight for the last second. Time has dropped out of your body like a birth. It is done. A smile, fluttering like a butterfly looking for the flower of the face, leaves the room. Steps fade. You are kept in until she, or they, are out of reach of a desperate hand through the bars separating day from doom. Then back to your cell or back to work. You aren't present, of course. You chew it this way, you take it out and breathe it in all over again, and then you chew it that way.

Tonight, back inside, an office cleaner will come and report what he saw where you couldn't see – who brought her, what they looked like, how long they had to wait, what the officers mumbled among themselves – and maybe he will tell you that he 'scored' a few cigarette ends in the visitors' waiting room, real Gitanes. 'Strong stuff, hey?' He would ask whether she's your daughter. You would say yes. He would inquire, 'The oldest one or the littlest?' You would tell him where to get off. 'The oldest one, of course! What do you take me for, an old goat?'

And then I would retire and have a long chat with my old companion, Don Espejuelo from Pretoria, who was with me even in the days when I dwelled in the valley of darkness with a nothingness head. He would smooth down his grey hair and rub his chin with slender fingers to hide a cynical lip-twist. He would engage me in a conversation about culture. Or try to get me to define the ethics of resistance – in the No Man's Land context, naturally – or to identify the elements of a South African identity. There may be silences. There will certainly be silences. The moon outside the bars will be curled like a cold white caterpillar, but the cold white light will be copious nevertheless, and white and cold the inundated world. Don Espejuelo's eyes will be closed to slits against the acrid smoke of the cheap snout he used to roll his pills (cigarettes). 'Homesick?' he would ask. Crack a joint. 'Home? What home? Where . . . ? What a debilitating concept. Fool! Fool!'

INSERT

It is certainly true that the whole process of punishment, the inordinate insistence upon punishment, the proliferation of prisons, the amplification of the concept and its applications until you have a penal universe, an alternative world, a culture of darkness – it is certainly true that all this ties in with the Protestant ethic. I don't know off-hand of any other culture where you are, as in No Man's Land, born guilty to die guilty except (very rarely: Heaven is a tight joint) when you are, provisionally and arbitrarily, saved by the Investerrogator. With luck (or if The Law does not cover enough ground) the Greyshits, His soldiers on earth, will desist for the time being from punishing or terrorizing you. The dichotomy is 'guilt'/freedom. Where freedom does not exist except as a subversive idea.

It is not only the cadre within which you evolve. The dichotomy has its objective existence also inside you. You are guilty even when you do not yet know of what. You are the mirroring of your environment with all its broken monkeys. Where freedom does not exist except as a subversive idea.

It can be said that we have to do here with real democracy. You are a consciousness-generating, surroundings expanding force, the way the termite is. You are a twinge of the Conscience. And the Conscience, the great Justification, is the *State*. The State *is* in reality the earthly shape and the terrestrial abode of Him, the Interstigator. And Minister Krüger said, 'The highest good is the security of the State.' (Can we allow the killing of God? Let us all unite to combat evil . . . which dwells within us. . . . To suicide, citizens!)

The State lives inside you. You are its condition. Except that the State is pure though jealous. Thou shalt have no other idols or urinations or blots. There will be no dissidence. You will not prostrate yourself before any other idea. Who else will be able to punish you? What other security can compare with the foot on the neck? There is no freedom (*that* is a fart of the heart) – there can only be guilt in its million convolutions and revelations. There can only be the twitching of many moustaches.

But the celebration of guilt can only take place in secret places. That too is part of the ethic: the need to hide, the need to pretend. It could be that other cultures, at other times, made a public display of their intimate rites – that they broke and burned their heretics on the market place. We, in our twisted ways, have to be subtle. We are not to be known, we can only be raped. We have built the mazes, the high walls from behind which we stare at the blocked-off sky. We take with us the images. We have to go down corridors, we have to have keys, we must shout and plead at the gates for guardians to let us through . . . to lead us ever deeper into the inner sanctum. To where the noose of the penitent waits. To where the altar of the State is erected. In the final heart of loneliness. We are the wind and we are the birds, and the singing, singing of the rope.

It must be like a wall. Very often – no, all the time really – I relive those years of horror and corruption, and I try to imagine, as I did then with the heart an impediment to breathing, what it must be like to be executed. What it must be like to be. Executed. Hanged by the passage of breath and of words. Sure, I remember the ritual preparations, the singing of those in 'the pot', the final leave-taking a day before when the weeping and the wailing of the mothers and the wives reverberated through the sections, surmounting even those high barriers which separate the bereaved from the doomed, and how the Black 'condemns' would regroup in the corridor after those last visits to return singing to the 'pot', the cell of the condemned ones, stamping their feet, rattling their chains and raising their voices in a rhythm of life and of sorrow so intimately intertwined that it could only be a dislocation of the very notion of the body of God; sure, and the next morning then when the cool light of daybreak envelops the prison and it is still dark in the tunnels, the voices behind the wall breaking with the poignancy of warm, breathed harmonies, the bursting of the pomegranates, the breaking of the fast and the rapidity of exhalation, and then the indecency from man to man of handcuff and hood and rope and trapdoor – the earth falling for ever away: we are the wind and we are the birds, and the singing, singing of weighted ropes. . . .

Yes, of course. And yet I don't know. You have made of my mind a misery of images which I shall never be able to express.

It must be like a wall, I say to myself. One must come to it like a white wall beyond which the unimaginable resides. Beyond which you must imagine the silence of the minotaur.

I think of the occult powers which deliberate death. I think of how they erect that wall and my thinking is like bricks which will be covered with plaster. Because the judgment and the killing is the work of men. There is probably subtlety there. The expiation, the weighing, the sending off to the abattoir, the words about the neck – these must have been refined to the gestures of lifting an eyebrow and moving a pen. They must experience a deep, reverberating pleasure in *deciding* death. The means is the murderer. In this way does writing destroy reality, to replace it. I close my eyes and I cannot face the darkness. I cannot go to sleep except if I fall behind the membranes of my eyelids. Like a wall soundlessly giving way before nothingness. I imagine. I go. I position myself on the edge of the precipice, on the lip of saying, and I jump. Or the earth lurches to steepness and starts crumbling and shifting: I cling to plants which tear and become limp in the grip of my hands. And then the hazy views recede before the opening up of majestic vistas – all the past is there, and all the future and the never-changed and the never-same which is always the same, the immense green patterns of sorrow. Where freedom does not exist except as a subversive idea. A falling, this falling, *forward* into the void.

Then also the dreams come. By night, when darkness has descended like a veil so that the eyes can be open like the looking of mirrors, then the dreams return. . . . I enter this tall building, this tower which has no windows or apertures; weighted down, heavy with the pack of a parachute on the back and straps constricting my limbs; into the lift where many red buttons indicating unidentified stages are flashing; another conscript there, a poor sod, a fellow. 'How long?' I ask him; 'Two years,' he says; and us not knowing whether we are going up or down; but we emerge on the flatness of an endless roof under a canopy of so many pale stars; we walk stiffly; to departure; we are pilots about to be shot off into nowhere; and we turn around – there's no lift shaft behind us, no stairwell, no door: no going down ever again . . . .

We are moving from prison to prison; in fact, we are to be released, we are released already; and are being transported in a lorry along a road crossing many high bridges; the wind, like ropes, singing, so that it moves our hair and flutters through our garments of prisoners, over many high bridges; far below us the sorrowful pattern in green and brown patches (and spirals and whorls) of prison compounds and lands where pumpkins are cultivated; old Charlie – we are free now – old Charlie is worried because he has no clothes for freedom; will his freedom be restricted? where will he go? we argue, he says no, he must go back for clothes to be discharged with – how else can one enter the world except through the skins and the rags of anonymity? – and he jumps from the back of the truck; I see the wind bulging the clothes of his confinement as he twirls, falls, spirals back to earth; and my throat is sore and swollen with tears because I see, far below, how the ants receive old Charlie like so many words, of how he will never be let go of again. . . .

I am free now; yes, I'm on my way in a car – to an airport? wedged tightly between two quiet moustached civilians on the backseat; in front, the grey-haired conductor with the jowls, the emissary of the highly-placed person; who will take me to the destination where freedom starts; I have my own clothes now, the suit unfamiliarly tight; up and over, and down a steep incline then so that it gets darker; is it raining darkness? a river at the bottom that we must go through? people in the valley? are they shouting? a riot? throwing stones? and the blind windows shatter like a splurge of silver tears, dribbling, coursing; already we are rocking; we shall never reach the end of the road. . . .

I am so hungry; the building is huge: it is a palace made of glass, which may shatter at any moment, disappearing with us when boundaries are effaced; I live in it as in a dream; there is a throng of I's, of convicts all lining up for food; pumpkin-and-potatoes; but *boere* walk down the line, grabbing hold of our dixies and throwing the yellow food on the floor; and they laugh with ruddy faces and teeth shining through the moustaches. . . .

They tell me to come to the office and they give me back my own clothes which feel so strange to the body; I'm to be transferred, they say, but they give no further explanation; and I find myself on my way back to Big House; many prisoners in the truck, an old friend of years ago too – old One-Eye Longtimer; how much we have to tell one another! but do you know why they're taking me, I ask him; surely because they want to release you, he says; if not, why else the clothes? but nobody says; nobody knows the troubles I have; and arrived there in the yard we are told to wait to one side; warders on a raised platform processing so slowly those to be discharged; Arselow among them, fatter than before; names are called out, mine not among them; what shall I do, I ask One-Eye – do you think it's good to ask? because as long as you're ignorant the worst will be postponed – and he assures me that I ought to – after all and if not, I can only be there to be freed; up I go; to speak to Arselow; who smirks and says, 'Ah yes, ah yes now; you just be patient – we have special plans for *you*. . . .'

It is the time of freedom – all to be released; the day is dawning like a sigh in the trees across the river; all go, all go; darkness recedes; quickly now, all ready, go! go!; I see them going, crossing the yard which is already growing its shadows, disappearing in the trees across the river, a singing in the air; I see them going, they are gone; the place is empty; all I need to do is get these bloody clothes on; now, I try; I try; my limbs are growing more and more dumb; I try; I'm getting caught forever in sleeve and in leg; already the outside is fading. . . .

4

Some Angels

Back to my cell. And the mountain a haze of flames. But for the time being the mountain is entirely in the mind.

And the mind produces its own darknesses. Darkness floods the dreams and taints the waking moments. Mind flooded by anguish. The darker it grows, the tighter it is wound, the more obscurantist and superstitious it is too.

I have retained a pig-eared pack of cards somebody let me have during my detention period. At night, in that slice of time between lock-up and lights out, I squat on my bed and I pack out the cards. Pale faces look up at me. I've started to ration my smoking – one pipe in the late morning and two after lock-up. So I can tamp down the tobacco now, and light a match. In the dark it doesn't taste the same. I've never truly learned the rules of solitaire but it doesn't really matter. In this way I can stretch the probabilities without having to sustain the knowledge of cheating. I lay bets against myself: if I succeed in 'playing out', it will be a good omen. And I go on and on, trying to succeed. The failures I forget about immediately, saying to myself: I wasn't really ready yet, that last game was only a dummy run. The mind trying to move the mountain. Groping blindly for interstices, for faults in the façade – desperate, like the rat in its cage sniffing at every crack, gnawing at every hole, for *any* form of escape. I can't lose and I can't win. If I succeed in my endeavours, then I'm jubilant. If I fail: well, who believes in these superstitions anyway? This is what Don Espejuelo tells me when he enters my cell. He makes a few acid remarks. He shakes his head. He chuckles. But I go down deeper into darkness.

Sometimes I continue playing long after the light has been turned out. I shuffle the pack and give myself the chance of drawing any card. Spaces are bad luck – especially the ace of spades. It makes me think of Big Chief Sitting Bull. Of death.

Hearts are fine. Particularly the nine of hearts. It means my lady love is thinking of me. The meaning of the other colours I have forgotten. I re-shuffle and draw and I say that the number on the card will correspond to the number of years left before there's a chance of release. If it's too high, I make it months. Or I translate it as being the number of days before I shall get a letter from Lady One. And when everything fails, when it is dark all over and the lettering on the cards is even blacker than the gloom in my cell, black like old coagulated blood, then I can at least remember the saying: unlucky at games, lucky at love.

The ears become the most important sense organs. You use your ears the way a bat employs its radar – to situate yourself, to detect danger, to find some security in this environment you cannot escape from. You learn to interpret the sounds and the sudden silences, the banging and the rustling; by listening you unravel the rhythm of daily activity. Voices you hear repeatedly take on shape and colour, become personalities. There are some people, like the 'condemns', whom I never saw – and yet I still have the impression that I knew them intimately.

(But at other times you wake, you listen, and the rumours you hear are indecipherable. Your ears lead you up blind alleys – they do not interpret. The noises confuse you. They are the exteriorization of your confusion. You want to shout to identify yourself, to pin yourself down. What is this? Where am I? Am I awake? Your silence is sucked through the bars. You fight for sense. At the bottom end of the mirror-smooth corridor you hear Pablo Casals sawing his cello into sad brown sounds. Rats as big as police dogs pad from cell to cell, smelling the cracks. As they rub along the walls their fur makes a whirring sound. Your mind lives outside you. The whole world has burned down.)

The warders shout at the convicts and they shout at one another. When on night shift, they don't even respect the sleep of those about to die, exhausted by this waiting for death. Why should other people sleep when *they* have to work? Their mouths are filthy and the wit is poor. Perhaps they are only pretending to be real he-men so as to survive in these circumstances of decay and degradation.

Sometimes you hear them hollering from one guardpost to the other, insulting each other's forebears, vilifying their origins.

'Your mother just threw you away when you were born,' one would intone with glee, 'and then she raised the afterbirth instead!'

'Nah, and you?' Number Two responds. 'Your father shat you out on a stone and that's where your mother found you!'

'Why don't you go and suck the elastic of your old grandmother's bloomers?'

'*Your* grandmother doesn't even wear them! You have to suck her bloody old cunt!'

'Your father's prick, man!'

'Look here, I'll come and chop a hole in your chest so that you can cough.'

'And I shall climb down your throat and shit on your heart, man!'

'I shall kick your child off.'

'I shall clout you on the head to make you fart and then I'll give you another one *because* you farted, you pig!'

And so it would continue endlessly. They thought it funny to try and put you off your food. When one was brought some mess of indeterminate origin for lunch and inquired after its nature, the answer was apt to be, *'Poes, pap en rape'* (cunt, porridge and radishes). Or when there was a hanging earlier during the day you might be told that you're going to be served some minced *kaffir* pricks.

Gradually I got to know the *boere*. There was Nit Arselow as always, cock of the coop, proud of his skill as a boxer. In the office he had two pairs of boxing gloves and it was his entertainment to don these and invite some prisoner to a 'friendly' bout. There was his elder brother, Ghries, a strong man who played rugby for the 'Prison's' first team. (The brothers Arselow hailed from the Marico district along the Botswana border – Bosman country.* In their area, they said, Blacks still had to dive off the road when the 'old master' (their patriarch) passed by, and any wrongdoing was punished by beating them with a length of barbed wire. 'The *kaffirs* only respect you if you keep them in their place.')

There was Daaf the cricketer – fat belly, thumbs hooked in his

*Herman Charles Bosman (who'd spent a few years, during the early 1930s, in Big House for manslaughter) a South African author whose archetypal 'poor White' farmer characters lived in the North Western Transvaal.

belt. With Buggerit – a truly impish fellow always up to some trick or other – Daaf would spend his time in the yard, throwing a tennis ball around. A less experienced fellow warder (such as Lucky the Pimp) would at times be invited to join them, only to be told that he's 'throwing the ball like a small puppy trying to learn how to fuck'.

There was Turkey, the red-headed young turnkey from the Kalahari, stupid as an egg but quite touchy nevertheless, avid not to be made a fool of, living in his own world of imagined heroics, pacing the yard or the passages, oblivious to the rest, pointing a finger at the wall and making pistol-shot sounds with his mouth. (Later, during my second trial, they gave him a real pistol and a private suit and had him sit among the spectators, presumably to squash in the egg any attempt at escaping I or my friends may be hatching.) There was Droopers, fat and jolly and obsessed by sex. He was from the Western Transvaal where, he said, the land is so flat that you can see your pension come crawling on its belly towards you from a long way off. There was Sampie, not so young any more, homosexual and suffering, with a good baritone voice, who used to sing on his rounds and sometimes, when he took pity on you, would throw down a morsel of *biltong* from the catwalk.* There was Sucker Snor who was caught one hellishly hot Saturday afternoon, snoring away on his back on the catwalk, stark naked, with his gun next to him and by his head a blaring portable radio. There was Irons van Wyk, the body-builder, who never wore shorts because he had delicate feelings about his thin legs. There was Soutie (Salty), the red-neck, the only English-speaking *boer*, who got caught up – it was alleged – in one of my escape attempts. There was Badweed, cap tilted over one eye, avid for money, always playing the horses, reading the sky and the stones and anyone's utterances for portents of winning (always just one out in his combinations), who actually offered to help me make a break if I would arrange for R20,000 to be deposited in his account. And there was Lucky the Pimp – of whom I shall have more to say by and by.

Gentlemen all, Mr Investigator. Pious too. On a Sunday they will be dressed in their best, and off to church. Believe in God,

**Biltong* – wind-dried meat, originally of game, now often beef. A way of preserving meat the colonists adopted from the indigenous hunters.

fatalistically. The end of the world is nigh. (I knew a warder who would answer to any remark one might make about the weather, the unseasonal cold or the early heat, the wind or the smell of snow, 'It's all written in the Bible that there will be signs and omens during the final days. . . .') Gargantuan meal for Sunday lunch, of course – potatoes with rice and pumpkin and sweet potatoes to go with the meat and the other vegetables. Perhaps, if 'mummy' is accommodating enough, a taste of nooky in a darkened back room. (They all call their wives 'mummy'.) Nit Arselow was so keen on promotion – which he could obtain only by cringing and hard slogging, as he sadly was passed by when intelligence was doled out – that he made sure it was marked in the 'incidents' book when he came to visit the prison on a Sunday evening. For conscientiousness beyond the call of duty. With his blue suit and his watered-down hair he would move through the sections, his little three-year-old daughter on the arm. Was it to taunt us, love-starved for the voice of a child, behind our bars? Or could he not afford to take her to the zoo?

I'd forgotten old Smizzy, Mr Investigator. How could I do so? He was such a perfect specimen! A stutterer, red face ruined by acne, ill-fitting dentures getting in the way of his tongue. His father was in the Service, as were two uncles and his father-in-law. His only brother had been a warder as well, but he'd accidentally killed himself playing Russian roulette in the barracks when bored. Smizzy's wife had been employed by the Department as a typist. His son? The little boy was interested only in becoming a guardian of people one day, he said.

You will find much in-breeding there. They live in the compound. They have to, to be on stand-by. And they never earn enough to live elsewhere. (There are special units – of fellow-warders – who, when the sirens summon them, will raid their houses at night to make sure that they don't have Black servants illegally 'sleeping in'.) Their whole life is that of the prison. They adopt the stance and the accents of their charges. The old ones will tell you that they have done 'the coat' (indeterminate sentence), when they have been in the Service for fifteen years or more. When they leave on holiday it is to a bungalow in another prison compound.

One sees young fellows of sixteen (fifteen even) arriving in the

Service, not shaving yet, the caps still sliding over their brows. Are they happy? Well (they say), it's a safe job – you can't be sacked; and at least there's a good pension waiting for you. They were never going to make it through school. One is born not for happiness but for a guaranteed pension after sixty. The real reasons are probably that in this way they escape military duty on the border, that it is the only 'uniform' branch they could get into without any qualifications, that they are from a poor rural background, that it has become a family trade. And where else can a young dimwit obtain some self respect by being given (armed) power over people?

During my time I've met some warders who should definitely have been in an institution for the mentally retarded. On their shoulders they all wear, in polished brass, the letters GD–PS – standing for *Gevangenisdiens – Prison Service*. They themselves, with a total disregard for spelling, read it as *Geduldige Poessoekers* (Patient Cunt Hunters).

Among the prisoners you will hear many crude and derogatory jokes about warders. Such as the small boy asking his father whether a homosexual couple of men can also produce children together, and the father answering, of course, where else do you think the *boere* come from? Or the one about the father coming home from the first day of work in the new place of work he'd just been transferred to, only to be told by his son that the neighbourhood minister or priest had been around during his absence on a contact-making visit, and had asked what line of work the father was employed in then. 'And what did you say?' 'I told him you play the violin in a whorehouse, Dad.' 'What! How could you tell such a terrible lie?' 'But, surely I couldn't say you're a prison warder, could I?'

The warders can also sometimes laugh at themselves. One of them told me the story of the farmer who was suffering terrible depredations from a troop of baboons among his crop of stones. Everything was tried to scare them off – nothing worked. A reward was offered to him who could succeed. And a young fellow presented himself and went down into the lands to talk to the baboons. The farmer, sitting on his *stoep*, followed the proceedings through his binoculars. The youngster called the baboons together and apparently addressed them earnestly.

Suddenly they all burst out laughing, holding their tummies, rolling in the dust. The speech continued and now, as one man, they were weeping bitterly. But all at once, lo and behold, they jumped up and ran hell for leather, tails between the legs, right over the range of hillocks, never to return. Well, when the victorious young candidate came to claim his recompense, the farmer was evidently most curious to know what happened. 'I told them that I'm a warder,' the fellow explained, 'and they all laughed. Then I told them what I earn and they cried with sadness. So I told them I'd been sent to enrol them in the Department of Prisons!'

5

Back in my Cell

Prisoners have unexpected and inventive ways of communicating. In C3 the 'Springboks' (the escapees) were housed, as also were all those sent up to the Hills for special punishment. They were lying in single cells, one next to the other. There must have been about ten of these down the one wall. When the man in, say, No. 1 cell wanted to talk to his mate in No. 10, he would shout 'Telephone!' down the passage. No. 10 would empty his toilet bowl; No. 1 would do the same, removing all the water with his mug, and they would then stick their heads down the porcelain pots. It is surprising what an effective, resonant channel can be established in this way.

People would send messages to one another, or tobacco, or maybe some other illegal article, by means of 'cables'. Any length of string would do: a thread picked patiently from your blanket, shoestrings and belt tied together – and this cord, with the buckle or a hook of some kind at one end, would be shot out through the slit between your door and the floor. Your neighbour meantime would be doing the same. You soon learn how to perfect the art of casting and fishing in such a way that the ends of these cables overlap and hook. Contact! Once the link up is made the rest is easy – provided that a warder doesn't come across the goods lying there in the corridor, and you on all fours with the lifeline in your hands. One gets to learn their rhythms too, at what moments of the day they are not likely to be passing through – and besides, the end cells act as 'early warning posts'.

People would send messages from cell to cell by hammering against their toilet bowls or on the separating walls. When taken to the office or to the bathroom one would leave a little note maybe, or some 'snout' and 'scratches' (tobacco and matches) somewhere, on a ledge or in a crevice or hidden in the cleaning materials or even in the food, knowing that your mate going down the same road will surreptitiously collect. It even happened that a prisoner would catch and tame a mouse, and using bread or some other delicacy as bait, the little animal would be taught to go from one cell to the other, again with some *dagga* or tobacco strapped to its body.

Nearly any part of the body of man or beast can be used for hiding and transporting illicit articles. In Beverly Hills it happened that a prisoner would wrap his small share of smuggled *dagga* in silver foil, tie a string to it and swallow it with one end of the string around a tooth. People would tape hacksaw blades to their bodies. I myself was caught once with a book stuffed down the front of my pants and I passed many a tense moment at some gate with a newspaper cutting in a shoe or inside my underpants, or even a complete (stolen) newspaper underneath the jacket down the back and into the belt. I once saw a young Black convict being caught after having smeared peanut butter all over the parts of his body which were covered by his clothes (Blacks aren't entitled to eat peanut butter, but have to carry the big drum of peanut butter from the lorry in the yard into the stores. Can you imagine how strong the temptation must be?)

The most popular carrying bag, or hidy-hole, is of course the anus. When something is hidden away there we say it is 'bottled' – the anus in prison slang is called the 'bottle and glass' after the Cockney rhyme for 'arse'. Mr Investigator, it is absolutely eye-popping when you see what objects can be hidden there: blades, knives, letters, money – which is then called *holpond,* translating literally as 'arse pound'. Anything you can think of, always wrapped in plastic. These 'banks' are important in the black economy of a prison. In Pollsmoor, for instance, the cooks and some privileged cleaners had quite a racket going. Blacks were getting nearly no meat at all. But if they had money they could buy a dixie of pork for R1. This money was collected by runners and smuggled, as *holpond,* to the roof where the tailors were installed. There this money would be washed and ironed ('dry-cleaned', as by the Mafia in the outside world), the *boer* in charge would take his cut, and the rest would be used, *inter alia,* to buy young prisoners with, for R15 each. (The money was given to the warrant officer responsible for deciding in which cells prisoners would sleep. Young first-timers would be raped, and *wyfietjies,* 'little females' made of them.)

The warders know about these hiding places, naturally. The

'span' (teams) going out to work in the workshops, when coming back at night, will be searched from top to bottom. It is called the 'balls parade'. If in doubt the warders will have you frog-jump with legs spread wide apart. And if it is suspected that you are carrying something up your rear end, they will have you internally searched, which in our language is referred to as being 'finger-fucked'.

Clothes too are excellent hiding places. I remember now, when I was sent to the 'bomb' in Pollsmoor – that is, the punishment cell – for having contravened the Prisons Act, I carefully undid the seam of my jacket the night before and secreted away an amount of very rough salt that I had managed to have smuggled to me from the kitchen. The food you get in the 'bomb' is neither salted nor sugared, and every day I would undo a small length of the seam to get at the life-giving salt. ('Bomb', by the way, is a good example of typical prison linguistic ingenuity: in the old days one was fed only rice water when in the punishment cell – rice water had the association of India, India of Bombay, and Bombay became simply 'bomb'.)

In the same way the cell itself is one huge hiding place. In the 'bomb' it will be absolutely empty during the day – with neither blanket nor mat inside, just the empty toilet bowl and your Bible – and still one succeeds in finding some crack in the wall, some slit in the floor, some protruding ledge around the window, the rim of the toilet bowl itself, to hide your precious, minute split matches, or your little twist of tobacco.

Here is where you learn all about the usages of toothpaste. It can serve as glue: in the 'bomb' a 'connection' (friend) managed to get some 'twak' (tobacco) to me be sending the *boer* to my cell with his Bible, the only reading matter allowed. Between two pages a minute quantity of tobacco was glued with the paste. Or it can be the paste you use (mixed with soap) to camouflage a crack in the wall in which you have something hidden. It is even a seasoner: the only way to get the tasteless 'bomb' food down is to eat toothpaste with it. Some prisoners use it, with ink, as paint for their artworks, which they then sell.

The cells, and your person too, are of course regularly submitted to a 'skud' (a search). At any moment of the day you could expect the *boere* to burst into your cell, or you would hear the dull thumps and thuds of a neighbouring cell being 'ramped'. Once they're gone you will hear fellows inquiring from one another whether so-and-so or such-and-such has 'survived'.

'I say, did Oldface survive?'

'Ja, it's cool, man. No sweat!'

Nearly anything can be used as a weapon. In the Cape area, for many years now, the Black prisoners have had no handles to their spoons – the reason being that these could be sharpened for use as knives.* The metal of the fittings around the light bulbs, the strips holding down the neon tubes, the tin dixies out of which we ate – all of these could be, and were, used as lethal instruments. One could take a sock and collect as much soap as one could get hold of, of the rough big green blocks with the consistency of stupid brains, and stuff same down the sock; left to soak for a while it makes an excellent cosh. Or you would tie the end of your towel to your tin mug and fill that mug to the brim again with soap: you have something particularly dangerous to hit with. A weighted-down garment can serve the same purpose. Ropes are fabricated to strangle people with. Poisons are concocted. Finely broken razor blades may be hidden in your bread. A blanket can be used for smothering you. (It is often employed, thrown as a hood over the victim, so that he cannot see who or how many hit him.) But the knife remains the favourite means, the mythical instrument. When a gang condemns someone to death, the tool – the knife – will be indicated. It is to be left somewhere by someone designated by the *kring* (circle: the commanding council) for the use of the executioner. It, the knife, is called a 'coal', because it is said that it will be burning hot and can only be quenched by blood. There is urgency. The killer has to go and pick up his coal, and *move* with the thing in an ecstasy of

*The result was that Blacks, humiliatingly, had to eat their food with their fingers. Vangat and Witnerf particularly had the habit of punishing the community for the transgressions of a few. We Whites had all our beds taken away because two 'awaiting trials' used the transversal slats of one bed for grappling hooks, attached to sheets, with which they escaped. Spoons have handles now again, for a bureaucratic reason. Every year there's a general stocktaking. Steel implements have no admitted lifespan. But spoons without handles have to be condemned by the conscientious stocktaker. And condemned spoons – Head Office demands – must be sold as scrap metals . . . at the weight of complete spoons. Dilemma! Hence handles are no longer cut off.

initiation. People are killed that way month after month. But the violence is not always directed at others. In the Hills I learned for the first time how long-timers would maim themselves in sheer desperation. If they could fabricate or get hold of anything that would cut, they would sever the tendon just above the heel, never mind if it meant being crippled for life. There were blokes who would wrap toilet paper tight around their legs and then put fire to this. There were people who would steal Brasso and find the means of injecting themselves with it. If nothing else worked, one could procure a needle and thread, impregnate the thread with one's own excreta and then insert this under the skin by means of the needle. Left there for some time it was guaranteed to rot the flesh.

Some people provoked gangrene. Others perforated their own ears. Others again would smash their hands against the cement walls. One young convict, who could not have been much older than twenty-one or twenty-two, was in Beverly Hills with a spoon in his stomach. Young Burns, the keen quack, showed me an X-ray taken of the insides of the spoon-swallower where you could very clearly observe the whole thing, except for perhaps an inch or two missing from the handle. And this was not the first spoon he had swallowed either. It was claimed that he had had a homosexual affair with a warder in Zonderwater prison, or that he had been raped, and that was the cause of his transfer to the Hills. He had in fact been given further punishment for making 'false' accusations, they said, and it was clear that he had been moved to Maximum Security in an effort to squash the affair. The spoon-eating was to protest against all this. You kill yourself because you sense that they are trying to kill you. It is finally a matter of acceptance. (In the quiet of the night you could sometimes hear a grown man weeping in his cell.)

The various forms of self-destruction are all just efforts to attract the attention of someone or to escape from the horror of being in Beverly Hills – to be moved to some hospital section in another prison for instance. Another favourite way out, if I may call it that, Mr Investigator, was to eat blades. The desperate prisoner would ingurgitate a number of broken razor blades, wrapped in toilet paper, with the hope of getting these down without shredding himself to ribbons inside. 'Blade eating' provoked intense abdominal pains and after investigation by the doctor one would normally be permitted to go to the sick ward, or perhaps even be taken to 'outside' hospital. Naturally there were some who miscalculated and in this way deaths were provoked. I remember how one young prisoner died in Pollsmoor, horribly bleeding to death internally. . . . But this opens up the whole chapter of suicides proper, which perhaps need more attention.

Mr Investigator, suffice it to say that when that dark bell tolls, when you yourself become one enormous muffled sound of mourning, anything at hand can be used for making the final transition: hanging by belt or by shirt or by strips of blanket twisted into a noose, cutting the wrists or making slits under the armpits or slicing through the main artery of the neck, or carefully hoarding or buying or stealing enough pills to constitute a lethal dose, jumping from the bunk head-first on to the concrete floor. . . . You will not believe how many different ways, how many different roads, lead to the escape of death.

Meanwhile the royal highway of execution was used unremittingly. Martin the Brain died. Johan and Skollie were taken up hand in hand. At the last Skollie tried to thwart the course of events by asking for the case to be reopened, claiming that he was the sole killer and that Johan was entirely innocent. But it didn't work. And I'm afraid that, fond as he might have been of Johan, the intention was not to save his life, but to gain a few more weeks – another day, another hour – for both of them. They died. Skollie, so I had been told, was tattooed from head to toe. I wondered afterwards how long it would take for the blue body-writing to fade from the corpse. . . .

Lying in my cell I was obliged, as we all were, to assist at the horrible final leave-taking, since sounds from the visiting cubicles flooded the corridors – the wailing of the wives and the mothers, the screaming perhaps of a baby who had, exceptionally, been allowed into the prison for that last visit. Johan and Skollie, before leaving that fatal morning, each sent me a cigar. The deed was accomplished. They became silently reverberating bells I was let out in the yard. The tomato bush planted in one corner of the well-like space had small dew-speckled fruit (as red as flesh), which I was to pick and give to Arselow. I stole one and ate it and felt the incredible taste of redness, knowing that never again would Skollie or Johan eat anything else except earth.

More and more I got to know the *boere* and the other prisoners through my ears. In my mind they took on shape, each with his own history. Cocky was hanged in silence and indifference. I can't even tell you what he was like, since I never heard his voice. He was there for having raped and killed one or several small boys, and the warders were always teasing him cruelly. ('What would you say to a little boy now, Cocky?') From what I heard about him later, it would seem that he must have been at the very least a mental case. Without a word he went up to heaven.

Some arrived anonymously and left anonymously for death. Sparks moved into Death Row and shook the fibreglass roof with his exuberant diabolical laughter. Lasher came and started fighting for his life. When I left he was still in Death Row and by then he was trying to convince the authorities to allow him to have a hair transplant. (I don't know whether he eventually had to settle for baldness, but I heard that he came to within a few days of being hanged before his sentence was reduced to imprisonment for life.)

Every Friday night, lying on our bunks, we could listen to Stefaans, off at one end of the prison, doing his weekly nut, entertaining us with his songs: always starting with 'Sarie Marais' and then going on to 'Roll Down the Barrel'. He had a slightly hoarse, urgent voice. I could imagine him behind his bars, bellowing his songs to the empty passage, or maybe lifting his head to the high ceiling like a dog howling its primordial fears at the moon. He would be cheered wildly by everybody else in the prison – we were the world's most enthusiastic audience – and some *aficionados* would scream for an encore. But that was the extent of his contact with his fellowmen.

Time passed. Time itself became the grey matter of my existence. I would surprise myself sometimes on my bunk, having been there perhaps for hours in a supine state, staring up into space, not knowing what I had thought or whether I had thought anything at all. We call that condition *kopvriet* (eating head). During one period in the Hills an outside span came in every day to paint the walls and the railings of the catwalk. The team must have been made up of old apes, long-timers knowing the ropes and the aisles and, as I learned for myself in due time, these old prisoners get away with murder (in a manner of speaking).

Perhaps they fitted in so well with their environment that a type of symbiosis between them and those who are their keepers came about. (Old prisoners fade into the walls. But there is also an unspoken complicity among old *langanas* to 'break in' young warders; to shape them to the needs and the laws of the environment – our world; to corrupt them. The old Coloured *bandiete* particularly have the knack of sapping the *basie* (little master) with an ostentatious submissiveness, until he is entirely in their power. In No Man's Land the white skin is the most effective rotting agent.)

The painters could not have been too closely supervised. One grizzled old fellow, with uncountable folds in his face, hissed down at me from the catwalk. He wanted me to exchange one of my cigars, a Toscani that I still had left from my period of detention when Yolande managed to get a few packets to me via Huntingdon, for something 'very special'. Some of the 'real stuff', he said. We solemnly agreed. The next day, like a cat, he was back. Hiss! Hiss! 'Hey, Whitey!' (Every White prisoner is called Whitey by the others.) Down he snaked his cable. An old bird will always have a cable tucked away somewhere in his body. (Also, somewhere on him, a rudimentary 'lighter' consisting of a bit of burnt rag – which ignites easily – in a hand-decorated tin, and a minute chip of flint dissimulated perhaps in a button.) I tied my cigar to his cable, he hauled it up and then chucked down into my cell a good thick *zoll* of Transkei *dagga*. (I walk through pastures of green peace. . . .) From any businessman's point of view he had made a stupid deal – his *dagga* must have been worth at least ten packets of cigars – but he was happy and so was I.

I already told you, Mr Investigator, that I had started making the acquaintance of some warders. (They are also known as 'guardian ghosts' or 'alligators'.) One day when I was in the bathroom for my ablutions, Arselow was summoned to the office and I was left in the care of the catwalk *boer*. This individual tried to squeeze part of a particularly ugly face through the narrow opening of the window looking down into the bathroom and started whispering at me. He wanted to know whether I was indeed Breytenbach. A metaphysical question admittedly, but I took the risk of saying yes. He said that, actually, he originated from the same part of the country as I did, and then he introduced himself. I said, 'Ah, yes?' He said, 'Yes, ja', and furthermore made it evident that if I needed anything done, any favour, he would be at my disposal. The scenario was repeated several days later, this time in my cell, and bit by bit Lucky the Pimp impinged upon my consciousness. He didn't like the Service, he said, and they couldn't stand him. And he didn't like the Transvaal. How could he, coming from the Boland? And it was a shame the way they kept me like a dog, locked up by myself. He would go mad if it were him. And I must be really dangerous, hey, because they weren't even allowed to talk to me. But he didn't care, he said. I could talk to *him*, he said, he was okay. Only, I mustn't tell anybody, else he'd be in the shit.

He was indeed not a pretty boy: he had the quality of which it is said in the Cape that it is not a question of being so *big*, but built in such an *indecent* way. He had the irritating habit of shuffling his bridge of false teeth around the mouth (like a petrified curse), taking it out, squinting at it and licking it clean. And he was sloppy – the headband around his cap was filthy. He gave the impression of bursting out of his tunic and his shorts were too tight. His shoes were seldom clean. No wonder he was always in trouble with the officers. But I was going mad, Mr Investigator. Anybody willing to talk to me was welcome.

Another young warder on night shift would, after carefully checking out that nobody could hear us, engage me in a game of chess – he standing on the catwalk peering down and I making the moves for both of us. He was, he said, the champion of the Pretoria Prison Warders Chess Club, and to my satisfaction I beat him. But the one who constantly came back was Lucky the Pimp, and always he had questions. Fat with curiosity, like a cat. To establish an aura of 'confidence', or to impress me, he would tell me tall tales about trips he claimed to have made through Africa as a hunter or in the Namib desert as a diamond smuggler. He had the imaginary life of a cheap novel. He said that he'd read my books, particularly *Om Te Vlieg* (In Order to Fly), for which he invented new episodes and a far-fetched ending: the late lamented Panus who dies by suicide in my mind, in Lucky's book ended up by joining the Air Force. And, of course, he was endlessly inquisitive about my past.

There you see me, Mr Investigator, standing hands behind the back, peering from the depths of my well, or pacing the floor because it is winter and cold, and listening to this young fool on the angel's gallery – talking to him, talking him to death, talking death to him: that is what is known as 'the valley of death'. Only, it is not a valley, it is a cell. He was willing to forward letters – in fact, he provoked the situation which would make it possible. So I wrote to my wife, to Jim Polley, to André Brink, to my publishers suggesting the creation of a grave for the unknown poet, to Tom and to Dick and to Harry, to Schuitema even. With the pencil stub he'd smuggled in I started making drawings and sending these out too. The Pimp could scarcely conceal his disgust when I gave him another love letter or drawing to carry out. Obviously the channel was supposed to be used for hard political matter, not romantic slush.

Marius Schoon had arrived in Beverly Hills in the meantime, together with T. The two of them were coming to the end of their twelve-year sentence.* They were now to be released and therefore separated from their comrades in Local for the last few months so as to blunt the contact between 'inside' and 'outside'. Lucky the Pimp informed me of their presence. Marius, it would seem, had withstood quite well the corrosion of dead time, but T. (the Pimp explained) had gone round the bend. He would spend his days lying on his bunk, intermittently smoking thick *zolle* rolled in newspaper, squinting through pebbly eye glasses at a book. He wore an eye shade which he'd fabricated himself from cardboard and elastic. Sometimes one could hear him howl in the night. . . . Years back, twenty years ago now, I used to share a flat with Marius in Cape Town, and all the time that he'd been in prison he'd been in my mind too, so now we were exchanging letters, carrying on old ideological arguments or just gossiping. The exchange was illegal obviously – the Pimp was the postboy.

The Pimp was not the only one with whom I had this type of contact. There were other contacts best not mentioned. I remember, however impossible it may sound Mr Investigator, obtaining some rum one night from Soutie. Soutie, with his kind heart, had managed to smuggle in the liquor which he was feeding by

*They had been members of the African Resistance Movement (ARM(and sentenced for attempted sabotage which had been masterminded, in fact, by a Security Police *agent provocateur*.

means of a plastic tube through the wire grid masking the door to a 'condemn' due to be executed the next morning, and I got some of it also. I remember how it flooded the veins of my head like a sun rising after years of ice, and how anxiously he tried to *ssshhh* me because I was singing and dancing with myself in an ecstasy of letting go. There were others for whom, in exchange for a few sweets, I would make – from a snapshot – a drawing of a girlfriend or write a letter. One or two, from their unspoilt young *boere* hearts, were willing to forward signals of life, cries of desolation, to the outside world. The head of the prison must have discovered that things were leaking out. He tried to trap one of these warders by convincing a prisoner on Death Row, with only a few weeks left to live, to strap a tape recorder to his body and to provoke the suspected warder into talking about taking out letters. The *boere* – policemen, detectives and warders – just love *trapping* the suspect, or the innocent for that matter. They would go to inordinate lengths to *provoke* a crime, and South African jurisprudence does not provide for the possibility of the accused being protected against trapping. I've often wondered what could possibly have motivated the prisoner, at such a late stage in his life, to allow himself to be used as bait.

And then the Pimp – which in prison language doesn't mean the procurer, but the one who tells tales, the betrayer, the tattler – took off his hat, squinted around, and started whispering at my window, with a leer so wide that his gums showed up pink, about escaping . . . and my mind took up the embroidery which constitutes the dreams of all prisoners. It was nice to lie there in the dark, hands tucked under the armpits, and to scheme about sawing through bars, climbing over walls, stealing cars and breathing the killing air of freedom. I shall not tire you with all the harebrained plans, Mr Investigator. One of the nicest versions was that the Pimp would get hold of the keys of my cell while on night duty, unlock me, and hide me in the gallows room where the bodies are cooled; I was to stay there until the shift changed and, when going off duty, he would have stolen around the back of the building with an extra uniform to whisk me away. But I am going too fast – forgive me. Much of what I'm mumbling about now was invented and was consecrated as 'reality' only during the course of the second trial.

Did I know that Lucky the Pimp was planted on me? Yes and no. *No* to the extent that one is always in the dark and one is always hoping for the impossible to be provoked into happening, for the crack in the inevitable. Your world is so small that there are no longer any limits to it: the walls receive, the mirrors cloud over, you do not know who you are, or whom you can trust, or even, sometimes, what really happened to you. *Yes* because the man so obviously faked a life; he was so entirely unreliable, so desperate to impose himself, to stay as close to me as he could get. I would be in the yard for exercises and he would be responsible for looking after me; he'd come up as close as he could and ask me to tell him again that story about the comrades outside. In the natural course of swinging my arms and bending I'd move away from him. And he would follow, sweating, bothered. It was practically as if he was saying, 'Please talk into the microphone,' the way I am talking now into this microphone, Mr Investigator. It was so obvious and somewhere in the ruins of my mind I naturally knew it, and I was feeding him ridiculous information. I think I wanted to see how far it would go and if it would rebound, I wanted to know what they were up to, and *who* was up to what (since Skapie Huntingdon was still coming to see me 'normally' all through this period), and in any event some signs of life were meanwhile penetrating the walls. I was going mad.

Gradually, I think, the Pimp and his controllers realized that I knew what they were up to; the game was no longer worth it. He disappeared for a while. He had been down to the Cape in the meantime, taking letters for me. Then, one Sunday, he turned up again. It was quiet. The silence of desperate men lying in narrow cubicles breathing their bitterness and their imprisonment. The sounds one heard might as well have been in your own head, the washing of violinists, the slow shattering of mirrors. Not a soul about. Must have been in the region of two o'clock when suddenly the door giving on to the main corridor leading into my section opened. No voice. Me up from the bed, ears hurting from listening behind the opening in cell door covered with wire mesh. Who? And Lucky sneaking up, unlocking me. Held out a pistol to me, butt first, whispering urgently – *here now is your chance quick all is safe there's no one around look I've got the keys you can go go go!* But I had been warned, Mr Investigator, between the lines of another letter. Throw up your arms all ye who enter here; you are now going into the valley of oblivion. And the chilly foretaste of death was now coursing down my spine. Remember what happened to George Jackson when they shot him, supposedly because he had a pistol tucked away in his Afro hairdo? Time locked in silence. A million years. Man, God's gift to creation. And to history. I knew that if I touched that weapon I'd be *morehond*, carrion, I'd be a gift to the maggots and the worms. I refused. He insisted. I refused. And he left. That was the last time I was to see him until we met again in court.

Silence. Brigadier Slappes, commanding Pretoria Prison Command, when coming by on inspection, insisted upon informing me that I could apply for the privilege of writing an 'extra letter' if ever circumstances merited it. Irons van Wyk unexpectedly gave me a printed document entitled: EXTRACTS IN TERMS OF THE PROVISIONS OF SECTION 85 OF THE PRISONS ACT, NO.8 OF 1959 AS AMENDED. In retrospect it was clear that 'they' were preparing their case. Was I going to plead ignorance? They could show that I was informed of the rules and of the punishment. Was I suffocated by not being able to communicate with my people? I had kindly been offered additional privileges. . . . Not long after I was called into the office and a big, bluff, red-eared major of the South African Police, and ex-sportsman of national renown, making it clear that he was not of the Security Branch, read out a series of very serious charges to me. It was to be terrorism all over again.

INSERT

For the dream is saying to some extent that the flying dreamer's native land is inaccessible to him.

One comes such a long way before one dies. The alleys you have to move through – the sky also has its passages which merge with a memory of blue – form the intricate skeleton of a labyrinth. You enter, you dwell, maybe you emerge. Flying with the birds signifies that one will dwell with men of foreign nationalities and with strangers. You who come out are free, and yet there is the you which disappears into the twists of mindless mind-seeking forever. Who comes forth then? Is there really a you? Isn't there, in the final instance, only an amorphous but all-encompassing investigator? You hover over the red ruins (which look like a child's watered-down sandcastle from up here) and you search for the you, in the same way that *it* has always been waiting for you. The one is the liberator of the self. I imagine an I.

Sometimes you are cock-sure. You stride into the barber shop and you flop down in the big leather chair and you clap your hands (the low morning sun comes glinting over the paving stones and the walls, deeper, searching for shadows, to pale them in a bath of luminosity) for the foam and the blade. Then someone else walks in, flitting by its reflection, and executes you with a single shot in the temple. Reverberating. Creating corridors. And you sit there with foolish eyes and mouth agape, sprawled as if flying, bathed in blood, staring at the sprawled and gaping dead man in the mirror.

I write about South Africa – which is the quintessential No Man's Land. 'Owning' is usurpation. There will be much killing of the image. Reality is that the illusion will be executed. I write to no one, inventing an I who may mouth the words that I can neither swallow nor spew out – they are the stones of the labyrinth, with the mortar of silences. Too weak, too weak.

When you die a traitor you will be buried with a stone in the mouth. Like a tongue. Never trust a South African. It cannot be helped: in whichever direction you argue, you will always be faced by the outcome – the System is historically defined and conditioned, and the people come like words from the belly of the System. It cannot change by itself. It is structurally impossible for those who are bred from it to modify the System significantly from within. The *structure* must be shattered by violence. And violence will be blind because its eyes will be useless from the despair of having seen too much . . . of never having truly seen anything at all. . . . The land shall belong to no one. Not even to the deads.

What then? You must go on, even if you lose yourself along the way. I do not know whether what I aim for will be any better but I do know that this is unacceptable and that it will have to be destroyed to make it possible for the *other* – maybe better – to take its place. And I know I am lazy . . . my knees are weak . . . I genuflect so easily. . . . The temptation is to remain in the labyrinth which finally offers the security of the known. I have unceasingly to pull myself up by the bootstraps. My arms get tired from pretending to be wings.

It must be done: there can be no turning back; there is no self to turn back to. You must resist, you must become and remain aware, painfully – ignorance is the only sin – and work out the clues to the ethics of resistance which will not paralyse you. Beyond flying or dreaming or walking. You must move against the death-producing System which is a structure, knowing that your flight and your search is a *process* (the way all living structures are), becoming that which you are: a metamorphosis.

From meaning to mind. From maiming to meaning. King Minos of Crete, it is said, wanted a sign from the gods that his kingdom was limitless. He built an altar to Poseidon to pray for this. *If only I knew that I have no end.* Poseidon sent Minos a spotless white bull, without the stain or birthmark of either question or answer, commanding him to offer the bull to the gods. Doesn't it make sense? How else can you remain certain except by letting go of certainty? But Minos had a destiny: he cheated, preferring to slaughter a poorer doubt so as to deify the beautiful white proof (like an unwritten page) of his immortality. Poseidon took revenge by having Pasiphäe, Minos's wife and possession, fall in burning rear-end love with the bull. How was she to satisfy her love? At the king's court there was the man who had the mind which produced a knowledge of structures and of processes. Of prisons. Daedalus. He built for her a hollow wooden cow in which to hide (it was covered with real cowhide, since nothing is as illusory as the real) and which could be covered by the bull of whiteness when in rut. In this laborious way the Minotaur was born, black and ungodly – and needing young virgins to survive (was it avenging itself or its mother?). Minos was destroyed by the living sign of his limitlessness, but he had to accept it as his offspring: the bull, the son of Minos. On his orders Daedalus constructed, near Knossos, the labyrinth in which the half-god was to be hidden. The Minotaur is I.

The rest you know: how a half-mad Minos had Daedalus and his son, Icarus, put in chains; how Pasiphäe freed them and helped them to escape; how Daedalus, with his bees-wax mind, made wings for them both; how they managed to find the loops of dawn before the vengeful Minos and his fleet; how Icarus flew too close to the sun and plunged to earth in a plume of smoke and was buried on the island of Ikaria; how the grieving Daedalus (who could satisfy the lust of a woman wanting to destroy her man by sleeping with his bellowing soul, but could not bring sense to the mind of a man who wanted to die in the light) found refuge with King Kakalos on Sicily; how Minos searched for him high and low and tried to entice him to come out of hiding (be it in cow or labyrinth or foreign court) by appealing to his intellect (and the intellectual is always blinded by brilliance and by words), offering a reward to him who could pass a thread through the spiral conch; and of how Daedalus did it by tempting an ant, with a thread attached to its body, to find its way through a small hole in the labyrinth to the honey at the other end; and how eventually (out of gratitude for the reward which Daedalus graciously gave to his protector) King Kakalos had his two daughters take Minos to bathe, where they flayed him alive with boiling water . . .

And the Minotaur? Never mind. That is freedom. The I is out. It is outside the walls. For if it doesn't need walls, it is not a Minotaur. If it can be written about, it doesn't exist.

6

Up, Up and Away!

I was taken to the Pretoria Magistrate's Court and charged under the Terrorism Act, with a series of alternative charges under the Prisons Act. They threw the book at me. I was accused again of wanting to overthrow the government violently, of attempting to recruit people from prison and wanting to send them abroad to Russia for training in terrorism, of having tried to escape with the purpose of committing acts of terrorism in the country – notably that of destroying the tunnel in the Du Toit's Kloof pass between Worcester and Paarl, and blowing the Language Monument to hell. If I may open brackets here, Mr Investigator, so early in the proceedings, *that* is perhaps the one accusation to which I should privately have liked to plead guilty. The granite penis erected against the flank of the mountain above Paarl, that finger in the eye, is an abomination, and not only an insult to anybody's aesthetic feelings but also an incredibly obtuse and insensitive and arrogant insult to the non-Afrikaner people of South Africa. I close the brackets, for pity's sake. I was, furthermore, accused of having smuggled out writings and drawings. Down in the court cells I was approached, or accosted, by two gentlemen unknown to me. They introduced themselves as solicitors – Andrew Williamson and John Brand – and said they'd been appointed from abroad, by my wife, to defend me. I must admit, Mr Investigator, that my heart leapt with joy. Whether they were competent or not I could not yet know, but at least they weren't brought to me by the Security Police.

The case was remanded and referred for summary trial to the Supreme Court. I learned later that they had done everything possible to prevent my friends and family from knowing about the date and the place of the trial, thus making it difficult for the lawyers to contact me. . . . They were right. I was in such a bad state that I would have pleaded guilty to anything to get it over and done with. Upon being whisked away from the Magistrate's Courthouse I noticed on the steps my three loyal friends, the Musketeers (the publishers of Taurus) who came just to let me know that someone out there was still supporting me. From a distance they showed me the cover of a recently published selection of my poetry with the title of *Blomskryf*. Under such circumstances poetry seems a rather unrealistic and futile pastime. I doubt if poetry was going to save my neck; it might well have become the very noose.

There was not much to be joyful about. It seemed that they, the forces of law 'n' order, were going all out this time to finish me off. I found out at a later stage that bets were being laid by police and prison officials on whether I'd be getting the rope or not. The purpose of these completely far-fetched charges seemed clear: on the one hand to finish the job which had been started with the first trial and incidentally also to discredit me even more thoroughly than had been the case before, and as far as possible to implicate and to smear some close friends or associates. But this trial was going to be a different kettle of fish. They were going to have to do battle.

True to his word, Andrew Williamson very soon afterwards came to look me up in prison. With him he had a barrister, Ernesto Wentzel. Things looked black indeed. We studied the charge sheet carefully and I was asked by Ernie to recapitulate as thoroughly as I could all the events leading up to the present trial. Now, in retrospect, I know that Andrew Williamson, who is first of all a competent lawyer and who subsequently became a very loyal friend, and Ernie Wentzel, who had had enough experience trying to do the impossible for the politically accused, were most pessimistic about our chances. They also quickly discovered that I was not in a very healthy state of mind, so that they had to fight on three fronts – trying to build up a coherent defence, which in the end turned out to be devastating; trying, secondly, to help me pull myself together and find a means of psychological survival; and, thirdly, working through the court case and the preparations for it to have my conditions of detention ameliorated, and in general fighting the Prison Department and the Security Police directing the game from the shadows.

The State was not going to be cooperative; it was going to be difficult for the lawyers to prepare a proper defence. Andy and Ernie would arrive and I'd be allowed to see them in a room put aside for legal consultations. I would then go through my exhaustive recollection of the small imbecilities from which the accusations were fashioned. Ernie would roll his eyes to the ceiling and say, 'Dear God, you *know* that we are not really against your government. Tell that to the colonel, please man. I want this to go down on the tape *clearly*.' And his belly would erupt in gurgles. (As we say in prison: he's laughing like a whore who's just found a bag full of pricks.) We all knew that our consultations were registered by their ubiquitous microphones. Legal consultations are to be made available to a prisoner as soon as he's going through the processes of a court case, without the presence of any State official; the observers stand watching from behind a glass panelled door to make sure that documents do not get tucked into sleeve or trouser leg.

It was only later that I realized how worried Andrew and Ernie must have been about my condition. They joked and laughed (and they were good at hiding their concern about me), but they saw the implications clearly and they were utterly decided to fight this one as best as they knew how. It was going to be a clear political trial, no punches pulled. I must mention, Mr Investigator, that if I had any affection for you – which you must allow me to have after so many days and so many nights – I would wish for you after your death to end up in the same place as Ernie Wentzel. Because if it's heaven it will be made all the more agreeable in his presence, and if it is hell he would make even that 'possy' seem so funny that you will hardly notice your environment for the wheezing and the cackling.

They soon suggested that we should have a third person for the defence. They explained that for this type of case it would be advisable to have a senior counsel take charge of the court proceedings. And thus they brought along Johan Kriegler whom I now met for the first time. He's not a big man, but ram-rod straight; intensely nervous with a kind of cold but very intelligent concentration, just barely holding his passions in check; a broad forehead, blue eyes which never waver, and then suddenly rather prominent front teeth with a space for whistling between them so that when he finally smiles it transforms his face into that of a naughty kid.

He chain-smokes and if you watch you will see that his hands are trembling slightly – a small indication maybe of the pressure under which he lives. You see, Mr Investigator, he is that rarest of all Afrikaners: a completely honest man, profoundly inspired by humane principles, and this despite whatever political beliefs he may hold. It was far more difficult for me to explain and to convince Johan Kriegler of my innocence than it would be later when I was actually confronted by the judge. His questions were not only relevant to the actual events but he also probed whatever motives he may have sensed in my convictions. I assume that he must have analysed as far as he could, perhaps in consultation with the others, my character and my life and my history. I won't know what his ultimate assessment was, but I do know that from the moment he agreed to defend me he never once went back on his ferocious commitment to my cause. I could not have asked for a better defender.

Even beyond the needs of their meticulous preparation, the legal team understood well the effects that solitary confinement had had on me and so they invented more reasons to come and see me regularly in prison. The fact that Williamson was in daily contact with Yolande helped still more. At first they arrived with briefcases stuffed not only with legal documents but also with all kinds of delicacies – homemade sandwiches, flasks full of coffee, sweets. Unfortunately the feast was rapidly stopped by the prison authorities. It would seem that fattening up the man who may be going to the gallows is not looked upon kindly by the powers that be. Sometimes they would come in on a Sunday and we would sit around the table and play Scrabble. The poor young warrant officer on duty one Sunday on the other side of the glass door was invited in to be a fourth for a game, and he promptly ended up winning. They also insisted on visiting the cell, the corridors and whichever area could be described as germane to the trial. Ernie, who had seen the inside of prison as a detainee, was particularly cutting in some of the remarks he made to the Head of the Prison accompanying them.

Towards the end of May 1977 the trial started. I was taken to court every day in a convoy, with handcuffs on and a warder (very often Arselow) in the back of the closed van with me. In the front there would be two armed warders and we would be preceded and followed by two cars carrying more warders in private clothes. I had my own private clothes back too – that was one pleasure. What an unfamiliar feeling to be wearing soft material, as unfamiliar and as sad as it was to be driven through the streets of the town. To see – through a small and dusty bulletproof window – life flowing through shops and office buildings; to see people with laughing faces and people carrying bags and people striding sternly. Court cells were as depressing as ever. The box in which I had to sit upstairs was an enormous one, obviously enlarged to accommodate the mass political trials that were going on during all those years. Once I was escorted from court to the prison at the same time as a lorryload of Black politicals were being driven back. Our van followed their lorry – a truck with its windows covered over with wire mesh. They must have been quite cramped, standing up during the trip. But all the way, right across the town, one hand stuck out through a hole in the mesh and a defiantly clenched fist was held out as a gesture and as a salute to the Black people quietly watching from the sidewalks. Remember this image, Mr Investigator: a Black captive, no personal future except perhaps death or long years on Robben Island, the arm is thin but the fist is resolute and it points forward – the struggle continues!

The State had built its case around Lucky the Pimp. I cannot for the life of me imagine what led them into this error; surely they must have known that the man was a liar and a megalomaniac. True, they did not expect me to want to defend myself, or else they were getting so sure of themselves that they thought they could get away with this *mise-en-scène*.

If I may sum up the events the way they became evident during the trial, I should say that at a fairly early stage after my first conviction it was decided to plant the Pimp, and perhaps a few other warders also, on me. Lucky the Pimp, having fairly regular contact with me, was to report immediately after every talk we had (or that he imagined we'd had, or which he'd invented) to his handler – a sad warrant officer in the Security Police, with thin shanks and striped socks and the run-down face of a travelling salesman – who was now coming to the end of his career. Together the two of them sat down at night and wrote up what I was supposed to have told the Pimp. The Pimp had been issued with a tape recorder (just like a real spy, man) but standing as he was, 10 to 15 feet above my head in an enormous reverberating concrete hollow, the tapes were entirely useless. Even sidling up to me in the yard with the machine taped to his breathing body did not much improve the quality of the sound. The Pimp was not satisfied by doing only what he was told – he showed some initiative of his own – but on the whole their idea was to get me to make contact, or to renew contact, with whomever I felt close to outside prison, and in so doing they were going to be able to trap a certain number of other supposedly subversive people. It had to be even more dramatic, so the Pimp was to come along with the idea of escaping. He was to claim that I had recruited him for Okhela, that I actually enroled him during some mumbo-jumbo ceremony in my cell – all in all the type of junk one finds in very cheap spy thrillers. To explain how it came about that he 'switched sides', how he started informing the police, he invented a visit from some mysterious, raincoated, green-hatted fellow speaking with a thick Dutch accent. This super-agent knew exactly where to track him down; he came right into the prison compound, and said that the passports for the Pimp and myself were ready (he let the Pimp have a peek: they were green, with 'Botswana' printed on them) and that the route for our escape had been worked out. And – thus spake Lucky the Pimp – the man said that if he (the Pimp, that is), did not abide by the plans, 'we' would know where to find him (frowned eyebrows, gnashing teeth, 'Know what I mean?') A threatening visit, your Honour. At this time Pimp caught such a *skrik* (fright) that he promptly lost all faith in me and my cause and he contritely remembered his devotion to State the Father, State the Prime Minister and State the organs of the State present everwhere, and he promptly reported to his superiors. To Big Brother. Yes, m'lord, he indeed saw that communism was coming to rape his mothers and to use the toilet bowls for wash basins. (Those are the distinguishing traits of a terrorist.)

He was exhibited in all his pristine innocence on the witness stand. In newspapers published during that time you will see photos of the Pimp showing off his pistol and his rifle and his determined sneer because, he said, his life was put in danger of death by my comrades, my fellow terrorists. Johan Kriegler settled his gown on his shoulders and in that quiet, penetrating, but absolutely merciless way of his, tore Lucky the Pimp to hums and to haws. I think the poor young man ended up being afraid to yes-sir or to no-sir when asked whether today's day was Monday or Saturday. To some questions he had no answer at all so that Kriegler would allow silence to do its own demolition before softly suggesting, 'But Mr Groenewald, all we want is a simple *yes* or *no*;' and Mr Groenewald, the Pimp, desperately scrutinizing the ceiling for help from above, knowing somewhere by now that he's utterly lost, whether he brays or whether he bleats.

At the outset the State team was confidently backed up by a number of self-satisfied security policemen and Brigadier Dupe of Prisons, but as the destruction job on Lucky the Pimp continued the State people drifted off with their tails between their legs to leave unfortunate Warrant Officer van Rensburg sitting there all exposed. The case for the State was led by the assistant Attorney-General of the Transvaal, a certain Mr Jacobz whom I referred to as 'Klip', meaning 'stone', because stone will never be diamond no matter how long and how often you rub it. The beak presiding was Mr Boshoff, acting Judge-President of the Transvaal Supreme Court. I came away with a fair respect for Judge Boshoff: his intelligent eyes behind very thick glasses didn't miss much and he obviously had at his disposal an incisive, legally trained mind. The State pulled a few other witnesses from the hat, more in an attempt to make good for the failure and collapse of the Pimp than anything else. A general in the Prison Department, called Bliksem, appeared on the stand to try to prove that I had actually worked on plans not only of escaping myself but also of helping at least one other White political prisoner, held in Local, to take the gap. For that purpose, Bliksem swore, I had obtained a map of Local Prison drawn by Marius Schoon. Johan Kriegler had no trouble at all in destroying this amateurish effort at smearing me. But the *boere* are tenacious and their communal imagination knows many twists and plots and figments. Bliksem was followed to the witness stand by Beau Brummel himself, he of the one green and the one brown eye (and both of them evil) who set about, in an entirely unsubstantiated way, to link me, through So-and-so now living in London, with certain acts of sabotage that had been committed in Natal roughly during the period covered by the charge sheet, but Johan Kriegler immediately questioned the admissibility and even the validity of such testimony and had the man removed.

At some point during the trial my lawyers demanded to be allowed to listen to the notorious tapes which the Pimp had made. Quite a nice outing it turned out to be. I had to be present. We were taken, under escort of course, to the buildings of the CSIR outside Pretoria. The Council for Scientific and Industrial Research is, theoretically at least, an independent research organization. In fact it operates as a think-tank for the Government and, more specifically, for the security forces. We were led to a sound laboratory and a nervous researcher started playing the tapes to us. Kriegler and Wentzel, alert and scrupulous as ever (and how tiring it must be to have to fight the system, within which you are obliged to operate, every inch of the way!), insisted on hearing the originals and not – as the red-faced official tried to explain – the 'cleared-up versions'. We listened to the originals and it was evident that the transcripts made must have been sucked from the common thumb of Humpty and Dumpty – Warrant Officer van Rensburg and Lucky the Pimp. What was more illuminating, though, was that we suddenly heard on these tapes, very bell-like, successively the voices of Jim Polley and of Yolande. Evidently the Pimp had been down to Durban where Polley was laid up in hospital after an operation (having had his pubic hair trimmed, he would say), and coming across as clear as daylight was the attempt made to get Polley involved in the thickening plot, the escape escapade. The tape of Yolande was obviously made with the intention of compromising her, to have her admit to passing material via Lucky to me. We weren't supposed to have heard this material and now they weren't going to be able to use it.

It was decided that I myself would take the stand. The lawyers had used the trial as an excuse to oblige the authorities to allow me to read my own book, *'n Seisoen in die Paradys (A Season in Paradise)*, ostensibly because we would need it as evidence. (It was the first chance I had to read it after its publication, with a few cuts, the year before. The copy I was now given had been through the hands of some prison censor; in the margins, referring to heavily underlined passages, were comments like: *attack against the church*, or *subversive!*) Kriegler now guided me through parts of the book again, to establish the background to the events leading up to my return and my arrest and also to permit me to reiterate my political beliefs, or my moral ones, or my conception of ethics if you prefer. But taking the stand also meant that I was willing to be cross-examined and the Klip, sensing that the case was slipping through his fingers and finding himself more isolated day by day, threw in everything he had to try to break me down or, by default, to stain me. It became a marathon confrontation. During the breaks the court stenographer, a friendly lady, would come and ask me to help her spell the foreign names and terms which came up during testimony. ('Would you be so kind as to help us get your death sentence written correctly, Mr B.?') I remember, as I stepped on to the witness stand, looking back and seeing Andy sitting at the table of the lawyers and of how his face went white first and then a blotchy red. It gave me courage, Mr Investigator, to see how a man who a few short weeks before this had been an entire stranger could now be so close as to be physically sharing my ordeal. My legal representatives were not just paid mouthpieces – they were profoundly sincere and just and humane professionals who needed, and who need, to fight injustice in whatever shape they encounter it, for the sake of their own consciences. (Although I'm amused by the professional distortion of the lawyer which has him say to the person in the shit: *we* shall do such and so; *we* are innocent. . . . And when the crunch comes it is *you* who return to prison and *I* who go on to the next we!)

Klip tried every trick in the book. I don't think it worked at all except that it was very tiring and sometimes confusing. Kriegler had warned me not to be tempted in making grandiose statements but to stick strictly to simple answers, and Ernie had told me that the real reason for their act was their need to discredit me at all costs. True, when nothing else worked the prosecutor – in a *coup de théâtre* – had me read to the court the letter I had written at Huntingdon's behest to Withart, in which I had offered my collaboration. Johan Kriegler rose calmly and asked me whether it had ever been my intention to work with the police. I said no. Of course it had been a clumsy attempt at manoeuvring the *boere*. And that was that.

As during the first trial a foreign jurist attended the court proceedings as an observer. It was to be expected that there would be an inordinate amount of interest from the media, even from the South African Television. During the pause for lunch the prison van would go and fetch food for me from 'home', from the prison. This I would wolf down and then sit on the one chair in the middle of the cell under the glaring light, waiting for the circus to resume. The same aged, idiotic functionary was still in charge of the dungeons. The one I was in had no toilet. I had to hammer against the door to alert the shuffling old man to my needs. But when there were no warders present he was afraid to let me go to the toilet and I had to piss my anguish against the wall of my cell, like a dog. In the well of the courtroom I would daily see a few loyal die-hard friends, chafing perhaps under the impotence of not being able to help me in any way. There was present also an old man who warmed the cockles of my heart. I noticed him sitting near the journalists, not far from where my brother sat, looking intently at me, and I did not know who he was. He seemed like an old hobo, just come in off the street, thin, sickly, unkempt. I one day read the movements of his lips as he said to the person next to him, 'He does not recognize me.' And then I was told by Ernie Wentzel during the intermission that it was Dirk Opperman the poet, he who so many years before used to be my teacher at the University of Cape Town; that he had been very seriously ill rather recently, left for dead, but that he had returned to this problematical earthly paradise of No Man's land after being in a coma for several months.

The two opposing sides entered their final pleas – the State asking for severe punishment and the defence adroitly dismantling the rickety structure that the Security Police and the prosecutor had had the effrontery to produce for the judge. They simultaneously brought the spotlight to bear on the conditions under which I had been kept for the foregoing two years. The teams had had enormous legal tomes carried into court. These with slips of paper marking passages were piled on their tables. *The law is.* The judge suspended proceedings and swept out. I was escorted down and then brought back up again. The court was crowded. In the doorways sat teenage typists who had forced their way in, munching their sandwiches and giving me bold looks. The judge was deliberating, the judge has deliberated, the judge is here! *Stand up in court!* Judge Boshoff looked through his glasses and started reading a long, carefully balanced text. Lucky the Pimp sat, grinning sheepishly, next to his girlfriend. As long as they talk about you, you exist. Among the audience the armed warders were scattered – Turkey looking like a stubborn red spot trying to merge with a white background. During this peroration I had to stand. Being talked to. Eyes all over me and my clothes like a swimming of flies. Silence in the head. Silence in the court! Life rumbling by in the streets outside. Sweet life. Yolande in Paris (or London?) waiting for the outcome. People eating somewhere. People in death's cells. Couples mating. And so the judge found me not guilty of the heinous crimes; he found me innocent on all the charges barring the last alternative one – that of having smuggled out the letters and the drawings which had been produced in court. (Which was just as well, Mr Investigator, since once having been evidenced it meant that they were saved.)

Johan Kriegler hid his emotions by making a big thing of taking off his gown, folding it, packing it away. Ernesto Wentzel laughed until his face shone, took off and polished his glasses and then laughed some more. His unruly curls were neatly cut: he was off to another political trial in Namibia. Sisyphus! Andy Williamson came and grasped my hand with a flushed face.

Down in the court cells Kriegler embraced me and said, 'Now behave yourself like a good Afrikaner and a good Frenchman.' Some court officials actually came down to congratulate me and to wish me the best. So also did a few of the journalists who had been in court every day, particularly during the nearly two-week period of my cross-examination. As the witness box was next to their press table, they had tried – until stopped – to position newspapers on the table in such a way that I could read them. The judge sent down a messenger to ask what ought to be done with the R300 that had been used in evidence – the R300 which Lucky the Pimp had obtained from André Brink during a foray to Grahamstown when, directed by Brummel, an attempt was made to compromise the Professor. It was legally mine, the judge maintained. I asked the lawyers to have it returned to the donor.

(Thinking about the money brings back the farce of the meetings between Brink and the Pimp. I was told of how, when the Pimp went down to Grahamstown on the second occasion, the two of them got into Brink's car and drove to a secluded spot outside town, presumably the better to conspire. But Professor Brink had by now become suspicious: as they got out of the car the tape recorder that he had hidden away under his seat fell out with a clatter. Embarrassing moment, surely, particularly since the other recorder carried by the Pimp was still turning in its silences for tapewords. . . . And Kriegler's words about being French remind me now of how, during the trial, an official translator was summoned to render from French into Afrikaans one of my illegal letters to Yolande. How we argued! Like fishwives! This translator from the Security Police and I could not agree on the Afrikaans term for the French *con*. Here we were, in the middle of this court case with all its momentous implications, having an undignified semantic tiff. As so often before, Johan Kriegler had to suggest a solution. Why not, he said, render it as *doos* – which literally means 'box' in Afrikaans. A rather hermetic way of referring to the female part. . . .)

It was over. For the last time I walked out to the van with my bangles on. Back to prison. People going after their private concerns in the streets. No more private clothes now. No more stolen smiles exchanged with friends in the gallery. Back to four walls, a floor and a light bulb on high. A few days later I was suddenly told one morning to get my possessions together and, without knowing my destination, I was booked out of the Hills, put in a car with a Prison Department colonel and whisked down to Local Prison where the other White politicals were kept. There I had to go through all the procedures of being booked into prison again from scratch. My perfectly good Maximum Security clothes were taken away and I was issued with exactly the same outfit, but now belonging to Local. I was lectured and admonished and told that my hair was too long; then taken into the maze – so different from, and yet so similar to, that of the Hills. Finally I met my fellow political inmates. They were all already busy at their various tasks. The place looked OK. There was a big courtyard where they had planted a rose garden and where they even had a miniature tennis court. My first job was to walk around the courtyard stooped, picking up cigarette ends. Just *look* busy, one of the convicts advised me, but don't finish up the work. One should never liquidate work lest you be given some more.

In a workshop where he was engaged upon making furniture I was introduced to Moumbaris and immediately we started exchanging some words in French until stopped by the supervisor.

I was shown my cell, told about the rules specific to Local, promised (in a whisper) some illegal coffee by the prisoner acting as storeman and general handyman (the cells had hot water!), taken to the dining room, which came as a surprise because there were real red peppers and even some reproductions of paintings on the walls, and also well in evidence, a sound system donated, I was told, by Helen Suzman, which made it possible for the prisoners to listen to records of their choice from time to time. This was going to be much better! This was going to be just great! Back outside my hair was roughly clipped, short around the ears and the back, by an old shivering prisoner. I think it must have been Kitson. It was time for tea, which was taken outside. I met Goldberg and all the others,* and I could transmit to them the latest news (which I had picked up during my trial) about political cases. Then, even before lunchtime, I was summoned back to the front offices and without a word of explanation taken through the whole rigmarole in reverse: booked out, divested of my Local clothes, taken back to Maximum. In the space of half a day I was back exactly to where I started from. The deception was enormous.

To this day I don't know what caused this inexplicable forth-and-back. I can only imagine that the fact of my being able to communicate with another prisoner in a language they would not understand may have scared them, or else it was one more control experiment. Perhaps they were testing someone or something.

At last, a few weeks later, came the day for my transfer. I had not been told where to, no, nor when, but I was confident – after the publicity given to my conditions during the trial – that I would be transferred eventually. Thus, one morning, Arselow told me to get ready. Turkey got hold of some cardboard boxes because in the meantime, Mr Investigator, I had been given

*Arthur Goldberg – a White South African who is, with Nelson Mandela, a co-founder of *uMkhonto we Siswe*, and is serving a life sentence.

permission to study. Not that it helped any: although enrolled at the University of South Africa for a correspondence course, I was not going to be able to fulfil my tasks since it took them the best part of the year to let me obtain the books necessary for my studies. (In any event, a year later the permission to study was to be withdrawn from all political prisoners and it was only going to be reinstituted towards the end of my time. And then I could not benefit as I wanted to study Zulu, which was not allowed.

I packed; I looked around my absolutely bare cell for the last time; I crawled in under the bunk and scratched my name in the wood underneath; and then, in the early afternoon, I was taken out for the final time through the front entrance, handcuffed, and put in the back of a van. It was 10 July 1977. I had been in Maximum Security for nearly two years and now I was off into the wild blue yonder, not knowing whereto, but anywhere was going to be an improvement on this. Not many of the people who were in Maximum Security when I arrived were still alive. They had been executed in the meantime. I was saved. Priapus, the god of gardens and birds and of thieves, no doubt wanted me to survive so as to be able to confess to you, my dear dead I.

I was not sorry to see the last of Pretoria. Indeed, I swore then – as I still swear today – that never will I freely set foot again in Pretoria. Let that bloated village of civil servants and barbarians be erased from the face of the earth. . . . The van was escorted by an unmarked car in which Brigadier Dupe himself took a seat. We left. These transfers are supposed to be discreet matters, sir. The warders accompanying you wear private clothes – in fact, they look very often as if they were going on a hunting expedition, with floppy hats, boots made for walking in the bush with, and very sophisticated firearms held at the ready. It was winter. The land was brown and grey. It was a dream to be driving along a highway with a slow darkening coming over the veld, seeing through the narrow slits of the slightly opened little back window of the van the headlights of private vehicles flooding the night. And then the moon. And realizing suddenly how bad my eyes had become over the years. Never stopping, Mr Investigator, moving at a fast pace. You have two or three blankets with you in the back. You have all your clothes on. They had given you a fair chunk of bread with maybe one or two hard-boiled eggs and some cold chicken. And you have two buckets in the back with you, which are now bobbing around, which you cannot secure – the one with water for you to drink, the other for your toilet needs. Your food has to last until you arrive at your destination, and as for your needs, these you might as well forget about since it is nearly impossible handcuffed, to do anything in that cramped space in which you cannot stand up.

We stopped at Leeukop Prison; we drove in beyond the inner walls and a number of shackled Black political prisoners were put into another van there. I could not see them but I could hear the chattering of the chains as they mounted the vehicle. Robben Island was their destiny. Misery and oblivion and fog and a salty wind. Sons of Africa. From there we left in a convoy. Somewhere during the night we stopped at Bloemfontein for fuel. A petrol pump attendant, grey with the cold, filled the tanks. Son of Africa. Men lying, quivering, wrapped in thin blankets, behind steel partitions. On into the night. Near Colesberg, I believe, we had a puncture and for the best part of an hour the van was immobilized on the side of the road. It started snowing. It does snow in the interior of the country in the winter. It was bitterly cold. On into the night. Driving through some of the towns you could see pink manikins in illuminated shop windows or sometimes other live little Black petrol-pump attendants, petrified by the cold, with Balaclava hoods nearly entirely covering their faces, staring at these prison conveyances. Could they know that there were people inside? They must know; they know everything; they are born with the wisdom of the oppressed. In the country, when you see convoys of people moving across the land to their doom, you *know* they are there. You cannot see them. And you on the inside, you know they are there on the outside, and you cannot communicate with them. Your heart thuds; they shuffle their feet. They feed their eyes. We are all blind.

Light caught us somewhere in the Karoo. Maybe Beaufort West. The expanse of the land all around, Mr Investigator. The beauty of it, Mr Investigator. The glory, yes. It was building up in me. We were going South. I was going to see the mountains, sir, and I now saw the Karoo unfolding. I remembered how, when I was very small, we used at Christmas time to drive down to the seaside in an old lorry, and I recalled the excitement of the strange land. Sometimes we see things for what they are, stripped of all adjectives. I was singing anything that came into my head, Mr Investigator; it was pouring out of me, all the broken filth of Pretoria. I sang of rock and hill and bush and lizard and moon. I sang to my Lady One and to the ghosts of ancestors. I even sang for you. Of the breathtaking prehistoric beauty of the desert; and of the madness of conquerors and the humiliation of the oppressed. Up and up we went over the Hex River mountains, Matroosberg with its white cape of snow glistening in the sunlight, and far below in the valleys the green fertility, the silver snake of the river, the bare orchards with branches like children learning to write Chinese characters. It was home – a home that would never be home again, which I had become alienated from forever. But the alienation was not from the earth, which I still recognized, with which I still felt at peace.

We stopped in Worcester, just off the main street. I could hear people walking by; I could hear the laughter of labourers going to work. Some warder must have gone across the street to buy cool drinks or food. And on. On we went. Du Toit's Kloof, high up above Wellington, my old home town. Ah, it was too much.

We arrived, after driving through the outskirts of Cape Town, at some place that I'd never heard of nor even suspected the existence of: a big prison compound lying in the lee of the mountains where they run into the sea at Muizenberg. It was in the late afternoon of 11 July 1977. We drove right into the building. I was unlocked after twenty-four hours of being cramped and chilled. But I was happy. It wasn't so cold there, close to the sea. Arselow, who had been riding shotgun in the van, took me through some passages to an office and immediately I was struck by the different smells and by the hum and buzz of many voices. Obviously there was much less discipline here. The place was dirty. This was the Cape. I was shown, or rather taken, into the reception office which was well inside the building, and told to wait. Now at last my handcuffs were taken off. I could rub my limbs to get the circulation going. Behind the counter there was an old sergeant with a rather ridiculous moustache, hair cut short but parted, glasses, pretending very hard to be occupied. It was Pollsmoor – that was the name of the place – Pollsmoor, Cape Town.

An enormous plate of food was brought to me in this office. It had been prepared with quite a lot of oil. Such is Cape prison cooking – excessively so. Time buzzed like a fly. The sergeant, scared obviously to take any initiative, not knowing what to do with me, had me waiting. Other *boere* walked in and around me, looking me over curiously. All over there was a much more relaxed atmosphere. In the Cape things are not taken quite as seriously. Head Office is far away, in the north. An officer entered. The beginning of a belly like a soccer ball. And perfectly mad, bulging blue eyes.

'Ah, yes, so you are Breytenbach. Yes. Yes.'

INSERT

The year is nearly done. Already big dark-green pine trees are appearing in front of public edifices and on certain street corners, festooned with silver bunting. When I climb the stairs I can look, across the wall separating the courtyards, into rosy interiors. People wrapped in heavy coats and scarves move through the rooms; they pause in front of the windows, looking out for an instant upon the blind night; they have the slightly stooped shoulders of exiles from some totalitarian state. Memory.

I have travelled through many countries, I have visited many cities over the last months. I have carefully taken the thought of you with me on my journeys. I have seen the land sweeping by, white and virginal under a crisp layer of frost. (Wraiths of fog seeping from hollows.) I have seen the sun glancing off spires and domes and tall blocks of flats as the day became flatter and weaker. Often I have tried to establish for myself what it was – or is – about prison that is the most typical. That will sum it up. Tell me, sir, I then ask. People say, *how did you survive?* I say, *I did not survive.* People say, *but prison is a clear instance of opposition, of resistance.* I say, *resistance, if that is what you want to call survival, is made up of a million little compromises and humiliations, so subtle that the human eye cannot perceive them.* You know it, I know it. . . .

Prison, for me, is the absolute stripping away of all protective layers: sounds are raw, sights are harsh, smells are foul. The scars are there, like tattoos on the mind. You are reduced to the lowest common denominator – being alone (and scared and weak to the point of being suffocated by a self-disgust) whilst always surrounded by others. Don't trust. Never softness. The consecration of the worst in human nature. What do you gain? You lose all sense of importance, of hierarchy, of standards and of norms. Things are as they are. A dusty wall is as beautiful as a fresco painted by Brother Angel, a broken leaf has as much value as a bar of gold. Stars are ships emitting waves of sound. No more attachment. Death is clarity. Setbacks are experienced with a body-consciousness. Walking erect becomes the purpose of walking. Walking becomes a matter of moving hips and legs. What do you risk? To project yourself to the mountain. To make of the mountain a myth. To hear the voices in the earth and to lose yourself in memory of sky when the morning is fresh. When you have forgotten about the aches of night. To fly.

For years, right up to the end in the Shu Ch'un T'ang, I used to come awake at night with a shock, sitting bolt upright in my bed, and always I'd be looking to my right where I expected Hoang Lien to lie, or my brother Sebastiaan. The whole body is one mind, and how permanent are the imprints of memory on the mind! I last shared a room with my brother at the age of ten! Every night the mind would crawl back into the protective shell of remembered security; each morning would bring the stiffening taste of bitterness. . . . And when I came out, away from the maze – here, so far from No Man's Land – I found myself running through the streets of winter at five o'clock in the morning, tasting the tears of helpless despair. I am not in exile. I am travelling. What is it I keep on running away from?

I have looked at the possibility of suicide. Oh, nothing spectacular, you know. But coldly, like a professional for whom the essential sense is in the breaks and in the silences, for whom there can be no ethic beyond that of continuing to walk with awareness, of going beyond. There is no elsewhere. I have thought about how it would be to die in one of those monstrous, chromed Zurich toilets. Leaving traces of blood on their shiny surfaces – how impure! Or vomiting at last, with black gloves on, in front of one of Karl von Piloty's sublimely ridiculous paintings in Munich's Neue Pinakothek. Smashing the dark glasses when falling. Making death so small. . . .

But always, wherever I've been, however hard I ran, whatever the temptations of oblivion, I've kept up my intimate questioning of you, Investigator. I've asked you to listen to the twittering of the birds in trees becoming barer with the cooling of the year. And I kept on trying to give you a free face. A name. I have seen you as the Minotaur, which is the I, which does not exist since it is a myth. . . . I see you now as my dark mirror-brother. We need to talk, brother I. I must tell you what it was like to be an albino in a white land. We are forever united by an intimate knowledge of the depravity man will stoop to. Son of Africa. Azanians.

We must launch a dialogue. I must warn you that the system by which we're trying to replace the present one will grind us down, *me and you*, as inexorably. I must tell you that I cannot hold my criticism, my disaffection, in abeyance; that I cannot condone your (our) agreements and compromises – not even tactically. I love you too bitterly for that.

I hear you chuckling, you who are Black. . . .

7

I Was in Pollsmoor

Witnerf, the mad major, looked me over with his bulging blue eyes. I was in Pollsmoor. It was quite late in the afternoon when I was finally processed through the books and handed clothes which had the number 4 stencilled on every item – meaning that they belong to Pollsmoor Prison, White Section. I also now belonged to Pollsmoor. I was further given a sheet, and pillowslip, a towel, a tube of toothpaste, a toothbrush and soap, and taken up three floors through many corridors and locked grilles to the section for White male prisoners and into my new cell, which was enormous compared to what I had been used to. Joy of joys – in one corner of the cell there was a large washbasin with hot and cold water and a shower and a toilet bowl. A low wall separated this area from the rest of the cell. (In due time I would spend time at night behind that low wall, pretending to stare vaguely at the door and the corridor where the *boere* patrolled, my knees half-bent with an open – illegal – newspaper balanced upon them: they couldn't see it, but I was avidly feeding the mind with politics and sports and small ads!) There were two tall, narrow, barred windows in the one wall actually giving on to the outside. I had a bed, I had a small table, a chair to go with it, and several lockers built into the walls of the cell. I had in reality quite enough room for my few possessions as the cell I was in normally held up to sixteen prisoners when White and maybe as many as thirty or exceptionally even more when Black.

But back to the window, Mr Investigator: I could actually see one part of a mountain! True, only the beginning slope, but it was something, a landmark, life outside uncontaminated by prison existence, a limit to the void, to nothingness. I couldn't believe my eyes. It became dark and I imagined that with the dusk I could smell through the windows (which I could open or close myself) the faint aroma of magnolias or perhaps even gardenias.

This was really the Cape then: memories came flooding back of that other night when I had met Paul somewhere in this same region and we'd gone walking through a sleepy suburb, smelling the intimate gardens and hearing the wind groaning in the oaks. Here from my cell I could surely, I thought, if I really tried hard enough, get a whiff of the sea. My sleep must have been filled with moonlight. This was paradise, Mr Investigator.

When I woke up seagulls were really flying over the prison, dropping their scissors-like squawks and screams in the concrete walled-in courtyards. Indeed, when I pulled the table close to the window and climbed on top of it I could just barely make out in the distance a thin but unruly blue ribbon. The sea. The limitless ocean. Looking at Antarctica.

Pollsmoor is situated in one of the most beautiful areas of No Man's Land – perhaps of the world. It lies nestled in the shadows of the same mountain chain which at one extremity is known as Table Mountain. Here in this part of the peninsula it finally runs into the ocean with the effect of creating a micro-climate. Wind there is enough of – the so-called 'Cape Doctor'. It became a constant companion during the months of the year – in fact it was a bench-mark by which the progress of the year could be measured. But that which particularly marked me and made me was the mountain: my companion, my guide, my reference point, my deity, my fire, my stultified flame, and finally – like a prehistoric receptacle – the mould of my mind, my eye, my very self.

The prison compound itself covers a large area which previously used to be several farms and a race track. It is confined partly by walls studded with watchtowers and partly by wire fences. These contain four separate prisons consisting of a large building called Maximum Security (which is where I now found myself), a series of single storey barracks-like constructions called Medium Prison, and two more modern constructions called the Female Prison and the Observation Station. A few years later the Female Prison would become Pollsmoor White Males and the women were to take over Observation. (When the day of moving came the White Males, each with his possessions slung in a bundle over his back, were herded on foot to the new home by warders with dogs and guns – all except me: I was taken there in a slow-moving closed conveyance. In the new place we found minutely scrawled graffiti of the most outrageous obscenity.) There are furthermore the houses – with the well-watered gardens – and the blocks of flats for the warders and their families, the administrative buildings, the recreation halls and the club buildings for the staff, their rugby fields and their swimming pools, and quite extensive farmlands where vegetables are grown.

Immediately beyond the boundaries of the prison community and towards the mountain there were private farms, some with cows so that we could hear the lowing of the cattle, and some with vineyards. On one of the farms they must have had a donkey because for a long period I used to listen every night for the lonely braying of this animal. Somewhere not far off, towards the sea, there were suburbs leading eventually to Muizenberg, which is a popular seaside resort. Some houses were built very close to the walls separating us from the outside world. There were many trees both on the terrain and beyond it, including palm trees and a number of gigantic bluegums. An old prisoner later told me of how, in earlier years when only Medium existed, they had to clear the grounds so as to build the other jails from scratch, and how they had to take out these big bluegums 'carrots an' all'.

I was now for the first time inserted in a prison community. I saw other prisoners trotting by my two little windows giving on to the passage, one on either side of the door, and some of them actually stopped and talked to me – although it was forbidden. I was like a monkey that had been brought back to the jungle, Mr Interviewer, hanging on to the bars, trying to attract any passer-by's attention. Pollsmoor had (has) a normal prison population of 4,000–4,500 people of which maybe 200 at any given time would be White, or rather whitish – since we were now in the Cape where population groups merge into one another. (The intake would rise spectacularly when the bulldozers had been at their periodic dawn feast of shanties made of cartons and jute and tin, and hundreds of squatters would be swept off the Cape Flats and brought to prison in lorries.) The staff – warders and various tradesmen working either in the workshops or on the fields – add up to about 300. Usually there'd be also between twenty and twenty-six dogs with their dog handlers. These (the Alsations, not the *boere*) were kept in fenced kennels situated just behind the building I was in. Whereas the dominant or prevalent sound of Pretoria, particularly at night, was the constant who-hooting and huffing of trains being shunted around the station yard not far from Central, the Cape will always be marked for me by the insistent growling and yapping and barking of dogs at night. Whenever the siren sounded the dogs would take up the echo in a chorus of howling.

But one soon got used to that. We lived in a universe of sounds which became our allies – the sad night birds, early every morning the wild geese raucously on their way back from the marshes near the sea to the mountain, the wind, the dogs, the guinea-fowl living free among the cabbages and the radishes; and the man-made sounds: the hissing as of an ocean liner of the big boilers situated above the kitchens of each of the buildings, the 'cat' – as the siren is known – sometimes going off in the night to summon the staff back to the prison buildings because there had been an escape attempt or a murder or gang warfare in the cells, the footsteps and the jingling of keys, the clinking of those who were chained and who moved under escort through the corridors, and the whimpers, the whispers and cries and curses of prisoner and of keeper.

To this I now had added the vision, a real vision even if impaired, of the blue sky and the sun and the tree tops bending, of pigeons coming to perch on the water towers, of first light paling (impaling and embalming) the morning star, and always – at the turn of a corridor, dimly observed, or, when you were out in the yard like an enormous voice standing over you – the mountain. The mountain with its richness of clothes as the seasons came and went.

The very next day Brigadier Dupe, who had escorted me from Pirax, came to fetch me in my cell and took me three floors down, plus one more, until we were actually below ground level, to a large artificially lit area which was the General Stores. This was where I was going to be employed for the rest of my stay in prison. Here I was to spend my daylight hours. The staff stood to attention as we entered.

Over the years some would be transferred to be replaced by others, but a core of two or three members never changed. There was Bles, with his shining bald pate, puffing away at his pipe; there was Pinocchio next to him, small and sinewy with a tooth missing (but a smile taking its place) and big ears and very rough hands scarred and stained by his passion for angling; there was Oom Flippie, grey-haired, drunk, pouchy eyes, a spare tyre bulging over his belt and a very smart moustache with long ends jauntily curling – these he would incessantly stroke and twist and he would profit from the movement to pick his nose at the same time. Others would come later: Wagter Basson with the long nose and the sad eyes; Cripple with his plastic container of thin white sandwiches (he never gave me any); Matthee who spoke with the slow enunciation of the Namaqualand people; Captain du Preez, blind but too vain to wear his glasses, never working, cursing the Department; Molemouth the smuggler who had had an open-heart operation; Duimpie who took a sadistic pleasure in hurting *bandiete*; Sergeant Japes, red-faced and huge, who had a full time personal *agterryer* (a tame prisoner acting as orderly) to carry his little suitcase with the coffee flask inside; Mad Mips who had a permanent erection and who was always on the go to fetch sandwiches (he always gave me some); Stargazer the half-wit who lacked three fingers on the one hand, who had been forbidden to work with prisoners because of his infantile but violent temper, who one day beat a prisoner to a pulp, butting him again and again with the head.

I was the only prisoner employed as clerk in the General Stores. I was to be told later that I was in fact the only prisoner in the Republic of South Africa officially working in an office, and that special permission for this had to be obtained from the Civil Service Commission. In reality a large part of the office work in all the prisons is done by convicts. During all my years there it sometimes did happen that other White prisoners worked in the Stores as tea-boys or as cleaners, but the White *boere* preferred having Blacks there. It is a constant theme among them that they'd much rather deal with Blacks and Coloureds than the Whites who only give them trouble. Perhaps they feel less free to use violence with Whites. I can imagine, sir, that the relationship between White warders and White prisoners is far more ambiguous than the apparently simple master–slave hierarchy you will find between White and 'non-White'. At this level the *boer–bandiet* relationship is a violent one. *Boere* are always practising their proudly acquired karate blows on the *mugus*. When one is caught having stolen some food or a shirt, the warder would beat him up – it was easier, it was said, than having the man charged for theft because that necessitated writing out statements and appearing in a kangaroo court. Corporal punishment was in any event also officially part of the system – one could be sentenced to a maximum of six 'cuts' at a time, with a light or a heavy cane (depending on your age). You would then be stripped naked and strapped, spreadeagled to the 'mare', a three-legged easel-like structure, something from the Middle Ages, bolted to the floor of the central hall. A protective cloth would be tied over your kidneys, and the blows meted out, with great relish, in the presence of a medical orderly.

Over the years I got to know quite intimately some Black or Brown prisoners working in the General Stores. As they had far more freedom to move around than I had they would find ways and occasions to communicate with me, even though this was expressly forbidden.

In this way I met Voetjies, a man of all trades and all wisdom, and a master at manipulating *boer* and *bandiet*. He had already been in prison for twenty years, as a multiple murderer. He had actually been condemned to death and had spent time in the shadow of the gallows before being reprieved. He had escaped once, ten years ago, had committed some more crimes while cruising, had been recaptured and sentenced to more time. We called him Voetjies or Foots or Toes because he had cancer of the big toes and wore special shoes. Already bits of his toes had been amputated. This didn't stop him from running down his prey and knocking the unfortunate fellow senseless with fist and with forehead. (He was exceptionally strong and combative.) The cancer, he said, was provoked by stones falling on his sandaled feet when he was breaking boulders in the notorious prison of Barberton in the north. As these injuries were never treated properly, they eventually became malignant. He in fact ran the General Stores, and he was a walking information bank on prison lore and laws and myths and history. He had no hesitation in grassing on his fellow prisoners – he did so, judiciously, to retain the favours of his masters (whom he despised) and he betrayed me on several occasions. He was infinitely resourceful in obtaining the means for satisfying his three basic lusts: *dagga*, sex and power. And he was a dealer and a power broker.

I worked in a specially built glass-enclosed cage erected in the middle of this big storeroom so that the warders could keep an eye on me at all times. (No other staff member – not even an officer – coming to the Stores in the course of his work was allowed to talk to me. Towards the end the Brown warders weren't supposed to even enter the space where I worked. What did the higher-ups fear? Collusion? Contamination? I don't know.) In one wall there were the normal narrow windows giving on to a courtyard which at one end was closed off by two huge steel doors painted blue. These gates gave access to a street running down one side of the prison. Here the lorries delivering foodstuff or whatever to the prison had to enter. The windows in my part of the room were therefore painted white, so that I could not look out on the yard, and subsequently welded shut – I suppose to make it impossible for me to smuggle anything in or out to someone working in the yard.

When I needed to go to the toilet I had to obtain permission from the officer in charge in the stores and I would then be accompanied by a *boer*, who had to have the rank of sergeant at least, deeper into the prison itself, where a special toilet was made available to me. Since this toilet was in fact in the Black section, I was daily exposed to their conditions. Over the years I was plunged, despite the most careful measures taken by the authorities, into the complete prison universe, populated both by Black and by White. Always there were teams of Black or Brown prisoners on their knees in the passages, moving rhythmically and in unison forwards or backwards over the gleaming cement. Each had a floor-brush and pads made of old blankets under the knees. A *voorsinger* (or choir leader) would be standing up front, improvising a song, and the group would repeat the refrain or the key words, or sometimes just hiss or say *ja-ja* or make funny little sobbing noises, and at the same time sway their shoulders and shuffle their knees. And so the group would proceed or retreat as one brushing body. The leader's song – if you listened carefully – would often be a running commentary on the conditions or the daily events. (*The foodsafree. Ja-ja. The sleepsafree. Ja-ja. The fucksa-free. Free-ja. So why-ja moan. Moan-ja. Here comesaboss. Boss-ja. Sobigbigboss. Isbig-ja. So step aside. Ja-ja. Good morning basie. Ba-ja. Workashit. Sshit-ja.*) The activity is known as *gee pas*, to 'give the pace'.

Often warders with yelping dogs on leashes were rounding up groups of convicts. There would be bedlam – screaming and cursing. When it came to meal times the long lines of poorly clad prisoners (nearly always barefoot and moving in crouched positions with their hands clasped before them because of the chill in these corridors, even in summer) would fetch their plates – on which the rations had been dumped pell-mell – on the trot. Run, grab food, run. Up by the kitchen the dixies would have been set out nearly an hour beforehand. On meat days small chunks of pork would be floating in the watery or oily sauce covering everything. A White *boer*, Sergeant Nogood by name, was often on duty there, guarding the rations. And as often I saw him methodically going from plate to plate, fishing out and eating the morsels of meat. (Not out of spite. Maybe he considered it his privilege, as a perk. Maybe he was just hungry, or greedy. Certainly he would consider that the authorities were just spoiling the 'dogs' by letting them have meat.)

The smell in those nether regions was indescribable. There were always far too many people. The single cells would house three men each – one on the bed, one under the bed, and one on the available floor space – and they would have to use the toilet bowl for washing purposes. Once, after a ritual murder when the victim had been laboriously decapitated with tiny penknives and his head exhibited on the window sill for the night (to grin at the passing warder who kept on telling him to go to sleep), it came to light that the cell which normally had room for perhaps twenty people had held forty-seven convicts – and not *one* was willing to testify to having seen the execution! There were never enough warders to allow people to have showers. Everyone was involved in some physical labour – often hard and dirty work, as when spans of Blacks were used to unload and carry in lorry loads of flour – and always on the double. Clean clothes were issued only on Sundays, for inspection. Blacks were given one small tube of toothpaste a month and three or four squares of toilet paper a day. People awaiting trial had it even worse – no change of clothing, since they kept and wore the clothes they were arrested in until sentencing, which may be a year or more in the coming. The sections had to be fumigated regularly to combat lice and other vermin. Groups of juveniles, from six or seven years of age to fourteen (a 'fourteen' is a short-timer, someone doing less than eighteen months, just there 'to dirty the dixies'), would be using the same facilities as the men and being raped in the showers. So there was the pervasive stench of unwashed bodies, old half-clean clothes, stale food – 'lightened' from time to time by whiffs of the tear gas used to control a cell when there had been a riot or a gang fight. Germothol, a disinfectant, was highly prized: diluted with water, it would be sprinkled parsimoniously in the cells just before inspection to make them smell 'clean'.

David was another one of the Coloured prisoners whom I met at work. But he was in for trouble. He was quite a few cuts above the average *skollie* (petty criminal, thug) – he had worked in the Municipal offices of Bellville as an accountant when caught and convicted to six years for fraud (he needed the money to send his daughter to university, he said). He wore glasses and good false teeth and was well-spoken, and because he was so obviously educated he was sent to work as a cleaner in the Stores. Trouble number one and break-in number one: he made the error of addressing a White warder as *meneer* (sir) and not as *baas* (master). 'A *meneer* is a *kaffir* preacher, you black arse; *I* am a *baas*!' was the lesson shouted at him. Then, within the space of three weeks, he was destroyed. By his fellows. With the *boere* assisting, laughing. You see, he thought he could be a *mister* (they said). First his glasses were broken – only one lens to start with, and a few days later the other one. Then he had to cough up his teeth, which disappeared. Simultaneously he was *slukked** when he tried to wangle a deal or two for some extra food or smokes. His formerly neat appearance soon became something of the past. He had tried so hard to keep his station, but the others took away his clothes and gave him patched ones in return. When sweeping out the office he would linger as long as he dared to near my workplace, and weep uncontrollably. His efforts at stealing some of the *boere's* coffee and sugar were clumsy. He was hungry. Then he

**Slukked* – from the Afrikaans *sluk*, to swallow, meaning to be taken in, to be cheated.

was caught on his knees behind a stack of bags, praying myopically and toothlessly, but fervently, and Bles had Voetjies beat him up for shirking work. And the last I heard before he disappeared in the murky gang-controlled inner jails was that he had been sodomized, that it had been decided to make a woman of him. He stood on the carpet before the *boer's* table that morning, asking to be protected against his tormentors, saying that as a married man he did not want to go through that particular hell (already cringing, and saying *baas* three times in the same sentence), and the *boer*, annoyed at this freak who spoke so much better than *he* ever could, advised David to 'take a man – it will make you strong and it's good for constipation too. Look, you should have thought about this before becoming a prisoner. And who the hell do you think you are anyway? A *mister*?'

Upstairs, after the initial weeks of cautious observation, I was allowed to stand in line with the other White prisoners when going to fetch my food or when falling in for inspection in the outside courtyard. (On the foodline the Brown cooks would wink, quickly give a clenched-fist salute, and try to slip me an extra dab of butter.) I was fetched for work early every morning immediately after breakfast, brought back upstairs for lunch, fetched again for the afternoon session and returned at night. We had to move through a large number of locked gates each guarded by a warder whose sole duty it was to man that point. After a while I learned that whenever I was escorted through the prison it had to be according to a pre-determined plan upon which Smoel, the security officer, had indicated with arrows the route to be followed. I had to be accompanied by at least two *boere*. Before leaving the Stores the security officer had to be informed by telephone that we were now setting off for my cell (in the same building!), and due to arrive within so many minutes.

My work was that of an ordinary pen-pusher – making inventories, entering on ledger cards the articles we had in stock, booking out to various sections whatever they needed in terms of cleaning materials or food or clothes and generally helping the storemen do what they were supposed to be doing. The supervision never slacked off. In later years the Stores were moved to another building in the compound; I would then be taken the 100 yards there in a closed van under escort of an armed warder, and a *boer* with dog had to be present when I got into or out of the vehicle in closed courtyards; the guardposts were also alerted so that they could train their guns on the passing van. Madness! But gradually my workload increased. I think there is a natural tendency for the bureaucrat to push off as much work as he can on to his lackey. In due time they lost control over what I was actually doing: I could have swindled the State out of millions by falsifying figures or making ghost entries. Regularly I was asked to rectify errors – shortages, surpluses, thefts – by cooking the books. Towards the end of my stay the Prison Department's activities were computerized and that went for our work in the Stores too. It was quite a challenge to learn how to prepare the material that would be fed into the computer system. I had to come to grips with codes. Since the work interested me – this visualizing of information, and the sense of being a small part of a bigger brain – I ended up being perhaps the only one in our Stores who understood to some extent what was going on. I'm sure there was serious resistance among the Stores staff to the very idea that I might be released, as they would then have to blindly grope their way through the work which they in their laziness had let me take care of.

A little while longer, Mr Investigator, and then my confession is done. Not that I'd have told you everything – there are stories of spies in the beginning and cowards at the end that I haven't even touched upon. And if I were to introduce you to all the people I met in boop, and tell you their anecdotes, we'd be going on for ever. No, a short way more, and then I'll be out of it forever.

The prison community can be cut up in many different ways. The basic racist classification enforced in No Man's Land applies to prison also. First there were the 'Darkies' – that is how the Blacks are referred to. Most of them originated from the Eastern Cape and were therefore Xhosa-speaking, but many had been living in the Western Cape for several generations and they would thus speak Afrikaans also. Then you had the *Gamme,** the

**Gam* – Ham, the son of Noah, who the *boere* say, was cursed to have slave descendants because he had laughed at his father's drunkenness.

Coloureds, mostly from the Cape area – and 'Coloured' could be anybody from white to black. Then there were the 'Whiteys', again from European pale to indigenously mixed brown skin.

However, if you want to understand anything about the prison universe – a world apart with its peculiar castes and culture and language, its own reality, in fact – then you have to know something about its constituent components. You will find that in the Cape particularly, prison life is run by gangs. The three major formations are the 'twenty-sixes', who specialize in money matters – they monopolize the network of smuggling, buying and selling; the 'twenty-sevens', who are the men of *igazi* (meaning blood), and that means that they are the professional killers, the executioners and nothing else; and the 'twenty-eights', who practise and idolize homosexuality as a way of life, the masters of sex, the procurers, the *maquereaux* – they who provide the rest of the prison population with *wyfietjies* (little women) whom they fabricate by rape and by corruption.

There's much rivalry (and murder) among the gangs and each has an internal structure and a division of tasks expressed in military terms and, ironically, also in legal ones; they have their 'judges', their 'prosecutors', their 'courts', their *tekeners* (draughtsmen, signers, writers) whose only job it is to sign the death orders; there are 'generals', 'colonels', 'captains' and 'soldiers'. Normally you only rise through the ranks by committing specified acts of violence: sticking a knife into a warder, for instance, is worth instant promotion to 'colonel', and the insignia will be tattooed on your shoulders. A gang general is indeed somebody with vast power, to be saluted when passed in the corridor.

The *kring* (the circle), governing council, will decide upon a death. Once its decision has been carried out, parts of the body of the victim may be eaten ritualistically. (Pause here, Mr Investigator, and consider how structuralized alienation has brought about a society of cannibals. These men eat human flesh as rats will devour each other – for similar reasons – and not because it has ever been 'traditional' anywhere. Don't try to shrug it off by saying 'they' are not like 'us'. Don't go and look for so-called Cultural so-called Differences . . . When you decide to release these confessions, Mr Investigator, you will have smoothly combed prison spokesmen denying *en bloc* the veracity of what I'm telling you. They will be sitting in smart offices, far away from the stinking death lying in the cells, and their civilized mouths will produce bureaucratic appeals to your 'understanding' – how frail is human nature! – by admitting to exceptions which have all been investigated, with the guilty ones punished. Will you be taken in? I'm telling you that what I'm describing is *typical* of that mirror which the South African penal universe holds up to the Apartheid society – and that it is *inevitable.*)

Of course, there are some people who do not belong to a gang. They are called *mumpatas*, meaning 'sheep'. Being a *mumpata* unfortunately does not safeguard you from being chosen as a victim. These gangs have links with outside ones operating in the Cape area, such as the Scorpions or the Mongrels, but their prison existence is far more organized and important than life on the streets. (The one is just a continuation of the other.) Originally they were born of the convicts' desire to stand together and fight for certain privileges: they still refer to themselves as *wetslaners* ('those who hit the laws' but also 'those who hit with the law, who constitute a law') – an indication of their original cause for existence. But this aspect of Prisoners United is now in abeyance.

I could relate to you many blood-curdling incidents of gang warfare, gang murder, gang anthropophagy, gang rape. It would have to be a confession of its own. Why do the authorities 'allow' these gangs to exist? Because it is finally of little importance to them if prisoners want to exterminate one another. At the heart of the South African prison system is the denial of the humanity of 'the other', and in that it is only a reflection of the larger South African cosmos; that is why those wielding power, they who believe themselves to be superior, are inevitably moral decadents; that is how and why they inhabit No Man's Land. Naturally there is some collaboration between the *boere* (White or Black) and the gangs since the gang leaders take over the disciplinary functions of the warders to a large extent.

Whites too belong to these gangs; you recognize them by the distinctive tattoos around the neck – a miniature gallows, a bow tie, a pair of dice (because they also 'walk with the number', i.e. belong to a number gang) or by the etched stars on the shoulders. There also you have ritual murders. White too would open up the belly of the victim, take out the heart, the liver, part of the innards – to eat them. We are talking of social climate, Mr Investigator. Of staunchness and of despair. Of 'laws'. It is grotesque. It is the dialectic, the revelation of the interaction of man with his environment pushed to its most awful and degrading consequences. I could tell you of people I saw who had their penises cut off at the roots; of the red stars I saw against the wall of a passage, rhythmically every few yards for more than a 100 yards, where a victim who had been knifed in the heart had run, spouting blood from the pierced pump – clinging to life until he had none left. I could tell you of a cell I saw with blood-encrusted walls, the spray from cut veins soaking a mattress, of the flies and the ants. I could tell you about people bludgeoned to death with the hammers used for crushing stones; about people left to die in epileptic fits, their medicine withheld from them; about people left absolutely naked in bare cells; about people being transported from court in a prison truck, everyone singing to cover the sounds of the execution of one suspected of having turned traitor, and again of how the head would be sliced off and come rolling out when the 'can' arrives at its destination and the doors are unlocked. I could describe to you how an informer is killed slowly, his stomach cut open with small blades made from the flattened filtertips of cigarettes, and his intestines taken out while he is still alive – to be laid out in lengths all around the cell – how such a man will beg for death. The earth is grey.

The *boere* could tell you of how you have to be careful, when shooting a *bandiet* attempting to escape, to have the body fall *inside* the walls – *that* is allowed; if it falls *outside*, you have to go through the bother of an inquiry and maybe even face manslaughter charges. And while you're at it, ask them to tell you how excited some of them are when they can provoke two prisoners to commit unnatural sex acts for them to watch and comment upon.

To me the measure of the self-contained and ritualistic nature of prison mores is its self-destructiveness. Some convicts would do everything possible to be condemned to death, and bathe in the glory of being a 'rope', of going up, of becoming part of prison mythology. Worse even, infinitely worse, is the way in which the fellow-prisoner victim nearly always collaborates with his executioners. The killing often takes place over several hours. So trapped is the prey, so much a part of the rites, that he will often assist at his slow death with open eyes, trying to muffle his cries and his sobs. Acceptance! Home at last!

Apart from the ubiquitous major gangs there are smaller ones too: the so-called 'Big Fives' for instance. To be a Big Five in prison lingo is to be a pimp, somebody who squeals on his mates, who reports to the authorities – a stool pigeon in other words. This function is recognized in prison life to the extent that a small gang will be formed proudly calling itself the Big Fives. In the North there's the Air Force, the equivalent among Blacks of the White Springboks. Each gang has its own emblems and its own way of 'picking up' – the signs made by the fingers of the hands to communicate and to indicate what gang one belongs to.

More permanently perhaps you will recognize in the prison community certain categories of people. You will see the *lanies*, the tough ones, the leaders, those who cannot be broken down – more often than not doing a very long sentence. You do not cross swords with them. (I had the good fortune of being under the protection of a *lanie* or two – to offset the spies and the pimps circling around me.) There will be the dealers, trading in drugs, money, groceries, books – you name it, somebody will have part of that market cornered. There are the bookies with whom you place your bets. You can certainly play horses regularly – you will find people running up incredible debts, losing or winning fortunes in prison, and of course sometimes losing their lives when they cannot pay their debts. (Yitshak was reduced to being a baker – making for sale or on command innumerable 'boop puddings' from left-over bread and hoarded jam and peanut butter, in an effort to reduce his betting debts of, at one time, 150 packets of cigarettes and nearly 70 packets of tobacco.) You thus have *boop* millionaires, people with a fortune in the prison context, obviously worthless outside. You will find the pimps. You will find the 'hawks', also known as *ringkoppe* (meaning 'ringheads') – these are the male partners of the homosexual concubinages. They are the hunters. ('Ringhead', quite apart from its obvious sexual visualization, also refers to a member of the Zulus' council of elders who wear rings around their heads.) You have the *laities*, the little ones or the 'female' ones, the 'women' in a homosexual relationship; but it can also just mean the young ones or the small ones. In the same order of ideas and indicating the various 'types' you will find in the predominantly homosexual community, there are *poephol pilots* or *hol buddies* (*poephol* being 'arsehole'); you have *moffies* and 'rabbits' and a more refined specialization in the 'grocery rabbits', the subservient and opportunist ones selling their graces for food.

There will be other categories, defined either by the social status or origin of the inmates – such as the *lallapype* ('pipe-sleepers', those who are so poor that they'd be sleeping under culverts outside), the *maplotties* (those who live on small free-holdings or plots around the big towns), the *vlamslukkers* or *bloutreinryers* ('flame-swallowers' or 'riders on the blue train' being those who are reduced to drinking methylated spirits, which is tinted blue in South Africa), or the most distinguishing feature of their condition in prison. In this way you have those called the 'chains', convicts who wear chains either because they have been condemned to death or because they have tried to escape or have been recaptured or because they are considered particularly dangerous – these chains are worn day and night so that you hear them turn over in their sleep with the click-click-click of iron links. You have the 'condemns', even in Cape Town where they will be kept for some time before being removed to Pretoria. There are those called the 'fives', indicating the Jewish prisoners (the name may have originated in Cockney slang); there are the social cases, the down-and-outers, the very old or the very poor who have no income and no means of raising any and often no family outside – the 'socials' will normally be the skivvies of the others, their servants doing the washing and the ironing, cleaning the cells and doing odd jobs for tobacco or for a few sweets every month. (Some of these ancient outcasts were on their last legs when they came in. It would be the final station before death. After two or three days they would go into fits of terror, a private hell, delirium tremens. They would see dogs skulking in corners and bloody children and toads raining from heaven. They'd be calling out the names of long-buried and forgotten relatives. Happy Botha arrived after having burnt down the White Horse Hotel in Long Street; he never remembered a thing about that. Percy Runner had to be stripped of his rags when he was admitted; I remember seeing his clothes in a bucket in the courtyard, and the lice floating on the water. He was released and found dead in the Public Gardens two mornings later.)

You have *roebane* (robbers) and *trassies* (transvestites, some very beautiful and provocative, exciting the fellows no end), and 'grubbies' (gluttons, those who go digging in the rubbish bins for throw-away food) and *howwe* (the lot taken to court) and 'hard labours' (sentenced inmates) and 'coats' who are *langanas* (long-timers) and GBHs (sentenced for assault with grievous bodily harm) and *jollers* (those who really lived it up outside) and *rokers* (pot smokers).

Skommel, a toothless youngster who worked as cleaner in the *boeres'* office in our section, had tattooed on his back (I give it to you, Mr Investigator, exactly the way it was written – look after it well):

A roker-boy came home one night
And found his house without a light
He struck a match to go to bed
When a sudden thought came to his head
He went into his daughter's room
And found her hanging from a beam
He took his knife, and cut her down
And on her breast, these words he found.

My love was for a roker-boy
Who smoked his *dagga* just for joy
So dig my grave and dig it deep
And plant some *dagga* at my feet
And on my breast a turtle dove
To show the world I died for love.

Now all young sheilas bear in mind*
A roker's love is hard to find.
If you find one good and true,
Never, ever, change it for a new.

(Skommel had worked in the outside world as a steward on the trains. Coffee, to be really good, had for him to taste like 'Railways

**Sheilas* – young girls in slang.

coffee'. He told me a visually funny but very sad story. During the course of his duties he once inadvertently opened the door to a compartment to announce lunch or dinner. Inside he found only one occupant: a woman, not so young anymore, wearing a fur coat. She was on her back, her dress lifted high, having her small lapdog do something to her. At the sudden sight of him the poor lady got such a fright that she chucked the beast out the open window of the moving train!)

There are naturally also real women in prison, although we never saw them. They are called the 'flat ones', or 'scissors', or 'slits'.

In general we, the prisoners, were known in the Cape as *bandiete* or *mugus* or *skebengas* or *skollies*. The warders remained, as ever, *boere*.

In the Cape, however, I came across a new category: racist Whites refer to Coloured people as *Hottentotte* or *Hotnots*, which is a pejorative term; now for the first time I heard Coloured warders being talked about as *Hotnotboere*.

My own situation gradually improved in some ways, Mr Investigator, although there would also be sudden clamp-downs for reasons which I did not always understand. When three White politicals escaped from Local in Pretoria I returned to my cell to find more, and more complicated, padlocks securing my inner grille and my outer door and the gate to the courtyard where I was taken for exercise. But in fact the security set up never changed. I shall never be trusted, it doesn't matter how long I live, or where in the world I find myself. I know, Mr Confessor, that what I have to tell you will be read avidly by the Greys and all the other *boere*, and that they will find by hook or by crook or by cowboy the means to avenge themselves. In due time there will be 'revelations'.

But that is for later. That will be the postscript. For now I must underline that I was never considered a normal prisoner. Witnerf laughingly confirmed this to me. 'We know you,' he said, 'if you're given half the chance you'd be flying out the window.' Thus it happened that a special crew of *boere*, dressed in battle greens, would go at night and search my place of work from one wall to the other. Poor Bles, who was personally responsible for me, found himself in murky waters because I had been allowed to work with carbon paper. 'Can you not see,' Witnerf told him, 'how dangerous this may be? Don't you realize that he can multiply political pamphlets and stow them away in these parcels so that they get distributed all over South African prisons?' Tch, tch, how stupid of me never to have thought of that possibility myself. We did indeed handle many parcels containing the clothes of people who were continuously transferred from jail to jail across the country. In the same way the sheet of blotting paper on the table where I worked during the day was carefully removed every night and the wee doodles or jottings that I whiled my time away with were photocopied to be forwarded to the Security Police for analysis and study.

What a cumbersome industry just to look after one person! They had to keep a multitude of books to record my activities or their observations of same. A daily report had to be written by my supervisor at work and this had to be summarized in a weekly and then a monthly account. The same held for the section sergeant. Every morning I was given an impressive ledger to sign, in which whatever requests or complaints I might have had were noted, as also the ultimate reactions to these. The idea, I assume, was to keep their record with the International Red Cross straight. Then there were several other books which I was not supposed to be aware of, but which I did find out about through my 'agents' (if I may call them so): one in which the sergeant or warrant officer responsible had to note daily the fact that my cell had been searched – ceiling, walls, floor, bathroom, pipes, bed, cupboard – and that no holes were found, no gnawing, nothing hidden; or if anything hidden, what it was, where, etc. A book of et ceteras. These entries had to be signed and countersigned by superior officers. Next there was a book entitled 'Incidents: Security Prisoner'; again the poor bastard on duty had to jot down whatever I'd done or said in the course of the day or the night – anything out of the ordinary perhaps?, the people whom I might have talked to, what I talked about, and if nothing of the kind, that too had to be testified to. Did I have a request that necessitated a written report? Write it out in duplicate, please. Again these would be filed and commented upon by the security officer or the head of the prison.

Now, from all this material a weekly extract had to be made. I once saw (quite illegitimately) the instructions pertaining to these weekly extracts issued by the Officer Commanding. It was specified, for instance, that any untoward gesture ought to be noted. Has the prisoner given the Black Power salute at any time? I presume that these summaries were duplicated and forwarded to the concerned intelligence organizations.

After some time I obtained permission to play chess (the permission was soon to be cancelled), which I was very happy about until I learned from one of my partners that he had been sent specifically to try to get me to talk politics.

Enough, Mr Investigator, you know enough by now. I think that you have always realized far better than I do what this is all about. What I'm attempting to say is that my alienation as a subversive criminal is permanent; nothing can ever bridge the gap between the authorities of the Afrikaner tribe and myself. And I accept this and I would not be happy otherwise, because I do not consider myself to be an Afrikaner. To be an Afrikaner in the way *they* define it is to be a living insult to whatever better instincts we human beings may possess and struggle to maintain.

Nevertheless, given this background of utter and permanent distrust, prison life did become progressively more relaxed. It took some time but ultimately I was occasionally allowed to walk the yard with the others. Even if you managed only to exchange a few words spread over the whole day or over several days, these added up to a conversation. It is vital to be in contact with other human beings. More important, Mr Investigator – as Don Espejuelo explained to me – more important than the banality of physical relationships is the deeper need for showing tenderness or kindness to another human. Man is born with the capacity and the imperative need to care for others.

Over the years I'd made some very good friends. Some I knew only for a short period before they were released or transferred, others deceived me or became enemies, and all of them have since become robed in the fog of time (despite the fact – allow me to mix my metaphors – that I now regurgitate them in words); but it doesn't matter: they made it possible for me to talk and to laugh, to situate myself, to give little presents, to learn about the final loneliness of human fate.

In this way I became friends with Cone, who was doing time for fraud. I was to exercise all by myself over lunchtime but

P. Cone soon joined me; since he was suffering from a heart condition the doctor prescribed extra exercise for him and the only available time for that was when I was in the yard. He was a leading cause for my being sent to the 'bomb'. I had been caught on two previous occasions with illicit newspapers in my possession (two catches out of twenty I considered not a bad average) and sentenced first to three meals, that is, deprived of food for a day and locked up in a small cell, and then to five days' 'bomb'. During the period when I knew Cone, Major Witnerf had taken away all our library facilities because one convict in his cussedness had torn up a book. Cone, being an orthodox Jew, had been permitted some religious works; I on my side had finally obtained the permission to be allowed some books on Zen. One day after discussing religion in the yard during our walk, I promised to lend him one of my books. This was found in his cell and we were both accused – he of having an article which he was not entitled to and me of trying to proselytize, that is, to subvert a fellow prisoner. Witnerf, who acted the presiding magistrate, let off Cone (because of his heart) with the suspension of some of his privileges; I was sentenced to ten days' isolation in the punishment cell, and to spare diet. (The kangaroo court imitated the real outside court in that sentences were cumulative. Smoel once judged three chaps for talking to one another on the food line; they appeared before him successively: the first got five days, the second ten, and the unlucky third accused a full fifteen. 'What?' Smoel said. 'Another one? This must stop somewhere!')

I mentioned before, Mr Investigator, that this food punishment is quite refined and worked out, reputedly, by dietary experts. Over ten days, for example, you will be on 'spare diet' for four days – meaning that you will be getting a small, carefully measured quantity of absolutely dry unsalted maize porridge without sugar or milk in the morning, one cup of unsalted soup made from some indistinct soup powder for lunch, and again the same porridge in the late afternoon. That is all. You may drink as much water as you wish. Then two days of half-rations – the normal food but rigorously only half the quantity; one day of 'full' and back again to 'spare'. Thus your starvation and your hunger will be dosed. You lose weight fast. The doctors collaborate by giving you a cursory glance-over before you go in, to declare you fit for punishment. You may only do thirty days at a time. If you've been sentenced to more you are allowed a break of ten days before recommencing. You're naturally also deprived of all smoking material, books and any company. You may receive neither letters nor visits during this period. I knew one incorrigible youngster, called Dampies, who spent 217 days of his eighteen months in prison in the hole.

During my third 'bomb' stretch – I had five 'internal discipline' convictions in all – the prison cook accompanying the 'bomb' *boer* to ladle out the crud actually tried to help me by slyly introducing some sugar *underneath* the porridge, and he added several minutely rolled smokes as well. In return he would, when the section was quiet, sneak up to one end of the barred corridor and over a distance of twenty yards hoarsely whisper his poems at me. I was to give my 'expert' appreciation. He was an Australian – his father actually a consular official in Cape Town. Alas, his sugar trafficking was discovered and he was promptly flung into the 'bomb' too, not far away from me. The poetry! The poetry!

I now started running and exercising regularly. In Pretoria I had continued doing *Zazen*, some yoga, and even *Tai-Chi* in the confined space at my disposal. Now I grabbed any chance I could get hold of to jog round and round the inner courtyard. (I once worked out that, had I been going in a straight line, I would have been halfway up Africa by the time I was released.) The Red Cross arranged for me to be given shorts and had insisted to the authorities that I should have half an hour exercising a day. My feet became quite tough. I learned that one must discipline oneself very strictly if one wants to survive. There must be the basic physical commitment of trying to remain fit, of listening to your body, of taking care of it (as Buddha had said) the way you would look after a sick man, not allowing it to go to flab and to apathy as happens to so many people behind the walls. You must furthermore discipline yourself intellectually by stealing with ears and with eyes, attempting in all possible ways to feed the mind. And you have to impose a moral discipline upon yourself, sensing and avoiding the crude simplifications and dichotomies the authorities try to have you conform to. Always remember the simple truth that denying the humanity of the person facing you is a sure-fire way of diminishing yourself. Keep away from the slothful slotting of 'them' and 'us'. I'm not talking about moral rectitude – it is an exigence of awareness, a consciousness tool for survival.

In passing I shall only refer to a few of my fellow inmates; the others – too many to mention – the night folk, the people of midnight populating No Man's Land penal universe, you will have to read about in *Pi-K'uan*.

I should mention Jerry Fox, the Slovakian. In his dishonesty he was true to himself and without any illusions about the nature of man or the essential nature of being a prisoner. Could there be a difference? He had done time before in Czechoslovakia, for smuggling people across the border. He had really worked in a salt mine; he had known Novotny; and he was appalled by the lack of solidarity among South African prisoners. 'Never ever again trust an ex-prisoner,' he said in his atrocious English. 'The spring will be broken. To survive he would have had to compromise. The weakness remains.' In South Africa he was living by his wits – in fact, he was pushing his prison sentence under an assumed name. (The 'real' Jerry had died in the Namib desert.) Outside he preferred the company of Coloureds even though he did not quite understand their language or their customs – and he didn't trust them either. He was constantly smuggling – being in the metal workshop helped – and I shared in the spoils.

Through Jerry I met the Tampax Kid, a young Afrikaner who had studied theology at the University of Stellenbosch. That one was the archetypal Afrikaner crook: looking you straight in the eye, bravely suffering his predestined fate, attending all the religious services, and capable of stealing your underpants while you're having a shower. (Captain Sodom had finally forced me to hand in my private underpants, threadbare by then; I was provided with the voluminous Santa Marias which pass for underwear in boop.)

The Tampax Kid, alias Mighty Mouse, had a penchant for the knife in the back. One lunchtime he came to my cell with a message from one of the 'chains', van Nickerk (considered to be a high-security risk), who – so Tampax breathed – wanted to escape and take me with him on condition that I would arrange for passports to leave the country once we were outside. I still believe it was a trap, carefully prepared by the little runt. When the thing became known, as it nearly immediately did, he wanted to be transferred to an easier prison because, he claimed, van Niekerk was going to beat him to death with his chains. Maybe he was also angling for some time off. Then arrived the day for him to be let loose and he came to my cell to swear undying fidelity with his hands on the Bible and tears in his eyes. Jerry Fox was there also, laughing derisively. I told the Mouse that little fable of Scorpion wanting to cross the swollen river and asking Frog to take him to the other side, and Frog being coy, saying that he's not dilly in the head, that Scorpion will sting him to death in mid-stream, of how Scorpion scoffed at this reticence declaring that he would do no such thing as it would assuredly entail his own water-death too, so please; and of how they then set off and how, halfway across, Scorpion did jab his sting into the docile flesh of the amphibian, who gurgled as they started going down to death. 'But why, why? Now you will also die!' And Scorpion answering 'Yeah, glub-glub, I know. But I can do no else. I'm glub-glub *made* this way.' I told this to the Tampax Kid, asking rhetorically how it could be any different since the Afrikaner is a product of the system which he has produced. No, he swore, he would never do anything to embarrass me.

Three days later Witnerf himself stormed with all his bullies into my cell and took everything apart; he even painstakingly probed my chess pieces with a needle. It was only afterwards that I learned that the Tampax Kid had gone to a national weekly newspaper with the story, splashed over the front page, of my being involved with van Niekerk, the bank robber, in an escape attempt. I learned that he'd even been paid for the story.

Often we had foreigners with us. Some were illegal immigrants – the Japanese would be with the Whites, the Chinese did their time with the Coloureds. We had several Yugoslavs – they seemed to have monopolized a part of the underworld. There were quite a few Portuguese, of course. Skippie – named thus because of a gloriously sinking three-master tattooed on his chest – one of them, was always going on a hunger-strike, being sent to the 'bomb' because of his hunger strikes, and then going on another hunger strike because of the unfair punishment. Sometimes he came in as a White, sometimes as a Coloured. Eventually he was declared permanently mad and referred to Valkenburg, the madhouse.

I met one Spaniard. He was called Jesus. Small of stature he was, dignified and portly, and speaking a consonantless French. He became a barber in prison. And he played a mean, if dithering, game of chess. To my chagrin, he had me fooled and off the board in less than twenty moves. He was disgusted with South Africa and was leaving as soon as he could, even if it meant walking on the water.

There were Poles and an Austrian pastry chef and fractious Germans. There were Greeks – nearly always in for contraventions of the Foreign Exchange Act. In one instance we even had an Iranian, condemned to death (he had killed some Indians in a shoot-out over drugs). In the middle of the night he would get up with a clatter of chains echoing down the corridor to start chanting his morning prayers to Allah.

Americans and Israelis never stayed very long – theirs were the only two governments with the prerequisite influence to have their nationals repatriated rapidly. In Big House up north – people who arrived from there told me – there was Kozlov, the Soviet spy, moving quite freely among the other prisoners. The extreme rightist Italians were also kept there: I remember one transfer arriving in Pollsmoor with a (private) T shirt bearing the legend: *Paracadutisti 'El Alamein' Pantere Indomiti* under the drawing of a snarling black leopard. The shirt was the fruit of some swop with one of the Italians.

Several Britishers came and stayed. A few were hitmen or specialized gangsters sent into South Africa on a quick in-and-out mission, and then the out got fouled up. One sympathetic Englishman I became friendly with was Tuchverderber. Before being sentenced for a farcical currency offence he had been a prosperous factory owner, but now his whole life was ruined. As they were going to deport him from South Africa upon completion of his sentence, he was obliged to sell his baronial mansion and his Mercedes Benz at ridiculously low prices. He still had money though, and the influence which money brings, and this he used judiciously to bribe the *boere* – amongst others Major Sodom – to bring in all kinds of sweets and fruit. From these I profited too, Mr Investigator. Yes, for a while I even had peanut butter for my bread. (I was then not yet allowed any purchases. Only A-Group prisoners may do so. Prisoners normally attain A-Group status after six or nine months of their sentence, 'politicals' only once they've done half their time – whatever the length of their sentence.)

The one Dutchman I got to know during my stay was Keulder, a big man with a lot of hair down his back. Keulder had quite a harem going. His weakness was for strapping young Afrikaner boys. These he would corrupt with favours. Tony, one of the sad-eyed Greeks sharing a big cell with him, recounted that the love sessions could be quite embarrassing. He (Tony) told of how he'd wake up in the middle of the night (he slept badly – dreaming of his wife and of boats) and be forced to listen to Keulder and the favourite boyfriend of the moment making love under the blankets. (Remember that the other ten people were all lying there, side by side on the floor.) And, he said, they'd be making the sounds of people slurping up tinned food. There could be no love *in petto*.

In Pollsmoor I also met Galgenvogel, the Hungarian exile, a big nob in the South African drug trade. He was a cultivated man who had studied for the priesthood until the discovery of Kierkegaard had opened his mind to darkness and to bitterness. His fingers were black from smoking and he had the racking cough of a thinker. His chess wasn't bad (it was certainly better than his chest), but occasionally the veneer of cultivation would crack and the real Galgenvogel would emerge to launch himself in a veritable philippic against mankind or even to get involved in some bloody bout of fisticuffs with another miserable specimen (nearly always a German). He lost all his fights. He also lost the appeal against his conviction. Then he lost his wife (or mistress). He lost a few tobacco-stained teeth. He played bridge for tobacco, and lost. He was not really a winner.

And all the time escape attempts were going on. People tried to 'make a break' or to 'kick out'. Stinkfoot solemnly greeted some of us by hand while we were up on the walled-in roof where the library was, scaled the wall and tried to climb down the outside. We were four floors high. They found him sitting on a ledge like some ungainly bird with cold feet, brought him back to earth, chained him and posted him to Pirax. Afkop and Nel got away as far as a house in the neighbourhood where within half an hour they tried to 'scale' (steal) a car, making such a racket that they were immediately recaptured. They were brought back in chains and savagely hit and kicked by the *boere*. (The *boere* refer to this exercise of baton-whipping and stomping as a 'carry-on'.) Swart Piet Vangat, drunk as a lord, came to my cell window to preen and to bluster, 'See how we got your chums?' People tried to have themselves carted away to freedom with the rubbish bins or the bags of washing. The only successful breaks were from court, or when chaps were taken to hospital or to an outside specialist, or from the train during a transfer, or running away from the fields when working in the agricultural span. These would be mostly Coloureds.

One White was arrested upon his return from abroad, on a trumped up charge. A year went by and still his case wasn't heard. So he 'threw sick' (feigned a malady), was taken to Groote Schuur Hospital, and took the gap. He was caught within the hour. The prosecution dropped the original charges against him, admitting now that it had all along been a matter of mistaken identity, but for escaping from custody he was jailed for a further nine months.

One ancient 'blue-coat' got away nearly by accident. I met him after he'd been recaptured and brought to Pollsmoor. He told of how he was being transferred by train from somewhere to Sonnies (Zonderwater) and how the warders with him were having a profound philosophical conversation with a bottle and that bottle's descendants. Arriving at Germiston station the coat asked for and obtained permission to make a quick phone call to his old wife. To give her some instructions about his pension. He got off. They'd given him a few coins. He entered the telephone booth. And was a long time in establishing the damn contact. The South African telephone system is not quite what it ought to be. The train hooted twice and slowly left the platform. And Hurry Harry, as the old man was known, all of a sudden found himself left in the lurch. He went outside to the main road and decided to catch up with his two guardian angels by hitching a lift. But, he said, no cars wanted to pick him up. There was very little traffic going the way he was heading, and maybe he looked a bit too much like an old prisoner. So he walked across the street and by and by found somebody willing to take him, but oh dear, going to hell and gone in the opposite direction. He was footloose for many months – he had meanwhile started a transport business – before they caught him again for driving an overloaded lorry.

During this outside time (this walkabout) he had written a letter to the Prison authorities to say he was just having a break, sir, and would be back soon-soon, and that they shouldn't be too angry with the two deep-thinking warders.

Some people broke out because they felt that not enough attention was paid to their griefs. One fellow was so upset at not being allowed to have an interview with a senior officer that he escaped from Zonderwater and made his way to Vermeulen Street in Pretoria, to Prison Head Office, to complain to the Commissioner himself.

And quite a few times I found myself involved – without knowing anything about it – in some far-fetched escape scheme. Once I was taken down to the commanding officer's sanctum and, in the keenly head-bobbing presence of his senior staff, accused of being the moving mind behind a planned escapade which included my having prepared passports and having bought a boat lying offshore ready to take me and my fellow conspirators to the distant shores of freedom of Never Never Land ready immediately lets go go go!

I remember how all the prisoners were once gathered in the big yard to be told by an officer what the advantages offered were for pimping another prisoner. If you were instrumental in uncovering an escape attempt you could get a reward of up to R30 paid in on your name, plus/or a reduction of sentence not exceeding nine months. As Lofty, one of my fellow *langanas* pointed out loudly, this was an open incitement for the short-timers to try and shop us. It's just not fair, Lofty said.

In retrospect it all sounds quite funny. Even at the time Tuchverderber and I agreed that if we ever survived, we would one day, looking back, remember just the hilarious bits. In such a way does the human memory try to escape from itself. But it wasn't so pleasant then, I can assure you. I remember how I one day realized with a shock that my nerves were shot to bits.

A squad of *boere* with their excited dogs came charging in unexpectedly. It was a shake-down. We were all chased from our cells and up a long corridor with both ends blocked off. We were thereupon body-searched individually before being led back to the cells which were similarly cleaned from top to bottom. Apparently they were after the copy of a key that they believed someone had succeeded in making. I had in my pocket once more a folded strip of paper. What was scrawled on it? The beginning of an undying poem? A reminder to tell Mr Investigator one day of this incident, or of that one? Let it be. . . . I literally went to pieces at the thought of them finding it on me. The violent reaction – the loss of control – took me by the throat as if by surprise. I stood with my back against the wall, shivering. Without my knowing it they have succeeded in making of me an unpredictable risk.

White long-term prisoners used to be held in Victor Verster Prison near Paarl, but in 1980 that institution was closed down for them, and they were all brought over to Cape Town. That is how I got to know Shorty, an old wrinkled monkey of a man, and Dennis, his right arm, who looked like a wiser version of Claude Lévi-Strauss. Shorty had been in prison ever since the Second World War. In reality he had passed straight from the Army into prison. When given half a chance he would harangue us with a rousing speech steeped in the sentiments and expressions of his war years. He was the permanent secretary to the Sports Committee which was really just a cover for the prisoners' mafia – collecting donations supposedly for buying sport equipment or something extra for Christmas, but in fact fed into the smuggling circuit.

I also made a friend of the head cook, old Angel. He was a bald-headed man with one gammy leg, and lovely, rosy gums. He had some nasty stains on his arms and his face, which turned out to be cancerous. I can't remember what crimes he was doing time for (inadvertently selling stolen cars, I think), but the source of all his problems was alcoholism. He had been inside before for something to do with bankruptcy. Life was a fuck-up to be lived unobtrusively and looked at steadily through thick glasses. His teeth he lost to a policeman's baton. (Those rubber batons are called *donkiepiele*, 'donkey pricks'.) His leg was the result of a car smash in Namibia. He used to work on a boat. He once went to Argentina but returned after a week because he found the hotel room stuffy. He dreamt of telepathy and astral journeys and was so rigorously honest that he sometimes wrote only three lines to his mother – his only correspondent – because he had nothing to say. During one of his fits of delirium tremens he was introduced to a small gentleman living on his shoulder. This gentleman, seemingly, never left him again. Angel was shy about his appearance. When I teased him too cruelly about his vanity or his death-wishing commercial schemes, he would react in a diffident way by telling me that he himself didn't mind much but (softly) that the little fellow on his shoulder (who was of a grumpy disposition) didn't take too kindly to all this ribbing.

Every once in a while, on a Sunday, Angel would produce a magnificent set of flashy false teeth which he had bought from a fellow convict. These did not fit, they were too big, and when he wore them he could not eat – but he would don his best suit of prison greens or his starched white cook's outfit, polish his glasses, and suddenly present himself with these grinning dentures in the face. These altered his appearance and his enunciation so completely that even his eyes seemed to pop behind his glasses. Indeed, so different was he then that I pretended not to recognize him. On such days he was known as Professor Hans Smilinks.

Angel lived in a wonderful world of sweet sadness. He must have been one of the only people ever turned away from a whorehouse in Lourenço Marques because his sexual appurtenance was found, after short-arm inspection, to be too awe-inspiring. He used to talk to the flies on his wall. He it was who introduced me to Reti, the god of retribution, by whom all long-timers swear. Somewhere up there in the lands of clouds and of bliss is a living force who will for sure wreak revenge on our enemies for all the miseries they have subjected us to.

Perhaps, once in a blue moon, one got some earthly recompense too. Angel was on occasion employed, years before, as a prison cook during a big week-long show in Pieter-Maritzburg where the Department also had a stand. Cooking was hot work. He had already bribed a *poisan* (a Black warder) to provide him with a bottle of wine, but when the latter refused to organize the first bottle's mate, Angel decided to do justice by himself. It was two o'clock and stifling. The officer in charge had taken off his uniform and, stuffed stiff, had lain down for a nap in the next room. So Angel borrowed his uniform, plus a portable radio belonging to a warder, and left for town. He was even saluted on his way out! In town he sold the radio and then ensconced himself in the coolness of the first bar he came to. It was late that evening when he finished the last of the money and – in an absolute stupor by now – told the barman to please phone the Prison Department to come and fetch him.

There are many more angels, Mr Investigator. I knew Jood, a fisherman by trade, who had spent perhaps twenty years of his life in prison. He was old now, reduced to shuffling, and suffering from rheumatism. His time in the yard he would spend looking for bees, which during certain seasons got blown over the roof and were too weak to fly away again; these, if they were still alive, he would catch and have them sting him, because he believed bee stings to be a cure for his aches.

I knew Franz, the gentle killer with the background of a trained psychologist. During his trial he pleaded with the judge to give him the rope, but his pleas fell on deaf ears and he had to be satisfied with a twenty-year sentence. Already this had been increased because of an unsuccessful escape effort from Victor Verster Prison. Franz told me in a clinical fashion, what it was like to kill someone, to shoot him at point-blank range and to watch death come over his eyes like a cheesecloth. He had felt nothing, he said, but he knew that he had smashed something essential in himself. Towards the end of my time in prison Franz tried to commit suicide out of sheer desperation when his young lover was released. This young lover, Romeo, was going to stay on in the Cape Town area. To break the link between outside and inside the authorities now suddenly threatened to remove Franz to Pretoria where – so he said to me – he was sure that his soul would be killed, and he didn't want to become a vegetable. His family was also in Cape Town; he had some of his books with him; and he was under the care of Zorro, the visiting outside psychiatrist. So Franz one night slit his own veins at the wrists and in the armpits. Quite by accident he was saved before bleeding to death. Zorro insisted that he should not be left in Pollsmoor. The authorities agreed but they wanted their pound of flesh by punishing Franz for the unsuccessful suicide, sending him to the 'bomb' for thirty days. Then, at the end of that period, they lured him into an office under false pretences, jumped him from behind, overpowered him and handcuffed his hands behind his back, chucked a few possessions in a carton, and shanghaied him to Big House. Thou shalt go and kill thyself in another command.

I met Hottie, the champion grubby of the whole of Pollsmoor: thin as a rake, but with an insatiable appetite. Hottie was so deeply in debt buying food off others, gambling in an attempt to pull even, irrevocably sinking deeper in debt, that he too tried to make an end to his days when his creditors started putting pressure on him. But it was a half-hearted effort. He was not so sure of the eating facilities in the other world. (Maybe he knew too much about decomposition, having been an undertaker by trade outside.) He cut his wrists and then tried to rouse his neighbour in the next cell. The neighbour, Trevor Universe, a fanatic body builder who treasured his sleep to increase his strength, snarled at Hottie to shut up and die but for God's sake to let him sleep in peace. Hottie found himself in the 'bomb' where he made matters worse first by writing a 'stink letter' (of outrage) to the Head of the Prison, because of which he was then charged and convicted, thereupon by going on a hunger strike in protest, whereupon he was charged anew – and then he got so frustrated that he attacked the first *boer* he could find with a sharpened spoon. It happened to be a pathetic warrant officer known as Chicken Breast.

Hottie was not to be in circulation again before Christmas. It was a pity that, because with a syndicate of accomplices I had started grooming another birdie, known as Skew-Eyes, who naturally had an unnatural appetite, with the aim of organizing and end-of-the-year eating championship in which the first prize would have been a huge pot of porridge. We were banking on our candidate with his nearly divine ugliness putting the other camp's – Hottie – off his stroke.

There was a high percentage of killers among the long-timers who came over from Victor Verster. In general they were the ones with whom I got along best; they were normally quiet and reserved, and at least not as totally dishonest as the robbers, the fraud artists, and even the rapists. A special connection with whom I shared some of the monthly delicacies (his boyfriend made nice puddings) and who joined me in my daily exercises in the yard, was Moineau. He had been the leader of the unsuccessful break-out from Victor Verster in which Franz too had been involved, and in the process he was shot through the cheek with the bullet lodging in his nose. The *boere* left him lying in his blood for an hour before they carted him off to hospital. Moineau was one of the *lanies* of our prison, an exceptionally gifted sportsman and a strong fighter. It was his dream to leave prison before he was too old, and to become a sports instructor or trainer. His problem was his ambivalent sexual urges, or the problems of self-acceptance and adaptation caused by those. (His victim had been an unfortunate drunken pederast.) Despair was darkening his mind. Already he had had his once fine body covered by tattoos, and regretted it (with slogans one sees so often in jail, like *Death Before Dishonour* and *I broke my mother's heart to please my friends*). Probably he will kill again and end his days in the darkness of prison, or throw his life away in a desperate run for freedom.

I got to know Alf, a sixty-year-old bull of a Portuguese. He was doing the coat for theft and had already been inside for nearly ten years, but he kept his body in excellent shape. He didn't smoke, didn't drink coffee, didn't smuggle, had no boyfriends, never asked for any favours, and maintained the principle of never talking to any warder in any circumstances – even when they addressed him – and further refusing to compromise or to collaborate in any way with their social workers or their parole boards or their chaplains or their shrinks. Repeatedly he was punished for refusing to see these parasites. I think they were quite afraid of him.

Quite often one came across ex-policemen or ex-warders in prison. (We also had with us, briefly – because their sentence was a sham – some of the mercenaries involved in the débâcle of the attempted Seychelles *coup d'état*. And towards the end the first convicted religious objectors to military duty started coming in.) One of the ex-coppers was a certain Onslof, formerly a detective-sergeant on the drug squad. His crime was stealing state evidence and bringing it back into circulation by selling it. He tried very hard to become acceptable to his ex-victims, and he was not really such a bad fellow. His speciality for earning some credit in prison was to embellish the penises of the inmates. From the plastic handle of a toothbrush or from perspex he would fashion little pearls. With a blade he would then make a small incision in the loose skin around the organ of the client to insert a 'pleasure bead'. Left alone the slit would close up in due time (theoretically that is, because some of the wounds sometimes did fester), and the bead would stay there forever. Some people, as he himself, had as many as nine of these mobile knobbles situated around their penises. It was, so he told the credulous folk, an unfailing way of giving excessive pleasure to one's sexual partner. Hottie had disagreed vociferously. He had been quite upset at the idea; according to him it was calculated to hurt the receiver and ultimately to provoke cancer.

Another of my friends was Mac who was at that time already pushing two coats for an accumulation of minor crimes and several escapes. In fact, I became involved with him in another ludicrous effort. We arranged (paying two packets of snout) for him to be knocked over the head by a fellow prisoner. The idea was to have him transported to outside hospital from where he was to run for it and ultimately come and arrange for me to do the same. So he was discovered lying with a messy scalp on his cell floor, ostensibly in a coma. They took him to Groote Schuur Hospital where the doctors tried to revive him. They directed light beams into his pupils and were baffled by the fact that the eyes contracted normally, but when they pulled out some of his chest hairs with a tweezer he never budged. Unfortunately for Mac and for me, he had been shackled to the hospital bed and when he saw that they were going to keep him tied down, be it until he died, he opened his eyes and ended the game.*

I must admit that I had been mixed up in some other improbable schemes. Barns, upon release, promised that he was going to return one misty night and get on to the roof of the prison (I just had to have something white fluttering from my window) to force apart the bars with a jack. We had agreed on a code; I never heard from him again. Jerry, once free, was going to arrange for me to obtain enough soporific to put out the *boere* in the General Stores at the time when he proposed coming by, with someone else in a delivery van using the pretext of bringing foodstuff to the prison. Blackie, also due to go, said that he had worked out a way

*At the time of confessing this (December 1983), Mac – who had broken out on several previous occasions, by absconding from the dentist or diving, handcuffed, through a train window – was on the loose again. This time he escaped in the company of an ex-policeman. Mac is a gentle, humorous bloke, not given to violence, but the newspapers (and the police informing them) are creating an atmosphere of terror which would provoke and justify the shooting to death of the escapees if ever they are cornered. As far as I know he is still free. . . .

of returning with a Coloured accomplice, both of them disguised as prison officials, to kidnap me at the moment when I was transported from the prison to my place of work. Needless to point out that none of these flights ever got off the ground.

Eventually I also got to know another terrorist, a man of the extreme right called Van der Westhuizen. He had been arrested with a real fanatic, Beelders, and convicted of taking potshots at a political leader of the Progressive Federal Party, of disrupting their political meetings violently, and of destroying property of government opponents. After being sentenced to five years and seven years respectively they had been brought to Pollsmoor prison. Immediately after their arrival I was warned by some of my 'spies' that they were threatening to *katang* me, meaning to wipe me out. We were never in the same section. Not many months later an intermediary – another one of those ex-warders now a prisoner working in the kitchen – came on their behalf to the door of my cell with the suggestion that we should escape together. They would provide the means of getting out, I was to procure travelling papers and undertake to make them acceptable to the overseas world. Of course I turned down this silly idea. Surely they would have slit my throat within half an hour of us being outside the prison walls. Or was this just another attempt by the authorities to bait me?

One Saturday afternoon a second emissary, also a kitchen boy, a German doing nine months (unfairly, he protested) for having shot and killed a Zulu on his farm, came with the same proposal – and warned me to watch out. Well, the German must have been looking for a reduction of sentence because the very next Monday I was suddenly brought back from the General Stores and taken into an office to be confronted by Swart Piet Vangat and his officers accusing me of having wanted to escape with the other two terrorists. The matter, Vangat intoned pompously, had been brought to the attention of the Minister himself. He, Vangat, had just come from the Buildings of Parliament. He had, he said – pointing with a fat index finger at his black briefcase – he had *documents*!

The German pimp was promptly released. Beelders and Van der Westhuizen were transferred to Pretoria the same day; they were obviously not going to be bothered in any other way. But of course the authorities were going to try to make out a case against me. Nails Van Byleveld came, supposedly to investigate the matter. Nothing came of it.

A year passed and Van der Westhuizen was brought back to Pollsmoor, this time to be put in the same section as I was. Yes, Mr Investigator, I even got to sympathize with him. After all, we were now objectively in the same situation. He told me that he had broken all links with Beelders. Beelders, he said, was an out-and-out Nazi with serious identity problems, first because he had difficulty with his homosexuality, and secondly because he was not sure of being a White. It was rumoured that he – a White supremacist – was in fact Coloured! Van der Westhuizen related to me how the two of them, with others of their extreme-right organization, had been directed by the Security Police as heavies or as thugs to go and terrorize suspected opponents to the government of No Man's Land. They would be summoned, he said, to an outlying police station (such as the one at Blaauwberg Strand), often by Van Byleveld who was their handler, and given instructions to go and burn out the motorcar or put fire to the house of so-and-so at such-and-such an address. The alarm would be given, the fire brigade and the police would be called for, but miraculously they would always arrive too late or go to the wrong place.

Van der Westhuizen also told me that Beelders had confessed to him that he'd been the one who assassinated Rick Turner, shooting him to death before his wife and daughter through the window of his own sitting room. He had relayed this confession to the police, Van der Westhuizen said, and a laborious inquiry had been launched.*

It is all coming back in bits and pieces, Mr Investigator. I am vomiting words, I have the sour taste, I'm trying to hold on to the thread. These things surface from somewhere intimate, and yet I do not know them. If I were to know my own nature well I should be knowing universal nature. I discovered gardens. I was

*Other well-informed sources claim however that Rick Turner was killed accidentally by an English mercenary who was hired by the then BOSS to give Turner a fright. . . . Maybe Van der Westhuizen was trying to do Beelders in, maybe Beelders was indulging in fantasy, or maybe Van der Westhuizen was. As for the inquiry – I'm sure it was never intended to be completed.

living in a cemetery for horses. I went screaming down passages of darkness. I was going ever deeper into the labyrinth. See here, I hold it in my hands. I have the black gloves. And silences. Salient incidents remain like shards in the mind. I dare not remove them from fear of provoking a bleeding that can never again be stopped. (This is a confession, not a saga.) I don't know if I have a mind. I dare not look into it – it is so sore. I'm tired of talking to you. I lie down on the floor for a rest and to look at the roof window full of daylight and the invisible stars beyond, it brings back memories, and I get up to continue confessing. I sing into the microphone. A coldness has come over the world. A brittleness too. This morning I was up in the dark to watch the windows nearly imperceptibly growing blue: and the morning star glittering above the buildings. Memories are made of this. Look how dark it still is when you rise at 5.30 in the morning, or a little earlier when you want to cross your legs and kneel facing the wall inhaling and exhaling the flow of emptiness. Even earlier when you stood on your head in the darkness and Warrant Officer Donkey, on night shift, came by and asked you all manner of silly questions through the barred window. 'You must finish your shit now, Breytenbach,' he said. 'It is not worth it. You have caused enough shit.'

See how dark it still is when you are let out into the yard to line up for work. See the matrix of stars. Know that they will not fade but that your eyes will soon be saturated and blinded by light. Smell the new day, the waking mountain. Hear the wind of daybreak. See, when they come in the van to fetch you to work, the spotlights washing the façades of the prisons – and look, outside Medium in that alley between two high wire fences the hundreds of prisoners squatting there in the glare with their hands on their heads, to be counted before going off in a shuffle-trot to their tasks.

I shall continue. I shall remember Nyoka, the vain young warder (who claimed to be a Catholic) making it his ambition to humiliate me, turning over everything in my cell, taking my so carefully collected half jug of jam and spreading it out on the floor to walk in it and to wipe his shoes on the blankets he's ripped from the bed. He had his hang-ups, Nyoka. The homosexuals fascinated him the way a bee is bemused by flowers. He would summon one of them to the office and have him describe minutely the ways of sodomy. Often it would be Marlene who had to give the story of the ring and its variations. 'She' was in exactly because of repeated more or less public acts of sodomy outside, and often said that for 'her' to be in prison is rather like locking up an alcoholic in a bar. Poor Nyoka – vanity fair! – so carefully combing his hair, his face pale from the repressed tension.

It was due to him that many of the moffies ended up working in the kitchen. One of the chosen ones was called Gatiep. A nasty job. He used to sell food to the hungry by having them commit fellatio with him – to satisfy his desire for having someone kneeling before him. Days. Nights. More nights. A darkness and people moaning in their sleep. Warrant Officer Donkey at my window. 'What are you doing at this hour? No man, Breytenbach, you must leave your shit be now. You must come right!'

I shall remember Sergeant Prins who had to look after me during exercise periods. For him I felt true affection. He was another one of life's eternal losers. All he ever really aspired to was to be on a farm of his own, among his horses and his sheep, and here he was whittling his life away in prison. He confided more of his private life to me than he'd ever do to anybody else. A simple man looking for understanding. Still, if he had been ordered – after knowing me for five years – to take me out, stand me against the wall and shoot me, he would have done so. With tears running down his cheeks. But he would have done so.

And there was the death of Paine. He had come in suffering from thrombosis; his legs were of a nasty blue colour with the varicose veins standing out in ridges on them. In the winter it would still be bearable because the medical stockings he had to wear were covered by long pants. Came the summer however, and we all had to dress in shorts. He was very upset; he asked consistently for permission to be allowed to keep on wearing his longs, to hide the ungainly stockings, but this was refused. The friction between him and the *boere* built up. Early mornings, immediately after breakfast, the medicine trolley would come round and those needing medication would line up. Paine was always in the queue, of necessity. He just had to be given his daily pills. One *boer* particularly, Muller by surname, would go for Paine; every morning while he was waiting in line he would pester him, taunt him, accuse him of being a shirker, mock his legs, do everything possible to make the man's life a misery. One morning Paine exploded and chucked his dixie of hot porridge at Muller's face. Muller dragged him off to the office, a few other warders hurriedly arrived, and Paine was obviously given a very bad hiding. Paine was then taken to the 'bomb' section without any of us seeing him and we learnt later – from someone who happened to be doing a 'bomb' stretch at that time – that Paine had knocked several times on his cell wall during the following night, that he had also called out for help. The next morning he was found dead. Verdict: heart attack.

Attack of the heart, Mr Investigator. Listen. I must tell you this too. Listen. Early on during the month of April 1978, Witnerf one night entered my cell to tell me that my mother, Ounooi, had died.

She had been to visit me on several occasions since my arrival in Pollsmoor Prison. The year before it even happened once, on my birthday, that I was called into Witnerf's office to find Hoang Lien and my mother and my father there. For one brief minute I was allowed to embrace them. As she put her hands around my shoulders, my mother said, 'Klong, I thought I'd never touch you again.' And her lips quivered. The last time I saw her was perhaps two weeks before the fatal heart failure. Johan Kriegler and John Brand had come down from Johannesburg to discuss some legal matters with me, and my parents – hearing that the lawyers would be there that day – drove into the city from Onrus, where they then lived, to see them; hoping also that they might be allowed to see me. Their request was denied. (You should have thought about the security of the State before bringing such children into the world, old woman. . . .) But as I was taken from the consultation room down the mirror-smooth passage where the offices are, back to my cell, I passed in front of an open door and glimpsed my elderly parents sitting there in the small waiting room. They were looking at the wall opposite them. She was holding a handbag, he was holding a hat. When did they become so grey? They did not see me and I was not allowed to stop.

Now Witnerf came in. It must have been seven o'clock. For the first time I saw him dressed in civilian clothes – a rather garish and outdated, blocked jacket, and some vulgar private shoes. I think the shoes were two-toned, black and white. He had just been riding a motorcycle, he said. The wind, wow! His son also wanted to have one when he grew up. ('Boys will be boys, you know.') Then he invited me to sit down next to him on the bed, and he announced the death to me. He must subsequently have given me a heart-lifting talk. I don't remember anything of it. He asked me whether I wanted something to make me sleep and I said no. He might have touched my hand. He left and I found myself in this big cell, in a kind of neon loneliness.

It was all abstract. In my mind my mother had been dead for years. I would never *experience* her death. I knew that she had died but I would never *know* that she's dead.

The warders were probably instructed to keep me under observation, or maybe they were just curious to see how I would react. For whatever reason two of them remained outside my windows, staring in at me. I had nowhere to go, Mr Investigator. I could not stay on the toilet forever. There was not a single nook, no hiding place, no nothing. There was nothing.

I turned my back and hunkered down in one corner of the cell with my arms around my knees to cry in privacy.

During that period the lights were never switched off in Pollsmoor's cells. You slept and you woke at two o'clock or four o'clock, not knowing what time it was. I often tied a rag around my eyes in an attempt to get some darkness. Now, with the cloth, I was at least oblivious behind my eyelids. I could talk to my mother.

Swart Piet Vangat himself passed by the next day to look at me through the window. I had not been taken out for work. It was quiet in my cell; I was doing slow *Tai-Chi* movements. Death is just a continuation, a walking on to the other land, a slightly modified rhythm, a deeper space. Vangat called me out and took me down to where the Commissioner, General Du Preez, sat in an office. I was told that my family had requested permission for me to attend the funeral, but that this had been turned down. Later that same afternoon I was taken downstairs again and was now informed that I would indeed be allowed to go to the funeral, but, as Du Preez said, it would be under the strict escort of senior officers; and he added that as my eldest brother Jan would be present at the grave too they had no qualms: if ever I tried to escape, he said, I shall have the shit shot out of me. (I'm trying to translate verbally the crude words he used.)

My family was allowed to come and visit me the next day. My father was withdrawn, silent, looking at me with an immense sadness. My sister was there with him. The following morning it was the turn of two of my brothers, Jan and Cloete, and – as could perhaps be expected – I was shown into an office to meet them without any supervision. Later that afternoon I was told that the decision to have me attend the funeral had been reversed again. It was over and done with. My mother was put into the earth in the cemetery overlooking the village of Hermanus and the sea.

I don't know whether she died happy or unhappy. Does it make any difference? I only remember that she had had a marvellous life, that she had listened to the music of that life, and that towards the end it had been made sombre by an unnecessary anguish. She was like a bird nevertheless, always optimistic.

Around me life was continuing. People mutilating themselves. People finding the most impossible means of drugging themselves. At one stage someone working in the fields came across some *malpitte*, the seeds of an indigenous weed (*Datura stromonium*). These he brought back and they were eaten by a few inmates. A characteristic of *malpitte* (madness pips) is that they cause the mind to hallucinate. For more than a week those who had partaken of the pips were indeed mad. One of them had his eyesight impaired permanently.

Vangat left Cape Town and was replaced by Brigadier-General Charles de Fortier. He was another type of person altogether – straight, honest, humane. My father still came to visit me every month and then just sat there, silently. He could not go on living all by himself in the house at Onrus; he wasn't even eating properly or regularly anymore. So he moved over the mountain to a boarding house in the Strand. Then he became ill. It was decided that he should go to live with my sister in Grahamstown. He came to say goodbye, holding his hat in his hand the way the old people do on formal occasions. De Fortier had the gate separating us unlocked so that I could embrace him. I have very seldom seen my father cry.

He left and soon after arriving in Grahamstown he had a stroke. He has been partly paralysed ever since.

Sometime during 1980 I was suddenly granted permission to start listening, in the Stores where I worked, to taped news and taped music. With the snorting and the shouting going on all around me the conditions were atrocious, but at least if I bent my ears close enough to the tape recorder I could hear a voice giving me the censored news of a few days previously. Connection, Mr Investigator. Somebody just like me talking into a little machine, confessing, confessing. Illegally of course I had managed to stay abreast of the news events to a certain degree. What was earth-shattering, what was fantastic, what was like an electric shock shaking my carcass – was the music. I shall never forget the first time I switched on the machine: there was silence, then a hissing noise, and then the opening bars of Bach's Brandenburg Concerto going right through my head. You will never hear anything like it, Mr Investigator. *Nobody* has ever been music the way I was then. Perhaps my body itself will never again be just an extension of the vibration of sounds.

The *boere* unfortunately also understood the value that music could have in such a context and spitefully they would take pains to ruin the cassettes either by taping the music at the wrong speed or, after my repeated requests for classical music, sending me hymns lustily sung on a Sunday evening somewhere in the church. I was told by one of the officers to whom I complained that it was much worse on Robben Island. There the politicals once had to endure the same record being repeated for weeks.

Communication with the outside world remained difficult and limited: to the end the powers that be tried to keep it secret that I was actually in Pollsmoor. Some people did manage to receive permission to come and see me. Dirk Opperman, the poet, arrived one day. Despite his weak condition he had himself brought from a hundred miles away. He assured me that I was still alive as a poet, that there was interest for my work among the students, and said that it would be fatal for me to break entirely with the Afrikaners. Soon after he was also to suffer a paralysing stroke.

On two occasions I'd written letters to Opperman (after obtaining permission) to thank him for a volume of poems he'd sent me. These never reached him. They were just stolen by either the Prisons or the Greyshits. But I threatened to lay a charge of theft when they held back one of Yolande's life-giving monthly letters. So Smoel brazenly turned up on a Sunday afternoon with it, claiming that he'd had to go himself to the Post Office where he'd found it on the floor! (The prison censor's dated stamp was carefully snipped off!)

Smoel left for the Island. Saayman took his place, a huge pig of a man, subservient to his superiors, bullying – violently at times – the prisoners, but above all lazy and incompetent. He was also just a liar. His conception of censorship was to 'lose' the incoming letters, or to hold back mine and then to have me rewrite them to his specifications. I wrote to Yolande once lyrically praising the talents of some chocolatiers – Bernachon in Lyons, Corné de la Toison d'Or in Belgium, etc. (it was getting on for Christmas, my mind was sweet with absences) and when she wrote back asking how I knew about these things I answered admitting that I'd always been an initiate of the Secret Order of Chocolate Lovers but that I could never tell her this as it was supposed to be a secret. So Saayman launched an inquiry; he wanted to know exactly what 'politics' was hidden in these codes. . . .

Frederick van Zyl Slabbert came to see me. Although he is the leader of the official Opposition I don't think it was that easy for him to arrange for the visit. (They tried to discourage him by telling him that his visit will have to be in the place of a family one.) He listened attentively to whatever I had on the heart. Only afterwards was I to realize how particularly kind he'd been to Yolande, making it possible for her to pursue her efforts to have me liberated. He is a discreet, efficient man, always following up on the initiatives that had been started.

Thanks partly to him I was now also allowed to receive the visits of a man of letters. Professor Kharon from the Afrikaans department of a university in a neighbouring town was allowed access to my manuscripts, and afterwards we could discuss these. For the first time since nearly seven years I now talked literature to an enthusiast. For me it meant that these writings were resuscitated from the dead. Kharon is an intelligent man, with wide-ranging and sensitive literary interests. The exciting experience was that I could talk about really important matters to someone who would disagree absolutely with what I'd done with my life and with the notions which had inspired me. Despite these differences, although I was a *bandiet* (and would remain one in my mind) and he a man moving in the vicinity of the powerful, sniffing the heady scent that I would find nauseating, I could sense a true affection developing between us.

More time passed. I built time itself into my system by running, by *Zazen* and by *Tai-Chi*, by escaping through the walls and walking up the mountain to smell spring with its first warmth being wafted down from the trees growing on the slopes. I knew that attempts were being made in the outside world to have me released, that even in the inner chamber of the ruling circles there were dissident opinions, but I did not believe in any of it. I also learned that Mandela had been moved from Robben Island to Pollsmoor together with Sisulu and one or two other political prisoners doing life sentences. A special cell had to be built for them on the roof of Maximum Security. And since some of the expert builders were White prisoners, acquaintances of mine . . . I knew that area well anyway; when we were still housed in Maximum it used to serve as our library.

Working in the Stores I was involved in equipping Mandela and his comrades with clothes and furniture, and I did so with tremendous glee, I can assure you. The *boere* so obviously hated having to find proper clothes and yet they had no choice because everybody was scared of the repercussions if Mandela complained to the Red Cross. ('Just give me a pickaxe handle and leave me alone with the bastard,' Bles growled. 'He thinks he's too big to stink? He's just a *kaffir* like the rest of them. All he needs is one good bashing and there will be no more of this *mister* business. It is the only language a *kaffir* knows and appreciates!') Brigadier de Fortier had the Stores on the jump. He insisted – as always – that things be done correctly and promptly. The storemen tried to frustrate his directives by passing the buck to the *boere* on the Island who were supposed to have sent clothes along with the prisoners. The Department was obliged to let the prisoners have the privileges they were expressly entitled to. But *never* would they be accorded a minute or a word or a potato beyond the precise allowances and instructions.

It is not clear yet why Mandela and the five others were transferred to the mainland. I know that the Prison Department intends eventually to close down Robben Island – it has become too expensive to keep it up, to continue transporting water and food there. (The island's own water is brackish, unfit for humans.) Perhaps the authorities want to move the leaders to even more secure (and dehumanized) institutions: there was talk of a new prison being built for that purpose near Kimberley and the maximum security sections of Leeukop and Pretoria Local have also been reconceived and rebuilt. The real intention however was probably to cut Mandela off from his own – to stop the Island being, as it had become, the 'Mandela University'.

Christmas would come and go. It was always the most nakedly horrible time of the year. But there were compensations. We would be allowed to buy, with our own money, 1lb of fruit, cake and sweets each. For these orders we would prepare weeks in advance. One had to be astute; in conjunction with one's friends one would spread the orders to obtain as large a variety as possible. We'd also willingly give up our sugar rations and our milk rations for the weeks preceding the day so as to make it possible for the cooks to prepare something special. And always there would be that one extra letter allowed in and out.

How could I be with my people? I put myself in a letter. . . . One year, towards the end of my stay there, the letter that I'd sent out to Madame Bubi never arrived at its destination. It was the only present I could give her – how else was I to try to make a grey European festive season somewhat less sad? The letter naturally had to contain 500 words only. Not one more. (The letters handled by Saayman would reach me with a pencilled – '25 words too many'.) I had counted my words carefully, I always count my words carefully Mr Investigator, I have an angel with a drawn sword before my mouth (albeit a drunken one), but without a word ever being said it was just gobbled up by the administration. Maybe it is still lying in a file somewhere; perhaps even now some security expert is trying to work out the coded message. Will he see the light? Will he find the key which will make it possible for White, Christian South Africa to turn back and at last remake History? Will the dark doings of the communist mind be laid bare for all to see? Will the hard-working secret hero finally get his well-deserved promotion? Don't stop now! Please read on. . . .

If you may only write 500 words you have to make a draft. I

found that draft again, Mr Investigator, tucked away among the drafts of monthly grocery orders. It was there with the odds and the ends that I managed to leave prison with. Please permit me to reconstitute it here.

Now it is again nearly Christmas. Would you be so kind as to pass along the belated missive to her ladyship? Please allow me to bring my humble present at last:

Once upon a time long ago in 198- there was a bandit with only one heart who lived in Nosemansland. Where he planted words for a living, hoping finally to make some grow sense whose odour may please the masters who are most particular in such smatters. It was very dry in Nosemansland. It was dry during the day and even drier at night and when it rained the rain was dry, but the masters sniffed and snoofed and said, 'Nosesmell is better than smell which may not be very noce.' So that the bandit with only one heart was (100) *really risking the unnecessary in doing what didn't have to be done. But that is not the point. The point is that he had a dream which kept on getting longer (because it was a longing dream) about One Lady who lived far far away in another world called Pararis. Lady One was an u'bbi. The amu'bbi (ecoli u'bbiti), as everyone knows, have nam-nam knees and small noces although they may make quite a noise when they feel like it. This Lady One was very beautiful – not just for an u'bbi but altogether urbi and orbi – even though somewhat ecleccentric.* (200) *She used to wear a veteran fur coat and bicycle shoes of different colours – also other clothes when these fitted; and as an alibi for buying sold rags and riches and plasticpalms in a blue swimmingpool. She also had a mother, Munch, and many many friends (not for sale). And she collected rings and cameras to take pictures of friends wearing rings with not for sale either but for steal exclusivement.*

So the one-hearted bandit (named Huan) went with a plea to the masters. He bore with him some words which he intended to break open hoping the (300) *scents would sway them in the absence of sense. Bulbnose referred him to Snout and Snout to Gallowsnoose and Gallowsnoose to Mose and Mose to Snovel. Snovel snorted, 'I can make no decision because Beak only decideth and he cannot because actuhelly's smother-wise occupied committing udder heartpatients to the infinimity of asylums so I must make the nositions for him. What exaggectly is't you whish to probosce?'*

'Please sir (Huan sad with 'eart in 'and), Isumever wish to memograte to Pariris for this heart's very sore from longing for Lady One. Had I but two it wouldn't mutter but this-one beats (400) *terribly from missing. It goes miss-a-moomph miss-a-boo-by. Listen. Please.'*

'What matter of nosesense is this?' (snarled Snovel). 'Knose alone knows I expiacted all kinds of batty scense but not those! Your word-shaveworms, my friend! You want to go to anozzle world? That den of thieves, anarchists and mad plumbers?'

*'But please, sir, there b-also goldenlight and planetrees and treeplanes (whether moony or not) and clouds and houseplants. And this heart aches because it belongs to the dream which belongs to Lady One who belongs in the dream. The ache is of the heart, not of the dream, and for fivehundred worlds** it aches because she etc., and since she etc., I don't want to split her personality (though she's a twin) and therefore must etc. Where the heart goes I go etcetera.'*

'Fine phrases, but juiceless' (Snovel sneered). 'Whatfor this wordthsickness? My noes are my noes. Go back to your dream. Don't come noise around here. And whatta-whatta-whatta-whatta.'

So time became past tense. With the passing of time more time passed away untillit was the deadtimetimes (but not quickly enough even if it's known that the longer the time the quicker it goes . . . like a dream). (512)

Eventually Huan could take nomore, afraid that the heart may come to belong to the ache. It was then the season of kindnose, blessé to the world and pearce to mankind. (Also when people spoke funny – like falseteethsticking to chewing gums.) So he applicated to Bulbous who scent him to Snoot who scent him to Galloresneeze who scent him to Mouse who inscent him to Snivel.

'Sir,' (he pedaled) 'since I know it is against your primciples to let me go – although I'm rerabbitated – and you cannot howmever (532) *much you may want to because only Beak can do that and nosesing can move Him (nor tide nor time) as He believes that any move must surely crumble Nosemansland into heartspace and the danger of beauty, and it being now Crossmast and I having no sother present to present to Milady except this one heart belonging to her and wishing to reunight her with*

*Mr Investigator, when I got so far did I throw all caution to the wind to continue, and was the letter then sunk by its specific weight? In fact I'm redoing the draft here: I know that I did cut back the lost letter to 500 words, and to incomprehensibility? (50)

sa-id somesing to pull up her nose at so that it may grow and become like unto ours' (this he advanced so that Snivel may take nosice) 'and I muzzle delay but hurry! hurry! time's runnin just like wordels from a broken throat – please, may I not thenetc.?' (563)

'Well,' (sighed Snivel) 'allwright, howsomever, wrub it up in no smore than 500 whatta-chatta.'

Which, Lady One, is why you receive today one battered habitat of ventricles and tubes (the ache and the sadness I'll keep as echoes) – with ardour I hope not malodorous or malheureuse.

INSERT

sempre più oltre

How does one survive? I did not survive. This is important to point out. True, there is a sum of attributes which can be called by name. 'Come out, Breyten Breytenbach!' you may want to call; and from the gloom, wrapped in words as if in cheesecloth, Bangai Bird will emerge. (He has the smell of writing on him; he is utterly deconstructed to stuttering utterances.)

It is important that you consciously (I'd be apt to say 'personally') assist at the putting down of the I. That is if you wish to parry destruction, to unsurvive. (As if 'survival' were going to inquire after your wishes!) The I not only as a concept of (para)physicality, as a screen of illusions, as a hole-ness – but in its most mundane manifestations.

You are the way; the walking and the walk, not the walker. The I which blocks the view must disappear by 'deconception' for a sense of movement to be actualized – a feeling of metamorphosis. And if you are furthermore a weaver of shrouds – well, then you can be the spaceman.

Does it sound too clever to be true? One mustn't be like those who always simplify 'reality' by attempting to understand it. One must live it; one should flow with the rhythm. You develop an awareness of the living structure – of that which is constantly *doing* itself: the patterns, the dialectic, the breaking points, the *limits* which are only the outer edges of pages and pages of silence, the relationships, and then where you lose all comprehension as the earth tilts away from you. Such is the structure of understanding.

But it is important to know that you are nothing. And to search without ever stopping, be you awake or withdrawn into the wakefulness of sleep, for the hairline cracks, for the gaps and the unexpected moments of deep breathing, for that space which is created by alleys and by walls.

Power is a totalitarian concept. To realize that you are marginal is of itself a way of making distance your own, of becoming as permanent as an ice block going downstream, of disregarding coercion. It is to come upon an interstice of freedom.

Once you have moved into the territory of the enemy and beyond the hindrance of oppositions, once you have been totally isolated and undone – then you will find the most permanent comfort in humble things: the ants and the flies you always tried like a madman to kill from some hang-up about sanity, the blotched tattoo on a back which someone has erased by redesigning along the same lines with Steradent, that fluff of wool in the corner, a cloud, a tin, the hoarse cry of panic slicing through the night, the boot on concrete, the smell of the septic well, the mountain, the mirror – like reminders of the limitlessness these things have a terrible one-by-one beauty.

Prepare yourself for the interstices of freedom. It requires a discipline, a directing of the sum of attributes. The better prepared you are, the more chance you will have of finding them. Knowledge becomes intuition. You will experience the mountain because you will *be* it. When you walk, walk! When you sit, sit! And there will be nothing that can take hold of you.

8

This is How it Happened

This is how it happened: during the month of May 1981 it was made public by the spokesman of the Minister of Justice (and other fancies) who in turn acted as the mouth of the government (which exist only as delegates of the State), that a certain number of prisoners would benefit from an amnesty to celebrate the twentieth anniversary of the glorious Republic of South Africa. Violent robbers, murderers and specifically political prisoners were excluded from this measure of mercy. Sir, I was shown my name on page one of a national newspaper the morning amnesty was announced: there it was said that it had been decided, for love and kindness, to set so many free, but among those *not* getting any time off only my name was singled out.

However, about a year later, in May 1982, the government piloted through Parliament an amendment to, I assume, the Prisons Act, which henceforth would entitle the Minister of Justice, by way of the Commissioner of Prisons, to accord a remission of sentence and/or parole to political pariahs. *Any* prisoner in South Africa, whatever his sentence, could now be released at the discretion of the Minister acting on behalf of the Cabinet of Ministers and basing his decisions on the advice of the Prison Department and other interested or concerned organizations such as the Security Police and the Department of National Security. A board of advisers to the Minister was created, consisting of a few academics and senior civil servants, to review the case of each political prisoner individually. Like all the other politicals, I was read the copy of a declaration of the Minister in Parliament, spelling all the above out in answer to a question from the Opposition, and it was stressed that the rulers had decided upon this in their own wisdom and not on your bloody life because of any pressure exerted from wherever, and especially that any political exploitation of the intended relaxation would jeopardize it immediately, if not sooner. Shorty, knowing more about these matters than any *boer* ever would, came to inform me that Head Office in Pretoria had 'pulled' (demanded) my file. He winked, showed a rotten tooth and assured me that it was in the bag – when *they* pull a file it's a sure sign that some little luck is in the offing. 'Just watch it!'

So what? I didn't believe any of it. I could not afford to. I had more immediate concerns. It was all just another sick joke, I thought.

Later that year a certain number of Black political prisoners were indeed released before their time was up, but those benefiting from these measures did not include any of the better-known national resistance leaders. Still, this apparent loosening up of the political repression pertaining to prisoners inspired some people to renew their efforts to have me liberated. Newspapers started speculating. One or two Afrikaans papers even asked in editorials that the government should reconsider my situation.

Over the years people never stopped showing their support for me, approaching the authorities with petitions and pleas on my behalf. About some of these *démarches* I learned only after I was let out. I have in my possession now, for instance, the copy of a letter my father received from the then Prime Minister, Big Chief Vorster himself. It would seem that my father had written to his holiness about my case quite early on during my purgatory. Vorster had answered saying that he did not feel free to be of any assistance to my father and advising him to be consoled by the fact that he had another son, Jan, an Afrikaner hero. He went on to illustrate his point by referring to the precedent of General Christian de Wet who was a Boer hero, and his brother, also a general, called Piet de Wet, who after two years of fighting had gone over to the British. Yes, Vorster said, unfortunately we know from history that within the same family we can have a hero and a traitor.

The successive Ministers of Justice and of Police had either refused to receive any delegation wanting to plead my cause or else they had given them the cold shoulder and the runaround. Jimmy Krüger, 'that ridiculous little man' responsible for the forces of repression at the time of my sentencing, was downright uncouth to any such instance approaching him. Never as long as he is alive, he swore. And he often added that he'd love to see all dissident writers behind bars. Le Grange, he of the low forehead, the large hands and the mean wit, was hardly an improvement on his predecessor. Yolande has told me of how she once, unassisted by anybody, fought for me with two ministers at the same time – Schlebusch and Le Grange. Schlebusch was obviously the more humane of the two, but he was over-shadowed into (perhaps an embarrassed) silence by the hard and intransigent Le Grange. Now there was a new broom at the ministry called Coetsee. From what I heard of him, and according to the estimation of professional minister-watchers, Coetsee at least had (and has) the laudable intention of ameliorating the conditions of political prisoners and maybe of speeding up the release of some among us. (But oh! where will he find the strength to do it?)

You must understand, Mr Investigator, that this 'humanization' arrived at a time when the Whites felt more sure of their own powers (truly draconian) than ever before. One can see that they thought it to their advantage to try to improve their image with the outside world. It furthermore must have become obvious to the more sophisticated among them that releasing a few mangy politicals was not going to bring the Republic crashing down around their ears.

The political considerations were clear. But just as clear was the fanatical opposition to any let-up emanating from the sadly misnamed intelligence community and the Security Police. The decision to let me go must have been in the making for at least a year; until the very last moment strenuous efforts were made by people like Huntingdon and Brummel to stop it from happening. Yes, they were exerting pressure on their own boss, they would even try to blackmail him in their bitter commitment to keeping me cooped up. What do you do when your own dogs make it difficult for you to pretend to be the master? I tell you, Mr Investigator, there is real fear among the politicians of the monster they have created.

The actual decision to let me go must have been the result of an accumulation of approaches made to the authorities and of careful opinions expressed either publicly or in private by influential groups of individuals. The French government, by way of Monsieur Plaisant, their envoy to Pretoria, continued asking their

South African homologues to release me; PEN International as also PEN groups in various European countries and America asked for the same thing; writers both abroad and in South Africa would at various occasions signal their concern. Allow me to point out here that Amnesty International had nothing to do with my release or the conditions of my imprisonment. Friends and colleagues in Holland and in Paris had formed committees to support me; when they approached AI for help they were turned down because I 'did not conform to their definition of someone incarcerated for his beliefs and opinions'. In a similar way the French MRAP *(Mouvement contre le racisme, l'anti-sémitisme et pour la paix)* dropped me like a hot potato – evidently at the behest of the South African Communist Party or their local comrades. You must know that behind the façade of the noble struggle for human rights there are sad marionettes for whom it is an ideological game. AIDA, a recently formed international group of concerned artists, did try to help in their own way.

There were, I've since learned, more far-fetched efforts – involving senior politicians of at least two European countries and some African ones in behind-the-scene manoeuvres – to arrange for an exchange of prisoners from which I could have benefited. Still along the same lines of cloak-and-dagger footwork, a colleague of mine, originally from the United States, told me of a rather funny incident. His uncle by marriage is a senior CIA official. In desperation my colleague, who had had no contact with this family member, finally wrote a letter asking him whether 'they' couldn't do something to obtain my freedom. Apparently this uncle (or this godfather) responded by saying that 'they' would look into the matter. He thereupon confirmed some time later that they did indeed look into same and that he would let the young whippersnapper know if their looking encountered anything worth looking in or into. Who looks shall see, through keyhole or by spy satellite. My colleague heard nothing more until the morning after my release when he had a mysterious phone call from Washington and the voice of this unknown uncle asking whether he'd seen the news: 'And are you satisfied now?'

No, Mr Investigator, I do not believe for one hilarious instant that my liberation could be ascribed to the intervention of the

CIA. It is much more likely that an opportunistic attempt was made by this official to take some credit for something that he or 'they' had nothing to do with (rather in the way that certain barren journalists invented the story that I might have been released in exchange for the French providing South Africa with another nuclear plant!). What *is* true, though, is that there certainly were influential members of the ruling Nationalist Party in South Africa itself who discreetly tried to point out, in inner circles, the possible benefits of such a step.

The last bit of the puzzle I wish to show to you is that I had agreed with Yolande that legal proceedings should be initiated by the lawyers who represented me – but on their own behalf – in order to make public the fact that certain promises had been made to them in return for my pleading guilty and my foregoing a political trial in 1975. Pieter Henning was the moving force now. We were nearing the end of 1982. Hoang Lien was in South Africa on a biannual visit; her visa was about to expire and she was due to return to Paris on 5 December. Ten days before that I learned from her that I was about to be visited by Johan Kriegler and John Brand, to finalize our strategy for the intended proceedings. Brigadier de Fortier then came to see me and told me to ask my wife to have the visit cancelled. He suggested that my case was now under active reconsideration by the powers of heaven and earth and that any legal proceedings or visits even from my lawyers could only adversely affect any pending decision. My gut reaction was not to take any heed of his advice, knowing that the Prison Department would shamelessly walk the extra mile, would use any imaginable excuse and argument, however dishonest, to prevent any embarrassment to themselves. After all, my birthday – which would have been a fine occasion for them to make a gesture – had come and gone with Yolande already in the country (especially with that hope in heart, I subsequently heard), and nothing had happened. Yes, 25 November came and went: nothing more happened. I was now entering the eighth year of my sentence.

Then came 1 December. I'd gone out to work as normal. It was a Wednesday. Madame la Générale was to come to say goodbye on the Thursday before returning to Paris.

That morning, it must have been about half past eight, Thick

Saayman the security officer, suddenly pitched up at the Stores and said he was taking me back to the prison to appear before the Board. Appearing before the Board is a six-monthly ritual: a committee consisting of the head of the prison, the psychiatrist, the officials responsible for you at work and in the section, sit to review your conduct and your position and your dashed hopes. They very evidently had no mandate materially to modify the sentences of politicals, but we all went through the motions anyway. Smiling. I had just recently seen the Board and couldn't understand how come I was to pass before them again so soon. Saayman had me get into his car, for once without any escort, and off we went. He drove right by the prison and continued on down the road. Looking at me he said, 'I bet you must be asking yourself where we are going now.' And I said, 'Yes, I am, but it's no use asking you because you will not tell me.' He said, 'Right you are.'

Right I was, Mr Investigator; it could have been my execution or the circus – listen, whatever was due to happen would be 'normal'.

He took me to a house I didn't know, asked me to enter it, and there was Brigadier de Fortier in civilian clothes. The two of them talked about the weather and the price of eggs. After that de Fortier invited me into his bedroom and asked me to try on one of his safari suits. I did as I was asked. It fitted rather well, even if I say so myself. He also handed me a pair of shoes, but the socks we could do nothing about. I kept on my prison ones. My own outfit I left lying on his bed. Cinderella was ready for the ball; the detainee was ready for another interrogation session, or a further trial, or to be put on show for a foreign newsman. De Fortier asked Saayman, 'How does he look?' Saayman said, 'He looks all right, Brigadier.'

His wife arrived, offered us some coffee. Their little dog came to sniff suspiciously at my legs. (What – a *bandiet* in the *baas*'s house!) Then de Fortier announced that it was time for us to leave. Saayman was no longer there. We got into the brigadier-general's car and left the compound in the direction of Cape Town. Not a word, Mr Investigator – no, don't say a word.

De Fortier, by nature a kind-hearted man, said, 'Look, I'm sorry but I'm not allowed to tell you anything. Just stay calm.'

We glided along the highway to the heart of the city. He was talking to me. My mind was divided between mumbling yes-sirs and oh-officers, and the etched experience of drinking in the passing sights. It was so long since I'd lost all notion of movement in a motor car. I saw seventy-eight trees draped in a finery of flowers, eighteen women in aprons in their backyards, hundreds of people wearing civvies, vehicles and a mountain. As we rose and came across the neck above Groote Schuur Hospital, descending now along De Waal Drive into Cape Town itself, the brigadier slowed down to allow me to feast my eyes on the magnificence of Table Bay spread out at our feet.

In the City we drew up before an imposing hotel whose existence I'd formerly ignored and got out. De Fortier said we were perhaps a bit early and that we should just stand there. I was invisible. No, not a word, Mr Investigator. Then he glanced at his watch and said maybe we had better start going in all the same. We entered the lobby of the hotel. I walked on his right. I did not open doors. People passed by us without taking any notice. He exchanged a few words with the receptionist behind the counter, who directed him to a lift.

We flew to the eleventh floor. On that floor there were only two doors leading off a small foyer. He now knocked on the one which had a little name plate identifying it as 'Concordia'. A man with a belly and a waistcoat opened the door. It was the Commissioner of Prisons in his own body. He had obviously spent the night there: the bed was unmade. He smiled, said, 'It's good to see you're on time,' and led us to the second door, on which was written 'Felicia'. (These must be bed nests for the recently or bogusly wed.) The same ritual, the deferential knock and the cough. The door was opened and the Man himself, much shorter than I expected him to be, invited us to step into his parlour. His bed was newly made. I think he was there only for that meeting.

No, don't ask, Mr Investigator. I have undertaken not to tell you. That is why I call him the Man. We sat down and the Man inquired whether we would like coffee or tea, or something stronger perhaps? He rang for room service. They discussed the price of eggs and the weather. As if this was the most usual mid-morning male tea party. An elderly Black gentleman in a white jacket (who sees without looking and without observing) brought in a tray of cups and teapots and instant coffee and hot water, and left. This went on for a long time. I could not hear the traffic in the streets below.

Then the Man turned an inquisitive eye on me and started putting what we shall now call hypothetical questions. What, he asked, what would be my itinerary if ever I were to be released from prison? Did I intend to stay on in the country? What was my attitude to the authorities going to be? Clearly, he had to master some arguments which he would afterwards have to present to his colleagues. The meeting, I sensed, was to be hush-hush. I wondered from whom he was hiding (the Security Police, perchance?). The third clear, though unspoken, message was their fear that my possible release could mobilize anti-government forces. It was evident that if they were to release me, they would want to give the outside world the impression that there were no strings attached. No, Mr Investigator. Although there must have been some message that they tried to convey to me. Basically I think it boiled down to: if we release you, it would only be if we were sure that you would not rally the dissidents (students and intellec-chals) around you; that you would not embarrass the government by insisting on staying in the country with your wife. . . . All of the foregoing was presented in a carefully wrapped package of political blah-blah: the possibility of change in the country, the need to strengthen the forces of reform, the resistance to reform from certain quarters, the difficult passage to be franchised by those in power at the moment because if you want to beat a dog any stick will do and how easy it is to upset the apple cart.

My answer was simply that I would want to get away as far from this country as possible and to rejoin my wife in Paris to continue my writing and my painting, that I had a life to catch up with, that I could not expect it of my wife and myself to stay in South Africa even if things were 'normal', as we'd always be 'in the eyes', that I'd like to be allowed to return to it from time to time because my father was aged and infirm and my heart beat for him, and oh but your land is beautiful, that I think I know what could be waiting for me abroad, the pitfalls, the tunnel vision of exile, the temptations of simplification, that much moral outrage covers political string-pulling and twisted patronizing, or ethical ineptitude, that man uses man, that I could only tell what I know, that I will be solicited by many who don't care a damn really about South Africa, the land of hope and of tragedy, that I could not say that I have been physically tortured, no, because it is not true. No, I did not make a speech. I did plead for other prisoners. I did say that any man after five years in prison is no longer a man. The Man was shocked at my prison language.

I did not believe for one moment, Mr Investigator, that anything could come from this interview – however extraordinary and off-beat it might have been. I had had too much experience of their penchant for fun and games, of their cruelty; and in any case, I had long since become far too conditioned by prison life to expect it really, fundamentally, to change. But I was and I am too well-trained a prisoner to leave without trying to score. So I profited from this once-in-a-lifetime chance to ask the Man if I couldn't please have a 'contact visit' with my wife the next day, that is, the day of her departure – a visit without intervening glass panels and talk boxes, breathing the same air (in the attentive presence of a *boer*)? Can heaven be any better? Will my heart not burst with joy? He promised to look into the matter and let me have an answer soon enough.

It was time to go. There was nothing to be had there. I left with de Fortier. We drove back along the road we came in on. Again he slowed down to let me have a last look at the sea; he even invited me to turn down the window to get the smell of the salty wind. He warned me against the danger of building up false hopes based on the interview we'd just had. Sea-mews wheeled over the car. He told me to stay cool. He made me understand that he personally would be relieved if something positive came out of all this. There were brilliant green trees against the lower mountain. He understood, he said. If they were to ask him, he'd say.

Back at his house I went through the same procedures in reverse – taking his clothes off, thanking him for their use, no smell of mine in there, putting my own back on, feeling much more familiar, feeling all me-ish, and Saayman came to pick me up and took me back to prison. I was not to talk to anybody about what had happened. My concern was now whether the cooks had kept my food or, as so often happened, whether some fink had stolen it or sold it to a grubby. This was where life was at.

I returned to work in the afternoon. Nobody noticed any difference. There was no difference. Afternoon. Evening. In the evening I wrote a letter to Yolande. It was never mailed. Here it is now. This is how it happened.

Private Bag X4
7965 Retreat
1st December, 1982

I thought of writing to you tonight – even though I'll be seeing you tomorrow for the last time this trip, before you return to a wintry Paris. I wanted to hand it in tomorrow early, before seeing you, so that it may wing away and get to you there in the cold not too long after your arrival. Something white to go with the ice on the windowsill.

But tonight there's madness. I feel that the mind, with its turmoil of emotions, is speared. A restlessness penned down. Forgive then the meandering sentences, the broken thoughts. Often I wondered: what would happen once the day of release were at hand; not afterwards, not from there *on*, but immediately before. One must come to a point, *faire le point aussi*. One must take stock surely, of the years spent in this situation. What will the essential be at that moment? What shall I take with me? And will I remain clear?

I don't know whether that moment has arrived. Despite what happened today I cannot permit myself to hope. It would be too horrible (for you and for me and for us) if nothing came of it. Like climbing down from the stake, half consumed by the fire. Now I don't know whether your visit tomorrow is to be the last of this series – or the first of a never-ending kind, with liberation a stretch of the fingertips away. We shall soon know.

Despite what occurred today. I cannot tell you about it in full. I dare not. I love you. The day was big and blue and burnt. How incredibly beautiful the surroundings of the city! With what majesty the mountain folds its contours, tumbles its growths along the lower slopes. It accompanies one into town, it is a moving presence. And then, in the city, once the car stopped, I felt in my head and my chest that peculiar smell of sea and harbour, and other street odours too. I love you. People were passing by on the pavements, crossing arteries and squares – women with slim backs and freshly moving limbs, men lingering in front of shop windows – and all blissfully unaware of the fire crumpling me. But enough of that for now. I believe I know how an extra-terrestrial must feel if he were to land here.

On the edge of the night. Late last night the moon was slow and full – all bone and silk. I pulled and pushed until it was framed in the long thin space of one of my windows open upon the dark. How sweet and how serene and how overpowering. I had to press my palms together and bow. A premonition bird-swift then, a prayer nearly, a praising. It was indeed the Buddha's belly. And later this afternoon – upon returning from the city, the dream not yet dislocated, something of leaves going up in ecstasy – I couldn't stop running round and round the inner yard; I had to perspire, I wanted tiredness to unflutter the birds; and when they called us in ('time, gentlemen!') the sun was still aloft, silver, incandescent, fierce, alone, pure: I felt obliged to stretch and open my eyes to it so that I came into the dark interior with a blind whiteness deep-eyed as temporary memory. Tonight (I think) it's overcast. No moon in any event. I'm not looking for it.

When all is shrivelled, what remains? I love you. It's a stupid expression – inadequate, cheapened a million times, endlessly in all possible ways. The courtly tradition of the knights of yore. Illusion. But what else can I say? I must embody it in its most ordinary and shallow and common form. When what I want to say is that I'll never come to the end of you. Your natural *pudeur* wants to make you tell me to cease. How dare I *étaller* thus what is intimate to us? Let the world know because it will never know!

All these years you came closer to me, ever more precious. And I know you less now than I ever did. You are so strong it is a mystery to me. You are so terribly fragile. And yet you fought, more tenacious than a tiger. You are timeless: from how far you've come! Lives and lives away, the flower opening endlessly. But you are so young. You are too beautiful. Sometimes I'm jealous that others may see the sadness and the lilt of your beauty. Then again I *want* to show it to the whole world. Were you or I to die tonight our togetherness will surely continue, just as it has forever been. (Agreed – you don't have to remind me – I abused it, but we were different people ten years ago and we shall continue changing. Growing closer.) How else must I say it then?

It is late now. From the small insects flying in through the open window it would seem that rain is not too far off. To perish all mangled and crushed. The prison is quiet. Or as quiet as it ever gets. A cough now and then, a sigh too loud. Outside is alive with sounds. Dogs. Nightbirds. A car very far away. Other clean mountain-noises perhaps. All these years you came and you supported me. You gave me of your strength and I survived. I died and you were there waiting. I was in my grave and you wrote to me. Perhaps tomorrow; perhaps from then on it won't be too long anymore. The terror must fade. The husk of alienation and hurt will be shucked.

One day we shall be free. We shall walk down a beach and we shall enter the water. We shall sit at a table. The sun will be in your eyes. Your hair will fall, black and straight, over the half of your face. One day. Maybe soon. Will you turn my salad, please? We shall bicker and argue and sulk even, and we shall be happy. Maybe not too far off in the future?

Thank you, young lady. You know it. Understand – I had to write, for you are the star I carry with me from here. You are my memory. You are there, coming, going, every present. Here I am with you.

Goodnight, my sweetness, my secret love

Then came 2 December. It wasn't raining. Radiant sun outside. Hot. The head of the prison was called Reindeer. He was in the dining hall that breakfast. Was I to go out to work, or should I stay in, I asked him. 'Yes. Why not?' But I was expecting a visit, I said. 'Well, we shall see.' And I happened to have seen the brigadier the day before – the major wouldn't by any chance know whether my request for a contact visit had been granted? 'No, we shall see.'

I was fetched for work. Everything was 'normal'. No, Mr Investigator, neither earthquake nor volcanic eruption, no fire-fingers running along the black mountain. Weather even, chance of wind rising towards midday, temperatures in the eighties, no storm warnings: early summer in No Man's Land. People were being shunted off to court. Somewhere someone was trying to nick his best friend's tobacco. Somewhere a bird hanging on to the bars to steal a look outside. Old men squinted at the sun.

About an hour after arriving at the Stores the phone rang and de Fortier instructed the *boere* not to let me return to the prison until he had been to see me. Ninety-three minutes later he turned up, accompanied by Professor Kharon. They took me into an empty office, the brigadier put his hat on a table, and the same questions pertaining to a hypothetical eventuality were put to me. I gave the same reassuring and finally non-committal answers. (See previous pages.) The two of them left, ostensibly to make contact with 'Pretoria' (by telex?), and I was told to wait.

I continued working. The twelve o'clock siren howled, echoed by the dogs. It became time to go in for lunch and nothing happened. The *boere* were cursing because two of them now had to stay on duty to guard me. I was cursing because I was missing my lunch. It meant two irregular lunches in a row, maybe even a no-lunch. Things were going too far.

More or less at one o'clock the two messengers returned. Again they summoned me to one of the empty offices, but there they found Bles eating words from the telephone. Hand signals were made, and as he feigned incomprehension his line was summarily cut and he was sent out.

De Fortier then turned to me, took off his cap and said, '*As from this moment you are free unconditionally.*'

Two things happened, Mr Investigator: my ears immediately went dead – I could hear nothing but the distant silence – maybe the blood had risen to my head; and a thought slashed my mind: *fuck it, there goes my Christmas order!*

Then I thought: *free*. Then I thought: *what a joke*. Then I thought: *if I don't say anything, it may come true*. I was at the window. A white cloud pursued its quest for silence above the mountain.

I looked at de Fortier and to my astonishment saw tears in his eyes. I said, 'What time is it, please?' He said, 'It is now fifteen minutes past one.' Kharon stood behind him, not knowing what to do with his hands or his paleness.

Thereafter things were speeded up as in an old movie, Mr

Investigator. God had spoken to the Prime Minister who had spoken to his Minister of Justice who'd spoken to his Commissioner of Prisons who'd spoken to the Officer Commanding Pollsmoor Prison Command who now summoned and spoke to the head of the Male White Prison, saying, 'Look, this man must be transferred to Pretoria immediately. Nobody is to know about it. How long do you need to get everything ready? Whom do you have that you can trust absolutely? How many members do you need to get him through the books? I give you exactly three-quarters of an hour.' And Major Reindeer, white as a sheet, jumped to attention and with three stretched fingers to the peak of his cap bravely swore, 'Three-quarters of an hour, sir! One sergeant, sir! Trotter Truter, sir! I think. Sir!' (It had been specified that the Department was keeping my release a secret. At least for a few days. The staff was to be given the impression that I was being shanghaied to Pirax. From there, God the State alone knew what might happen. One or two of the *boere* gave me funny, penetrating looks. Did they guess? But they were afraid to take-taste the thoughtword 'free' on the tongue lest it become a curse blighting their careers till doomsday.) We needed cardboard boxes for my possessions (study books). And so the head of the prison spoke to the sergeant in charge of the packing facilities at the Stores who took me out into the backyard where he spoke to the Prisoner in Charge of Cardboard Boxes, Rags and other Cleaning Material. God's divine intervention nearly trickled away in the sands of reality right there when the lowly *mugu* turned away his head to spit, rubbed the spittle into the earth with a toecap, grinned, and reported, 'Sorry, *baas*, we ain't got no boxes.'

I was escorted back to prison. On foot! I walked in the front door! Kharon rapidly lent me the R50 needed to pay the outstanding fine Judge Boshoff had imposed during the second trial. Despite Reindeer's brave undertaking, all the sergeants present in reception had to get stuck into the books in the gigantic task of processing me through them. I was given my manuscripts. Counted. Sign here. These I clasped under my arm. No way was I going to leave them. In the cell my locker was cleaned out rapidly and, as will always happen in that type of institution and situation, my fellow prisoners, those who just happened to be around, the halt and the lame and the permanently 'off work' and the *slimmetjies* who knew every trick and feint, such as Shorty, immediately sensed that something was up and as rapidly they were there to score, to profit from whatever largesse there might be. 'You won't be taking that flask, will you now?' Or, 'How's about leaving us some snout, I say?' Dougy came along with Shorty to help carry the books. Commiseration. Solidarity. 'So they're moving you? Trust the bastards – always up to something evil!'

I shall waste no more time now, Mr Investigator. I looked round my cell in which I left most of my bric-à-brac, none of it of any importance. All that mattered was the manuscripts under my arm. If I could not take them with me I was going to refuse to leave the premises. Don Espejuelo came and crossed my palm with his, and with his lopsided smile said, 'Just remember – *un fascista es una nada, hombre.*'

I was taken to the administrative offices, smuggled in a back door there, given an outsize apricot-coloured suit and some private shoes provided by the Stores (all long-timers having to face the free world get clothes and money), and bundled into a car driven by Professor Kharon.

Kharon took me to the house where Yolande was staying with friends. She had by then been informed by a spokesman of the Department not to come to the prison that day but to wait at the house for a phone call. She knew no more than that. Not a word. The house is situated in a suburb called Newlands. At first we got lost, and when the professor eventually found it he went to see if there were any other people present before allowing me to enter. There I was, left all by myself in unfamiliar, borrowed clothes in a car on a suburban street. The thought, Mr Investigator, crossed my mind to get out there and then and make a run for it, uphill downhill, to freedom! To find a hole in the ground. I could escape! But the forces of custom held me back. Who knows what unseen *boere* were lurking behind the trees? I did, however, work up the initiative to step out of the car and stretch my legs on the sidewalk. The door in the wall surrounding the house opened and Yolande emerged. She saw me, stopped in her tracks, and asked, 'What are *you* doing *here*?' (Well, that of course was a long story.)

We were immediately taken by Professor Kharon to his house,

where we were to discuss means of leaving Cape Town. From the time we arrived there I was absent to the world. Even before that. I remember only flashes of what happened. I saw the mountain bowing low. I heard the sea cheering. We entered the house of the professor as if in a dream and I asked him if we could open the windows. (For weeks wherever I went I felt the need to open large all doors and windows.) I recollect being embarrassed, afraid nearly of the tumult of objects in the building; of being scared that I might bump my head against the unfamiliar ceilings; of instinctively lifting my feet very high. Outside the one window there grew a loquat tree, its branches darkening the roof. Yellow fruit were ripening on those branches. Small fires grow up to be big conflagrations. With the evening meal we drank a local wine, Fleur du Cap. Did I taste it? I don't know. Did I taste anything? At odd moments, yes.

The plan, their plan, became evident. I was to stay on in Cape Town, or in South Africa at least, for a decent period to create the impression in the public mind (the public mind being a creation of the media) that I was entirely free, and Yolande meanwhile was to return to France, where I would eventually join her. But she would have no part of that. Nothing at all. No, not a word. Kharon, a man of traditional and conservative Afrikaner stock, did not expect this opposition; he especially did not take kindly to it coming from a small, non-Afrikaner woman. 'Understandings' were being questioned here. Commitments to higher-ups. The poor man – after the tension of the previous days, and his own emotional investment, he must have felt thwarted. So he raised his voice the way patriarchs and prophets do. But when he raised his voice she told him that she would not be spoken to in such a fashion (had I been with it, I could have told the unfortunate man so before, heh-heh) and that he was to contact the minister and tell him that we were leaving together that Sunday. It was up to them to make the necessary arrangements. She would not wait another day. His argument that she had waited for more than seven years and surely a few days extra would make no difference was rejected with the answer that it is exactly because it has been seven and a half years that she would not wait a minute more.

(Her fears and those of some friends too, never expressed publicly, were that I would be, upon release, a walking target for some White fanatics, be they manipulated by the security hounds or not.)

From time to time Kharon went into the next room to phone, leaving us alone to discuss these matters and options of momentous import and then she would shake me to try to convince me that I too could now make decisions and stand up and participate. Alas, all to no avail, Mr Investigator. For too long have I been in no condition or position to decide for myself about anything pertaining to my life.

Many phone calls were made. (The next days would be strung together by phone calls.) The lady imposed her will. (My inclination, informed by a deeply imprinted fatalism and fear and superstition would probably have been – don't letsh rock ze boath.) We returned that same evening to the house of Yolande's friends where we spent the night and went through a hilarious version of the old-fashioned bedroom farce. I did not yet exist officially. I was still in prison. Nobody was to know. We had to keep up appearances. The girl working in the house, who got to know Yolande quite well, was not to find a man in her bedroom the next morning. She knew that Yolande's husband was where so many Brown husbands habitually went, and what a shame and a shock it would have been to find the lady comforting herself with another presence. If, on the other hand, she recognized Yolande's husband – well, that would have meant having an escapee on their hands! And then? So I had to tiptoe about, and kept being shooed away.

Morning came.The glory, sir, of sitting in a big garden under a huge tree and the even huger sun. Birds fluttering. Blue dome. Soft morning sounds. I borrowed the host's clothes. Wrote a note or two to particular friends whom I couldn't see from fear of compromising them. A girlfriend of the lady's came to say goodbye to her and I had to run upstairs and hide in the room of the son of the house. A boy's kingdom. Model aeroplanes. Stones. Scientific experiments. Books. Comics.

It had been agreed that I'd be allowed to go and say goodbye to my father in his hospital in Grahamstown (it was the one favour I insisted upon) but Hoang Lien was not permitted to travel in the country with me. She was to fly to Johannesburg and wait for me there.

It was now Friday, the 3rd. This is how it happened. We separated. A police captain came to Kharon's house, walked in, bared a shiny set of dentures in what he must have wanted to have pass for a friendly smile, clicked his heels, bowed, presented a hand and immediately pointed out that he's not from the Security Branch. We drove into Cape Town. All by myself I had to go into a pharmacy to have photos taken for a passport. I had been given money to pay for these, and dropped most of it on the pavement in my clumsiness at handling such unfamiliar things. My fingers could not yet read coins. A Brown vendor on the corner was singing the praises of his fruit and immediately incorporated a friendly warning to me in his sing-song. No need to throw it away, he sang.

We had lunch at Kharon's and that same afternoon we left Cape Town in his son's Alfa Romeo. This was the start of the death journey. I was a mummy sitting there looking at the horrendously beautiful country rushing at us. The road going along the south-east coast crosses the mountains enclosing False Bay; from up there I looked back on the Cape smoking in the distance, Stellenbosch a little deeper inland, Somerset-West and the Strand strung along the ocean. I was seeing everything for the first time. I was seeing everything for the last time.

The road branches away to the interior before you reach the hills around Hermanus. There my mother lay in her grave, close to the come-and-go movement of the waves, her hands folded, looking with an eternity eye at the blue haze. She would have laughed with joy until the tears came to her cheeks. She was living for this day too.

Kharon talked and talked. We stopped to buy dried fruit. In Swellendam we stopped to fill up with petrol. Every time we stopped he would go off to make a phone call. Our progress had to be followed hour by hour. I wandered around, waiting for him. Through a window giving onto the street I saw an old man still employed at making harnesses for horses, working with awl and gut. Poplar trees and green canyons. My parents' people traditionally lived in this region. No one left. Not a word, no. Must be cemeteries for horses up there.

We drove by Heidelberg and then Riversdale where Oubaas had had a farm when I was small. We stopped in the town. I had spent part of my school years in Riversdale. We went into a bar for a quick drink and were accosted by a drunken client draped over his chin, and informed us that he was a warrant-officer in him or else fight him right now on the sawdust in that corner. Friday night blues. He lisped, tried to stop the ss-es from dribbling over his chin, and informed us that he was a warrant–officer in the Prisons Service. I didn't know whether to laugh or to run, Mr Investigator. He would not recognize me, I knew, because he would never expect to see me there (one only recognizes that which you expect to recognize), but if he did, surely he would pull out his pistol and shoot both my knees off immediately.

On and on we drove. In the town of George, electoral seat of the Prime Minister himself, we dined. We asked our way to the nearest eating place from two brazen teenage tarts. Maybe young country whores. Dark place. Bad food. Bad service. Bad wine. Kharon went to phone. A moon flowered above the horizon. The full one of a few nights ago. A lifetime. How come I'm still up at this hour? The night sergeant has long since switched off the lights. Wonder what people are doing – Moineau, Piet, Oldface, Dougie, Pimples, Stinkfoot, Pa, Skommel, Nefesj, Jakes, Ampie, Ghana, Goodbye Charlie. . . . Sea somewhere on our right. Moon must have eaten butter. Yellow orb. Warrior, its body rubbed smooth and shiny with butter, rotting, but as cheeky as ever. In dark glass bowls and scales starfruit are put out, kind with kind. Come judgement day and the mango will be separated from the pear and from the fig. Blood yellow. The land, primordial, ancient, unchanging, shifting by. In the distant hills must be the blown away graves of captains and of shepherds. Stars sucking up a thin light. Men leading men must have shouted at the sun here. Land singing nakedness.

We spent the night in a hotel at the top end of the main street of Humansdorp. If you were drunk, you could wend your way from hotel to hotel down the hill to its foot, where the sea was a distant rumble and slosh. Tired now. Kharon went to make a call. Also went to ask(?) something at the blue-lamped police station. (I believe he had a special dispensation from the minister to drive as fast as he wanted to.) We shared a room. I still had on my jail underpants. (I walked by waters of unrest, in unfamiliar hotel rooms I lay me down.)

Then it was 4 December. Up and away early. It's the early worm that catches the bird. We left for Port Elizabeth. Imperceptibly the land changed. The moon was blue and the country singing a lonely barrenness. We crossed dry riverbeds. Along here the land is so poor that it will eventually be ceded to the Blacks. We passed by the intriguing nameplates delimiting the emptiness. *Gamtoos* (an ancient Khoi word); *Mondplaas* ('Mouth Place' or 'Mouth Farm'); *Voorstekop* ('First Head' or 'First Hill' perhaps) belonging to a farmer called Emile van Papendorp.

From Port Elizabeth I called my sister in Grahamstown – just like that, out of the blue, I too could use the telephone! – to warn her that I was on my way. In the booth reading the instructions on how to telephone, in both languages. (Quiet! Quiet now, my heart!) And ssshh. And to ask her to have our father brought to her house for the meeting. I could not show my face in public. I was not released yet. No, not a word.

Then we waited in front of a bottle store for nine o'clock, for official opening time. In fact, we walked in just before nine but the Indian owner lifted admonishing eyes to the clock on the wall. In South Africa we all respect the law. *The law is.* I wanted to take at least one bottle of good wine to celebrate with my father the return of a lost son from the land of swines, to pour a small libation for the gods. It was already hot, man! In Port Elizabeth there are crumbling houses. Some have Chinese characters traced on the façades. I saw a centre for martial arts. Years ago, in the dim past when I was involved in the activities of Atlas and Okhela, we had a code name for South Africa/No Man's Land/ Azania: we referred to it as 'Elizabeth'. Do you want to hear more, Investigator? (You old voyeur, you.) Stay with me. Stay with me till the end.

On the pavement before the shop a Black Father Christmas sat steaming already in the early morning heat. He had on a red woollen suit. Hot, man! He had pulled down below his chin the white cotton-beard attached by an elastic band around his ears. I could not help but go up to him to touch my own white-tipped one, and say: 'Ah, but I have a *real* one.' At which he responded by: 'Ja, good morning, *baas*', and promptly put his own back in place again.

We arrived in Grahamstown. We looked for and found Rachel's

house. Kharon diplomatically went off to phone from somewhere in town, leaving me time, that first time, that time which cannot be wrought in words, leaving me time to enter and to see my father. He was sitting in the living room wrapped in a blanket and his eyes were very alive and black and fully aware. His paralysed hand was hidden under the blanket. With the other one, the left one, he grasped me. There was still strength left in that arm. But I could see the praying-mantis thinness of the limbs, the stillness, the low flame quivering now over the ashes. His mouth was soft. And he wept unashamedly. He tried to talk to me. He mumbled pain and happiness. My sister explained that he had not been able to pronounce any word at all up till then, but now he spoke my name and even a few more syllables. He said, '*Klaar*!' (It is *finished* now, it is *past*.) And then he clicked his tongue in frustration at not being able to continue. His eyes never left my face. His eyes are there forever. I live with my face lifted to his eyes. Every once in a while he would say, '*Magtag*.' (It means 'damn'; it could also mean 'powerful'.)

Rachel had asked André Brink, to help bring Oubaas to her house (asking a male nurse might have raised suspicion). And he had deduced quite correctly that I was coming.* He now walked in and announced that it had been arranged that we should all have lunch at his place. There was a slip-up there. I had only three hours left to see my father. I was selfish. But I could understand that my sister was overtaken by the events. Kharon walked in too, and the two professors – they are not quite bosom-friends – circled one another with bristling neck hairs. And so we all went up the hill to fetch a pail of water, to Brink's baronial mock-Moorish mansion overlooking the domain of Grahamstown. Yes, Mr Investigator. Now, for the first time in my life, and surely the last time too, I had the privilege of carrying the old one in my arms from the car up to the house. This big sunburnt man with the dark hair striding across the fields of my mind – how light he had become! How small had he shrunk!

*Quite by chance a newspaper which had asked for my release six months earlier chose this day to contact the Prison Department, to follow up on their request, to ask if any decision had been made. The Prisons spokesman went into stasis – when in doubt bury thy head – and requested the reporter to call back later. The newsman, suspicions now thoroughly roused, called Brink to ask whether he, perhaps via the family, had picked up a scent somewhere.

We lunched and we swam in the lord's swimming pool. My sister cut up my father's meat into edible pieces. My father was ill at ease. He was ashamed at being out in his pyjamas. When one has lost so much one doesn't want others to see. He had no choice. The wine was good. The food was good too. The two professors circled one another warily. It was time to fly. It is always the time to go. Time, gentlemen. Not a word. We left. No, not a word.

Kharon drove me back to Port Elizabeth from where I was to catch the connecting flight to Johannesburg. I had a final request: to take just one dip in the sea. We stopped off at a beach outside the city. Kharon had an extra bathing costume in his car. Look, that's me running into the waves there. Look, it is a green wave with white foam, and there's another and another. See how the years are of no consequence. See how carefree (because over the edge, nonexistent) that me is when touching and smelling the ocean, how integrated in time. Look at the little stones in the sand. Now I am human. That is what the garden is all about: the stone which is not there. That is why a poem is about words.

I found that we were inadvertently swimming in a part of the ocean reserved for Blacks only; emerging from the waves I was surrounded by small Black children who saw nothing wrong with this Whitey being in the water with them. Ignorant little bastards – haven't they learned about Apartheid yet? I was still damp in my clothes when we arrived at the airport.

There I had a tug-of-war with the security personnel, who wanted to take away my briefcase of manuscripts. *They* were looking for bombs and *I* was hanging on to the fragmentary scenario of my identities. The lone and rather ridiculously exposed controller/observer sitting behind his newspaper in the middle of the departure hall looked on from a distance. I said goodbye to the good Professor Kharon, who was utterly exhausted by then and who probably still had to go and make a phone call. I left. The plane banked over the glistening land, rose until it became small, and flew through the vast halls of arms of cloud castles to Johannesburg.

At the foot of the passageway I was approached by a modishly dressed young fellow with longish hair. The pistol in his waistband was making an obnoxious bulge. The slightly older obligatory partner was hanging back in the crowd there, his glance flitting from face to face. The youngster introduced himself as being from the Prison Department, delegated as a measure of courtesy to render any assistance I might need. Will you hide your mirth, Investigator? Don't be a fool! Sure, I know – I'd just spent more than seven years in the inner chambers of the Other World, I was raised by hand you may say – and never could a prison-*boer* be that suave, never would he be allowed to wear his hair that long. But that didn't matter. We shall play hide-and-seek till the skies cave in.

He escorted me through the little-known byways of Jan Smuts Airport with Partner dutifully bringing up the rear. If I had had any Gauloises I would've offered him one, for old times' sake, but I had given up smoking too. I told him about the queries from the newspaper to Brink. He frowned.

He led me out to where a middle-aged gentleman was waiting in an unmarked car parked unobtrusively some distance away from the exit. I was introduced to Major Somename, also from the Prison Department, yes. But when his young subordinate related to him the story of the bungled stall leading to awakened interest from the press, he exploded, saying, 'The Prison Department never told *us* anything about this!' He took me to the house where Yolande was waiting. (These secret cars cruise so nicely!) As we arrived he remarked upon a vehicle parked nearby. 'Funny, that wasn't there just now. . . .'

We went in. He met Yolande and her friend, the gentle and shy Ukwezi. He sniffed around a bit – you can't teach the tricks of an old dog – and then left us alone.

Time was of no more importance. Everything was dying, everything reborn. What was left of the previous night's moon now swam like a shimmering dolphin in the pool. I joined it. We fried meat outside. Tang of smoke in eyes. A festive tablecloth. The food was good, the wine was better. It was deep and red. I started to taste things. No, no word. Here the heart is getting thin.

The telephone rang and Major Somename asked if he could come by. He just happened still to be working. An old horse, you know, what? He sniffed around some more. No, he wouldn't eat anything, thank you. Well, just one glass then, if you insist. Never do it on duty, you know. He needed a photo for my application for a French visa (which was going to be granted that night). And wondered whether I minded very much just signing this statement. It was a typed page saying that I'd been released and that I was leaving the country of my own free will. That I held no grudges against the South African government. Give – I'll sign. Give more! I'll sign anything. I signed.

He also said that the Prison Department was now going to confirm that I'd been freed, but they would say that we had gone on the Saturday night flight. He left. We laughed. The phone rang again: an excited journalist informed Ukwezi that I was out of prison and that we were already winging our way to Europe. We laughed some more. Then we slept. The moon stood guard above the dark pool and the trees and the house. Here the heart is getting thin.

Then it was Sunday, 5 December. This is how it happened. Yolande packed the bags. Ukwezi in the background, smiling. Unexpectedly John Brand turned up for breakfast. (But it seems that Yolande had called him.) Stupefaction. What a beautiful day. The doorbell went. Major Somename. He was to take us to the airport. Gave me a passport with a valid visa inside. They were actually going to facilitate our going!

Little traffic on the road to Jan Smuts. Major Somename talking about the weather, and had we noticed how expensive eggs had become? Ukwezi and John Brand following in another car. Airport. Someone from the French embassy to take charge of us. Major Somename solemnly saying goodbye now. Must be off, he says. Huntingdon had said, years ago, smiling sarcastically, that he'd still be taking me to the airport one day. Maybe he was there. Maybe I just didn't see him. I didn't look. *Chef d'escale* of UTA there. Very friendly. No trouble weigh-in, check in. Ukwezi with Sunday papers. Announcing my release. Must be something in that. John Brand very tense. Monsieur Plaisant the ambassador, with book. I sign. I have to scratch through. I cannot spell simple words.

This is the true story of what happened. Embrace Ukwezi. Embrace John Brand. Now the heart is going thin. Monsieur Plaisant's wife is suspicious because he left the residence so early on a mysterious mission. In the distance, trying to merge with the background, Major Somename. Looking away embarrassed when I wave to him. Through customs. No one looking for Galaska. *Cheb d'escale* UTA downstairs opening bottle champagne. Other employees coming by murmuring encouragement, good show. Everybody already in the aeroplane. Go up steps. Beautiful summer's morning. Now the heart.

Take-off. High in air above land. More champagne offered discreetly. Compliments of personnel. Africa underneath, slipping away, my love. Confusion when food tray arrives: can't remember how to use knife, fork, in what order dishes. Use spoon only, so long. So long. Not a word, no. Africa going. Yolande, Lady One Hoang Lien's hand in mine. Then she flakes out. To sleep the sleep of the very,very tired. I plug in the earphones. Handel: *Concerto pour orgue en Fa Majeur; 'Le coucou et le rossignol.'* We are to arrive at Roissy–Charles de Gaulle at 21.40. It will be raining. It is done. . . .

Pretoria/Pollsmoor/Palermo/Paris, 29 December 1983

Notes

1

A Note on the True Confessions of an Albino Terrorist

Die woord is 'n engte. The word is a narrow; a slip of land between two dark oceans; a tongue. The word is also a confinement. Yet it is the only way that I know, the only space. I realize now that the preceding document is in itself for me an interstice of freedom.

I had to write it. I had to purge myself, and this I had to do before memory itself becomes obscured by the distortion of time. If I say 'purge' it may imply that there are events – that I myself have done things – which are improper, which I ought to be ashamed of. It is true: I am not a hero; I am not even a revolutionary. In retrospect I should have done this or that – with support, in a slightly different context, if I were better prepared, if I were less naïve, I would have done so maybe. It does not matter now. I don't believe in trying to change the past, except to the extent that a forever changing future continually throws another light on that past. Mutation continues. What will I do next time . . . ? But I tried also not to paint myself prettier than I am.

Even without the aspect of personal appraisal (is it provoked by pride?) there is the filth – the degradation of human relationships imposed on one within the interrogator–detainee or warder–prisoner context – that one has to get rid of if one wants to go on living. As for myself – I feel that there are areas that will never be alive in me again, but I had to digest and transform that period of alienation before I could turn my back and go on to what is unfolding. Life is good. Survival is also a choice. It is important to walk on.

I had to write it. That is, I dictated it. The document itself took shape from the obsessive urge I experienced during the first weeks and months of my release to talk talk talk, to tell my story and all the other stories. It must have been rather horrible for him or her who happened to be victim to my vomiting. So I was advised to talk it into a tape. This procedure defined the inner structure and tone of the book. Inevitably it then also became the story of doing a book. More – it had to become the reflection of a search for what really happened, and for the identity of the narrator. It is by walking that you learn to walk. It is by being, which invokes questioning, that you discover *being*.

My wife typed the tapes. I used her transcripts as 'rough copy'. These I would blacken, add to, delete from, change about – and she would retype a clean version for me to go over again if needed. Therefore I was in the first instance, in all intimacy, talking to her; telling her all which I'd had to hold back over the years. Without her it could not have been done.

My account of what happened is neither objective nor complete. I consciously left out much that I knew about, or now know about; all the outside moves and happenings. Others will have to complete the story if they feel called upon to do so. I don't think there is any total objectivity ever. There must be however, I believe and I try, a constant attempt at remaining fully aware under all circumstances, which again means that there are choices to be made and responsibility to be taken for the awareness and for the choices. I have attempted as closely as possible to describe only that which I experienced or saw. Some of it will be considered hearsay by a court of law. But a prisoner is not a scholar. We are all subject to the fantasies of our world which is – consciously – being deprived of the checks and balances of an open environment. Yet I tried always to remain clear and to penetrate to a feeling for truth in what I heard and learnt from others. (When you are forced to live forever on the *qui-vive* you develop an instinctive appreciation, a gut evaluation, of those you meet.)

There may well be mistakes in the text – minor ones of names and dates. Some that may look like mistakes I have put in on purpose: those concerned will understand. And some 'errors' may still provoke revealing reactions.

In some instances I have used the real names of the people involved, mainly because it would have served no purpose to camouflage them. In many other cases I have modified or replaced the names – but behind every name there's a real person, and you may rest assured that the people concerned will recognize themselves. In one case only did I split one person by making two 'personages' of him. It was a natural thing to do. And I have not 'invented' or transposed any event. It will be clear to the reader that I often emit opinions or allow myself judgements. These are my own.

It was not my intention to take revenge on a system or on certain people – at least, I don't think it was. We are too closely linked for that. In the same way that the ideology of Apartheid is only an aberration – a stillness – of what is potentially present in all of mankind, the butchers and the interrogators are not monsters but people like you and me. That is what makes them so horrible and so pitiful. And that is exactly why we must continue condemning and combating their acts. I believe that the torturer is as depraved by his acts as the one who is tortured. We will be fools and mere objects of history if we go looking for the causes of depravity in 'human nature' only. We make society and society makes us, all of us. But there are certain fabrics once torn that cannot be mended again; certain transgressions that can never be condoned.

It was my intention to produce a political text – if it turned out to be more 'literary' than expected it can only be because I couldn't help it. It is the lability of the job, it is the seductiveness and the *life* of the word. But the two approaches are not all that far apart.

When you are interested in prison accounts as a genre you will soon see that prisons are pretty much the same the world over. It is rather the peculiar relationship of power-repression which seems immutable, wherever you may hide. And when you scratch a little bit you will see that our century is stained by large scale and institutionalized acts and even policies of brutality in growing areas of the world. The tolerance is less; totalitarianism is on the increase. Never before has it become so all-important for all of us – especially for the most 'ordinary' citizen – to struggle with all the inventiveness at our disposal against the dehumanization of man. The least all of us can do – the marginal ones, the outcasts, the displaced persons, the immigrant workers, citizens of our various countries – is unite to expose *all* the intelligence services and the spy organs and the security or political police and the secret societies of the world. Pipe dream! So much for universality. Still, if what I had to describe is of any documentary value it can only be because I tried, as a White African who has had the privilege to enter into a world known only too well by the majority of South Africans, to paint as *fully* as *possible* my view of *that* society as it exists *now*.

I want to dedicate this book not to Mr Investigator, but to the multitude of detainees and tortured ones and prisoners in the land of my birth, and not only to the 'politicals' but also to the 'common criminals'; and with a kind thought to some of the poor bastards who lead their twisted lives defiling mankind by extorting and oppressing and punishing and ruling in the name of 'security'.

2

A Note on the Relationship between Detainee and Interrogator

The detainee and the interrogator both know that there is, obscurely, a measure of ritual involved in their relationship, a ritual as old as the history of human intercourse. Perhaps because in a specific kind of power set-up people will go through the moves in very similar ways. There are predictable reactions to objective conditions. The needs and the gestures and the effects of the relationship seem to be permanent: There is the struggle for domination – to have the other do what you want him to do (for the relationship seem to be permanent: there is the struggle for job); there is the effort to destroy – because the opposing forces are irreconcilable, or because there is the pathological human curiosity for killing, for altering permanently, or just 'to see', or because the dismantlement has revealed *vis-à-vis*, a brother-I, a mirror-image or only a miserable human-conditioned pile of flesh and faeces which is unbearable and needs to be done away with; there is thus already the tendency to identify with the other (and the roles can be inverted) and the blind desire to force a solution to and a resolution of the irreducible contradictions – precisely because you cannot accept the (self)-image revealed to you, nor the knowledge that never the twain shall meet.

And yet this twilight zone of jerking or being jerked according to the specifications of preordained roles, this macabre dance, this fatal game (because there are certainly elements of a game present) should not obscure the fact that the situation and the steps and the rules are always personalized and localized and in no way can the players be exonerated from their responsibilities. Knowing that human congress has always been sullied by this destructive and self-destructive *face-à-face* does not take away from the horror of it.

It must be repeated that the phenomenon is not indigenous to certain countries or cultures or political systems only. Africa knows it, you will encounter it in Chile and Vietnam and Italy and Russia and in Northern Ireland: wherever there are political dissidents and 'terrorists'. The process – employed in the name of 'security' – which involves the mutual destruction of human dignity, seems to be an integral part of most police and specialized agency methods. The really powerful reject these gutter ethics with their lips only: compromises and corruption have led to *de facto* condonation. It is as if they wish to say, 'what right have *you* to appeal for purity when *we* have been obliged to dirty our hands! Life is not a rose!' It would seem furthermore that there is no religion or structure of public mores strong enough to eradicate, or even to contain, the custom. Its virulence has nothing to do with backwardness and with ignorance; more advanced technologies have merely brought a greater sophistication to the methods employed.

The interrogator will be someone who looks and behaves as if *normal*. He will lead an unremarkable family life. If he is a doctor or a psychologist he will probably also have a mundane practice to look after. He will be Mister Everyman. These people are not monsters: they have no reason to feel ill at ease in society; on the contrary, they know that they are tolerated and accepted by the powerful. They may even fondly believe that they are implicitly supported by the so-called silent majority. They will at most consider theirs to be 'a necessary if dirty job'. They have to *simulate* their normality obviously. What happens in bare rooms where all time has been twisted is not just dirty work – it is the heart-rending flowering of evil which will profoundly modify all the actors.

This much you, the detainee, will *know* in advance: that the interrogator disposes of a panoply of powers, which include the 'right' and the willingness to kill you (it is signalled clearly: not for nothing have well over seventy South African people over the last decade been done to death in cells by the security forces); the 'right' and the desire to maim you, because you must be destroyed; the 'right' to manipulate and to circumscribe your environment – physical or moral – in terms of food, space, isolation from and contact with the world, family pressure, privileges offered or withdrawn; the 'right' to mould time because he regulates it, he plays with it, he has an unlimited amount at his disposal. The interrogator's power is absolute and having the detainee know it is his most efficacious weapon, but ultimately it rots him utterly.

The prisoner will inevitably end up confessing. There can be no doubt about that. His only leeway can be to hold out, desperately, for time. He may have to decide *when* to safely let go, about how long he can hold out, how many false confessions he can make before cracking, how to remain *conscious* (if not sane) in the coils of his inventions and his lies and his hallucinations. He will be raped. His problem is to realize it, to handle it, and to know that it is the humanity he shares with the aggressor that is being raped. He must also realize that the damage done is permanent.

The self-disgust of the prisoner comes from the alienation he has been brought to. That in which he participated (because the mortification lies in that he is forced to participate in his own undoing) will play havoc with his conception of himself and it will forever modulate his contact with other people. He will have the leftover knowledge that he has been used as a tool, that he was coldly and expertly manipulated, that he was confronted with his own weakness. Worse, far worse, that he ended up looking upon his tormentor as a confessor, as a friend even. This development is so profoundly unnatural that it makes him sick of himself.

The two of you, violator and victim (collaborator! violin!), are linked forever perhaps, by the obscenity of what has been revealed to you, by the sad knowledge of what people are capable of. We are all guilty.

The deception flowing from this realization is destructive to the extent that one is a prisoner of one's own illusions about human conduct. To reduce a person to a weakness of babbling, to confuse him in private and to parade his humiliation publicly, constitute a sickening spectacle which affects the whole society. It is an abasement which cannot be undone again. Humans are fragile. It is not difficult to bring out the worst in man. Respect and dignity are also matters of make-believe. We need to maintain the illusions if we intend to cohabit in a civilized way.

The horror is that this mobid relationship makes no sense, it can finally have no purpose beyond that of being a catharsis for the interrogator. You can never destroy the image because you cannot efface consciousness.

With the struggle for some freedom intensifying as it is bound to, there is not the slightest chance that those in power politically will want to lay down guidelines to guarantee the dignity of the detainee and the interrogator and thus to sanitize public life. It is not sure that they could call off their dogs even if they wanted to. And they don't want to. It is therefore incumbent upon all of us who are concerned to provoke a public exposition and debate of the issues, and to arrive at a code of conduct to be adhered to when faced by the police and the secret agents. It will be another way of strengthening the political and class consciousness we still lack. A mistake which is often made by our South African militants is to assume that we are cleverer than the police, that we can out-manoeuvre the 'hairybacks' and the 'rock spiders'. that we don't need to report fully on *any* and *all* contacts we may have had with the masters. Our weakness has always been (apart from the infiltrators among us) the arrogance which makes us blind to the fanatic commitment and the determination and the intelligence of the minority in power and of their executants.

3

A Note on South African Prisons

Any society – so Winston Churchill declared on occasion – can be measured by its attitude to its prisoners.

At the risk of emitting a series of platitudes and pious wishes I'd still like to make the following simple remarks.

Prisons only serve to create prisoners. If society views prisoners as its outcasts, its anti-social elements, then they will indeed become and remain that. Penal reform, the treatment of prisoners – these are not the problems of specialists but of concern to everybody. The solution to crime is one of social consciousness to be solved by the whole of society.

In South Africa the prime motivation when dealing with those found guilty in terms of laws promulgated often for the protection of sectional or class or ethnic interests, is the notion of punishment. It moves from the premise that you can educate or rehabilitate a person by punishing him. You don't. You may break him: you strengthen the reasons that brought him to the predicament he is in. A fellow prisoner, Kenny van Niekerk, once said, 'Whereas no man should break the law, the law must not break man either.'

There are obviously people who are, knowingly and willingly or not, dangerous to society. No judge should be allowed to decide about their fate all by himself. And when such a person is removed from the company of his fellows there is no reason why he cannot be kept in a humane fashion in decent surroundings. The individual life, as an expression of the whole of which we are all part, must be inviolate. When the State executes someone (murders him in a reflex of barbaric revenge) it is a destruction of freedom; it is a negation of the dignity of man, any man; it is also an admission of its own incapacity to improve the social environment.

Who are the people ending up in South African prisons? From

my observation the first remark must be that many of them ought never to have been there at all. (To show you how repressive the South African legal system is: from a population of not yet 30 million there are on a daily average more than 110,000 people in the gaols without counting the detainees, those awaiting trial, those in reformatory institutions, those who have been 'endorsed out' or dumped in distant rural camps, those in work colonies.) The laws governing Apartheid – the pass-laws for instance – based on purely racial criteria, account for a large percentage of prisoners. (They are however not regarded as 'politicals'.) There are many who must be described as socially feeble – the old bums, the vagrants, the weak-minded. There are many for whom the basic problem is alcoholism. But all seem to suffer to a certain degree from social disfunction and maladaptation, or from an immature or impaired sense of reality. The attitudes of irresponsibility and selfishness, the need for affection – these may well be the end results of an insufficient preparation for adult life, or weak or broken or hostile family ties. The individual functions badly and aggressively with reference to his social unit, but the 'fault' is not necessarily his or his only, and the way to a solution must in any event be found by all involved.

What is that world like? It is one of repression and of baseness where the lowest instincts prevail; it is a world of humiliation and whore's values; it is a world where the harshest forms and expressions of racism are institutionalized; it is a world with its own culture – language, customs, laws, myths, structures; it is a world of promiscuity, of closeness in fetid cells, of living in the clothes and the beds of others, of greyness, of losing all sense and appreciation of beauty until only sentimentality is left; and it is also a world of fancy where you will encounter the generosity of make-believe – people extending to one another the courtesy of accepting their lives as invented – and never any trust or confidence. It is the incarnation of split perceptions.

South African prisons are overcrowded. There are people who for petty crimes end up doing long sentences with hardly a comma or a semi-colon from time to time. They exist only in terms of the prison world – outside that they would be nobodies. Cheek by jowl with them you find the youngsters coming in for the first time. The effects of isolation from everyday life, of marginalization, are intensified. It is not that prisoners are particularly antisocial, but that they are obliged to constitute a social grouping of their own, another society because of the prevailing inclination of the larger community to hide its problems behind walls, because of the separateness of prison life, the distillation and the concentration of the weaker elements. The confused ones, those who feel rejected by the 'normal' world, are confirmed in their alternative way of life. The weak become weaker. No wonder then that recidivism should be so rampant.

It is said that we inherited our archaic legal notions from the British. Certainly our administrative practices, and to some extent the ideology informing these, are a legacy from our colonialist past. (The local contribution can be seen as a cruel Calvinist and racist twist to these notions.) It is unrealistic to even dream of doing away with the stays of incarceration corseting the South African nation. But it is all-important to keep on pleading for the realization that solutions can only be found along the way of communal responsibility, once we move away from the atavistic attitudes of punishment and of revenge, once we move away from the alienating concept of leaving prison matters in the hands of the penologists and the criminologists, once we move away from the totalitarian stance that the State (or the Party) will judge and decide and regulate.

At the moment incarceration still means breaking the fragile ties the prisoner may have had with his family and with society at large. Everything must be done to reinsert the prisoner, to help him readapt to the outside community. Those having the care of prisoners should go out of their way to *multiply* and to *diversify* the contacts with the outside world, in an atmosphere of mutual respect. Training programmes should be pushed much further and should involve outside experts. Why can prisoners not go through the regular apprenticeship periods outside, under supervision (as would be normal) of craftsmen and tradesmen and trade unionists? Everything must be done to involve 'outside' agencies and concerns in the attempt to find a collective solution to the problems of 'crime' – without necessarily making everyone a warder. The prisoner needs to know that he is doing something useful, with initiative and responsibility. He must be paid a decent wage for the work he will be doing and he must be given the normal (but so important) right to put that money at the disposal of his outside dependants.

Inside you will often hear the reflection that only a prisoner can rehabilitate himself. Well-meaning psychologists, sociologists or social workers cannot do so. The key, to my mind, is not obedience and acceptance, but a critical awareness and social responsibility. Everything ought to be done to help awaken, strengthen and reward initiative, responsibility and maturity. There is no reason finally why inmates cannot run their own affairs and their own institutions. The prisoner needs to feel that he has a grip on his own fate. A nefarious side effect of living in a totalitarian structure is that you become lazy, apathetic, content with the commonplace. A conscious effort must be made to go against the grain. Why not allow outside teachers to come and direct classes in prison? Why not allow publishing houses to donate their works to prison libraries? Involve them! Why not permit prisoners to take care of one another – to share whatever expertise they may have – through discussion groups and classes? Why not allow them to establish a trade union, involving also ex-prisoners outside? It could be named SAPU: South African Prisoners Union, later to be abbreviated to APU only!

4

A Note about Torture in South African Cells and Interrogation Rooms

By now it is sadly no longer necessary to prove that torture is practised by South Africa's police and security agents. There have been too many deaths they could not camouflage, or did not want to hide. Regularly, during security or political trials, there will be 'a trial within the trial', usually held *in camera*, when the presiding judge or magistrate has to consider allegations of torture raised by the accused. Enough affidavits have been made and testified to by those who survived. Ever more often too there are examples of the police authorities settling out of court the claims of criminal law detainees who had been assaulted or tortured by their agents. (The police are unhappy with such procedures: money the State has to pay out in this way will then be recuperated by deduction from their salaries.)

The methods employed (they have been described repeatedly) will be anything from sheer brutality and bestiality – hitting with fists and batons and anything that will concuss but not burst the skin, kicking, stomping, burning with cigarettes, pushing down stairs or out of windows – to the more 'refined' ones employed elsewhere in the world, too – strangulation by putting a wet sack or a plastic bag over the subject's head, holding the subject's head under water until he drowns or loses consciousness (the 'submarine'), beating the subject while he is being twirled hanging handcuffed from a stick in the fold of his elbows or his knees (the 'aeroplane ride'), beating the soles of his feet with batons and with canes, applying repeated electric shocks by electrodes attached to the subject's extremities or his sexual parts or his nipples ('telephoning' or 'playing radio') – to the more patient and slower forms – depriving him of sleep and/or other physical relief, having him stand in a certain posture for hours on end, having him squat on his haunches or sit with legs outstretched for days and nights. To this must be added the various forms of mental coercion – isolation, calculated confusion, false confessions, etc. Even more horrifying are reports filtering down from 'the border' (Namibia, Angola, and other neighbouring countries subject to incursions from the South African Defence Force) of Military Intelligence interrogators, aided by medics, using drugs or in some cases the withholding of painkillers from the wounded, to 'break' their captives.

A few remarks need to be made:

(1) Brutality, police assault, torture – these methods are much more widely and freely used than we ever thought. Time and again I have met prisoners who were beaten, shocked, half-smothered, half-drowned – sometimes in a nearly off-hand fashion, sometimes because the police wanted specific information quickly. According to my informants this is standard procedure with the Murder and Robbery Squads, particularly those of Brixton in Johannesburg and Woodstock and Athlone in the Cape. Some of these prisoners could show the physical marks and scars on their bodies. Many of them seem fatalistically to accept this as 'a risk of the job'. To give you an example of the casual horror: F., an ex-sergeant in the South African Police, now a prisoner, told me of how he assisted one Sunday afternoon at the torturing of a Black detainee. Not because they wanted information from him, but because the men on duty were bored, because they wanted some amusement, maybe also because the *kaffir* had to be kept in his place. They had the prisoner undress completely; they then emptied his cell of everything except a blanket; the cell was hosed down, the blanket soaked in water too. The naked prisoner was then locked in the wet cell and the blanket, through the bars of the door, connected to an electric current. The fun was to see the man trying to climb up the electrified walls.

(2) There is nothing – no ethics, no moral or religious code – restraining the political or criminal police in their absolute power to do with and to the detainees what they want. These attitudes and actions are tolerated in the never-contested climate of racism where to be a Black or Brown or Indian

prisoner in the hands of a White (or subordinate Black or Brown or Indian) policeman means quite simply that your humanity is reduced to exploitable weakness. These attitudes and actions are exacerbated by a siege mentality having to oppose a 'total response' to what they paint (and at least some of the painters must know that the picture is false) as a 'total onslaught' against South Africa. They furthermore justify these actions in terms of a crusade against communism, Marxism, nihilism, atheism, permissiveness, liberalism, immorality and pornography. The higher-ups in fact cover up for this policy by their feigned ignorance. The only impediment the torturers do have – and they are unhappy about that – is the bother of red tape in the case of death. F. explained to me that it is better not to be in an office where someone is put to death: it means having to write out statements in triplicate, and probably answering questions. A waste of time.

(3) Revealing the assaults and the torturing has not inhibited those involved. Public inquests cause some discomfort. The actors may be photographed with their short hair, their dark glasses and their tight smiles. They may be transferred to another area. (That is the risk you run when you're stupid enough to be caught at it.) They continue their careers; are often promoted. (Not so in the Prison Department – in Pollsmoor I knew an officer whose promotion had been held back, or so he believed, because he had been involved in the killing of a prisoner.) Magistrates do not allocate blame to the torturers when they preside over an inquest. How could they? Whom should they believe? Dead men don't talk, and survivors – being 'terrorists' – are *ipso facto* 'unreliable witnesses'. Magistrates normally conclude that death must be ascribed to this or to that accident for which nobody can reasonably be held responsible. No outcry has yet succeeded in inflecting the basic thrust of the repressive interrogation system which is to maintain a calculated atmosphere of terror

(4) Not only are these acts not disavowed in practice – the 'anti-terrorist strategists' *want* their opponents to know that, when captured, they will be brutalized. The clearly signalled intention is itself part of the strategy. They believe that it is a simple matter of 'them or us', and, cynically, that the ends justify the

means. They also believe that foreign rulers and investors, despite hypocritical sounds of disapproval of necessity made from time to time, do in reality understand their politics.

(5) Torture is spreading in South Africa. Security forces in the supposedly independent Bantustans have been taught well by their masters. The same methods are now part of the arsenal of police and army units in the Transkei and particuarly the Ciskei – and are used there with enthusiastic abandon.

(6) The only forces which could oblige the South African torturers to scale down their actions to within 'defendable limits' would be the 'sympathetic' foreign powers: the United States, Britain, West Germany, Canada perhaps, France maybe. No pressure in that direction could reasonably be expected from South Africa's allies – Taiwan, Israel, some Latin American countries.

5

A Position on the Struggle for the *Taal* (being Afrikaans)

Afrikaans is a Creole language. (For this contention I'll be eaten alive by Afrikaans linguists and historians.) It evolved in very much the same way or conditions that other Creole languages came about (such as the French spoken in the West Indies or in the Indian ocean area, or as pidgin English), and for similar reasons.

The Afrikaner establishment's historians and academicians, the lords of culture and of tribal identity, pretend that Afrikaans is the youngest in the family of Germanic languages. They need to say this because they must accentuate the European heritage and predominance with all its implications of cultural-imperialist 'superiority' not yet disavowed. But to be African is to be a bastard. The heart of Africa is metamorphosis.

True, Afrikaans (which is just the Afrikaans word for 'African'!) developed largely from the seventeenth century's seafarers' Dutch and other dialects spoken in the Low Lands. The language, however, was born in the mouths of those – imported slaves, local populations – who had command of no European tongue and who needed to communicate in a *lingua franca* among themselves; who had to be able also to understand the Master. Not for nothing was it referred to as 'kitchen Dutch' for so long.

In its structural simplifications it was influenced by the language spoken by the Malays; in its vocabulary by those of Khoi-khoi and Blacks.* One can trace to some extent the proliferation of diminutives, the shifts in sound and in meaning, the repetitions – so typical of Creole evolution.

In its present sociological context and political impact Afrikaans

*Khoi-khoi literally means 'people of the people', the way the 'Hottentots', so named by European colonists, referred to themselves.

bears the stigma of being identified with the policeman, the warder, the judge and the White politician. Afrikaans is the language of oppression and of humiliation, of the *boer*. Official Afrikaans is the tool of the racist. That is why the majority of South Africans mock and nearly instinctively reject the *Taal*. But this is not entirely true. Afrikaans is not even now the exclusive property of the Whites – already it is spoken by more so-called Coloureds, and in one form or another by a larger number of Blacks, than there are Whites in the country. Attempts are made continually to 'regularize' Afrikaans, to purify it from foreign contamination and to teach it in its academic form, and already the language which is spoken in township and prison and in the army, on fishing-boats and in the factories, has escaped entirely from the control of the Afrikaners. In that shape it is a virile medium, ever being renewed, which so far finds but little reflection in the writing.

To be an Afrikaner is a political definition. It is a blight and a provocation to humanity. Afrikaans, however, is a means of communication intimately interacting with the specific characteristics of South African life and history, and enriching the land in a dialectic of mutual shaping.

Does a language, of itself, have only one political meaning? Surely not. It is true that the Nazis used the German language to impose their ideology. But Goethe and Heine wrote in German too. So did Brecht. A language is what you want to make of it. Insofar as it reflects conventions prevalent among the people using it, it obviously will be associated with the dominant cultural precepts and pretences of those people. Their attitudes may infect the language itself. I believe there are still traces to be found in modern German of the Nazis' attempt to 'Germanize' the language. And it is revealing to see how Solzhenitsyn is trying to 'cleanse' Russian of words of foreign or tainted origin. In Afrikaans too, words still currently used have been accorded a definitely derogatory racist content. But it is possible also to express alternative concepts in the language.

To me it is of little importance whether the language dies of shame or is preserved and strengthened by its potentially revolutionary impact. Of course it will be a loss if it were to die: a language is a living organism, not just a reflection of life, but also a precursor and a crucible thereof.

But I most certainly do not agree with the need to wage a struggle for the survival or the imposition of Afrikaans. Those who do so are, to my mind, objectively strengthening the ideology of the White rulers. They justify their power monopoly (and the accompanying oppression of others) in terms of their so separate and so specific cultural identity, which can first of all be indicated only by Afrikaans.

Similarly I have felt for some time now that the attention paid to the contestation of Afrikanerdom, within limits of loyalty and fealty, by the so-named *Sestigers* (writers of the 1960s), the self aggrandizement and the bloated self-importance of these authors, have helped entrench the reactionary forces in the country. This happened first of all because the debate around and by the *Sestigers* obscured the far more important political issues of the time (suppression of Black parties, impoverishment of the majority, militarization and 'securization' of the country, the start of aggressive military foreign policy), including the wiping out of a decade of Black writing which was of greater significance for the future than the 'existentialist' deviations of the youngish Afrikaners; and secondly because the charade was foisted upon the world that *Sestiger* dissidence (as for that matter White dissident writing at present) could influence the political future, could effectively alter the set-up, could expose the real implications, could translate *the* South African reality – so much so that it was not seen that the *enfants terribles* were endowing the Afrikaner establishment with a greater suppleness to resist real transformation, and simultaneously serving as lightning conductors to close the eyes and the minds of people to the true death (and hope) moving deep down through the land. The tragedy is that with the pretensions of being 'open' we closed more doors, erected new walls, blinded more eyes. It could be argued that it wasn't done consciously. I'm not so sure. Besides, ignorance is no excuse. And neither is arrogance. (White writers – of the 'liberal kind' – are in reality just getting a personal kick out of flaunting some tribal taboos.)

During the early part of 1976 I wrote the following poem. It is not prophetic – but it shows that even in isolation behind prison walls one sensed to a degree the atmosphere that was to lead to the Soweto uprising. It was smuggled out at the time and later published in an English translation done by Denis Hirson. The following is a new translation.

THE STRUGGLE FOR THE TAAL

CLEAN AS THE CONSCIENCE OF A GUN

MIROSLAV HOLUB

We are old.
Our language is a grey reservist of a hundred years and more
with fingers stiff around the triggers –
and who will be able to sing as we sang
when we are no longer there?
As we did when alive we will spurn the earth
and the miracles of the flesh which grows
throbbing and flowing like words –
It is you who will serve as bodies for our thoughts
and live to commemorate our death,
you will conjure up tunes from the flutes of our bones . . .

From the structure of our conscience
from the stores of our charity
we had black constructions built for you, you bastards –
schools, clinics, post offices, police stations –
and now the plumes of black smoke blow
throbbing and flowing like a heart.

But you have not really understood.
You have yet to master the Taal.
We will make you repeat the ABC after us,
we will teach you the ropes
and rigours of our Christian National Education . . .

You will learn to obey,
to obey and be humble.
And you will learn to use the Taal,
with humility you will use it
for it is we who have the sunken mouths
poisoned with the throbbing and flowing of the heart.

The Struggle for the Taal

You are the salt of the earth –
with what will we be able to spice our dying
if you are not there?
You will turn the earth bitter and brackish, glinting
with the sound of our lips . . .

For we are Christ's executioners.
We are on the walls around the locations
gun in one hand
and machine gun in the other:
we, the missionaries of Civilization.

We bring you the grammar of violence
and the syntax of destruction –
from the tradition of our firearms
you will hear the verbs of retribution
stuttering.

Look, we are giving you new mouths for free –
red ears with which to hear red eyes with which to see all
pulsing, red mouths
so you can spout the secrets of our fear:
where each lead-nosed word flies
a speech organ will be torn open . . .

And you will please learn to use the Taal,
with humility use it, abuse it . . .
because we are down already, the death rattle
throbbing and flowing
on our lips . . .

We ourselves are old. . . .

6

A Note for Azania

The temptation, when writing about No Man's Land/Azania, is to pour forth visions of apocalypse. Or to give way to the temptation of trying to be a prophet. Or both.

At the end of the book is a reproduction of the Okhela–Manifesto as we proposed it in 1975. Much water has run into the sea since then. Also some mud and blood. The Apartheid state is for all practical intents and purposes stronger now than it was then. The authorities have dismembered the country further, creating the Frankenstein structures as excrescences and expressions of their policies which will profoundly affect the reality of a new Azania beyond liberation. One can say of those in power that they are not only actively ensuring their own doom (in an orgy of self-fulfilling repression) but that they are also sowing enough dragon teeth to make the ultimate reconstitution of a viable state most problematical, if not impossible. In this, as also in their aggressive destabilization of the other regimes in southern Africa, they are enemies of the future, foes of humanity. Is it because they cannot help themselves, like the scorpion stinging to death the frog? Or are they in all consciousness destroying the future of all the South Africans?

The Manifesto's analysis of the possible role to be played by Whites in the struggle for liberation is probably still fairly valid. But it must be remembered that we proposed that line of action with specific people and conditions in mind, and that it flowed from certain experiences and chances we then had. All that is past now. In a sense the political struggle is at present even more polarized along ethnic lines; in another for the first time in years we assist the attempt to find communal and non-racial forms of political expression, as with the recent creation of the Union of Democratic Forces.

The shifting sands of time have created new patterns. I remain as convinced as ever that majority rule will eventually come about and that South Africa has the potential – human first of all – of becoming a great country in accordance with its natural beauty and its richness in history and strategic resources. I am sure also that the contribution of its experience to mankind, distilled in the struggle, will be of enormous value. But I fear that the price to be paid – in the cruel game directed and enforced by those now in power – will be exorbitant; the suffering will rip the country asunder and create generations of blindness, bitterness and hate. Are we not heading for an ungovernable Lebanon-type situation where killing will be the only form of communication?

The African National Congress – or some organization still called the ANC for I am now projecting my mind into the distant future – will eventually rule the country. What's left of it. Judging from its practices in exile, inside the organization and towards other South African political groupings, its alliances and its ideological examples and commitments – it is conceivable that the present totalitarian State will be replaced by one which may be totalitarian in a different way, and intolerant of alternative revolutionary schools of thought, more hegemonic but minus the racism. As things stand now the External Mission, in the grip of the dogmatists, will be stronger than the ANC inside the country, and probably they will shut them out in an ensuing power struggle. This is my personal view.

And yet there is no other way. How can we advance unless we destroy racism? I don't believe that enough Whites of the ruling caste can be influenced to become humane and thus obviate a dragged out civil war. They are captives of the system they still create and maintain. Racism and corruption have alienated them too profoundly. (And their White critics are just dogs yapping behind the hill.) They are conditioned by the ignorance and the fear they generate. Their power monopoly must be destroyed if we want to have even the smallest hope for change. I don't believe the Western powers are really intent upon using their leverage to prevent a war (they are even now allowing the South African rulers to wage war in Angola) despite an increasing awareness of the complexities and the interdependence of North–South relationships – and the extent to which a South African conflict will bedevil these relations. The short-term interests of the Western powers are too profitable for that. (War and unrest are lucrative too.) And I don't believe there's any chance of the ANC transforming itself into a free democratic organization. (It is 'free' and 'democratic' now in the double-speak, Orwellian sense.) It is the victim of its friends, its history, and the conditions imposed on it by the struggle for freedom in an arena controlled by a cruel and criminally irresponsible adversary.

So what do you do as an individual, as a writer perhaps? The implications of the unfolding drama are too momentous for you to afford the luxury of 'tactics'. Holding back, hiding your game, is a form of paternalism and disdain for your fellow South Africans. You have to try by all means to see justly and clearly. You have to speak your mind directly. Fight your own fear: 'they' handicap you by the fear they instil in you. Guilt and all wishy-washy or breast-beating sentimentalism engendered by guilt – these are out. Leave that to the judges and the preachers. Don't be a preacher or a judge. You are an African. Assume that fully. Solutions must be found *within* the country, *with* the people, *all* the people. Nobody is clean. No heaven exists. Combat dogmatism. Try to force a dialogue, try to keep it open, along lines of honest recognition of differences in background and forms of struggle. Self-knowledge is not self-abasement or self-rejection. Don't be manoeuvred into defeatism. Strive for the growing realization, through heritage and through struggle, of one South African cultural identity composed of an incredibly rich variety of sources and expressions. Promote tolerance. Don't expect it of yourself or of others to be a hero. Don't judge people. But remember that to transform is to fight laziness, your own first of all. Be patient and realize that there will *never* be a perfect society *anywhere*. Move on. If you are a writer, watch out for the words – they are traitors! Be pliant and weak when you have to. Cry if you must. Try not to go to prison; it's never worth it. Survive, so as to continue to struggle. Try to see it as a continuous *process*, not a rigid goal or structure. Realize that ruptures can be flashes of comprehension. Do yourself a selfish favour: if you want to remain whole, recognize the humanity of your enemy. But recognize also that there are irreconcilable interests. Don't make a fool of yourself by killing him. No cause can justify the destruction of life.

After all, we are all blood brothers and sisters.

Thirteen poems

from the outset*

from the outset of the poem we are once more
as at all times before
at the end of all time

look
here I come on my way
out of a savage wasted region
taking what there is for creed
I come to blow on life's coal-ash
I come with my gallows gladness
and a knapsack full of words for the day
when the mouth is dumb as dust
a sheath of swords reddening to rust
to feel for the fish and the worm
squirming in the earth
pyramids full of the roots of words
verses mirrors of soil and steel
from a black and bitter land
where the word is voicefruit and tonguefood

with swordwater and bulletjuice in my veins
riding a mount
my body has no need
of me now
soul in hand
sighs leaving the anus

**Note:* All the poems in this section have been translated from Afrikaans by Denis Hirson.

the spirit moves me
not to meditation but reflection
not to vision but recognition
the veil stripped
and I come out of a black and savage land
or can I really be here?

for to come or to go
both mean staying the same

plagiarism

a man made himself a poem
for his birthday the sixteenth of the ninth –
o, not a fancy affair with room and rhyme
and rhythm and iambs and stuff, or a soundless rustling
or a bone to pick or other poetic knicknacks –
not under such meagre circumstances as at
present, mountain-sucking-eyes, steady hours, tree-with-stars,
wife and sea gone – almost
all elements sadly lacking;
still, there were certainly odds and sods around –
he scraped and scrounged, aped what he found
and tried to turn the leftovers
into something with his breath –
even in the desert the tongue has its shade:
first then the man himself, hump on his shoulders –
old humpskull, bumptious baboon,
(but ruin already alive in his seed – that's part of Death's art)
and then the fine hairs on his hands, and the fly
(rechristened Stalin) since it really is a cloud
in the be-all of a cell, and some further words thrown in for free –
the sixteenth of the ninth brought him
to sinews and blessings, ten against one, pins and puns –
and running out he had to bring his pants
into the poem – the short khaki ones
worn away by so many, stitched up with purple cotton
here at the waisted parts like an appendix scar
the stigma partly grown into the skin, and the spoon
with 'maximum' stamped (chewed?) into the handle wrought
of unblemished steel, to help get him to the end of the line
('I am defiled! defiled!') (with a dying flourish he spooned out the thought)

and then there was the ant dragging its body-one-leg-broken
which strayed in from who-knows-where,
and like punctuation when sense is absent
the memory-of-love

having used up everything to hand
he wrapped it circumspectly in fresh paper
meaning to write it out neatly later that evening
but when around nightfall he unfolded the present
the damned paper had already gobbled up the poem;
and the man gripped his hump and humphed a groan:
'my poem, my poem – now what will I have to show for my birthday the sixteenth of the ninth!'

(from the Otherplace)

snow falls thick

Snow falls thick flaked in my sleep
and white the coast and white
the forbidding sea – a dismal walk
through scourmarks, rustle and crunch, strokes slanting down.

Of grey cement
the deserted towns.
Of grey cement the streets and trees
hung with droplets
like small microphones
that catch the grey and make it loud.

Our neighbours are in the waterpipes' splashing
the hairy windowpanes, eyelashes
over the wet of the iris. Into
the white eye of your laid out body
I will descend. Your teeth are tiny snowmen.
I will diminish in the lens.

There are sentries
with black tongues – tongues
like the festering moon – and silver
machineguns
in the neck between the torn sea
and the bottomless snowfields of the interior:
a border post –

there is life

there are christs spiked against trees
prophets in the wilderness seized with fits
worshippers whose eyes bud under the sun
buddhas on one side conversing with figs

there is life greening in the clouds
and dolphins that shred through waves
the seagull's swerving gutlean shriek
the scragginess barefoot against the mountainflanks

behind magnifying air the crater's firespeech
slopes of snow like silences shifting
when heaven cracks open hairline wide
and out come black legends the swallow the dove

there are bones that bind the earth
and delight that breaks through transience
I might be a blunderer a crazy daydream
I will still grow rich on day's bright beam

the scales flamed throughout the night
I too might once have been a prisoner
but here the heart's pulsing contract is made
clear: a hundred years from now we will all be naked

do you still remember

do you still remember when we were dogs
how we used to trot
on sore little paws
through all the tunnels and sluices of the city
streets of flapping yellow sheets
across cobblestones mud banks loose planks
and leafy avenues
canals which even the rats never knew
do you remember how low down we kept to the ground
and how exhausted we grew
with flabby bloodlimp rags for tongues
and how we panted hard uphill
right through hedges glass walls shafts of concrete
past the fearsome knots of streets and spurting traffic lights
fundaments cellars cesspools and sewers where the self-slaughtered
still kicked in the breeze
with day and night but a dulling of the eye –
then we arrived at old Master R's quarters
where we could eat and smoke and drink
vodka for me and *tchai* for you
and sugary cookies for us both

and our knowledge of the city
no one else could know
that it was in reality
a rhythmic intertwining flow

do you still remember when we were dogs
you and I, best beloved?

your letter is delightful . . .

your letter is delightful, larger and lighter
than thoughts of a flower when the dream
is the earth of a garden,
                                        as your letter opens
there is an unfolding of sky, of word from the outside
of ample spaces,

I slept in green pastures
I lay on the ridge of the valley of the shadow of death
during the last watch of the night
listening to the condemned
being led down corridors underground,
                                              how they sing,

their breaths in their mouths
like residents
about to quit a burning city, how they sing
their breaths like shackles,
                                            how they sing,
they who will jolt from obscurity to the light
they who will be posted to no destination,
terror fills me at the desecration

the table before me, in the presence of my enemies,
is bare; I have ash on my head,
my cup is empty,

I fled to your letter, to read
that the small orange tree is a mass of white blossoms
opening with the sun,
I could smell it on the balcony,
                                                I can smell you
more delicious, lighter than thoughts of a flower
in this dismal night,

I will be suspended by the sky of your words,
allow me to live in your letter
all the days of my life

envoi,
your letter is delightful, stretching out lighter
than thoughts of a flower when the dream
is the earth of a garden,
                                            as your letter opens
there is an unfolding of sky, of word from the outside
of memory,

he will remember . . .

he will remember –
mornings before daybreak, the city dressed in grey
and the distant droning sprung from no visible source –
cantering hooves? an ants' nest, a flood –
restful warm back in bed,
the steaming bowl of tea and slither of bread
and then, rain flicking against an ice-cold glass face
on the pushbike through the misty canyons of the city
past trees that swell and drip and glitter with wetness
all the way to the *dojo*, (only later does the sun bark like a dog
in a courtyard)
the cool black folds of breath,
the inward tumbling stillness,
and now, from deep in the belly –
Maka Hanya Haramita Shingyo:

he will remember –
the rough work-clothes of cronies drinking in the bistro,
the greeting, clickety-click of words against each other
and knives, and the red blush on the white napkin of light
through the glass of wine, the beefsteak, green salad,
soft meeting with the eyes of friends
and now, to work!
the smell of fresh canvas and turpentine

he will remember –
flames glowing in the dark dreamed eyes
of the woman curled before the fire in the hearth,
journeys measured out in days by the twisting of mountains
so white the eyes feel naked, and down
between ricefields through goldspeckled Sienna evenings
he will remember how the woman goes looking for shells
where the blue sea brims
at the rim of the desert where the wind
blows soundlessly, and is peeled black

he will remember –
the wild moon like a glowing hand
from the ocean turning silver palm trees
to nothing but small feathered tongues while the shadows
well up of their own free will, blotch,
bear forests, and quack

he will remember
how for one measureless second
the sun flutters like a blood-streaked bird in his fingers
and then soars up like a wall reaching higher
than any rampart or prison's narrow now:

ghja tei, ghja tei, hara-so ghja tei,
bô-ji so wa-ká:

Hanya Shingyoooo . . .

metaspecks

when I climbed onto the chair
to wipe the southeast wind's gold dust
from the high windowledge
I saw in the sliced space behind the tungsten bars
that passes for an opening
two swallows hanging playfully in the dusk air
caught and released by turn in the dying earth's brightness
like leafboats from the endless blue heavenly bluegum tree
free, free, free
as they careened and heckled between fire and dream;
and there is life in the metabolism between eye and flight
around the spinning smoke-bound bow
my ladyfriend, my sister, my wife –
each hour since the making of the earliest sign
has been a rite of giving and taking –

in the middle of the night

in the middle of the night
the voices of those
to be hanged within days
rise up already sounding thin
with the terror of stiff ropes –
we each bear like shadow
                    thrown over our thoughts
the noose, or a cancer, or shattering glass
(and yet: grim the consciousness
that men's lives must be intentionally measured out
and emptied – or left brimming till the last?
like gulps from a glass)
                    what difference does it make
if you kick the bucket like a *bandiet* shot into space
or wearing silver socks, a cigar stuck between your chops
on a border or in the ice-box-ocean
sounding like old reeds on the air
or in a gloomy room somewhere –
while alive we all bear the great divide
and shadow inside us
                    the knowledge

and all at once (in the middle of the night)
a remembered image breaks through the white wall:
a rider on his horse stilled for an instant
in the rain that spatters silver
as he fords a river
one gloved hand flung up in nonchalant salute
standard Western cavalry outfit
(but a smile like a trout
                    displayed under glass)

what Matinee Buffalo Bill is this out of the blue
caught in which of memories' webs
(in front of a TV set and a fire while rain lacquers the tiles)
now (why?) dragged up
branded strangely to be shaken
onto the retina of the imagination
(while rain drips like dead blossoms
onto the roof)

and so too this unexpected shameless joy
that I can think of you despite it all
you stay close to me
in the immense coupling and death of consciousness
o my wife

(while gulp by gulp shadowvoices are drained
in the middle of the night)

when my mother was

when my mother was dying
I had to wade and flay through the seething current
to reach her where they had laid her out
on her bedstead in the yard: shimmering yellow
the sun stroked the arcadian scene
playing on the halfcircle of faces of old
deceased uncles and forefathers who sat
sucking peacefully at pipes to blow out carols of smoke,

strong and healthy she was under the white sheet
her eyes full of light and rounder without glasses
her plump arms moving with clarity
to bless and deliver the last messages
(only some tired grey hairs had already come loose):
visions of how everything would turn out fine and that she
was at rest now with *inter alia* Matthew and Mark left and
right the two old-timers indeed stood,

and she also kept on calling me by the name
and did not recognize me

but I had to get back before the authorities
suspected my escape in the current's
whirling rush I began to sink
and further down teeth chattering washed between banks
(finally engulfed?)
somewhere beyond farmlands where mudspattered
grain elevators slash heavenwards where haystacks
rot and turnips are swallowed up by the earth,

as they strained at their leashes I heard the stinking
dogs their throats clogged with cries of excitement

release

I arrive on this first day already glistening bright
among angel choirs: far and wide the feathered folk sing psalms
and my face smells marvellous and my hands
are embalmed – did I not store the leftover oil away
for years with precisely this meeting in mind?
I will lie very still holding in my glee
so as not to bump the earth on this last lap of the journey

dance the dust up my beloved – why the dullness in your eye?
let friends pick sprays of laurel leaves
and twine them into garlands of green victory
and don't anyone mourn or the coffin will shake
because I am yours now cleansed of all disgrace
yours where dolphins wheel soft as wind in the palms
yours turned entirely free in the gardens of the night

the return

in rue Monsieur-le-Prince
coming down the same side as the Luxembourg gardens
on the left, where the twigs are set on fire by the evening sun
as it nests in the trees
the same side as the Odéon theatre
a honeycomb of freedom
as long ago now as May sixty-eight,

in rue Monsieur-le-Prince
is the restaurant where we will meet
at precisely nine o'clock
you will recognize me, I'll be wearing a beard once again
even if it is of cheap silver
and the Algerian boss-cum-cook
with the moustache nesting in his red cheeks
will come and put his arms full of bees around my shoulders
saying
alors, mon frère – ça fait bien longtemps . . .

should we order *couscous mouton* for two?
I can already taste the small snow-yellow grains
and the bit of butter –
and a bottle of pitch dark Sidi Brahim
smacking of the sun and the sea?
and then what would you say to a *thé à la menthe*
in the flower-decked glasses all scalding wet?

listen to that same wind calling
through the old old Paris streets

you're the one I love and I'm feeling so good!

‘to live is to burn’

Andrei Voznesensky

entirely luminous and still: to live is to be consumed
like this summer day’s delight; to renew now
and always praise for the earth’s onward rolling, supple foliage
of the brushwood, waterslopes, tongues of stone, birds’ charmed
heart-notes spun
to light chain linking stillness to stillness; how entirely lush
the mountain, sun-caked, naked – only one plume flourishes
white already, where wind will soon swell fine pipe sounds
and streamers; and in their cycle’s fullness, the seasons turn
around
heaving old worm-like wrinkles from the womb – see, we each
drive what passes, upright as the mantis, hands bleaching
at the reins of death’s wagon. prayer by prayer our way meshes
and marks us, cool skeleton cupped in the daywear of flesh

burn, burn with me, love – to hell with decay
to live is to live, and while alive to die anyway!

Okhela – Manifesto

OKHELA–MANIFESTO

Draft proposal submitted to militants for comment and/or amendment*

Paris, June 1975

I. *The Nature of the South African Struggle:*
– struggle for national liberation and socialism against settler colonialism, capitalism and imperialism – the question of race and class – prevailing conditions or needs for theory based on revolutionary practice – contradictions in South African society – call for the destruction of the Apartheid state –

II. *Traditions of Struggle and the African National Congress of South Africa:*
– formation and development – alliances – armed resistance and the *uMkhonte we Siswe* – international solidarity and the *External Mission* –

III. *Present Perspectives and Demands Facing the Liberation Movement:*
– Black militance, the SASO and BPC – Black workers' organizations – problems of rallying to a concerted programme for national liberation –

IV. *Problems of Identification with the Liberation Struggle:*
– Black militancy and White activists – forms of struggle as determined by social and economic differences existing objectively inside South Africa –

V. *Role of White Militants:*
– conditions, possibilities and limitations springing from a scientific class analysis – national and international contacts –

VI. *Commitment to the Liberation of Women*

VII. *Creation of OKHELA:*
– international solidarity and lessons in internationalism – conception of needs of developing struggle – legitimacy derived from the *African National Congress* –

*I took this document with me to South Africa in July 1975, with the intention of discussing it with our contacts there. It was found by the Security Police and used in evidence during the first trial in November 1975.

VIII. *Demands on Organization and Structures of OKHELA:*
– national liberation as first stage – internationalist and anti-imperialist outlook – clandestinity and security –

IX. *Our Aims:*
[Fourteen aims, a – n, listed in full below]

UNITY THROUGH STRUGGLE
POWER TO THE PEOPLE

I. *The Nature of the South African Struggle:*

The struggle for liberation in South Africa is a complex one – complex because of the history of the country and the diverse origins of its people; complex because of the nature of the forces involved in the struggle and those whom we combat; complex because of the international, political and geographical position of South Africa.

The nature of the struggle can be read on many levels: it is the struggle of the Black majority against the White minority for national liberation; it is the struggle of an indigenous people against settler colonialism and as such is part of Africa's continuing attempts to free itself from the results of colonialism; it is the struggle for socialism against a *strongly entrenched capitalist state* supported by world imperialism – and therefore it is a struggle with internationalist dimensions; it is finally a class struggle with the class divisions overlying the racial dimensions to a large extent. This struggle expresses itself politically, economically and also culturally since it touches upon national, racial, group and class identities.

These apparently divergent but interlocking aspects of the struggle make it essential to understand the role that each group, be it of race or of class, is called upon to play, and to define the grounds upon which each group can engage the combat. We, the South Africans, must still forge a comprehensive understanding of the reality of our conditions and a theory which will encompass the aims and the need for freedom for all the people – but this theory must be developed in the struggle itself; it will grow from our praxis and in turn define the latter.

As for the conditions under which the struggle is being waged, they are those of extreme repression, exile and a partial dislocation of the forces for liberation and transformation. On the other hand though, the conditions are also those of a growing awareness and a more perceptive application of our own power, and the increasingly strong international solidarity with our cause.

We, the South Africans, have a rich history of resistance from which to draw our lessons and our inspiration. It is important for us to understand these experiences, to draw the correct conclusions, to apply the lessons learnt and to take the initiative for a change.

The profound contradictions within the South African society must explode; the interests of oppressed and oppressors can never be harmonized; the super exploitation of the urban and rural proletariat has become insupportable; the alienation of the Blacks and the accompanying dehumanization of the Whites can no longer be accepted; the Apartheid state must be destroyed.

II. *Traditions of Struggle and the African National Congress of South Africa:*

At this point in our history we believe that the short term goal of our struggle is the liberation of the territory of South Africa and the seizing of power by the Liberation Movement representing the people of South Africa. To this we are committed as South African patriots. For us the tradition and the existence of resistance are embodied in the African National Congress and the various political and labour organizations allied to this movement.

The ANC was formed in 1912 in an attempt to give national expression to the claims of the oppressed and exploited and disinherited people of South Africa, to oppose and counteract the doctrines of racism upon which the newly established South African state was based. The ANC rapidly developed into a mass movement with a democratically elected and representative national leadership putting forward the demands of the African people for equality and dignity in a reasonable and responsible manner.

Despite the fact that the ANC could claim to represent the majority of South Africans, Britain consecrated the colonial conquests of the settlers and in accordance with her own imperialist interests handed over power to the local White minority. Imbued by the ideals of non-violence, the ANC led the resistance to this state which denies the birthright of the people.

From very early on also, the ANC in alliance with the SACP and the trade union organizations gave expression to the interests of the working class.

When the all-White Nationalist Party came to power in 1948 it laid the blueprints for the rationalization of exploitation and for the ultimate dismemberment of the country. The national presence of the ANC reached a high point during the 1950s with the existence of the Alliance of Congresses grouping organizations representing all the different ethnic groups and the South African Congress of Trade Unions (SACTU). Reflecting the developing demands and the working class consciousness of the people, the Congresses mobilized nationally through successive stay-at-home campaigns and national strikes.

The growing strength of the Congresses as mass protest organizations and the unsuccessful attempts of the illegitimate State's authority to break the spirit of struggle – at the abortive 'treason trial' – culminated in the banning of the ANC, the disbanding of some other organizations and the brutal repression and hounding of the freedom militants.

uMkhonte we Siswe – the military wing of the ANC – came into being in the early sixties. The *External Mission* of the ANC had already been established and sent abroad where international solidarity work was started through its creation of national Anti-Apartheid Movements in several countries. These developments showed:

a. the need for a visible part of the leadership to be seen continuing the struggle and to represent the South African people abroad; and
b. the need for the ANC to transform itself from a mass protest movement into an organization capable of carrying on the struggle in all its forms – and particularly the armed struggle and underground work; and
c. the broadening of the struggle against Apartheid by isolating the illegal regime internationally and at the same time broadening the international support base for the ongoing struggle at home.

The ANC was called upon not only to survive under difficult circumstances but also to start transforming itself structurally to face up to the new situation; to maintain, carry forward and strengthen traditions of resistance. This is an ever continuing process.

III. *Present Perspectives and Demands Facing the Liberation Movement:*

Exile, imprisonment, bannings, the need to reorganize the structures – all of these brought about a temporary dislocation of the work of the Liberation Movement inside the country itself.

During the sixties and the early seventies – filling the relative vacuum – a new generation grew into the struggle, propounding the ideas of Black militancy. The forms the struggle took were defined on the one hand by the restrictions imposed by the authorities and on the other hand by the need to assert or reassert the Black identity both culturally and politically.

At first the forums of self-assertion and self-reliance were the campuses, cultural and religious bodies. Black students broke away from the NUSAS and formed SASO; UCM and the BPC came into being. Early during the seventies the focal point of the struggle moved into the field of labour. The Black working class became aware of its growing power. The impressive series of strikes spreading to all sectors of the economy, organized and controlled by the workers, led to the formation of new trade unions and the revitalization of others. The students and the workers – two vital sectors of the population – were and are defining their means of struggling.

If these means of resistance and mobilization were seen to be less decisive than expected it is:

a. because of the repressive machinery of the state;
b. the lack of political cohesiveness among the various organizations with the accompanying danger that the trade unions for instance, will become ensnared in a purely 'economic' approach;
c. the imperfect coordination of the struggle inside and outside; and particularly
d. the fact that all struggle must be built around a drive by the Liberation Movement to wrest political control and central power from the minority.

IV. *Problems of Identification with the Liberation Struggle:*

The rise of Black militancy and the creation of autonomous Black organizations forced White activists to reassess their position and role not only in racial terms but also in that of class. The hitherto paternalistic approach of the Whites became exposed and was rejected. It became evident that the Whites themselves are in need of liberation but that national liberation will have to be fought for under the leadership of the Black movements. It became obvious that the function of the Whites is not to confuse themselves with organizations expressing Black consciousness and aspirations, but rather that they should turn to how best to assist the struggle of the majority for national liberation.

It became progressively clear that unity among revolutionary groups, whose forms of struggle are defined by the economic and social differences existing objectively in the country, can only be achieved in the struggle as a concerted programme under the leadership of the Black liberation movement.

The first step in this direction was the way in which White students turned their attention and efforts towards helping Black trade unions establish themselves. A second step is the way in which some sectors – areas of church and of culture – are, as Whites and in terms of their professional and moral interests, starting to organize against the reactionary power of the State. A third step will be the participation of White organizations in all forms of revolutionary struggle as led by the ANC.

V. *Role of White Militants:*

We believe that a clear conception and application of the role that Whites can play demands a thorough definition of our conditions, possibilities and restrictions springing from a scientific class analysis. We believe that the first priority of a revolutionary is to find what she or he can do taking into account the history of his or her people, the objective conditions which define his or her class, the effectiveness she or he must strive for and the national and international contexts within which the struggle is unfolding.

VI. *Commitment to the Liberation of Women:*

We furthermore recognize the political, economic, educational, legal, sexual and commercial exploitation of women in law, practice and attitude as being a tool to perpetuate the capitalist system and maintain the status quo.

We believe that the total liberation of women, as defined by women themselves, is a fundamental necessity for the victory of the revolution.

VII. *Creation of OKHELA:*

Over the years many White individuals have joined the struggle for liberation in one form or another. One foyer of activity became the international solidarity work of the *External Mission* of the ANC which, since it meant working with and among progressive forces in other countries, in turn strengthened the awareness of the anti-imperialist nature of our struggle.

Flowing from all the above developments and in terms of a

clearer understanding and conception of the needs that the developing struggle indicates, and based on the experiences of a few comrades, it was decided to create an organization of White South African militants called OKHELA. This organization is called upon to play a specific role within the National Liberation Front being constituted.

We derive our legitimacy from the African National Congress who requested us to form this organization.*

VIII. *Demands on Organization and Structures of OKHELA:*

The conditions under which the struggle is fought make it imperative for us to be clandestine so as to be effective. The needs of clandestinity, security and effectiveness define the structures and the functioning of our organization.

Our immediate objective is to participate in the national liberation of South Africa which in itself is lifting the first barrier barring the road to the revolutionary transformation of South African society.

We are present and active both inside and outside the country; our outlook is internationalist. We are profoundly aware of the anti-imperialist and anti-capitalist nature of our struggle.

IX. *Our Aims:*

a. To provide *'invisible support'* – materially and politically – to the Liberation Movement.
b. To develop the tradition and means which will enable us to fulfil our special role, to build our organization to be both flexible and resilient, an organization which can take the initiative for action and 'create the facts on the ground'.
c. To acquire all the necessary techniques and experiences for underground struggle – logistical support, information, communication, etc; to accumulate these experiences, transform and adapt them to our needs; and to transmit them by having the necessary training facilities.
d. To be a political and practical 'training ground' for White militants.
e. To assist the Liberation Movement develop its methods and forces so that a strong liberation front can be established grouping an alliance of all the forces for change, be they representative of ethnic groupings or political formations.

*This is not true. In fact the office-bearers of the ANC, with whom we were in contact, could not and did not encourage us in the name of the ANC.

f. To consciously and ideologically develop the ideological grounds upon which we as White South Africans can become fully participant in the revolutionary struggle; to build a base on these grounds.
g. To work with and to coordinate progressive forces abroad supporting our cause.
h. In doing so to bring about a more progressive political commitment to our struggle and to channel the manifestations of this support into the country.
i. To develop the means of gathering political and economic intelligence without which we will be blind; to develop the most effective ways of using this information.
j. To develop the means of protecting our organization from the enemy and of assuming responsibility for our own safety and security.
k. To develop all the possibilities for support to militants in distress.
l. To develop all possibilities for defensive and offensive direct action.
m. To continuously evolve programmes – in terms of our objectives and strategy – which can advance the struggle, and the structures needed to accommodate these programmes.
n. In all of these ways we contribute towards the treasured ideals of the South African Liberation Struggle.

UNITY THROUGH STRUGGLE!!

STRUGGLE FOR POWER!!

ALL POWER TO THE PEOPLE!!

Index

CLEOPATRA AND ROME

CLEOPATRA AND ROME

Diana E. E. Kleiner

The Belknap Press of Harvard University Press
Cambridge, Massachusetts, and London, England · 2005

Printed in the United States of America

Library of Congress Cataloging-in-Publication Data

Kleiner, Diana E. E.
Cleopatra and Rome / Diana E. E. Kleiner.
p. cm.
Includes bibliographical references and index.
ISBN 0-674-01905-9 (alk. paper)
1. Art, Roman—Egyptian influences.
2. Cleopatra, Queen of Egypt, d. 30 B.C.—Influence.
I. Title.
N5763.K58 2005
932′.021′092—dc22 2005041015

For Alex the Great

and in the belief that one inimitable person can change the world

CONTENTS

I hope it's true about the Queen, and about that Caesar of hers too.

—Cicero, *Letters to Atticus,* Puteoli, 11 May 44

PROLOGUE

FROM CARPET TO ASP

Cleopatra is one of the most famous women who ever lived. Even though she was the last of a dynasty of seven Cleopatras, we think of her as if she were unique. The most beautiful and celebrated actresses of all time, among them the divine Sarah Bernhardt, the incomparable Vivien Leigh, and the legendary Elizabeth Taylor, have vied to portray her on stage and screen. Several civilizations lay claim to Cleopatra, and even today there are few unfamiliar with the queen's dramatic death at the prick of an asp (Fig. P.1). In fact, the remarkable image of this spectacular woman lying on a couch expiring from a self-inflicted wound haunts all subsequent versions of her story; the death by suicide of this great queen remains one of history's most climactic moments.

Cleopatra's life may be glimpsed through a series of such sensational events. These episodes seared themselves into the minds of her contemporaries and into the memories of later generations. What is most striking is that each of those defining moments had to do with Rome. The convergence of Cleopatra and Rome near the turn of the first century was a momentous rendezvous with the destinies of three Romans—Julius Caesar, Mark Antony, and Octavian Augustus. Cleopatra's most unforgettable moments appear to have been shared in turn with this trio.

Since the full panorama of Cleopatra's life is lost to us, we attach great importance to these incidents, which serve as tantalizing clues to what must have been fuller accounts of Cleopatra's interaction with Rome's

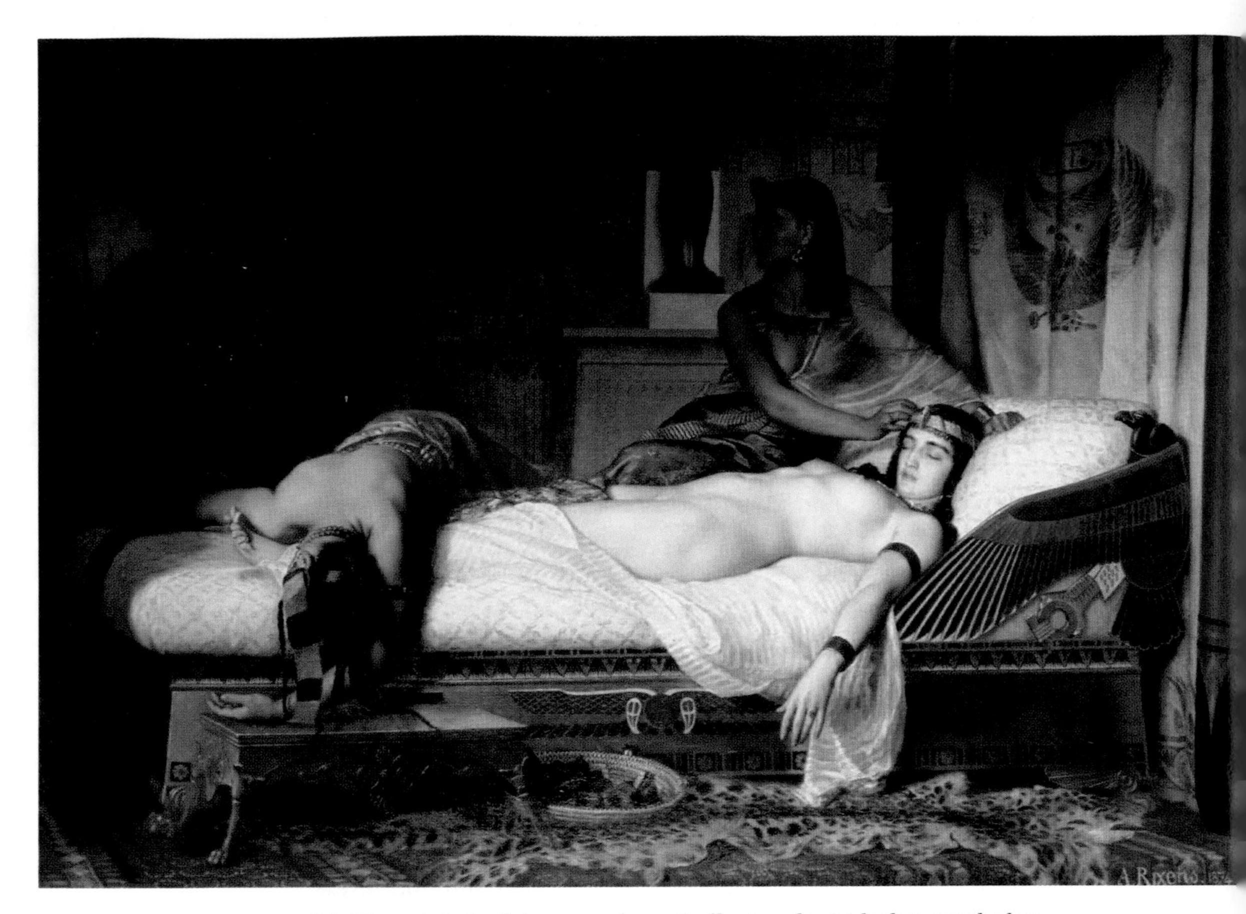

P.1. Cleopatra's death by asp, a dramatically staged suicide that was the last spectacular event of her life.

leaders by Livy and other contemporary historians writing in the second half of the first century B.C. In what little survives of their work, there is scant reference to Cleopatra and to her dealings with these three men. Although Caesar mentions in his *Civil War* his visit to Alexandria in 48 B.C., and one of his officers describes the subsequent Alexandrian War, the dictator's liaison with Cleopatra is absent from their narratives. Little of significance is added in extant excerpts from the autobiography and other writings of Nicolaus of Damascus, one-time tutor to Cleopatra's children.

What does endure is the callous but vivid language of such preeminent Augustan poets as Virgil, Ovid, and Propertius. Their poems reflected their own censorious view of Cleopatra, branding her a "licentious harlot" and worse; their verse was also intended to cater to Augustus and appeal to his supporters. Deliberately provocative, these words were unforgettable and helped to make Cleopatra a compelling personage who captured the imagination of later historians and biographers such as Dio Cassius, Plutarch, and Suetonius.

It is to those later historians that we owe the major episodes and all the other details that have since defined the life of Cleopatra VII. These authors and several others were active many years after the deaths of Cleopatra and her contemporaries and based their versions on a variety of earlier sources, some more reliable than others. Although a few of these writers may have been fastidious recorders of events, there were some who surely exaggerated the facts for dramatic effect, still others may have embellished incidents as propaganda or to achieve other objectives. For these reasons, their veracity has appropriately been questioned.

The key episodes are pivotal and are never less than high drama. In each instance, Cleopatra seems to be orchestrating the event. Cleopatra didn't merely stroll on to the world stage; she purportedly hid in and was then deliberately unfurled from a "carpet" (or, in Plutarch's version, bed linens),[1] emerging in Caesar's presence and instigating one of history's most famous liaisons. Afterward, Cleopatra did not just voyage by sea; she apparently floated effortlessly down the Nile, with an attentive Caesar by her side.[2] Cleopatra's encounter with Mark Antony at Tarsus was not a first chance meeting but seems to have been a carefully arranged tryst.[3] We don't know for certain whether Cleopatra and Antony had met each other before Tarsus. Appian mentions the rumor that

Antony had fallen in love with Cleopatra when he served under Aulus Gabinus in Alexandria,[4] but no other source comments on this infatuation and even Appian doesn't state that the general and the teenager actually met. If they had, their acquaintance might have been renewed when Cleopatra was in Rome. Whether or not they knew each other, Cleopatra appears to have coordinated the Tarsus event to make an impression. Dressed as Venus and with boy Cupids at her side, she arrived in style, enveloped in a perfumed mist and accompanied by melodic cadences (see Fig. 7.1).

Even Cleopatra's death by asp seems to have been meticulously calculated.[5] She probably thought it was better to perish in her homeland and by Antony's side than be paraded as a captive in Octavian's Rome triumph. The last time Cleopatra had been in Rome, she was honored as Egypt's monarch and housed in Caesar's private villa across the Tiber. It is unlikely she would accede to going back enslaved and in chains. It might be said that Octavian got the better of her by displaying her effigy in his ostentatious parade. Yet, even as an effigy, she appeared "with an asp clinging to her," as described by Plutarch—that asp the vehicle of her last self-empowered act—and accompanied by her children, Alexander Helios and Cleopatra Selene.[6]

Plutarch and Dio Cassius are our best sources for the life of Cleopatra, but it must always be kept in mind that their intent was rarely strict reportage. Plutarch, for example, was more interested in revealing moral character than in narrating life stories and thus arranged the subjects of his biographies in parallel Greek and Roman pairs (Antony, for example, was matched with the third-century Macedonian King Demetrius Poliorcetes). Such conceits lent themselves to hyperbole, since they relied as much on colorful anecdote and rumor as on hard fact.

The historian Erich Gruen doubts the authenticity of Cleopatra's most memorable moments and attempts to dispel what he thinks are some deeply entrenched "myths" about Cleopatra. He suggests that she was unlikely to have rolled out of bed linens, that she did not cause Caesar to transform his Roman dictatorship into a Hellenistic monarchy, that she did not enter Rome in the kind of Hollywood splendor featured in Joseph Mankiewicz's 1963 movie epic (Fig. P.2), and that she did not remain at Caesar's villa in Rome for eighteen months. He focuses on the length of

P.2 Although Cleopatra may not have entered Rome in as dazzling a way as Elizabeth Taylor, she made an indelible mark on the city during her sojourn at Caesar's villa.

the Roman sojourn and replaces what has been widely viewed as an uninterrupted stay with a reasoned scenario for two visits to Rome, first to reinforce a treaty between Egypt and Rome and later to underscore Cleopatra's claim to maintain an intact Egypt and Cyprus in the light of a potential Roman reorganization of the eastern provinces. There is much to recommend this hypothesis: as Gruen points out, there was an established tradition for such royal visits and entreaties. Gruen is also likely correct that Cleopatra did not participate in an ostentatious entry into Rome, although she and Antony spared no expense in a later triumph in Alexandria.

Plutarch and other ancient writers glamorize Cleopatra and feature her flair for the theatrical, a likely reflection of her desire to unify the wealthy and cultivated Egypt of her Ptolemaic ancestors with a Rome that had become the ancient world's premier superpower. Cleopatra is placed at the epicenter of these encounters with Rome and is depicted as staging them for maximum impact and effect with a succession of Rome's foremost leaders.

The famous account of the bed linens is a case in point. Plutarch relates the story and emphasizes not only Cleopatra's cunning in carrying it off but also the strong impression her coyness made on Caesar (see Fig. 5.4). Exiled by her brother, Cleopatra needed a stratagem to enter Alexandria. Her game plan was ingenious and bold; to keep from being detected and to amplify the element of surprise, she enlisted the help of a single aide. "Taking just one of her couriers, Apollodorus the Sicilian, she boarded a small boat and landed near the palace at dusk. Unable to think of any other way to enter unnoticed, she lay down full length in a bed-linen sack, and Apollodorus tied the sack up with a strap and carried it through the gates to Caesar. Caesar, it is said, was immediately taken with this trick of Cleopatra's and the coquettish impression it made and, becoming more so through getting to know her and her charm, resolved to reestablish her on the throne with her brother."[7]

Whether or not this story is true, Cleopatra's post-sack affair with Caesar introduced him to a breathtaking Alexandria with impressive scholarly and artistic accomplishments and a library overflowing with books. The pair's romantic and triumphal barge trip down the Nile exposed Caesar to Egypt's countryside treasures—its pyramids silhouetted

P.3. The artistic dialogue between Cleopatra and Augustus was to turn out to be more enduring than her love affairs with Julius Caesar and Mark Antony.

against unending sand, its quixotic sphinxes, its grandiose and lavishly decorated temples and mortuary chapels, and its imposing statues of the pharaohs and their consorts (see Fig. 5.5). Caesar's contact with these creations was likely one of the elements that galvanized him to want to build an Alexandria on the Tiber, although an Alexandria that possessed a decidedly Roman look.

The intensity of the contact between Cleopatra and Rome apparently inspired ancient writers to try to capture that interaction. They may have embellished the story, but these authors revealed an interactive dynamism between an Egyptian queen and a group of elite Romans that was also reflected in contemporary art and architecture. If we examine these stories along with surviving material evidence, we find indications that Cleopatra's persona and the art she commissioned with Julius Caesar and Mark Antony had a dramatic impact on Augustus at the very moment when he was revamping Roman society and creating a pictorial language to express that transformation. The dialogue among these elites, with visual arts the medium of communication, permeated a wide variety of cultural activities in the age of Augustus and continued after Cleopatra's death—a dialogue much more important for understanding the age of Augustus than the fine points of chronology or whether Cleopatra was wrapped in bed linens or a carpet (Fig. P.3). A plausible case can be made that Cleopatra and her monuments made a profound contribution to art in the age of Augustus, and my aim is to try to do that here.

Cleopatra died young and in a dramatic way. Like other politicians and celebrities who have more recently come to early and memorable deaths (for example, John Fitzgerald Kennedy, Marilyn Monroe, and Diana, Princess of Wales), Cleopatra likely became in death even more than she was in life. She was immediately mythologized in a series of literary and historical vignettes that highlighted what were seen as her foremost qualities. These attributes—loyalty to country, political shrewdness, clever intellect, and personal attractiveness—were, however, broad enough to be used by her contemporaries and future generations to express their own agendas.

Augustus, as Cleopatra's immediate successor in the new Roman province of Egypt, took the lead and remade her in his own image, as have subsequent "admirers." The more iconic Cleopatra became, the more she seemed unique; in post-antique times she became the proverbial empty vessel that could take on the requisite form of the day. Each subsequent generation has had its own Cleopatra, and her name has become synonymous with the supreme femme fatale. Most recently, for example, there has been widespread speculation that Cleopatra may have been a black woman either by birth or symbolically because she suffered oppression, exploitation, and miscegenation. Since Cleopatra was a Macedonian Greek, this hypothesis is highly unlikely, but it exemplifies how historical personages who become icons can be utilized to reflect the intellectual or spiritual aspirations of later individuals and cultures.

Although Cleopatra was unquestionably a remarkable woman in her own time, most written praise of her was subsequent to her death and thus subject to hyperbole. Dio and Plutarch, for example, mention Cleopatra's literary skills, praise her facility with languages, and supply other details that may have been fictionalized or at least exaggerated. As incredible as she may have been, Cleopatra did not take the ancient world by storm. She did not burst on the scene like Minerva, full grown from the head of Jupiter, and play the part of master puppeteer, with Caesar, Antony, and Octavian as her pawns. Nor was she malleable putty in the masculine hands of individuals more interested in the wealth and resources of her country than in her. Cleopatra, Caesar, Antony, and Octavian came together in the natural course of human history because they were contemporary leaders, although each had a defined political and personal agenda. Yet those who might argue against Cleopatra's significance in the second half of the first century B.C., dismissing her as the political and sexual plaything of Rome, underestimate her impact. Cleopatra stood out among other women of the late Hellenistic period who had affairs with Caesar or Antony. She became a celebrity, whereas Eunoe, queen of Mauretania and wife of King Bogud, with whom Caesar supposedly had a liaison, is largely unknown.

Cleopatra's skill as Egypt's monarch in both the domestic and international spheres led to her ascendancy, but it was also her personal charisma and her use of visual culture to relate her story that contributed to her lasting influence. Above all, her interaction with Augustus ensured her fame. Augustus seems to have recognized that Cleopatra's dramatic passing could mark the momentous cultural shift from the Hellenistic world to the Roman Empire. That Cleopatra was at the core of this convergence demonstrates that a single flamboyant personality may be capable of accelerating a situation that is already decades in the making. The queen's death was not an end but a beginning, one that reinforced Augustus's overarching vision of a fully Roman realm. Cleopatra and her life, captured in a series of vibrant episodes, became a starting point for a wide variety of appropriations by Augustus and his contemporaries that established a paradigm for cultural conversion. Augustus used Cleopatra and her art so creatively and with such nuance that she entered the Roman lexicon with ease and soon became so seamlessly interwoven with the Augustan ethos as to become indistinguishable from it.

The collision of Cleopatra of Egypt and Octavian Augustus of Rome on the world stage was one of the greatest historical encounters of all time, even though the naval battle off the coast of Greece that marked that conflict was itself not particularly noteworthy. While Rome's dominion over Egypt after that engagement is well known (it became a Roman possession), the profound mark that Egypt made on Rome has not really been acknowledged. Some scholars have documented a wave of Egyptomania that swept through Rome after the Battle of Actium, but it is presented as a fashion surge rather than a revolution. From the time that he became aware of her, Octavian was impressed with Cleopatra and either consciously or subconsciously appears to have allowed her outlook and art to have a significant impact on his own.

Cleopatra likely made an impact on Augustus because she was a powerful woman with the will to make commanding monuments. Inspired by Egyptian pharaohs and Greek kings, she followed in the footsteps of her Ptolemaic predecessors. Like them, she built and restored temples and covered them from top to bottom with a profusion of scenes depicting the requisite Egyptian obeisance to the gods. Cleopatra's monuments paid homage to her Macedonian lineage and displayed an Egyptian pedigree. She assimilated herself to divine alter egos such as Isis and Hathor and commissioned a temple at Dendera that positioned her and her son as the masters of Egypt.

Yet Augustus had conflicting feelings about Cleopatra, as he did in general about women and foreigners. On one hand, he mounted a successful and devastating propaganda war against her. On the other, he recognized that her celebrity could be useful to him as a foil for his own ambitions. Instead of annihilating Cleopatra's image, Augustus allowed her gilded statue in Rome to stand in the hallowed presence of his own patron goddess, Venus Genetrix, like a kind of trophy of war.[8] He had Cleopatra's pearls placed in the ears of another statue of Venus,[9] and in a striking display of appropriation typical of Augustus, his name was inscribed on her temple at Dendera. Acts like these suggest that Augustus used Cleopatra's images and accoutrements to underscore his mastery over her and her kingdom. At the same time, Augustus assimilated Cleopatra's aura and found it useful to incorporate Cleopatra and her view of the world into his own vision for Rome. This coalition occurred at the time of Augustus's foundation of the empire and his codification of an art that can truly be called Roman. It seems fair to say, then, that there is more of Cleopatra in Rome than Augustus's propagandists would ever have believed possible.

Privileged Romans, like our main protagonists, spoke to one another and recorded some of those words in texts. As elite members of their respective societies, Caesar, Antony, Octavian, and Cleopatra were highly educated, articulate, and fluent in more than one language. They read widely and appreciated literary and historical writing. It was completely natural for each of them to want to leave a written account on a valued subject for posterity. Conversing with one another was easy, but they surely recognized that only a small number of their peers could read what they wrote or appreciate its subtleties. The real challenge was finding a way to reach the audience of largely illiterate Romans, Macedonians, and Egyptians of their day.

In Rome, most of those who could read and write, only about 10 to 15 percent of the population, were members of the ruling elite. The Egyptian lettered were also primarily members of the ruling class, including the scribal bureaucracy. Such widespread illiteracy meant that messages requiring broad circulation to a Roman or Egyptian audience were best transmitted through a vehicle other than text. The most direct and effective way to communicate was through visual means, including staged public appearances where the planners and participants had full control over the setting, the script, and the costumes.

Such pageantry was long practiced by the ancients, but it was embraced with special enthusiasm in the second half of the first century B.C.

Notable happenings were staged in Rome and the East that showcased Caesar, Antony, Octavian, and Cleopatra, who created the major events of their time, participated in them as they unfolded, and celebrated and memorialized them in art thereafter. These episodes appear to have been presented to diverse audiences in blatantly different ways, making use of what was judged in each situation to be appropriate imagery. In Rome, for example, Caesar portrayed Egypt as a conquered nation that could be exploited for its wealth, while in the East, he and Cleopatra depicted Egypt as a willing participant in a mutually beneficial merger.

Caesar's triumph over Alexandria was celebrated in Rome, along with three other military victories, all nominally over foreign foes. The quadruple triumph through Rome was an extraordinary parade, complete with floats containing chained prisoners and piles of valuable spoils. Exotic captives from a wide variety of locales were witnesses to the magnitude of Caesar's victories. The booty was a signal to the spectators that such bounty would be used to improve the lives of Roman citizens by providing them with new or renovated buildings for public discourse and for daily business and commerce. Caesar's subjugation of Egypt and entrance into an alliance with the Ptolemaic dynasty were publicly announced in the Alexandrian part of the triumph by including Cleopatra's sister Arsinoe as a manacled participant. Her identification was proclaimed by an accompaniment of panel paintings depicting the mighty Nile River and the legendary Alexandrian Pharos aflame.

In contrast, Cleopatra and Caesar's barge trip along the Nile (see Fig. 5.5) highlighted for an Egyptian audience the reestablishment of Cleopatra's monarchy after her recall from exile and her new and powerful alliance with the leadership of Rome. The splendiferous appearance of the barge, with its expensive and colorful gems and textiles, was meant to underscore the significance of the event. The vessel that bore Cleopatra to her subsequent meeting with Antony at Tarsus was equally ornate, decked out in purple and silver, fit for the goddess she came as. Cleopatra's apparent wealth and that of her country were undoubtedly accentuated not in order to gloat but to make manifest in easily recognizable terms that Egypt had much to offer as the country entered into an alliance with another powerful and protective Roman. Cleopatra was assimilated to Venus, an association that highlighted her sexuality—another asset that would lead to an invaluable coalition with Rome, whose legendary ancestor Aeneas was the son of Venus. Cleopatra's unions with Julius Caesar and Antony were presented not only as personal relationships but also as public mergers that furthered the political agendas of the pairs and benefited their nations.

However spectacular and memorable they may have been, such events were nonetheless ephemeral. That we have written evocations of them is invaluable to understanding the age of Cleopatra—the queen's political and personal objectives and those of her Roman contemporaries. Cleopatra, Caesar, and Octavian all had their eye on posterity and shrewdly realized that what could preserve these fleeting occurrences were written or visual documentaries that might take the form of selected vignettes. These would enable those citizens who had missed Caesar's triumph or Cleopatra's voyage, or who had been there and wanted to relive them, to access them again. There is no material evidence that visual documentaries of these happenings were produced in the first century, although Caesar's textual account of his Gallic Wars might suggest that this kind of visual narrative existed in ancient times. What has come down to us are what might be described as excerpts. These excerpts are not literal ones—the kind that would become ubiquitous in subsequent Roman art (the emperor leading his troops into battle, sacrifice after victory, the emperor's triumphal entry into Rome)—but abbreviated references to momentous events in the form of buildings, coinage, statuary, relief sculpture, and painting. The content of these was often more subtle than the staged pageants, and careful consideration was given to the intended audience. It is these works of art and architecture that became the essence of the visual dialogue among Cleopatra, Caesar, and Antony, and that were appropriated by Augustus after Cleopatra's death.

What is explored above all in this book is a magical moment in history when a gifted group of elite men and women—Octavian, Caesar, Antony, Cleopatra, and also Octavian's sister Octavia and his formidable wife Livia—came together and changed the world. They also activated ambitious succession plans that ensured dynastic continuity through their children. It might be argued that an examination of the ways in which privileged people with royal or patrician pedigrees and enormous political clout interacted with one another is elitist and even outdated. In recent years, historians have increasingly turned their attention away from studies of "great men" and their accomplishments to the ways in which entire groups or classes of people, many of whose names and personal histories have not come down to us, have shaped political events and social change.

A new and more revealing approach would investigate the kind of synergy that is sometimes created between a powerful elite and a vibrant and upwardly mobile multicultural society. Vast numbers of slaves were transported to Rome in the mid-Republic and were supplemented by significant numbers of additional captives from Caesar's Gallic Wars. These slaves came from both eastern and western colonies and had diverse ethnic and religious backgrounds, as well as varying levels of education and professional expertise. Their immigration forever changed Roman society, especially since most of their descendants became Roman citizens.

Cleopatra was herself a foreigner and viewed as one by Augustus, who was initiating a complete transformation of Roman culture. Augustus's society was one in which slaves, foreigners, and even elite Roman women were considered inferior. He enacted laws to keep women "in their place." At the same time, for reasons of political expediency, Augustus provided Octavia and Livia with unprecedented freedom and power. His attitude toward Cleopatra was equally ambivalent. The tension between the repression of the rights of women, foreigners, and slaves and their concomitant power is one of the fascinations of this period and allows a concurrent exploration of a small number of elites and a large faceless and nameless group of foreigners and slaves.

There was a powerful trickle-down effect under Augustus: the ideology of emperor and empress, as well as the form of their art, had a significant impact on that commissioned by freedmen and slaves. More difficult to understand, but no less significant, are the individual professional contributions and artistic predilections of this other class of Roman patrons. What complicates matters further is that it was the non-elites who were the architects, artists, and artisans of the period and who played a significant part in creating the visual language that gave concrete form to the imperial family's political and social agenda.

Cleopatra's and Rome's defining moments were also revealed through surviving works of art. While some of these monuments effortlessly divulge their secrets, the meaning of others has been lost over time. Yet what remains clear is that Cleopatra had a lasting impact on Rome, especially in the visual arts, and set in motion what became a dynamic dialogue with the visual culture of Augustan Rome. That a female sovereign of Egypt influenced the art of Rome in so profound a way has never before been considered because Cleopatra's personal myth and iconic status, kept alive by ancient writers like Plutarch and Dio Cassius, and later by Shakespeare, rapidly took on an existence that outgrew her art. Furthermore, the monuments that Cleopatra commissioned with Caesar and Antony were not confined to Alexandria but spread across Egypt and the East, gracing such non-Egyptian locales as the Acropolis of Athens. This dispersal made those works more difficult to characterize, and the situation is complicated further by their low rate of survival.

If past is truly prologue, it is not only the remnants of history and literature that have preserved the essence of ancient history's greatest female star. Cleopatra also comes alive in surviving works of art and other remains of what was once an opulent material culture. No visual detail is too insignificant to add to the picture, and a wide variety of works of art and architecture commissioned by both elite and everyday patrons provide valuable evidence. The more conventional representational data are found in urban plans, temple complexes, forums, altars, cult statuary, honorific portraiture, villa paintings, tombstones, coins, seals, and more. Yet the materiality of the clothing, perfume, and especially the hair styled to perfection for such ephemeral occasions as triumphal processions and barge cruises also amplifies our understanding of Cleopatra's contribution to Rome.

The surviving literary and historical vestiges of Cleopatra may not all be accurate, but the monuments, portraiture, and even the strands of hair, frozen in marble flawlessness, provide plausible evidence for the life and art of Cleopatra and their impact on a Rome that was beginning to free itself from the shackles of a powerful Hellenistic past. It is this visual culture that best chronicles Cleopatra's legend and requires further investigation. As we shall see, some works of art openly herald Cleopatra's supremacy; others subtly disclose her impact on the sphinx-like Augustus, whose complex response to the queen made a subtle but indelible mark on the art of Rome at the critical moment of its inception.

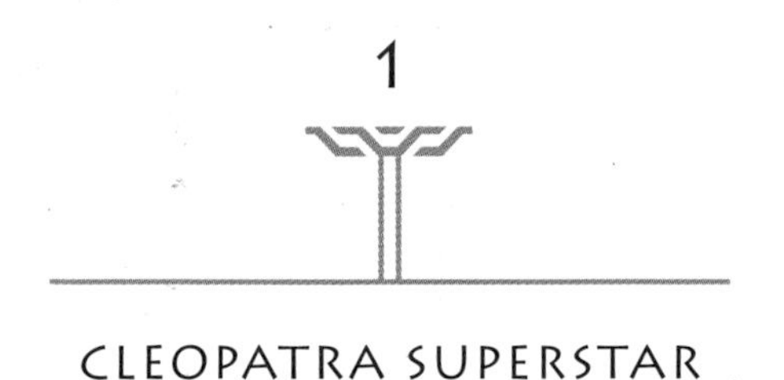

CLEOPATRA SUPERSTAR

Cleopatra's death by asp, reenacted in Augustus's triumph in Rome, was instrumental in elevating her to superstar status. Yet despite her renown, the fundamental outline of the life of Cleopatra VII Philopator may be narrated in a few sentences. She was Queen of Egypt. She allegedly rolled out of bed linens into Julius Caesar's life. She had a highly publicized affair with Mark Antony. These liaisons led to children with both men, one of whom was Caesar's sole male heir, Caesarion. Antony and Cleopatra lived the high life in Alexandria and were treated as celebrities in Asia Minor and Greece, rewarded with gifts and statuary depicting them as deities. Their fame did not protect them, however, from the wrath of Octavian Augustus. Octavian defeated the famous couple at a naval battle at Actium off the western coast of Greece. As Octavian entered Alexandria, a series of miscommunications between the lovers—each thought incorrectly that the other was dead—led to their successive suicides.

These basic facts have been told and retold, in simple and embellished form, in books, plays, films, and animation, with the result that it is no longer easy to distinguish fact from fiction and to discover who this woman really was (Fig. 1.1). Any attempt to reveal her is complicated not only by the vast collection of later interpretations but also by the exceedingly biased picture of her painted by Augustus and his propagandists.

That Cleopatra was the most powerful woman in the ancient world's first century B.C. cannot be contested. That a Roman triad as formidable as Caesar, Antony, and Octavian were in turn captivated by her is a strong tribute to the queen's compelling personality and authority. A recreation of Cleopatra can go only so far, however, and it is challenged at every turn by partisan historical and literary accounts and by the disappearance of most of ancient Alexandria and the majority of Cleopatra's portraits and monuments. Nonetheless, the historical and material remains that we do have tell a remarkable story.

Since this is a book about the art of Cleopatra and Rome, my objective is not to give a full history of Cleopatra beginning with her earliest experiences and culminating with her sovereignty of Egypt. In any case, others have already effectively recounted the chronology of Cleopatra's life and accomplishments. That said, any attempt to interpret the material remains of the first century B.C. must be informed by a historical and literary context, although for these purposes the facts do not have to be examined in strict chronological order.

1.1. Cleopatra with wig and vulture headdress in a portrait found near the Sanctuary of Isis on the Via Labicana in Rome, likely made when she was in Rome with Caesar.

What is important to keep in mind is that Cleopatra's unwrapping before Caesar was not synonymous with her birth. Cleopatra came from an eminent and wealthy family; as the daughter of Egypt's pharaoh, she inhabited the center of Ptolemaic power. She was tutored by Egypt's leading scholars and had access to the "great books" (scrolls in those days) in the famed Library of Alexandria. She traveled extensively with her father, who took the opportunity to mentor her in the ways of their dynasty.

Cleopatra thus had an eventful life before Julius Caesar and Mark Antony came on the scene, and her illustrious family had a history separate from Rome's. Cleopatra's Egypt was its own empire, but it was distinct from Egypt's Old, Middle, and New Kingdoms. Cleopatra was not Egyptian but Macedonian, and she followed a succession of strong and influential Macedonian women who ruled Egypt beside their Ptolemaic husbands.

In fact, the Ptolemaic dynasty had a far more illustrious past than that of Caesar, Antony, and Octavian, tracing its lineage, not biologically but foundationally, to history's grandest Macedonian—Alexander the Great, a man whom every first-century Roman leader tried to emulate (see Fig. 8.1). Alexander founded his urban namesake, Alexandria, in 332 B.C., as the basis for governance of all of Egypt. Sophisticated enough to know that respect for Egyptian culture and the heritage of 3,000 years of pharaonic leadership would further his objectives, Alexander acquiesced to being crowned pharaoh and received the appropriate royal titles and insignia. After his death in 323 B.C., Alexander's empire was dispersed to his loyal commanders, with Egypt eventually assigned to a man named Ptolemy, who was pronounced king. Ptolemy I Soter was a childhood friend of Alexander and a notable general. He was also a writer, even a propagandist, who hoped to record the heroic life of his distinguished mentor as well as his own.

Like the legatees of most great men, Alexander's successors warred with one another for supremacy. Over the next half-century, Macedon and the Seleucid and Ptolemaic empires came out on top. Even without other contenders, all three remained rivals and each vied for Greece, Syria, and Palestine, with varying degrees of success. Their competitiveness reached a peak, however, in the cultural and artistic sphere, as they attempted to outdo one another's libraries and palaces. When it came to lavish and conspicuous consumption, the Ptolemies had no peer. While Ptolemy I Soter's court was probably fairly simple, ostentation became the norm among the later Ptolemies. *Tryphe* or magnificence was their goal, and some of the Ptolemaic dynasts gladly took on weight, amplifying their physicality as a way of publicly embodying the plentitude of their reigns. Caesar was impressed by what he saw at Cleopatra's court, and Antony was able to luxuriate there in an incomparable style; life was bountiful among the Ptolemies, and they embraced it with ebullience.

The establishment of the Ptolemaic dynasty by Alexander brought considerable stability to Egypt. The city of Alexandria grew apace, and other regions of Egypt, especially an area in the north called the Fayum, became increasingly populated and even urbanized. Under the Ptolemies, there were probably about three million people living in Egypt. Ptolemaic governance was based on an administrative structure that had stood the test of time—thirty centuries of pharaonic rule. It was a substantive and strict bureaucracy that was, in a sense, largely established at the whim of the Nile River. The Nile's annual flooding needed to be managed both at the uppermost levels of government and locally along the mighty river's path. It was this overflow and the fertile land it created near the river's edge that allowed Egypt not only to feed its large population but also to export ample amounts of grain to Rome. Wisely, the Ptolemies did not dismantle a successful bureaucracy but rather made slight alterations that were appropriate to the current situation. A hieratic and rigid organization placed Cleopatra and her brothers at the apex, in the same position as their pharaonic and Ptolemaic forebears. The Ptolemaic adjustments involved empowering Greeks in the uppermost administrative levels and even in the countryside, and restructuring the country's agricultural and craft production to produce greater revenues.

Egypt's Macedonian Greek heritage also made it an integral part of the Hellenistic world. Egypt emerged from this small but significant reorganization as the wealthiest of Alexander's dynastic spin-offs and lasted the longest. Even when it fell to Rome, Egypt had the distinction of becoming imperial property rather than a more traditional province. Augustus kept his new possession close to his vest by entrusting it only to equestrian leadership—equestrians being the distinct order of knights between the senate and the plebs—avoiding senatorial stewardship in a post as critical as Egypt.

To say that the governance of Ptolemaic Egypt was a Macedonian family affair is an understatement. Probably inspired by the union of the mythological Egyptian sister and brother, Isis and Osiris, brothers married their sisters. The practice aimed for familial loyalty and gave the Ptolemaic princesses an authority that ancient women did not always possess. All the brothers were Ptolemies and the sisters Cleopatras, Berenices, and Arsinoes. Royal titles emphasized heartfelt family ties. *Philometor* and *Philopator* meant mother- and father-loving respectively, and *Philadelphus* brother- and sister-loving. Ruling fathers routinely selected their son as successor before their own demise and also married their choice to the boy's sister. This incestuous merger ensured predictability in succession, although it did not always prevent treasonous behavior among family members.

The land of Egypt was the Ptolemies' possession, making them the overseers and primary beneficiaries of the country's agricultural output. Grain production, bolstered by the annual flooding of the Nile, was prodigious and made Egypt the most significant grain producer in the Mediterranean. The resulting wealth not only augmented Egypt's power but also made the country a target for would-be world rulers. The Ptolemaic penchant for monopolies did not lessen under Cleopatra, and its reach was impressive. The products that supported many of the daily needs of the Egyptian populace (papyrus, wool, salt, cloth, perfume, and oil) were manufactured under the management of royal factories and with royal licenses. Still, local artisans and merchants worked in these places and benefited from Egypt's transformation into a cash society and the concomitant circulation of a substantive coinage. The introduction of an official coinage in Egypt was revolutionary because of the belief that gold belonged to the gods, not to commerce; coinage thus would not have been possible without a Greek leadership.

Blessed with a spectacular harbor at Alexandria, the Ptolemies enhanced it with a remarkable lighthouse (see Fig. 5.1). They gathered enough scrolls to create the ancient world's largest and most comprehensive library, adjacent to a museum for teaching and learning (Fig. 5.2). Each Ptolemy added a new edifice to the dynasty's palace, creating a structure that meandered endlessly.

The Ptolemies also devoted considerable resources to building and rebuilding temples and to supporting related libraries and museums, underscoring the power of the priestly overseers of these temples. Membership in the Egyptian priesthood offered status and the potential for a leadership position in the Egyptian hierarchy. The priesthood was a hereditary enterprise and under Cleopatra the high priests of Memphis were influential, especially one Pshereniptah. Otherwise, there was not much in the way of an Egyptian aristocracy.

These priests officiated at cult sites honoring traditional Greek divinities as well as Alexander the Great and the Ptolemaic dynasts. At Alexandria and the city of Ptolemais in Cyrenaica, a Ptolemaic possession since the third century B.C., members of eminent families held the priesthoods, their primary duty being participation in processions commemorating deceased kings and queens. While it was Cleopatra and her brothers who were regarded as the genuine intermediaries between the Egyptian gods and the Egyptian people, it was the priests who were charged with maintaining the order of the Egyptian universe and ensuring the continued beneficence of the gods. Worship of these gods was not the monopoly of temple culture but also occurred in the privacy of homes and in professional and private guilds and clubs.

Since the Ptolemies possessed the breath of divinities, a close connection was established between them and the Egyptian priesthood. The Ptolemaic dynasts were one with the pantheon of Egyptian gods and therefore shared with them the interior space of the temple. What this meant is that Cleopatra was a genuine goddess from her birth and shared that standing with other family members. It may well have been priests who taught Egyptian to the young girl to demonstrate that she was a goddess with a common touch, the ancient equivalent of the "people's princess," in contrast to her predecessors, both male and female, who spoke only Greek.

The royal burial ground was already situated near the palace in the reign of Ptolemy I. Its purpose was to house the remains of the members of the newly founded Ptolemaic dynasty. Ptolemy I, however, quickly acted to turn it into a hallowed shrine and tourist destination. What better way to make Alexandria a magnet than to locate Alexander's tomb within the city walls? That was easier said than done, however, since Alexander's corpse was already on its way to Macedon. In a bold move, Ptolemy hijacked the corpse and had it triumphantly transported to Alexandria. Possessing Alexander's body was like having a magic talisman that would cast its special aura on all subsequent Ptolemies. The drawing power of Alexander's tomb continued into Roman times. Augustus made a pilgrimage to see it, and his obsession with the establishment of a dynasty owes much to the Ptolemaic model.

Cleopatra was born to Ptolemy XII in 69 B.C. In the well-established brother-sister tradition, she married her two brothers, Ptolemy XIII and XIV, in succession. These were essentially marriages in name only. Both

1.2. Cleopatra's father, Ptolemy XII Auletes, appears in this image as a Hellenistic king wearing a royal diadem that may suggest his assimilation to the god Dionysus.

boys were younger than Cleopatra, in fragile health, and apparently without her intelligence and verve. Cleopatra must have recognized that these boy kings did not have the machismo to make it in the competitive arena of ancient world politics and surely realized that she would have to ally herself with a different breed of man if she truly wanted an empire worthy of the great Alexander.

Significant interaction between Egypt and Rome predated Cleopatra's sovereignty. Sulla was instrumental in placing Ptolemy XI on Egypt's throne, but he was quickly overthrown. Cleopatra's father, Ptolemy XII, was chosen by the Alexandrian court to succeed him. While his full name with titles was Ptolemy XII Theos Philopator Philadelphus Neos Dionysos, his nickname was Auletes or the flute player, signaling his obsession with the arts and his relationship with Isis, whose favorite instrument was the flute (Fig. 1.2). Ptolemy XII appears to have been married to his sister, probably Cleopatra V Tryphaena ("the opulent one"), about whom little is known. She seems to have died within a year of giving birth to Cleopatra, possibly after producing Cleopatra's younger sister, Arsinoe IV. She also supplied Auletes with two older daughters: another Cleopatra, who briefly became Cleopatra VI Tryphaena, and Berenice IV. Cleopatra's two half-brothers, who were to become Ptolemy XIII and XIV, were born to Auletes's second wife, whose name is not recorded.

While together Auletes and Cleopatra V seem to have led a high life that drained resources from Egypt, one of the couple's highest priorities was maintaining friendly relations with Rome. Neither their extravagant spending nor their flirtation with Rome was well received locally, and the Alexandrians summarily expelled Ptolemy XII. Since Rome had Ptolemy in its pocket, considerable Roman effort and expense were put into restoring him to power. It suited Rome's leadership to have Auletes as its pawn, and the situation was relatively stable until Pompey the Great, fresh from a major victory over the Seleucids, decided he wanted to take on the Ptolemies (see Fig. 8.3). Pompey's objective seems clear: Roman possession of Egypt and its boundless treasury would fortify his power base. Pompey's fellow triumvirs, Caesar and Crassus, were, however, similarly motivated, and as the three men jockeyed for position they canceled out each other's attempted appropriation of Egypt for Rome. Yet another ambitious Roman, Cato the Younger, was successful in Cyprus, which was ruled by Auletes's younger brother, also called Ptolemy, who committed suicide after his devastating loss.

Auletes was immediately blamed for losing Cyprus. Seeing the handwriting on the wall, he grabbed the treasure and headed for the island of Rhodes, leaving most of his family behind. To signal continuity, his eldest daughter, Cleopatra VI Tryphaena, was appointed queen. Her authority was not clear-cut, however; in some regions of the country his second daughter, Berenice IV, was considered in charge. Although that turn of events was advantageous to the two sisters for the time being, it was Cleopatra who got to see the world with her father. She accompanied him to Rhodes, then to Athens, and finally to Rome. It has been speculated that while in Italy she must have resided in one of Pompey's villas, perhaps the one nearest Rome's greatest Republican sanctuary, that of Fortuna Primigenia at Palestrina. The sanctuary cascaded spectacularly down a mountainside, which must have given it at least a superficial similarity to Egyptian religious complexes. More significant was the sanctuary's honoree, a goddess who, like Isis, was favored by women but also appealed to travelers like soldiers and sailors. Scholars have even noted the association in Italy of Fortuna with Isis Navigans, that is, Isis—whose many aspects encouraged assimilation—as goddess of seafaring.

Cleopatra and her entourage of women attendants thus must have been acclimated to female cults in Italy. They deepened their understanding of the impact that female goddesses could have when Cleopatra was welcomed at the Temple of Artemis at Ephesus, where she and Auletes stopped on their way back to Egypt. Even though Auletes's treasure was depleted, he paid obeisance to the goddess by funding ornate ivory doors for her temple, one of the seven wonders of the ancient world. His religiosity was, however, diluted by his ruthlessness once back in Alexandria. While his wife appears to have died of natural causes, Auletes ordered the murder of his eldest daughter for trying to usurp his power. Although this deed allowed Auletes to regain jurisdiction over Egypt, it bankrupted both his authority and his treasure and initiated a personal decline from which the king never recovered.

Auletes's loss of physical strength and political resolve created a power vacuum that his remaining children attempted to fill. The wheeling and dealing that must have ensued among the Alexandrian power brokers and with the authorities in Rome is difficult to assess. What seems clear is that Auletes hoped to be succeeded by his eldest living daughter and his eldest son. In reality, however, these two were rivals with different supporting factions. Although Cleopatra was older and more competent, the patriarchal proclivity of Ptolemaic society led to joint rule.

It is ironic that Cleopatra's political alliance with Rome began when she supported Pompey the Great's war against Julius Caesar (see Figs. 8.4 and 8.5). In 49 B.C. she supplied Gnaeus Pompeius with ships, forces, and corn, which Gnaeus sent on to his father. Rumors of a liaison between the younger Pompey and Cleopatra are reported by Plutarch, but this hearsay is not confirmed elsewhere. Cleopatra probably bestowed largesse on the younger Pompey in return for his father's support of Auletes, not because she was having an affair with him. Caesar pursued Pompey and waged war against Ptolemy XIII for harboring him. Weakened by Caesar's attack but not wanting to give his sister a chance to take advantage of this debility, Ptolemy expelled Cleopatra. During her expatriation, Cleopatra stayed in Arabia and Palestine where she attempted to raise an army. Support for this effort is attested by contemporary coins minted with her portrait in Ascalon. Once she had amassed a substantial force, Cleopatra stood up to her brother. Before anything definitive could happen, however, a momentous clash between Pompey and Caesar took center stage.

Pompey was defeated by Caesar at Pharsalus in Thessaly in 48 and fled to Egypt. Upon his arrival there, he was stabbed to death. Caesar restored Cleopatra's power by reinstating her on Egypt's throne. By now Cleopatra and Caesar were lovers, and Cleopatra parlayed her personal alliance with Caesar into a compelling political one that enabled her to expand her influence outside Egyptian borders. Her power was solidified when Cleopatra became the mother of Caesar's only son, Ptolemy Caesar or Caesarion, in 47 B.C. (see Fig. 9.7).

After Caesar's death in 44 B.C., Cleopatra entered into a political alliance with Mark Antony that was even more far-reaching (Fig. 1.3); she consolidated it further in 41 by providing Antony with twins, Alexander Helios and Cleopatra Selene, whom he recognized in 37. A third child and second son, Ptolemy Philadelphus, was born to the couple in 36. While Cleopatra promised to back Antony in his military encounters and to provide money and supplies, Antony saw to it that part of the old Ptolemaic empire, including Cyrenaica, was returned to Egyptian sovereignty. In 34 B.C., Antony and Cleopatra appropriated additional "donations," which consisted of all the lands once ruled by Alexander the Great, and Antony appointed Cleopatra and her children to govern them. Cleopatra thus became "Queen of Kings," and her son Ptolemy Caesar "King of Kings." Their domain was not only Egypt but also the entire empire, east and west of the Euphrates, and including Cyrenaica.

These generous gifts put Antony's loyalty to Rome in doubt—the Roman senate, in fact, refused approval—and Octavian capitalized on Antony's new autocratic bent. A vicious propaganda war between Octavian and Antony ensued, with Antony and Cleopatra taking refuge in Asia Minor and Greece. The couple likely thought that Cleopatra's enormous wealth and formidable army and fleet would protect them; Antony relied also on support from senatorial friends in Rome. Nonetheless, when the contents of Antony's will (which may well have been fabricated by his enemies) were revealed first by former confidants and then to the senate by Octavian himself, the balance of the propaganda war shifted dramatically toward Octavian. Even though they already had suspicions, the Roman people professed shock to learn that Roman holdings had been bestowed on Cleopatra, that Antony had recognized Caesarion as Caesar's son, and that Antony intended to be buried in Alexandria rather than Rome. The populace demanded war. Octavian readily acquiesced to public opinion (an opinion he helped promote) and met Antony and Cleopatra on the seas near Actium. The result was a momentous victory for Octavian and the double suicides of Antony and Cleopatra in Alexandria.

This brief sketch of Cleopatra's interactions with the two Pompeys and

1.3. A playful Cleopatra drops her pearl earring into a goblet while she and Antony dine at Tarsus and strategize about a lasting alliance between Egypt and Rome.

with Caesar and Antony provides the known facts. More challenging is to try to assess just what it was about Cleopatra that made her so special. Supreme self-confidence, fostered by a sense of history and duty, must have been an important factor. She cannot have helped feeling that she, rather than her brothers, was responsible for maintaining Egypt's greatness and seeing that it was perpetuated. Her identification with Isis was also clearly a major asset. Although Cleopatra was considered a genuine divinity in Egypt, her sacredness elsewhere was not a foregone conclusion. Yet, independent of Cleopatra, the cult of Isis was gaining ground in the West because of the goddess's appeal to merchants and sailors throughout the Mediterranean. The acceptance, even adoration, of Isis made her human counterpart easier to worship. While Cleopatra knew that her Ptolemaic sisterhood had achieved positions of authority held by few women in the ancient world, she was acutely aware that she could not fulfill her destiny without a partnership with men. Recognizing that her brothers were unlikely to be up to the task, she wisely sought to establish alliances with Rome's male stars. She was undoubtedly able to discern that Rome was a cut above the Seleucid Empire and Macedon. Given that Cleopatra's death and the incorporation of Egypt into Rome were simultaneous events, it can be argued that the queen's overarching mission failed. Cleopatra's impact on Caesar, Antony, and Octavian, however, was so profound as to have altered the trajectory of Roman art and architecture. In that sense, she unquestionably succeeded.

As for her personal attributes, Cleopatra appears to have been a vibrant and attractive woman. She was intelligent and spoke several languages, including, as we have seen, Egyptian.[1] In fact, she was the first member of her dynasty to recognize the importance of being able to converse in the local language. Cleopatra seems to have demonstrated deep concern for her people and was solicitous with regard to their material and spiritual needs. They appear to have returned her affection. The ruthlessness that has been attributed to her must be evaluated in the context of the long tradition of Ptolemaic family politics, where ruthlessness was rife. Furthermore, her ambitions for herself and her country appear not to have been ignoble, and there is evidence that her affection for Caesar and Antony was sincere.

Cleopatra's Roman paramours were two of the most powerful men in the ancient world. That the world's most powerful woman was attracted by and attractive to two of the world's most powerful men is not at all surprising. Although Cleopatra was apparently aware of the advantage of these unions, there is no reason to believe that the Queen of Egypt traded sexual favors for political gain. Nor is there firm evidence to suggest that Cleopatra had affairs with men other than Caesar and Antony. She was involved with each in turn, not at the same time. Since flagrant infidelities were not the norm in the Ptolemaic court, Cleopatra's behavior was in keeping with that of her royal counterparts. Indeed, Cleopatra's monogamous behavior provides an interesting contrast to the overt adulteries of women of the court circle of Augustus, including the emperor's daughter Julia and granddaughter Julia the Younger.

Given Cleopatra's intellectual attainments and facility with languages, it is possible that she wrote treatises, opinions, or other documents. Caesar was a writer, and it could not have escaped Cleopatra that men who mattered recorded their deeds in texts that could outlive them. Numerous writings are attributed to Cleopatra, who was also known for her clever puns. After the queen's death, many literary works were associated with her; she was also credited with an essay on weights, measures, and coinage and others on cosmetics, alchemy, and medicine, especially gynecology. If these are indeed reflective of the kinds of things she might have written, they provide valuable evidence on what were identified as Cleopatra's interests and talents by her contemporaries. The treatise on cosmetics was widely quoted by Roman writers and is especially interesting in light of a cosmetics workshop that was found at En Boquet near the Dead Sea. Constructed by Herod the Great, it came under Cleopatra's jurisdiction when the area was presented to her by Antony.

While these writings on cosmetics and the female reproductive system may speak to Cleopatra's femininity, others on business, farming, and magic have a decidedly masculine cast. Whether or not they were written by Cleopatra, these attributions indicate that her intellectual powers were widely recognized and her expertise respected. They underscore the fact that Cleopatra and her peer group recognized the value of words, especially prose, that could outlive them. Given this impact made by words, we can easily assume the same or more for the impact made by the visual arts, including architecture.

2

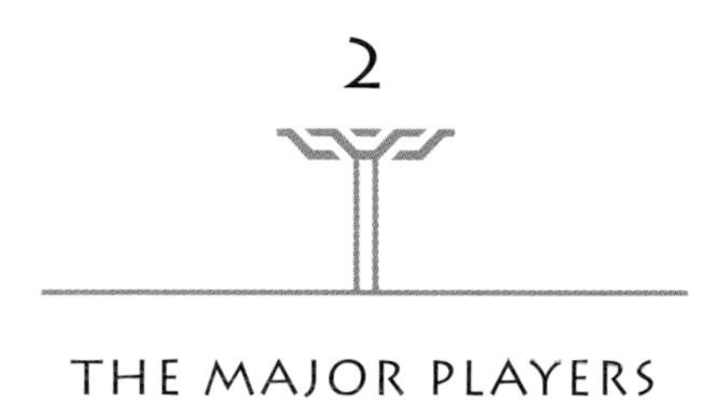

THE MAJOR PLAYERS

The primary protagonists of *Cleopatra and Rome* are among the most colorful historical figures of all time. In addition to Cleopatra herself, there were five major players in the story that underlies this book: an epileptic dictator with an eye for young foreign female sovereigns; a brilliant military commander who drank too much; a woman so virtuous that she raised the children of her husband's mistresses; a pregnant but ambitious ingénue who married her second husband while carrying the child of her first; and a ruthless opportunist determined to rule Rome and an empire. The potent chemistry of this group ignited the ancient world and catapulted them to superstardom. From that elevated perch, this intriguing sextet had a momentous collective impact on Rome and on western civilization.

Princeps Femina: Livia Drusilla

Since Roman women could not hold public office, Livia Drusilla's power was different in kind from Cleopatra's, but nonetheless compelling. Cleopatra had inherited a position that put her in charge of a mighty kingdom with an illustrious past, and she enhanced her influence further by entering into political and personal alliances with Caesar and Antony. Livia's base of authority was her membership in a formidable patrician family, the Claudians, with political clout in Rome. Born in 58 B.C., Livia must still have been a child when she realized that she could never be a public official (see Fig. 18.2). Nonetheless, Livia apparently had the vibrant intelligence, strong will, and cleverness to take advantage of a series of affiliations with men in order to position herself as a major force in Roman public life. As was traditional for elite Roman girls, she married for the first time at age 15 or 16. The marriage was certainly arranged by her family for political gain.

Livia was first betrothed to Tiberius Claudius Nero, a man with a public profile. Quaestor or public officer in 48, and a commander of Caesar's fleet in the Alexandrian War, Claudius Nero settled veterans in Gallia Narbonensis, one of the four provinces into which Augustus divided Gaul after the hostilities were over. He belonged to a group of elite men who in the period after Caesar's death found themselves having to choose whether their allegiance was to Octavian or Antony, as the two rivaled each other for supreme power. Tiberius Claudius Nero opted to speak in favor of rewarding Cassius and Brutus for their assassination of Caesar, and in the war that took place in Perusia, the modern Italian hill town of Perugia, he sided with Antony's brother Lucius Antonius rather than with Octavian. After fleeing Octavian's successful foray, Claudius Nero attempted to foment a slave uprising and then fled to Sicily to join Sextus Pompeius; Livia and their infant son accompanied him. Apparently never having the acumen to back a winner, Claudius Nero later affiliated himself with Mark Antony in Greece.

Nevertheless, after the Treaty of Misenum between Octavian and Pompeius was signed in 39 B.C., Claudius Nero returned to Rome. A magnanimous Octavian appears to have forgiven him for his lack of support but, in return for absolution, requested what might be described as significant compensation. While Octavian may not have admired Claudius Nero's political sensibilities, he approved of his taste in wives. Octavian wanted to marry Livia Drusilla, and in 38 he convinced Tiberius Claudius Nero to divorce her—even though she was, at the time, pregnant with their second child. Livia wed Octavian, and Drusus was born three months later. Whether Livia had anything to say about this arrangement is not known, nor is it clear whether she knew then that whatever ambitions she had could be better realized with a man with the political perspicacity of Augustus. The personal alliance between Livia and Octavian was to have extraordinary repercussions for the history of Rome.

2.1. Livia, presented like a Greek goddess on the Ara Pacis Augustae, was a formidable force in Roman public life.

Augustus was as paternalistic as other men of his time. In fact, he was more so, instituting strict behavioral rules for Roman women. These promoted marriage, discouraged adultery (*lex Julia de adulteriis coercendis*), and encouraged childbirth (*lex Julia maritandis ordinibus* of 18 B.C., emended in A.D. 9 by the *lex Papia Poppaea*). By rewarding motherhood, these laws helped Livia to achieve an authority that no woman in Rome had enjoyed before (Fig. 2.1). Livia was adopted into the Julian family in Augustus's will. A majestic title was her reward: she was designated *Augusta,* the female equivalent of her husband's *Augustus.* After Augustus's death, Livia was afforded numerous other honors and privileges. She was allowed to sit with the Vestal Virgins in the theater, and she was freed from the legal guardianship required for all Roman women.

Despite all these tributes, Livia was not able to acquire as much influence as she apparently would have liked during Augustus's principate, and she redoubled her efforts to position her elder son Tiberius as Augustus's successor. Upon Tiberius's eventual ascent, Livia was able to enhance her own position as mother of the *princeps* or emperor, which gave her a high position in Roman public life that was recognized by the senate. The message that it was motherhood that had elevated her still further was not lost on an admiring public.

Livia made Augustus's marriage and moral codes work for her. Since the laws underscored women's primary roles as keepers of the household and producers of children, especially male heirs, Livia, as the mother of Tiberius, became the supreme head of the imperial family or *Domus Augusta.* Nonetheless, Livia's relationship with her ruling son was tempestuous. The ancient sources make it clear that the two had a falling-out and that at Livia's death, Tiberius refused to have her deified.

First Sister: Octavia

Octavia, Octavian's sister, was, like her brother, the offspring of Gaius Octavia and Atia (Fig. 2.2). Seven years older than Octavian, she married Gaius Claudius Marcellus in 54 B.C. and together they produced three children—two Marcellae and a Marcellus—before his death in 40 B.C. Although Mark Antony had been married three times by 40 B.C. and had already fathered twins by Cleopatra, Octavian apparently viewed him as an appropriate husband for his sister. The union of Antony and Octavia as a seal for the pact among the triumvirs at Brundisium (modern Brindisi on the Adriatic coast) was uppermost in Octavian's mind and was probably more important to him than the marital happiness of his sister.

The newly affianced pair spent the first two years of their marriage in Athens and had two daughters together—Antonia the Elder and Antonia the Younger. Octavia, probably only too well aware of how tenuous her hold was on her new husband, worked tirelessly to maintain his association with her brother, but the two men's differences widened. Octavia continued to try to keep them aligned, and her intervention appears to have contributed to the pact between Antony and Octavian at Tarentum (modern Taranto in the south of Italy) in 37 B.C.: the triumvirate was renewed for another five years. Octavia's effort was not rewarded, however; Antony left alone for the East and for Cleopatra, by whom he immediately had another son. Never one to miss gaining the strategic upper hand, Octavian put politics over his sister's marital discord and, in a ploy to embarrass Antony, sent Octavia with troop reinforcements. As Octavian had surely expected, Antony rejected this gesture and forbade Octavia to travel beyond Athens. Octavian, undoubtedly delighted at this turn of events, took the public posture of deep offense and attempted to convince his sister to divorce Antony. Yet Octavia's stalwart devotion to their children gave her pause and the divorce did not occur until 32 B.C., and then only because Antony instigated the separation.

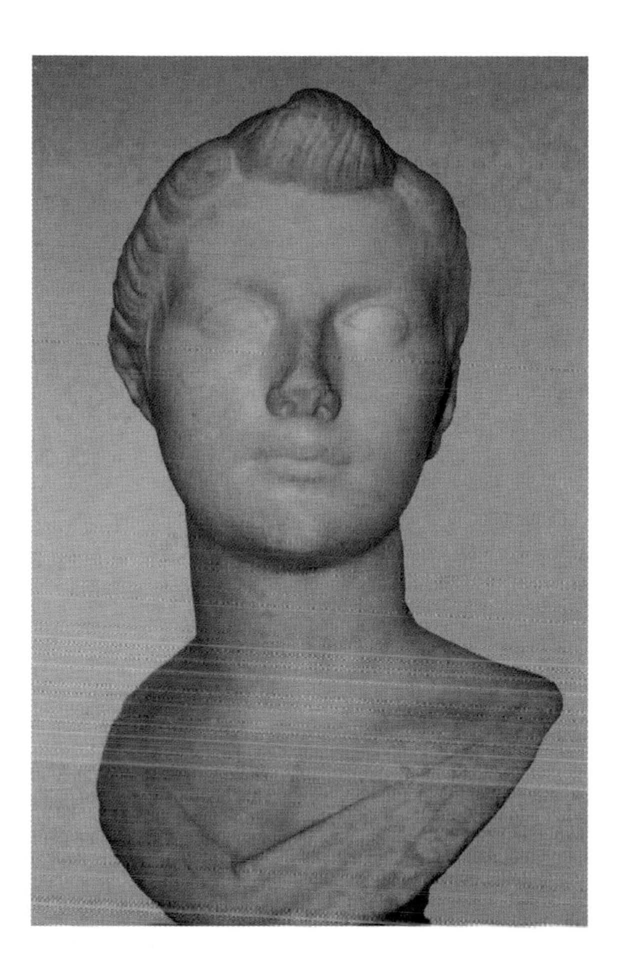

2.2. Octavia was famous for her beauty and her virtue, but she also had a steely determination to make her marriage work and to keep the Empire united.

Up to her death in 11 B.C., Octavia was highly regarded for her stoic virtue in the face of such a public humiliation and admired for her single-minded devotion not only to her biological children but also to those Antony fathered with other women, including Cleopatra.

The Dictator: Julius Caesar

Gaius Julius Caesar was born with the proverbial silver spoon in his mouth (see Fig. 8.5). Scion of a patrician family, his way in life was made easier by abundant financial resources and invaluable connections. His father was the quaestor Gaius Julius Caesar and his mother, Aurelia, was the daughter of a consul, namely Lucius Aurelius Cotta. Predictably, the influential Lucius Cornelius Cinna arranged a marriage for Caesar. Along with his daughter Cornelia, Cinna gave him the position of *flamen dialis,* the most distinguished of the Roman priests or *flamines,* associated with particular gods. Caesar was an effective military tactician and was able to accumulate victories in Asia, including one against the forces of Mithradates VI Eupator of Pontus, one of Rome's most formidable enemies in the first century B.C. These military accomplishments resulted in the reward of a *corona civica,* a very high honor bestowed on soldiers who had saved the life of a Roman citizen in battle.

Family connections continued to benefit Caesar, resulting in his co-option as a *pontifex,* a priest from the most illustrious college of priests in Rome, in 73. Assumption of this office was accompanied by a return to Rome and appointment as quaestor and as *tribunus militum,* a military tribune with consular power. Several opportunities allowed Caesar to practice his oratorical skills, including prosecutions of former supporters of Sulla and public orations at the funerals of his wife and his Aunt Julia. Their spectacular funerals, carried out with the traditional pomp and circumstance of such patrician ceremonies, provided Caesar with an opportunity to craft a public family saga. He took advantage of the situation, using his aunt's descent from gods and kings to underscore subtly his own. He pointed to the aristocratic pedigree of her biological family and those they married, including Gaius Marius, the husband of his father's sister Julia. After Cornelia's death, Caesar married Pompeia, granddaughter of the illustrious military commander Lucius Cornelius Sulla.

In the spirit of the Republic, Caesar and Pompey each took on different commands. Pompey's had the happy consequence for Caesar of removing the great general from Rome. With Pompey abroad, Caesar could concentrate on establishing an alliance with Marcus Licinius Crassus, Pompey's enemy. Crassus supplied the financial wherewithal and Caesar the political strategy. In addition, Crassus's resources underwrote Caesar's work as aedile, or ministerial superintendent, as well as his oversight of the Via Appia in Rome. Caesar was not beyond doing what was necessary to make his way in Roman public life. Bribery led to his being appointed chief priest. Soon he added the designation *praetor,* chief Roman magistrate and aide to a consul, to his *cursus honorum,* or professional résumé, and he rapidly became a man of true authority in Rome.

Always the strategist, Caesar knew that having a new wife would enhance his consulship. He used as an excuse to divorce Pompeia the bold attempt by Clodius Pulcher, disguised as a woman, to participate in the rites of the Bona Dea or Good Goddess, an Italian divinity worshipped primarily in Rome and environs, which Pompeia oversaw. His next wife was the well-known Calpurnia, daughter of the consul Lucius Calpurnius Piso Caesoninus, a marriage that was part of an alliance among Caesar, Crassus, and Pompey, who married Caesar's daughter Julia. The merger also gave Caesar Illyricum, the Indo-European territory beyond the Adriatic Sea, and Cisalpine Gaul, now northern Italy, to which the senate added Transalpine Gaul, a large region stretching from the Pyrenees and the Mediterranean coast of France to England and from the Atlantic coast of France to the Rhine River and the Alps. Caesar took advantage of an uprising by the Celtic tribe of the Helvetii to take control of all of Gaul, a heady victory that encouraged him to think he could accumulate the resources and stature to become a formidable political force.

Caesar's ambition was further fueled by the craving for power of other male aristocrats who rushed to his side with visions of conquest and ample booty, as well as by a desire for the celebratory parade or triumph customarily bestowed upon victorious Roman generals. These single-minded members of a Caesar-centered elite wrought havoc on the people, economy, and environment of Gaul, displaying their spoils in Caesar's ostentatious triumph of 46. A million Gauls were allegedly killed, and another million enslaved. This triumph was preceded by another spectacular military engagement—the invasion of Italy and the declaration of civil war. Caesar defeated Pompey at Pharsalus in Thessaly. Pompey then fled to Egypt, where he was murdered. Caesar's pursuit of Pompey to Egypt was a fateful one, as Caesar became embroiled in adjudicating a local conflict over kingship and personally involved with Cleopatra. The result of the latter entanglement was their son, Caesarion. A subsequent victory in Africa culminated in the quadruple triumph of 46 in Rome. Another triumph soon followed as a result of Caesar's victory over Sextus Pompeius at Munda in Spain. Caesar's accumulation of triumphs positioned him as the supreme Roman general, with prime events to celebrate and valuable booty with which to fund them and build commemorative monuments.

The years from 49 B.C. were marked by a series of consulships and dictatorships, culminating in the title of dictator for life or *dictator perpetuo* in February of 44. However, Caesar's dalliance with absolutist governance that compromised republican values led to a rift between him and his fellow aristocrats. This split and the concern of these nobles that Caesar would be an absent leader as he prepared for departure for war against Parthia, an empire stretching from the Euphrates to the Indus Rivers, may have been factors that led to his assassination in the Senate House in Rome on March 15 of the same year. Another interpretation posits the opposite—that Caesar's aristocratic murderers were motivated by fear that the dictator would democratize Rome and strip them of their influence.

The fact that Caesar was driven to compose numerous books on the Gallic and Civil Wars, several of which survive, is a testament to his hope that his version of these events would be the one that would tell his story to posterity. The will to leave a written record was matched, in material terms, by his ambitious building program in Rome.

Commander in the East: Mark Antony

After Caesar's assassination, Calpurnia presented her husband's papers and 4,000 talents to Mark Antony (Fig. 2.3). By 41, Antony had also, in a sense, inherited Cleopatra. In that year, the pair met at Tarsus, a fateful encounter that was followed by a winter spent together in Egypt, resulting in the birth of their twins, Alexander Helios and Cleopatra Selene. Initially this did not alter the trajectory of Antony's military and political career in Rome.

Antony had been born the son of Marcus Antonius Creticus, probably in 83 B.C. Some of his youth appears to have been wasted through dissipation, but he was nonetheless able to distinguish himself sufficiently as a cavalry commander in Palestine and Egypt to subsequently join Caesar in Gaul. He became quaestor in 51 and then tribune. Caesar had enough confidence in Antony to have him oversee Italy while he himself was on campaign in Spain. At the Battle of Pharsalus, Antony commanded Caesar's left wing. In 47, he was Caesar's *magister equitum* (every dictator had such a representative of his choosing), and his consular colleague in 44.

After Caesar's assassination, Antony and Octavian vied to take over Caesar's authority. Each had his supporters, and there were oppositions and reconciliation between the two. They became triumvirs, along with Lepidus, in 43 and proscribed their enemies in 42. Cleopatra cannot have helped being concerned about the coalition of Octavian and Antony in 42, especially after Caesar was proclaimed a god on January 1, 42 B.C. Whatever hopes Cleopatra may have had for Caesarion's future interests in regard to Rome must have been dashed when Octavian took on the mantle of the "son" of a divinity, or *divi filius*. On the other hand, Antony most definitely caught Cleopatra's eye. She appears to have known him already, and that acquaintance may have been renewed in Rome when she resided at Caesar's villa. The alliance remained intact into 41 B.C. as Octavian and Antony defeated Caesar's murderers, Cassius and Brutus, at the Battle of Philippi in Alexander the Great's native Macedonia. This momentous encounter brought fame to both men and led to their division of the empire, with Antony responsible for the oversight of the eastern part, as well as Gaul.

2.3. Mark Antony embraced life with remarkable passion as he dreamed of merging Rome and the East and of ruling that empire in concert with Cleopatra

Antony's interlude with Cleopatra in Egypt and the birth of their children in 41–40 did not deter him from agreeing to marry Octavia (of his three earlier wives, Fulvia was notably one of the most politically active women in the Republic). As we have seen, his purpose was to solidify the treaty he signed with Octavian at Brundisium and to concretize the division of the empire into east and west. Antony and Octavia went east together, and Antony's forces repelled the Parthian invasion of Syria. The agreement at Tarentum led to a renewal of his alliance with Octavian, perhaps giving Antony the confidence to leave Octavia home when he renewed his affair with Cleopatra—a resumption that resulted in the birth of their third child, Ptolemy Philadelphus, in 36.

The blatant re-emergence of this relationship at a time when Antony was married to Octavian's sister may be variously interpreted. What would compel Antony to risk his alliance with Octavian and put himself in danger of renewed enmity? It is conceivable that their long history of war and conciliation was an unalterable pattern. Cleopatra's personal allure may well have been irresistible, but it is also plausible that her political and military clout in the East was a powerful lure and provided Antony with the self-assurance to thumb his nose at Octavian. While Antony granted Cleopatra much by expanding her kingdom in turn, he withheld other lands that belonged to such critical allies as King Herod of Judaea. At the same time, he may have become carried away by a romantic vision of himself and his consort overseeing a kingdom in the East that would rival and perhaps even overcome Octavian's in the West.

Antony and Cleopatra played their roles to the hilt; they undoubtedly enjoyed dressing up as Osiris and Isis, joined in a divine merger that stood for the unification of Asia. Antony annexed Armenia in 34, an event marked by his and Cleopatra's Alexandrian version of a Roman triumph in which not only their children but also Caesar's son Caesarion participated, dressed in the local costumes of the lands they were destined to inherit.

In the meantime, Octavian was not standing idly by. Lepidus had fallen by the wayside, and Octavian celebrated a major victory against Sextus Pompeius. At the same time, Octavian was beginning to wage a brutal campaign of propaganda against Antony, who was providing him with just the ammunition he needed. The clash between the two intensified when some of Antony's staunchest supporters left Rome. Antony's response to Octavian's invective was to divorce Octavia, an event that Octavian had foreseen and had prepared for by granting Octavia *sacrosanctitas,* endowing her with a near sacred aura. When the marriage dissolved, Octavian shrewdly used the personal slight against his sister as a legitimate reason to retaliate by making public what was purported to be Antony's will, a document that revealed that Antony intended to be buried with Cleopatra in Alexandria and to bequeath Roman lands to their offspring. Octavian annulled Antony's power and declared war against Cleopatra, making Antony a traitor for allying himself with the enemy of Rome.

The theatricality of these events should not be underestimated—several strong-willed men and women striding across their respective world stages in east and west, staking their claims and counterclaims. Moreover, they were dressing appropriately for the occasion and even, in some cases, taking on the appearance of carefully chosen divinities to underscore their points. As we shall see, some of their posturing was memorialized in art and took place in monumental stage sets built for the occasion and for posterity. Dramatic military encounters ensued. Cleopatra's financial resources and forces buoyed Antony up initially, but his Roman support base continued to hemorrhage, largely because of his affiliation with the Egyptian queen. The star-crossed pair succumbed to Octavian at the Battle of Actium, and Antony committed suicide at the very moment when Octavian entered Alexandria.

While these general outlines of Antony's life are well known, they are contaminated by the vengeful propaganda attack waged by Octavian who, as the winner, left the written record. As far as we know, Antony left no written account of his life or accomplishments with the exception of a brief pamphlet, entitled *On His Drunkenness,* responding to Octavian's vitriolic attack on his person and life-style.

Master of the Universe: Octavian Augustus

Both ancient sources and modern appraisals indicate that, despite his placid and even bland appearance in his deliberately idealized portraiture, Augustus was a cautious, clever, decisive, and ruthless man driven by the desire for extraordinary fame in his own day and the wish to establish for posterity a larger-than-life reputation (Fig. 2.4). Although Augustus was capable of close attention to detail, he was a man of broad vision who pictured nothing less than the complete alteration of Roman society. His carefully crafted political ideology was based on military supremacy, the establishment of peace, ostensible restoration of the Republic, and

2.4. Brilliant and uncompromising, Octavian sought to change the course of Rome's destiny in a way that owes more to Cleopatra than he is likely to have admitted or even realized.

moral reform. Augustus's achievement outlived him, but that achievement is, for all intents and purposes, the one he fashioned himself because Augustus presented his own version of his accomplishments to posterity. In fact, it can be argued that Augustus manipulated the entire record of his principate to his own advantage. Nowhere is this better illustrated than in the *Res Gestae*, the emperor's personal account of his accomplishments, begun early in his principate but completed just before his death and entrusted to the Vestal Virgins, along with his last will and testament and the directions for his funeral. The original version was to be inscribed on bronze tablets in front of his mausoleum, and numerous other copies in both Latin and Greek were carved on the walls of temples of Augustus (and Roma) in the provinces.

Since Augustus's *Res Gestae* was a personal account, it presents his own interpretation of historical events. For example, Augustus credits himself alone with the victory over Caesar's assassins at Philippi. His decision to suppress any mention of Mark Antony's indispensable contribution to the success of that military venture was undoubtedly influenced by the later enmity between Augustus and Antony that culminated at Actium. In fact, it should be noted that Augustus chose to mention none of his other enemies, for example Sextus Pompeius. Furthermore, he does not allude to his biological parents or his wife. Family matters were for the most part suppressed. He refers often to his adoptive father (Julius Caesar) and his adoptive sons (his biological grandsons Gaius and Lucius Caesar), as well as his close confidant and adviser Marcus Agrippa and his adoptive son and successor, Tiberius. The focus of Augustus's account is the wars he won, his diplomatic victories, and his foundation of new colonies. He mentions his building programs, especially his public works. He lists all the titles bestowed on him, all the positions he held, all the monuments erected in his honor, including the Ara Pacis Augustae, and all the tributes he bestowed on Gaius and Lucius. Indeed, the very title, *Res Gestae* (literally, "things accomplished"), proclaims the document as Augustus-centric and underscores its author's obsession with ensuring that these impressive accomplishments would outlive him.

Augustus starts his story when he is 19 and beginning to raise his army. Of course it began much earlier than that, and those first stages had a profound impact on what was to happen later. Augustus was born in Velitrae in the Alban Hills to an interesting set of parents—Gaius Octavius, a *novus homo,* or the first man in his family to reach the Roman senate, and Atia, the daughter of Julius Caesar's sister. Through them, Octavian had access to the senate in a junior position, and to the dictator of Rome as one of his closest male relatives. The way Octavian ascended through the ranks was indeed dazzling. When he was a mere boy of 12, he delivered the funeral oration of his maternal grandmother. By the time he was 17, Caesar had crafted his last will and testament, designating Octavian as his adoptive son and heir.

After Caesar's assassination, Octavian may have already harbored ambitions to become master of the Roman world, but it took him a while to achieve his goal. Politically shrewd, Octavian moved forward with dispatch to honor his adoptive father and court Caesar's friends, especially his military veterans. These actions led to strife between Octavian and Antony, temporarily resolved by the foundation of the triumvirate, which included Lepidus. This pause in Octavian and Antony's power struggle left Octavian time to settle other scores and achieve other goals. He defeated Antony's brother, Lucius Antonius, and Antony's wife Fulvia at Perusia. Land confiscations and proscriptions followed, with Octavian demonstrating little mercy. With an eye to the political benefit of the right union, Octavian married Scribonia and then Livia, and gave his sister Octavia in marriage to Mark Antony, confirming their treaty at Brundisium.

This internecine warfare led to Octavian's realization that he needed to vanquish a foreign enemy to gain legitimacy, and he turned his attention to the Illyrians. Not able to achieve much success there, he altered his approach and began to wage his carefully calculated propaganda war against Mark Antony, characterizing Antony as un-Roman and immoral. Both denigrations were closely related to Antony's relationship with Cleopatra who, as a foreigner, was considered both alien and libertine. Octavian effectively caused Italians to fear Antony's pro-Egyptian stance, and Italy rewarded Octavian with an oath of loyalty in 32. Hand in hand with powerful and devoted generals like Marcus Agrippa, Octavian won important victories over Antony, none more significant than the Battle of Actium in the next year. This complete defeat of Antony and Cleopatra not only demonstrated Octavian's prescience and patriotism but also left him with full coffers and a new imperial protectorate, courtesy of Egypt.

Appointed consul in 31, Octavian arrived in Rome in 29 and celebrated an over-the-top triple triumph, closed the doors of the Temple of Janus to signify the achievement of peace, and began a revival of the commonwealth or *res publica*. He also embarked on a strategy to transform Rome from a city of brick to one of marble. His achievements were greatly appreciated and celebrated by the conferring of numerous titles, not the least of which was that of *Augustus* in 27 B.C. By bestowing this designation on him, the senate was publicly acknowledging that Octavian was sacred in the religious sense and worthy of worship—an appropriate finale for the man who would be "king."

A SYNERGISTIC SEXTET

The lives and loves of this striking sextet were inextricably bound. Cleopatra had affairs with Caesar and Antony and provided both with children. Livia was married to Augustus. Octavia was the sister of Augustus and married to Antony. Cleopatra was an ally of Caesar and Antony and the enemy of Augustus. Cleopatra was famous for her liaisons that were not officially recognized as marriages in Rome. Livia became the idealized icon of Roman womanhood, as expounded in Augustus's moral and marriage legislation. Octavia was the devoted mother who cared for all of Antony's children, even his daughter by Cleopatra. Cleopatra was the most powerful woman in the ancient world—a queen of Egypt—who shared children with two of Rome's most authoritative and influential men and who was in direct opposition to a man who in the end proved even more powerful and influential. Livia and Octavia held a more subtle authority granted them by the very *sacrosanctitas* or inviolability that was bestowed on them by Octavian as a weapon against Cleopatra.

Several members of this group came to colorful ends. Caesar was murdered in Rome in 44. Antony took his own life in Alexandria in 30 B.C., the same year as Cleopatra's dramatic suicide by the bite of an asp. Octavia, in contrast, died of natural causes in 11 B.C. Augustus lived to the age of 76, passing away, also of natural causes, in A.D. 14. The formidable Livia outlived them all, not dying until A.D. 29, fifteen years after Augustus and nearly seventy-five after Caesar. Thus this sextet dominated Roman political life for approximately eighty years.

In some ways Livia is the most interesting of all three women because her ascendancy was the most surprising. Cleopatra was born to her position and was pursued by men to whom she could offer not only her own exotic person but also the tradition and power of Egypt with its financial and human resources. Livia was something of an innocent bystander, a young pregnant woman of elite status who caught Octavian's eye, but who seized the moment to take charge of her own life and large ambitions. Upon hearing of her husband's intention to make Octavia sacred, she apparently cajoled Augustus into granting her sacrosanctity as well. Augustus had no choice but to accede to her wishes. The legal edict was enacted in 35 B.C. Livia's sacrosanctity, like Octavia's, was accompanied by extraordinary privileges—freedom from legal guardianship and the opportunity to access her inherited wealth to do with as she saw fit. Livia was granted the power of choice. And with the freedom of choice came the opportunity to become all that she could, though still within the confines of Roman society that saw women as subservient to men. When it came to what mattered most, Augustus and Tiberius were still in charge.

What these men had in common was their will to record their accomplishments in written and material form. They were aware that such records would not only lead to fame during their lives but also ensure *memoria* after their deaths. Neither Livia nor Octavia appears to have left written accounts, although some are attributed to Cleopatra, but all three women bequeathed buildings and works of art to posterity, emphasizing that their story was best told through visual means. While the commissions of their paramours are quite well known, the women's monuments have not received as much attention, perhaps because they are fewer in number and less well preserved. Nonetheless, those that survive tell the story of a trio of strong women who left an indelible mark on Rome.

3

THE SUPPORTING CAST

Cleopatra and Rome's supporting cast is made up of an eclectic circle of family members, close friends, and political and military associates of the major players. In many ways, this coterie was as eccentric as the prime-time actors. It consisted of an adulterous princess with a penchant for ribald jokes, rebellion, and perhaps even conspiracy; a confidant of the emperor who was an inveterate builder of monuments bearing his name; a gastronome who built Rome's first private swimming pool; a literary patron who supported women poets; a pair of spirited youths who imitated their grandfather's hairstyle and handwriting and dressed up like Trojans; and a melancholic recluse who seems to have grown to dislike his mother but who was partial to gorgeous islands. All of their lives were intertwined with that of Augustus, and some of them may have been aware enough of Cleopatra's personality and art to acknowledge them in their own lives and monuments.

FAMILY MEMBERS

The Sinner: Julia

Julia was the only child of Augustus, born to him and Scribonia in 39 B.C. (Fig. 3.1). On the very day she was born, Julia's parents divorced. Augustus and Livia, who married in 38, lost no time in situating Julia in Augustus's house, seeing to it that she was properly trained in weaving, spinning, and other appropriate skills. Her upbringing was strict. She was still

3.1. **Julia, a woman of spunk and wit, was Rome's quintessential "bad girl," whose adulterous affairs caused her father Augustus to banish her to a desolate island.**

a child of 8 when Augustus defeated Antony and Cleopatra at Actium. At that time, both Cleopatra and Livia must have seemed to her larger than life. In 28 B.C., when Julia was only 11, Augustus attempted to establish his moral and marriage legislation, but an unwilling aristocracy rejected his foray into transforming Roman social life. Julia would eventually bristle under the constraints that Augustus was beginning to formulate for Roman women.

When Julia was still a baby, the search began for the man who would eventually be her mate. Already in 37, Marcus Antonius Antyllus, the eldest son of Mark Antony, was viewed as a potential choice. Antony claimed that Augustus intended to have Julia wed Cortiso, the King of the Getae, a Thracian tribe, but the spread of such a rumor may have been mere gossip on Antony's part and an attempt to legitimize his own relationship with the foreign Cleopatra. When Julia reached the marriageable age of 14 in 25 B.C., she was betrothed to her handsome and promising young cousin, Octavia's son Marcus Claudius Marcellus. The match was ideal, and Augustus had high hopes for his talented young nephew and son-in-law. Tragically, Marcellus died two years later.

In 21, the grieving emperor compelled his close friend Marcus Agrippa to divorce his wife Marcella and become affianced with Julia. The marriage produced Gaius and Lucius Caesar in a timely manner, giving Augustus two new male heirs. Julia and Agrippa also had two daughters, Julia the Younger and Vipsania Agrippina (Agrippina the Elder). A third son, Agrippa Julius Caesar, was born after Agrippa's death and was thus referred to as Agrippa Postumus. With her production of so many children, Julia must have seemed, in those years, the very embodiment of Augustus's marriage laws, which were finally passed in 18 B.C. Nonetheless, her marriage to an older man and her frequent pregnancies must have led her to miss the relative freedom of her youth, and she began to engage in adulterous affairs. These illicit liaisons appear to have been very well known.

After Agrippa's death in 12 B.C., the most appropriate husband for Julia, certainly from Livia's point of view, was the empress's elder son Tiberius, who was obliged to divorce his beloved Vipsania Agrippina (daughter of Agrippa and his first wife, Attica) in order to marry Julia. While the partnership appears to have been successful at first, despite the death of their one child in infancy, Tiberius and Julia were soon estranged. Tiberius may have missed Vipsania, and Julia's passion was probably a poor match for Tiberius's cooler disposition. Julia's adulterous behavior may have contributed to Tiberius's decision to leave Rome in 6 B.C., although it was not the principal reason. Her husband's absence from the capital only gave Julia more independence; her adulteries increased, and she became careless about any attempt to conceal them.

Although Augustus may have been aware of the situation sooner, he publicly acknowledged his daughter's transgressions in 2 B.C., when Julia was 38. Details of her assignations were reported in contemporary and later histories (Seneca, Tacitus, Suetonius, Dio Cassius, Velleius Paterculus). Julia was reputed to have had many lovers with whom she engaged in a wide variety of sexual practices. She allegedly lived out her fantasies against the backdrop of the best-known monuments and statues in Rome, even some of those belonging to her father's building projects. Trysts occurred at the rostrum in the Roman Forum, with meeting times posted at one of Rome's most famous gathering places— the statue of Marsyas.

Augustus was disgusted with his daughter's behavior, which ran counter to the tenets of his moral legislation. He also needed to protect his political flank, which may have been jeopardized by Julia's activities. Some scholars continue to believe that the morals charge eventually brought against Julia was a cover-up for something far more serious—Julia's involvement in a conspiracy against her father. Augustus divorced Julia from Tiberius, banned his only child from Rome, and exiled her to the desolate island of Pandateria. Her mother, Scribonia, voluntarily accompanied her. While many scholars have accused Livia of encouraging Augustus to banish his spirited daughter, there is no evidence in the ancient sources that this was in fact the case.

On Pandateria, Julia was allowed no luxury, not even wine. Augustus did relent enough to allow her to leave the island for Rhegium on the Italian mainland but, as if her banishment were not enough, Augustus publicly declared through a codicil to his will that, at her death, Julia was not to be buried in the family tomb—the Mausoleum of Augustus. Tiberius was equally harsh, keeping Julia confined and cutting off her allowance. The latter stipulation left her without food, and she consequently died of malnutrition late in 14, the same year as her father.

Julia's lovers suffered similar fates. Some, among them five men of aristocratic status (Velleius Paterculus lists Iullus Antonius, Tiberius Sempronius Gracchus, Cornelius Scipio, Appius Claudius Pulcher, and Titus Quinctius Crispinus), were convicted (they may or may not have had trials); others were banished. Iullus Antonius was either executed or committed suicide.

A distinction has been made thus far between elite men who left written records of their accomplishments and elite women who probably did not. Julia fits somewhere in between. She was an intelligent and well-educated young woman to whom Macrobius attributed a sharp wit.[1] In his *Saturnalia,* Macrobius stages an imagined dinner party where the sophisticated guests contemplate Virgil's work but also share humorous stories, some purportedly Julia's. Not surprisingly, the stories about Julia center on her physical appearance, what kind of clothes she wore, and how she arranged her hair; her relationships with men as a daughter, wife, mother; and how she wielded power and managed finances. The challenges Julia faced as the daughter of an emperor are highlighted, and it is clear that she rose to the occasion with self-confidence and humor. When asked, for example, by a close friend why she wasn't as frugal as her father, Julia retorted: "He forgets that he is Caesar, but I remember that I am Caesar's daughter." One of Julia's most famous witticisms concerns her equally celebrated adulteries. Those who were well aware of her infidelity marveled that, despite all her affairs, Julia's children resembled their father Agrippa. Julia is said to have explained this with the words: "Why, I never take on a passenger unless the ship is full."

If these jokes actually issued from Julia, they provide a rare glimpse into the mind of a woman who rejected the limitations of her strict upbringing and was not afraid to speak her mind or behave in a nonconformist way. If other writers fabricated Julia's jokes, their intention may have been to present Julia as an imperfect woman whose failings were in strong contrast to the moral behavior of the upright Livia.

These jokes underscore the complexity of the relationship between this particular father and daughter, as well as more generally between the *paterfamilias* and *filia* in Roman society. Was Julia a bright and carefree girl who relished the role of imperial princess and a marriage to the handsome and promising Marcellus? Was she disillusioned to find that fate instead sacrificed her to a series of loveless alliances with men who were chosen by her father from his own close circle as part of his quest for a family dynasty? Did the relentless pressure of producing male heirs inure Julia to the pleasures of motherhood?

The historian Amy Richlin effectively argues that the Romans used women as political icons—Livia as the paragon of wifely and motherly virtue, a producer of children, a modest and dutiful woman; and Julia as an example of a woman's potential for bad behavior, someone who was promiscuous and lascivious in dress and comportment. At the same time, the case of Julia is an especially complex one. It was only after her marriage to Marcus Agrippa produced Gaius and Lucius that Augustus publicly celebrated Julia as the mother of two potential heirs in an official series of coins struck in Rome—an honor not bestowed during their lifetime on any other woman in Augustus's family circle. Yet despite this tribute, Julia fell fast and hard from that peak. Her exile of 2 B.C. must have been especially difficult for a woman who had earlier loved attending parties and practicing her clever repartee with aristocratic peers.

The Chosen: Gaius Caesar

Since Augustus had no biological sons, the status of his eldest grandson, Gaius Julius Caesar, is difficult to overemphasize. Son of Julia and Marcus Agrippa, Gaius was born in 20 B.C. and adopted by Augustus as his son in 17 B.C. when he was only 3 years old. Augustus put all the hopes and dreams for the future of his principate and Rome on this toddler and his infant brother, Lucius Julius Caesar. The fact that Livia's oldest son, Tiberius, retired from Rome in 6 B.C. probably attests to his perception that the ascendance of the grandsons signaled his own lack of opportunity for promotion. Tiberius was apparently on the mark because a year later when Gaius assumed the *toga virilis,* the toga that marked a boy's introduction to public life, the boy became heir apparent. Gaius's status was indicated by his designation as consul, his admission into the senate, and his recognition by the equestrians or *equites* as *princeps iuventutis.* From this moment on, the title came to signify that a probable successor had embarked on public life.

When he was 19, just the age Augustus had been at the beginning of his own rise to power, Gaius was married to Livia Julia, usually called Livilla, the daughter of Nero Claudius Drusus and Antonia, and was invested with proconsular power and sent to the East. His authority was clear in A.D. 2 when he deliberated with a Parthian king and appointed a Roman king of Armenia. The latter act, not surprisingly, led to a revolt that he suppressed. Gaius's good fortune expired, however, at Artagira where he was seriously wounded in a siege. He died a year and a half later in Lycia on the journey back to Italy. It was the 21st of February in A.D. 4, and Gaius was only 24 years old.

The Spare: Lucius Caesar

Lucius Julius Caesar was the second son of Julia and Marcus Agrippa, and his personal and professional trajectory followed that of his brother. He was born three years later than Gaius, in 17 B.C., at which time Augustus adopted both boys as his sons. Thus, in the case of Lucius, his welcome into the world was as the son of the emperor of Rome. He assumed the *toga virilis* in 2 B.C. and was immediately invested with all the same honors as his elder brother. He suffered the same misfortune: he too died outside of Rome, in Massalia (now Marseilles), while on his way to Spain. It was the 20th of August in A.D. 2. Lucius was only 19.

The Outcast: Tiberius

As the elder son of Rome's first empress, Tiberius was probably disappointed that he was passed over by Augustus for adoption as his son, especially after 6 B.C. Even after Augustus was dead and his will was read in the senate by a freedman, it was clear that Rome's first emperor turned to Tiberius only as a last resort. The will's preamble stated: "Since fate has cruelly carried off my sons Gaius and Lucius, Tiberius shall inherit two-thirds of my property."[2] This proviso was hardly a ringing endorsement for Tiberius, who must have been dismayed since there was little in his early life to suggest anything but success.

Born on the 16th of November 42 B.C. to Livia Drusilla and Tiberius Claudius Nero, Tiberius was only 4 years old when Livia, pregnant with his younger brother Drusus, divorced his father to marry Octavian. How close Tiberius's ties were to his biological father is not known, but this turn of events must have been dramatic. Tiberius was immediately drawn into the orbit of Rome's most ambitious and gifted politician. At a young and impressionable age, Tiberius could not have been anything but dazzled.

Tiberius's proximity to Augustus privileged him and provided entrée into a life of public service with prestigious appointments. Before he turned 20, Tiberius served with Augustus in Spain and was appointed quaestor in 23 B.C. From then on, he could boast a succession of accomplishments in various venues around the empire. He bestowed the Roman stamp of approval on King Tigranes in Armenia; he restored Roman honor on the Rhine after an earlier disastrous defeat; and he and Drusus conquered the Alps. This cycle of success continued into the next two decades as Tiberius oversaw military forays into Pannonia, the Illyrian outpost south and west of the Danube River, Germany, and Illyricum, located beyond the Adriatic. In 7 B.C., he was sent on an important mission to Armenia, being granted in advance tribunician power (the right to call the plebs, or Roman citizens who were not patricians, into assembly and encourage resolutions) as well as *imperium*, or supreme power, in the East.

Tiberius did everything Augustus asked him to do, even divorcing his cherished Vipsania Agrippina to marry the emperor's daughter Julia. This was a great personal sacrifice, and it is therefore no surprise that Tiberius was devastated when Augustus's young grandson and adoptive son, Gaius Caesar, was appointed to an early consulship. Tiberius departed Rome for Rhodes in 6 B.C. He nursed his wounds on the spectacular island and then attempted a comeback by returning to Rome in A.D. 2. Tiberius's effort had no impact, however, and it was only in the year 4, with both Gaius and Lucius dead, that a resigned Augustus adopted his stepson as his son and heir. At the same time, to ensure that the succession remained in the family, Augustus adopted Agrippa Postumus, the last son of Julia and Agrippa, and Tiberius adopted his own nephew, Germanicus Julius Caesar. Tiberius finally realized his hope to be named Augustus's successor.

Tiberius had relied heavily on his mother to keep him in Augustus's good graces. Even during his sojourn on Rhodes, Tiberius expected Livia to lobby on his behalf for titles and honors. Once Tiberius became emperor, however, he had less need for his mother and their relationship deteriorated. When the senate voted Livia the title *parens patriae* or "Parent of the Country," Tiberius vetoed it. He refused to attend Livia's funeral, forbade her deification, and annulled her will. Tiberius's anger toward the woman who had borne him and who had supported him so staunchly provides insight on how some of his disappointments in life had led to disillusionment, even though they were interspersed with some notable achievements.

It is difficult to assess Tiberius's state of mind as he became emperor of Rome at Augustus's death in 14, but whatever it was, he publicly honored Augustus because it was the prudent political thing to do. If he couldn't win his stepfather's devotion, he could at least take advantage of the achievement of Rome's first emperor, positioning himself as a "son" who would follow his now divine father's policies.

Although this seemed like a smart game plan, Tiberius's early wins were a thing of the past and he blundered through a series of missteps and misfortunes. Some were not of his making—mutinies, revolts, economic uncertainties, and serious grain shortages. Tiberius's morose personality isolated him, and his unwillingness to open the purse strings made him increasingly unpopular in Rome. In addition, his family and the Roman populace preferred Agrippa Postumus and Germanicus. As the question of the succession raged again in Rome, Tiberius, never one to confront his demons or his enemies, retreated first to Campania in west central Italy and then to the island of Capri. There was public rejoicing when he died in March of the year 37.

FRIENDS AND SUPPORTERS

The lives of other prominent patrician men were intimately interwoven with those of the main characters. There are several close male friends and supporters of Augustus whose lives, political careers, building programs, and desire for eternal fame were so intertwined with those of Augustus that his place in the world is difficult to assess without understanding their motives and accomplishments. Primary among these are Marcus Vipsanius Agrippa, Marcus Valerius Massala Corvinus, and Gaius Maecenas.

The Best Man: Marcus Agrippa

The relationship between Augustus and Marcus Vipsanius Agrippa was one of the most enduring and significant of the emperor's life (Fig. 3.2). Augustus was born in 63 B.C., Agrippa in the same year or possibly the year before or after. Agrippa's family was not well known but had substantial means, and early on Agrippa recognized Octavian's rising star and attached himself to it. Out of affection and perspicacity, Agrippa aided Octavian after the shocking murder of his adoptive father Caesar by helping Octavian to form a private army, prosecuting Caesar's assassin Cassius, and participating in a war against Lucius Antonius. These acts were rapidly followed by Agrippa's ascendance through the elite man's résumé or *cursus honorum*. He became, in turn, tribune of the plebs, senator, urban praetor, governor of Gaul, and magistrate or aedile. In addition, Agrippa performed feats of military valor by suppressing a rebellion in Aquitania in Gaul, winning important naval victories at Naulochos and Mylae in Sicily, and participating in the Illyrian War.

Agrippa was a naval commander at the Battle of Actium and deserves recognition for his forceful contribution to Antony's downfall. Octavian's confidence in Agrippa's leadership skills and loyalty is attested by Octavian's decision to leave Agrippa and another friend, Maecenas, in charge of Rome during his post-Actium absence from the capital between 31 and 29 B.C. After Octavian's return, Agrippa's political profile in Rome remained strong. He led a purge of the senate, held a census, and became consul for the second and third times. Agrippa had married Caecilia Attica in 37 B.C. It is not known what became of her thereafter, but we do know that Agrippa married Augustus's niece Marcella in 28, probably because of the strong bond between the two men. When in 23 B.C. Augustus fell ill and was simultaneously embroiled in political controversy, the emperor once again demonstrated his trust and unwavering personal af-

3.2. Childhood friend of Augustus, effective military commander, and great builder, Agrippa left a major mark on Rome and the provinces.

fection for his longtime comrade by granting Agrippa his signet ring. This gesture meant that Agrippa could sign important documents in Augustus's absence. The bond between the men continued to grow stronger and resulted in Augustus's granting the hand of his only daughter, Julia, to Agrippa. The pair married in 21 B.C. after Agrippa's divorce from Marcella. While his first two wives had produced only daughters, Agrippa and Julia had not only two additional daughters together (Julia and Agrippina) but also three sons (Gaius and Lucius Caesar and Agrippa Postumus).

Many more honors followed. Agrippa was granted proconsular power in the eastern part of the empire, tribunician power, and *imperium.* He celebrated the Secular Games in Rome in 17 B.C. and thereafter left Rome on a second expedition to the East, where he established good relations with other powerful world leaders such as King Polemon of Pontus and King Herod of Judaea. A revolt in Pannonia took Agrippa there in 12 B.C., but he became ill and died on the way home. As a man whose power was almost as substantial as Augustus's own, Agrippa was granted a major public burial and was laid to rest in the Mausoleum of Augustus.

Like Augustus, Caesar, and other powerful and ambitious men of the time, Agrippa wanted to leave a written record for posterity. He wrote an autobiography and a geographical treatise, neither of which survives. The latter was to be used as the source for a colossal "map" (possibly text-based) that was to be installed after his death in the Porticus Vipsania in Rome. Agrippa's interest in geography and mapping was matched by his urge to benefit Rome and the eastern and western provinces. At the same time, it was not lost on him that building durable monuments was a way to ensure a lasting reputation, and he embarked on an ambitious building campaign in Rome and the provinces.

The Supporter: Marcus Valerius Messalla Corvinus

Marcus Valerius Messalla Corvinus was also a national figure of stature in the age of Augustus. Like Caesar, Antony, Octavian, and Agrippa, Messalla was a man who craved fame in his lifetime and wanted to make the kinds of contributions to public life that would accord him a lasting reputation. In the manner of his famous contemporaries, he recognized that one of the ways to accomplish this was to leave a written record of his deeds as well as grandiose public monuments made of durable materials. Thus Messalla wrote his memoirs and commissioned several public buildings in Rome.

Messalla began, as did so many other elite men of his day, by making his mark as a soldier and commander. He participated at Philippi on the side of Cassius yet, after Cassius's defeat, swore allegiance to Antony, and then wisely switched to Octavian. Messalla joined Octavian's propaganda war against Antony by preparing pamphlets against him. He then served as consul with Octavian, and took part in many of the most significant military encounters of the day—the battle against Sextus Pompeius, the war in Illyricum, and, most important, the Battle of Actium. Messalla subdued Alpine tribes, was active as a commander in Syria, governed Gaul, and celebrated a triumph in Rome.

After distinguishing himself militarily, Messalla followed an elite man's *cursus honorum* by becoming in turn urban prefect, augur or diviner, arval brother (named for offering public sacrifices for the fertility of fields), and *curator aquarum*. In the last of these roles he oversaw Rome's water supply, an exceedingly important position at a time when new aqueducts were being built in the city. Messalla was a shrewd politician who is probably best remembered for proposing in 2 B.C. that Augustus be given the title "father of his country" or *pater patriae*, an honor held a half-century earlier by Marcus Tullius Cicero.

At the same time, Messalla prided himself on being a man of culture. He tried his hand at writing poetry as well as philosophical and grammatical texts. Moreover, he had a gift for recognizing literary talent greater than his own and gathered around him a coterie of intellectuals and writers. He may well have had the motive of finding someone who would honor him in his writings, and he was rewarded with the *Panegyricus Messallae.* Tibullus and Ovid were members of his intellectual circle, as was his niece and ward Sulpicia.

The Patron: Gaius Maecenas

While Messalla appears to have hoped that his literary friends would honor him in their poetry, Gaius Maecenas apparently encouraged members of his intellectual circle to honor Augustus and his new regime in their verse. Maecenas's group included such literary stars as Virgil, Propertius, and Horace, as well as others who are today less well known. That Maecenas encouraged these friends to uphold Augustus and his vision is not surprising. Maecenas was one of the earliest and staunchest supporters of Rome's first emperor, and his power in the age of Augustus came from this friendship and not from a rise through the military and political ranks.

Although he fought at Philippi, Maecenas did not follow this military expedition with a life of predictable public service. Instead of holding a string of increasingly important public offices, he worked with Augustus to accomplish critical alliances, such as Augustus's marriage to Scribonia and the pacts at Brundisium and Tarentum. Even though Maecenas never became a magistrate or senator, he possessed authority in Rome, even standing in for Augustus when he was absent from the capital. Augustus's own supremacy benefited Maecenas, likely contributing to the latter's vast wealth. Maecenas's spectacular house on the Esquiline in Rome, which could be seen from a great distance, had a magnificent panorama of the city, a famous turreted wall, and Rome's first private swimming pool. At his death, Maecenas bequeathed this splendid possession to Augustus. Surviving epitaphs attest that Maecenas oversaw large numbers of slaves and freedmen, and much is known about his lavish lifestyle. He was fond of such exotic dishes as baby donkey, relished expensive wines, and favored luxurious textiles brought to Rome from great distances.

For a brief time, in the midst of these high-living, often reckless, and invariably ambitious men and women with their tastes for poetry and architecture and politics and power, the Egyptian queen appeared like a comet from a distant mythical world. We do not have enough detail on Cleopatra's sojourn in Rome in the mid-40s to know exactly how long it was, whom she met, and what impact that interaction might have had. Nor do we know with certainty how Cleopatra's contemporaries and immediate successors perceived her larger-than-life reputation, or what other personalities and events may have motivated them instead. While it is somewhat speculative to posit that Cleopatra sparked elite contemporaries into a dialogue with her persona and her art, it is certainly possible that her visibility, notoriety, and exoticism made her a touchstone for others who wanted to cross traditional boundaries.

We have seen that Julia was such a pioneer. While still in her formative years, Julia may have heard enough about Cleopatra to admire her spirit and strong sense of self. Like Cleopatra, Julia was well educated and clever and greatly enjoyed engaging with Rome's most elite men. Cleopatra's fervent nationalism, so intimately intertwined with her personal liaisons, may have given Julia the idea to wed her many affairs to her conspiratorial stratagems. Agrippa acquired Cleopatra's taste for empire building, made manifest through great public works and temples; and Gaius and Lucius recognized that to be princes like Caesarion or Ptolemy Philadelphus was risky but potentially rewarding. Maecenas and Messalla, like Cleopatra, got pleasure from the finer things in life and brought the construction of opulent domiciles in Rome to an art. They also doubtless admired Alexandria's cultural life and shared Caesar's vision that Rome could be as civilized as that city.

While such speculation may seem far fetched, surviving material remains suggest that such inspirations were not beyond the realm of possibility. At the very least, Cleopatra was at the core of a visual dialogue that crossed nationalities and countries and became the foundation for Roman art.

4

THE PROFESSIONALS

The material remains left by Cleopatra and Rome demonstrate the synergy between sovereign and slave in the late first century B.C., an interaction that made possible the transformation of ideas into everything from hairstyles to architecture. Since hairdressers and architects took direction from queens and empresses and their most highly placed advisers, their creations contributed to the political and cultural landscapes of Alexandria and Rome. While it is difficult to document with certainty the specific contributions of the workers in Rome, some of whom were well-educated professionals brought to Italy as prisoners of war, a broad picture of imaginative collaboration emerges from surviving visual clues.

Given her status as a queen, Cleopatra's entourage was surely that of a monarch. Texts from Egypt on papyrus and potsherds used for writing, or *ostraca,* provide extensive information about Ptolemaic and Roman Egypt, although not enough to reconstruct the full range of Cleopatra's court. What can be discerned is that Cleopatra appears to have had a large retinue to attend to her personal needs, and some of her political advisers and priests were highly placed and visible enough that their names have come down to us, for example her prime ministers Hephaestion (52–51 B.C.), Protarchus (51–50 B.C.), and Pothinus (48 B.C.). Cleopatra also had a cupbearer and a personal physician named Dioskorides Phakas.

A full staff was likely called into service when the queen wanted to take a barge trip or journey to Rome with Caesar or go to Tarsus to meet Antony. Cleopatra surely had access to personal attendants who would pack her belongings, escort her, dress her, arrange her hair, accompany her activities with music, and the like. When Cleopatra wanted to honor Caesar or Caesarion with edifices at Alexandria or elsewhere, she would have had designers and artisans to turn her ideas into architecture. Some of these hairdressers and builders were talented enough to make their own suggestions, some of which were doubtless adopted.

As a very well educated woman and one who took pride in scholarly activity at her beloved Library and Museum, Cleopatra likely relished the access she had to the finest astronomer and the best mathematician of the day, namely Sosigenes and Photinus. We can even speculate that Cleopatra's interaction with Photinus was substantive because he called one of his primary works *Cleopatra's Canon*. The strength of her interest is underscored by her introduction of these men to Caesar when he was in Alexandria, an encounter that enlarged the dictator's intellectual and architectural ambitions for Rome.

Alexandria under Cleopatra appears to have been half the size of Rome under Augustus—a city of 500,000 people in a country of 3 million. Alexandria was a multicultural milieu, although the diversity seems to have been less pronounced than Rome's. The population of Egypt under the Ptolemies was primarily a ruling elite of Macedonian Greeks, of which Cleopatra was the foremost example, an Egyptian priesthood and scribal bureaucracy, working-class Egyptians living in the capital, and Egyptian peasants in the countryside. There was also a significant Jewish population, especially in the city's delta region near the palace.

Slaves were not as numerous in Cleopatra's Egypt as in Augustus's Rome, and those who were there worked primarily in domestic settings, with a small number involved in agriculture on country estates. There was doubtless some friction in Alexandria between a privileged foreign elite and a poor and subservient local domestic force, but there were surely some fruitful collaborations and occasional intermarriages. Most of the slaves worked in the royal palace or in businesses under the jurisdiction of the ruling family, like Cleopatra's wool-working factory, providing occasions for the queen to interact with some of her slaves. Since Cleopatra spoke Egyptian and many other languages, she could actually converse with her staff. Michel Chauveau has pointed out, however, that the Greeks and Egyptians of Cleopatra's day lived in "parallel universes," with minimal interaction and little reciprocity. In addition, there is evidence that slaves in the royal palace occasionally fled their bondage.

The connection between Rome's first empress, Livia, and her slaves and freedmen was likely closer than Cleopatra's. The household staff of Livia and other members of the imperial family may be reconstructed from epitaphs from the Monumentum Liviae, a subterranean sepulchral site on the Via Appia in Rome. Built toward the end of Augustus's principate to house the cremated remains of over a thousand individuals, the columbarium, run by an association or *collegium* of slaves and former slaves, was still in use after Livia's deification in A.D. 41. It was excavated in 1726. At least ninety of the slaves whose remains were placed there appear to have belonged to Livia herself. Others, laid to rest elsewhere, would have been employed in the many houses outside Rome owned by her and Augustus. The columbarium's contents demonstrate that the empress, almost like a queen herself, had a large and highly specialized staff that was well organized and had a clearly articulated chain of command. Slave ownership was a sign of great wealth and high social status in Augustan Rome. That Livia owned and oversaw a formidable domestic workforce indicated that she had status and power at home but also the opportunity to interact with her employees.

Livia's residence in Rome, the so-called House of Livia where the empress resided after Augustus's death, appears to have been overseen by a steward; his job was to manage the sizable crew of workers who had responsibility for the maintenance of the facilities, the cleaning of the domicile, and the preparation of food. It has been conjectured that there were at least 55 different kinds of jobs. Even though Livia was a woman, the majority of her staff were men. Some were slaves, others freedmen. There was a full contingent of building and maintenance workers, including surveyors, builders, carpenters, plumbers, marble workers, carvers, gilders, glaziers, and painters. Among them were craftsmen of exceptional skill such as metalworkers, goldsmiths, silversmiths, furniture makers, jewelers, and perfumers. Grounds attendants included the gardeners, grooms for horses, chariot overseers and drivers, and litter-bearers. A watch person was assigned to every key domestic space—the doors, atrium, dining room, and sleeping chambers. Since large numbers of visitors and petitioners seeking imperial favors came to the house, staff members were assigned to issue invitations and shepherd the visitors through their itinerary.

The women on Livia's staff, both slaves and freedwomen, were largely responsible for the more intimate details of her life. The empress had female attendants who aided her in the personal activities of dressing and arranging her hair. Other assistants saw that her garments and accessories were carefully cleaned and stored. In her employ were wool spinners, menders, washers, and shoemakers. Livia even had an aide to set her pearls. There were also workers who supervised the empress's possessions, among them furniture, pictures, and family portrait busts. The empress had a masseuse, escorts, messengers, a caterer, cooks and bakers. There was staff to deal with the family's financial matters, including the maintenance of records and accounts and the performing of secretarial services. In addition, a professional cadre of doctors and teachers saw to the medical and educational needs of the empress, her family, and her slaves. These included resident general practitioners and specialists, midwives and wet-nurses, and teachers for the imperial and slave children alike—the latter receiving a somewhat different and more vocational education, probably from a separate set of pedagogues.

The historian Susan Treggiari, who has done a masterful job of reconstructing Livia's household staff, points out that a Roman woman had a special responsibility for organizing, overseeing, and protecting her family's house and its possessions, an accountability made explicit in later Roman times by her ownership of the keys. In some cases, in fact, the property belonged to the woman and she had a relatively free hand in administering it, usually with the aid of a trusted freedman as steward. As Treggiari shows elsewhere, most of the extant documentation on the urban staff of elite families is provided by epigraphical evidence from the subterranean tomb or columbarium of Livia's slaves and freedmen and the columbaria of other members of the Julio-Claudian family as well as two other early imperial families, the Statilii and the Volusii. There is no manual on desirable household staffing or management that has survived from Roman times, and no preserved register with a complete list of the members of an extended urban family. The surviving epitaphs of workers provide the name of the deceased, his owner, and his profession, for example: *Gemina l(iberta) Augustae ornatrix*—Gemina, freedwoman, hairdresser of the *Augusta,* that is, the empress.

The slaves and former slaves of Livia's domestic workforce were at the bottom of a hierarchical social pyramid that had the nobility at its peak. Beginning in the third century B.C., these slaves were brought to Rome as part of a massive Republican wartime expropriation of human life, booty, and highly valued art and artifacts. Monumental buildings were also savaged for plunder. Sulla commandeered columns from the Hellenistic Temple of Olympian Zeus in Athens for Rome's Temple of Jupiter on the Capitoline hill, and numerous other Roman generals followed his lead.

Many of the newly enslaved men and women were highly educated professionals, some of whom came from civilizations more advanced than Rome's own. Augustan Rome was home to about one million inhabitants and, as such, was a vibrant melting pot with a distinctive multicultural society. People of diverse backgrounds—speaking different languages, practicing different religions, preserving different customs—came together in a fertile mix. Since the only professions an elite Roman man was permitted were politics, the military, and owning and managing estates, other careers were left for slaves. The best educated and most skilled of these were physicians, lawyers, businessmen, writers, architects, artists, musicians, and so on. Even though Rome was a slave-owning culture, it was also a society that was upwardly mobile. Slaves with lucrative professions could amass sufficient financial resources to purchase their freedom. Others were freed in their patrons' wills. Children of freedmen and freedwomen who were born after their parents' manumission were themselves considered freeborn.

What is especially interesting is the frequent interaction and interdependence of the elite and the non-elite in the age of Augustus. As noted, Augustus and Livia had hundreds of slaves, who were buried en masse in underground chambers like the Julio-Claudian Columbarium II of the Vigna Codini on the Via Appia in Rome. Some of these slaves lived with the emperor and empress in their palaces and villas and raised their children and grandchildren. Some cured the maladies of the imperial fam-

4.1. A Roman sculptor, probably a slave or former slave, completes the portrait of a woman client.

4.2. The income the baker Eurysaces earned from selling bread to the Roman army allowed him to build a tomb for his wife that egotistically featured his own professional accomplishments.

4.3. This female poultry vendor was one of many non-elite women in Ostia and Rome who worked as shopkeepers.

4.4. Slaves and freedwomen helped Octavia and Livia arrange their "power hair" and invest it with fashionable flair and political impact.

ily and tended their financial affairs. Some designed their architectural commissions; others positioned and carved the stone. Some slaves surely painted the walls of imperial residences with vivid figural scenes and landscapes that encapsulated the family's personal history and the dynasty's public mission. Others undoubtedly worked with Augustus and Livia to shape their political and social ideology into visual form, not only in monumental architecture but also through sculptured portraits and images on coins and cameos. A funerary altar in the Vatican Museums showcases a sculptor putting the finishing touches on the portrait of a woman who has apparently been posing for him and inspects his handiwork (Fig. 4.1). Some of Livia's domestic slaves were hairstylists. It was these talented women who helped the empress create a new coiffure, with deliberately arranged curls and waves, at her request to present her as a patriotic and virtuous Roman woman.

Since these individuals came from a wide variety of backgrounds and cultures, their impact must have reflected their diversity. The increasing importance of slaves and freedmen is attested by their insinuation into every phase of imperial governance by the end of the Julio-Claudian period. Claudius's closest and most trusted advisers were the freedmen Narcissus, his secretary, and Pallas, his treasurer.

There were likely two million slaves in Italy in the Republic, roughly 35 percent of the population. Those brought in during the military conquests were, for the most part, settled in agrarian communities. Yet they were increasingly placed in domestic settings, many of which were country estates; others were situated in urban enclaves. As the conquests waned, the slave supply was continued through slave dealers or through local breeding practices.

Over the years, scholars have presented conflicting views of the Roman slave system. Some suggest that the relationship of masters to slaves was one of mutual and respectful interdependence, with a strong prospect of eventual manumission; others, most recently the historian Keith Bradley, paint a bleaker portrait of oppression and exploitation. As Bradley points out, there is not enough evidence to provide us with a complete picture of the working and personal lives of Rome's slaves, and we do not have the slaves' counterpart to the rich literature of the contemporary elite. What literary record there is belongs to the slave owners and dealers. Any written testimony left by slaves is in the form of epitaphs; these were liberally carved on their tombs and make important and interesting reading today. While they are, for the most part, formulaic, they reveal something of the values and dreams of these individuals. Although Bradley may be right that this group constituted an involuntary labor force, the close ties that were surely formed between slave and free in the intimacy of the Roman household must have allowed personal alliances to be forged. These bonds might have led, for example, to creative collaboration between the *domina* and her personal dresser or hairstylist. For this reason, it is important to attempt to envision where such partnership might have evolved and thrived.

Most slaves and freedmen of the working class, of course, had no direct contact with the ruling elite. An account of the lives and professions of this group can best be gleaned from surviving sepulchral inscriptions that provide at least a partial picture of daily urban life. Many slaves and freedmen, as mentioned, were professionals serving as doctors, lawyers, or teachers. Others were workers and were employed as builders, silversmiths, goldsmiths, metalworkers, jewelry designers, businessmen specializing in the export of products ranging from bricks and terracotta lamps to cheese and wine, butchers, bakers, cobblers, furniture designers, dockworkers, bath attendants, and salesmen (Fig. 4.2). Although the majority of such workers were men, women were involved in some of these activities and were well represented in such professions as clothing and jewelry manufacture. Some women ran shops or served as saleswomen (Fig. 4.3). Others ran brothels and inns. Women were especially active as hairdressers (Fig. 4.4). Those who worked commercially catered to women who could not afford a private hairstylist.

There were, however, a fair number of slaves and freedmen who had direct and frequent contact with the imperial family while serving as domestic employees. Some of these were women. The constant interaction they enjoyed may well have led to a collaboration that had a significant impact on the creation and enactment of imperial ideology. Of course, individual contributions are difficult to assess, as is an individual staff person's geographic or ethnic origin, both of which might have determined in part the character of that contribution. Yet no assessment of the visual language employed in the art of Cleopatra or Rome would be complete without attempting to evaluate the essential participation of slaves and former slaves, both as creative partners and as emulators.

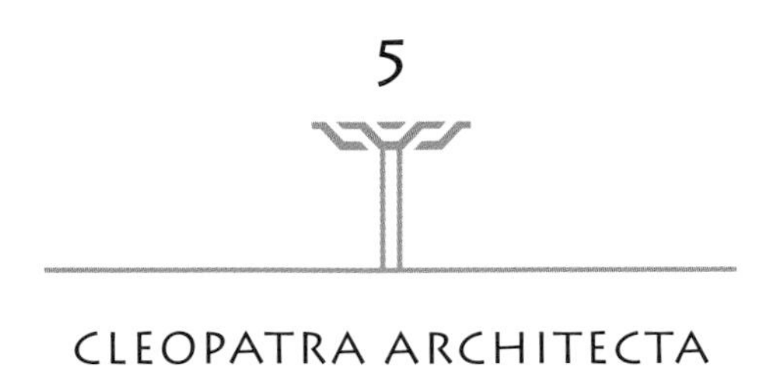

5

CLEOPATRA ARCHITECTA

Cleopatra was as sophisticated as her forebears in the matter of urban planning and architecture. She doubtless thought the Egyptian people would acclaim her if she maintained and enhanced Egypt's urban centers and provided her citizens with buildings in which they could conduct their public and private lives with ease. As Queen of Egypt, she was expected to do no less, especially because she was in a long line of kings and queens who had provided such amenities. At the same time, she was undoubtedly shrewd enough to recognize that presenting the Egyptian populace with the kinds of gifts that were likely to endure physically would ensure lasting fame for her.

There was an illustrious history in Egypt of building cities and supplying them with monuments, beginning with the pharaohs, whose temples and sphinxes remained in Cleopatra's time the most distinctive characteristic of the Egyptian landscape. Then under Alexander the Great, who conquered Egypt in 331 B.C., the country's most important city began to take shape. Alexander's plan was to establish a city at the western mouth of the Nile River and to have it serve as the locus of a Greek colony. It would bear his name and would be the first city in Egypt to possess the appellation of its founder and not that of a god or mythological creature. The site Alexander chose was the nondescript seaside town of Ra-Kedet, or Rhakotis in Greek. It was in 304 B.C. that one of Alexander's Macedonian generals was selected to locate a dynasty there. In the course of two decades of rule, Ptolemy I Soter established a thriving kingdom in the area, and when Alexander's body was brought to Alexandria for burial, the city became the kingdom's capital. The presence of Alexander's remains gave the city a sacred status and made it a potent symbol in the ancient world. Not surprisingly, Greek settlers comprised the largest population group in Alexandria, followed by Jewish inhabitants and a native Egyptian population. Greek politics, language, customs, and religion dominated because of the preponderance of Greeks, but over time the interests and practices of these diverse peoples mingled.

Under Ptolemy Soter and his descendants, including Cleopatra, the seacoast village became a sophisticated metropolis of 500,000 inhabitants. Until the late first century B.C. when it was overtaken by Rome, Alexandria was the largest city in the ancient world. Its setting was an auspicious one, with its natural protective boundaries: the Nile, Lake Mareotis, and the small island of Pharos, connected to the city by a causeway. It was located not only at the juncture of a major sea route, but also at the crossroads of caravan trade routes from Europe, Africa, and Asia. Goods from all over the world thus made their way to Alexandria, and the city thrived in large part because of such active commerce. The frequent exchange of products also ensured the intermingling of the latest ideas and technologies.

Whereas significant portions of Rome survived the centuries, Alexandria's fate was different. The great urban center has long since disappeared, and we need to rely on the geographer Strabo's description of the metropolis in 24 B.C. for a sense of its original appearance. The city was planned by the Macedonian architect Deinokrates, who designed it as the traditional grid favored in Hellenistic and early Roman town planning. The municipality, with its public buildings and private residences, was laid out in this way and announced by the island of Pharos with its multistoried lighthouse, visible from a great distance. Begun at the instigation of Ptolemy I Soter in 290 B.C., and inaugurated by his son Ptolemy II Philadelphus, this landmark building, the prototype for all later lighthouses, was designed by the Greek architect Sostratos from Asia Minor. Although the structure, victim of a fourteenth-century earthquake, no longer survives, its appearance was recorded on coins, paintings and engravings (Fig. 5.1), and in mosaics, among them one on the walls of San

5.1. The legendary Pharos of Alexandria, one of the Seven Wonders of the World, remained a celebrated symbol of the city in Cleopatra's day.

Marco in Venice. The Pharos of Alexandria was, in fact, long the city's symbol and remained so under Cleopatra.

Alexandria had two harbors, and the city center was the site of its major public buildings—the market, theater, and law courts, the gymnasium and racecourse. Like any ancient metropolis, Alexandria also had many religious structures. While most of these were dedicated to the gods favored by the Ptolemaic dynasts, among them Dionysus, Poseidon, and Serapis, several honored the goddess Isis, preferred by the Macedonian queens. In addition, temples were built to commemorate the cults of Alexander and the Ptolemies. The Ptolemaic palace and gardens, constituting a fourth to a third of the city, were situated in the royal quarter close to the Mediterranean Sea, as were the tombs of Alexander and of the founding dynasty. It was this seafront that disappeared beneath the sea in the fourth century A.D. after being devastated by a series of earthquakes and ravaged by powerful sea waves.

Over the past decade, the city and its harbor have been extensively explored through ambitious land and marine excavations, under the leadership of such archaeologists as Jean-Yves Empereur and Franck Goddio. These investigations have allowed a better understanding of the metropolis, its harbors, and its public buildings, as well as the daily lives and funerary commemorations of its inhabitants. In addition, Goddio's team has been exploring the sunken royal quarter of Alexandria for the past several years and has mapped this region using global satellite positioning devices. It is here that Cleopatra would have resided and welcomed Caesar and Antony. According to Strabo, the palace would have dominated the city and contained the administrative core of the Ptolemaic dynasty as well as the residence. The palace's vast size resulted from the many additions made to it by the successors of Ptolemy I. Near the royal quarter was the island of Antirhodos (Pharos), part of a peninsula named Lochias, and a harbor that was built or restored under the Ptolemies.

From the very day of Alexandria's founding, Ptolemy I Soter was determined to establish the city as a lively intellectual center. One of his goals was to create a museum, literally a place dedicated to the Muses, or *Mouseion,* near the palace where intellectual and artistic activity could thrive. The Museum's attractive walkways, fountains and gardens, research halls, dining and seminar rooms were designed to encourage intellectual exchange. Administered like a religious institution, it was directed by a priest of the Muses who gathered a community of up to fifty erudite men from around the ancient world, whose study there was largely subsidized by the royal treasury or even sometimes by public funds. In return for their privileged tax-free condition and the kind of job security afforded today to tenured faculty, the members often served as tutors to the royal family and other Alexandrians. Among those who did scholarly work at the Museum were mathematicians, including Euclid and Apollonius of Perga; scientists, philosophers, rhetoricians, and geographers, such as Eratosthenes and Claudius Ptolemy; astronomers like Aristarchos and Hipparchus; physiologists, including Herophilus; and poets such as Theokritos and Kallimachos.

The Museum's greatest asset was its proximity to the public library of Alexandria. Ptolemy was equally ambitious in his plan for that enterprise, which was founded around 300 B.C. or not long after. With the support of the king and that of his son, relying on the intellectual expertise of the son's tutor, Demetrius of Pharelon, former tyrant of Athens and student of Aristotle, the Library rapidly became the largest and most comprehensive collection of texts in the ancient world (Fig. 5.2). By the time Cleopatra was old enough to read, the Alexandria Library contained over 400,000 scrolls.

Egyptian works were, of course, well represented, but what gave Ptolemy's library its international flavor was the king's aggressive acquisition of Greek texts. Ptolemy's agents, flush with cash, made offers that couldn't be refused, and on the rare occasions when they were, the agents seized the texts anyway. Not surprisingly, the oldest works were the most highly prized, and the dogged Ptolemaic search for these resulted in a burgeoning business in counterfeit editions. Under Ptolemy III, the one library with its many rooms and porticoes became two. The main one was part of the palace complex and served the scholars of the Museum, while the secondary library was located in the Sanctuary of Serapis further from the royal residence. The Library had a large and busy staff, including scribes funded by the Ptolemies whose scholarly activity ensured that the Library at Alexandria was not only a repository of the world's great books but also a place where seminal philological work took place. The Director, appointed by the king's court, was an intellectual celebrity and was sometimes also asked to tutor the royal children.

5.2. Scholars at work in the hall of the great Library of Alexandria, a magnet for lively intellectual activity in the age of Cleopatra.

Such an eminent academician tutored Ptolemaic princesses alongside their brothers. The fact that Cleopatra was well educated speaks to the high level of the education of women among the Ptolemies. Indeed, the scholarly life of the Alexandrian Library was not entirely confined to men. Although it was men who were associates of the Museum and had access to the court and ruling patrons, women scholars were not invisible. Specific names are preserved, foremost among them Hestiaia of Alexandria, a grammarian who wrote a monograph on whether the Trojan War had been fought around the city she knew as Ilium.

Ptolemy I and his dynasty envisioned themselves as Hellenistic successors to Alexander the Great and also the scions of the Egyptian pharaohs, who were noteworthy builders, especially of temples and tombs. In fact, the Ptolemaic period marked the final great era of temple construction in Egypt. Located at sites such as Dendera, Edfu, Kom Ombo, and Philae, these Ptolemaic commissions were either renovations of or additions to earlier temples, or new temples based on traditional types. Temples were popular building choices for the Ptolemies because they were microcosms of the Egyptian cosmos, with an established hierarchy consisting of the gods, the king, the community, and those who had passed on to the next world. These sacred sites were the location of a struggle between Egyptian order, or *ma'at,* and chaos, or *isfet.* This clash took place in divine or royal cult complexes, where both gods and kings were honored but where they were alternately the primary focus of cultic practice. The walls, traditional facade pylons, and columns of both kinds of temples were covered with hieroglyphics and figural scenes that recorded pictographically the theology of the temple and its cult ceremonies. This imagery became especially abundant in those temples built by the Ptolemies and by Rome.

Cleopatra's father, Auletes, restored several temples and thus achieved a reputation as a major builder. While some have disappeared, remains of others are still visible at such Egyptian sites as Edfu, Dendera, Kom Ombo, and Philae. In some cases, Auletes's benefaction was minor: walls were repaired and pylons added. His most significant contribution was the restoration of the Temple of Amun-Re at Karnak, an important site for the Ptolemies because they, like the pharaohs, asserted that they were descended from Amun-Re. Worshippers were not allowed to enter these temples but instead had to imagine the interiors and the rituals that would have taken place there. In order to acquaint them with the cult and rituals, many of the exterior walls were carved with figural scenes. At Ombo and Philae, for example, Auletes was portrayed in the act of defeating his foes, a scene that had a long history in pharaonic art.

Cleopatra would have witnessed such architectural projects from an early age. This exposure would have made apparent to her that she was in a long line of pharaohs and kings who had the opportunity and responsibility to undertake building programs and feature scenes of their exploits or their interaction with the gods. Cleopatra's brother and first husband, Ptolemy XIII, would surely have come to the same conclusion and, as his father's oldest son, would have had even more reason than his sister to depict himself in his father's image. When the pylon towers of the Temple of Horus at Edfu were carved, the imagery included the ubiquitous set piece of two large facing figures of Ptolemy smiting his enemies in the presence of Horus and Hathor (Fig. 5.3). Most of the temple was older than Ptolemy was himself; construction had begun in the late third century B.C. Like most Ptolemaic temples, its plan and cultic functions mimicked those of the temples of an earlier pharaonic Egypt.

Although Ptolemy is portrayed on the pylons as king, the temple's pictorial program centers on the myth of Horus, the falcon god who possessed divine powers and served as protector of the pharaoh. As reigning dynast, Ptolemy was the governing force on earth and the container of the royal life force or *ka* that was transferred from one pharaoh to the next. He bore Horus's name, sat on his throne, and thus guaranteed political and cosmic order. While the scene of Ptolemy triumphant over his foes dominates the pylon imagery, the rest of the scheme centers on the divine triad of Horus, Hathor, and Harsomtous. They, and other deities, are depicted in creation and foundation scenes, battles, and daily and special ritual enactments. The king and queen are sometimes present, usually bringing appropriate offerings to the gods. These depictions cover walls and columns, leaving little unoccupied space. This profusion of decoration is a hallmark of Egyptian temple architecture under the Ptolemies and the Romans and has been aptly described as a locus for cultural identity and memory. Ptolemaic temples, like that of Horus at Edfu, have a panoply of components that are comparable to those in earlier Egyp-

5.3. Ptolemy XIII, Cleopatra's brother, vanquishes his enemies while Horus and Hathor look on.

tian temple architecture—pylons, courtyards, sanctuaries, hallways, and storerooms. Some contained birth houses that celebrated the delivery of the child in the divine triad as well as the king's divine descent. Ptolemaic additions to the temple were a pronaos screen wall, a columnar entranceway, and a central sanctuary. There were also spaces for a wide variety of additional activities such as workshops, scribal offices, and visiting rooms. The kind of scholarly activity that took place at the Museum and Library in Alexandria also happened in many of these temples, attesting to the high regard for scholarship that permeated Ptolemaic Egypt. Excerpts from some of the texts were displayed on the temple's walls.

When she became Queen of Upper and Lower Egypt at the age of 18, Cleopatra was prepared to follow in her father's footsteps. That her reigning consort was her 10-year-old brother Ptolemy XIII ensured that she was likely to maintain the upper hand. While it was natural for Ptolemy to be depicted in his father's image at Edfu, Cleopatra, like queens before her, also built and restored major Egyptian monuments. Her apparent talent for statecraft matched her architectural prowess and she, more than her brother, took the lead. With the help of a knowledgeable and supportive staff, Cleopatra issued the customary orders and edicts and, just like Caesar in Rome, received petitions and dispensed justice.

This is not to say that everything proceeded smoothly. In fact, the opposite was increasingly the case. The most disadvantaged Egyptians were rendered more needy still by a succession of famines. The Egyptian bureaucracy was becoming bloated. Plots against Cleopatra were rife within her own family: her brother had come under the influence of three advisers unfriendly to Cleopatra, and even her youngest sister, Arsinoe, maneuvered to replace her as female sovereign of Egypt. The former sturdy Egyptian currency was losing its potency in the world market. All of these circumstances conspired to put Egypt at the mercy of an increasingly powerful Rome.

Despite these enormous challenges, the young Macedonian monarch acted rapidly, forcefully, and with considerable success. Cleopatra devalued the Egyptian currency in order to make Egyptian exports more competitive abroad, and encouraged religious reforms that appealed to both the priestly elite and indigenous Egyptians. Most important, she maintained the risky alliance with Rome, in which she offered those who led it her country's natural assets and, in some instances, her own formidable personal ones. This ambitious attempt to wed two nations and underscore their bonds by establishing a strong personal alliance between their leaders was not unique; in fact it was fully in keeping with a long practice common from the beginning of the Hellenistic period. Yet the personalities and policies of the particular individuals involved made these alliances particularly electrifying.

What the young queen undertook was the quintessential balancing act. Cleopatra apparently resolved to continue an association with Rome that would support the superpower's expansionist aspirations while allowing Egypt to maintain a strong and independent national identity. How the queen handled Egypt's currency is a striking illustration of this policy. As a gracious nod to Rome, Cleopatra looked to the silver content in the Roman denarius to set the standard by which Egypt's currency was measured. She decreased the quantity of silver in Egyptian drachms to match the weight of the denarius, using this as an opportunity to take measures to restore Egypt's fiscal health. That Cleopatra was serious about this endeavor is underscored by her decision not to mint any gold coins at all but to increase the production of the less expensive bronze currency.

Although every decision Cleopatra made was vital, not every judgment was sound, and there was ample room for miscalculation. In fact, Cleopatra erred from the very beginning by choosing to back Pompey rather than Caesar. It was an understandable choice because Pompey had already demonstrated that he was a strong ally of Egypt. Nevertheless, Cleopatra apparently failed to notice that, as he crossed the Rubicon, Caesar was gaining visible strength. Cleopatra was walking a tightrope in Egypt as well. Her provision of soldiers and supplies to Pompey was not well received and weakened Cleopatra's support among her people, creating an opportunity for Ptolemy and Arsinoe to mount an insurrection. This uprising was severe enough to cause Cleopatra to flee Alexandria. Losing access to some of her own troops, she was forced to add mercenaries to her legion as she attempted to regain authority. Cleopatra's ability to assemble an army in such a short time was, in any case, an impressive achievement for a fugitive queen. While she was marshaling her new forces, fate intervened. Pompey, newly vanquished by Caesar at the Battle of Pharsalus, looked to his former Ptolemaic friends to provide refuge in his hour of need. Ptolemy and his advisers were politically astute enough to side with Caesar. They murdered Pompey and presented his decapitated head and signet ring to Caesar.

Caesar is reported to have wept openly at the sight of all that remained of his fellow Roman. Still, he relished his achievement as victor or *triumphator* and proudly entered Alexandria with his soldiers. The city's inhabitants did not share Caesar's sense of accomplishment and rose up against him, causing casualties among his troops. Politically astute, Caesar quickly assured the Egyptians of his commitment to the sovereignty of Egypt, a promise first made to Auletes and now extended to the former king's children. Ptolemy was immediately appeased, but Cleopatra was considerably more cautious. On one hand, she questioned Caesar's trustworthiness, but on the other, she recognized that her brother and his advisers were disloyal. Knowing full well that she was not likely to prevail, she had to make a pragmatic choice and opted for Caesar. It was at this moment that Cleopatra was alleged to have returned stealthily to Alexandria, hidden in bed linens. If the story is true, it emphasizes the continued ingenuity and flair of Egypt's queen, whose unwrapping before Caesar must have been a carefully constructed, dramatic, and memorable event devised to win his support at a crucial time (Fig. 5.4).

Caesar and Cleopatra immediately became lovers. Caesar announced that as executor of Auletes's last will and testament he would honor the joint rule of Cleopatra and Ptolemy. Furthermore, in a display of good faith, he returned the island of Cyprus to the youngest sibling (the future Ptolemy XIV) and Arsinoe so that they would have their own kingdom to oversee. While that might have been enough to bring the royal pair contentment, it apparently wasn't, at least for Arsinoe; she worked ceaselessly with the elder Ptolemy and his wily advisers to turn public opinion against Cleopatra and her Roman consort. Initially their efforts were effective. Before long, they provided one of Ptolemy's aides with a contingent of troops to attack Alexandria and initiate a full-fledged civil war.

The confrontation raged for months, with the two sides alternately gaining the upper hand. At first Caesar and Cleopatra saw to it that Ptolemy was kept in the palace, but eventually they decided to release him. As the fighting spread toward the harbor, Caesar ordered that the Egyptian and Roman fleets under his and Cleopatra's jurisdiction be set afire, rather than have them fall into enemy hands. That conflagration spread and engulfed part of the city, purportedly damaging even the famed Library of Alexandria. Whether part of the main Library was involved or only the book warehouses on the docks may never be known; the ancient sources, among them Plutarch, Dio Cassius, and Ammianus Marcellinus, offer conflicting versions.

As Caesar and his army pushed Ptolemy's troops back toward the Nile, those soldiers were eventually forced to flee. Among them was Ptolemy himself, found shortly thereafter drowned in the Nile. Ptolemy's golden breastplate was claimed as Caesar's trophy and displayed to the Alexandrians, who now recognized that they had a new master. They prostrated themselves in front of Caesar and begged for clemency. It was the end of March in 47 B.C., and Cleopatra, who had been bound to Ptolemy in the traditional Egyptian brother-sister marriage, was officially a widow.

As protocol needed to be followed, Cleopatra married her younger brother, who became Ptolemy XIV. Fortunately for Cleopatra—and for Caesar—the younger Ptolemy was only 10 years old. Arsinoe was still a threat and was consequently sent to Rome as a prisoner and paraded in Caesar's triumph of 46 B.C. Still mindful that he had to protect Cleopatra's safety, Caesar provided the queen with a large contingent of Roman guards. He also rewarded those among the Egyptians who had stood by him during the civil war in the hope that they would continue to be loyal to Cleopatra.

Caesar and Cleopatra had much to celebrate and must have thought that a triumphant procession down the Nile in the spring of 47 would highlight not only their alliance but their combined authority as well. It might also be hoped that the populace would delight in their union and enjoy the pageantry (Fig. 5.5). The triumph must have been quite a spectacle: the royal barge did not travel alone but was joined by 400 additional ships. Caesar's objective was surely to flaunt Rome's military might and, by so doing, awe the Alexandrians into obeisance to Rome. To fortify Rome's superior rank, he also established several of his legions as an oc-

5.4. Cleopatra is revealed to Caesar when Apollodorus unwraps her from bed linens, the first key episode in her interaction with Rome.

5.5. Cleopatra and Julius Caesar float together down the Nile, an unforgettable journey that was to have a momentous impact on the art of Rome.

cupying authority.[1] Cleopatra was too shrewd, however, to allow Caesar to dominate the event. She knew that the Alexandrians would also likely interpret the voyage as a reenactment of the famous annual Festival of the Reunion of Hathor and Horus, when Hathor departed her temple at Dendera and sailed upstream to meet Horus at his temple at Edfu, stopping along the way to visit other deities. At the same time, the procession was a visual expression of the fact that Egypt was now a Roman protectorate. The journey also gave Caesar an opportunity to see the sites and to benefit from the explanations of scholars brought along to edify him.

Cleopatra was descended from great builders, and Caesar must have developed on his own a similar inclination. He had already traveled extensively with his army engineers, who skillfully built bridges, camps, and places for sacrifice whenever they were needed. His military forays had brought him into contact with splendid edifices around the world. In addition, Caesar must have felt the weight of peer pressure. His Republican compatriots were commissioning major structures in Rome, and as a recent *triumphator,* Caesar was also expected to initiate projects to benefit the capital city.

While competition with his Roman peers may have first fueled Caesar's interest in monumental architecture, it is hard to imagine that Cleopatra and Caesar, as they came to know each other more fully, did not discuss their shared taste for grandiose architecture both as an aesthetic addition to their respective capitals and as a purveyor of their power and ideology, alone and collectively. Though still a young woman, Cleopatra was born to rule and was secure in her intelligence and facility with languages. She was certainly also comfortable with the pharaonic and Ptolemaic traditions that made commissioning buildings and statues a matter of course. She had around her an entourage of highly educated and skilled political advisers, priests, astronomers, architects, and the like, who were there not only to counsel her but also to see promising projects through to completion.

For his part, Caesar must have been profoundly affected by the sights and sounds of Egyptian politics, social life, religion, literature, science, and art that he experienced in the months he spent with Cleopatra in Alexandria. An ambitious and visionary man, Caesar doubtless thrived on the contact with this intelligent and articulate woman and the brilliant scholars in her circle. He also experienced in Alexandria the heady rush of autocratic rule so natural to Egypt but alien to Republican Rome. While dictatorship was a Roman institution, and circumstances in Rome prompted Caesar to accept that office, it is possible that his firsthand experience with Ptolemaic practice was also influential. And it seems likely that other ideas made their way via Caesar from Alexandria to Rome as well: Cleopatra's astronomer Sosigenes, for example, appears to have introduced Caesar, and through him Rome, to the 365-day solar calendar. Caesar's exposure to the ancient waterway that joined the Red Sea and the Mediterranean may have inspired him to cut his canal through the Isthmus of Corinth and to embark on other large-scale public projects, including the draining of the Pomptine Marshes and Lake Fucinus and the construction of a highway running from the Adriatic across the Apennines to the Tiber.

What could have made more of an impression on Caesar than the sepulchers and sphinxes of the pharaohs and the museums and libraries of the Ptolemies? Caesar knew as well as anyone of his day that texts could survive as long, if not longer, than monuments. A writer himself, Caesar doubtless admired the comprehensiveness of the Alexandrian collection of great books, as well as the massive edifice that protected them and announced their erudition to the world. Caesar's mind must have been awhirl with the potential benefits of introducing such wonders to Rome.

It was in Egypt that Caesar was introduced to luxury, conceivably greater than any he experienced elsewhere. Although the epic poet Lucan was staunchly anti-Caesarian, leaving us no choice but to assume that his assessment of ostentation at a banquet Cleopatra prepared for Caesar was hyperbolic,[2] the details are not entirely out of keeping with the reputation the Ptolemies had for extravagant entertaining. The feast took place in a banqueting hall that Lucan says was as large as a temple: "Its fretted ceilings were encrusted with precious stones, and its rafters heavily plated with gold. The walls were marble, not merely marble-faced; pillars of sheer agate and porphyry supported the roof; and the entire palace had an onyx pavement. Similarly, the great doorposts were solid ebony, not common timber with an ebony veneer; these costly materials, in effect, served a functional, not merely a decorative, purpose. The entrance hall was paneled in ivory, and its doors inlaid with tinted tortoise-shell, the dark patches concealed by emeralds. There were jewel-studded couches, rows of yellow jasper wine-cups on the tables, bright coverlets spread over the sofas—mostly Tyrian purple repeatedly dyed, and either embroidered in gold, or shot with fiery threads of cochineal in Egyptian style. The tables were rounds of citrus-wood, supported on gleaming elephant tusks—Caesar never saw anything so fine even after his conquest of King Juba."

Caesarion was born on June 23 in 47 B.C. This had already been a momentous year for Caesar and Cleopatra, and the birth of their child might well have underscored not only the effectiveness of their personal union but also that their alliance could continue into the future in the person of their son. Caesarion's birth and the promise of his life were celebrated in works of art that Cleopatra commissioned in Egypt. As her first son and heir, Caesarion was a potential future king of Egypt, making Cleopatra not only Queen of Egypt but now possibly also the mother of a sovereign-to-be. The power she possessed, as dynast, was now even further strengthened by her motherhood. Cleopatra's beauty and sensuality were thus enhanced by her fertility. As she followed her father's and brother's lead as a builder and restorer of major Egyptian monuments, Cleopatra is likely to have thought about how best to portray visually the bond between herself and her son. It is not surprising, in view of the infant's dual heritage, that Cleopatra was assimilated both to Isis, who became patroness of the Ptolemies after Alexander the Great's establishment of the dynasty, and to Venus, the divine progenitor of Caesar's Julian family. Right after delivering Caesarion, Cleopatra commissioned coins depicting herself as Isis/Venus cradling Caesarion (Horus/Eros) in her arms. Furthermore, it is likely that those viewing contemporary statuary of Isis and Horus, often with Horus seated on Isis's lap, would have immediately thought of Cleopatra and Caesarion.

By the time Caesarion was 3 years old, both of Cleopatra's brothers and co-rulers, Ptolemy XIII and XIV, were dead—the latter, according to Josephus, poisoned by Cleopatra herself. Caesarion was designated Ptolemy XV. Since every king of Egypt was associated with Horus during his lifetime and Osiris after death, it was time for Cleopatra to begin to think about how to have Caesarion portrayed on the visible pylon walls of a great Egyptian temple. As noted earlier, scenes of kings assimilated to Horus, shown smiting their enemies and appearing before the gods, had a long history in the art of the pharaohs, and the Ptolemies had themselves similarly portrayed. Ptolemy XIII, with Horus and Hathor as his carved witnesses, was shown slaying his foes on the walls of the Temple of Horus at Edfu (see Fig. 5.3).

Even though Cleopatra did not shy away from military confrontation, neither did she allude to it at Edfu or in the major Egyptian commission of her reign, the Temple of Hathor at Dendera. At Edfu, a diminutive Caesarion is well protected by huge falcons at the temple's entrance. The relief sculpture on the outer wall of the Dendera temple does not depict either Cleopatra or her new co-ruler Caesarion smiting enemies; they are shown in peaceful concert with the deities of Dendera. Caesarion is por-

5.6. Cleopatra, in the horns and disk headdress of Hathor, and Caesarion, wearing the double crown of Upper and Lower Egypt, sacrifice to the Egyptian gods Hathor and Ihy on a frieze from the temple at Dendera.

trayed as the principal ruler, nearest to the gods, with the queen close behind, separated from him only by his diminutive toy-like *ka* (Fig. 5.6). While Cleopatra is depicted as a bare-chested kilted pharaoh in an Egyptian stele now in Paris (perhaps this image was originally meant to be her father; see Fig. 9.1), her role as mother to the pharaoh is foremost in the imagery at Dendera. Cleopatra's presence in this scene underscores her dual function as pharaoh and mother of the pharaoh, substantively enhancing her authority. Furthermore, the Dendera temple was dedicated to Hathor rather than to Horus—a choice especially sympathetic to Cleopatra, who was assimilated to the goddess and to Isis.

The substructures of the Temple of Hathor at Dendera have been attributed to Auletes, whose name is inscribed in the foundation walls, probably laid in 54 B.C. Since Cleopatra completed the temple, the choice of relief scenes can be attributed to her. After Cleopatra's death in 30 B.C., Octavian made Egypt a Roman province, entering Alexandria in triumph as Caesar had done sixteen years earlier. Augustus's decision to have his name inscribed at Dendera near the paired relief portraits of Cleopatra and Caesarion was striking and surprising. So too was his decision not to dismantle the temple but allow it to stand and even to enhance it by adding walls to the *naos* and completing the Temple of Isis. Augustus's Julio-Claudian successors followed his lead, as did subsequent emperors through Marcus Aurelius—a tribute to the temple's importance in the life of Egypt and to the continuing respect there for the last Ptolemaic queen. This is significant because these Roman imperial patrons rarely hesitated to eradicate portraits or inscriptions in Rome and elsewhere.

The exterior walls of the Temple of Hathor at Dendera are carved with a multitude of crowded figural scenes depicting the divine pantheon of Dendera. The dyarchy of Cleopatra and Caesarion appears twice on the temple's 100-foot rear exterior wall. The two scenes mirror each other, as was traditional for the representation of such royal personages. Although Caesarion was probably no more than 14 when the relief was carved, he appears as an imposing pharaoh wearing an elaborate headdress and offering incense. Behind him is Cleopatra, also in headdress with *uraeus,* the representation of a rearing cobra that protected pharaohs, and carrying Isis's attributes of rattle or *sistrum* and *mnet.* In both scenes, the regal pair face five deities to whom they make offerings—Hathor, Horus, Harsomtus, Ihy, and Hathor again on the east half, and Isis, Harsomtus, Osiris, Horus, and Isis again on the west half. The divinities back up against one another and are separated by a monumental head of the temple's goddess, Hathor. The emphasis on Hathor and Isis again suggests a Cleopatra-centric approach to the design of the temple's visual imagery. An adjacent temple to Isis further merged the two deities.

It is worth noting that one of the most prominent events in the calendar of Upper Egypt was the Festival of the Beautiful Embrace, the union of the two great divinities, Hathor and Horus. The divine marriage was enacted by transporting an image of Hathor by barge to the great Temple of Horus at Edfu, a procession depicted in reliefs and described by accompanying texts on the temples at both Dendera and Edfu. While the Egyptians practiced brother/sister marriage and Cleopatra was legally wed to Ptolemy XIII and Ptolemy XIV, she was also the mother of Ptolemy XV and thus, since he was Caesar's son, she might be construed, at least in Egyptian eyes, as the "wife" of his father, Julius Caesar.

That Hathor and Horus lived separately and required annual reunification had resonance for a "marriage" (or, at least, a political merger, which produced a biological heir) between a sovereign of Egypt and one of Rome. Although the matrimonial link between Cleopatra and Caesar had produced Egypt's new male monarch, mother and son could oversee Egypt without Caesar's presence just as Hathor, without Horus, could guide Dendera. Caesar's absence, both in actuality and in the temple reliefs, was not a liability but a circumstance that only consolidated the affiliation of the royal and divine pairs. Since Horus was also the divine child of Isis and Osiris, their assimilation to Cleopatra and Caesar might also have been inferred. While such allusions might have been frowned upon in Republican Rome, they were traditional in Egypt. The temple's location, subject matter, style, and explanatory hieroglyphs and cartouches confirm that the Dendera reliefs were intended for an Egyptian audience, and it is therefore possible, even if not provable, that such references were aimed at those who were sophisticated enough to appreciate them.

Caesar and Cleopatra collaborated on at least two building projects in Alexandria. The fabled city's virtual disappearance, however, has deprived us of significant remains of either of these edifices. One of them, the Caesareum, is mentioned by Strabo and was described in some detail in the mid-first century A.D. by Philo of Alexandria. The Caesareum was likely begun by Cleopatra and Caesar in 48–47 B.C., although some posit that the queen erected the building in honor of Antony. Philo records the structure's notable location overlooking the harbor and describes its unroofed precinct, colonnades, banqueting halls, and landscaping. The large enclosure or *temenos*, with porticoes around its inner perimeter, may have been based on earlier temple enclosures such as the one honoring Ptolemy III and Berenice at Hermopolis Magna (third century B.C.). A later structure of similar plan in Cyrene dedicated to Augustus suggests that the design was subsequently adapted for buildings celebrating the imperial cult, especially in the Greek-speaking world. Caesar built a similar building bearing his name a few months later in Antioch (also not preserved), and John Ward-Perkins has convincingly argued that the plan of the Caesareum may have been one of the inspirations for the design of Caesar's Julian Forum in Rome.

Augustus completed the Caesareum as part of his Egyptian building program. Augustus's penchant for mixing his Egyptian and Roman metaphors led him to place two obelisks at the entrance to the edifice. These Egyptian pillars thus marked the gateway to a precinct that appears to have honored the cult of the emperor, not only Augustus but also his divine father Caesar. Furthermore, Augustus must have known that the obelisks were originally dedicated to the Egyptian sun god Re at the Pharaoh Tuthmosis III's Sanctuary at Heliopolis. By removing these obelisks from their former Egyptian locale and inserting them in a new Roman context, Augustus was emphasizing his alliance with Rome's sun god, Apollo, and signaling Rome's dominance over Egypt. Both obelisks ("Cleopatra's Needles") still survive, having been moved in the nineteenth century to London and New York.

Julius Caesar's personal ambitions and aspirations for Rome were as grandiose as those of Cleopatra for herself and Egypt. As work began on the Caesareum in Alexandria, the dictator was already putting into action his plan for the redesign of Rome. Some of Caesar's ideas were formulated in the course of his Egyptian sojourn and were profoundly affected by his affair with Cleopatra and their collaborative building projects. Their relationship provided not only companionship but also, in his case, entrée into Alexandria's sophisticated world of erudition and art, statecraft and bounty. Cleopatra put Egypt's riches at Caesar's disposal, invaluable resources that further enabled his expansionist dreams. In turn, Caesar provided Cleopatra with protection. The might of the western world's most powerful man and the force of his nation could ensure that Cleopatra stayed on Egypt's throne. In fact, leaving Egypt for a sojourn in Rome with Caesar was risky for the Egyptian queen. Whatever enemies she had at home were at liberty in her absence to foment dissent. At the same time, she knew that lack of proximity to Caesar might jeopardize their relationship. Unlike Cleopatra, Caesar had had many affairs, and she was not the only foreign woman of authority with whom an affiliation might provide political and strategic gain. Caesar's name was linked contemporaneously, for example, with other sovereigns such as Queen Eunoe, wife of his ally Bogud, King of Mauretania.[3]

Despite the political peril, Cleopatra joined Caesar in Rome in 46. She brought Caesarion with her and also her brother/husband, Ptolemy XIV. Their large retinue included the requisite staff, but also the kinds of intellectuals and artists Caesar had met in Alexandria. In that same year, Caesar was appointed dictator for ten years, and late in the year he left for Spain. It is unclear whether Cleopatra resided in Rome during his absence or returned to Egypt (probably the latter), but it is likely that she would have wanted to be in Rome upon Caesar's triumphant return from the victory at Munda in 45. Since the paternity of Caesarion was hotly contested in Rome, Cleopatra may have hoped that she would become pregnant again by Caesar and give birth to a second child in Rome. Such a delivery might have made a genuine marriage possible. In any case, rumors about an impending wedding between the two and a potential move of the capital from Rome to Alexandria appear to have swirled around the city following the Spanish conquest, although this hearsay was emphatically contradicted by Caesar's actions.

A less personal reason for Cleopatra's second visit to Rome has been suggested by Erich Gruen. After vanquishing his foreign foes, Caesar could turn his attention to various reforms, including the possible annexation of Egypt and Cyprus as Roman provinces. If Cleopatra wanted to forestall such an appropriation, she had to plead the case in person and may have done so, according to Gruen's theory, in 44 B.C. The idea that Cleopatra's return to Rome had more to do with preserving the heritage of her Macedonian forefathers than with her wish to have another child with Caesar would seem to be bolstered by the fact that, already in September 45 B.C., Caesar had provided Rome's Vestal Virgins with his will. The document made no provision for his biological son Caesarion or for Cleopatra. Instead, it highlighted Caesar's intention to adopt as his son after his death his grand-nephew Gaius Octavius, and to provide the youth with three-quarters of Caesar's substantial estate. In early 44 B.C., Caesar was appointed dictator for life.

Despite his public display of *Romanitas,* Caesar was planning an ambitious campaign to conquer Parthia, with tangible human and financial resources supplied by a number of dependencies, the wealthiest of which was Egypt. In return for such assistance, Cleopatra would solidify her supremacy in Egypt and her personal alliance with Caesar. Caesar's dramatic assassination on March 15, 44 B.C., canceled their plans and hastened Cleopatra's return to Egypt (Cicero referred in his letters to her departure as a "flight"). The queen entered Alexandria with Ptolemy XIV by her side but soon realized that her co-ruler and teenage brother was a liability. Caesar's will had been read in Rome, and Octavian was declaring himself Caesar's sole heir. Ancient writers like Josephus and Porphyry suggest that Cleopatra murdered her brother. If that is true, her motive was clear—to situate Caesarion on the throne of Egypt as her co-ruler. The 3-year-old boy was proclaimed Ptolemy XV and given the designation "God Who Loves His Father and Mother" *(Theos Philopator Philometor)*. While this title spoke above all to an Egyptian audience, it is conceivable that Cleopatra also saw it as a subtle reference to Caesar's paternity and a gauntlet tossed to Octavian, whose familial connection to Caesar was more distant and thus more tenuous. That Octavian was fully Roman was, however, an effective equalizer.

Cleopatra's maternal bond with her son served as the locus of her political agenda and was highlighted in art that she commissioned in Egypt. Although at Dendera, Caesarion was depicted as being more mature and powerful than he actually was at that time, there were other commissions that featured his birth and associated it with the birth of Horus to Isis. *Mammisi* or birth temples were small sanctuaries appended to larger ones that celebrated the birth of the child in the divine triad; they also made reference to the divine descent of the king. These birth temples were a Ptolemaic and Roman phenomenon in Egypt but found their prototypes in the birth rooms of New Kingdom temples, the earliest example of which dates back to the fourth century B.C.

The Egyptian *mammisi* possessed elaborate birth cycles carved in relief. One of Cleopatra's commissions was the birth temple at Erment, near Thebes (now destroyed), where Horus, beneath the sacred scarab, was depicted as being born to Isis in the presence of a multitude of divinities. Amun-Re, the goddess Nekhbet, and Cleopatra were shown witnessing the event, while numerous divinities, among them Isis, suckled the baby. It would have been natural to think of the birth of Caesarion when viewing such nativity scenes of Horus. The theology of the divine delivery incorporated that of the royal birth in a way that made them essentially indistinguishable. Cleopatra went a step further when commissioning relief sculpture for the Shrine of Hermonthis in Upper Egypt. These scenes combined the birth of Horus, a traditionally popular theme, with the delivery of Caesarion, an innovative portrayal of a current event. As the first extant scene in an Egyptian context to represent the parturition of a royal prince, the Hermonthis scene was not only bold and unprecedented but presumably meant as an official proclamation. Since Horus was expected to avenge the death of his father Osiris, Caesarion's birth might have heralded the expectation that he would similarly avenge Caesar's murder.

Because Octavian had reserved that task for himself, the Hermonthis reliefs may have been viewed, at least in Egypt, as challenging Octavian's filial role. It is possible that Octavian heard that Cleopatra was advertising in Egypt Caesarion's claim to be the biological son of Caesar, a message at variance with Octavian's assertion that he was the slain dictator's only legitimate heir. Since Octavian was expressly designated as Caesar's heir in the dictator's will, it is unlikely that he worried about the images Cleopatra was projecting to the Egyptians. Yet it is possible that these themes—the nativity of an exceptional baby and the portrayal of a very young prince with his royal mother—may have entered Octavian's consciousness, to reappear before long in the visual repertory of his own child-oriented relief sculpture in Rome, especially the Ara Pacis Augustae.

In this way, the commissions of Cleopatra *architecta* were influential not only for Caesar but also for Augustus. It is significant that Augustus, like Caesar, built monuments in both Rome and Egypt that traced their heritage to Cleopatra. I will try to make the case that the Ara Pacis was in part a visual dialogue between Augustus and Cleopatra; and it is incontrovertible that Augustus added his name and portrait to the queen's temple at Dendera. In fact, Augustus turned up in Egypt in the most extraordinary places. For example, at the *mammisi* at Philae, Horus is shown being born and nursed in the presence of none other than Augustus; the emperor is depicted as a pharaoh bearing the gift of a pectoral for the infant. Augustus may not have been unduly worried about Cleopatra's or Caesarion's legacy in Rome, but he appears to have been very interested in taking their place on Egyptian soil, not only in name but also by using tried and true Egyptian visual strategies.

6

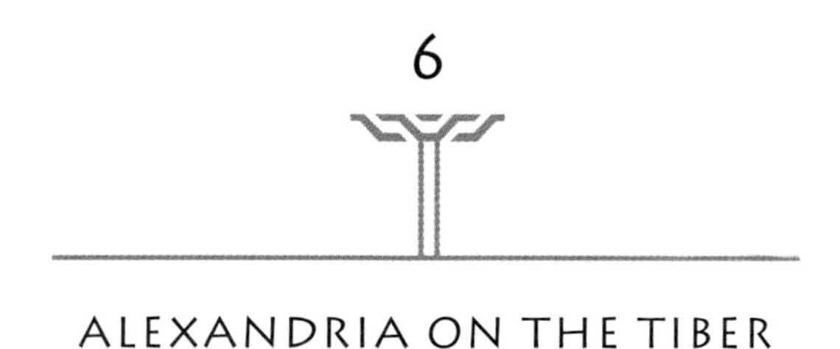

ALEXANDRIA ON THE TIBER

Julius Caesar was a military tactician and colonizer before he became a builder. Campaigns in Asia, Gaul, Spain, Africa, Britain, and elsewhere introduced him to diverse civilizations with a wide range of religious and social customs as well as to the buildings, statues, and paintings that made concrete these different views of the world. Whether modest or monumental, these works of art could not have failed to make an impact on the ambitious Roman leader bent on making his mark. Caesar's military success enabled him to seize some of the works he favored, at least those that were readily transportable, and to convey them to Rome both as valuable plunder and also as prototypes for a new Roman art. Intense competition was arising in Rome among Republican friends and foes, who no doubt recognized that the valuable booty they amassed abroad could be exhibited or rapidly translated into funding for building projects through which they could celebrate and measure their relative accomplishments.

Prior to 48 B.C., Caesar's building activity, which some believe was begun as early as the late 60s, centered on the restoration of memorials to illustrious relatives and the building of monuments in important public spaces. Not one to think small, Caesar set his sights immediately on one of the most significant communal locations in Rome—the Forum. While his agents were accumulating prized property in the city center to allow the expansion of this space, a fire in 52 B.C. at the sepulchral pyre of Publius Clodius destroyed various basilicas and curias. This fortuitous event allowed Caesar and other moneyed men with military victories under their belts to rebuild these structures. In addition, the booty from Caesar's Gallic campaigns provided him with the wherewithal to replace the Basilica Sempronia with the Basilica Julia, named for the Julian family.

By the time of the completion of this project, the dynamic between Caesar and Pompey the Great had been forever altered, and the two proud generals met each other at the historic Battle of Pharsalus. In a display of great bravado, Caesar had vowed before the confrontation that if triumphant, he would dedicate a temple to Pompey's own patron goddess—Venus Victrix. When the goddess obliged him with a victory, he decided to rethink the Forum project. No longer was he content with the expansion of a space that had had a long string of miscellaneous patrons. Instead, he envisioned a space he could call his own and conceived a separate forum with a prominently positioned temple to Venus Genetrix, the progenitor of the Julian family. That the Forum also aggrandized Caesar was not lost on the Roman populace, nor was it meant to be.

By 46 B.C., Caesar had a lot to crow about. He celebrated five major victories in one year (Gallic, Alexandrian, Pontic, African, Spanish), including the quadruple triumph of 46, which gave him the status and even the duty to erect public buildings *ex manubiis* (from the spoils of war). Diane Favro connects the events of 46 and the ensuing booty with Caesar's construction of a stadium, a temporary hunting theater, an artificial lake for sham naval battles, and improvements to the Circus Maximus and Roman Forum. She effectively describes how he used those projects and the two monumental structures already underway—the Basilica Julia and the Julian Forum—to compete with other powerful men of the day. He had already formed mutually beneficial political alliances with some of them; others were hostile rivals.

Caesar's commissions were part of a major building program in Rome that included imposing a structured plan on what was then a disorganized city center. This project called for the remodeling of the Campus Martius with an emphasis on the Roman Forum and the renovation of its two basilicas as well as construction of a senate house and a speaker's platform. While some of the choices of building types presumably reflected Caesar's sense of what was appropriate to a given site within a distinctive Roman city, others were the result of their patron's competitive bent. Favro points out that Caesar hoped to build a theater to rival Pompey's and that his Temple to Venus Genetrix vied with that of Pompey's to Venus Victrix. The Basilica Julia responded to the Basilica Aemilia across the main space of the Roman Forum. Caesar also downgraded some of the commissions of his rivals by destroying or renaming them. A notable example was Caesar's rededication of the great Temple of Jupiter Optimus Maximus on the Capitoline hill. Caesar accused Sulla's supporter Quintus Lutatius Catulus of embezzling building funds and thus justified replacing Catulus's name on the temple with his own.

The architectural discourse in Rome from the 60s to the early 40s B.C. essentially took place among elite men who had achieved military successes. Whether or not elite women participated in this conversation has not been fully explored. Yet, even though monuments honoring women were certainly built in the late Republic, there is as of now little evidence that elite Republican women were active art patrons like their husbands. The likely explanation is that it was war and the consequent booty that generated occasions for memorials and the funds to realize them, and women were not actively engaged in military campaigns. Left tending the domestic domain while their husbands were abroad, women for their part accumulated a *cursus honorum* of household virtues, for which they were duly honored. Julia, the young daughter of Caesar and wife of Pompey, for example, was celebrated for her potential as a mother when she was interred in the *Tumulus Iuliae* after dying in childbirth.

While elite women in Republican Rome were not yet commissioners of major monuments, some foreign women were. Cleopatra was primary among them, and it is highly likely that she and Caesar shared plans for architectural projects when they were together. That togetherness was relatively intense between 48 and 46 B.C., when Caesar resided with Cleopatra in her palace at Alexandria, installed her with two consecutive brothers as joint ruler of Egypt, cruised with her down the Nile, fathered her child, and hosted her at his villa in Rome. Even though Caesar's Roman building projects had been instigated long before his personal involvement with Cleopatra and would surely have continued without her, it is hard to believe that the two did not discuss architecture's power to articulate a leader's vision in her time and to preserve it for posterity.

It was thus at this juncture in Caesar's career as a builder that Cleopatra was likely to have become a factor. In just a few years Caesar had defeated Pompey, celebrated numerous triumphs, conducted love affairs with more than one queen, and fathered a son with one of them. Although he was already in his fifties and in ill health, suffering from headaches and epileptic seizures, Caesar must have felt as potent as ever in his life, and energized to think further about the redesign of Rome. His return to Rome in 46 B.C. coincided with Cleopatra's visit to the city. Whatever her reason may have been for coming there, she did not arrive alone but with her latest brother/"husband," her advisers, and most significantly, with Caesarion. Even if Erich Gruen is right that the primary reason for her visit was to shore up her alliance with Rome by formal recognition and a new treaty, and even if she arrived without any fanfare at all, once she was there she could see the Rome of Caesar for herself.

Cleopatra's presence at the fashionable parties of the Roman elite is attested in Atticus's letters to Cicero. There is every reason to think that Caesar's commissions after 48 B.C. were influenced in some way by his Egyptian consort and even by their ambition and taste as a "couple." Suetonius characterizes their relationship as a close one: "Among his [Caesar's] mistresses were several queens—including Eunoë, wife of Bogudes the Moor . . . The most famous of these queens was Cleopatra of Egypt. He often feasted with her until dawn, and they would have sailed together in her state barge nearly to Ethiopia had his soldiers consented to follow him. He eventually summoned Cleopatra to Rome, and would not let her return to Alexandria without high titles and rich presents. He even allowed her to call the son she had borne him 'Caesarion.'"[1]

Cleopatra's contribution to Caesar's Rome is not easy to prove; there is no incontrovertible evidence, and thus there is room for speculation. Furthermore, even if Cleopatra's impact was significant, as I believe, it remains one among many influences on Caesar as a leader and as a patron of the arts. Like other rulers in authority, Caesar courted public favor; both the sponsored entertainment and the building projects of the period are evidence of his frequent nods to different groups in society. Caesar delighted the Romans with impressive spectacles and continued to vie with his rivals by building structures that were grander than theirs, even replacing their names on projects with his own.

Even without Cleopatra, Caesar apparently favored self-aggrandizement. The Romans supported this inclination in Caesar by funding additional monuments in his honor in order to gain his support. At about the time of Cleopatra's arrival in Rome, the senate voted Caesar a residence where he could live on state property. In addition, the house was allowed to have a pediment or *fastigium*, an architectural element normally reserved for kings and gods. The honorific *fastigium* was appended to an otherwise relatively unpretentious domicile. While modest houses were the norm for aristocrats in Rome in the late Republic, more palatial villas were favored in resort locales. At such places outside of Rome, for example his estate at Nervi, Caesar is likely to have wanted to compete with his peers and thus needed no prod from Cleopatra to favor luxuries.

According to Suetonius, "Contemporary literature contains frequent references to his [Caesar's] fondness for luxurious living. Having built a country mansion at Nervi, from the foundation up, one story goes, he found so many features to dislike that, although poor at the time and heavily in debt, he tore the whole place down. It is recorded that he carried tessellated and mosaic pavements with him on his campaigns." In addition, Suetonius notes, "fresh water pearls seem to have been the lure that prompted his [Caesar's] invasion of Britain; he would sometimes weigh them in the palm of his hand to judge their value, and was also a keen collector of gems, carvings, statues, and old Masters."[2]

In 46 B.C., the senate decreed that a bronze statue of Julius Caesar was to be set up in front of the Temple of Jupiter Optimus Maximus on the Capitoline hill, underscoring Caesar's mastery of the world. Caesar also began to be associated with Romulus, founder of Rome. Other honorific statuary was commissioned and installed in visible public places at the very time when Cleopatra was in Rome. She cannot have failed to notice these statues, and surely saw this development as a natural one that paralleled Ptolemaic honorific statuary. In view of her heritage, Cleopatra may well have interpreted the sudden profusion of Caesarian statuary as a sign that Caesar was on the cusp of achieving the kind of monarchical rule she enjoyed in Egypt. But Caesar's political antennae were keen, and he realized the only title he could prudently accept was *parens patriae*, or parent of his country. This title put him in a mutually beneficial covenant with Rome, making him the father who was obliged to care for his charges.

Caesar saw as one of his responsibilities the enhancement of Rome as a world-class urban center. It should be clear by now that Caesar's extensive travels and firsthand experience of such cities as Antioch and especially Alexandria fueled his ambitions to make Rome grander still. Hostile rumors, which were probably fabricated, highlighted Caesar's dissatisfaction with Rome and suggested that he might even transfer the capital to Troy or, more likely, Alexandria.[3] Yet Caesar's ambitious building activities in Rome would seem to tell a different story. As Suetonius points out,[4] Caesar wanted each and every one of his commissions to be the largest or greatest in the world—the Temple of Mars, the Library (to rival that in Alexandria), the Saepta, the Circus. Moreover, Caesar opened the quarries at Luna (modern Carrara) on the northwest coast of Italy to provide appropriate building stone for his constructions. He improved the port facilities of Rome and Ostia to receive the gray-veined white marble, as well as the gorgeous multicolored and variegated marbles from around the Mediterranean that were becoming increasingly popular in his circle. Although Caesar's time in Alexandria was spent primarily in dealing with civil strife, he was certainly exposed to the sophisticated opulence to which he had become accustomed at Cleopatra's court, and the impression it made on him may have motivated him to duplicate it at home.

Despite Caesar's exposure to the Ptolemaic proclivity for restoring earlier pharaonic temples, he did not make renovating Rome's temples a high priority. Diane Favro suggests that Caesar's self-promotion took precedence over urban redevelopment and that he therefore focused on building new edifices in specially chosen districts. Constructing a public library was, however, important to Caesar. His assassination canceled those plans, but a loyal partisan, Asinius Pollio, made the dictator's well-developed concept a reality. Flush with spoils after a successful military exploit in 39 B.C., Pollio allocated those resources for a library adjacent to the Roman Forum. Like the Library at Alexandria, Pollio's was divided into two parts—not the main and secondary collections of the Egyptian prototype, but the distinct Greek and Latin libraries envisioned by Caesar. This new arrangement served as the basis for all later Roman libraries.

Caesar was interested above all in Rome's greatest and most visible public space, the Roman Forum, and the adjacent space where he had already begun the construction of a second forum, this one to bear the

6.1. One of Caesar's goals was to make Rome a vital commercial and cultural center in the image of Alexandria, his reorganization of the Roman Forum, especially the western end as seen here, was a significant first step.

Julian family name. Caesar began building the new forum with the spoils taken in Gaul, and allotted more than a million gold pieces for its construction. While embarking on both of these projects, Caesar could not have failed to think of the Caesareum in Alexandria, both in its individual glory and its situation in the marbled splendor of the city at the mouth of the Nile. Caesar's alterations to the Roman Forum were dramatic. The unruly central space was regularized with ordered axes, and a spanking new pavement was installed (Fig. 6.1). Along the main axis were the two monumental basilicas, still under construction—the Basilica Aemilia and Basilica Julia—both very tall to mask the surrounding buildings and establish the forum space as distinct from the rest of the city. The western end was broadened to accommodate the Tabularium, and at the same end Caesar constructed the Rostra or speaker's platform. The Rostra was centered on the main spine of the forum and thus was discernible from a distance. The platform's visibility was enhanced further by its ornamentation with the beaks of captured ships. The dais also displayed recently repaired statues of Sulla and Pompey. Nearby was the Senate House or Curia Julia, built by Caesar and bearing his name. The Curia was provided with two doors in its rear wall to serve as a passageway from the Roman Forum to the brand-new Forum of Caesar.

Although the Forum of Julius Caesar was thus accessible from the Roman Forum, it was essentially walled off, creating a special world removed from the city around it. It consisted of an open rectangular space with colonnades and shops along the side and a large marble temple at one short end. The temple had a platform in the front that imitated Caesar's Rostra in the Roman Forum next door. It was dedicated to Venus Genetrix, the Venus of Caesar's august Julian line. The family traced its lineage back to Aeneas and Venus, providing ample reason for Caesar to select her as the goddess of his forum temple. There may have been other reasons as well: this was the same Venus Genetrix to whom Caesar had promised a sacred place if she supported Caesar in his war against Pompey and Pompey's patroness, Venus Victrix. In fact, Venus was the goddess of choice for Republican generals with military victories, but she also had resonance for a Roman dictator involved with an Egyptian queen who was assimilated to Venus's Egyptian alter ego, Isis.

The concept of Caesar as a divinity had no support in Rome, though the fact that he was descended from a goddess gave him special status by association. Cleopatra, however, was worshipped as a deity in Egypt and was likely also viewed as such in Rome after Caesar placed a gilded statue of her in the temple's cella next to the image of Venus Genetrix. By so doing, Caesar transformed his forum from a public space used by a growing Roman populace for daily business and matters of law to a tribute to his authority in Rome and the Mediterranean, and to Rome's alliance with Egypt through its equally powerful Queen Cleopatra.

While, as a goddess, Cleopatra found her appropriate place next to another divinity inside the temple, the Julian forum proper contained statuary of her Roman partner. For this reason, it is hard to imagine that their well-known liaison was not brought to mind to those who came here to conduct business. Among the statuary in the forum commemorating Caesar was an image of him in battle gear as well as a likeness of his favorite horse, located directly in front of the temple to Venus.[5] The latter was noteworthy because the hooves resembled human feet.[6] A portrait of Caesar appears to have been added as the horse's rider after the dictator's death. Once he was divinized, Caesar had the status to join Venus and Cleopatra inside the temple, which is exactly what he was allowed to do by his successor. So that his divine status would not be missed, Caesar's statue was provided with a star above his head.[7]

As we shall see later, the gilded image of Cleopatra in this temple may have portrayed the queen with Caesarion, which would have meant the boy was presented not only as the son of a foreign queen and the "little Caesar" of his Roman father, but also as a descendant, in a sense, of Alexander the Great. No one in Rome had a pedigree that grand. Caesar's statement of alliance with Cleopatra and Caesarion may have been a somewhat reckless one, as it might have been interpreted as jeopardizing the very fabric of the Roman family and its normal inheritance rights. Of course, all of these possible interpretations are uncertain. Alexander was a favored soul mate among other powerful Roman Republican men, who also modeled themselves after the famed leader, and in the end Caesar chose Octavian, not Caesarion, as his rightful heir.

Caesar's close association with the sacred domicile of Venus and Cleopatra in Rome is underscored by the details of his funeral, probably planned by him before his death. His funeral procession wound its way from his residence to the Rostra in the Roman Forum and included magistrates carrying a gilded model of the Temple of Venus Genetrix on top of an ivory couch. A detail he was unlikely to have prepared for in advance was the display of his bloodied garments in the model's *cella*.[8] Caesar was cremated in the Roman Forum and his remains placed with his daughter's in the Tumulus Iuliae. Julius Caesar was now history, and Cleopatra had no choice but to follow their shared dream for the unification of Egypt and Rome alone.

7

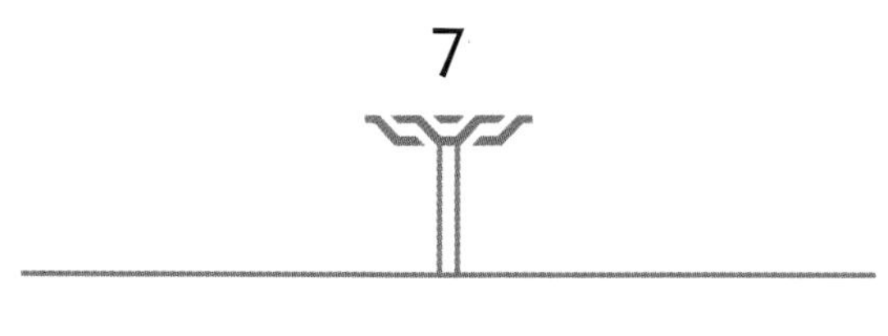

LIVING THE INIMITABLE LIFE

The death of Caesar was not only a personal loss for Cleopatra and a threat to her son's future but also a political nightmare. Caesar's murderers, Cassius and Brutus, came east. Octavian had a rightful claim as Caesar's adoptive son. Mark Antony believed that Caesar had wronged him when he chose Octavian as his heir. Even Cleopatra's half-sister, Arsinoe IV, appeared hostile and would have been happy to replace her sister as Egypt's queen. Fortunately, Caesar's supporters and his assassins were at odds with one another. The former officially joined forces by creating the Second Triumvirate, comprising Octavian, Antony, and Lepidus. Concurrently (on January 1, 42 B.C.), Caesar was proclaimed a god at Rome, which immediately conferred on Octavian the powerful status of *divi filius*—son of a god. Octavian's godlike standing made him a more formidable rival, but Caesar's divinization also conferred a godly aura on Caesarion.

Cleopatra had to choose, and it is not at all surprising that, despite her mistrust of Octavian, she opted to side with him and Antony rather than the murderous Cassius and Brutus. She was apparently so galvanized at the thought of warring with the two assassins that she herself commanded the first ship of her fleet. Inclement weather and seasickness prevented her, however, from making a dramatic stand against Caesar's foes, and she returned to Alexandria just before the Battle of Philippi. At least she had adeptly chosen to side with the winners. Antony proved to be a worthy leader of the Caesarian side, and both Cassius and Brutus fell through suicide in the Macedonian battle. Mistrust of Lepidus led to his marginalization, and the victors, Octavian and Antony, divided the empire between them. Antony received the wealthy eastern provinces, thus ensuring future official dealings with Egypt and its queen, and providing proximity to the Parthian empire. He hoped to take up where Caesar had left off and crush Parthia.

Antony reveled in his victory and his newfound potency in the East. He immediately journeyed to the lands over which he had oversight in order to shore up his power and to begin to amass through taxation the financial resources he needed to support his troops. He appears to have relished every minute and to have taken advantage of every opportunity. When in Greece, for instance, he became an initiate of the Eleusinian Mysteries. Not all was pleasurable, however. Antony flexed his military muscle here and there, most significantly in Judaea where he settled an uprising by putting King Herod in charge. Although not divinely associated with Caesar in Rome as Octavian was, Antony soon made up for this in the East, where he was heralded as the new Dionysus. He also fancied himself as the heroic Hercules. Antony's fondness for attractive and singular women led him to affairs not only with notable Roman women (some of whom he married) but also, like Caesar, with exotic provincial queens, such as Glaphyra of Cappadocia. Some of his Roman women were quite formidable, especially his wife Fulvia. Antony, in his forties in 41 B.C. and thus a full twenty years older than the youth Octavian, recognized that if he was to wage war against the Parthians he, like Caesar before him, needed Cleopatra, then 28, as an ally and supplier. He invited the queen to meet with him at Tarsus in 41.

Plutarch vividly describes the momentous meeting between Antony and Cleopatra,[1] conjuring up Cleopatra's magnificent royal barge with its gilded exterior and hoisted purple sails being propelled forward by the brisk activity of silver oars, rowed to the cadence of harps and flutes. The scene was faithfully illustrated by Giovanni Battista Tiepolo in celebrated Venetian frescoes in the Palazzo Labia, executed in the 1740s (Fig. 7.1). One thing the painting cannot show, however, is the perfume that accompanied the meeting, its fragrance so intense that it reached the shore. Cleopatra herself was adorned as if assimilated to both Isis and Venus arriving to meet Dionysus. She reclined languorously beneath a canopy of gold cloth while being fanned by comely boys dressed as Cupids. The barge was steered and the sails were raised by Cleopatra's maids, wearing the costumes of sea nymphs and graces.

That Cleopatra traveled with Caesar and to Antony by barge is hardly remarkable; the only two options for travel were by water and by land. What is noteworthy, however, is that Cleopatra invested her ocean excursions with carefully chosen costumes, divine associations, expensive textiles and jewels, music, and exotic essences. These adornments dramatically set her expeditions apart from ordinary tours by sea, suggesting that she hoped to be viewed as if she were a deity in a celestial vessel. Boats had long been sacred in Egypt. Ritual ships, stored in temples, were used to transport images of gods from one religious site to another. These divinities were usually accompanied on their voyages by priests and sometimes by the pharaoh with his wife and children. The sides of the portable shrines that carried the cult statues were adorned with the royal participants' names in cartouches and other explanatory hieroglyphs. The roofs of the shrines were decorated with a frieze of *uraei* or rearing cobras, whose job it was to safeguard the enclosed images.

Having arrived in Tarsus in splendor, Cleopatra responded to Antony's invitation to dine on his vessel with a summons to her own ship. She feted him with four days of lavish banqueting, a scene that was also recreated by Tiepolo as part of his Cleopatran extravaganza (see Fig. 1.3). The dynamic duo were perfectly matched, and they soon became lovers. Cleopatra returned to Egypt, appealing to Antony to join her there. Later in 41, he answered her call. The dazzling charisma of Cleopatra, the seductiveness of Alexandria with its remains of the mighty Alexander, and the riches of Egypt proved the same lure to Antony as they had been to Caesar. Antony pledged to spend the winter months there, but the intended brief sojourn lasted a full year. And what an extraordinary interval it must have been.

It is interesting to speculate on whether Cleopatra saw her relationship with Antony as an attempt to recapture the political and personal magic

7.1. Cleopatra arrives at Tarsus and alights from a gilded barge with purple sails for a meeting with Mark Antony, a meticulously arranged event.

she had experienced with Caesar, or as a unique union. Although both men had the authority of Rome at their core, Caesar had been older and more focused in his ambition for fame. Antony was somewhat closer in age to Cleopatra and apparently more fun-loving. Antony's association with Dionysus was apt; he enjoyed good parties and fine wines. With a group of Alexandrian elites at their side, Antony and Cleopatra immediately set out in search of *amimetobios,* that is, the "inimitable life."[2] An inscription of 34 B.C. in the Greco-Roman Museum in Alexandria even heralds Antony as "the Great Inimitable." While Antony's enemies may have circulated embellished details of these activities, they are not out of keeping with a high life long enjoyed by the Ptolemies. From Plutarch we learn that these inimitable friends feasted on plates encrusted with jewels, played whatever games were *au courant,* such as dice, and went fishing and hunting for exotic animals. They lived life to the hilt, as if each day were their last, even naming their dining club the *synapothanoumenoi,* "those who are about to die together." All of this was done in a grand style and doubtless in a spirit of delight and theatricality. This is not to say that Antony was superficial or without intellect; it is unlikely that the brilliant Cleopatra would have spent time with him if he had been.

In fact, while in Alexandria, Antony frequented the great Library and attended lectures and seminars. As Caesar had done before him, he toured the impressive and unforgettable sights of Egypt. However, Antony and Cleopatra's inimitable life together was not to last. Like Caesar, Antony had set out to destroy the Parthians, but while he was in Alexandria, they grew stronger still and became a significant threat to Rome as they spread into Asia Minor and the Middle East. The Parthian incursion into Judaea was especially serious, forcing Herod to seek protection in Rome. Still fervently duty-bound, Antony departed Egypt, but not without leaving his mark on the queen. Six months later Cleopatra delivered their twins, fittingly named for the sun, Alexander Helios, and the moon, Cleopatra Selene. The inimitable couple had produced two inimitable children. While Caesar's paternity of Caesarion was questioned by some, no one doubted that Antony had sired Alexander and Cleopatra. Caesarion was now blessed with two half-siblings who, like him, were at once Macedonian Greek and Roman and heirs to the kingship of Egypt.

All of these significant events transpired while Antony was still married to the formidable Fulvia, a Roman woman with enough self-confidence to encourage a rebellion against Octavian, perhaps to gain favor with her wayward husband. It was not successful. Fulvia fled with her children to Brundisium and then Greece, heartbroken by the loss and by Antony's infidelities. Fulvia fell ill and died at Sicyon; her demise was followed by a reconciliation between Antony and Octavian.

In 40 B.C., Octavian and Antony reaffirmed their alliance with the Treaty of Brundisium. This pact again certified Antony's authority over the East, a dispensation clearly advantageous to Cleopatra. But other decisions at Brundisium pleased her less, especially the one that made Herod the king of Judaea, Samaria, and Edom. Despite Antony's well-known affair with Cleopatra, Octavian chose to seal the treaty by offering his sister Octavia in marriage to Antony. There is perhaps no better illustration of marriage as a political act among the Roman elite.

Octavia was widely praised for her beauty and virtue, a pleasing combination, and the merger quickly produced a daughter, Antonia the Elder, born in 39. The new family journeyed to Athens. Antony was no less himself with Octavia than with Cleopatra, enjoying the epicurean life in Greece as he had in Egypt. In his role as Dionysus, Antony hosted sumptuous repasts and festive celebrations, and he was mystically united with the city's goddess, Athena. His joyous mood must have been buoyed up further by the success of his armies in Parthia, which sent him word of compelling victories.

Nonetheless, tensions with Octavian began to build again, especially after Octavian's marriage to Livia in 38. A serious rift between the two men was narrowly averted by Octavia's intercession on her husband's behalf, and in 37 the triumvirate was renewed at Tarentum for another five years. Antony was not honorable enough to express his gratitude to his wife for her advocacy by respecting their marriage, even though she was pregnant again. Instead, he recklessly flouted his independence by precipitously departing for Egypt to renew his liaison with Cleopatra. Whether he did so to secure resources for additional excursions against the Parthians or out of love for his Egyptian consort, or whether these and other reasons overlapped in his mind, is impossible to know. Whatever the case, his action demoralized his wife and ensured Octavian's wrath.

A jubilant Cleopatra, with their twins in tow, met Antony in Syria. While Roman law did not allow him another wife, Egyptian legislation permitted polygamy, and the pair were married in an Egyptian ceremony in Antioch. The newlyweds revived their inimitable personal life, continuing to recognize that their political strength rested on mutual support. At the same time, both were cunning enough to know not to lay all their cards on the table. Cleopatra did not finance Antony's Parthian campaigns without exacting real estate in return. Antony was experienced in making deals with client kings in places like Judaea, Cappadocia, Pontus, and Galatia, and he was therefore shrewd enough not to give Cleopatra everything she asked for. Nevertheless, Antony rightly viewed the Egyptian treasury as a highly desirable asset and, in order to enhance his access to it, granted Cleopatra parts of southern Syria, Ituraea, and the Island of Cyprus.

When, in 36, Antony left for a Parthian engagement, Cleopatra departed with him. But she was pregnant with their third child, and decided before long to turn back. Ever the shrewd monarch, she returned in style, stopping along the way to view her new property acquisitions. Escaping assassination by Herod while crossing Judaea, she made it safely back to Alexandria, where she gave birth to Ptolemy Philadelphus. While Cleopatra was joyously celebrating the birth of her third son, Antony was experiencing demoralizing defeats at the hands of the Parthians. The loss of Roman life was staggering and Antony barely held on, rescued only by supplies and funds contributed by Egypt's queen. At Antony's behest, Cleopatra even delivered personally clothing for his troops in Syria. Cleopatra did what she could to shore up Antony's effort by forging alliances with neighboring countries and thus recovering some of the land Antony had been forced to relinquish.

While Antony was losing ground in the East, Octavian was rapidly ascending in the West, wresting Sicily from Sextus Pompeius and Africa from Lepidus. Octavian continued to have ambitions to rule the entire Roman world and took full advantage of Antony's affair with Cleopatra. Seeing that Antony was in desperate need of ships, troop reinforcements, and funding, Octavian sent all these to him with Octavia as their personal escort, even though Roman women were not usually so dispatched. This was a brilliant tactical move on Octavian's part, and to make it even less attractive to Antony, Octavian offered troop contingents of only 2,000 men. While devoted to his sister and publicly hoping she might regain her husband's affection, Octavian expected Antony to refuse his offer. Octavian was in a winning situation. If Antony accepted his largesse, it would reunite him with Octavia. If he spurned these gifts, Octavian would be justified in waging legal war against a fellow Roman. Antony notified Octavia that he would not meet her, and she was dispatched back to Rome.

At first, it seemed as if Antony had made the right choice. Even with the shattering Parthian defeat, Antony was able to get himself back on his feet by achieving a rapid victory over King Artavasdes of Armenia and securing Armenia as a Roman province. As was customary with such conquests, Antony acquired notable plunder, with which he embellished Alexandria.

Grateful to have an achievement to celebrate after the embarrassment of Antony's Parthian rout, Antony and Cleopatra played their good fortune to the hilt. In 34 B.C. they staged the Alexandrian version of a Roman triumph, with the Ptolemaic display of the king and his dynasty and the blatant Roman exhibition of war spoils. At the parade's head, Antony rode in a chariot as if a traditional Roman *triumphator.* In this Alexandrian venue, Antony cast modesty aside and appeared in the full panoply of his divine alter ego, Dionysus, a masquerade that would not have been any more acceptable in Rome than the Alexandrian triumph itself. As in Rome, enemy hostages walked alongside Antony's chariot. These included the manacled Artavasdes in golden chains and the rest of the Armenian royal family. Not to be outdone, Cleopatra, splendidly outfitted as Isis, was ensconced on a gilded throne, from which she received territorial gifts for herself and her children from Antony. The striking tableau must have impressed the people of Alexandria, who participated in the revelry as they shared in a bounteous banquet.

The pageantry did not end there. It culminated several days later when Antony made official his truly momentous bequest to Cleopatra and his offspring. In a public assembly, he proclaimed that he was apportioning Cyprus, parts of Syria, Armenia, Medea, Libya, Cyrenaica, Phoenicia, and Cilicia, the so-called "donations of Alexandria," among Cleopatra, Caesarion, Alexander Helios, Cleopatra Selene, and Ptolemy Philadelphus. The procession had augured these gifts. In Plutarch's description of the memorable event, he relates how Antony had "brought forward Alexander in Median dress, including a tiara and upright Persian headdress, and Ptolemy in boots, a cloak, and a *kausia* bearing a diadem; the latter was the dress of the successor kings of Alexander, the former that of the Medes and Armenians. When the two children had embraced their parents, an Armenian guard circled one, a Macedonian the other. Cleopatra both then and at other times when she appeared in public, took the holy dress of Isis, and was treated as the new Isis."[3]

Bronze statuettes now in New York and Baltimore depicting a boy as an Armenian prince may be Alexander dressed in the costume of his new possession (Fig. 7.2). Wearing the tunic and leggings and the elaborate pyramidal tiara of Armenian royalty, Alexander's likeness may have been carried with others in the Alexandrian triumph and later deposited in a temple devoted to the cult of the Ptolemies. There is every indication that Rome was aghast at the presumption of Antony's Alexandrian triumph and his unlawful bequest of these properties to his illegitimate wife and children. Statuettes of those very children in the attire of that largesse, especially the self-confident 6-year-old youngster with his outstretched right arm, taking charge of his domain, must have seemed to Octavian and others as an insulting affront. Only four years later, the tables had turned. In 30 B.C., this very same Alexander Helios was captured in Alexandria and sent with Cleopatra Selene and Ptolemy Phildelphus to live in Rome with Octavia. Not long after his arrival, the boy had to suffer the indignity of parading in Octavian's triumph over Cleopatra. The procession of Cleopatra's children, whether in Alexandria or Rome and whether authoritative or powerless, marched into Octavian's consciousness and later surfaced on the monument that codified the Augustan family that supplanted the Ptolemaic family—the very special Ara Pacis Augustae.

Antony's momentous bequest, meant to shore up his own authority and that of his Egyptian family, was a sign that he, like Caesar before him, had embraced a form of autocratic rule, acceptable in Egypt but not in Rome. Octavian was quick to seize upon the event as evidence that Antony was no longer a loyal Roman.

For her part, Cleopatra had once again been an effective mentor. Through her tutelage of the man in her life she was able to achieve her

7.2. Alexander Helios wears the costume of the recently annexed Armenia, a new possession granted him by his father, Mark Antony.

ambition—to restore the kingdom of Egypt to what it had been in pharaonic times; indeed, to extend it even further. There was, however, one critical difference: Egypt was no longer an independent nation but a Roman protectorate.

Ongoing friction between Antony and Octavian eventually escalated to a propaganda war, complete with brutal invective and invidious rumors on both sides. Octavian raised his indignation about Antony's affair with Cleopatra to a high art. Ignoring his own frequent peccadilloes, Octavian expressed public outrage at Antony's intimacy with Cleopatra. Suetonius records Antony's clever response: "What has come over you? Do you object to my sleeping with Cleopatra? But we are married; and it is not even as though this were anything new—the affair started nine years ago. And what about you? Are you faithful to Livia Drusilla? My congratulations if, when this letter arrives, you have not been in bed with Tertullia, or Terentilla, or Rufilla, or Salvia Titisenia—or all of them. Does it really matter so much where, or with whom, you perform the sexual act?"[4]

As they sparred with one another, Antony and Octavian each selected a divine sponsor. Antony's was Hercules and Octavian's Apollo, and contemporary art depicted the gods and also their alter egos at odds with one another in terracotta relief sculptures that decorated Apollo's temple on the Palatine (Fig. 7.3). As the slander reached its peak in 33 B.C., Cleopatra and Antony settled for the winter at Ephesus in Asia Minor. Protected by a vast army and fleet, the largest controlled by one man since Alexander the Great, they attempted to live a normal life, with Cleopatra conducting her queenly duties. Ephesus was an appropriate place to do this: though now under Roman provincial jurisdiction, it had powerful Ptolemaic bonds, having belonged in the mid-third century B.C. to Ptolemy II Philadelphus. Antony and Cleopatra remained optimistic that they would prevail in the inevitable face-off. Two of Antony's most resolute backers had just been elected to the senate in Rome, and many other senators openly sided with Antony. Antony's military prowess and Cleopatra's treasury still looked to be unbeatable. From Ephesus, the pair visited Greece, stopping in Samos and Athens in 32 B.C., continuing to weigh their options and strategize about their ambitions for the future. Like conquerors in the West, they extracted booty along the way with the intention of further embellishing Alexandria. The great Library, for example, may have received a vast addition of 200,000 scrolls at this time.

7.3. Octavian and Mark Antony, disguised as their alter egos, Apollo and Hercules, battle for the Delphic tripod on a terracotta plaque from the Temple of Apollo Palatinus.

It is said the scrolls were appropriated by Antony from the Library at Pergamum, and were supposedly presented by him to Cleopatra as a replacement for those lost in the fire of 48–47 B.C. The veracity of Antony's bequest has been questioned, however; Plutarch reports that Gaius Calvisius Sabinus, a friend and supporter of Augustus, probably invented the scandalous gift to defame Antony in the court of Roman public opinion.[5]

During the Ephesus sojourn, Antony's senatorial friends in Rome continued to support him staunchly. Nonetheless, Antony's reputation was dealt a fatal blow when two of his former confidants released the contents of his will, recently entrusted to the Vestal Virgins. Octavian was able to secure a copy and, eschewing the customary confidentiality, revealed the contents to the senate. In this document, Antony recognized Caesarion as Caesar's son, confirmed his "donations," and asked to be buried in Alexandria with Cleopatra. The veracity of this document is highly suspect because its terms and their disclosure were simply too convenient for Octavian. Even the professed shock of Romans at its revelations seems somewhat staged, since Antony's public behavior surely signaled his intentions. It was remembered that Caesar had had the decency not to forsake his Roman roots when he chose as his heir his Roman grand-nephew Octavian rather than his biological son Caesarion, while Antony had the audacity to do otherwise. Antony's perceived betrayal of Rome was greeted with public calls for war with Egypt.

The enthusiastic welcome that Antony and Cleopatra received in Athens must have buoyed their spirits and inflated their self-confidence. Unlike the Romans, the Athenians accepted both of them as divinities and honored them as a couple by placing paired statues of them as Isis and Osiris in Athens' most hallowed place, the Acropolis.[6] Wintering in Patras on Greece's western coast, they felt secure with troops loyal to Antony lining the shore. The spring season, however, brought with it a fierce attack from Marcus Agrippa in the south, causing Antony and Cleopatra to flee northward, where Octavian awaited. Octavian effectively blockaded the naval fleet of Antony and Cleopatra. On the second of September in 31 B.C., the combined forces of Cleopatra and Antony tried to break that blockade by charging Octavian's fleet. That the star-crossed pair escaped with 60 ships is a tribute to their courage. The loss of 170 of their ships gave Octavian the right to claim victory.

Cleopatra, always a resourceful dissembler, tried to make light of their loss. She shrewdly recognized that her enemies would take advantage of any perceived weakness. Acting as if nothing had happened, she returned to Egypt with ship prows bedecked with garlands and accompanied by a concerto of victory odes. Once there, she ruthlessly ordered the assassination of prominent opponents who were rejoicing in her Waterloo and seized every available treasure, even those that came from sacred sites. She wisely fortified her forces and searched for new allies.[7] Once Antony joined her in Egypt, Cleopatra felt secure enough to go for the jugular. The queen taunted Octavian with a reality that she must have known haunted him. No military victory could make up for Octavian's foremost shortcoming: the inability of his wives Scribonia and Livia to produce a legitimate male heir. In that arena, Cleopatra and Antony were peerless. And what better way to prove this to the world than to throw a party—a princely festival to celebrate the coming of age of Caesarion and Antyllus, Antony's elder son by Fulvia. Surely such a dynastic display would verify that Caesarion and Antyllus were the lawful successors of Caesar and Antony.

Cleopatra's scheming was all for naught. All the festivities in the world were no match for Octavian's military might and the fact that Cleopatra and Antony had become virtual prisoners in the city of Alexander the Great. While troops closed in from all sides, Antony made one last gallant stand. The final days of the inimitable pair were as tempestuous as their lives, and it is hard to determine what really happened. Did Cleopatra offer to abdicate and Antony to retire? Did Octavian encourage Cleopatra to take her own life, or did he profess love to the queen in order to deter a royal suicide? Was the message that Antony received that Cleopatra had killed herself a chance miscommunication or a deliberate fiction? Even Plutarch, who described Cleopatra's death, noted that "the truth about the manner of her death no one knows."[8] Plutarch reported that one of Cleopatra's two servants, who loyally perished with her, used her last breath to declare that the manner of Cleopatra's self-destruction was "fitting for one descended from so many kings."

Much of the human tragedy, and the dramatic events leading up to it, can be inferred from contemporary architectural undertakings—or, in Antony's case, the significant lack of them. As we have seen, Rome in the 40s B.C. was embellished with the building projects of a group of elite patrons flush with the substantial resources that accompanied military accomplishment. Strong feelings of responsibility toward Rome and its adornment caused them to acquire real estate and hire architects and artisans. As Diane Favro has pointed out, the patronage of these buildings divided along political party lines, with the followers of Antony and Octavian associated with distinctive projects.

While Antony's followers commissioned triumphal monuments in the Campus Martius and Octavian set his sights on the Roman Forum, where he attempted to regularize the site and to complete the edifices begun by Caesar, Antony himself failed to grab the brass ring. By the 30s, Antony was focused on the eastern empire and on Cleopatra and their children; as far as Rome went, he did not commission monumental architecture but only dabbled in the enactment of municipal laws that prescribed building maintenance and traffic regulation *(Lex Julia Municipalis)*. Whereas Octavian chose to erect marble edifices substantiating his claim to be Caesar's son, Antony eschewed such projects in favor of focusing on what he viewed as Caesarion's more legitimate claim for his patrimony. Antony's lack of interest in contributing to the construction of urban Rome in the late Republic offended his countrymen and made the rumors that he intended to transfer the capital to Alexandria more believable. Favro rightly observes that Antony lost out to Octavian in Rome by not capitalizing on the "power of place."

Although Antony seems to have been more interested in living in the present than in building monuments for posterity, his friends and partisans in Italy appear to have commissioned a scattering of monuments that featured him as a great commander in the manner of Alexander the Great. One candidate is a marble relief block now in the Vatican Museums, found in the Sanctuary of Fortuna Primigenia at Palestrina, a city loyal to Antony (Fig. 7.4). The slab appears to have been decorated with relief sculpture on at least three sides and may have served as the socle of a monument that has long since disappeared. One relief depicts a flotilla headed by a battleship, which is emblazoned on the bow with a crocodile. Such an insignia must have belonged to Antony's Egyptian fleet, bankrolled by Cleopatra. The hint of an infantry on the left side suggests that Antony was as skilled a commander on land as he was on sea. The relief was probably carved in the years before Actium (37–32 B.C.), when Antony was chief officer in the East and allied with Cleopatra.

Another loyal and proud proponent of Antony was commemorated with an exedra tomb at the beginning of the Via Appia in Rome around

7.4. Mark Antony's ambitions in the eastern part of the Empire are celebrated in a relief from a monument commissioned by one of his partisans.

35 B.C. The honoree was probably Publius Ventidius Bassus, a general and devotee of Antony, who is represented in a curved relief now in the Museo del Palazzo dei Conservatori at the very moment of victory over an eastern barbarian. That Bassus had the right stuff and prevailed in a fitting manner is attested by the presence of Honos, personification of honor.

While Antony's supporters commissioned works on Italian shores, the "power of place" for Antony resided in the East and especially in Alexandria. Nonetheless, even there, Antony didn't seem to recognize that his lifetime authority rested in part on what he built and that such monumental projects would help ensure lasting fame. It is also notable that Antony, unlike Caesar and Octavian, had no interest in recording his accomplishments in a written document. Even in Alexandria, Antony apparently did not aspire to build an edifice to rival the Caesareum of Caesar and Cleopatra, nor even a monument to Caesarion and Cleopatra like the one at Dendera. Antony chose to live life to the fullest in the here and now, focusing on the power of experience rather than that of architecture.

8

ERSATZ ALEXANDERS IN EGYPT AND ROME

We have seen that Cleopatra was one of those rare individuals who was special in her lifetime but became an icon after death. Her fame centered on her accomplishments and was reinforced by her personality and appearance. Evidence for her deeds and her looks is preserved in the historical and literary records, with one or the other taking precedence as she was imitated and reinterpreted over time. As the emphasis shifted back and forth, Cleopatra became a touchstone for two very different kinds of women—the powerful monarch and the seductive femme fatale. After her dramatic suicide at a young age, it was the second of the two images that appears to have become the essence of her myth. This is not just because she was a woman; even famous dead men have become known more for their physical attributes than their accomplishments, as their bodily parts took on the power of talismans. Perhaps the best twentieth-century example is John Fitzgerald Kennedy, whose mythology is made up as much of his youth, casual elegance, and hair as his PT 109 exploits, stirring speeches, or tragic assassination. In other words, style is as integral a part of such imagery as substance.

In the ancient world, Cleopatra's only rival for this level of celebrity was Alexander the Great. Alexander's thrilling exploits, striking good looks, and untimely death were the perfect recipe for lifetime fame and for posthumous adoration and emulation. As the quintessential general and leader, Alexander was already depicted as a hero during his life-

8.1. The charisma, striking good looks, and energized hair of Alexander the Great established an iconic prototype for portraits of leaders who strove to follow in his footsteps.

time. Surviving statuettes, like that with a lance in Paris, and portrait heads, for example the marble head from Pella in Macedonia (Fig. 8.1), show Alexander with a set of what had become canonical features: youthful nude body, dramatically upturned neck, large luminous eyes, and—the pièce de résistance—a glorious head of hair that was raised over his forehead in a kind of off-center pompadour or *anastole,* flowing back in long electrified strands. Many of these images became extremely well known, not just because their subject was widely admired but also because the most talented sculptor and painter of the day, Lysippus and Apelles, respectively, created his likenesses. Death made Alexander an icon, and his greatest accomplishments as hero were rapidly intertwined with his newly achieved divinity. In his posthumous portraiture, Alexander was depicted as a genuine god, often invested with divine attributes such as the diadem, lion or elephant skin headdress, ram's horns, lightning bolt, aegis (breastplate with head of Minerva), and star.

These amplified images multiplied on coins and in statuary and were widely circulated around the Hellenistic world, crossing civilizations and becoming the benchmark for portraits of male leaders of the lands ruled by Alexander's lieutenants, among them Ptolemy I Soter of Egypt, who was depicted on his coinage as a duplicate of Alexander. A portrait of Ptolemy on a silver tetradrachm of 305–285 B.C. from the Alexandrian mint, now in the Yale University Art Gallery (Fig. 8.2), emphasizes the way these lieutenants adopted the mantle of their leader. Ptolemy affects the upturned neck, wide eyes, and energetic mane of his mentor. However, these men rarely adopted Alexander's look wholesale, instead se-

8.2. Ptolemy I Soter's coinage advertised to the Hellenistic world that by taking on the wide eyes and energized hair of Alexander the Great, he aimed to be as inspired as his mentor.

lecting details that, when added to their own likenesses, invested them with a special aura. Since Hellenistic culture continued as a force in Republican and Augustan Rome, Alexander remained the preeminent role model for ambitious Roman generals and politicians, especially those with military ventures in the East.

PORTRAITS OF THE PTOLEMAIC KINGS

Above all, Alexander's power was visually invested in his hair, especially the trademark *anastole*. Those who wanted to reference Alexander in their own images were especially drawn to that feature. The Ptolemies were just as enamored with Alexander's allure as anyone else in the Hellenistic world, and taking on the attributes of a man who was entombed in their backyard made perfect political sense. Nevertheless, Ptolemy I was perceptive enough to realize from the start that his new dynastic portraiture should, above all, underscore the unbroken line from Pharaoh to Ptolemy. His local subjects would be comforted to know that he and his fellow Macedonians were not usurpers but brothers, united by a common heritage. Furthermore, he needed to communicate with them in a visual language that they could understand. Ptolemy acted immediately to ensure that the images of him carved or painted on divine or mortuary temples looked Egyptian. Wisely, Soter's fourteen successors, the last of which was Ptolemy XV Caesar (Caesarion), followed his lead. At Cleopatra's Temple at Dendera, for example, Caesarion is portrayed wearing the traditional Egyptian headdress and carrying appropriate Egyptian attributes. He is presented in concert with his mother and with the Egyptian pantheon of deities and is depicted in the rigid hierarchical style favored by the pharaohs since the Early Kingdom (see Fig. 5.6).

The Egyptian mode was also normally used for statuary and portraiture of Ptolemaic dynasts, especially that which was intended for a religious or quasi-religious context. A basalt portrait of Ptolemy I with distinctive pharaonic headdress from the Egyptian Delta, now in the British Museum, is an example of this trend. Yet this time-honored mode was increasingly blended with a Hellenistic style that became the common pictorial language of the Greek East after Alexander. Often, the two traditions were merged to form a new and distinct mode of representation that incorporated features that came out of the orbit of Alexander's images.

That fusion is well illustrated by portraits of Ptolemy I Soter in Copenhagen and Paris. They depict their subject with features that Ptolemy shared with his family—round face, prominent eyes, and short hair—but also exhibit the twisted neck and upturned head that were the hallmark of portraits of Alexander the Great. The Copenhagen head, found in the Fayum and probably a posthumous portrait of Ptolemy, is also carved with a distinct linearity that reveals its indebtedness to the marble-carving approach that was characteristic of Egyptian art of the twenty-fifth and twenty-sixth dynasties.

Ptolemy XII Auletes

Cleopatra's father, Ptolemy XII Auletes, was also depicted in both the Egyptian and Hellenistic styles. The Egyptian mode is attested by a granite portrait, identified by Zsolt Kiss as a portrait of Auletes on the body of a sphinx. The statue emerged in October 1998 from the waters of the Alexandrian harbor near the sunken site of what was the royal palace of the Ptolemies. The statue was one of two sphinxes, the other with a portrait of an unidentified Ptolemaic king. Both were probably displayed in a temple to Isis on the island of Antirhodos; columns, granite blocks, Isiac statuary, and other objects that probably belonged to that structure were also discovered. Auletes wears the traditional Egyptian headdress and stares straight ahead—an immutable symbol of the pharaonic tradition. The milieu must have been so Egyptian that Augustus dared not alter it when he came on the scene. A black granite head of Octavian Augustus, also found at the site, offers additional intriguing evidence that the emperor wisely left the dynasty intact, placing his own images among the Ptolemies rather than fully replacing their dynasty with his own. Octavian apparently wanted to present himself as the legitimate successor to the Ptolemies, not as a usurper.

The granite sphinx with the features of Auletes was not an aberration. Many other Egyptian-style portraits of Cleopatra's father were commissioned, as were images of him in traditional Egyptian scenes, for example a relief from a sanctuary at Euhemeria in the Fayum depicting Auletes worshipping the sanctuary's crocodile deities. Other portraits of Auletes were crafted in the inspired Alexander mode. This is not surprising since the Alexander ruler portrait was an image that spoke to the Greek segment of Egyptian society and to a wide and cosmopolitan Hellenistic world. A marble head said to be from Alexandria and now in the Louvre (see Fig. 1.2) has been identified as Auletes because it bears a striking correspondence in profile to the king's numismatic portraiture. That the subject's nose, lips, and chin are intact makes verification easy and also allows comparison with portraits of Cleopatra. The resemblance between

Auletes and Ptolemy I Soter (Fig. 8.2) is also noticeable; it must have been accentuated not only because of familial resemblance but also to emphasize the links between the dynasty's founder and his successors. The plastic rendering of the face and hair and the twist of the neck are Hellenistic features. In addition, the head was originally completed with plaster, a technique that was practiced in workshops in Egypt in Ptolemaic times. The Ptolemies, like the Romans, often remade their portraits, and the Louvre head of Auletes is an example of that practice. The art historian R. R. R. Smith suggests that this portrait of the king was recarved between the time Ptolemy returned to Egypt to resume his kingship (55 B.C.) and his demise in 51.

A bronze bust of Auletes, now in a private collection, depicts him with the same facial features as those of the marble portrait in Paris. Yet here his tousled locks are intertwined with a diadem with shoulder-length streamers, ivy, and the horns of a bull, which associate Auletes with Dionysus and explain the origin of his name. It was Ptolemy XII's reverence for Dionysus that resulted in the appellation "the flute player," or Auletes. He was also called *neos Dionysos*. While the Roman Dionysus was at first assimilated to the Egyptian Osiris, he came over time to be associated with a culture of luxury or *tryphe* highly prized at the Ptolemaic royal household, especially in the first century B.C.

PORTRAITS IN ROME

Images of Alexander the Great were a vital part of Rome's visual culture in the first century B.C. and could be readily viewed by would-be Roman world conquerors and the general populace in public forums and also in porticoes that served as museums. Pliny, Statius,[1] and other ancient writers describe sculptured and painted portraits in Rome of Alexander as a boy, a general on horseback, in a triumphal chariot, and in concert with his father Philip, the Goddess Athena, the personification of victory (Nike), and with the twin brothers and heroes, Castor and Pollux. Alexandria, Ephesus, and other major cities in the East visited by Roman generals during campaigns abounded in shrines and other cultic locales that must also have had prominent statues of the great general. There was no end to pictorial sources for Roman leaders in search of a role model.

Pompey the Great

Pompey openly embraced the magic of Alexander and was the first Roman to receive the epithet *Magnus*. Bestowed on him by his troops in 81 B.C. after a short conflict in Africa, the title intentionally linked him to Alexander the Great and was overtly inscribed on coins. In his subsequent triumph in Rome, at which time Sulla made the designation official, Pompey was to be transported in a chariot drawn by elephants, further underscoring his connection to Alexander.

Plutarch indicates that Pompey imitated Alexander's melting gaze and wore his hair brushed up over his forehead in Alexander's characteristic *anastole*.[2] Pompey's portraits on coins struck after his death by his sons, a terracotta head in Stuttgart, and two surviving marble portraits, now in Copenhagen (Fig. 8.3) and Venice, confirm this intended association primarily through the configuration of the hair over the forehead. Nevertheless, significant differences—Pompey's small squinting eyes and bulbous nose—demonstrate that Pompey insisted on being depicted with his own facial features, rendered in the objective, even witty way that was characteristic of the portraiture of distinguished elite men in late Republican Rome.

In antiquity, Pompey's marble portraits would have surmounted full-length statues. These were probably based primarily on stock body types that came out of the Hellenistic repertory, some of which were made more dramatic by pronounced neck and body torsion.

Julius Caesar

Caesar was exposed to the same Alexander imagery in Rome and the East as Pompey and was aware that Pompey had taken on Alexander's mantle in his name and portraiture. Caesar and Alexander were themselves linked in antiquity. Plutarch, for example, places Caesar next to Alexander in his *Lives*.

The portraiture of Caesar is both revolutionary and complex, drawing on a variety of ideas and models; among the latter were Jupiter, Romulus, and Alexander. Nonetheless, the references to Alexander were subtler than those used by Pompey and thus harder to characterize. Caesar was never addressed as Caesar the Great, and he is depicted as balding rather than with full undulating locks. It is nearly inconceivable to imagine that anyone would mistake a man with a receding hairline for a divinized

8.3. Pompey the Great was another neo-Alexander, affecting the Hellenistic leader's trademark hairstyle and "melting gaze."

Greek hero with an abundance of serpentine curls. Caesar preferred his own no-nonsense military haircut and appears not to have imitated Alexander's melting gaze. And yet, Caesar took on a panoply of attributes that had already become associated with Alexander and other Hellenistic kings, among these the wreath and diadem; the aegis, lightning bolt, and lance of Jupiter/Zeus; and the astral symbolism of a king made god. These appear on lifetime and posthumous coins portraying Caesar with stars, globes, and other suggestive paraphernalia, and in a terracotta relief in Rome that depicts Caesar with a lance and being crowned with a diadem by a flying Victory figure.

If Caesar hoped to be seen as a world-conquering hero, why did he not appropriate Alexander's power hair? If Caesar had asked his portraitists to depict him with Alexander's tousled mane, they would have done it. That choice was Caesar's to make. Although Roman rulers, however enhanced through cosmetics and dress, had no choice but to appear in public as they were, they could commission bronze or marble images of themselves in any manner they wished. Few Roman subjects, especially those in the provinces, would have seen the ruler in person, so he was free to fictionalize his imagery. In fact, in an age where there was more visual than verbal literacy and when public pageantry presented carefully crafted tableaux that constructed events and molded opinions, portraiture was an especially significant and malleable vehicle.

We can't know for certain what motivated Caesar to display his balding head in his portraiture. We do know that he was self-conscious about his lack of hair and that he tried to compensate for it. Suetonius remarks: "His [Caesar's] baldness was a disfigurement which his enemies harped upon, much to his exasperation; but he used to comb the thin strands forward from his poll."[3] As Suetonius continues, he provides a helpful clue: ". . . and of all the honors voted him by the Senate and People, none pleased him so much as the privilege of wearing a laurel wreath on all occasions—he constantly took advantage of it." Caesar thus replaced power hair with a power wreath or diadem; the diadem conjured up the divinized Alexander.

If this headdress was indeed a crown, it might have elevated Caesar more than hair could do, and it had the added advantage that Caesar could appear as the war hero he was in imagery that allied him with his loyal troops. The crown theory has viability if it is aligned with another that suggests that Caesar was about to take on the title of "king." Suetonius remarks in particular on the title: "This open insult to the Senate was emphasized by an even worse example of his arrogance. As he returned to Rome from the Alban Hill, where the Latin Festival had been celebrated, a member of the crowd set a laurel wreath bound with a royal white fillet on the head of his statue. Two tribunes of the people, Epidius Marullus and Caesetius Flavus, ordered the fillet to be removed at once and the offender imprisoned. But Caesar reprimanded and summarily deposed them both; either because the suggestion that he should be crowned King had been so rudely rejected, or else because—this was his own version—they had given him no chance to reject it himself and so earn deserved credit. From that day forward, however, he lay under the odious suspicion of having tried to revive the title of King; though, indeed, when the commons greeted him with 'Long Live the King!' he now protested: 'No, I am Caesar, not King'; and though, again, when he was addressing the crowd from the Rostra at the Lupercalian Festival, and Mark Antony, the Consul, made several attempts to crown him, he refused the offer each time and at last sent the crown away for dedication to Capitoline Jupiter. What made matters worse was a persistent rumor that Caesar intended to move the seat of government to Troy or Alexandria, carrying off all the national resources, drafting every available man in Italy for military service, and letting his friends govern the city. At the next meeting of the House (it was further whispered), Lucius Cotta would announce a decision of the Fifteen who had charge of the Sibylline Books, that since these prophetic writings stated clearly: 'Only a king can conquer the Parthians,' the title of King must be conferred on Caesar. Because his enemies shrank from agreeing to this proposal, they pressed on with their plans for his assassination."[4] What we learn from Suetonius is that Caesar was flirting with this title at a time when he was supposedly considering shifting the capital from Rome to Alexandria and when he was embarking on eastern campaigns in Parthia—in other words, while he was involved with Cleopatra and when he was contemplating mastery over the part of the Hellenistic world that had been Alexander's.

If Caesar rejected Alexander's flowing tresses and "melting gaze," what did he do about the king's youthful complexion? Alexander was young, even at his death. Caesar was by this time middle-aged and epileptic. He chose to be himself, siding with his troops and fellow elite Romans, including Pompey, who favored the realistic style then in vogue. Caesar's deeply creased face and long, lined, scrawny neck are apparent in his sculptured and numismatic portraits. This matter-of-fact portrayal of an aging Roman luminary was refreshingly honest and in keeping with a growing late Republican trend toward rendering a subject's face with a super-realism or verism, which grew out of the Roman penchant for factual recording. This factualism paralleled Roman ancestral practice that focused on documenting the variable idiosyncrasies of the human visage. Indeed, among Republican Romans of distinction, wrinkles and crow's-feet were not to be shunned but to be worn with pride, as they signified that their bearer was an experienced and wise member of elite Roman society.

One reason Caesar's portraiture was revolutionary is that he was audacious enough to mint coins with his own image in Rome, and during his lifetime. Prior to this, official moneyers were permitted to place the portraits of illustrious but deceased relatives on the obverses of the official Roman coinage, as was done by Pompey's sons. What Caesar did was an astonishing act in Republican Rome. It can only have been viewed as such and must have struck observers as another example of Caesar's soaring ambitions, possibly fueled by his increased familiarity with the imagery of Alexander and other foreign kings. Whereas coins with lifetime images were not allowed in Rome, they had been manufactured in the East from the time of Alexander the Great; Alexander's Ptolemaic successors had long adhered to that practice. Caesar's decision to embark on such a

8.4. This candid portrait of an aging Caesar is groundbreaking because it was the first to depict a living ruler on the official Roman coinage.

course is in keeping with his overarching political objectives and, as we have seen, with his ambitious urban planning, but it is also possible that he received Cleopatra's encouragement in this matter. We know that she was in Rome when he made the historic decision. Caesar's numismatic self-imaging occurred first in 44 B.C. and was an event of such significance that it necessitated a senatorial decree. The advent of contemporary portraiture on the Roman coinage was accompanied by the concurrent depiction of recent and ongoing events.

In his first lifetime portrait on the official Roman coinage, the famous denarius of 44 B.C. from the series struck by Marcus Mettius (Fig. 8.4), Caesar wears his laurel wreath low on his forehead. He doesn't shrink from being depicted with a receding hairline and deeply etched cheek and neck wrinkles. In fact, it is likely that he saw these incised creases as a

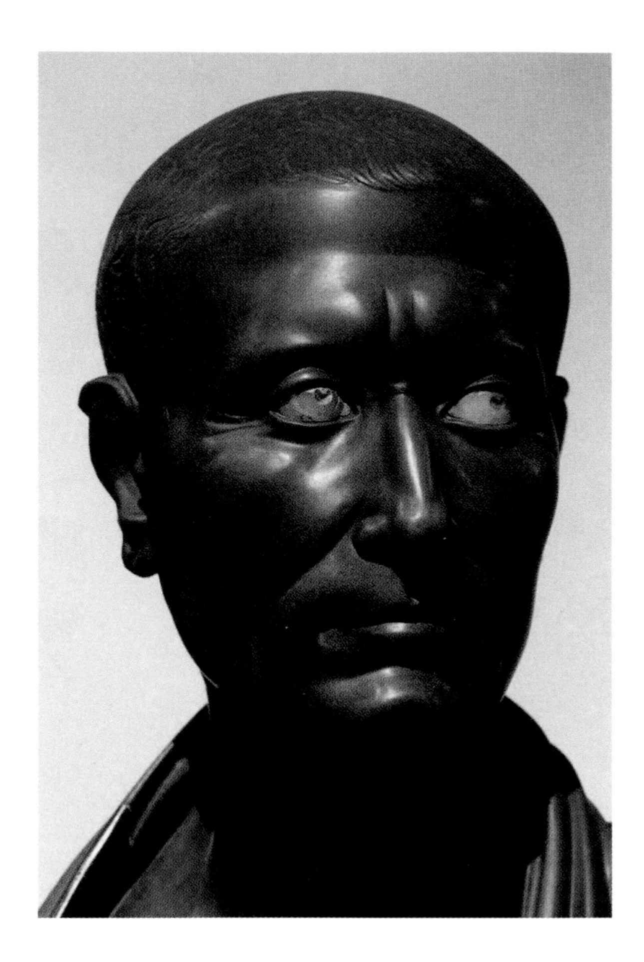

8.5. Cleopatra may have been the commissioner of this green diabase portrait of Caesar based on the revolutionary Mettius coin and intended for display in the Caesareum at Alexandria.

sign that he had thought hard and done much. It was an effective image, apparently free from pretense and affectation.

Once Caesar had struck coins with his own image, the special possibilities of such self-representation became apparent to other Roman leaders; the practice took hold and was immediately used to advantage by Antony and Octavian in lifetime portrait imagery. What emerged was portraiture that was often self-fashioned by the subject (although, of course, produced by a professional artist and paid for by the senate or a private benefactor) and thus likely to be intertwined with that person's political and personal agenda. In this way, Roman portraiture became a vehicle for the transmission of policy and often provides today a key to interpreting that policy.

Caesar's approach to portraiture was always multifaceted, and its references to historical events and to heroes, gods, and various Greeks and Romans are difficult to decipher fully today. There is, however, some tantalizing literary evidence that Caesar might have sometimes been assimilated to Alexander. The late first-century A.D. poet Statius notes that Caesar's forum in Rome featured an equestrian statue of Alexander the Great, by the Greek sculptor Lysippus, and that Alexander's portrait had been replaced by one of Caesar.[5]

If Caesar's bronze and marble portraiture did indeed reference Alexander, few clues remain. Most of Caesar's surviving portraits were posthumous creations, with the possible exception of the head of the dictator now in the Castello di Aglie in Turin, which may be a late Roman copy of a lifetime portrait. Strikingly similar to the Mettius coin, but without the protective wreath, the marble head is an unabashedly veristic rendition of Caesar as he was—furrowed brow, lined jowls, striated neck, and receding hairline.

In the months following Caesar's assassination, the grieving Cleopatra commissioned an image of her deified lover for the Caesareum in Alexandria. A head of Caesar, now in Berlin, made of a green diabase stone that is only quarried in Egypt may be this very portrait (Fig. 8.5). It is a striking likeness of Caesar based closely on Caesar's lifetime image of 44 B.C., preserved in the Mettius denarius. The dictator is represented with thinning hair, prominent crow's-feet, and a deeply creased jaw and neck. Deep furrows line his brow and the area between his eyes. The incised pupils and irises add intensity to the veristic portrait. When Cleopatra memorialized her dead paramour, she revealingly chose not to depict him as a divinized Alexander (unless an attribute that alluded to Alexander is now missing) but as a man who, despite his dalliance with Ptolemaic autocracy, wanted above all to remain Roman to the core. Caesar's resolute devotion to Rome is nowhere better expressed, and this portrait demonstrates that Cleopatra understood that even though Caesar absorbed the cultures of other places, including Alexandria, and even sometimes took on the aura of Alexander, he remained a loyal Roman. The politics of Roman portraiture was a balancing act that Cleopatra was sophisticated enough to comprehend and to use to her own advantage, much as she staged her public events and orchestrated her own imagery.

Mark Antony

Antony's long service in the East and his marriage to Cleopatra made him even more susceptible than Pompey and Caesar to the allure of Alexander the Great. In fact, Antony made taking on a series of heroic and divine identities look easy. As these alter egos became seamlessly intertwined with Antony's self-image, they helped to shape and define his life and his interactions with his fellow triumvirs, soldiers, and wives, especially Cleopatra. The associations were so transparent that it is relatively easy, even now, to track Antony's links with Caesar and Pompey (through a shared use of the veristic style) and with Hercules, Osiris, Dionysus, and Alexander, whose traits and attributes he adopted as they became advantageous. It is also important to note that Antony likely selected personae that would appeal especially to an eastern audience, since the eastern part of the empire became his primary venue.

At the time of Caesar's assassination in 44, Antony was his consular colleague. Immediately after the murder, the mint master Publius Sepullius Macer struck a series of coins with a portrait of a veiled Antony wearing the beard of mourning. A similar portrait, without the veil, was struck in Transalpine and Cisalpine Gaul in 43, this one with a portrait of a laureate Caesar on the reverse. As Cleopatra grieved for her lover in Alexandria, Antony mourned his close colleague in the West, and works of art that reflected this grieving process were produced for public view.

Antony's coinage in Rome and Gaul had counterparts in the eastern empire over which Antony had jurisdiction. Client kingdoms in the eastern Mediterranean declared their allegiance to Antony by striking silver, and especially bronze, coins with his portrait, beginning in 42 B.C. Antony and his advisers followed Caesar's lead and chose the veristic Roman portrait type as the vehicle for Antony's self-imaging, but they gave it a special twist by incorporating some of the qualities of Antony's divine alter ego, Hercules, a hero also favored by Alexander and conjured up in the coin portraits showing the king with a lion skin headdress. Plutarch emphasizes Antony's Herculean appearance, highlighting the masculine massiveness of his face and features.[6] Both the western and eastern numismatic representations depict Antony with a square face, thick neck, prominent Adam's apple, and the crooked, down-turned nose of a well-worn fighter. He had more hair than Caesar and was portrayed accordingly. It is arranged in comma-shaped locks over his forehead and grows long on the nape of his neck.

Antony's supporters in Rome and the eastern client kingdoms courting his favor probably commissioned numerous sculptured portraits of their Herculean hero. Paired statues of Antony and Cleopatra were erected in Athens and elsewhere, and Cleopatra probably honored her husband and their children in Egypt, as she had Caesar and Caesarion. As victor, however, it was Octavian who got to decide which portraits would survive and which would disappear. While Octavian allowed Cleopatra's portraits to continue to be displayed, he had Antony's proscribed. That act must have all but ensured the disappearance of Antony's portraits in Rome, although loyal partisans and devoted family members may have concealed some for posterity. Egypt had become Octavian's personal possession, so he had jurisdiction there as well. Nonetheless, affection for Antony remained strong among some supporters and Antony had many more descendants than Octavian, making likely a few commissioned portraits of him as part of later family genealogies.

A search among surviving portraits of the first century has not yielded any heads or statues that seem incontrovertibly to be Antony. One of the more promising contenders is a green basalt head in the Bankes Collection (the National Trust) in Kingston Lacy (see Fig. 2.3). The subject possesses a solid masculinity accentuated by a cubic massing of the planes of the face, a distinctive nose with down-turned tip, and a conspicuous Adam's apple. The hair is full and arranged in comma-shaped locks across the forehead. The fact that the portrait was found at Canopus in Egypt is further substantiation that the basalt head likely portrays Antony.

Antony's group portrait with Cleopatra in Athens depicted the pair as the Egyptian gods Osiris and Isis, but the temptation to be portrayed as the fearless Hercules or the awe-inspiring Alexander (who was also supposedly descended from Hercules) must have remained overwhelming. As he pursued the "inimitable life" with Cleopatra, it is unlikely that Antony allowed traditional Roman modesty to stand in the way of self-expression and self-imaging. It is not hard to conjure up a majestically muscled Antony in the guise of Hercules. Moreover, a statue in Cairo displays what may be Antony as Alexander and Jupiter. The statue, of Egyptian manufacture, depicts its Roman subject as a sturdy man with athletic build and a massive square face consistent with Antony's numismatic likeness. The man's aegis, draped over his left shoulder and decorated with a Medusa head, and the scepter he likely held in his left hand indicate that he is depicted in the guise of Alexander with a lance. The body is based closely on a celebrated statuary type created by Lysippus, who was also the sculptor of Alexander's equestrian statue in the Forum of Caesar

In view of Mark Antony's later acculturation into the luxurious lifestyle of the Alexandrian court, it was natural for him to choose Dionysus as a patron god. As we have seen, Dionysus was long favored by the Ptolemies, who saw him and the concept of *tryphe* (magnificence) as one and the same. With his own devotion to the "good life," Antony could not help but feel a special affinity for Dionysus, who had the added attraction of association with Alexander and with a variety of other Hellenistic kings. Antony had already acquired the official title *Neos Dionysos* in 41 B.C. in the Asia Minor city of Ephesus. There he paraded in the god's garb, carrying Dionysus's *thyrsus* or staff, and surrounded by participants wearing the costumes of the satyrs and maenads who usually engaged in such Bacchic rites.

While Antony may have eschewed the "power of place," he, like his Roman compatriots Pompey and Caesar, was enticed by the aura of gods and kings—taking on their identities as a mantle that made him a worthy counterpart to an Egyptian queen. Among the various guises that were possible to put on, Alexander's was the most seductive and perhaps the most appropriate for men with Alexandria on their minds.

9

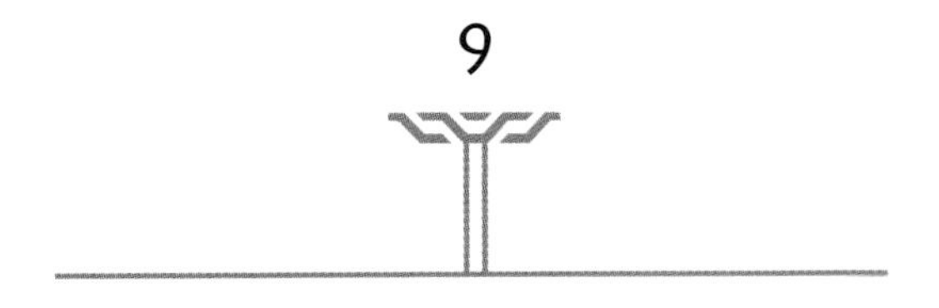

"QUEEN OF KINGS": CLEOPATRA THEA NEOTERA

The Ptolemies showcased their elite women in their art. Ptolemaic queens were regularly represented on the official coinage and in portraiture, usually paired with their husbands. R. R. R. Smith speculates that their prominence made them likely models for Hellenistic portraiture of women in the East, both royal and non-royal women alike. The Ptolemaic queens were portrayed in a highly idealized style with broad cranium and narrow delicate chins, unlined faces, rounded lips, and almond-shaped eyes. Their hair was waved or more often arranged in a series of overlapping sections that resemble the outside of a melon; this was designated the "melon hairstyle" *(melonenfrisur)* by German scholars.

It was thus very much in the natural course of things that numismatic and statuary portraits of Cleopatra were commissioned. The commencement of Cleopatra's co-regency with Ptolemy XIII, when she was around 20, marked the official debut of her public imagery. Just as the portraiture of Auletes and the other Ptolemies was based on that of the dynasty's founder, Ptolemy I Soter, so too was that of Ptolemy XIII. Cleopatra's portraits were similarly rooted in prototypical images of Egypt's earlier Ptolemaic queens and princesses—the many Arsinoes, Berenices, and Cleopatras.

The accident of Cleopatra's birth had placed her at the center of power and was something to be relished and capitalized upon. There is every indication that she maximized her opportunities and did so with grandeur and style. As we have seen, Cleopatra's barge cruises were carefully orchestrated, with nothing left to chance; and even her spur-of-the-moment flourishes, like presenting herself to Caesar in bed linens, were intuitively dramatic and effective. She also undoubtedly realized that these events could be reinforced in the public mind if they were referenced in durable materials like granite and bronze. Images of the queen were thus commissioned for placement in key public spaces and buildings in Alexandria as well as other cities in Egypt and abroad. Some portrayed Cleopatra with one of her reigning brothers, others with Antony, and still others with her children. There is no way of knowing in what quantities they were produced.

What we do know is that little of this portraiture has survived. Some of it disappeared through natural causes—the same earthquake and high waves that damaged Alexandria. Other statues in cities like Athens or Rome came to comparable natural ends. Still, the very low survival rate suggests that some of what may have been a relatively large output was not only lost but may have been deliberately demolished. In the age of Augustus, the Romans, almost certainly aware of what was already an established Ptolemaic practice, experimented with what would become the imperial right of destroying or remaking images of defeated opponents or out-of-favor predecessors. Even the Ptolemies, who were driven to recast portraits primarily because of the scarcity of marble in Alexandria, were sometimes politically motivated to remake discredited rulers into their successors.

Octavian Augustus had credible political and personal reasons for the public condemnation of Cleopatra and Antony and the concomitant destruction of their imagery. He had been waging a successful propaganda war against Cleopatra and Egypt for some time. And yet, astonishingly, the extant evidence suggests that Octavian not only preserved Cleopatra's imagery but also frequently enhanced it with his own. As we have seen, Octavian added his name to the Temple of Dendera and placed his granite portrait next to that of Auletes at the Isis temple on Antirhodos.

Although Rome under Caesar and Augustus began to produce lifetime portraits of its leaders, that imagery did not take on the cultic proportions of the long-established tradition for ruler portraiture in Egypt and Macedonia. During her lifetime Cleopatra was paid homage as a member of the royal couple, and she was also venerated after her death. Depictions of her on temple relief sculptures were accompanied by such epithets as *thea philopator,* the goddess who loves her father. On coins of Mark Antony, the title *thea neotera* (the younger goddess) associates Cleopatra with Hathor/Aphrodite. Other titles are equally elevating. In an inscription that was carved on the Temple of Isis at Philae in the fourth century A.D., a scribe named Petesenufe claims to have overlaid a wooden statue of Cleopatra with gold, the kind of reverence due a genuine goddess.

Even though evidence for the portraiture of Cleopatra is meager, what survives is revealing. Plutarch, writing decades after the queen's death, describes her as intelligent and charming but not as the breathtaking beauty we know from twentieth-century cinematic Cleopatras: "For her beauty, as we are told, was in itself not altogether incomparable, nor such as to strike those who saw her; but to converse with her had an irresistible charm, and her presence, combined with the persuasiveness of her discourse and the character which was somehow diffused about her behavior towards others, had something stimulating about it. There was a sweetness also in the tones of her voice."[1]

When Caesar was in power, images of Cleopatra in Rome depicted her as queen, goddess, and mother. Caesar honored her as the Queen of Egypt by placing her statue in the temple in his forum in Rome. This act was no small matter; Caesar certainly didn't privilege every visiting foreign dignitary in this way. Furthermore, the temple that housed Cleopatra's image was not just any temple. It celebrated Venus Genetrix, the progenitor of Caesar's Julian family. In this special context, Cleopatra may also have been considered a goddess since she was an incarnation of the Egyptian Isis and in the temple closely associated with the Roman Venus. This same statue celebrated her as a new mother, whose child was the son of Rome's Caesar and possibly even depicted in the same temple statue. She was also advertised as "little Caesar's mother" on bronze coins of her and Caesarion intended for an eastern audience. With Antony, Cleopatra became a true partner who shared dominion over the eastern empire. As such, she played Isis to his Osiris.

The surviving portraits of Cleopatra seem to fall into three general categories. The first (Type 1) depicts Cleopatra in the traditional Egyptian mode and was predictably selected for use in conventional Egyptian settings such as the Temple at Dendera. The second (Type 2) represents Cleopatra in Hellenistic Greek manner, in keeping with a format and style customary for princesses in Macedonia and other eastern kingdoms. This type appears to have been the most widely distributed and was used for coins and portraits in Egypt and the eastern empire. A third (Type 3) appears on the reverse of Roman silver coins (denarii) struck by Mark Antony; this type exhibits a more blatantly realistic style that was unusual for women in late first-century B.C. Egypt and even in Rome.

When Cleopatra commissioned images of herself and Caesarion for the walls of the Temple at Dendera, a structure wholly in the pharaonic tradition, she apparently asked the head designer to require the stone carvers to depict her and her son in the conventional Egyptian style (see Fig. 5.6). In this way she followed in the footsteps of her father Auletes, who opted to be portrayed as a pharaoh in monuments on Egyptian soil. A stele now in Paris, originally from Egypt's Fayum region, highlights the seamless transition from one pharaoh to another (Fig. 9.1). Although the kilted sovereign, with the double crown of Upper and Lower Egypt, was probably at first intended as Auletes, the recarved inscription refers to Cleopatra as devoted daughter *(thea philopator)* and thus magically transforms Auletes into his offspring. Looking very much the model male monarch in strict profile and with royal insignia, it is the 17-year-old Cleopatra who presents the nursing Isis with two spherical vases at the high point of her own life, her accession in 51 B.C. At home, the Egyptian style remained the most appropriate choice.

The Egyptian type was also suitable for the statuary of Cleopatra in Alexandria and the rest of Egypt. Local audiences would be reassured that their new monarch was in the line of Ptolemaic queens as well as being the successor of her father, the Pharaoh Ptolemy XII. This Egyptian statuary type of Cleopatra has remained elusive because there are no surviving examples with inscribed rear pillars; the authenticity of the sole extant inscription, on a marble statue in the Metropolitan Museum, has been questioned. Furthermore, the Egyptian type has not been aggressively sought by scholars because inscribed coins show the queen in the Macedonian/Hellenistic style, leaving virtually undetected a group of Egyptian statues that may represent the queen. The speculations of the few scholars who searched for the Egyptian Cleopatra were not widely accepted, leaving the Macedonian queen in ascendance.

9.1. Cleopatra's assumption of the monarchy in 51 B.C. led to the recarving of the inscription of this stele, which transformed a masculine monarch into a new Egyptian queen.

Now, however, a sensational breakthrough by Sally-Ann Ashton has led us to the Egyptian Cleopatra. Ashton has grouped together statues of a late Ptolemaic queen wearing a triple *uraeus,* the representation of the protective rearing cobra. These portraits had previously been associated with Arsinoe II, even though Arsinoe favored a double *uraeus,* signifying her oversight of both Upper and Lower Egypt. Ashton has now demonstrated the connection between these images and a portrait on a blue glass intaglio in the British Museum that almost certainly depicts Cleopatra VII. Similar to Cleopatra's portrait on Greek-style coins, the intaglio likeness nonetheless shows the queen crowned by a prominent Egyptian headdress with triple *uraeus.* The crown is especially grand and has clearly been accentuated by the artist, who wanted to make sure that the recipient of the precious glass gift did not miss the fact that it had come from the queen herself. Ashton has associated this intaglio portrait with various statues of a Ptolemaic queen now in St. Petersburg, San Jose, Paris, Turin, and New York. All belong to full-length statues depicting their subject in a long diaphanous garment and an elaborate tripartite wig, arranged behind the woman's ears (Fig. 9.2). The statues in St. Petersburg, San Jose, and Paris are purely Egyptian, with the arms-at-side pose and such royal Egyptian insignia as the bar, ankh (the hieroglyphic symbol for life), and lily scepter. The two in New York (at the Brooklyn and Metropolitan Museums) possess some Hellenistic Greek flourishes, including corkscrew-curled hair and a knotted garment. The statues in the Metropolitan Museum and St. Petersburg depict the women with a cornucopia, a single Greek type in the former and the double cornucopia of Cleopatra's coinage in the latter.

Cleopatra was undoubtedly clever and daring enough to come up with the triple *uraeus* concept. The transition from Arsinoe's two to Cleopatra's three *uraei* must have represented more than the queen's attempt at establishing her individuality, and Ashton conjectures on Cleopatra's possible objectives. Since Arsinoe's two *uraei* referred to the kingdoms of Upper and Lower Egypt, Cleopatra's third *uraeus* may well have had a geographic connotation. Perhaps it referred to the Seleucid Empire that was absorbed by Cleopatra and Antony. It may also have designated the triple rule of Cleopatra, Caesarion, and the divine Julius Caesar, or that of Cleopatra, Caesarion, and Mark Antony, although this possibility seems

9.2. A statue for an Egyptian audience presenting Cleopatra with the triple *uraeus,* an insignia that may have symbolized her aspiration for the union of Upper and Lower Egypt with Rome.

less likely because neither Caesar nor Antony ever ruled Egypt. The third *uraeus* might refer to Auletes, underscoring Cleopatra's bond with her father as *Philopator.* Alternatively, the three cobras might be the kings in Cleopatra's title "Queen of Kings," a designation she received at the time of Antony's Donations of Alexandria. The Donations provided Cleopatra's three sons (the three kings) with eastern kingdoms and proclaimed Caesarion "King of Kings." Cleopatra, as "Queen of Kings," was thus Caesarion's equal but more elevated than her other children in a Ptolemaic monarchy that now oversaw an expansive eastern empire.

Since the precise date of these statues cannot be ascertained at present, it is impossible to know exactly when Cleopatra adopted the triple *uraeus* as her personal insignia. Nevertheless, the overarching goal of her art, whether she commissioned it alone or with Caesar and Antony, was to link Egypt and Rome, and that mission might allow a fuller understanding of the queen's adoption of a tripartite badge. Her dominion was to be not only Upper and Lower Egypt but also Egypt and Rome (supporting the theory of the third *uraeus* also having a geographic connotation), a dynamic union achieved through her alliances with Caesar and Antony, with Caesarion serving as the biological bridge. I interpret Cleopatra's triple *uraeus* as her assertive retort to Octavian's triumvirate. That neither Caesar nor Antony ever ruled Egypt was to a woman like Cleopatra a minor obstacle to be brushed away with a wave of her hand. Of course, it must be kept in mind that the statues of Cleopatra with triple *uraeus* were intended for an Egyptian and not a Roman audience. It is hard to know whether the average Egyptian viewer would have seen such a meaning in the new tripartite insignia. Still, Alexandria's alliance with Rome had by then a long and highly visible history. Cleopatra's Egyptian subjects had been treated to a variety of evanescent but memorable montages featuring the union of Egypt and Rome, especially Cleopatra's barge trip with Caesar and her triumphal procession with Antony. It is not impossible that the triple *uraeus* signaled more of the same.

At least one clay seal impression, from Edfu, now in Toronto, depicts Cleopatra with tripartite wig and other Egyptian accoutrements; other Toronto seals represent the queen in a manner that could only be described as Hellenistic Greek. Cleopatra's official coinage, initiated in Alexandria in 47/46 B.C., also portrayed the new queen in the manner of the blue glass intaglio and deliberately associated her with her Macedonian female predecessors, also queens of Egypt. It is revealing that Cleopatra chose a Greek rather than Egyptian form of self-imaging for portraits on a circulating currency. While an Egyptian appearance would suit the locals, an international audience presumably called for a more cosmopolitan look that was exemplified by the universality of the worldly Hellenistic style.

Like earlier Ptolemaic queens, Cleopatra is portrayed with an unlined visage and a melon-like coiffure in these Hellenistic portraits. Although it cannot be proved definitively, it is likely that most of Cleopatra's sculpted portraits outside of Egypt were carved in this Hellenistic manner. It was not only a style long associated with the Ptolemies but also represented an approach to the portraiture of women that had already become the accepted convention around the Mediterranean.

At least fifteen different issues of bronze and silver drachms and tetradrachms with Cleopatra's portrait were struck in Alexandria, Ascalon, Orthosia, and Antioch, beginning in the early 40s B.C. Hans Baldus and Agnes Brett have divided them into two main types: the "Alexandrian" type and the "Syro-Roman" type, corresponding to Types 2 (Hellenistic) and 3 (realistic) above. R. R. R. Smith speculates, rightly I think, that each of these two types is closely tied to Cleopatra's political and personal agenda at the time the coins were first struck.

The Alexandrian type was created not long after Cleopatra and Ptolemy XIII came to the throne of Egypt and was embossed on silver and bronze drachms at Alexandria and tetradrachms at Ascalon. Some coins with that type continued to be circulated until Cleopatra's demise. These coins depict the queen's head and shoulders and present a young woman with large eyes, full lips, and a small chin—features that she shared with Auletes. Her skin is taut and youthful, and her hair is sectioned in the melon coiffure. She wears a broad hairband or diadem. The subdivided hair is arranged in a generously rounded bun at the back of her neck, the strands of which appear to have been tightly braided. The many soft tendrils that escape from the coiffure around the forehead and ears are neatly curled.

The Syro-Roman type was created a decade or more later, appearing first in 37 B.C. on silver tetradrachms minted at Antioch (Fig. 9.3). These coins continued to be manufactured until Cleopatra's death. A larger and more formidable portrait of the queen is displayed on one of the coin's faces. Cleopatra is depicted almost to the waist and manifests a commanding presence and force of character not apparent in the blander Alexandrian type. She looks older, has a thin neck, which serves to accentuate her long prominent nose, has a strong jaw, and wears a conspicuous necklace that may have been a gift from Antony. The portrait is less flattering, but it is unflinchingly powerful and exudes a kind of masculine authority that is shared by Antony in his likeness on the coin's other side. Smith suggests that Cleopatra is "meant to look Roman" in this portrait type and was intentionally presenting herself as a Roman client queen rather than a Hellenistic monarch.

The year 37 coincided with Antony's Donations, and the new coin type may well have been chosen to commemorate those bequests. The verism of Cleopatra's Syro-Roman type is striking in its strength as an image. It is also noteworthy because Cleopatra is portrayed in the Roman mode more suitable for Roman men than for women—a frank style favored by Roman Republican generals and senators of note, rather than the softer, more idealized style that was normally reserved for their spouses. By making this choice, Cleopatra and Antony undoubtedly wanted to present a strong and united front. This approach is underscored by their selection of this potent imagery and their decision to maintain it on official Roman denarii, struck between 34 and 31 B.C. in support of their Actium campaign, with portraits of Antony on the obverse and Cleopatra on the reverse (Figs. 9.4 and 9.5).

While the majority of these official coin portraits depict Cleopatra alone, an interesting series of copper coins struck in Cyprus beginning in 46 B.C. portray Cleopatra suckling the infant Caesarion, as Isis nursed her son Horus (Fig. 9.6). Their production was instigated by Caesarion's birth, which seemed to herald an even stronger alliance between Rome and Alexandria—an association emphasized by the double cornucopia on the coin's reverse. The correspondence of the image of the goddess and her offspring to Cleopatra and Caesarion was not lost on Cleopatra's countrymen.

Cleopatra and Caesarion were linked on these Cypriot coins and also at Dendera, and it is likely that paired portraits of mother and son were also displayed in Egypt, especially after Caesarion became Ptolemy XV. Egyptian-style portraits of the boy survive, although they are not definitively identified since they are not inscribed and might also be the boy kings Ptolemy XIII and XIV. At Edfu, Caesarion was flanked and protected by giant falcons. In a statue now in Brooklyn (Fig. 9.7), Caesarion has a bare chest, wears a kilted skirt, and holds a pair of bars. His broad cranium and cap of hair with locks across the forehead link him with the Julian family in Rome. Similar comma-shaped locks emerge from the Egyptian headdress worn by Caesarion in a portrait from Karnak, now in Cairo. The fact that the inscription on the back pillar was erased is further evidence that the portrait probably depicts Cleopatra's son; the inscription may have been obliterated by an Octavian who had no use for a potential competitor for the divine Caesar's heritage.

Although Cleopatra and Caesarion were celebrated on the official Alexandrian coinage, no extant evidence confirms that Cleopatra and Caesar were honored in paired portraits, either in Alexandria or in Rome. If they were, Alexandria would seem the more likely location. Cleopatra had provided the new Caesareum with a portrait of her Roman lover. Was one of her portraits placed at his side? If so, one would expect a statue in the Greco-Roman mode. And yet, surprisingly, it was Rome that was the location of one of the most audacious portrait juxtapositions in the history of Roman art—the statue of Cleopatra in the Temple of Venus and that of Julius Caesar in the forum that contained the temple. While not side-by-side, these statues of Cleopatra and Caesar were arranged with what seems like such a clear political and personal agenda that they suggested that Caesar might have been on the verge of marrying the queen—a shocking event that, if true, was canceled by his murder.

That statues of Caesar were scattered around Rome in abundance was to be expected. The dictator's likeness turned up in all the right and most visible places—the Roman Forum, the Capitoline hill, and in many of the major temples of Rome, especially those of divinities like Quirinus, Clementia, and Venus Genetrix, with whom Caesar had a personal connection. The dispersed statues depicted Caesar in a number of different guises and with a variety of attributes, but the statue in his new Julian Forum depicted him in cuirass, the first public statue of an armored general in Rome. In the same forum was a majestic equestrian statue of Alexan-

9.3. This forceful portrait of a masculine Cleopatra depicts her at half-length, with a striking necklace that was probably a gift from Mark Antony.

9.4. Antony is depicted here in a strong and frank portrait that was one of a pair with an equally formidable likeness of Cleopatra, signifying the alliance between Egypt and Rome.

9.5. This portrait of Cleopatra breaks new ground because it portrays her as a forceful woman dynast and also links her to Mark Antony on an official Roman denarius with a non-Roman agenda.

9.6. Cleopatra nurses her infant son Caesarion on a coin that the Egyptian people would have interpreted as a joyous sign that Egypt had a new prince, though one with a Roman pedigree as well.

9.7. This statue presents Caesarion's dual parentage, signaled by his kilted Egyptian skirt on one hand and his Julian cap of hair on the other.

der effectively transformed into one of Caesar. While these two statues were situated in the forum proper, Dio Cassius and Appian described a gilded statue of Cleopatra located in the Temple of Venus Genetrix, the focal point of the Forum of Caesar.

According to Appian, writing in the second century, Caesar had "erected the temple to Venus, his ancestress, as he had vowed to do when he was about to begin the Battle of Pharsalus, and he laid out ground round the temple which he intended to be a forum for the Roman people, not for buying and selling, but a meeting place for the transaction of public business, like the public squares of the Persians, where the people assemble to seek justice or to learn the laws. He placed a beautiful image of Cleopatra by the side of the goddess, which stands there to this day."[2] Similarly, in the late second or early third century, Dio Cassius noted: "Cleopatra, though defeated and captured, was nonetheless glorified, in as much as her adornments repose in dedications in our temples and she herself is seen in gold in the Shrine of Venus."[3]

Thus both writers claim that a statue of Cleopatra was placed in the temple's *cella*, but when that occurred is in dispute. Scholars agree that Appian states it was Caesar who placed the statue of Cleopatra next to Venus's in his temple, an event that obviously had to happen during the dictator's lifetime. More controversy surrounds Dio's language. Most recently, Erich Gruen has suggested that Dio lists the gilded statue as one of several trophies of Cleopatra placed in temples in Rome after the Battle of Actium. Although Dio clearly states that, after Cleopatra was defeated and captured, she was nonetheless glorified because her adornments (presumably such personal relics as her clothing, headdress, pearl earrings, and Isiac attributes) were placed as trophies in various temples around Rome, and it is fair to assume that these personal items only became Roman property after her death, the phrase "and she herself is seen in gold in the Shrine of Venus" can be variously interpreted. In contrast to Gruen, I think that while Dio confirms that Cleopatra's statue still reposes in the temple, he does not state categorically that it was a trophy or that it was recently acquired. The statue might well have been placed there by Caesar and allowed to continue to repose there by Augustus, who at the same time was scattering other Cleopatra paraphernalia in additional religious settings around Rome. The further attraction of this explanation is that it is consistent with the similar evidence supplied by Appian and Dio.

If Caesar was indeed the statue's sponsor, he probably placed it in the temple around 46 B.C. He chose to situate it right beside that of the temple's cult goddess, Venus, as befitted a queen who was closely associated with Isis and Hathor, while his own images were outside in the forum. Cleopatra's residence was thus the abode of the gods; Caesar's domicile was in the realm of public service, in the midst of the bustling activity of the forum's market and community life. Cleopatra's image was golden and thus otherworldly, while Caesar's images, whether bronze or marble, were geared for battle and administrative challenges in this world. In this way, the lovers seemed to inhabit different domains. Yet it is hard to believe that the cognoscenti in Rome in the second half of the first century B.C. would have failed to make a connection between Egypt's "goddess" and Rome's dictator. Still, despite his grand ambitions, Caesar was politically shrewd enough to know that he could go just so far in the climate of Republican Rome. While he couldn't shout his personally perceived divinity from the rooftops, he could take advantage of his association with his divine ancestress, Venus Genetrix, and his royal *amorata*, Cleopatra. That said, he may have gone a bit too far, and such behavior may have had an impact on his eventual downfall.

We know a fair amount about what must have been the famous portrait of Cleopatra in the Roman Temple of Venus Genetrix. As a sparkling celebrity in Rome in the mid-40s, queen of a world power, and Caesar's consort, Cleopatra attended social events in the capital city that were chronicled in Cicero's *Letters to Atticus*. Caesar had wed the highly respected Calpurnia in 49 B.C., so his Egyptian sojourn and, even more, the arrival in Rome of a foreign queen whom Cicero dubbed "that Egyptian woman" and their son must have fascinated but also rankled the aristocracy. Whether or not the ostensible reason for Cleopatra's sojourn in Rome was the business of reaffirming Egypt's alliance with Rome, her presence there apparently brought her together with those at the upper echelons of Roman society. A sense of the "Roman" Cleopatra comes through in Cicero's letters. The author never refers to Cleopatra by name, but only as "the Queen." Despite his lack of regard for her, Cicero clearly attended events at Cleopatra's Roman residence. These were likely to have been literary salons for distinguished intellectuals of the day. Caesar, concerned about appearances, did not allow Cleopatra and Caesarion to inhabit his domicile in downtown Rome but settled Cleopatra and her retinue in one of his villas across the Tiber. Nevertheless, whether she was encountered in soirées at that villa or at dinner parties in the city center, everyone who was anyone in Rome was surely paying careful attention to Cleopatra and commenting on what she looked like, what she wore, and how her hair was arranged. All of those impressions must have had a profound impact on how contemporary elite women saw themselves and their role in Roman society.

Those who partied with "the Queen" had an opportunity to formulate their impressions at first hand, but other Roman citizens would have seen "that Egyptian woman" only in staged appearances, if any were arranged. That a gilded portrait of the Egyptian dynast resided in the Temple of Venus Genetrix must have been known around the capital city, as was the fact that she stood next to Venus, the temple's patron goddess. However, few people would have actually seen this spectacular statue because the temple's main room or *cella* was reserved for the priesthood. Caesar's images, on the other hand, were surely seen by those who frequented his forum. One can readily imagine the chatter that would have ensued there about the famed statue of the dictator's lover that stood inside the temple in an honored position near Venus herself, although it is something of a mystery why Cicero never mentioned it in his voluminous letters. Perhaps the man who couldn't face committing Cleopatra's name to writing also chose to block out the glimmer of her effigy.

The golden glow of the statue of Caesar's mistress can only be imagined. A pale but illuminating reflection is preserved, however, in a Parian marble portrait of Cleopatra, found in 1784 at the Villa of the Quintilii on the Via Appia in Rome, and now in the Vatican Museums (Figs. 9.8 and 9.9). It was probably made between 40 and 30 B.C. The portrait can be identified as Cleopatra by its striking similarity to the numismatic images of her in the Macedonian mode. The marble version has the same profile with the same physiognomy, the same hairstyle, and the same broad hairband, probably made of gold and worn by many of Cleopatra's queenly predecessors.

The head is now placed on a statue of a draped woman to which it does not belong, and one can merely speculate on what kind of body type Cleopatra's portrait originally rested. Since the marble head was found in

9.8. This marble copy of the head of Cleopatra, now in the Vatican, is probably based on a gilded statue of the queen commissioned by Julius Caesar for his Temple of Venus Genetrix in Rome.

9.9. The residual marble on the left side of Cleopatra's face suggests that she was originally depicted with Caesarion on her shoulder, an image of mother and child that became influential in Augustan Rome.

Rome, it was probably based on the famous lost statue of the queen in the Temple of Venus Genetrix. Even more significant is that the Vatican portrait provides evidence that the gilded statue of Cleopatra may have originally portrayed her with Caesarion. A depiction of "Little Caesar" appears to have been perched on Cleopatra's right shoulder, with his left hand resting on her left cheek. Small raised and uneven residual remains of marble can still be discerned on the Vatican portrait's left cheek, just below the left eye, and just below the left corner of the mouth, right where the baby's hand would presumably have rested.

This astonishing observation was made by Ludwig Curtius in 1933, and was supported by others; in a more recent publication, however, Eugenio La Rocca explains the excess marble as surviving points used in the Roman replication process. With all due respect to La Rocca's observation, the Curtius hypothesis would seem to be borne out not only by the marble residue but also by evidence for such a mother-and-child statuary type reflected in surviving Hellenistic terracotta statuettes from Rome and elsewhere. Additional support is provided by the likelihood that the cult statue of Venus Genetrix also portrayed the goddess with her son Cupid on her shoulder. If both mothers were depicted with their sons in Caesar's forum temple, it would have been highly significant and adds to the probability that Caesar was the commissioner.

If Caesarion was indeed depicted with his mother in this venerated temple, in a location not far from portraits of Caesar himself, this would have been exceedingly noteworthy in its day—so remarkable that it again raises the question of why there is no mention of the boy's portrait in surviving sources, and why, if it was there, Octavian let it stand after Cleopatra's death. We shall likely never know the answer to either query, but I think it is fair to say that the historical and literary records are so spotty as to be inconclusive. With regard to the portrait of Caesarion, two possible explanations come to mind. The depiction of Caesarion may have been removed from the gilded statue before it was described in the surviving sources, which would suggest that Octavian was happy to let Cleopatra's statue stand in the temple as an adjunct to Venus but that an image of Caesarion was unacceptable to him. Or, in the spirit of so much other Augustan imagery, the figure may have been generic enough—it could just as well be Cupid as Caesarion—to be interpreted in various ways and thus innocuous. Infants in Augustan art are notoriously difficult to decipher. Notable examples include the baby at the foot of Augustus's statue from Primaporta, variously identified as the child Cupid or the emperor's grandson and heir, Gaius Caesar. And what of the babies seated on the lap of the woman in the southeast panel on the Ara Pacis Augustae? The list of human and divine possibilities for those two children is endless and has never been satisfactorily explained. Since Augustan art was notoriously polysemous, and intentionally so, the image of Cleopatra and Caesarion would have readily fit into the Augustan lexicon.

It was this kind of complex visual imagery that sparked Augustus and his artists in their dialogue with Caesar, Antony, and Cleopatra. Augustus was clever enough to use these powerfully suggestive images as inspiration for and a foil to his own art. As the winner and only central character left alive, Augustus could effectively direct the message. His discourse was no longer with these individuals but with their monuments; indeed, which works of art were allowed to stand and which were destroyed was part of the conversation. Augustus proscribed Antony's images but let Cleopatra's statue remain in the Temple of Venus Genetrix. Augustus paraded Cleopatra's effigy in his Actian triumph. As we shall see, Augustus venerated Cleopatra's gods all over Egypt, replacing her in the line of Egyptian pharaohs and kings. Without a second thought, Augustus had Caesarion murdered but spared the children of Antony and Cleopatra. Once Caesarion was dead, he posed no threat to Augustus but was instead a useful symbol of Augustus's ascendancy as true heir to Caesar.

The statue of Cleopatra and Caesarion also spurred the discourse about dynasties. Caesarion was part of Cleopatra's family dynasty in Egypt; with the adoption of Gaius and Lucius Caesar, Augustus was also staking Rome's future on hereditary governance. The portrait of Cleopatra and Caesarion appears to have motivated Augustus to recognize the generative power of the family. It remained an inspiration almost two decades later when Augustus's Ara Pacis (Altar to Peace) began to be built in Rome; there Augustus's "sons" Gaius and Lucius Caesar are depicted in the lap of a motherly Venus-like goddess and in close proximity to their Roman "mother," Livia (see Figs. 15.2 and 15.4).

The marble head of Cleopatra from Rome shows the queen with a diadem, suggesting that she received her earthly power through Hathor and Isis. While it is possible that the diadem of the original gilded statue may have been enhanced with the regalia traditional for pharaohs since the Old Kingdom, we don't know for sure. The prominent marble boss at the center of the diadem, just above the midpoint of the queen's forehead in the Vatican replica, has been described as residual marble from the replication process, but I would suggest instead that it is the remains of what was originally the rearing female cobra or *uraeus* that protected the pharaoh and the land of Egypt. Although the *uraeus* was an ornament, it gave the impression, at least from a distance, of a topknot; I believe this served as the model for the creation by Octavia and Livia and their hairdressers of what was to become the Roman *nodus* hairstyle.

The significance of the Vatican portrait of Cleopatra cannot be overstated, not only because it replicates what must have been the most notable statue of Cleopatra VII Philopator in the West but also because it is only one of three surviving marble heads in the Macedonian-Hellenistic style that represent "the Queen." In fact, it is a special challenge to try to invoke the physical presence of one of history's most heralded women through a trio of Hellenistic heads (a questionable portrait in the British Museum is no longer associated with Cleopatra) and a cluster of coins. The statues and reliefs of Cleopatra in the Egyptian style are too generic to add further value. The Vatican Cleopatra is a pale, even frigid, reflection of the original cult statue in the Temple of Venus Genetrix, which must have been shimmering and full of life, perhaps with a playful Caesarion on the shoulder. Fortunately, the other two surviving portraits in the round—marble heads now in Berlin and Cherchel—are more sensitive renditions of their subject and help provide additional clues to the appearance and personality of Cleopatra.

The well-known portrait of Cleopatra in the Antikensammlung in the Staatliche Museum in Berlin captures Cleopatra's intelligence, character, and charm (Fig. 9.10). While based on the same prototype as the Vatican head, with a comparable physiognomy, melon hairstyle, and broad diadem, the Berlin head is smaller and the marble more softly modulated. There are also subtle differences in detail, such as the Berlin artist's decision to wrap the diadem higher around the head so that the entire ear is revealed and to treat the hairband as an entity separate from the bun.

The third marble portrait of Cleopatra was found in the harbor area of Cherchel (modern Algeria, but part of the Kingdom of Mauretania in Cleopatra's time) and is now in the museum on the site. It shares the same

9.10. This marble head is a more sensitive likeness of Cleopatra, but one that probably originated from the same portrait type as the Vatican head.

physiognomy, coiffure, and diadem as the Vatican and Berlin heads and must be based on the same Alexandrian prototype. As in the Berlin head, the diadem is flat against the head, leaving the ears free, but the hairstyle is unique: it is sectioned behind the diadem but is arranged in corkscrew curls across the queen's forehead in a distinctive manner. There is a break in the marble hair over the center of the forehead which suggests that something that was protruding must have broken off—possibly the *uraeus* of the Vatican head, or alternatively a topknot. Both Klaus Fittschen and R. R. R. Smith have convincingly suggested that this portrait of Cleopatra was one of three royal portraits from Cherchel that were found near the palace and were made for King Juba II of Mauretania (25 B.C. to A.D. 23), who had married Cleopatra Selene. Other scholars suggest that this head represents Cleopatra Selene rather than Cleopatra, although Cleopatra remains the more likely candidate.

The abundance of post-antique Cleopatras, imaged in paintings and film, lulls us into thinking that we know "the Queen." We imagine we recognize what she looked like, how she carried herself, and how she interacted with the men in her life. Our contemporary Cleopatra is a ravishing beauty, the ultimate femme fatale, whose clothing and black wig with bangs make her more Egyptian than Macedonian, more pharaonic than Hellenistic. It is profoundly unsettling to realize that much of what we think we know is really myth, and that Cleopatra's physical being can be glimpsed only through a small and incomplete number of antique remains. Yet, as we have seen, these scattered and varied fragments are surprisingly revelatory and, in the end, provide us with a balanced picture of the Macedonian princess, Egyptian queen, and Roman consort.

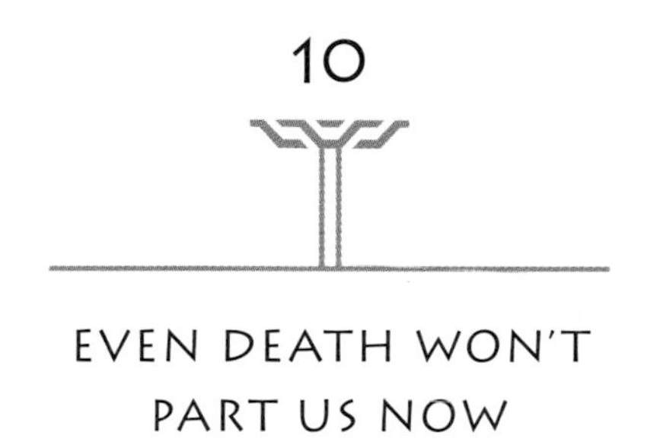

10

EVEN DEATH WON'T PART US NOW

Cleopatra's impact on Rome was much greater after her death than during her life. Even though she had been Octavian's principal foreign enemy and his propagandists had made much of his enmity toward her, she insinuated herself into his life and into many of the works of art he commissioned. In some instances, he appears to have been enticed quite willingly. In others, he surrendered unawares.

At first it seemed as if it was Octavian who adopted the strategy of seduction. Once he realized he was close to vanquishing Cleopatra and Antony, Octavian remained concerned that they might turn the tide militarily or, once they realized all was lost, decide to destroy their accumulated wealth. Rumor had it that Cleopatra was storing her riches in a tomb she was building in the Alexandrian royal cemetery and that she would not hesitate to torch it if her demands were not met. Since, from Octavian's vantage point, it seemed as if Cleopatra had already succumbed to the potency of Caesar and Antony and their shared vision of a united Rome and Egypt, Octavian conjectured that a profession of love from him might captivate her once again. Dio Cassius reports in his *Roman History* that Octavian "sent Thyrsus, a freedman of his, to say many kind things to her and in particular to tell her that he was in love with her. He hoped that by this means at least, since she thought it her due to be loved by all mankind, she would make away with Antony and keep herself and her money unharmed. And so it proved. In the meantime

[Octavian] Caesar took Pelusium [the easternmost city on the Nile and thus a convenient gateway into Egypt], ostensibly by storm, but really because it was betrayed by Cleopatra. For she saw that no one came to their aid and perceived that Caesar was not to be withstood, and most important of all, she listened to the message sent her through Thyrsus, and believed that she was really beloved, in the first place, because she wished to be, and, in the second place, because she had in the same manner enslaved Caesar's father [Julius Caesar] and Antony. Consequently she expected to gain not only forgiveness and the sovereignty over the Egyptians, but the empire of the Romans as well."[1]

Octavian had other motives besides seizing Cleopatra's wealth. Dio mentions that Octavian hoped above all to be able to capture Cleopatra alive so that he could transport her to Rome to appear in his triumph. His objective was not to trick her but to subdue her, so that she would be perceived as a genuine captive. But Octavian's scheming was for naught. By the time he reached Cleopatra, the poison of the asp had done its work and she was beyond resuscitation. Furthermore, Dio reports that when Octavian realized this he "felt both admiration and pity for her, and was excessively grieved on his own account, as if he had been deprived of all the glory of his victory." Cleopatra and Antony "were embalmed in the same fashion and buried in the same tomb."[2]

Octavian's distress that he couldn't parade Cleopatra at his triumph in Rome was alleviated somewhat by his display of her effigy and her children by Antony in that procession. But his frustration likely stayed with him and appears to have motivated him to continue to try to possess her.

Dio also describes the triumph in *Roman History,* with Cleopatra's effigy as the supreme trophy: "On the second day the naval victory at Actium was commemorated, and on the third the subjugation of Egypt. Now all the processions proved notable, thanks to the spoils from Egypt—in such quantities, indeed, had spoils been gathered there that they sufficed for all the processions—but the Egyptian celebration surpassed them all in costliness and magnificence. Among other features, an effigy of the dead Cleopatra upon a couch was carried by, so that in a way she, too, together with the other captives and with her children, Alexander, called also Helios, and Cleopatra, called also Selene, was a part of the spectacle and a trophy in the procession. After this came Caesar, riding into the city behind them all."[3]

According to Plutarch, the facsimile of Cleopatra conveyed in Octavian's cortege depicted the Egyptian queen "with an asp clinging to her," dramatizing her death.[4] While Octavian may have humiliated Alexander Helios and Selene Cleopatra by parading them through Rome as captives, their lives were spared. So too was the life of Ptolemy Philadelphus.

Antony's son by Fulvia, Marcus Antonius Antyllus, and Caesarion were not as fortunate. As their fathers' eldest scions, the youths were deemed a risk, lest they attempt to wrest power from Octavian. Octavian's ruthlessness was apparent in the way he slaughtered these boys. Antyllus was even engaged to Octavian's only daughter and had hidden in a shrine that Cleopatra had built for Antony. But the refuge of a sacred space provided no protection, and Antyllus was immediately slain. Caesarion, aware that his mother's death put him in immediate danger, fled to Ethiopia; at Octavian's order, he was pursued on the road and killed. Octavian did, however, smile on Antony and Octavia's daughters, his own nieces, and saw to it that Iullus Antonius, the younger son of Antony and Fulvia, received his rightful inheritance.

It is Plutarch who tells us that Octavian "could not but admire the greatness of her [Cleopatra's] spirit."[5] That admiration led him to issue the command that she and Antony should be buried side by side "with royal splendor and magnificence" in their beloved Alexandria. Cleopatra was 39, Antony in his mid-50s.

Octavian's admiration for Cleopatra's spirit must have been very great indeed. He decided not only to bury her in queenly grandeur in Alexandria but also to allow her resplendent gilded statue—perhaps depicting Caesarion as well—to continue to be displayed in the hallowed hall of the Temple of Venus Genetrix in Rome. To pay such honor to the image of the woman whom the poets from Octavian's literary circle had recently branded the "harlot queen of licentious Canopus"[6] represents one of the greatest about-faces in history.

Why did Octavian do this? Because he could not but admire Cleopatra's spirit? Because his divine adoptive father, Julius Caesar, of whom he was *divi filius*, had once been involved with Cleopatra? Because Egyptians and Romans believed that Cleopatra was a genuine goddess? Because having a statue of Cleopatra in the Temple of Venus Genetrix in Caesar's Forum in Rome reminded him that, however great she was, he was greater still to have vanquished her? Because even if he couldn't parade her in his triumph, he could display her effigy in that procession, and continue to exhibit it forever as a trophy of his conquest? It is unlikely that we will ever know. Plutarch's explanation for Octavian's decision not to destroy statuary of Cleopatra was a cynical one—that he was paid off—but when Plutarch provides it, he also reports that, in contrast to the fate of Cleopatra's Roman image, Octavian obliterated those of Mark Antony: "His statues [Antony's] were thrown down, but those of Cleopatra were left untouched; for Archibius, one of her friends, gave Caesar two thousand talents to save them from the fate of Antony's."[7]

The statues of Cleopatra that Plutarch refers to were probably images in Egypt, because Plutarch points out beforehand that Octavian gave orders for Cleopatra to be buried with Antony in Alexandria. But wherever those statues stood, mention of a payoff confirms that a decision about whether they and others like them should continue to be displayed after Cleopatra's death was a matter for discussion and perhaps even negotiation. In addition, it has been pointed out that two thousand talents was a significant amount of money in Augustan times, so sizable that it could have supported Octavian's army for a full year. Plutarch's citation of such a grand sum serves to emphasize Cleopatra's continued worth, which was sustained by allowing statues in Egypt and at least one in Rome to remain on view.

It is paradoxical that Octavian left the temple statue intact while, at the same time, choosing not to depict Cleopatra in his state monuments, even as the vanquished enemy. And yet, since Octavian's overarching goal was to present himself as the queen's "successor" in Egypt, that objective was more easily achieved if she remained a visible force, both there and in Rome.

As mentioned earlier, both Appian and Dio Cassius provide convincing evidence that the statue of Cleopatra still stood in the Temple of Venus in the second and third centuries A.D. We also learn from Dio that the gilded statue in the Temple of Venus was not the only prominent celebration of Cleopatra in Augustan Rome; some of her adornments were reposing elsewhere. Although leaving the statue of Cleopatra in the temple of Caesar's forum was an act of laissez-faire by Octavian, the placement of her pearls in the ears of a statue of Venus in the new Pantheon erected by Marcus Agrippa in 27–25 B.C. was a deliberate move on Augustus's part.

This statue of Venus stood beside one of Mars and near that of the divine Julius Caesar in the temple's main space, while other statues of Augustus and Agrippa were placed in the pronaos; the full group signaled that the temple honored the Julian family or *gens*. Here, too, Cleopatra's alliance with Julius Caesar could not fail to be noticed, nor her association with Venus—the patron goddess of the Julian family.

In his *Natural History* Pliny gives a detailed history of these pearls and how they came to be placed in Venus's ears: "There have been two pearls that were the largest in the whole of history; both were owned by Cleopatra, the last of the Queens of Egypt—they had come down to her through the hands of the Kings of the East. When Antony was gorging daily at recherché banquets, she with pride at once lofty and insolent, queenly wanton as she was, poured contempt on all his pomp and splendor, and when he asked what additional magnificence could be contrived, replied that she would spend 10,000,000 sesterces on a single banquet. Antony was eager to learn how it could be done, although he thought it was impossible. Consequently, bets were made, and on the next day, when the matter was to be decided, she set before Antony a banquet that was indeed splendid, so that the day might not be wasted, but of the kind served every day—Antony laughing and expostulating at its niggardliness. But she vowed it was a mere additional douceur, and that the banquet would round off the account and that her own dinner alone would cost 10,000,000 sesterces, and she ordered the second course to be served. In accordance with previous instructions the servants placed in front of her only a single vessel containing vinegar, the strong rough quality of which can melt pearls. She was at the time wearing in her ears that remarkable and truly unique work of nature. Antony was full of curiosity to see what in the world she was going to do. She took one earring off and dropped the pearl in the vinegar, and when it was melted swallowed it. Lucius Plancus, who was umpiring the wager, placed his hand on the other pearl when she was preparing to destroy it also in a similar way, and declared that Antony had lost the battle—an ominous remark that came true. With this goes the story that, when the queen who had won on this important issue was captured, the second of this pair of pearls was cut in two pieces, so that half a helping of the jewel might be in each of the ears of Venus in the Pantheon in Rome."[8] The way Pliny describes those earrings suggests that they were viewed as trophies of Cleopatra, seized from her after her capture and displayed as spoils in the Pantheon—an act comparable to parading her effigy through the streets of Rome.

After the death of Cleopatra, Octavian made Egypt an imperial protectorate. Egypt was not to be just any Roman province, but a special one. Even a senator couldn't settle along the Nile without Octavian's permission. Dio elaborates on this decision, because it came while Octavian was in Egypt attempting to convince Cleopatra to return with him to Rome. "After this, he [Octavian] viewed the body of Alexander and actually touched it, whereupon, it is said, a piece of the nose was broken off. But he declined to view the remains of the Ptolemies, though the Alexandrians were extremely eager to show them, remarking, 'I wished to see a king, not corpses.' . . . Afterwards, he made Egypt tributary and gave it in charge of Cornelius Gallus . . . he would not even grant a senator permission to live in it, except as he personally made the concession to him by name. Thus was Egypt enslaved."[9]

Why did Octavian decide to treat Egypt differently from the many kingdoms and civilizations that he was bringing into the orbit of Rome? The most likely explanation is that what made Egypt so enticing, not only to him but also to Caesar and Antony before him, was the country's vast and rich resources—its sheer wealth as well as its grain supply, so critical to the welfare of Rome and the rest of the empire. With Egypt an imperial protectorate, Octavian had entrée to the resources that Caesar and Antony had gained through Cleopatra and could also make certain that no Roman senator was in a position to gain access. The fact that Egypt had been Cleopatra's, and for a time Caesar's and Antony's, provided it with a special aura that surely made Octavian want to possess it all the more. Octavian wanted Cleopatra in his triumph, and he wanted her country to belong to him. In this way, Octavian would possess Cleopatra as she had already been possessed by his divine adoptive father and by his most illustrious Roman foe. Octavian would possess Cleopatra after her death, as he had not been able to during her life. Yet, in the end, it was she who possessed him.

11

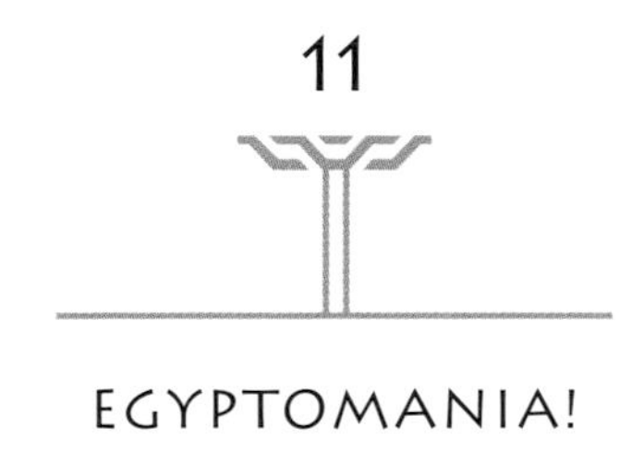

EGYPTOMANIA!

It was not only Cleopatra's Egypt and its grain that Octavian was after. Cleopatra's pearls were not the only trophies he coveted. He wanted to own Cleopatra's monuments—monuments that had inspired Caesar to redesign Rome. As Octavian contemplated his own renewal of Rome, he wished to punctuate his refurbishment with reminiscences of his Egyptian conquest.

After Octavian became Augustus, he began to transform Rome from a city of brick to one of marble. He decided that Egypt's singular marble obelisks with their exotic hieroglyphs would not only add an attractive profile to the skyline of Rome but could also serve as permanent monuments to his subjugation of Egypt. Augustus began to transport these Egyptian monoliths and set them up in key locations around Rome; he placed them in close proximity to many of his most significant monuments, such as the Ara Pacis Augustae and even his own tomb.

Although stocky monoliths were erected in Egypt during the Old Kingdom, what we think of today as the typical Egyptian obelisk was a New Kingdom phenomenon. It had a slender profile and was carved from a single block of stone, with a pyramid-shaped tip that was probably gilded. The obelisk commemorated the Egyptian *benben*, the primordial mound upon which the legendary phoenix *(benu)*, an incarnation of the sun god, was said to have perched. The mythological phoenix was worshipped at Heliopolis in Egypt as the incarnation of the sun god Re. According to

Pyramid Texts, when the Pharaoh died, the sun would strengthen its beams to create a celestial stairway or ramp, by which the deceased king would ascend to the heavens. The true pyramid can be seen to symbolize or represent this solar ramp, and the idea of the staircase is apparent in the design of the early step pyramids.

These obelisks undoubtedly appealed to Augustus not only because of their elegant monumentality but also because of their solar symbolism. Augustus was partial to the Roman sun god, Apollo. Now that Egypt was his, so was Heliopolis, the home of the potent Egyptian solar deity Re. Heliopolis abounded in obelisks and became a kind of quarry from which Augustus and his circle could make a selection. These lofty monoliths were also seen as the spoils of Augustus's Egyptian conquest. Even the illiterate in Rome must have been impressed by their size and aware of their heritage; the mysterious hieroglyphs may not have been decipherable, but they were immediately recognizable as Egyptian. For those Romans who could read, Augustus encouraged his designer to add a Latin inscription at the base honoring the sun and himself as the son of Divus Julius. For those who couldn't comprehend the full inscription, the Latin names would have been signs that Augustus was now master of Egypt. Augustus undoubtedly wanted those who saw the obelisk to make the connection between him and the royal kings who had earlier set up these monoliths.

In 12 B.C., Augustus instructed his soldiers to move red granite obelisks from Heliopolis to Alexandria and to place them in the Caesareum, as described by Pliny in his *Natural History*.[1] Whereas these obelisks were erected in Alexandria to honor Caesar, Augustus received the same distinction in Rome. In 10 B.C., Augustus imported two obelisks to Rome and had them set up in prominent positions. The first, now in the Piazza del Popolo, originally erected by Sethos I with additional hieroglyphs by his son Ramesses II (1304–1237 B.C.), was set up on the *spina* or spine of the Circus Maximus. The other, now in Piazza di Montecitorio and originally erected in the early sixth century B.C. by Psammetichus II, was made the *gnomon* or pillar of a colossal sundial in the Campus Martius (Fig. 11.1). As such, it was a significant part of the complex that included the Ara Pacis and the Mausoleum of Augustus. It was probably fitted with a gilded sphere surmounted by a short spire at its apex and appears to have been mounted on a stepped base.

11.1. This Egyptian obelisk was brought to Rome by Augustus in 10 B.C. to serve as part of a complex with his family mausoleum and the Ara Pacis Augustae.

Augustus's tomb in the Campus Martius was eventually embellished with two plain red granite obelisks. They stood a little over 14 meters high and were first described by Ammianus Marcellinus but not mentioned either by Strabo in his description of the tomb or by Pliny.[2] Thus these monoliths were likely placed beside the sepulcher in the later empire. Whether Augustus had planned for the pair of obelisks is not known, but even if he had not, their placement in front of his mausoleum in late antiquity demonstrates that Augustus's link with the possession of Egypt and Cleopatra was understood by his successors.

Although these iconic monoliths were potent symbols of Rome's tenancy of Egypt under Augustus, they were not the first Egyptian monuments in Italy. The cult of the Egyptian goddess Isis, introduced to Egypt by Ptolemy I Soter, had gained favor in the eastern Mediterranean in the fourth and third centuries B.C. As Isis's ritual began to be practiced along heavily frequented trade routes, appropriate sacred spaces were constructed on the Greek island of Delos and elsewhere. Merchants in Delos traded with those in the South Italian city of Puteoli, and just before 100 B.C. a temple was erected there to the Egyptian goddess. Other shrines rapidly appeared in Campanian towns such as Pompeii and Herculaneum. In the course of the second century, Isis worship spread from Delos to Rome, where it was not officially sanctioned through the first half of the first century. The years right after 50 B.C., however, saw a momentous shift, and the impetus may well have come from Cleopatra. As the living embodiment of Isis, she likely made the goddess fashionable among the glitterati of Rome. Isis was the ideal women's goddess—the guardian of women, marriage, maternity, fertility, and children. The triumvirs, Antony among them, dedicated a temple to Isis in 43 B.C. and another to Serapis, the Egyptian god who from the time of Ptolemy I was the state god of the Ptolemaic kings. It was through the Ptolemies that Serapis came to the attention of Roman emperors, who associated themselves with him especially in the second and third centuries A.D.

Despite the initial support of the triumvirs, the worship of Isis in Rome suffered frequent setbacks. Dio Cassius, Tacitus, and Suetonius record repeated crackdowns on the cults of Isis and Serapis by Augustus and especially Tiberius,[3] and it was only under the emperor Caligula (A.D. 37–41) that Isis was officially recognized in Rome.

The temple to Isis that the triumvirs dedicated was likely that of Isis Campensis in the Campus Martius, where it was adjacent to the Temple of Serapis; together, they were the Iseum and Serapeum. While the fortunes of Isis waxed and waned in Rome, it was not long before Antony was audaciously posing in statuary groups in the East as the Egyptian god Osiris to Cleopatra's Isis. Osiris, the god of death and resurrection, vegetation, and the Nile, whose identity sometimes appears to have overlapped with that of Serapis, was closely associated with the afterlives of pharaohs and kings. In Egyptian myth, Osiris was Isis's brother and husband (Egypt's brother-sister marriage was a reflection of this relationship), who impregnates her after his resurrection. She later gives birth to Horus (Harpocrates), who avenges his father and becomes an important force in his own right. Yet, in an incestuous turn, Horus rapes and beheads his mother. Vengeful and always resourceful, Isis cuts off Horus's hands in return.

This complex family saga found its way into the pictorial arts, primarily in the form of excerpts from the longer narrative. Like Isis sanctuaries in Egypt, those in Rome also needed Isiac décor. Suitable relief scenes, statues, and architectural embellishment (columns, capitals, and the like) were brought to Rome to enhance the sanctuaries, although there is no evidence whatsoever that a statue of Antony and Cleopatra as Osiris and Isis was among them. Additional works in the Egyptianizing style were added on the spot. Some were worked in Italian marble, others in hard, vividly colored stones from Egyptian quarries. Use of the latter necessitated skilled stone carvers, most of whom were probably Egyptians who came to Rome to take advantage of what was becoming a lucrative market.

Anne Roullet has studied the surviving Egyptian and Egyptianizing monuments of imperial Rome and has observed that the exports were of relatively recent manufacture, that is, from the time of the XIXth dynasty and later; that they were produced in Lower Egypt; and that they originally came from a religious context. The Romans who stole them were selective, choosing works that were characteristic of the Roman idea of Egypt—obelisks, small pyramids, sphinxes, lions, and gods with the heads of animals. Some were chosen at random, others from sites that were especially well known, and still others because they had royal insignia of special historical or religious import. Roullet posits that the latter were selected by Egyptian priests who themselves came to Italy to manage and officiate at the new Isiac temples. In addition, Egyptian artists may have made their homes near the temples where they could find work.

While Augustus's appropriation of Egyptian obelisks was a sign of his conquest of Egypt and his ownership of Cleopatra's legacy, the arrival of these highly visible monoliths in the capital inspired a taste for things Egyptian among wealthy aristocrats. Fashionable moneyed patrons, even in the imperial circle, began to commission buildings and paintings with an Egyptian flavor. These were plentiful in the age of Augustus, and the surviving examples far outnumber the Egyptian originals. Many, if not most, of these had little to do with promoting political objectives and everything to do with being in vogue. Some were near duplicates of well-known Egyptian pieces; others were entirely new creations, done in a manner that looked "Egyptian." Once again, the artists were probably Egyptian immigrants who worked for seemingly insatiable Roman patrons.

The intended contexts for these monuments varied. Those that were made for Isis sanctuaries were religious in intention, but those that reflected a frenzied and fashionable Egyptomania turned up in a wide variety of locations including cemeteries, circuses, villas, houses, and gardens. Gaius Cestius, for example, who died around 15 B.C., erected a concrete family tomb in the shape of a pyramid, faced with marble, outside the city walls (Fig. 11.2). An inscribed base in front of the tomb names Marcus Agrippa as one of Cestius's heirs. Like so many other Romans of his day, Cestius must have heard stories and seen paintings of the marvelous monumental pyramids that in Egypt served as the last resting places of Egypt's illustrious pharaohs. An elite family with grand pretensions could hardly do better than be buried in similar royal splendor—and how envious their peers would be if they were the first in their circle to do so. Commissioning art in the Republic and early empire, at least among the elite, was a highly competitive act, and Cestius's pyramidal sepulcher was not the only one erected in Rome during this period. Others rose on Roman funerary thoroughfares such as the Via Appia and the Via Flaminia; one of them was even identified in the Middle Ages as a tomb of Augustus's nephew Marcellus. This is impossible since Marcellus

11.2. Egyptomania permeated Rome after Augustus made Egypt a Roman province, setting the stage for Gaius Cestius to build a pyramidal tomb for his family.

was buried in the Mausoleum of Augustus, but the fact that such an association was even entertained provides further evidence that Augustus and Agrippa and their families were considered appropriate honorees for monuments in the Egyptian mode. The Tomb of Cestius, in excellent condition today, is far smaller than the pyramidal tombs in Egypt's Valley of the Kings and more closely resembles later examples, especially those of the New Kingdom at Deir el-Medina or in the Sudan.

Caesar and Cicero and other wealthy Republican patrons also vied with one another to see who could have the largest and most magnificent Egyptian-style garden. The goal was to create a complete setting that conjured up the Nile or some other exotic body of water, like the Euripus, a strait in Greece between Euboea and Boeotia. A canal would serve as the main focus of the garden, around which statuary was arranged. Outer walls might be painted with complementary scenes. The extensive garden of Loreius Tiburtinus at Pompeii had such a waterway, as well as a small shrine dedicated to Isis and statuettes of pharaohs and Egyptian deities. Such Egyptian-looking complexes were among the sources for the Canopus and Serapeum at the later Tivoli Villa of the emperor Hadrian.

Augustus was not a fan of eastern cults. How much this had to do with his conflicting feelings about Cleopatra is difficult to know. That conflict is made manifest in the existence of a small room in a building in an area on the Palatine hill that was right next to Augustus's house and thus probably part of the same imperial complex. This particular residential sector was the location of the domiciles of power brokers and trendsetters in the late Republic. Packed cheek to jowl, these dwellings belonged to Cicero, Quintus Lutatius Catulus, Sulla, Marcus Licinius Calvus, Hortensius, Mark Antony, and many others.

The chamber in this residence, called the "Aula Isiaca" because of its subject matter related to Isis, was long and narrow and had an apse on one end. Its walls were painted with Egyptian motifs such as situlas (water vessels), jugs, *uraei,* lotus blossoms, and sun disks (Fig. 11.3). One wall was decorated with a Nilotic scene including pygmies and a hippopotamus, another with a veiled priestess of Isis. Nearby was a painting of the ravishing Helen, daughter of Zeus and Leda and wife of Menelaus of Sparta, who was seduced by Paris and whisked off to Troy. Yet the Helen episode depicted in the Aula Isiaca is not the traditional one but a dif-

11.3. The walls of the Aula Isiaca on the Palatine hill were painted with water jugs, rearing cobras, lotus blossoms, and sun disks, Egyptian motifs similar to those on the walls of Cleopatra's temples and shrines.

ferent interpretation corresponding to the version of the poet Stesichorus, who related that it was a phantom who went to Troy while the real Helen remained in Egypt. The Palatine scene shows Helen disembarking in Egypt with her lover Paris. This adaptation of the Helen story must have been selected because it seemed especially relevant to recent Roman events, namely Cleopatra's illicit post-Tarsus affair with Antony. The boat resembles one of Cleopatra's barges with its royal retinue, including a girl with parasol to protect Helen from the sun and wind.

A small upstairs bedroom in Augustus's own house on the Palatine hill also showed the impact of the Egyptomania that was sweeping Rome after the emperor's annexation of Egypt. The room had multicolored compartments at the top of the south wall that were enhanced by large plants with intertwined *uraei* (rearing cobras) and Egyptian crowns. Since Augustus had triumphed over Cleopatra and Egypt now belonged to him, he must have seen himself also as the proud possessor of the visual imagery of his new holding. The royal *uraei,* potent symbols of pharaonic power and comparable to those at Cleopatra's temple at Dendera, were now his regalia to display as he wished.

This was not the only place in Augustus's domicile that alluded to Egypt's former queen. In a painting that once graced the House of Augustus and is now in the Palatine Antiquarium, a woman in a distinctive Egyptian headdress and garment, carrying a situla and a plate with cone-shaped loaf of bread, makes an offering. Nearby is a sphinx that may have crowned a pedestal or an altar. Livia's Palatine house also gave a nod to Cleopatra, or at least to her Egypt, now Livia's queenly domain. Egyptian crowns and solar disks, resembling those carved on edifices at Dendera, are among the ornamental motifs on the empress's dining room wall.

Livia's former slaves also had a taste for the finer things in Egyptian life, as attested by the Egyptian insignia that turn up in the underground burial chambers of her freedmen on the Via Appia. Marble plaques from these columbaria represent *uraei* interspersed with an Egyptian pantheon of divinities, among them Isis and Horus/Harpocrates. These symbols and personalities may have been selected for display by freedmen of Egyptian origin, but it is not inconceivable that freed patrons with other origins had developed a taste for things Egyptian while in Livia's employ.

While these Egyptian motifs might be described as more decorative than doctrinaire, other painted cycles narrated stories with Egyptian protagonists. These episodes were surely chosen because they had a resonance for their patrons that went beyond fashion. The interior of the Farnesina Villa, on the bank of the Tiber, was provided with frescoes on the occasion of Julia's marriage to Agrippa in 19 B.C. The villa was decorated with a familiar-looking naval battle and a painted frieze that represents the Egyptian pharaoh Bocchoris (720–715 B.C.), with his bodyguards, serving as a judge. A series of criminal cases are presented to him, and in each instance he renders a judicious judgment. All the better if the spectator associated Bocchoris's verdicts with equally sagacious acts of Augustus. From Augustus's standpoint, the union of his only child with his closest confidant was one of the high points of his life—one that called for an appropriate home in which to raise offspring. For her part, Julia perhaps wanted a residence that presented her as a princess who was the soul mate of spirited and exotic queens like Cleopatra, not upright Roman matrons like Livia.

Even though this momentous wedding took place twelve years after Actium, the tempestuous affair between Cleopatra and Antony was already the stuff of legend. While Julia knew only too well that her marriage to the aging Agrippa would be more like Cleopatra's liaison with Caesar than with Antony, she must have relished being as fertile as Cleopatra and having sons whose careers she could support. What we know of Julia's well-documented wit also suggests that she displayed a rebellious attitude toward her father. She may have enjoyed needling him by decorating her honeymoon hideaway with remembrances of the Cleopatra her father vanquished but never possessed. After all, it was Julia who dressed one day in a daring costume and the next in one that was exceedingly proper, taunting her father with the remark: "Why, today I decked myself for my father's eyes, yesterday for my husband's."

The Egyptian references in the paintings of the Villa Farnesina go well beyond the rearing cobras and modest Isis priestess of the Aula Isiaca. While in the latter building the Isis priestess is dressed in a proper white gown and matching veil, there is distinct flamboyance to the women depicted in the Villa Farnesina. The painted Isis priestess in the villa's Cubiculum B wears an elegant belted tunic and a sparkling sky-high headdress. She stares straight ahead, icon-like, but at the same time she dramatically feeds two rearing heraldic panthers from libation dishes. Another Isis priestess in Cubiculum B shakes her rattle or sistrum in front of two crowned owls that face her and call attention to her majestically towering crown. Cleopatra's self-confidence and consummate style may well have buoyed Julia's own sense of self and encouraged her to ponder the history of women, in which she was herself an important player. Julia opted to have her artist cover the villa's walls with paintings of other fantastic women. The goddesses Venus, Diana, and Selene, Cassandra, Dionysiac priestesses, victories, caryatids, sirens, modestly and immodestly draped women, naked women embraced by men, and women musicians are portrayed in landscapes and domestic scenes and in theatrical stage settings.

The Palatine venues were residential, although Roman houses were also places where business was conducted and thus locations for visual display. That the facade of the Temple of Apollo Palatinus was readily accessible is certain. Even there, at the abode of the emperor's favorite patron god, there were references to Egypt and to Cleopatra. These, however, were more subtle than blatant, and might have been missed by a less than astute visitor. Augustus built the temple adjacent to his own residence. In this juxtaposition, he followed the lead of Hellenistic rulers, who built sanctuaries next to palaces. Although Augustus vowed to build the temple after the completion of his military campaign over Sextus Pompeius in Sicily, construction did not begin until after the Battle of Actium. The temple was dedicated in early October of 28 B.C. The temple's cella had a cult statue of Apollo with his mother Leto and his sister Diana. What is more interesting, however, is the series of terracotta plaques found in excavations in front of the temple in 1968.

The composition of each plaque is the same—a central frontal figure or object framed by two figures or animals in profile. This suggests that a master artist was given the commission and that he designed all the panels, leaving the actual execution of each to the artisans in his workshop. Thus one would expect a clearly delineated subject matter, an overarching theme that would unite all the individual episodes. Since the temple was begun a few years after Actium and honored the god who had both sired Augustus and also gave him two military victories, the scenes most likely made reference to those situations and events. It is not surprising that myth was the chosen form of communication in these scenes: the prevailing language of art in the imperial circle of Augustus was not direct but presented even current events through the veil of myth.

It is this mythological veil and the early Augustan preference for indirection that makes interpretation of these panels so interesting. What seems incontrovertible is that Apollo is honored as divine father and ensurer of victory and Augustus is heralded as divine son and savior of Rome. Together they have realized a military and moral triumph over Cleopatra and Antony, underscored by the reciprocity of the father's temple and the son's house or *domus*.

The same message was delivered through the terracotta relief scenes, which were repeated again and again for emphasis. The key scene depicting the battle between Apollo and Hercules for the Delphic tripod is, for example, the subject of nine preserved panels. Apollo and Hercules, shown in profile, each grasp a leg of the central tripod (see Fig. 7.3). While the struggle seems evenly matched, the result is preordained because Apollo, protector of the tripod, will prevail. The victories decorating the tripod ensure his success. Since statues in Rome depicted Antony as Hercules, and Augustus was garbed as Apollo at dinner parties, it would have been obvious to anyone who saw or heard about these terracotta panels that the clash over the tripod was really the contest for Rome. The mythological saga was a perfect story line for Actium. Hercules (Antony) had committed an offense and sought absolution at Apollo's shrine at Delphi. Furious at receiving no oracle, he tried to steal the tripod but was halted by Jupiter's intervention. Apollo (Octavian) retained the tripod, but Hercules was sold to Omphale (Cleopatra) as a slave.

While the historic encounter pictured here features Apollo/Octavian and Hercules/Antony, Cleopatra was alluded to in the lotus blossom (Egyptian) decoration beneath the feet of the main protagonists. Furthermore, several other plaques depicting Isis rattling her sistrum seem to be a clear reference to Cleopatra's activity at Actium. A frontal Isis, with an elaborate hairstyle and an Isiac headdress, emerges from a flowering acanthus plant, framed by heraldic female and male sphinxes. In the best-preserved plaque of this type, the female figure appears to have portrait features, an elaborate coiffure, and wears a headdress with what may be a rearing cobra—the royal Egyptian insignia. Perhaps she is meant to be Cleopatra herself. If so, the head of the male sphinx, which has an unruly flowing beard, should also be identifiable and could be her father, Auletes.

Three other surviving plaques from the Temple of Apollo Palatinus depict the story of Perseus and the Gorgon. The terrifying Gorgon, capable of turning men into stone with just a glance, is represented frontally in the center of the plaque. The pubescent Perseus, resembling an Augustan youth and wearing his winged shoes, is depicted in profile at the left. He holds the Gorgon. Minerva, at the right, grasps the polished shield she has given Perseus for protection. The story relates that Perseus, since he couldn't look directly at the Gorgon, used Minerva's shiny shield as a mirror when cutting off the Gorgon's head. Perseus's journey to kill the Gorgon was an especially perilous one, but he prevailed. Would those looking at these panels have associated the monstrous female Gorgon, who could turn men into stone with her eyes, with the venomous Cleopatra of Augustan propaganda? Would they have seen Augustus in Perseus who, under the protection and with the gifts of the gods, outsmarted this formidable woman enemy?

Other plaques from the temple represent heraldic lion griffins flanking a candelabrum, and there are surviving antefixes with Silenus heads, elephant heads, and acanthus leaves. Nine panels depict two women holding flat baskets on their heads and flanking an incense burner. The central burner has a base with three female sphinxes, a detail that emphasizes the pervasive Roman interest in Egyptian and Egyptianizing artifacts after 30 B.C. In this example, both women wear their hair parted in the center, brushed back in waves, and fastened in a bun at the back of their necks. Two other very fragmentary panels depict two women decorating a central candelabrum.

Two additional plaques portray two women ornamenting a central pedestal or betile shaped like a phallus, to which are affixed Apollo's cithara, quiver, and bow. The woman on the right wears a tiara and has a coiffure that resembles that of the other women in the panels—parted in the center, waved, and with a big bun at the back of the head. Her face is idealized, with even features and an aquiline nose, and she resembles Livia in portraits where she is assimilated to Greek goddesses, such as on the Ara Pacis. The other woman is more exotic looking, has a more prominent nose, and wears her hair in tight curls around her face and in a long waved plait of hair that falls down her back. Her exoticism and curled coiffure are Egyptianizing, and it is interesting to speculate that she might represent Cleopatra facing Livia. If those identifications are correct, the plaque may signal that Livia has triumphed over Cleopatra as Octavian did over Antony, saving Rome and becoming Egypt's new queen. The presence of the betile would seem to support such an interpretation, since betiles were common in Ptolemaic art. In addition, the betile is featured in one of the sacred landscape paintings on a wall in the Room of the Masks in the Palatine House of Augustus—another link between the respective residences of Augustus and Apollo, as well as between Rome and Egypt.

Other Apolline subjects, like the tripod and griffins, decorated the doorway of the Temple of Apollo Palatinus. Propertius describes ivory door panels there that depicted the sack of Delphi by the Gauls in 279 and the slaughter of the children of Niobe by Apollo and Diana.[4] Augustus's defense of the Roman world and his avenging of Caesar's death may be alluded to in these scenes that ostensibly depict the deeds of Apollo.

Propertius also reports that the Temple of Apollo was surrounded by a portico and that statues of Danaus and his fifty daughters were displayed in between the columns.[5] At their father's behest, all but one of the fifty brides murdered their husbands—who may also have been depicted as equestrians—on their wedding night. Scholars have suggested that the Danaids are surrogates for Cleopatra. They were descendants of Io, who was sent to Egypt and produced a family that included the brothers Aegyptus and Danaus, who in turn fathered the fifty sons and fifty daughters depicted in the temple's portico. Furthermore, there has been speculation that the family feud stands for the civil war between Octavian and Antony. The fact that the Danaids obeyed their fathers but transgressed Rome may be a further parallel for what was viewed as Cleopatra's bad behavior. Three female herms, fashioned in black marble and found in the vicinity of the Temple of Apollo (now in the Palatine Antiquarium), may be a subset of the temple's original Danaid statuary group. That this assemblage was well known and imitated in its day is suggested by several bronze figures of women dressed in the peplos; these figures, which come from the peristyle of the Villa of the Papyri in

Herculaneum and are now in the Archaeological Museum in Naples, appear to be based on the Palatine prototypes.

In fact, the terracotta plaques from the Temple of Apollo have a larger number of female protagonists than male ones, reminding us of Cleopatra's power. The message of these relief scenes was that Augustus's conquest of a female fury at Actium underscored his success as Rome's savior, a victory made possible through the unwavering support of Apollo.

12

DIVINE ALTER EGOS

The intense rivalry among elite Republican men for the most compelling building project was matched by a more personal competition. These individuals vied with one another through the gods and personifications they chose as their personal gurus and family ancestors. The world according to Caesar, for one, included his Julian lineage from Venus Genetrix.

Privileged Roman leaders in the age of Augustus continued to take a cue from earlier Hellenistic dynasts, among them the Ptolemies. Every Ptolemy had his *ka,* an aspect of his personality that generated a life-giving force, and possessed godlike qualities that gave him the capacity to lead. These special traits were highlighted through the royal names or titularies that were attached to these dynasts. Cleopatra was the goddess who loves her father, *thea philopator;* and Auletes, as *Neos Dionysos,* possessed characteristics of his divine namesake. These titularies were not just honorific but carried ethical and religious obligations for the king to defend his country, look after his people, and revere his gods. Several strategies were used in Ptolemaic portraiture to emphasize the godliness of its subjects: they were paired with divinities whose identity was immediately recognizable, like Re or Horus; they were endowed with the headdresses or attributes of such divinities; and their statuary was made from a precious material or its surface was polished or gilded, in the manner of Cleopatra's statue in Rome.

Other Hellenistic kingdoms had similar approaches to royal portraiture, but such practices were not deemed appropriate in Republican Rome. Nevertheless, although the Romans eschewed divine titles and godlike statuary in Rome, they sometimes flirted with such associations in the eastern part of the empire where that kind of assimilation was firmly entrenched. And even in Rome, some subtle dalliances between leader and god infiltrated the visual culture of the capital in the first century B.C. Ptolemaic portraiture was one of several models for that of the triumvirs and their wives, and Cleopatra must have played some part in making it relevant.

It is not surprising that the greatest liberties were taken by Antony—he spent more time in the East than Caesar or Augustus, and he married a Ptolemaic queen and fathered three children who received their own royal titles and were portrayed in the traditional Egyptian manner. Yet while many works of art featuring Antony's divine associations, for example the Athenian group portrait depicting him as Osiris and Cleopatra as Isis, were intended for an eastern audience, others turned up in highly visible western contexts. Since only a small proportion of the pictorial imagery of this period survives, it is not easy to decipher the intended messages or to be certain for whom they were planned.

The Romans, like the Ptolemies, were mythmakers and effectively interwove their personal histories with the sagas of their divine benefactors. As Octavian and Antony played out their contest for supreme power on the stage of the ancient world, they turned to the gods not only as guardians but also to amplify themselves in the eyes of their supporters. Plutarch suggests that Antony's masculinity reminded people of the machismo of Hercules.[1] There were apparently statues of Antony depicting him with the well-muscled body and mighty club of Hercules. A carved stone from a ring, found at Pompeii and thought to depict Hercules with the face of Antony, suggests that Antony's supporters in Italy wore rings of their champion, which they may also have used as a seal. As Antony's life changed, so did his divine affiliation. When he entered Cleopatra's orbit, the rough-edged Hercules, so at home among the soldiery, seemed a less appropriate companion for an elegant and cultivated queen. Plutarch confirms that it was not long before Antony changed his costume, emerging in the East as the courtly Dionysus and making quite a public show of his new affiliation: "As Antony entered Ephesus, women garbed as maenads, men and youths as satyrs and Pans all sported before him. The city was filled with ivy and *thyrsoi* [poles carried by Dionysus and other participants in Bacchic festivities], with the music of the flute, syrinx [pipes], and lyre. All welcomed him as Dionysus bringer of joy, gentle and kind."[2]

As Dionysus, and also assimilated to the Egyptian Osiris, Antony was a perfect partner for Cleopatra, already a fetching fusion of Isis and Venus. Such guises readied the duo for their "inimitable life." Dionysiac costume parties were all the rage in the late Republic, some linked to solemn ritual and others somewhat more fanciful. The Dionysiac celebration painted on the walls of a room in Pompeii's Villa of the Mysteries preserves one such event, culminating in a scene of Dionysus reclining languorously in the lap of Ariadne.

Not one to be outdone by his opponent in the East, Octavian held his own soirée in Rome. The theme was a banquet of the twelve gods, with Octavian choosing Apollo as his alter ego. Although the party was a private one, word got out, possibly through a letter of Antony's, and caused a scandal, especially because the festivities took place during a serious food shortage in Rome. The day after, the word in the street was that "the Gods have gobbled all the grain" and, most important in this context, "Caesar is Apollo, true—but he's Apollo of the Torments."[3]

Octavian had long been in lockstep with Apollo. Apollo was widely viewed as Octavian's divine father,[4] and two times, first after his war with Sextus Pompeius in Sicily and then after Actium, Octavian vowed he would build a temple in Rome to his patron god. After the deaths of Antony and Cleopatra, the promise was finally realized.

As Octavian and Antony began to swagger in their respective surroundings as Apollo and Dionysus, Octavian made a fascinating decision. He needed an insignia that he could use as a seal for letters and dispatches. Antony had such an emblem, and so did Alexander and the Hellenistic kings. In the last years of his life, Caesar had a signet ring depicting an armed Venus, militarily potent but also recalling the nurturing mother of the Julian family. Furthermore, after his assassination, Caesar himself became a kind of good luck charm. Caesar's supporters may have worn rings with the dictator's portrait after his death and especially as a talisman in their campaign against Cassius and Brutus. An iron ring with a gilded portrait of Caesar, now in London, may have belonged to one of the triumvirs, even Octavian himself. Octavian may also have inherited Caesar's Venus seal. Before long, however, he chose his own insignia: a sphinx. This choice was noteworthy enough to be remarked upon by Suetonius, Pliny, and Dio Cassius. Suetonius gives the following description: "On letters of recommendation, documents, and personal letters he [Octavian] at first used a sphinx as his seal design, later a portrait of Alexander the Great, and finally his own portrait cut by the hand of Dioscurides; the last of these continued to be used by succeeding emperors."[5]

Here are Pliny's comments on Octavian's seal: "The divine Augustus at the beginning of his career used a seal engraved with a sphinx. He had found among his mother's rings two which were remarkably similar. During the civil war whenever he himself was absent his friends used one of these as a seal on letters and edicts which the conditions of the time made it necessary to issue; and it was a standing wry joke among those who received them to say that the sphinx had come bearing its riddles."[6]

Finally, here is the account of Dio Cassius: "He also gave to Agrippa and to Maecenas so great authority in all matters that they might even read beforehand the letters which he wrote to the senate and to others and then change whatever they wished in them. To this end, they also received from him a ring, so that they might be able to seal the letters again. For he had caused to be made in duplicate the seal which he had used most at that time, the design being a sphinx, the same on each copy; since it was not until later that he had his own likeness engraved upon his seal and sealed everything with that. It was this latter that the emperors who succeeded him employed, except Galba, who adopted a seal which his ancestors had used, its device being a dog looking out of a ship's prow."[7]

What is to be made of this choice? It may mean nothing at all, since Pliny suggests that Octavian discovered by chance two similar sphinx rings among the belongings of his mother, Atia. And yet what better mascot when facing the rattle-shaking Isis/Cleopatra than a demon with Egyptian roots? The sphinxes of Egypt were portrayed as reclining male lions with a pharaoh's head and false beard. The Great Sphinx at Giza probably depicts the pharaoh Khafre as Horus, honoring his divine father Khufu, who was identified with Re, the sun. In fact, Khafre bore the title Sa-Re, or son of Re. In Archaic Greece, sphinxes were female, and the type may have been transported to Greece via the East. Greek sphinxes were thought to be evil spirits who captured people and murdered them, and also soothsayers who specialized in riddles.

If Paul Zanker is right that for Augustus the sphinx was a symbol of the *regnum Apollonis* with oracular powers, Augustus's choice suggests that both Egyptian and Greek models were known and understood. Augustus would have favored a close association with Apollo. As he began to take on the role of Egypt's pharaoh, Augustus was also about to become Horus's representative on earth. At the same time, it is certain that Augustan artists were looking at Greek rather than Egyptian models when they fashioned a sphinx for Atia's rings.

Augustan seal impressions and coins depict a Greek type—a female sphinx, sitting up on her haunches, with outstretched wings. The Augustan artists, however, gave this Greek sphinx what may have been a decidedly Roman flourish. While in some specimens the sphinx's hair looks like a cap rendered in the severe style of Greek sculpture (480–450 B.C.), other examples show a coiffure that looks remarkably like Octavia's and Livia's *nodus,* with protrusions of hair in the center of the forehead and at the nape of the neck.

Cistophoric coins with portraits of Augustus on the obverse and the sphinx on the reverse were struck in the East between 27 and 26 B.C.—thus beginning in the year when Octavian became Augustus (Fig. 12.1). C. H. V. Sutherland thinks it is highly likely that these sphinxes are based on Augustus's seal, but he rejects any allusion to Egypt because of the Greek character of the sphinx.

To brand Roman coin reverses with the image of Augustus's signet ring, a sign of his authority, made perfect sense in the year 27; so did the choice of the sphinx, because it referred to Augustus's victory in a civil war and also over Egypt. Despite its Egyptian allusions, the choice of a Greek sphinx type by Augustus and his advisers is not surprising. First, the selection may not have been calculated since the sphinx motif decorated Atia's ring; second, Augustus's sphinx referred to Cleopatra's Egypt, and Cleopatra was a Macedonian Greek rather than an Egyptian; finally, though Augustus frequently appropriated Cleopatra's images for himself, he sometimes gave them a decidedly Greco-Roman twist. Whether Augustus's use of a sphinx seal was a reflection of Atia's taste or whether it was Octavian's deliberate appropriation of an icon of Egypt will likely

12.1. As emperor, Augustus sealed his first official letters with a signet ring bearing a Greek-style sphinx, just like the one on contemporary coins.

never be known. The fact that Octavian's second signet ring had a portrait of Alexander the Great might suggest that Octavian continued to favor insignia with Macedonian/Egyptian connections, but it may also have had nothing to do with Cleopatra. As noted earlier, there was a long-standing emulation of Alexander among Roman generals and statesmen before and independent of Cleopatra.

Nonetheless, more than a decade after the Battle of Actium, the sphinx remained a fixture of Augustan art. In the most famous surviving portrait of the emperor—the marble statue from Livia's villa at Primaporta (Fig. 12.2)—the shoulders are ornamented with heraldic sphinxes. The statue appears to be a copy of a bronze image of Augustus of around 20 B.C. When this particular statue was fashioned for Livia's residence, the decorated breastplate was added and the emperor was depicted as a *divus,* which he became after his death in 14 B.C. Augustus's bare feet reveal his divine status. Although most of the scene on the breastplate is devoted to

12.2. The sphinx remained a potent symbol of Augustus's conquest of Egypt even after his death, when sphinxes were carved on the breastplate of a statue depicting him as a god.

an episode depicting Tiberius receiving the Parthian standards, perhaps Tiberius's greatest moment, Augustus is already ethereal, having by this time been elevated above such temporal events. The scene of the return of the standards is featured in the center of the breastplate, but the ornamentation above signifies the emperor's entrance into a heavenly realm inhabited by personifications of the Sun, Moon, and Sky, as well as a pair of sphinxes. That the sphinxes are prominent and closest to the deified emperor suggests that Augustus's victory over Cleopatra remained paramount. The boy on the dolphin at Augustus's feet has been variously identified as Cupid or Gaius Caesar, or an assimilation of both. If it is Cupid on a dolphin, it probably refers to Augustus's victory over Cleopatra at Actium. If it is Gaius, he is intentionally as proximate to Augustus here as Caesarion may have been to Cleopatra in her statue in the Temple of Venus Genetrix.

The assimilation of Octavian, Antony, and Cleopatra to their divine counterparts was capitalized on not only to score points for themselves but also to malign one another through negative campaigning. Antony's compatriots might admire him when, as Hercules, he mightily swung his club, but when the club was brandished by Omphale instead, they would have felt nothing but shame. Hercules became a slave to the Lydian Queen as punishment for committing a murder, and she rendered him so feminine that he wore women's clothes and did their work. Plutarch thought that Cleopatra's disarming of Antony was comparable to Omphale's wearing Hercules's lion skin and pilfering his club.[8]

Fragmentary clay molds that depict the saga of Hercules and Omphale were probably also intended as pronouncements against Antony, readily interpreted that way by a public eager to take sides. Although the early Augustan silver bowl from which these molds were made has long since disappeared, the surviving impressions suggest that these narratives were common in the age of Augustus (Figs. 12.3 and 12.4). Their small size

12.3. Probably commissioned by a partisan of Augustus who favored tableware with politically charged themes, these clay molds cast Mark Antony (Hercules) as the effeminate tool of an empowered Cleopatra (Omphale with a club).

12.4. A scene portraying Antony and Cleopatra in the guise of Hercules and Omphale on this clay mold suggests that the couple's exploits were the subject of gossip.

made them attractive vehicles for spreading censorious gossip in the guise of everyday tableware. The scenes make fun of an effeminate Antony wearing a flimsy costume, his delicate skin protected by a parasol held by a female attendant, riding in a chariot led by centaurs. As he glances behind him, Antony catches sight of an empowered Cleopatra. She has a regal bearing and looks straight ahead, wearing Hercules's skin like a royal tiara. The club rests comfortably across her right arm as if it had always belonged there. While her attendant has a fan, Cleopatra is sturdy enough to need no protection from the sun.

These molds reflect Augustan partisanship and suggest that Cleopatra, in this case disguised as one of her alter egos, had authority over Antony. As we have seen, Cleopatra also had an impact on Augustus when it came to the visual arts. Through pictorial experiments like the scenes on these molds, Augustus came to realize that clothing imperial policy in the veil of myth, a practice that had a long and illustrious history in Greece, had a future in a new Roman art. That approach soon became the cornerstone of Augustus's Ara Pacis Augustae.

13

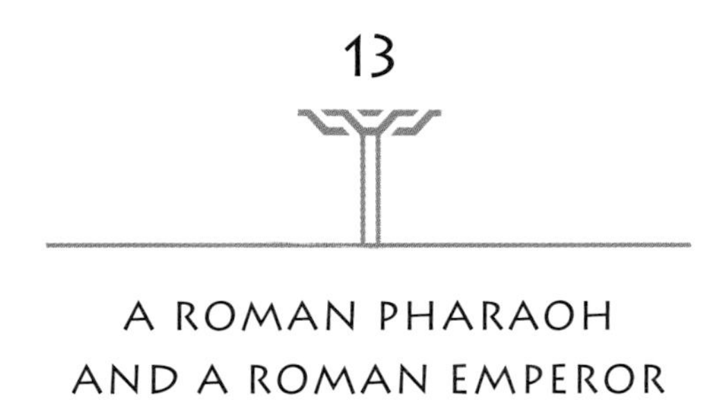

A ROMAN PHARAOH AND A ROMAN EMPEROR

Octavian became master of Egypt even before he became Augustus, and thus inherited the traditional rights of the pharaohs and their Ptolemaic successors. One of these was to celebrate the official cults and to be depicted as so doing on the walls of Egypt's temples. Both Augustus and the local priests had compelling reasons to maintain an unbroken tradition of building and restoring temples and decorating them with appropriate scenes and inscriptions. The priests were probably given the authority by Rome to continue with business as usual, but it is likely that Roman advisers, with close ties to the emperor's circle, were chosen as well to participate in mapping a general pictorial strategy for Augustus in Egypt. Although we will never know the names of those who participated in these discussions, it is very probable that the script that emerged owed a great deal to the aims and ideology of Rome's first emperor and reflected the fact that Egypt was not just any new Roman acquisition.

The Egyptian monuments that were built or refurbished during the principate of Augustus demonstrate that the plan was to preserve prevailing custom and portray the emperor in appropriate Egyptian costume, paying obeisance to the usual Egyptian pantheon of deities (Fig. 13.1). Augustus was depicted in strict profile and without much reference to his personal physiognomy, imparting the message that Augustus's ascendance to power in Egypt was in the natural course of things. Before long, Augustus was the star of an impressive array of narrative relief sculptures

13.1. After Cleopatra's suicide, Augustus replaced her as pharaoh in temple narratives all over Egypt. At the Temple of el-Dakka in Nubia, for example, Augustus makes an offering to Thoth, Shu, and Tefnut.

in Egypt that were begun immediately after that country came into Roman possession. Although Augustus could have authorized the destruction of Cleopatra's palace and temples, he let them stand in Egypt, as he did the gilded statue and assorted trophies in Rome. The meaning of this decision seems clear. Augustus and his advisers wanted him to be perceived as the legitimate overseer of Cleopatra's Egypt, who would guide it as Cleopatra and the Ptolemies had done before him.

It is noteworthy that Augustus's legitimacy as Egypt's newest "Pharaoh" did not extend to his wife Livia, especially since it was Ptolemaic tradition for the queen to be honored in art as the king's spouse or co-regent. While scholars are uncertain as to the nature of the political power of some of these Ptolemaic women, it seems likely that they were important participants in cult practice, as suggested by their inclusion in scenes that depict such activity. Yet the ritual scenes that featured Augustus as participant do not include Livia. As we shall see, however, Livia did find a place on the coinage of Alexandria, where she was featured as Egypt's new queen—an interesting ascendance that had no parallel for her in Augustan Rome.

Temple building in Egypt in Roman times followed the pharaonic and Ptolemaic pattern. Temples at important sites were rebuilt and expanded, while others were commissioned anew. All were constructed in the traditional Egyptian way with the same cultic components, decorated in a similar manner. Most of the main protagonists were the same as they had always been—the ubiquitous Isis, Osiris, Horus/Harpocrates, and so on. What did the emperor's advisers make of these foreign gods, so recently maligned by Augustan poets in their partisan support of Octavian over Antony? In the *Aeneid*, for example, Virgil describes Cleopatra trailed by a motley array of Egyptian deities with an animalistic nature—a strong contrast to the august stature of the core Roman divinities: "Never turning her head as yet to see twin snakes of death behind, while monster forms of gods of every race, and the dog-god Anubis barking, held their weapons against our Neptune, Venus, and Minerva . . . Mars, engraved in steel, raged in the fight . . . Overlooking it all, Actian Apollo."[1] Propertius called Cleopatra, whom he deliberately does not mention by name, "the harlot queen of licentious Canopus [who] dared to pit barking Anubis against our Jupiter and to force the Tiber to endure the threats of the Nile."[2] Whatever their opinion, these advisers made the strategic decision (or tacitly approved the choice made by the Egyptian priests) to allow Augustus to cavort with the enemy, so to speak, by having him present traditional gifts to the very deities who had recently stood behind Cleopatra and in opposition to the Roman state gods. While Augustus continued to have little patience for Isis in Rome, he was portrayed offering obeisance to her in a large number of sites along the Nile.

At locations in Upper Egypt, Augustus appeared again and again in the presence of Egyptian luminaries—humans who were gods, and divinities whose sacredness no one questioned. In an extraordinary twist, Augustus was portrayed as venerating those whom he had vanquished rather than as the conqueror receiving their acclamation, tribute, or reverence. At the Temple of Hathor at Dendera, Cleopatra's own temple where she had proudly presented herself not only as queen but also as the mother of the pharaoh Ptolemy XV Caesarion, Augustus was eager to leave his mark. The emperor appears in a wide variety of locations around the temple complex. In most of the relief scenes, he stands before the usual cast of Egyptian divinities and pays them homage. On each side of the doorway in the outer hypostyle, for example, Augustus offers an obelisk to the serpent-headed Hu, Horus, and Hathor, at the very time that he was transporting such monoliths to Rome as trophies. On the east exterior wall of the temple, Augustus participates in foundation and dedication ceremonies. He is shown departing the palace, measuring the temple, pouring sand in front of Isis, presenting bricks to Harsomtus, and offering the temple to Hathor and Horus. It was the rear wall of the temple that depicted Cleopatra and Caesarion, and it is therefore not surprising that Augustus wanted to join them there.

Cleopatra and Caesarion process on the lower part of the wall, where Augustus had his name inscribed right next to their likenesses (see Fig. 5.6). The double scenes flank a head of Hathor. On the left side, Caesarion, his *ka*, and Cleopatra approach the sequence of small versions of Harsomtus, Isis, Harsomtus, Osiris, Horus, and Isis. On the right, they advance toward a diminutive Ihy, Hathor, Horus, Harsomtus, Ihy, and Hathor. Augustus added a frieze of five scenes to the upper section of the wall, depicting him on the left before Isis, Harsomtus, and in front of Horus and Hathor. On the right, the emperor is represented with an image of Ma'et and small Ihy before Hathor and two figures of Horus. He also presents mirrors to Isis and Harsomtus. In this way, the rear wall preserved for posterity what must have seemed the unbroken line of succession from Cleopatra to Augustus, and proclaimed that it was Augustus who became emperor of Rome and also Egypt's pharaoh in place of Caesarion.

That Augustus made this temple his own is attested not only by his frequent presence in the temple's relief scenes but also by the later appearances of many of his imperial successors. All of the Julio-Claudians added their portraits to the display, as did the second-century emperors from Trajan to Marcus Aurelius. It seemed that inheriting Egypt as an imperial possession required Augustus's Roman successors to add their names and images to his on Cleopatra's temple. Just as the Egyptian queen's gilded statue in Rome remained an icon, so too did her temple in Egypt.

At the Temple of Horus at Dendera, Tiberius is depicted offering wine to Hathor and Horus. Claudius, holding scepters and sistrums, appears before various Egyptian deities, as does Caligula. Nero, followed by *ka,* leaves the palace and later offers such interesting gifts as a small model temple to Isis, a head-cloth with new year's wishes to Ma'et, and eye-paint to Isis and Harsomtus. The Flavian emperor Domitian offers milk to Hathor, who is suckling Horus. Marcus Aurelius appears before Harsomtus and Amun. Scenes of infant deities, primarily Horus, being suckled abound at Dendera, and the significance of the birth and nourishment of children was not lost on Augustus.

Thus the Roman emperors were taking up where the Ptolemaic dynasts had left off, with the Egyptian temple complexes becoming long-term projects that each new emperor augmented. Augustus was the first Roman emperor whose likeness was added to the Temple of Haroeris and Sobek Triads at Kom Ombo, a temple where Ptolemy XIII, one of Cleopatra's brothers, was honored as *neos Dionysos,* although earlier Ptolemies, Cleopatras, and the like were also celebrated there. Ptolemy appears over and over again in the traditional processional scenes, and one of the bases in the temple's court depicts Augustus with a similar entourage of deities. Later emperors from Tiberius to Marcus Aurelius once again followed suit.

The Temple of Isis at Philae was another Upper Egyptian temple that Augustus set his sights on. Both Augustus and Tiberius appear in scenes on a wall behind columns in the temple's court. The figural vignettes are familiar by now—the emperors making offerings to Egyptian divinities like Isis, Hathor, Osiris, and Horus. An upper register depicts Nero in like fashion. Trajan and Hadrian make appearances elsewhere in the complex. It is worth noting that this is another temple where Ptolemy XIII was honored as *neos Dionysos,* although his commemoration was hardly exclusive; he followed numerous earlier Ptolemies and Cleopatras who were also portrayed with the gods at the Philae Isis temple. The exterior west wall of the main temple also displayed Augustus and Tiberius in prominent positions. In the registers depicting Augustus, the emperor appears before the usual deities and is accompanied by Nile gods and field goddesses. The Temple of Hathor at Philae also featured Augustus, as did the Temple of Khnum on the island of Elephantine.

Some temples were built as new commissions by Augustus and his Roman successors. The Temple of Isis at Shanhur, a commission of Augustus and Tiberius, is a case in point. Since the project was their own undertaking, they might have had more leeway in the subject matter and design, but even here there is no divergence from the traditional. Augustus makes the same offerings to the same gods in numerous scenes on the entranceway to the sanctuary and in the sanctuary itself. The exterior represents Tiberius in like manner.

No area received more attention from the pharaohs and Ptolemies than Karnak on the east bank of the Nile. Auletes had been active there, and so was Augustus. Augustus focused on the southwestern group of temples, adding a room to the Temple of Khons, where he was depicted with an image of Ma'et before Amun, Ptah, the deities of the elements, and Hathor. It is not surprising that Augustus was also interested in the Temple of Apet at Karnak. Already begun by Ptolemy VII, this temple was augmented and further decorated by Auletes. Augustus's contribution was the exterior ornamentation of Sanctuary X.

In reliefs on the intercolumnar walls of the forecourt at the Temple of Isis at Dabod, located in Nubia in the Nile Valley above Aswan, Augustus is shown openly expressing adoration of Amun, presenting an image of Ma'et to Osiris, and offering victims and a vase to Isis. Osiris, Isis, and Horus receive incense and a libation from the emperor. Some of this activity takes place in the presence of Imhotep, the architect of Djoser's Step Pyramid and one of the few non-royal Egyptians who achieved mythical status and was revered as a great sage and even a god.

The emperor is depicted in relief sculpture making offerings to the usual deities—Horus, Isis, and Osiris—at other temples in Nubia. These include the Great Temple of Mandulis (a Nubian god) at Kalabsha, the Temple of Thoth of Pnubs (also Nubian), and the Temple of Augustus at Dendur, now in the Sackler Wing of the Metropolitan Museum of Art (Fig. 13.2). Dendur, like Shanhur, was a commission of Augustus, dedicated to the local gods Pedesi and Pihor.

13.2. In full pharaonic regalia, Augustus (at left) sacrifices to Thoth and Sekhmet at the Temple of Augustus at Dendur, today on view at the Metropolitan Museum of Art in New York.

I have suggested that what motivated Augustus to allow himself to be depicted with the posture, clothing, and headdress of an Egyptian king was his wish to be viewed in Egypt as the natural successor to the Pharaohs and the Ptolemies and their most recent queen, Cleopatra. Caesar and Antony had paved the way for a union of Rome and Egypt. It remained for Augustus to finalize the merger. He did so by making Egypt an imperial protectorate, a fact that was best expressed visually by the coalescence of Roman emperor and Ptolemaic monarch. Taking on the clothing and attributes of the Egyptian sovereign allowed Augustus to beat Caesar and Antony at their own game. While Caesar had been Cleopatra's Roman consort, and Antony played Osiris to her Isis, Augustus bested them all by becoming pharaoh. Egypt was his own private playground. Local deities who had once opposed him were now his supporters and benefited from his largesse, as depicted in temple relief sculpture all over Egypt. The repetitiousness of these scenes made them into a symbol of kingship (possible for Augustus in Egypt but not in Rome) rather than an accurate narrative of cult practice.

It would be misleading, however, to dismiss Augustus's assimilation to a foreign sovereign as a routine event—quite the contrary. While Augustus was a frequent actor in relief sculpture carved in the western and eastern provinces, he was customarily shown there as a clean-shaven and handsome Roman youth with a distinctive cap of hair. In these other provinces he was portrayed in a way that was particularly Roman, not as a foreign potentate paying obeisance to alien gods. In sculptured reliefs on major monuments from sites as far away from each other as North Italy (the Arch of Augustus at Susa) and Asia Minor (the Sebasteion at Aphrodisias), Augustus appeared as himself.

To make the transition of power in Egypt look seamless, however, Augustus became the new pharaoh and was portrayed as such in processional cycles all over the country. And on the official coinage of Alexandria, Livia was depicted as the new queen, although with a decidedly Roman appearance. Egypt thus had a special status, a unique position that distinguished it from all the other territories in the Augustan age. No other Roman province was identified as the emperor's property. It is apparent that Augustus wanted to possess not only Egypt but also Cleopatra of Egypt, with the objective not of destroying her but of owning her. He achieved this by putting himself in her place, taking over her status and her official activities. In a sense, Augustus became both Cleopatra's consort in the tradition of Caesar and Antony, and also her alter ego.

Augustus was a consummate politician and seems to have realized early on that he needed to tailor his message to his audience. He must have adopted this as his mantra: when in Alexandria do as the Alexandrians do, and when in Rome do as the Romans do. In developing this philosophy, Octavian had learned from Antony's fatal mistakes. It had seemed that Antony had it all, including a beautiful aristocratic wife who was the sister of a fellow triumvir. Yet he recklessly left her behind, tending hearth and home and conducting family business, while he cavorted with a foreign queen in decidedly non-Roman locales. Antony also squandered his special status as Caesar's protégé in favor of living the "inimitable life" with Cleopatra. Furthermore, Antony ignored the power of place, preferring worldly experiences to everlasting fame. "Let Antony be Antony" was Mark Antony's philosophy.

Octavian was apparently savvier than Antony, recognizing that he could make people believe what he wanted them to believe. To be effective in Egypt, Octavian shrewdly recognized that he had to become a pharaoh and, as we have seen, commissioned narrative temple relief sculpture that portrayed him in the act of offering obeisance to the Egyptian pantheon of gods. In Rome, of course, such images would have been sacrilege. There, Octavian rejected the pharaohs and Ptolemies as portrait models and substituted the more acceptable Alexander the Great. Octavian's immediate predecessors, Pompey, Caesar, and Antony, had been enamored of the King of Macedon's mystique and had already circulated around Rome images of themselves as nouveaux Alexanders. While Octavian ridiculed the dead Ptolemies in Alexandria as mere cadavers, he revered the deceased Alexander as a monarch with continued capacity to motivate. On his pilgrimage to view Alexander's remains, Octavian touched him as if he were an icon with magical powers.

That Octavian considered Alexander to be an apt model was smart but not surprising. Octavian was a youth when he began his rise to power and only 32 when he became master of the ancient world. Surrounded by elderly senators and following in the footsteps of an aging Caesar, Octavian surely recognized his youth as an asset that could be accentuated in his portraits. Searching the distant and recent past for archetypes, Octavian was drawn to the exuberant energy of Alexander. The fact that Alexander founded Alexandria with a Macedonian dynasty, of which Cleopatra was the last sovereign, perhaps connected the two in Octavian's mind. Cleopatra's youthfulness and vitality also made her a seductive model. Both Alexander and Cleopatra died when they were in their thirties, and Octavian must have learned from their example about the potency of youthful images frozen in time. Although he lived to be 76 years old, Octavian apparently decided that he would nonetheless be forever young, and the majority of his surviving portraits depict him as a virile man in his mid-thirties.

Octavian may in fact have viewed his military victory over Cleopatra and Antony at Actium as comparable to Alexander's world conquest. Octavian became master of Cleopatra's Egypt and Alexander's Alexandria. Having their rich resources at his disposal enabled Octavian to think in a grander way about rebuilding Rome in the image of Alexandria but also provided him with a wealth of symbolic currency. Cleopatra and Alexander were both buried in Alexandria, making it a sacred place.

While youthfulness was a hallmark of the portraits of both Cleopatra and Alexander, it was Alexander's likeness that served as the primary model for Octavian's first portrait type, created just after his victory at Actium (around 30 B.C.) and usually called the Actium type. Alexander's numismatic and sculptured portraits, still widely visible in Octavian's day, portrayed the Macedonian general in a flamboyant manner with wide, expressive eyes, a vivacious visage, and lively locks of streaming hair (see Fig. 8.1). After Actium, Octavian's authority was Alexander-like, making it appropriate for him to affect Alexander's dramatic toss of the head, mobile face, and full head of layered hair, as apparent in a marble head of Octavian in the Capitoline Museum (see Fig. 2.4). The deep creases between Octavian's eyes emphasize his determination as a military commander in the tradition of Alexander, and the studied disorder of his locks seems to demonstrate that he, like Alexander, was an inspired general.

Once he was settled into his principate, Octavian chose to tone down his portrait, stripping it of Alexander's dynamic energy and investing it instead with the immutable perfection of a Greek god. Apollo became Octavian's favored patron, and his second portrait type (named the Primaporta type after a portrait in Livia's villa at Primaporta) radiated Apolline beauty and serenity. It was an image carefully chosen to reflect a new message. For a Roman military commander on the rise, the consummate general Alexander had been the ideal role model. Now that Cleopatra and Antony were dead and Egypt was his, Octavian was free to concentrate on bringing peace to a world that had seen far too much bloodshed.

The Primaporta portrait type of Augustus, created around 27 B.C. and no later than 20 B.C., diverged from the Actium type in a number of significant ways (see Fig. 12.2). The abrupt torsion of the neck is gone, as are the deep creases above the eyes. The emperor is now the serene consolidator of the state rather than a resolute warrior. The activist locks of hair, tousled in the wind, are replaced by an immutable cap of hair with every strand in place. The likely model for this idealized image of the emperor is a famous fifth-century B.C. statue of a Greek athlete, the Doryphorus or Spear-bearer of Polykleitos; a fine Roman bronze copy of the head is now in the Archaeological Museum in Naples.

It was only in his last portrait type, known as the Forbes type, that Augustus relinquished his hold on the past. Probably created some time after the Primaporta type, the Forbes type, exemplified by a portrait in the Galleria Borghese in Rome, depicts Augustus with some of the signs of age. Creases near his eyes and mouth reveal the passage of time and his willingness to acknowledge it. That he was finally his own man underscores the confidence that his continued authority had conferred on him.

14

ROME ON THE TIBER

While Cleopatra's vital spirit continued to shine brightly in Egypt, its radiance was no less vibrant in Rome. The gilded statue in the Temple of Venus Genetrix, installed by Caesar, was gleaming still, and Augustus set out to continue and even enhance Caesar's renovation of Rome. His decision to do this was significant. Caesar had been by nature a great builder, and his relationship with Cleopatra and exposure to Alexandria had caused his ambitions to soar; he set out to achieve on the banks of the Tiber a blueprint for a new Rome that was unprecedented. The sights he had seen during his sojourn in Egypt and his barge trip along the Nile—the jutting profiles of the pyramids, the lofty heights of the obelisks, the opulence of variegated marbles—surely inspired him to revitalize Rome in the image of pharaonic and Ptolemaic Egypt. This is not to say that he engaged in wholesale imitation, however. Caesar was always aware of what was appropriate to Rome and what architectural and artistic vocabulary suited a city on the Tiber. What his Egyptian experience encouraged him to build were monuments that were large and impressive enough not to be forgotten, and structures that preserved for posterity not only the essence of the gods but also the deeds of their representatives on earth.

The ethos of the Republic was that triumphant generals were responsible for using the wealth of their victories to benefit the people of Rome and the city's urban fabric. Retrofitting Rome with new monuments and art to enhance them was a goal of all the Republican *triumphatore,* whose diverse interests and varied artistic predilections led to a vital but uncoordinated cityscape. Caesar was prescient enough to recognize that he needed to tame the ad hoc growth of Rome and encourage a more systematic urban plan. His pursuit of these goals was canceled by his death. The triumvirs, however, through their teams of advisers, architects, and designers, were ready as a group to fill the breach.

Together they "eagerly did everything which tended to [Caesar's] honor, in expectation of some day being themselves thought worthy of like honors."[1] (The dictator's deification in 42 B.C. was accompanied by a triumviral order to complete the Curia and to initiate a temple in Caesar's honor in the Roman Forum. Nonetheless, the triumvirs didn't throw themselves into this undertaking with equal vigor. Antony was willing to buy into a triumviral commitment but was too busy shoring up his eastern empire to fund additional projects on his own. Lepidus was tired and indifferent. It was Octavian who stepped up to the plate, recognizing the power of place and resuming the dictator's redesign of Rome on the kind of grand scale that would rival Alexandria. Octavian capitalized on his blood relationship to the dictator—a public relations ploy sanctioned by the gods, who ensured that lightning struck the Tumulus Juliae when Octavian entered Rome following Caesar's assassination.[2] Octavian concretized these claims by continuing Caesar's building projects, among them the completion of the Basilica Julia and the Rostra in the Roman Forum, as well as the construction and dedication of the Temple of Divine Caesar in the same locale. He also completed Caesar's Forum and Temple of Venus Genetrix.

Rivaling Alexandria by building Rome at Egypt's expense must have thrilled Octavian. It was his victory over Cleopatra in 31 and the absorption of Egypt into the Roman Empire in 30 that enabled Octavian to get Caesar's redesign of Rome up and running again. Like Caesar, Octavian recognized that what was key was a genuine urban plan and monumental structures that proclaimed Rome's place among the great cities of the ancient world. While Octavian wanted Rome to be as impressive as Alexandria, he also wanted the capital of his empire to be distinctively Roman. The objective was not to build Alexandria on the Tiber but a Rome that was more dazzling than its archetype. Replacing Roman basilicas and temples with Egyptian versions would have sent the wrong message. Commissioning temple relief sculpture depicting Octavian paying obeisance to Egyptian deities would have been political suicide. The Roman aristocracy had already demonstrated its uneasiness with the prospect that Caesar might move the capital of the empire from Rome to Alexandria, and Octavian was too smart to raise that red flag again. What would be acceptable was to scatter a few Egyptian obelisks and diminutive pyramids across the urban landscape as symbols of Rome's subjugation of Egypt.

Although the art and architecture of Augustus did not replicate Egyptian prototypes, it participated in a complex discourse with the art and architecture of Cleopatra, Caesar, and Antony. Even its existence was predicated on Egypt's wealth and position in the world. The only civic project that can be directly associated with Egyptian *manubiae* (funds obtained from the sale of booty) was the reworking of the Via Flaminia, as Diane Favro points out; but it was Egyptian plunder that made possible various architectural projects all over the city. These included the Curia and probably even the Forum of Augustus and the Temple of Mars Ultor. Favro notes that the private land on which both were constructed was purchased from these funds *(ex manubiis)* and that the source was likely the Egyptian treasury; the representation of the Egyptian god Amun in the upper story of the forum's side porticoes would seem to substantiate the connection.

Egypt's wealth allowed Octavian to eclipse other Roman patrons in the 30s. He had collected not only spoils from Egypt but also additional booty from Dalmatia on the east coast of the Adriatic, some of which was showcased in his triple triumph of 29 B.C. This three-day event was staged at the end of the summer and dramatically presented Octavian's victories in Dalmatia, at Actium, and over Egypt. Projects financed by the conquests of Cleopatra and Egypt—the Temple of Divus Julius and the Curia—were dedicated at the end of the festivities. The Curia was appropriately provided with an altar and statue of Victory; the spoils of Egypt and prows of ships captured at Actium were exhibited on the platform of the Temple of Caesar.

Favro distinguishes between Caesarian projects well under way and thus easily finished by Augustus, and others only in the planning stage.

Augustus rapidly completed the latter. They were intended both as memorials to his dead adoptive father and as permanent tributes to Augustus's authority to rule. Nothing was more intimately associated with Caesar's persona in Rome than the Julian forum, and it is therefore not surprising that Augustus moved immediately to complete it. Although Caesar had dedicated the forum prematurely in 46 B.C., it remained unfinished at his death. The large open rectangular space with porticoes and shops had Hellenistic prototypes and, in its overall design, was reminiscent of the Caesareum in Alexandria and a similar building in Antioch—a striking connection that must have pleased Augustus because it underscored the forum's descent from the great art of Caesar and Cleopatra. Augustus added a statue of Caesar to the forum complex in Rome and, as we have seen, allowed the gilded statue of Cleopatra in the temple to remain, a continuing reference to Augustus's power over her and, unwittingly, of hers over him.

Caesar's upgrading and regularization of the Roman Forum had been, in essence, an urban retrofit that took a jumble of Republican buildings and reoriented them so that they were more effective both individually and as a group. Augustus completed those that were not finished at Caesar's death and added a few new edifices to the mix. The Roman Forum reemerged as the capital's most vital public space under Augustus, who shaped its physical and political identity so successfully that it remained largely unchanged until the late third century under Diocletian.

While Caesar strategically allied the Roman Forum with the Julian Forum, he also recognized the importance of distinguishing it from its neighbor, and the Roman Forum began to be known as the Forum Magnum. The buildings added to this Forum Magnum by Augustus were carefully sited and had dedications that complemented those that were already there. The Julian Basilica and the Basilica Aemelia bordered the perimeter of the renovated portion of the Forum (Fig. 14.1). Both were Republican structures with long and illustrious building histories. By renovating them, Augustus simply followed in the footsteps of his forebears. Nevertheless, the emperor had an overarching agenda that separated him from earlier patrons. Augustus was less interested in restoring individual buildings than he was in a full renovation of the western side of the Roman Forum. His objective was to make the part of the Forum closest to

14.1. Augustus continued Caesar's renovation of the Roman Forum by restoring the Basilica Aemilia (shown here) and Basilica Julia and playing them off each other as a pair.

the Capitoline hill a microcosm of the Julian Empire, linked through a passageway to the Forum of Julius Caesar next door.

Augustus used the two basilicas as ramparts that shielded the Forum from the outside, creating a space that celebrated the world according to Julius Caesar and Octavian Augustus. In addition, Augustus coordinated the two disparate buildings with columnar screens that created the fiction that the same architect had designed them as a pair. The Roman penchant for "facadism" reached a pinnacle in this carefully orchestrated basilican duo. The Basilica Aemelia and Basilica Julia were sited along the long north and south sides of the Roman Forum. The Basilica Aemelia was proportionally smaller than the Julian Basilica, a problem already recognized by Caesar, who had lengthened its profile by erecting a senate house (Curia) next door. Augustus completed Caesar's Curia as the dictator would have wanted, providing it with a pediment, a portico, and a prominent inscription honoring Caesar. He displayed it in its final state on the official Roman coinage.

The east-west sides of the Forum were provided with structures that enclosed and regularized the central open space. Caesar had commissioned the Rostra or speaker's platform on the western side, not far from the Tabularium, an office building where state records and archives were kept, built by Quintus Lutatius Catulus during his consulship of 78 B.C. The Rostra or speaker's platform was left unfinished at Caesar's death but completed by Augustus (Fig. 14.2). Facing the Curia and regularizing it from the east was the Temple of the Divine Julius Caesar, dedicated in 29 B.C. The triumvirs had begun the temple in 42 B.C. as a sign of their communal mourning. It was a salute to their slain leader, whose body had been cremated on the site, and it complemented their bearded mourning portraits on contemporary coins. Octavian completed the temple and held games on the day of its dedication. He insisted that the final form of this sacred structure had to contribute to the newly reorganized space of the Roman Forum. For that reason, the Temple of Divus Julius was provided with a dais that mirrored that of the Forum's principal Rostra and was decorated with selected ships' beaks from the Battle of Actium.[3] While it is not surprising that Octavian was still relishing his victory over Cleopatra two years after Actium, it is fascinating that he chose to reference his conquest of the Egyptian queen in a monument marking his adoptive father's assassination. In what may have been a show of father-son rivalry, Octavian was once again boasting, with great public bravado, that he too possessed Cleopatra and her wealthy kingdom.

Octavian commissioned a colossal statue of Divus Julius, which may have been surmounted by a star marking his divinity.[4] Augustan coins portray the cult statue with a veiled head and a crooked staff or *lituus*, referring to Caesar's roles as chief priest of Rome and diviner or *augur*. The

14.2. Augustus's renovation of the Roman Forum had at its core the desire to present the space as a microcosm of the Julian Empire, with a new Curia (right) and Rostra (left) begun by Caesar.

same numismatic renditions depict the temple with a star in the pediment.

In his *Res Gestae,* Augustus boasts that he built or renovated 82 temples, among them temples of all of Rome's major state gods—Jupiter, Juno, Minerva, Apollo, and many lesser members of the pantheon. These were situated in key locations around the capital city: on the Palatine and Capitoline hills, in the Roman Forum, and so on. In fact, Augustus did not turn his back on any Roman divinity, asserting that he omitted no sacred sites "which at that time stood in need of repair."[5] Just as he paid obeisance to an impressive array of Egyptian gods in temples up and down the Nile, Augustus honored the Roman state gods in the capital by refurbishing their abodes.

Nothing conjured up Alexandria better than its great Library, fabled throughout the ancient world. Caesar had been impressed by Cleopatra's erudition, and it was in Egypt that he was directly exposed to intellectuals who frequented Alexandria's Library and Museum. That Rome should also have a renowned library was obvious, and Caesar was determined to see that one flourished on the banks of the Tiber. In order to give the library visibility and an aura of tradition, Caesar planned to build the structure on one of Rome's most illustrious hills—the Palatine. Although Gaius Asinius Pollio, a supporter of Antony, took up the gauntlet after Caesar's assassination and built Rome's first public library next to the Forum, it was Augustus who realized the dictator's dream of a learned edifice on the Palatine. Like its Republican predecessor, Augustus's version had Greek and Latin sections. In Rome's second public library, Augustus merged the dictator's reminiscence of scholarly days in Alexandria with the solidity of Roman political and social life. In addition, the emperor reflected his own ambition by locating the library next to a portico adjoining the Palatine's temple to his patron god, Apollo. That the temple to Augustus's solar patron was next to the emperor's own residence demonstrated that Augustus was always attuned to the personal benefit provided by such projects. In fact, Augustus was not content with a single new library; he added Rome's third library to the court of the Porticus Octaviae in the Campus Martius, which bore his sister's name and was dedicated to his son-in-law, Marcellus. The design of Rome's libraries was by now cast in stone: this one as well was divided into Greek and Latin components.

Self-interest must have also motivated Augustus when he decided to actualize Caesar's vow to construct a Temple to Mars that was greater than any other in existence. The warrior Mars suited Caesar's military objectives and achievements, a correlation that Augustus noted when he chose to dedicate the temple to Mars Ultor—Mars the Avenger (Fig. 14.3). It was the willingness of Mars to support Octavian's avenging of his adoptive father's death that led to the victory over Cassius and Brutus at Philippi and to the resultant construction of the temple. In this instance, Augustus was celebrating not only his own military achievement

14.3. Augustus fulfilled Caesar's vow to build a vast temple to Mars Ultor in Rome, a building that also commemorated Augustus's victory over Caesar's assassins, Cassius and Brutus.

but also Caesar's, and possibly also referencing male Ptolemies in Egypt like Auletes who liked to have themselves depicted smiting enemies in the thick of battle.

And yet, even though the temple in Rome celebrated Mars's vengeance, it wasn't this quality that was accentuated in the edifice's sculptural program. The very presence of Mars might conjure up military conquest, but it was his relationship with other gods, legendary figures, and personifications that was the primary subject of the pedimental sculpture and the statuary group in the temple's cella. Although the pediment does not survive, a depiction of it is preserved on a relief originally from the so-called Ara Pietatis Augustae, an altar commissioned by the emperor Claudius.

The relief depicts a bearded Mars at center stage below the apex of the pediment. Although he is bare-chested rather than armored, Mars does have some of the accoutrements of battle, including a helmet, a lance, and a sword in a sheath. He is accompanied by Fortuna, with her cornucopia and rudder, who brought him luck in war; Roma, goddess of the city for which he fought; Romulus, Rome's founder; and the reclining personifications of the Palatine, on which the city was founded, and the Tiber, on whose banks it flourished. Fortuna is immediately to the right of Mars, balanced on the left by Venus, with a small Cupid sitting on her left shoulder. While Venus was the consort of Mars, she was also the statuary companion to Cleopatra in the Temple of Venus in the Forum of Julius Caesar. The Temple to Mars was the centerpiece of a new Forum of Augustus, closely based in its architectural design on the forum of his adoptive father. As plans progressed for the sculpture that would decorate the exterior of the Temple of Mars, Venus was selected as a main protagonist. She was chosen above all because she was the patroness of the Julian family, but her juxtaposition with Cleopatra in the older temple is likely to have been noted. If that statue of Cleopatra indeed depicted her with Caesarion on her shoulder, it would have been an apt inspiration for the grouping of Venus and Cupid.

It is a chicken-and-egg conundrum to try to determine whether Cleopatra was mimicking Venus or Venus imitating Cleopatra, but it probably doesn't matter much. What is significant is that in Rome of the last several decades B.C., there was a rich vocabulary of visual signs and a highly charged pictorial discourse in which Caesarion might have been to Cleopatra as Cupid was to Venus. When Augustus was formulating his imagery, the power of the mother-child dynamic was doubtless not lost on him. After ordering Caesarion's murder soon after the Battle of Actium, Augustus began an aggressive search for male heirs that eventually resulted in the selection of Gaius and Lucius Caesar. By the time the Temple of Mars Ultor was dedicated in 2 B.C., depictions of small boys on the shoulders or beneath the skirts of their mothers could just as well have been allusions to Gaius and Lucius as they were to Cupid or Caesarion. Augustus was a master at encouraging his artists to create imagery with multiple meanings.

The statuary group inside the temple is also no longer preserved, but a reflection of it is captured in a relief from Algiers (Fig. 14.4). Mars is depicted here in full battle dress, carrying a lance and shield, and thus is more blatantly warlike than the Mars on the pediment of the temple. The Venus to his right, leaning languorously on a pedestal, is more sensual than her counterpart on the pediment. As in other depictions of Venus, the drapery slips off her left shoulder, and her costume is wrapped tightly across her abdomen and thighs to accentuate their fullness. Her right hand is placed jauntily on her outthrust right hip, and a piece of fabric swirls across the genital area, around her left wrist, and in front of the pedestal, falling on top of the head of a small naked Cupid below. While Cupid grasps a fold of the cloth in his left hand, he looks up at his mother and offers her a sheathed sword. She is not aware that this gift is hers, however; she is looking not at the boy but in the direction of Mars and another figure. Since it was Cupid who helped prepare Mars for battle, the sword is probably intended for Mars, delivered to him through Venus, thus allowing Venus to arm her man as Venus did Aeneas[6] and as so many elite Roman and Egyptian women did in the age of Augustus, among them Cleopatra and Octavia.

Although Mars is Venus's intended partner in the temple's cult statue, the relief is designed so that her true comrade appears to be not Mars but the man at the far right. He is youthful and beardless, with a naked, well-developed chest. His drapery slips very low, just barely covering the pubic area. A glimpse of his exposed left leg suggests full nudity beneath the falling mantle. The figure is widely identified as Divus Julius, that is, Julius Caesar after his death and divinization. This is not the epileptic, aging Caesar, with a bald head and deeply lined jaw and neck, but the god Caesar, totally rejuvenated with a full head of hair and a smooth face. Caesar's feet are missing in the relief, but the fact that Venus and Mars are standing on marble pedestals suggests that the figures should be read as

14.4. This relief from Algiers reflects a statuary group inside the Temple of Mars Ultor, depicting Venus, Mars, and Divus Julius

three statues on individual bases that together formed a statuary group. Since this group was originally a cult statue, it was accessible only to priests and special dignitaries, not to the public at large. Nonetheless, word must have spread rapidly when new cult images were dedicated, especially ones that celebrated revered divinities like Caesar, who was once human. What would people have said? That an aging dictator had come back as a god—young and vital? That he now resided in a realm with other gods such as Mars, Venus, and Cupid? That he had been reunited with Cleopatra and their son, "Little Caesar"? That the divine Caesar resembled his adoptive son Octavian, and that he was depicted with the same smooth face and distinctive cap of hair? That this youthful Caesar also looked remarkably like Gaius and Lucius? In the polysemic manner that became a hallmark of Augustan art, the youthful image of Caesar was probably meant to conjure up many of these associations. Although we cannot know which ones were considered, it is highly likely that Caesar's youthfulness in this statuary linked him in the minds of Romans with his "son" and his "grandsons," in a grand dynastic Julian chain that was created to rival Cleopatra's Ptolemies and other Hellenistic dynasties.

The Temple of Mars the Avenger was situated in Augustus's forum. Although the forum bore his name, it was more a tribute to his relationship to his divine father than to himself. While Octavian's bond with his biological father, Gaius Octavius, and his divine father, Apollo, were celebrated on the lofty Palatine hill with its divine and imperial residences and announced by an archway, the emperor's association with Caesar found its proper place in the center of Roman public life—in the forum that formed the locus of civic activity. It was Caesar, not Octavius or Apollo, who provided Octavian with his political legitimacy. The Forum of Augustus transformed that legitimacy into a solid urban entity that promised to link father and son in perpetuity. To ensure that bond, the Forum of Augustus was constructed adjacent to the Forum of Caesar; and even the design of the later complex was based closely on its prototype, with its open rectangular space, dominant temple, and embracing wings.

While Augustus lavished attention on what were now Rome's three forums—the focal point of the city's municipal center—he also undoubtedly recognized that if Rome were to rival Cleopatra's Alexandria, it needed the requisite urban amenities. To provide them, he turned to his friend and right-hand man, Marcus Agrippa. Agrippa was part of the imperial family; he had wealth; and he aspired to erect buildings that would compete with those of aristocratic rivals and ensure his own lasting fame—the perfect recipe for success in Rome in the late first century B.C.

Agrippa didn't disappoint. He plunged as vigorously into construction as he had into strategic planning and warfare. Beginning even before Actium and continuing until his death in 12 B.C., for about eighteen years, Agrippa was a prodigious builder, altering the landscape of the city of Rome as well as such far-flung Roman colonies as Nemausus (Nîmes) and Athens. In 33 B.C. Agrippa had been appointed aedile, and from that position he orchestrated a full-scale renewal of city services in Rome. This revitalization was intended not only to improve living and working conditions in Rome but also to convince the city's inhabitants that Octavian was their man. With private funds, Octavian and Agrippa set out to repair heavy-use public buildings and well-trodden streets. They increased the city's water supply and improved the aqueduct system so that water could flow freely in the municipal baths and fountains. To make sure that Rome's residents did not miss the point, they were provided with a year of free bathing privileges. As the ambience of Rome improved and its inhabitants were treated to what seemed like an endless series of public games (59 days in a row!) as well as bountiful supplies of such basics as olive oil and salt, Octavian handily won the support of the populace.

The new aqueduct system was composed of renovated Republican structures and Augustan additions, like the Aqua Julia, which took its name from the Julian family. These aqueducts fed many public establishments, among them a spanking new bath building that was built by Agrippa to his specifications. Begun in 25 B.C., the Baths of Agrippa were supplied by water from the Aqua Virgo. These Agrippan Baths were the first of Rome's great bath complexes, and their ancestry can be traced to earlier Italian bath structures such as those at Pompeii (Fig. 14.5).

When Agrippa died in 12 B.C., he willed his baths to the people of Rome. What Agrippa recognized from the start is that his bathing establishment needed a carefully orchestrated decorative program like the artwork that covered the exterior and interior walls of Egyptian temple and tomb complexes. As in the earlier Stabian Baths at Pompeii, the walls and vaults of the Thermae Agrippae were embellished with stuccoes. Sections done in terracotta were tinted with encaustic. The Agrippan Baths served as a showcase for plundered art from conquered territories as well as artworks created in Rome. Even the warmest rooms, the *tepidarium* and *caldarium,* which would seem ill suited to having painted walls, were covered with pictures. Sculpture was displayed around the bath complex; the highlight of the exposition was appropriately a famous statue of an athlete, the Apoxyomenos by the Greek sculptor Lysippus, which was set up in front of the structure.[7]

The Baths of Agrippa were part of an ambitious complex of buildings

14.5. Marcus Agrippa sponsored many public works in Rome, among them the baths that bore his name, the Thermae Agrippae.

that Agrippa commissioned in the Campus Martius in Rome, comprising the Baths, the Pantheon, the Basilica of Neptune, and the Saepta Julia, the enclosure where the Romans voted. Agrippa was here following the lead of Caesar, who had recognized the importance of this site and was likely the first who conceived of building the Saepta in that location. Whether Caesar actually began construction is not recorded, but it seems likely that Lepidus did some work there. Agrippa completed the Saepta in 26 B.C.

In its final form, the Saepta was a rectangular structure with colonnades on two sides. The design of the building made it especially well suited for the exhibition of art. Accordingly, it was used as a public gallery, although Augustus sometimes staged gladiatorial combats there. The purpose of the Basilica of Neptune in Augustan times is unknown, but it appears to have been more closely connected with the Baths than with the Pantheon. The Pantheon was considered such an important commission that a distinguished Athenian sculptor, Diogenes, was hired to make the facade's sculpture and the caryatids that carried the pediment. These caryatid supports in the form of maidens were based on those of the classical Greek Erechtheum's Porch of the Maidens, but were given a Roman sheen by supporting capitals made of gleaming bronze.

Whether Caesar had been inspired by his Egyptian sojourn when he conceived of the Saepta is not known, but the plan of a rectangular space lined with colonnades is similar to that of the Caesareum in Alexandria. Agrippa may also have had Augustus's Egyptian building projects in mind when he decided to erect a Pantheon in Rome, and both the Saepta and the Pantheon were built next to the Temple of Isis and Serapis.

Agrippa was well aware of Augustus's interest in the close association of dynast and god. Augustus was already dressing in private as Apollo, honoring the god through architecture (the temple on the Palatine), and even subtly combining the god's identity with his own (the temple's terracotta plaque with Apollo and Hercules)—all the while fully aware that he could go just so far in Rome. Although he didn't hesitate to cavort with all the gods on temple friezes in Egypt, Augustus was more cautious in Rome, inhabiting the human domain in his relief sculpture. Augustus's relationship to the full array of Roman deities was suggested more indirectly in the Pantheon's dedication to all the gods.

Dio Cassius reports that the Pantheon received its appellation because it contained many statues of gods and because its dome resembled the dome of the heavens. Writing in the late second and early third century A.D., and depending either on earlier sources or on personal knowledge of Hadrian's replacement for the building, Dio was apparently unaware that the Agrippan structure was unlikely to have had a dome. He did, however, know that Agrippa was responsible for the original Pantheon because he could read the inscription on the facade of the Hadrianic structure: M.AGRIPPA.L.F.COS.TERTIUM.FECIT (Marcus Agrippa, consul for the third time, made this).

Since we know Agrippa commissioned the Pantheon in his third consulship, it thus dates to 27 B.C., although Dio reports that it was completed by 25 B.C.[8] Dio further states that Agrippa wished to put a statue of Augustus in the building and thus make it an Augusteum—Rome's version, in a sense, of the Caesareum in Alexandria. When the emperor demurred, Agrippa installed a statue of Divus Julius instead but convinced Augustus to allow him to place statues of Augustus and himself in the temple's portico.

The Agrippan Pantheon also had a statue of Venus, leading to speculation that it was not only Augustus's divine adoptive father who was honored there but also Venus (the Julian patroness) and her consort Mars. Although the temple was dedicated to all the gods, a few of Augustus's favorites appear to have received special attention. Most revealing is the allusion in this temple to the era's most spectacular diva—Cleopatra. As noted earlier, half of Cleopatra's infamous pearl was placed in each ear of the temple's statue of Venus, the Julian family's divine forebear. Whether the assimilation of Augustus's godly patroness Venus and the Egyptian goddess Cleopatra was obvious to the Roman citizenry is difficult to assess, since only the priesthood was permitted to enter the temple. Nevertheless, in view of the Roman penchant for juicy gossip, it is highly likely that word would have spread rapidly that the Pantheon's Roman Venus was wearing the Egyptian queen's pearls, even if they were considered trophies of Augustus's Actium victory. In fact, the placement in the Pantheon of yet another Julian Venus initiated a fascinating dialogue between the gilded statue of Cleopatra in the Temple of Venus Genetrix in Caesar's forum and the cult statue of Venus with Cleopatra's pearl in the Pantheon. It is also not inconceivable that this dialogue was further expanded by an association in the Roman urban landscape between these statues and the city's Temples of Isis and Serapis, part of the same complex in Rome's Campus Martius. The triumvirs approved the structure in 43 B.C., and even though Augustus introduced repressions against the Egyptian gods and Tiberius is said to have closed down the Temple of Serapis and tossed the goddess's statue into the Tiber,[9] these reports may be exaggerated. What does seem clear is that the cult of Isis in Rome, firmly established by the principate of Caligula, would have been unlikely to become as entrenched in the fabric of Rome as it did without the impact of Cleopatra.

From this material evidence, it seems clear that Cleopatra was one diva who was in Rome to stay, and that she continued to fascinate Augustus, his closest associates, and future emperors. In 25 B.C., six years after

Actium, Augustus and his artists were still investing works of art with signs that continued to enliven a visual dialogue with "the Queen," a dialogue that may also have had a post-Augustan afterlife.

Renovated public spaces were ideal locations for the immense number of works of art that continued to be carted back to Rome by triumphant generals, Octavian and Agrippa among them. It was, however, Agrippa who first recognized that the Republican practice of using such booty to enhance personal holdings and to compete with aristocratic rivals was exclusionary. While it might puff one up with one's peers, it was hardly a practice that endeared an elite Roman to the Roman populace at large. Better to nationalize the vast store of famous masterworks so that they belonged to the Roman people and were a treasury of which they could collectively be proud. Octavian had seen firsthand that Alexandria under the Ptolemies had become a mecca for art and culture, a city where intellectuals studied in the Library and debated in the Museum. If all of Rome's art was the property of the state, it could be deployed in a way that would ensure maximum visibility and enjoyment, and, even more important, would provide an identity for the city that would be recognized far and wide. With such a transformation in Rome, it would be the equal of Alexandria, enabling Octavian to be master of the two greatest cities in the ancient world.

Although Agrippa's proposal to nationalize the state's collections was never officially legislated, he and Octavian went a long way toward making large numbers of artworks an integral part of the public urban fabric. By so doing, Octavian moved from an art of personal rivalry to one that had the potential to express a unified vision, and thus took a giant step toward creating a Roman empire out of a more diverse Hellenistic world. While Octavian might have moved in this direction irrespective of Cleopatra, it is quite possible that her world view was influential. Cleopatra and the Ptolemies, like other Hellenistic dynasts, had inherited a codified repertory of recognizable signs and symbols that they used in the service of their political objectives. When Cleopatra attempted to merge her Egypt with the Rome of Caesar and Antony, she likely also envisioned the unification of her visual language with theirs to create a universal visual dialect—one that would enable her and her consorts in turn to be masters not only of their individual domains but of the entire ancient world. The works of art they commissioned together bear witness to their attempt to define that shared idiom.

With Caesar, Antony, and Cleopatra gone, Augustus could proceed alone, but he surely recognized, as they did before him, that he needed a unified, not a fragmented, artistic dream. A cacophony of Hellenistic and Republican approaches would only confuse a populace and a world already inundated with a profusion of conflicting images. Rome needed both a unique vocabulary and a systematized collection of images that were readily understandable by an ethnically and culturally diverse population. Furthermore, the new Roman terminology could not appear Egyptian—that would have been anathema in the current climate—but had to combine Italic, Etruscan, and Greek elements with a new Roman vision to create a singular but identifiable lexicon.

15

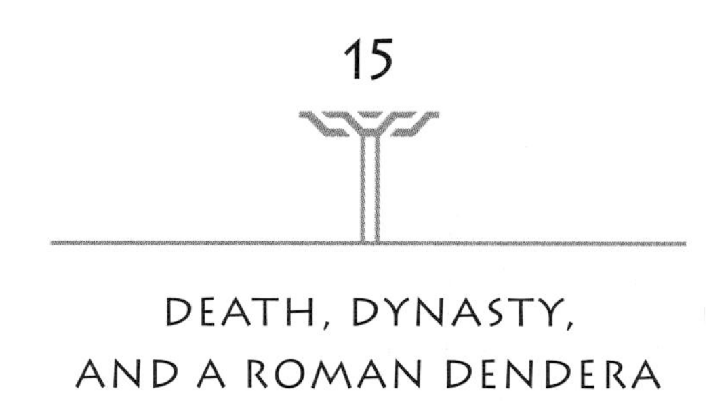

DEATH, DYNASTY, AND A ROMAN DENDERA

Agrippa's penchant for architectural complexes with public exhibitions of art and Augustus's articulation of a unified vision came together in what was unquestionably the artistic masterpiece of Augustus's principate the Ara Pacis Augustae. Begun a year before Agrippa's death, the Altar of Augustan Peace was not a stand-alone monument but part of a collection of several buildings, including Augustus's own mausoleum (Fig. 15.1).

Even as a young man, Augustus's health was not robust, and he was concerned about his longevity. For this reason, he quickly focused on finding an appropriate successor. Whatever he achieved would not have a lasting impact if someone with a similar vision were not in place to keep that dream alive. At the same time, Augustus understood that his legacy would be strengthened by a viable successor and also by the potent memory of his own achievements. These accomplishments needed to be imprinted in the memory of the Roman populace in a way that was not ephemeral. The pharaohs and Ptolemies provided ample evidence that both goals could be achieved. While hereditary dynasty was the chosen succession vehicle in Egypt, it was at that time an un-Roman institution, and Augustus searched among associates as well as members of his own family for a worthy heir. Augustus's succession plan took a long time to achieve, and he realized in the course of that long process that, whatever the outcome, monuments and inscriptions had the potential to keep his political agenda alive.

15.1. The Ara Pacis Augustae, the artistic masterpiece of Augustus's principate, presented the past, present, and future of Rome and the Julio-Claudian dynasty.

In Alexandria, Augustus had seen and must have been inspired by the tomb of Alexander and the new sepulcher for Cleopatra and Antony. Since Antony's burial in the East suggested an allegiance to Egypt rather than Rome, Augustus shrewdly used his own tomb as a mark of his loyalty or *pietas* toward Rome. Augustus surely recognized that building his mausoleum in Rome would not only provide a monumental sign that he had come, seen, and conquered, but also would signal that he was quintessentially Roman and would rest among his Roman family for eternity. He chose a site along the banks of the Tiber River, as a response to the rival Nile.

The Mausoleum of Augustus was planned as a family burial site so that Augustus and his own dynasty could be reunited after death like the Ptolemies. Augustus refused to view the tombs of the Ptolemies when he was in Alexandria, but he knew that they possessed an impressive family burial ground and this probably stirred his competitive spirit. Since these Ptolemaic sepulchers, located near Cleopatra's palace, are now buried beneath the sea, we know little about their appearance or whether Augustus was moved to incorporate any of their features. We also know little of Alexander's tomb, another likely touchstone for Augustus. The parentage of Augustus's mausoleum was clearly eclectic; even if there were Ptolemaic characteristics, they were combined with others in a tomb that had its own distinctive design. The mausoleum's round earthen mound was reminiscent of Etruscan tumuli (although, according to the first-century Latin poet Lucan, Alexander's tomb also had an earthen mound), and its stone perimeter and superstructure owed much to Hellenistic Greece.

Penelope Davies has convincingly demonstrated that Egyptian structures and building techniques were known and used as a resource by Augustus's architects. Drawing on Egyptian expertise in erecting tall structures like pyramids and lighthouses, Augustus's designers were able to make his tomb the tallest edifice in town at 150 feet, capable of supporting a hefty bronze statue of the emperor. Also inspired by Egyptian labyrinths, these builders provided the Mausoleum of Augustus with annular corridors that had indirect and thus somewhat mysterious access. Davies posits that Alexander's tomb may also have had a labyrinthine plan, the inscrutability of which may well have appealed to Augustus.

Augustus's tomb was begun in 28 B.C., not long after the Battle of Actium, and completed in 23 B.C. While constructing a glorious place for eternal rest was on the emperor's mind, he was fresh from his victory at Actium and mindful that his tomb might also serve as a monument to his most significant military achievement. Moreover, while Augustus's victory over Cleopatra and Antony began with a battle at sea, it culminated deep inside a sepulchral chamber. Dio Cassius reports that, in an attempt to deceive Augustus, Cleopatra had word sent to him that she had died.[1] When Antony by mishap received this news, he stabbed himself. While wounded, he heard that Cleopatra was still alive; he made his way to her tomb and was hoisted inside. Since his condition was fatal, Cleopatra also committed suicide. Augustus ordered that the two be similarly embalmed (in the Egyptian manner!) and buried in the same tomb, perhaps bestowing on the lovers a final, quintessentially Egyptian and decidedly un-Roman branding. While Augustus thus allowed Cleopatra and Antony an everlasting union, he likely wanted his own last resting place and that of his wife Livia to be a testament to military success, world sovereignty, and the bonds of legitimate Roman marriage.

With regard to its design, Augustus and his builders may have found agreeable models for the emperor's mausoleum in trophy tombs or cenotaphs honoring Alexander and other Hellenistic rulers. In terms of its siting, we do not know whether the Mausoleum of Augustus was first intended as an independent monument or whether Augustus and his planners, with significant input from Agrippa, were intending from the start to make it part of a complex. Even if they weren't, the idea must have soon occurred to them. Augustus and Agrippa were in the process of a major overhaul of Rome, and what would be a more significant location in the city center than the region that contained the emperor's sepulcher? It was at that very locale that a list of Augustus's achievements and his vision for Rome's future would be recorded for posterity. After Augustus's death, the entrance to the mausoleum was provided with two bronze plaques inscribed with the emperor's own words, his list of things accomplished, the *Res Gestae Divi Augusti*—"Divi" because Augustus, like Caesar, was transformed into a god at his death. Since the tomb provided for the entire imperial family, Livia would eventually rest by his side, as would Gaius and Lucius.

Expecting that divine status would eventually be bestowed on him, Augustus also probably wished to be associated for eternity with his victory over Cleopatra at Actium, since it was that encounter that paved the way for the foundation of the principate. The event was commemorated with an obelisk that was brought from Egypt and set up in 10 B.C. next to the Mausoleum of Augustus (see Fig. 11.1). In its Roman setting, the obelisk became the gnomon of a massive sundial, just the kind of timepiece that would have intrigued the intelligentsia of Alexandria. The Romans now had a wonder of their own, indicating that Augustus's Rome was the equal of Cleopatra's Alexandria. The new inscription at the base banished forever any association of the obelisk with the Pharaoh who had built it.

The hieroglyphs on the shaft were obviously Egyptian but could not be deciphered by the Roman viewer. What could be read was the Latin inscription at the base, certifying that Augustus, son of the Divine Julius Caesar, dedicated the obelisk to Rome's subjugation of Egypt and to the sun god. Even the illiterate could pick out the name of their leader and understand that this obelisk signified their emperor's mastery of Egypt.

Even before the obelisk was brought to Rome, work had begun on the Ara Pacis Augustae. What Augustus wanted to achieve was to situate that altar in an assemblage of structures that reflected his dominion over the western and eastern parts of the empire and made apparent that even the East of Cleopatra and Antony was now under his jurisdiction. Inspired by the Egyptian knack for creating a seamless synergy of temple and tomb and god and dynast, Augustus strove to make his Roman complex a similar composite of religion, sacred sepulcher, divinity, and sovereign.

Augustus's sanctified altar in Rome was ostensibly intended as a tribute to the emperor's achievement of diplomatic peace with Spain and Gaul. But Augustus was not a man who left to others the articulation of his vision for a reorganized Roman society. The consecration of the Ara Pacis on July 4 in the year 13 B.C. provided Augustus with an opportunity to present his grand strategy for Rome to the world. Although the treaty with Spain and Gaul cemented and furthered the Pax Augusta, the Augustan Peace had been achieved at Actium. The positive aftermath of that historic confrontation brought peace to a country that had been embroiled in a divisive civil war, one that was caused in part by a liaison with Cleopatra. In the decade and a half that had passed, Augustus had re-established Republican, religious, and family values, created a new form of governance, restored Rome's pride in its history, and continued Caesar's ambitious building program to translate Rome's newfound power and influence into tangible form.

The new altar was constructed near the Tiber, recalling Cleopatra's edifices on the Nile. It took three and a half years for a master designer and his artisans to translate Augustus's ideology into marble. It became clear before long that it would be desirable to dedicate the altar on January 30, Livia's birthday. On that day in 9 B.C., Livia turned 49—about a decade older than Cleopatra when she died, but now it was Livia's turn to be Rome's "Queen." Cleopatra may have held court in Caesar's Roman villa, and she had a Roman son by Caesar and two by Antony, but Livia had also been fruitful and multiplied. In fact, Livia surpassed Cleopatra by having four rather than three "sons," namely her biological offspring, Tiberius and Drusus, from her first marriage and Gaius and Lucius Caesar through their adoption by Augustus in 17 B.C. This adoption coincided with Augustus's marriage legislation of 18 B.C., in which special status was granted to women with three or more children. What we know today of that legislation does not make clear whether adoptive children legally counted toward this special status, but Livia, as empress of Rome, could likely claim it anyway.

Cleopatra had brought to Rome the concept of the authoritative woman monarch. While Roman custom did not permit bestowal of that kind of status on Livia, the empress's special rank in Rome was publicly alluded to when she was depicted in a relief portrait on the Altar of Peace. That this was an unusual event is underscored by Livia's appearance in the procession of the south frieze; there she is shown not with the traditional *nodus* hairstyle she helped popularize, with a roll of hair centered over the forehead, but with her hair parted in the center and arranged as if she were a Greek deity (Fig. 15.2; see Fig. 2.1). If Livia was going to compete with the diva Cleopatra, she too had to be a resplendent goddess.

The status of the Ara Pacis Augustae as the monument that best encapsulates Augustus's world view does not derive from its architectural form, which is traditional and even ordinary. The rectangular altar with doorways on the east and west sides was based on earlier altar design in Greece and Asia Minor. Its architectural plan resembles that of the fifth-century B.C. Altar of Pity or the Twelve Gods in Athens, and its extensive figural relief decoration is dependent upon that of the Altar of Zeus at Pergamum. It is the relief sculpture that covers every inch of the altar's surface that gives the monument its distinction and articulates Augustus's political and personal objectives. In this it is difficult not to see a reflection of Cleopatra's temple at Dendera.

Many scholars, myself among them, have maintained that the Ara Pacis owes much to sources in Periclean Athens and Hellenistic Pergamum. I continue to believe this is true, at least in part, especially with regard to the altar's architectural form. It now seems clear, however, that this is too narrow a perspective. It was Karl Galinsky who encouraged Romanists to see Augustan art as polysemous—as drawing on a multiplicity of sources, and also deliberately choosing signs and symbols that had more than one meaning. This observation has allowed scholars to be more open in attempting to understand the diverse sources that Augustus must have been drawing on when he began to craft his unified vision for Rome. The emperor was doubtless inspired by many of the same ideas and images that came to Caesar after he began his love affair with Cleopatra in Alexandria. Like Caesar, Augustus had a clarity of mind that enabled him to absorb these influences and transform them into something that was uniquely his own. What has been missing in the scholarly assessment of Augustus's sources is the part that Egypt, and especially Cleopatra, played. Nowhere is this clearer than on the Ara Pacis. I believe that the Ara Pacis Augustae became Augustus's Dendera.

At Rome, as at Dendera, the subject matter is peaceful procession and ritual sacrifice in which obeisance is offered to a contingent of divinities and personifications. This was the same role that Augustus or his advisers chose for him in art in Egypt, and it was the part Cleopatra played at Dendera. While male Ptolemies also performed this pacific role and were depicted in this way in their temple relief sculpture, they especially relished being portrayed in the act of smiting their foes. Cleopatra's father and brothers were shown slaughtering enemies on the walls of their temples (see Fig. 5.3); Cleopatra was not. Although Augustus was a world conqueror who had earned the right to be depicted in Rome as militarily potent, with vanquished enemies crushed beneath his horses' hooves, he chose instead to be portrayed in a solemn procession in honor of Pax, Roman goddess of Peace.

Like Caesarion at Dendera, Augustus is portrayed at Rome as the principal ruler, nearest to the gods and the altar. In Egypt, Caesarion is accompanied by Queen Cleopatra; at Rome, Augustus is followed by his queen-consort, Livia. At Dendera, Cleopatra is both dynast and royal mother. Livia is powerfully maternal on the Ara Pacis and is followed in the south and north processions by her biological sons, Tiberius and Drusus, and her adoptive sons, Gaius and Lucius Caesar (Fig. 15.2). While Cleopatra was assimilated at Dendera with Hathor and Isis, Livia was closely associated on the Ara Pacis with an array of female deities and personifications connoting beauty, sensuality, fertility, and domesticity. The controversy that surrounds the identity of the seated woman in the center of the southeast panel of the altar in Rome makes it likely that she is one of Galinsky's polysemous Augustan personae (Fig. 15.4). The figure is difficult to identify because she is every woman—as comely, arousing, and fecund as Venus, as placid as Pax, as bountiful as Ceres, Tellus, and Italia, and as much in possession of all these qualities as the empress Livia.

Just as Cleopatra and Caesarion appear twice on the temple's rear exterior wall at Dendera, the Augustan procession moves forward in two parallel lines. While Cleopatra and Caesarion make offerings to six deities—Hathor, Horus, Harsomtus, Ihy, Isis, and Osiris, animal victims are readied for presentation to Pax on the sacrificial altar frieze of the Ara Pacis. Other personifications and gods are also present—Roma, Mars, and perhaps even a composite of Venus.

That Augustus would mimic a beneficent Egyptian queen rather than a more macho Ptolemaic male sovereign is interesting and instructive. The male Ptolemies Augustus knew were weak and not worthy of emulation. Cleopatra had a powerful and seductive persona that had captivated Caesar and Antony, and indeed the world. She had been Augustus's primary enemy at Actium, and had been the target of his vindictive propagandists. Nevertheless, Augustus kept her alive, perhaps subconsciously, by drawing on her art as one of his primary sources for the Ara Pacis.

The participation of Livia and other women from the court of Augustus, including Octavia and Julia (probably on the north side; Fig. 15.3), in the sacred procession of 13 B.C. must have surprised viewers when the altar was unveiled in 9 B.C. Even more astonishing was the fact that these women were depicted alongside their men, as full players in the drama of Augustan politics and family life. In addition, their children tagged along, hiding behind their garments and pulling on their cloaks, providing a lively and captivating distraction from the solemnity of the occasion. Since there was no earlier example of such family groups in Roman Republican relief sculpture, scholars have looked to other models. More than twenty years ago, I suggested that the prototypes for the Ara Pacis families were those on classical Greek and Hellenistic gravestones. While I continue to believe that such models were known and imitated, I now think it is likely that Augustus was also inspired by a very different

15.2. The biological and adoptive children of Augustus and Livia follow them in procession, just as Caesarion was paired with Cleopatra at the Temple of Dendera.

15.3. Women and children of the Julio-Claudian dynasty accompany their men in this landmark monument that was part of a visual dialogue with the art of Cleopatra and her children.

15.4. One of the most famous women in Roman art, this female figure is the embodiment of every woman, whether empress, goddess, or personification.

group portrait—one that made his blood boil but also got his competitive juices flowing.

Mark Antony's women had received a good deal of attention in the 30s B.C., situated prominently on the official Roman coinage. Even Cleopatra turned up on Roman denarii. In addition, Antony did not hesitate to appear with Cleopatra in highly visible group portraits in Athens and other major eastern capitals. Not the least bit shy about their partnership, Cleopatra and Antony were presented as Isis and Osiris in Athens. While Antony had never been good at recognizing the power of place, he clearly understood the power of personality and the power of personal alliance. He instinctively saw that taking on the costume and mannerisms of Hercules or Osiris might elevate him to the divine level that Cleopatra had occupied since birth.

The impact of such paired portraits of Cleopatra and Antony was not lost on Augustus. Livia completed him as a couple, as Cleopatra did Antony. The emphasis on men depicted with their wives on the Ara Pacis may have been, in part, Augustus's response to the pairing of Antony and Cleopatra in art. The inclusion of portraits of husbands with their wives on the Altar of Augustan Peace was also a strategic statement on Augustus's part that Roman-style matrimony was the one true form of Roman union. Whereas Antony's marriages to the likes of Fulvia and Octavia had been legal according to Roman law, his marriage to Cleopatra was not.

The partnerships between men and women on the Ara Pacis are legitimate marriages that were sanctioned by the state and by the Roman pantheon of gods, in contrast to Antony's godless marriage. Lawful matrimony produces legitimate children, and the north and south friezes of the Ara Pacis depict an array of them. Caesarion, Cleopatra Selene, Alexander Helios, and Ptolemy Philadelphus may have been accepted in Alexandria, but they were considered illegitimate in Rome. No one in Rome regarded Cleopatra's son Caesarion as the lawful heir of Caesar. The children on the Ara Pacis were, however, fully legitimate, and deserved their prominent positions in the hierarchy of the procession. The north and south relief scenes on the Ara Pacis are the first in the history of Roman art not only to depict women as the wives of their husbands, but also to portray children and to include them in the important rituals of Roman religious life. I have long thought that children were included in the north and south relief scenes of the Ara Pacis because they make reference to Augustus's dynastic intentions and his marriage and moral legislation. I now also believe that children were important to Augustus as part of his rivalry with Cleopatra.

16

COMPETING WITH CLEOPATRA ON COINS

Livia, Octavia, Julia, and their families were displayed on the south and north friezes of the Ara Pacis Augustae for all in Rome to see. Cleopatra had made being a woman with a family an asset, and Augustus had every reason to match her maternal achievements with those of women in the imperial circle. While the Ara Pacis was Augustus's answer to Cleopatra's temple of Dendera in the capital, he used the official Roman coinage to advertise his message more universally by disseminating it around the empire.

Julius Caesar had already broken the ice by minting coins with his own image during his lifetime, making it perfectly natural for Augustus and the other triumvirs to follow in his footsteps. Octavian commissioned coins with his own portrait on the obverse in 43 B.C., Antony in 44. Both Octavian and Antony immediately claimed a close connection with Caesar by striking coins with a laureate Caesar on the reverse and their own bearded portraits in mourning on the obverse. As the two rivals continued to jockey for power in east and west, they issued coins that staked out their positions and advertised their political and personal alliances. The small size and easy transportability of these specimens meant that these messages were not only conveyed in Rome but also had the potential to reach the furthest frontiers of the growing empire. This evidence has some limitations, however, since most preserved coins are from hoards concealed during times of war or other catastrophes and never retrieved;

these do not necessarily correspond to historical, literary, or other material evidence. The large quantity of Hellenistic coins brought to Rome as booty and openly displayed in official triumphs, for example, has never come to light. The coinage that circulated tended to be carried by soldiers or used in trade, but the greatest monetary transfer was the result of state expenditures, presumably putting the leadership in the position of deciding which coinage they would distribute. In fact, the Romans centralized their official coinage more than any other preceding civilization, but nonetheless regional coinages remained common and might be struck in diverse locales by a general on campaign. Antony's mints traveled with him, and some of his coins seem to have been struck on the road, so to speak; others were produced in mints in major urban centers in the East.

Although Octavian and Antony put nearly identical images on their first mourning Caesar coins, their distinctive views of war and peace, nationalism and internationalism, women and family soon led to a divergence of approach in advertising those positions on the Roman coinage. Nowhere was this more apparent than in their attitude toward the women in their lives. Octavian seems to have used the Roman coinage primarily for self-promotion, choosing to depict women from his circle only when it suited one of two goals: establishing a hereditary dynasty and consolidating imperial power. Antony had similar political goals, placing portraits of three of his wives on his coinage to signal political alliances that would support his vision for a united eastern empire. What distinguished Antony from Octavian, however, were the occasional numismatic glimmers that indicated he was something of a romantic when it came to women. He was very modern in his recognition that men and women could collaborate in a way that made them stronger when acting as a team.

The portraits of Octavia, Julia, and Livia on the official Roman coinage in the capital and in Egypt presented to citizens at home and abroad the public image of the three most important women in Augustan Rome. These numismatic portraits were far more than physical descriptions of their subjects; they were used to articulate imperial policies and to highlight the female virtues expected of aristocratic women in Rome. Octavia, her husband's helpmate, and the very symbol of Antony's alliance with

Octavian, stood for devotion *(pietas)* and unity *(concordia)*. In addition, she was young, beautiful, and fashionable, having introduced the simple but distinctive new *nodus* hairstyle to the Roman repertoire (see Fig. 2.2). Julia was the fecund *(fecunditas)* mother of a pair of male heirs. Livia was the modest *(pudicitia)* Roman matron, united in harmony with her husband *(concordia)*, to whom she was dutiful *(pietas)*; she was also the mother of two boys *(fecunditas)*, and so upright that she became the very embodiment of chaste womanhood in Rome. Livia's assimilation to these virtues was so complete that under Tiberius, she was routinely associated with them on the official Roman coinage, assimilated for example with Pietas or Iustitia (Justice). Under Augustus, Livia was denied portrayal on the official Roman coinage in the capital, but she achieved a kind of pseudo-"sovereignty" on coins in Egypt.

While it is impossible to know for sure, it is likely that these women had some say about the way they were portrayed on the Roman coinage, and that they and their portraitists used as models likenesses of royal women on local Hellenistic coinages. They must have assiduously studied how these women were clothed, jeweled, and coiffed so that they might either emulate or reject them, depending on a wide variety of political and personal criteria. Cleopatra's notoriety, her affairs with elite Roman men from their own Roman families, and the queen's memorable sojourn in Rome doubtless made her an especially intriguing archetype. When they conceived of their own numismatic images, these Roman women were, in a sense, competing with Cleopatra.

Fulvia: The Possible Pioneer

There is no evidence that Antony's first two Roman wives, Fadia and Antonia, were depicted on the Roman coinage. Fulvia, whom Antony married in 47 or 46, may have been the pioneer; it is her image that has been tentatively identified on an official coin of 43 B.C. That this occurred only a year after Caesar's first lifetime coin portrait is remarkable and, if true, is a tribute to the force of Fulvia's personality, the distinction of her accomplishments, and, as we shall see, the influence of women like Cleopatra.

Fulvia was a formidable woman who had an unusual ability to use a series of marriages to become involved in the machinations of Roman politics in the 40s. All three of her husbands—Publius Clodius Pulcher, Gaius Scribonius Curio, and Mark Antony—interacted with Caesar, sometimes supporting him and other times not. Even Antony's relationship with Caesar was rocky at times. The intrigue was a perfect training ground for Fulvia, who increasingly developed her own allegiances. In fact, after Caesar's death, Fulvia backed Antony's faction against Octavian (even though by 41–40, Antony was already wintering in Alexandria with Cleopatra), and she became directly involved in one of the major events of her day—the Perusine War.[1]

In response to what Fulvia viewed as an illegal act by Octavian—the settling of some of his army veterans on land owned by other Italians—Fulvia journeyed to Praeneste, modern Palestrina, southeast of Rome, where she took up arms and issued military orders. Her collaborator, Antony's brother Lucius Antonius, in turn marched on Rome. Their attack was not successful. When the city of Perusia sheltered Lucius Antonius, Octavian captured it; Lucius surrendered in 40 B.C. Fulvia fled to Greece, where she died. Despite what Octavian must have viewed as Lucius's treasonous behavior, it was Fulvia who bore the brunt of the criticism. When the chips were down, elite Roman men usually backed each other up, often attributing their disaffection to the scheming of misguided women. Octavian and Lucius's estrangement was publicly attributed to Fulvia, and in his *Memoirs,* Octavian apparently suggested that it was Fulvia's inappropriate behavior that led to the Perusine War.

As Plutarch comments, Fulvia did Cleopatra a great service by familiarizing Antony early in life with a capable woman: "She [Fulvia] was not a person made to spin wool and run a home: despising the domination of a simple citizen, she wanted to dominate a dominator and to command an army commander. Cleopatra was in debt to Fulvia for the lessons of submission to women that Antony had learnt from her: she had made of him a tamed and trained man when he passed into Cleopatra's hands."[2]

Fulvia left to posterity a remarkable achievement. At the very inception of numismatic portraiture of living persons in Rome, she seems to have made the portrait of a Roman woman a viable subject. In view of the audacity of this act, Fulvia's portrait was partially disguised by melding her features with those of a well-known female personification—Victory, complete with wings. In 43–42 B.C., a *quinarius* with Fulvia/Victory

16.1. A daring image of Mark Antony's third wife, Fulvia, whose features appear to be assimilated to those of Victory; it established women as a viable subject for the official Roman coinage.

on the obverse was struck at Lugdunum in Gaul, where Antony had a mint. The head of Victory appears to have Fulvia's features and a distinctive Roman hairstyle, with a looped topknot and a tight bun at the back of the head. *Aurei* with similar portrayals of Fulvia/Victory were produced in Rome in the year 40 under the supervision of the mint master Numonius Vaala (Fig. 16.1). It is not known whether Vaala knew that he was striking coins with Fulvia's features or was unaware that she and Victory had been assimilated in Gaul, nor is it known whether the Roman populace recognized the daring of these images. It is possible that Fulvia's features were sufficiently disguised in both Rome and Gaul that few were aware that Fulvia had penetrated the male reserve of self-imaging on the Roman coinage. Nonetheless, when the Gallic *quinarius* and Roman *aurei* are viewed from the vantage point of what came after them, their bold innovation is immediately recognizable.

By the time Vaala released the Rome specimens, Antony was already in Egypt with Cleopatra. Fulvia was surely aware that she was matching herself as Victory to Cleopatra as Isis, and her topknot to Cleopatra's melon hairstyle—that is, she was competing openly with her rival for Antony's attention. While Plutarch may have been right that Fulvia had tamed Mark Antony for Cleopatra, it was probably Cleopatra who readied Antony to accept portraits of women on Roman coins.

Octavia: The Professional Power Broker

Fulvia was a true pioneer, setting the stage for Octavia's debut into public life and also into the visual repertoire of Antony and Octavian's imagists. What positioned Octavia so well is that she was important to both men: she was the glue that held them together and a sign of their alliance. Octavia was already well known in Rome as the widow of one of Rome's shining lights, Gaius Claudius Marcellus. Octavia and Marcellus had three children together, supplying Octavia with what was considered in Rome the appropriate number of offspring. Despite the rivalry between Octavian and Antony, Octavia's widowhood made possible an even stronger coalition. The marriage of Octavia and Antony was to serve as evidence that Octavian and Antony had reconciled, and by so doing ratified the treaty that the two men had signed in 40 B.C. at Brundisium.

Antony's and Octavian's attitudes toward the women in their lives are nowhere better indicated than in the way each chose to portray their political affiliation in art. To mark the treaty at Brundisium, Octavian commissioned coins that depicted him and Antony in paired portraits and also the more generic head of Concordia and the caduceus, symbol of *concordia,* with clasped hands. Antony also chose the former but replaced the latter in 39 B.C. with unprecedented paired portraits of himself on the obverse of the coins and Octavia on the reverse (Figs. 16.2 and 16.3).

From the point of view of women's history, this object is one of the most significant surviving coins from Roman antiquity. By coupling himself with Octavia on the official Roman coinage, Antony publicly recognized that a woman had been the driving force behind the rapprochement of two men. Octavia is not portrayed as Victory or a Roman goddess like Venus but is resolutely presented as herself. Widely acclaimed for her beauty, Octavia is depicted as a striking young woman wearing the Roman *nodus* hairstyle, with a bun at the back and soft tendrils on the neck.

Octavian rapidly abandoned the Brundisium issues and began to use

16.2. Mark Antony displayed his willingness to share the spotlight with the women in his life by pairing his portrait with that of his fourth wife, Octavia, after their marriage and the treaty with Octavian at Brundisium.

16.3. Octavia is portrayed as herself in an innovative coin portrait that showcases her beauty and represents her with the *nodus* coiffure that she appears to have invented.

his coinage to tackle other agendas, initiating his special relationship with Apollo and starting to showcase the temple he intended to build. Antony, however, continued to strike coins with the portrait of Octavia. This is perhaps not surprising. Antony was, after all, married to Octavia, and her continued appearance on the Roman coinage spoke to her lasting involvement in keeping Antony and Octavian reconciled. It is also possible that Octavia herself convinced her husband to allow these coins to remain in circulation. After all, for all her selfless virtue, Octavia likely felt some antagonism toward her rival, and the best way to keep their competition alive was to remain front and center and not let Cleopatra gain the upper hand in the realm of public opinion. Matching Cleopatra's coins with her own was one viable strategy.

Octavia succeeded in getting the two men to meet face to face in 37 and sign a new treaty, this time at Tarentum. This important event appears to be referenced in a coin of 36–35 B.C., of unknown provenance. On the obverse is the stunning presentation of the conjoined heads of Antony and Octavian facing that of Octavia. Nowhere is the image of Octavia as power broker better expressed. She is depicted alone and they together, emphasizing not only her singularity but also her influence. The Tarentum pact was not an empty covenant. Octavian received ships from Antony's fleet, and Antony secured legionaries from Octavian for his Parthian campaign. Even though Cleopatra was already very much a part of Antony's life, Octavia may also have attracted him. While the jaded view would be that she was merely useful to him politically, the coins attest that the pair may have had, at least briefly, something of a love match. Evidence for this is found in a series of coins struck by Antony in 36–35 B.C. depicting himself and Octavia in a highly romantic conceit: they are portrayed as Neptune and Amphitrite riding in a quadriga drawn by hippocamps, creatures that were composed of the head and forepart of a horse and the body and tail of a sea serpent.

Post-Tarentum, Octavia was still enough in love with Antony, or at least dutiful enough, to continue to work tirelessly on behalf of his coalition with Octavian. She masterminded another agreement that called for Antony to furnish Octavian with two of his naval squadrons in return for four of Octavian's legions. Antony made good on the promise, but Octavian did not. Octavia continued to intercede with Octavian on

Antony's behalf, but her frailty after the birth of her second daughter may have made her less effective. Antony was livid at Octavian's unresponsiveness and, in retaliation, left Octavia and Rome for Cleopatra and Alexandria. His anger and Cleopatra's personal appeal were not the only enticements; Cleopatra had the resources to supply Antony with the troops he was denied by Octavian. In addition, she had just provided Antony with a male heir.

While Octavia continued to be a loyal surrogate for Antony in Rome, his behavior in Alexandria was making her job exceedingly difficult. Not only had he by now sired two children by Cleopatra, he also publicly acknowledged his parentage and even made his offspring sovereigns of Roman lands. Octavian decided to make one last attempt at a reconciliation of the pair. In 35 B.C. he sent Octavia to Antony with troop reinforcements, but she was rebuffed. Antony requested and was granted a divorce from Octavia in 32, and in the same year (or even earlier) he struck coins that visually concretized his union with Cleopatra, who had since borne him another son.

Antony's decision in 32 B.C. to place portraits of Cleopatra on official coins of the Roman realm was shocking. Denarii with a portrait of Antony on the obverse and Cleopatra on the reverse were manufactured either at a mint traveling with Antony, or at Antioch (see Figs. 9.4 and 9.5). The coins even included Cleopatra's names and titles, a privilege that had been denied to Fulvia and Octavia. For Antony to use the official Roman coinage to advertise his political and personal merger with a foreign queen was an aggressive gesture that was surely meant to antagonize Octavian. This new denarius was also an unwelcome signal to the Roman people that Cleopatra was Antony's wife.

Julia: The Mother

Octavian was more sparing than Antony in his inclusion of female relatives on the official coinage of Rome. He seems to have been less inclined to acknowledge women as partners in his publicly commissioned art, with the exception of the Ara Pacis Augustae. As he fashioned a public identity, Octavian not surprisingly focused on the men in his life. Even Octavian's mother, Atia, seemed to have little to do with his birth. Octavian appeared, for all intents and purposes, to have been sired by a trium-

16.4. Augustus honored his daughter Julia and her sons Gaius and Lucius Caesar on coins that equated her maternity with Cleopatra's.

virate of men—his biological father, Gaius Octavius, his adoptive father, Caesar, and his divine father, Apollo. Octavian's hopes for the succession were set in turn on Marcellus, Agrippa, Gaius and Lucius Caesar, and, as a last resort, Tiberius.

While Octavian never struck coins in Rome with portraits of either Octavia or Livia (even though he recommended both for the right of public statuary), he did decide to honor his daughter Julia as the mother of Gaius and Lucius. In 13 B.C., the year of the consecration of the Ara Pacis, the moneyer Gaius Marius issued coins from the mint of Rome with portraits of Augustus on the obverse and a variety of reverse types, some with portraits of Julia. Thus Augustus repeated what Antony had done nearly thirty years earlier—a woman from the imperial circle was given a prominent position on the official Roman coinage.

One coin depicts a reverse group portrait of Julia, Gaius, and Lucius Caesar (Fig. 16.4). There is no attempt to assimilate her to a goddess or personification. The decision was to let Julia be Julia. As herself, Julia wears the *nodus* hairstyle, which became, as we shall see, a kind of badge of Roman womanhood. How else could Julia be imaged than as the ideal Roman princess who, just as fertile as Cleopatra, had given birth to two Augustan princes? Nearly twenty years after the Egyptian queen's death, Cleopatra and her art were still having an impact over image making in Augustan Rome; Julia's coins with her sons were strikingly reminiscent of those of Cleopatra with Caesarion. A wreath above Julia's head on the coin offers tribute to her greatest accomplishment—providing the emperor of Rome with heirs. The wreath is the oak crown awarded to Augustus for saving the life of a Roman citizen in battle; it signified that Augustus had saved many lives by restoring the Republic. The oak crown was to become the permanent emblem of imperial power, transferred on this coin by Augustus via Julia to Gaius and Lucius.

Livia: Cleopatra by Proxy

Even though Livia was the star of the Ara Pacis Augustae and was granted public statuary in Rome by Augustus, the emperor never minted coins in Rome with her portrait. This is no small matter, especially since it is highly likely that Livia asked him to do so. Augustus must have had what seemed to him a very compelling rationale for this decision, although it is difficult today to understand what that might have been. Since Augustus appears to have been motivated to advertise hereditary dynasty and imperialist expansion on his coinage, one can only assume that he didn't think a portrait of Livia expressed either of those goals. Julia was exploitable as the mother of two potential male heirs—indeed, she was a competitor to Cleopatra in that realm—but Livia was perhaps less so, although she took on the role of the dynasty's "mother" on the Ara Pacis. Where Livia could be useful, however, was in the arena of colonization. Once Egypt was made a protectorate, it was important to proclaim it as such. In Rome, Augustus decided to do this by means of coin imagery such as a crocodile and the legend *Aegypto Capta;* but in Egypt he made a different determination.

Augustus recognized that in Egypt he was minting coins for a people long used to being governed by a queen and most recently by "the Queen." Since Egypt was a protectorate that belonged to the emperor, any coins struck there would have been fully under his jurisdiction and privy to his directives, and he must have wanted to emphasize that fact. It was surely Augustus's direct order that resulted in the issuance of coins in Alexandria in 10–9 B.C. with Livia's portrait and the legend *Livia Augusta* in Greek. Augustus's decision to have these manufactured in Alexandria and not in Rome was a clever strategy to provide the Egyptians, recently governed by a goddess-queen, with a female replacement for Cleopatra. Augustus's message was clear and to the point—the Egyptians were now ruled by a Roman pharaoh and a Roman queen, and by the Julio-Claudian rather than the Ptolemaic dynasty.

17

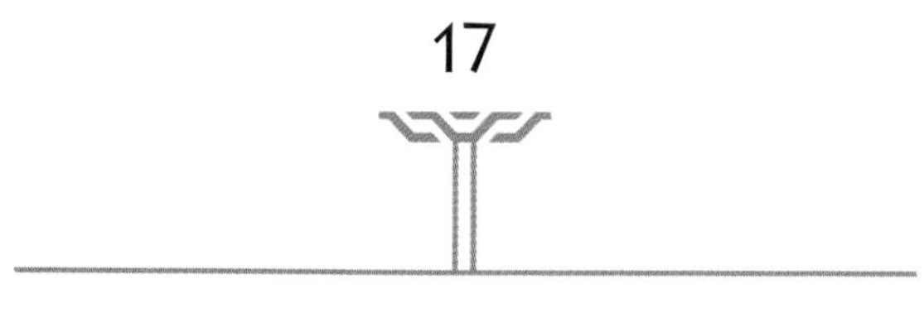

PRINCESSES AND POWER HAIR

While the coin portraits of Octavia, Julia, and Livia may be the purest expression of the public roles of these influential women, they were by no means the only one. Sculptured portraits of all three were also erected in highly visible public spaces in Rome and the provinces. Octavia, unlike her lesser-known sister of the same name, was commemorated with portraiture. The reason that she, and not her sister, received this privilege is that Octavia was a key figure in Roman public life. Such a position was accorded her primarily because of her marriage to important men and because she was actively involved in helping her brother form alliances that furthered his political goals. Above all, it was the direct result of the *sacrosanctitas* (sacrosanctity) that Augustus bestowed on her and Livia in 35 B.C. As we saw earlier, Augustus was motivated by his rivalry with Antony and his desire for jurisdiction over the entire empire. Octavia's sacredness would mean that any offense against her (for example, Antony's affair with Cleopatra and the birth of their children) would also be a transgression against the state, punishable by a declaration of war.

Dio Cassius mentions the *sacrosanctitas* law, but he doesn't indicate whether it was promulgated by the senate or was a triumviral edict.[1] In either case, it was very special, had no precedent, and was, in fact, so unique as to be confined to only these two women. It provided them with unmatched financial freedoms and liberated them from Augustus's sumptuary laws for women that regulated the wearing of ostentatious jewelry and the expenditure of large sums of money. Once Octavia and Livia were freed from those restrictions, they were in the position of Augustan men who could jockey for status and influence by making benefactions and building public architecture. The law also granted both of them the right of commemorative statuary, and likenesses of them were surely erected immediately upon its enactment. The appearance of these statues in highly visible locations in the city would have immediately announced the honor in the most public way possible. The new award also included tribunician *sacrosanctitas,* which was the part that conferred both privilege and protection as the honorees took on a more public role. The two women were now able to move around the city without a guardian and attend the theater and other municipal events.

Although they were not related, Octavia and Livia were portrayed in their new public statues as if they were sisters. In these sculptured portraits, the faces of both women are idealized and ageless, and their radiant oval visages are framed by hairstyles that are barely distinguishable from each other. Why would two prominent and wealthy women from different families who had access to the finest textiles, the highest quality cosmetics, and the most talented hairdressers want to look like twins? Both women were acknowledged beauties, and both had the self-confidence to establish fashion rather than follow it. Because of their sacrosanctity, both even had genuine authority in Rome.

There are two likely explanations. One is that Augustus's obsession with the succession and his lack of a son led him to emphasize familial connections in portraits of the imperial circle. In their portraiture, Marcellus looked like Augustus, as did Gaius and Lucius Caesar, and even Tiberius. Gaius and Lucius were Augustus's grandsons and Marcellus was his nephew, so they may indeed have resembled him, but there is no reason to think that Tiberius looked anything like the emperor. That they bore a resemblance to one another in their portraiture was meant to convince the citizenry that all were viable successors. That the female members of the imperial family were presented as if they were blood relatives also emphasized the idea of the imperial family as an indivisible unit. Furthermore, the conformity of Octavia's and Livia's portraits to a physical feminine ideal established that ideal as an objective to be aspired to by all Roman women.

Such homogeneity in female portraiture of the Augustan age makes distinguishing portraits of Octavia from those of Livia difficult today. As empress, Livia was depicted more often in portraiture, and those images of her that have survived have received more scholarly attention. While this is not surprising, it may represent a missed opportunity because Antony's coin series with Octavia's portraits establishes a framework for her portraiture that is lacking for Livia's. The likelihood that Octavia's coin portraits were associated with specific occasions provides them with a historical context and allows close analysis of the motivation for their commission.

Key political events involving Octavia were appropriate times for the creation of new portrait types—the signing of the Treaty of Brundisium (40 B.C.), the Tarentum Treaty (37 B.C.), and the granting of *sacrosanctitas* (35 B.C.). Octavia was also likely honored after her death in 11 B.C. That said, it is not easy to match surviving portraits to their numismatic counterparts. Moreover, contemporary coins depict portraits with striking variations, especially in the configuration of the hair. Rolf Winkes, for example, distinguishes Octavia's Type 1 portrait from Type 2, with the first type closely allied with coins of 39–36 B.C. and the second with an *aureus* of 39. Which of these two should be associated with the pact at Brundisium?

The best example of Winkes's Type 1 portrait is a marble head of Octavia from the Bergen Collection. Carved in late Augustan times, it must have been based on a model from the early 30s B.C. Octavia is portrayed with an oval face, pointed chin, large almond-shaped eyes, and small rounded lips. She is already depicted with the roll of hair or *nodus* over her forehead, waves of hair covering the tops of her ears, and a large rounded bun at the back of her head. One main strand of hair is braided and supported by two lightly twisted subsidiary strands. The primary braid is wrapped three times around the bun and secured. The rolling, braiding, and binding of the hair are significant because they emphasize the subject's modesty and chastity.

Type 2 is known from the quintessential marble portrait of Octavia from Velletri, and now in the Palazzo Massimo alle Terme (see Fig. 2.2). In this portrait, Octavia seems to have come into her own. She is less restricted, with a looser *nodus* and tendrils of hair escaping her coiffure along her forehead, above her ears, and on the back of her neck. A tight braid still emerges from the *nodus* on the top of her head, but it is narrower with less pronounced subsidiary sections. The braid is wound around the bun as in the Type 1 portrait, but in this case only twice. Octavia's face is similarly modeled, with the eyes somewhat less pronounced, and is instilled with a classicizing immutability that parallels Augustus's Primaporta type (see Fig. 12.2). The Type 2 portrait suggests that Octavia is comfortable in her own skin and has fallen naturally into her role as first sister and a very important person in Rome.

Octavia's type 3 portrait, known best not from a marble head but from the coin of 39, represents her in a manner comparable to Type 2, but with a smaller bun that rests lower down on the back of her neck (see Fig. 16.3). Might the more confident Octavia of Types 2 and 3 be the one who was granted sacrosanctity in 35 B.C.? Although this honor had a downside—it was a signal that she might be about to lose Antony once and for all—it was, at the same time, an unprecedented distinction for a woman. Octavia was strong and capable enough to take real pride in that accomplishment.

While determining which portrait type belongs to which event would be a major contribution to the history of the portraiture of elite Roman women, what is more important is the message that all of Octavia's portraits imparted. They presented Octavia as an attractive young woman who resembled her brother but whose physical beauty was only one component of her individuality. The idealization and serenity of her portraiture were suitable expressions of her good nature and her maternal devotion. What Octavia's exquisite visage did not reveal was the strength of her will and the determination of her actions. Her dynamic participation in Octavian and Antony's contest for world supremacy endowed her with a *gravitas* and prestige that were rare for a Roman woman.

Octavia's political maneuvering and domestic duties left her little time for fashion. Yet it was she who appears to have first conceived of a new hairstyle that was so clever and so perfect for the image of the new Augustan woman that it was rapidly adopted by empress and slave woman alike. Called today the *nodus* coiffure, it takes its name from the roll of hair that was arranged like a pompadour above the center of the forehead. This coiffure was created as a response to the hairstyle of the most stylish and notorious woman in Republican Rome—Cleopatra. Cleopatra was Octavia's rival, a royal diva who was serious competition for the affection and loyalty of Antony. For Octavia, losing Antony meant not only losing a prominent husband and the father of her children, but also severing her most significant link to her brother's political program.

With regard to her physical appearance, Octavia had two choices. She could either compete head-on with her rival and Egyptianize by lining her eyes with kohl or adopting the queen's striking melon coiffure, or she could highlight her own strengths, among them her patrician Roman features and slender frame. The latter was really the only option since Octavia was already widely considered the more comely of the two women, and an Egyptian appearance would not have been appropriate for Octavian's sister. Nonetheless, Octavia's refined beauty and noble bearing were no match for a monarch with a country, an army, and the vast resources of a royal treasury. Octavia could not brandish regal insignia like those in the possession of Cleopatra's family for generations. What Octavia did instead was truly ingenious. I think it is likely that she worked with her hairstylists to create a coiffure made entirely of hair that had the height and impressiveness of Cleopatra's *uraeus* (rearing cobra) without the ostentatious artifice. That is, Octavia conceived the *nodus* as a facsimile of the cobra made of hair rather than metal. At the same time, as a foil to Cleopatra, Octavia emphasized the coiffure's simplicity and saw to it that it remained braided and bound, reflecting the virtues of ideal Roman womanhood. While it could be argued that an attempt to improve on Cleopatra's hairstyle only called further attention to the Queen and was an ineffective tactic, Octavia must have struck just the right chord, because the shrewd and ambitious Livia began to wear the hairstyle herself. With the empress's imprimatur, the style took off like a flash.

Whereas Octavia's primary objective must have been direct competition with Cleopatra, Livia seems to have had more ambitious aspirations, using the new hairstyle to position herself as the paragon of female rectitude. She needed not just to present herself as the model Roman woman, but also to intertwine her person with the tenets of Augustus's marriage and moral legislation. One wonders what Julia must have thought of all this—the family rebel who chafed at the idea of conforming to Augustus's strict regulations for female behavior. After Augustus exiled Julia, in punishment for her multiple and widely known adulteries, there was a cessation of coin portraits of her, and no new statuary was commissioned. Since the senate did not vote Julia an official condemnation or *damnatio memoriae,* there is no evidence that existing portraits were formally removed from public view or destroyed. Nevertheless, the paucity of surviving portraits of Julia suggests that, if not deliberately damaged or mutilated, they were at least neglected and discarded.

Since so few depictions of Julia survive, her official portrait has to be reconstructed from various sources—less than a handful of marble heads, coins, a sword sheath, and even fairly mundane objects such as theater tokens. The words "Iulia Augusta" were inscribed on lead theater tokens found in Rome, also embellished with a profile likeness of Julia wearing the *nodus.* A bone gaming token from Oxyrhynchos with a *nodus* portrait of a woman is inscribed IOY IA. That so few of these have survived is a tribute to the success of Julia's unofficial condemnation.

We have already seen that groundbreaking coins depicting Julia with Gaius and Lucius, probably conceived under the influence of coins of Cleopatra with Caesarion, were minted in Rome in 13 B.C. (see Fig. 16.4). Julia is also depicted between Gaius and Lucius Caesar in a scene on a metal sword sheath in Bonn, probably used by one of Augustus's supporters. Since the three are portrayed in frontal portraits on the sheath, these likenesses are more revealing than their numismatic counterparts. Julia's round face is framed by wavy hair with a central *nodus.* The boys, who each lean inward toward their mother, are wearing military dress and have their hair in a style that closely resembles their grandfather's.

After Agrippa's death in 12 B.C., Julia and Tiberius were given no choice but to wed. Julia's adulteries increased after this, and Tiberius, also unhappy, left Rome in 6 B.C. By 2 B.C., Julia had been exiled and discredited. None of this turbulence is alluded to in the Roman coinage, either in Rome or elsewhere. A striking series of coins issued in Pergamum in Asia Minor between 6 and 2 B.C. depict Livia as Hera on the obverse and Julia as Aphrodite on the reverse. Both women wear the *nodus,* with Julia's even more prominent than that of the empress, and both have buns wrapped with braids. It is hard to imagine that these women found this coiffure fashionable after more than thirty years, and even harder to believe that they still had their hair so arranged. It is a tribute to Cleopatra and her continued impact on Rome that elite women were still depicted as if they wore the coiffure. Apparently the *nodus* had become so closely intertwined with the notion of the ideal Roman matron and of ardent national pride that hairstyle and concept were nearly indistinguishable.

Julia was probably depicted on the Ara Pacis, although the figure on the altar usually associated with her is now headless (see Fig. 15.3). If it is she, she is the first woman in the procession on the north frieze, while Livia is the first on the south side. Livia and Julia were thus paired on the Altar of Peace as they were in Pergamene coinage as the wife and daughter of the ruling dynast. Although separated by age, these women were similarly presented.

When Julia was in her heyday, touted as the woman who made Augustus's dynastic hopes a reality and singled out on the Roman coinage as the mother of all imperial heirs, numerous statues of her were made for wide distribution around the empire. These appear to have been especially abundant in the East, where Julia traveled with Agrippa between 16 and 13 B.C., just before the consecration of the Ara Pacis. It was in the East that Julia was even called "thea" or divinity, the same epithet that had been applied to Cleopatra.

While the official coinage was proclaiming Julia as Rome's first mother, the designers of the Ara Pacis were beginning to conceive of showcasing Julia as Livia's younger counterpart. These must have been heady days, even for the daughter of an emperor. Once a princess, Julia was now almost a queen. She had prevailed over Livia by giving birth to two boys who were now the emperor's heirs, and she was honored for her accomplishment on the coin of the realm. She had become so elevated that she replaced Octavia as Livia's companion in portraiture, and the two were even revered together in an Athenian cult. These honors gave Julia visibility in Rome and around the empire, a prominence that was unmatched at the time. With her status, youth, fertility, and intelligent wit, Julia must have seemed almost Cleopatra-like. Julia, more than Livia, had some of Cleopatra's spirit, and she was as notorious as she was famous. From Cleopatra and Antony, Julia learned what it meant to live the inimitable life. Romping around Rome with some of its most prominent male aristocrats and most gifted poets, she must have cut quite a figure.

Over the years, various marble portraits of young women with a noble countenance and a *nodus* hairstyle have been associated with Julia. These identifications are merely surmises because the portraits do not have identifying inscriptions and are not based on a common prototype. The association of these portraits with Julia is so tenuous that they cannot be used to shed further light on the emperor's daughter and her imagery.

Searching for Julia has now become a cottage industry, with some emphasis recently on marble portraits from Caere and Baeterrae. Elizabeth Bartman identifies them as portraits of Julia on the basis of a common prototype made at the time of Augustus's adoption of Gaius and Lucius. In the Baeterrae head, the woman wears a broad and somewhat flattened *nodus* with a central braid. The Copenhagen head has a similar braid but a shell-shaped *nodus,* providing a glimmer of Julia's party-girl frivolity. Yet these portraits depict a pudgy and dour young woman who may have the requisite Augustan almond eyes and rounded lips, but doesn't really resemble Augustus. Susan Wood's observation that she is a closer likeness of Agrippa and may be his daughter, Vipsania Agrippina, is compelling.

Catherine de Grazia Vanderpool has come up with a more spirited Julia in a portrait from the Julian Basilica at Corinth (see Fig. 3.1). The fact that the head was found in a major public building makes it more likely that it represents a woman of substance, probably from the imperial circle. The Corinth head depicts a woman of Julia's age with simple, forceful features—an aquiline nose, full rounded lips, and large almond-shaped eyes beneath perfectly arched brows that cast the eyes in deep and dramatic shadow. The woman wears the *nodus,* which is gently lifted above the rest of the hair in a manner resembling Octavia in the Velletri portrait (Fig. 2.2). Since this portrait is unique, it has not been widely accepted as Julia; but some scholars, most recently Rolf Winkes, think the identification has real merit, and I agree.

The dynamic among Octavia, Julia, and Livia in the last two decades of the first century B.C. must have been galvanizing as these women, all of whom had been touched in some way by Cleopatra, tried to figure out how to gain and wield power. Octavia had to confront her husband's very public affair with Cleopatra and the resultant children, some of whom she selflessly volunteered to rear. Octavia had tried to compete with Cleopatra when the queen was still alive, intervening with Octavian on Antony's behalf and amassing funds and equipment for Antony's military ventures. Despite her genteel upbringing, Octavia had a visceral reaction to "the Queen" that motivated her to use her sacrosanctity to achieve tangible results—her portrait on the Roman coinage and her invention of the *nodus* coiffure. As Augustus's sister, Octavia possessed real authority in Rome, which was further substantiated by her sacredness. It is not surprising that when Augustus was searching for a potential son-in-law and heir, he turned to Octavia's son Marcellus, whom he betrothed to Julia.

That Julia was Augustus's biological daughter gave her immediate cachet. In Rome, biology was beginning to become destiny, and even though Julia couldn't develop into a ruler, she could be an empress if her husband succeeded Augustus. She had three chances—first with Marcellus, then with Agrippa, and finally with Tiberius. An even better shot at bona fide clout was the likely ascendance of Gaius and Lucius. If either followed Augustus, Julia would be first mother. If the boys succeeded him at a young age, she might even be regent. Julia must have felt almost like Cleopatra—born into privilege and with the knowledge that she herself could rule, at least through the men in her life, and especially through her sons. With all of Rome potentially at her feet, Julia squandered the opportunity, preferring to fulfill her dreams in the arms of a different group of Roman men. Still, some of her lovers were highly placed aristocrats with whom she may have hoped to overthrow her father and achieve an even greater share of the Roman *imperium*. Like Octavia, Julia played politics, and it is possible that what she heard about Cleopatra's leadership skills and femme-fatale appeal may have inspired her. If things had turned out differently, Julia's relationships with elite Roman men, like those of Cleopatra, might even have led to mastery of the empire.

18

REGINA ROMANA

When Livia met Augustus, Octavia and Julia were already an integral part of his life. Livia also had her life, including a marriage, a son, and a second child on the way. Augustus viewed Livia's patrician lineage as a major asset to his quest for *auctoritas,* but she must have entered the union with eyes wide open. In Rome, marriage was rarely forever, especially for ambitious politicians. Octavia and Julia could count on their biological link to Augustus, but Livia was on shakier ground, knowing that any day she could become expendable. Livia's hold on Augustus was tenuous enough that she quickly needed a strategy to ensure her continued presence in the emperor's circle. She could have found no better role model than Cleopatra.

Livia probably recognized from the start that even Cleopatra acquired most of her authority through men. She was the daughter of the Pharaoh Auletes and ruled Egypt not alone but with a succession of brother-consorts. Cleopatra's alliances with Rome involved mergers with elite Roman men. Livia sought to solidify her own power, first through her husband and then by ensuring the succession of her elder son, Tiberius. Livia seems to have been single-minded in pursuing what was really a very simple plan, but one that was inspired by a consummate guide.

It is clear that Livia was gifted with the ability to recognize a good idea when she saw one, seize it, and then make it her own. Augustus built temples; so did Livia. Augustus and Agrippa erected porticoes; so did

Livia. Octavia was granted sacrosanctity by Augustus; Livia apparently convinced her husband to give it to her as well. Octavia invented the *nodus* coiffure; Livia adopted it and made it an internationally recognized hairstyle, worn by aristocrats and freedwomen alike. Livia never had portrait coins in Rome, but it was her face that replaced Cleopatra's on coins in Egypt. Seemingly not content to be only an empress, Livia became a kind of surrogate queen. She presented herself to Rome and the empire as the virtuous and modest Roman matron, Rome's consummate saint, an icon of ideal Roman womanhood and the antithesis of the sinner Julia. Yet Livia was far from modest, becoming the most powerful woman since Cleopatra.

Livia was savvy enough to take advantage of her situation, and she acquired bona fide influence at a time when women could not vote, hold public office, or appear in public without a guardian. Even though Augustus regulated the lives of women around Livia by promulgating strict moral and marriage laws that established firm guidelines for virtuous behavior and increased procreation, Livia herself enjoyed unprecedented freedom. She rejected guardianship, became a patroness of monumental architecture, and cleverly imaged herself as the symbol of her husband's new ideal Roman woman. Creating a dynamic public persona from the simple concept of the modest and chaste Roman mother would seem a conflicting and impossible goal, but Livia had the skills to achieve it. Livia looked to Cleopatra as one of a small number of formidable women leaders who had achieved genuine power in a man's world, and who continued to be celebrated for that success not only in her own country but also in Rome. By the time Livia was made sacrosanct, Cleopatra's statue had stood in the Temple of Venus Genetrix for almost ten years—a compelling and accessible model. Livia sought to craft her own trajectory of power, knowing that the designation of sacrosanctity would free her from most of the constraints under which Roman women lived. What made Cleopatra even more appealing as an archetype is that the Egyptian queen had also been a force against Rome that required opposition. For that reason, any dialogue Livia established with the art of Cleopatra would have the same kind of multivalency that Augustus was seeking in his own monuments.

Livia's union with Augustus catapulted her into a position of prominence and influence. She held sway as Rome's first lady and gained enhanced authority as mother of the second *princeps,* capitalizing on every privilege she could extract from her husband and son. Although Augustus set public policy, which may not have always corresponded to Livia's own personal beliefs, the empress found ways to circumvent this policy in her own life.

Livia established a record of influence and accomplishment that seems notable even today. It was Livia more than Octavia or Julia who truly succeeded in supplanting Cleopatra on the stage of the ancient world after the Battle of Actium because it was Livia's visage that replaced Cleopatra's on the Egyptian coinage. Feminine power was openly transferred from one woman to another, and all the world was invited to see it happen. Augustus acknowledged that shift by appearing in a double portrait with Livia on eastern coinage, mimicking a type used by Ptolemaic kings and queens.

Cleopatra vividly demonstrated that a woman in the public eye had the opportunity to weave her own narrative. Augustus was a mythmaker as well. Thus Livia could learn this art from two masters of storytelling. Even though she married Augustus while still pregnant with another man's child, Livia nonetheless transformed herself into the very symbol of chaste Roman womanhood. She astonishingly became the ultimate *univira,* a woman who married once and remained faithful to that one man. Although Livia and Augustus had no children together and Livia had only two by her first husband, she was presented to the Roman people as the consummate mother of Augustus's marriage and moral legislation, the mother of more than three children—a fiction made possible by Augustus's adoption of Gaius and Lucius Caear, making Livia their mother by association. This parsing of the truth exceeded anything ever attempted by Cleopatra.

Livia may also have learned from observing Cleopatra that it was not enough to be a human being, especially a woman, and that accumulating divine attributes was advantageous. Ptolemaic practice allowed Cleopatra to possess the aura of a genuine goddess during her lifetime, but Livia could only attempt to claim that status openly in the East. In Rome, she and Augustus had to be more circumspect. Yet Livia's sacrosanctity and the voting of public statuary provided opportunities to explore divine associations even in the capital, and thus Livia is unlikely to have objected when Augustus put a statue of her as his newly sacred wife in proximity to Cleopatra's in the Temple of Venus Genetrix.

Livia's public and private personae were not always one and the same. Like Cleopatra, Livia developed the capacity both to play to the crowd and to make things happen behind the scenes. Devoted to her elder son and his bright political future, she became first mother among mothers while, at the same time, plotting behind her son's back to share some of his imperial authority. As Rome's first empress, Livia was publicly revered and worshipfully imitated. What Livia wore and how she dressed her hair were matters of enormous interest, and her calculated personal choices about her wardrobe and her coiffure were underscored again and again as women from all levels of Roman society adopted her selections as their own. Aristocrats and freedwomen alike were depicted in their portraiture dressed like the empress and coiffed with variants of Livia's *nodus* hairstyle.

Surviving historical and literary sources provide an outline of Livia's life and attainments, but it is the material evidence that completes the contours of this formidable woman. These tangible data inform us of Livia's appearance, her bearing, her disposition and character, and her way of looking at and having an impact on the world in which she lived. The architecture she commissioned and the inscriptions that list her titles and donations provide a picture of her contributions to Rome. Like Cleopatra, she wanted to be a prodigious builder and to have her name and accomplishments preserved for posterity. In addition, she looked to statuary to present her persona in Rome and the empire, relief sculpture to describe her relationship to other members of the imperial family, coins to advertise the emperor's policies, and gems to articulate that same vision for a more selective audience.

Livia played a greater role than has previously been thought in the selection and formulation of her own imagery, as the following examples will show. Her unique position in Roman public life gave her the prestige to achieve this aim, but she also benefited from a general expansion in the production of imperial portraiture in the first century. This increased output included statuary of women, who had previously been largely excluded as the subjects of portraiture. As Rome's first empress,

Livia was empowered to create a new mode of representation for the *princeps femina*. Since there were no Roman models to emulate, Livia undoubtedly looked to the repertoire of images of classical Greek goddesses and Hellenistic queens and selected features that, when combined with her own facial traits, personality, and core beliefs, resulted in a portrait that would reflect the political and social ideology of Augustus. Cleopatra was doubtless one of the Hellenistic queens Livia studied, but she had to be mindful that while she could use the Egyptian sovereign as a role model for authoritative womanhood, she needed to make sure that the resulting portrait was viewed as the antithesis of Cleopatra's.

Although Livia's portraits were recognizable likenesses of the empress, their primary intent was not to depict a specific woman but to present the ideal Augustan matron, worthy of emulation. Despite their blatant artifice, Livia's portraits codified the image of empress and served as the archetype for portraits of subsequent Roman empresses and princesses, who either imitated them or deliberately rejected their most distinctive features. It is also worth noting that Livia's facial features were subsumed in an idealized veneer that was the chosen mode of representation for Augustus and other members of the Julio-Claudian family. Even though some of these family members were not biologically linked, their deliberate resemblance in portraiture was meant to encourage the viewer to think that they were. For this reason, the general type chosen for Livia's portrait is far more important than the subtle distinctions among types.

The official Roman coinage represents a nearly unbroken chronology of imperial policy and ideology, providing a chain of portrait types that constitutes our best evidence for the physiognomies and policies of all the Roman imperial dynasties. Furthermore, whether an empress is or is not depicted on the Roman coinage speaks to her authority or lack thereof. What is critical in any evaluation of the imagery of Livia is the recognition that Augustus made a deliberate decision not to strike coins with her portrait in Rome. He apparently did not want to suggest in the capital that his wife was that important. Augustus did, however, advertise Livia's consequence in the provinces, where he selectively issued portrait coins of her in appropriate locations such as Egypt. Tiberius reversed Augustus's policy, deciding that a close link with his mother was politically desirable. Beginning in A.D. 22, Tiberius issued coins in Rome with Livia's portrait to record important events and to associate his mother with a variety of personifications and divinities.

In view of Livia's forceful agenda, it is not surprising that she was honored with more sculptured portraits than was any other Augustan woman. In fact, a more complete material record survives for Livia than for Cleopatra. The amount of physical evidence is so vast that it is not easily categorized. As long ago as 1886 Johann Bernoulli compiled the first systematic list of Livia portraits, upon which all later scholarship has been based. Recent studies continue to divide Livia's portraits into four or five types—two or three created during her lifetime, one dating from early in the principate of Tiberius, and a fourth after Livia's divinization by Rome's fourth emperor, Claudius. In addition, many spin-offs were based on these prototypes.

Since Livia appears to have adopted the *nodus* coiffure as a badge of national pride and was apparently determined to work with court advisers and artists to make it a sign of women's morality in the age of Augustus, it is not surprising that all lifetime portraits of the empress in the round depict her with this hairstyle. While the chronological evolution of these three lifetime portrait types, known today by their find spots or present locations, has been arranged and rearranged by scholars, the most recent studies favor a sequence of the so-called Marbury Hall Type, Albani-Bonn Type, and Fayum Type.

In the Marbury Hall portrait type, epitomized by a portrait in the Palazzo Massimo alle Terme, Livia is represented as a serious Roman matron whose image has yet to break free from the confines of Republican portraiture, which depicted middle-aged women as they were (Fig. 18.1). While her face is wrinkle-free, she is not idealized. Her nose has a noticeable hook, and her lips are thin and tightly closed. The oval of the face and the almond-shaped eyes look more Augustan. The hair, rather than providing a soft frame for the face, is severely bound with a small, tightly rolled *nodus,* a single braid over the head, and twisted plaits at either side of the head. A small bun at the back of the head is tightly wrapped with another braid.

In the Albani-Bonn type, Livia has loosened up. A portrait of the empress now in Baltimore is an example of this type and portrays a softer and prettier empress. The oval face and almond-shaped eyes are still in evidence, as is Livia's distinctive nose, but her lips are more sensuously rounded. Livia has done away with the encumbering side plaits of hair in favor of soft waves that undulate above the tops of her ears, although a braid is fastened on either side of the head above the waves and on top of the head. The rest of the hair is gathered in a bun, which is wider than in the Marbury Hall type. The *nodus* is also broader, covering most of the expanse of Livia's forehead and made up of a thicker and flatter section of hair.

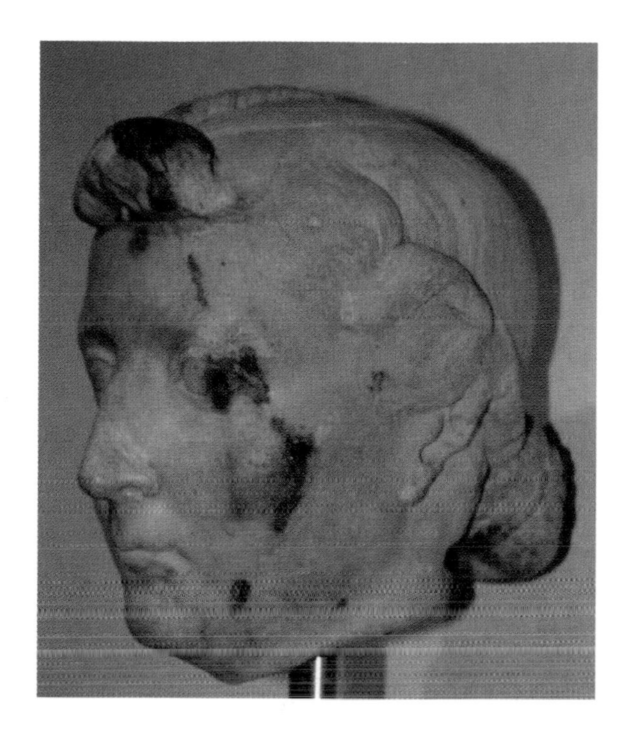

18.1. In Livia's earliest portraits, she is shown as young but not idealized and already coiffed with the *nodus* hairstyle.

It was in the Fayum Type that Livia's portraitist achieved what was to become the quintessential Livia likeness, and the one that was created to be the companion to Augustus's so-called Primaporta Type (Fig. 18.2; see Fig. 12.2). The type takes its name from the find spot, Arsinoë in the Fayum in Egypt, where the portrait was discovered together with marble heads of Augustus and Tiberius. Surrounded by husband and son, Livia is both empress of Rome and matriarch, whose offspring Tiberius has just been adopted by Augustus. Furthermore, she is strutting her stuff in Egypt, where Cleopatra once ruled.

The Arsinoë portrait, now in Copenhagen, has naturally progressed from the two earlier types. Livia is represented with the same oval face and almond-shaped eyes, but the forehead is broader, the chin more pointed, the eyes larger, the eyebrows more sharply defined. The hook of the nose is less pronounced, and the lips are smaller but still lush. The *nodus* has been toned down—it is a little less wide and a little less tall, and the waves are looser still. The side braids have disappeared entirely, although there is still a plait, now much flatter, on top of the head. The bun is smaller than in the Albani-Bonn type. The tour-de-force detail of this portrait is the tendrils of hair that escape from the coiffure on the forehead, around the face, in front of the ears, and on the nape of the neck.

They are a tribute not only to a highly talented artist but also to the empress's desire to be an approachable icon.

Livia looks younger in this portrait type than in the preceding two. This may have to do with the fact that it was at this time in her life that Livia's personal style really came together, but it may also demonstrate a deliberate decision on the part of empress and emperor to synchronize their images. In the Fayum group, both Livia and Augustus are younger and more idealized than in earlier portraits. They are better looking and resemble each other more closely than ever before. They are now truly cut from the same cloth—they have left Republican verism behind and have become symbols of their imperial roles.

The emergence of the Fayum portrait type as the canonical Livia portrait indicates that the empress and/or her portraitist clearly decided that the portrait type on which the Fayum portrait was based most successfully captured Livia's conception of herself. Furthermore, by grouping her with Augustus and Tiberius, it presented most effectively the role Livia played within the Julio-Claudian family and in Roman public life. And yet, in this assemblage, Livia's portrait was smaller in scale than the other two—a blatant demonstration to the spectator that whatever she had achieved, Livia, as a woman, did not possess the authority of her male counterparts.

18.2. The canonical portrait of Livia, portraying her as the beautiful and ageless icon of Roman womanhood with the simple *nodus* hairstyle that has by now become a badge of national pride and the antithesis of Cleopatra's ornate coiffure.

Although Livia appropriated Octavia's *nodus* and made it her own, investing it with a multitude of meanings, she was not a slave to this Roman hairstyle. When it suited her and when she had other objectives in mind, the empress did not hesitate to instruct the court artists to depict her hair differently. As a team was brought together to design and execute the Ara Pacis, both Augustus and Livia were probably involved in planning sessions. The monument was going to be consecrated in the near future, with the expectation that it would be finished in a few years and dedicated on Livia's birthday. The reliefs on the Ara Pacis were intended to encapsulate the history of Rome and the present and future direction of the Julio-Claudian dynasty. This monument would rival Cleopatra's temple at Dendera in its ambition and would be Livia's first opportunity to be a queen in Rome as she was already in Egypt.

As we have seen, the *nodus* coiffure included among its references Cleopatra's *uraeus* (rearing cobra). By now, however, that message seemed a little tired; the *nodus* had been around for many years, and even freedwomen were wearing it in their sepulchral portraits. Livia needed to do something dramatic, and she could not have chosen a better stage than the large marble altar in the Campus Martius, the first Roman monument that would include portraits of Roman women and their children (see Fig. 15.2). Furthermore, Augustus was already planning to bring Egyptian obelisks to Rome and to place one between his tomb and the Ara Pacis—a highly visible reference to the Roman conquest of Egypt and Cleopatra's demise. Livia was thus undoubtedly free to take a new direction. While Roman mores did not allow Livia to present herself as a diva, she could express in a subtle way that she had supplanted Cleopatra as Rome's "goddess."

On the Ara Pacis, Livia decided to unroll her *nodus*. She mined the repertory of earlier ancient art until she came up with an idea (see Fig. 2.1): she parted her hair in the center and wore it brushed back like a fifth-century B.C. Greek goddess, for example the so-called Farnese Athena in Naples, a Roman copy of a Greek statue of 420–400 B.C. This worked perfectly with what her husband and his artists had in mind. The altar's designers were themselves probably Greeks and had carved contemporary Greek divinities and maidens, including a replacement for one of the caryatids from the south porch of the Erechtheum in Athens of around 420–406 B.C., with the same wavy parted hair and long strands falling on the shoulders. Moreover, these same artists were probably already sketching the head of the female deity for the southeast panel of the Ara Pacis (see Fig. 15.4). She too would have wavy parted hair and long ringlets on her shoulders, as well as two bouncing babies on her lap. Assimilating Livia to her would underscore Livia's role as the supreme Roman mother. Mindful that an image of Cleopatra, possibly with Caesarion, still stood in the Temple of Venus Genetrix, Livia may have been especially enthusiastic about being shown on the Ara Pacis with both her biological and adoptive sons. It was the Ara Pacis portrait of Livia that established a new view of the empress, one that was to be the basis for portraits commissioned of her by Tiberius and also by Claudius.

Livia was often conceived of in partnership with one or more other imperial Roman woman, especially Octavia and Julia. The triumvirate of the wife, sister, and daughter of Augustus had an aura as special in that time as that of the trio of Octavian, Antony, and Lepidus. In a sense, the authority of these three women was invested in their femaleness rather than in their individuality. What is remarkable, however, is that Livia was as successful as Augustus at breaking through the constrictions of the group and striking out on her own.

19

FROM ASP TO ETERNITY

The politics, persona, and art of Cleopatra had a profound impact on Rome through the Queen's intense interactions in turn with Julius Caesar, Mark Antony, and Octavian Augustus. Cleopatra commissioned architecture and statuary with Caesar and Antony, but her most significant and lasting influence with regard to first-century visual culture was not on them but on Augustus, with whom she never shared a monument. Whereas Caesar and Antony sought alliance with Egypt, Octavian chose to appropriate the kingdom and to transform what had been Alexander's Hellenistic world into a markedly Roman one. Art was pressed into the service of Octavian's ambitious agenda, and a multitude of Hellenistic elements were among the strands woven into a distinctly Roman art that could not be mistaken for the art of any other culture. One of the most important Hellenistic threads in Augustus's new Roman fabric was that of Ptolemaic Egypt, which found its latest manifestation in the art of Cleopatra.

The shift from a Hellenistic to a Roman ethos was already happening before Octavian's rise to prominence, but it was he who accelerated the process by ramping up the Romanization of diverse Hellenistic kingdoms. By the time Augustus began to commission art in Rome and these new Roman provinces, he had already incorporated what he had learned from Cleopatra in a new Roman mélange. The Queen's influence was far-reaching; through the vehicle of Augustus's art, it was disseminated from the emperor through all levels of Roman society. While patrons of art from senators to slaves may have been aware of Cleopatra's impact in the late 40s and 30s B.C., identifiable reminiscences of Cleopatra and Egypt probably faded as her artistic contribution was increasingly melded with a thoroughly Roman culture.

Those in Augustus's immediate circle, among them Octavia, Livia, Marcus Agrippa, the Augustan poets, and even the imperial family's slaves and freedmen, were more likely than anyone else in Rome to have had some real knowledge of Cleopatra. While impressions made at dinner parties are fleeting, poetic stanzas and works of art have the potential to last forever. Both odes and monuments provide clues that allow a fuller understanding of Cleopatra and her influence on Roman art at the most critical time in its history.

For Octavia, Cleopatra must have loomed large as the ultimate rival. Although Octavia was the sister of a man who was the "son" of a god and on a trajectory to rule Rome, the Queen of Egypt was a formidable competitor for the affections of Antony. Octavia's notable loveliness was no match for a charismatic monarch who ruled the wealthiest country in the world and had unlimited access to armies and advisers. While Octavia fought hard for her man, enlisting the help and considerable resources of her brother, she eventually had to concede defeat. Octavia's reaction to Cleopatra had repercussions not only for her personal life but also for Roman art.

Without Cleopatra as rival, Octavia would have been less likely to create her own version of the power hairstyle. To win Antony back, Octavia might have done herself up in imitation of Cleopatra, but she chose instead to do her own thing. Along with her hairdressers, Octavia invented the *nodus* coiffure, probably the single most significant hairstyle worn by a Roman woman (see Fig. 16.3). Its importance was due not only to its adoption by Livia and its popularization by Rome's first empress, but also to the fact that it linked fashion with ideology. Once the *nodus* became a sign of Roman national pride and of the ideal Roman woman, it had the power to speak to contemporary elite and non-elite women, who adopted it in large numbers, as well as to Roman empresses and princesses not yet born. Freedwomen and slaves were depicted in art with the *nodus* coiffure, among them Vecilia Hila, manumitted by a woman patron

19.1. The inclusion of women and children in the art of Cleopatra and Augustus led to the commissioning of family group portraits among enfranchised slaves in Rome.

in the age of Augustus (Fig. 19.1). In addition, empresses like the second-century Sabina, whose hairstyle signaled her husband Hadrian's philhellenism, would not have realized that a coiffure could be invested with a political agenda were it not for Octavia's response to Cleopatra.

It was Pascal who speculated: "Had Cleopatra's nose been shorter, the whole face of the world would have been changed." Cleopatra modified Octavia's life and, with it, the objectives of Roman art. Antony was deeply involved with Cleopatra even before his political marriage to Octavia, and Octavia suffered the public humiliation of having her husband return to his exotic paramour even after their union and military support from Augustus. More devastating was Antony's decision to marry Cleopatra, a marriage that was not accepted by Roman law. That Antony decided to be buried in Alexandria rather than Rome was the final insult.

Even though Cleopatra was never a serious rival for Octavian's affections, Livia probably noticed that Octavian found "the Queen" useful in the war of words he was waging with Antony, and that her monuments were, among others, a source for the emperor's redesign of Rome. Livia was in all probability intrigued by Cleopatra's portraiture since her own newly acquired sacrosanctity brought with it the right of statuary. Livia was in the position to have a say, if she wished, about the kinds of likenesses of her that would soon be put on display. Since there were few Roman models to consult, Livia may well have turned to the images of elegant foreign queens for guidance. At least one of those queens was already celebrated in Roman settings: Cleopatra's gilded statue had been in Caesar's Temple of Venus since the mid-40s B.C., and in 32 B.C. Antony had put Cleopatra's portrait on the reverse of his Roman denarii (see Fig. 9.5). Both of these images emphasized that a woman's authority could be advertised as openly as a man's and demonstrated that dress and hairstyle might reinforce a woman's public status.

Livia may not have known that her husband feigned love for Cleopatra as a ploy when trying to capture her; a love note was allegedly delivered to Cleopatra by Augustus's freedman Thyrsus as a way of discouraging her from burning her treasury before Augustus could appropriate it.[1] But Livia would have seen or heard about the famous post-Actium triumph, where the procession included a reclining effigy of Cleopatra on a couch, complete with asp. Even a recumbent mannequin of "the Queen" was quite a spectacle, especially since her likeness was accompanied by the living results of her union with Antony, their children Alexander Helios and Cleopatra Selene. This sensational scene would have had an impact on Livia and indeed on the throngs of people who lined the streets of the city to get a glimpse of the vanquished number-one enemy of Rome.

Cleopatra's power as a woman and as a political icon could not have failed to fascinate Livia. The Queen was a woman so sensuous and so commanding that she could seduce a dictator, marry a prominent Roman, and even extract "professions of love" from Livia's own ruthless and rather frosty husband. To top it all off, Cleopatra had produced four biological children. If she had been Roman, Cleopatra would have won out over Livia in Augustus's litmus test for fertile and nationalistic Roman women—the production of at least three offspring. Livia had failed in this particular competition since she was not able to provide Augustus with children and had only two from her former marriage. To equal Cleopatra's achievement of four progeny, Livia had to add a pair to her production. When Augustus adopted Julia's sons, Gaius and Lucius Caesar, in 17 B.C. (many years after Cleopatra's death), this new state of affairs allowed Livia to claim them also as her own.

Well before 17 B.C., Livia had embraced the *nodus* hairstyle (see Figs. 18.1 and 18.2). Recognizing that Octavia was onto something and that differentiating herself from the dead Cleopatra was a desirable goal, Livia began to wear the simple but distinctive hairstyle, one that appropriated Cleopatra's regal insignia, the *uraeus*. Livia's ascendancy as empress put her in a position where she could take full advantage of the highly charged coiffure. While both Octavia and Livia were very visible in Rome and both were granted the right of statuary, the proliferation of portraits of Livia was remarkable. Livia became one of the most imaged women in Rome's history and certainly the ascendant female star of her day—although Augustus did not permit her to be represented either on official coinage in Rome or in imperial family group portraits in Italy.

Because Octavia's and Livia's inviolability provided them with financial freedom, they, like their husbands, could sponsor building projects. When they got started on this in the 30s B.C., Octavia and Livia were aware of what their husbands and male relatives had already done. At that time the porticus was a popular building type among elite Roman generals back from victorious campaigns and flush with booty, including splendid works of art by famous artists. These men needed places to exhibit their war trophies, and the porticus was an ideal solution: a covered columnar walkway where public collections of statuary, paintings, maps, or scrolls could be displayed. These buildings were, in essence, ancient equivalents of a museum or rare book library. Intellectual life was becoming as important in Rome as it had been in Alexandria, and vast resources were invested to make Rome a competitive cultural center. Architecturally, the origin of the porticus was the Greek stoa, a covered colonnade, and its design probably migrated to Rome through military men who saw such structures in Sicily. The earliest examples in Rome appear to date from the mid-second century B.C.; Augustus and Agrippa erected versions in the late-first century B.C. Augustus commissioned the Porticus ad Nationes, known for its statues honoring all nations, and Agrippa constructed the Porticus Argonautarum, the prize possession of which was a famous painting depicting the saga of the Argonauts.

Livia and Octavia doubtless aspired to be builders because that is what elite Roman men did, and the sacrosanctity of the two women helped to level the playing field. They lived at a time when the impetus for creating edifices was enormous. Augustus and Agrippa had embarked on major construction programs in Rome and abroad; marble was arriving daily from Luna on the northwest coast of Italy; triumphant generals like Gaius Sosius were embellishing Rome with the proceeds of successful wars abroad. With resources at their disposal, Livia and Octavia joined the competition and demonstrated that women in Rome could be builders on a grand scale. Cleopatra's achievements in this area could not have failed to impress them. The two women had likely heard that Cleopatra had commissioned an edifice in honor of Caesar that bore his name, as well as a complex at Dendera that proclaimed her son Caesarion's birthright and her own authority as mother of the new pharaoh. It is also noteworthy that the Caesareum in Alexandria, built jointly by Cleopatra and Caesar, was essentially a porticus, with colonnades around its inner perimeter. Caesar put up a similar building in Antioch, and both structures are thought to have been prototypes for the Forum of Julius Caesar in Rome. In view of all these associations, it is not surprising that both Octavia and Livia built a porticus in Rome. Agrippa's sister, Vipsania Polla, was also the sponsor of a public colonnade—the Porticus Vipsania, which was the home of a famous map and thus a frequently visited location.

Octavia's Porticus Octaviae linked her with her son Marcellus. It is possible that Marcellus began the commission; in any case, Octavia dedicated the structure in his honor after his premature death. Octavia's porticus was located next to the Theater of Marcellus, built by Augustus as a showplace to memorialize his nephew as his dead heir. The Porticus Octaviae was a multipurpose structure with a library, a school or *schola,* an extensive art collection, and gardens.

It was Livia more than Octavia, however, who appears to have recognized the power of place and understood that a public porticus had the potential not only to link her in perpetuity with her men, but also to benefit the general public and disseminate imperial policy. The Porticus Liviae, preserved on Rome's third-century marble map, was built on land that had earlier been occupied by the ostentatious House of Vedius Pollio, one of the wealthy aristocrats who competed with his peers to have the most extravagant life-style. Pollio left his flamboyant domicile to Augustus in his will, and Augustus dramatically razed it to the ground and gave the land to the people of Rome by allowing it to be developed as a public recreational area in Livia's name. This act was another step in Augustus's moral regeneration of Rome, in which Livia played a key role as the ideal Roman woman. Like Octavia's porticus, Livia's had splendid gardens and a noteworthy public art collection.

Just as Octavia and Marcellus were joint commissioners of the Porticus Octaviae, Livia and Tiberius collaborated on the Porticus Liviae. In the age of Augustus, the bond of imperial mother and son became increasingly important to both parties. Young men found that their mothers were diligent sponsors, and women discovered that they were more influential with their sons than their husbands. While no direct link can be proved, it is illuminating to note that in first-century Rome the earlier mother and son combination of Cleopatra and Caesarion may have continued to be displayed together in the statue in the Temple of Venus Genetrix.

Livia and Tiberius appear to have dedicated the Porticus Liviae in 7 B.C., possibly after the completion of Tiberius's German campaigns. Just as on the Ara Pacis, depiction of war was banished, even though it had been the catalyst of peace, and peaceful procession in honor of the gods was the focus. Livia dedicated a shrine in the center of the porticus that resembled Augustus's Altar of Peace and had the same goal—the celebration of *concordia,* the political agreement that follows a military victory and the marital harmony that unites the imperial family.

It was this very message of peace and peaceful procession that had been featured by Cleopatra at the temple of Dendera and that appears to have been adopted by Augustus as a subtle and effective way of alluding to, rather than portraying, the war that made peace possible. Cleopatra and Caesarion are depicted at Dendera in concert with the Egyptian gods, and Cleopatra is presented as both wife and mother. While Roman law could not conceive of women married to their sons, such incestuous relationships were the stuff of Ptolemaic dynastic life as well as Greek and Roman mythology. That Livia wanted to be associated with her son's German triumphs is not surprising because it afforded her the opportunity to share in his victory by proxy.

Harmonious marriage had been a useful theme for Cleopatra, as it might be for any woman commissioning art in antiquity. Livia also realized its value when she constructed a handful of temples in Rome. While this number was small in comparison to the eighty-two temples built or restored by her husband, it was significant for a Roman woman. As these structures went up around Rome, it is likely that Livia would have gotten a lot of pleasure from the realization that she was a great woman builder in the tradition of "the Queen" (there were no earlier Roman women to emulate in this venue) and that, like Caesar and Augustus, she was contributing to making Rome a major urban center in the tradition of Alexandria and other renowned Hellenistic cities. In fact, Livia knew her temples would be more effective if they were intertwined with Augustus's blueprint for the political and moral rebirth of Rome. For that reason, Livia's temples featured the Roman woman of the new social order, exalting Roman married life for an ideal woman whose behavior was positioned as the polar opposite of Cleopatra's.

The liaison of Cleopatra and Caesar, the unlawful marriage of Cleopatra and Antony, and the illegitimate (by Roman standards) children that were the result of those unions shocked Rome in the 40s and early 30s B.C. These scandalous events were still remembered in the age of Augustus. Livia appears to have had the dual objective of wanting to be as authoritative a woman and as great a builder as Cleopatra, but also to be the embodiment of her husband's new morality. Livia did not flaunt her sensuality as Cleopatra had done but was instead the model of *pudicitia* or female modesty. Even though divorced, Livia was fictionalized as a *univira,* a woman who married one man and never remarried. The *univira* was the heroine of Augustus's marriage legislation and very different from

Cleopatra, who had had incestuous (at least in appearance) unions with her brothers and son and an illegal marriage to Antony. Although Cleopatra was the mother of four children, it could be argued, at least in Rome, that her progeny were illegitimate.

Livia's temples no longer survive, but we know something about them from archaeological remains and literary citations. Ovid tells us that Livia restored the Temple of Bona Dea Subsaxana, maintaining that she did so in imitation of her husband.[2] The temple was associated with female fertility. The Temple of Fortuna Muliebris, noted by Dionysius of Halicarnassus,[3] was on the Via Latina in Rome and had an inscription naming Livia as the restorer. In both cases, only *univirae* were purportedly allowed to worship the goddesses or tend to their cult. Specific reference to the virtue of *pudicitia* is apparent in two other commissions by Livia: the Shrines of Pudicitia Patricia (Patrician Chastity) and Pudicitia Plebeia (Plebeian Chastity), both restored by the empress in about 28 B.C. Livia's involvement came about because Augustus needed a woman to revitalize the shrines and also embody the cult of Chastity. Livia filled that role perfectly.

Like other women of their age, Livia and Octavia doubtless had conflicting feelings about Cleopatra. On one hand, they could not help but admire her indomitable spirit and ability to get things done. On the other, they were as besieged as everyone else in Rome with the message that Cleopatra was evil incarnate. Bolstered by their own sacrosanctity, Livia and Octavia were able to participate in public life more actively than earlier Roman women and to have a say about the form and meaning of Rome's architecture and statuary. As buildings and portraits were fashioned with their input, the obvious forerunners were the artworks of the Hellenistic queens; none was better known in Rome than Cleopatra.

Octavia played politics by being the primary intermediary between Antony and Octavian and serving as the prize that bound the covenant between the two men. For her part, Livia capitalized on her sacred status, cast off her guardians, and used her substantial financial resources to go her own way. While sometimes using Cleopatra as one of their role models, these two women publicly opposed the queen by putting themselves forward as the archetypes of correct behavior, wearing modest clothes and a simple, tightly fastened hairstyle.

Livia and Octavia would have heard about the incredible paired portraits of Cleopatra and Antony erected in major cities in the eastern empire. Since rulers were routinely assimilated to divinities in the East, they would not have been surprised to learn that Cleopatra and Antony sometimes masqueraded in this public portraiture as Isis and Osiris. What is especially noteworthy is that the couple were depicted as partners, side by side. While Octavia no longer had a viable consort, Livia was no doubt enthusiastic about public pronouncement of her official partnership with Augustus. Roman custom would not allow the emperor and empress to be depicted in the costumes of gods, but the East was as wide open to Augustus and Livia as it had been to Antony and Cleopatra. There is evidence that paired portraits of Rome's first couple began to be produced for display in the East right after the Battle of Actium, turning up in cities like Ephesus, Samos, Mytilene, and Cyzicus. Octavia was also part of the Mytilene group. Similar assemblages grouped Livia and Octavia together, and Livia with Julia and Julia the Younger.

In Italy, however, imperial portrait groups did not include Livia during Augustus's lifetime, just as the emperor did not strike coins in Rome with Livia's visage. While it is possible that such portraits existed but have not survived (Elizabeth Bartman has pointed out that portraits designed for groups in the West were carved on separate rather than shared bases, making it more likely that they were later disconnected), this is unlikely.

The art of Cleopatra may also have served as a paradigm for the men who surrounded Augustus, even if they never actually met her, because her reputation and monuments outlived her. Marcus Agrippa, for one, was a naval commander at Actium and had proconsular power in the eastern part of the empire; thus he may have been exposed to Cleopatra's construction program in Egypt. Cleopatra's architectural collaborations with Caesar in Alexandria were still standing after her death. Furthermore, through his connection with Augustus, Agrippa was also likely aware of the impact the partnership of Cleopatra and Caesar had on Caesar's intention to redesign Rome. Agrippa's impressions of Cleopatra and Egypt were combined with others he gleaned elsewhere. When he, like other elite men in Rome, began to use architecture to ensure fame and a lasting legacy, the final product incorporated some of what he knew of Cleopatra and her art. Agrippa's ambitions were among the most visionary in Rome. He recognized from the start that he needed to provide Rome's people with daily amenities as well as glitzy monuments and thus was as energetic about erecting aqueducts and baths as he was in commissioning a temple to all the gods.

While Agrippa, like Augustus, focused on the capital city's vital center and remade it in a dramatic way, he was also patron to some of Rome's most important provincial cities, Athens primary among them. Greece had come under Roman sway already in the second century B.C., when Lucius Aemilius Paullus defeated the Macedonians at Pydna in 168. Twenty years later, Macedonia was made a Roman province. It was Lucius Cornelius Sulla who sacked Athens, celebrating his 81 B.C. triumph in Rome by displaying spectacular Athenian works such as a painting by the famed artist Zeuxis. Sulla also confiscated colossal columns from the Temple of Zeus Olympios in Athens, with the intention of using them to rebuild Rome's Temple of Jupiter Capitolinus, recently damaged in a fire. In their new Roman environment, these pieces of Athenian visual culture became powerful symbols of Roman hegemony in Italy.

In a deliberate move, Agrippa and Augustus also wanted to establish a pictorial equivalent for Roman supremacy in Athens, just as Augustus had done in Alexandria and across the Egyptian countryside. Agrippa wrested the Acropolis from the Hellenistic kings and queens who had most recently claimed it by commandeering a Hellenistic monument at the entrance to the Acropolis and making it his own. Agrippa appropriated the tall pentelic marble pillar originally erected in 178 B.C. to honor Eumenes II, king of the Kingdom of Pergamum, and transformed it in the last quarter of the first century B.C. into the Agrippa Monument by replacing the portrait of Eumenes in a four-horse chariot with one of himself. The pillar still stands; the statuary group has long since disappeared. We do not know what Agrippa did with the statues of Cleopatra and Antony as Isis and Osiris that also stood on the Acropolis. While it is difficult to speculate in this instance, we have seen that the Augustan approach in Rome and elsewhere was to allow Cleopatra's statues to stand but to proscribe Antony's.

It is likely that Agrippa and Augustus planned their seizure of Athens' Acropolis together. Although the once glorious Athens was something of a backwater in Roman times, the resplendent civilization it stood for remained highly prized under Augustus. Just as Augustus had taken Egypt for his own, he wanted Athens as another trophy. The fact that Athens had been under Antony's jurisdiction and that he and Cleopatra had spent time there probably made Augustus all the more acquisitive.

What mattered above all was to signal that Rome was taking on the cultural mantle of Greece. For that reason, the visual language of the monuments restored by Augustus and Agrippa in Athens was Greek. The small temple that Augustus built in 27 B.C. to memorialize his ownership of the Acropolis was at the northeast corner of the Parthenon (Fig. 19.2). It was dedicated to Augustus and Roma, the eternal embodiment of the capital city, a sign that Rome was now master of Athens. Though surprisingly modest in scale, the temple was made of Greek pentelic marble, with a sloping conical roof and nine Ionic columns that were almost exact duplicates of those of the nearby Erechtheum. One of the reasons the decision was made to reproduce the Erechtheum columns was no doubt expediency, possibly even lethargy. Augustus's architects were simultaneously working on the fifth-century Erechtheum, which had been recently damaged by a fire; when they needed to carve capitals for the new Augustan sanctuary, it was easier to stick with the decorative motifs of the Erechtheum. But the choice may also have been more deliberate.

We know that the Erechtheum's unique Porch of the Maidens caught the eye of Augustus and Agrippa, because they were both impressed enough to commission buildings in Rome with similar supporting women. When Augustus's artisans repaired the Erechtheum caryatids, even replacing one with a new Roman copy, they made plaster casts of the caryatids and brought them back to Rome, where they served as prototypes for new Roman versions. Exact copies of the caryatids, although in smaller scale, were placed on the second story of the colonnade of the emperor's forum in downtown Rome, and a second set supported the porch of Agrippa's Pantheon. Agrippa's caryatids were even designed by a Greek artist, Diogenes.

Also in Rome, and near the caryatids in Augustus's forum, Cleopatra remained resplendent in the Temple of Venus Genetrix. Cleopatra was even more valuable to Augustus dead than alive: she could be anything Augustus wanted her to be. Augustus paraded Cleopatra's effigy as a trophy in his triumph to underscore his mastery over a formidable enemy.

19.2. With the art and architecture of Cleopatra as one of his inspirations, Marcus Agrippa oversaw architectural commissions in Greece, among them the temple to Augustus and Roma on the Athenian Acropolis.

In order to avoid the impression of waging a civil war, Octavian had declared hostilities against Cleopatra rather than Antony, and it was she who therefore became the invincible vanquished. That Augustus had conquered the queen of the ancient world's wealthiest kingdom, who was closely associated with goddesses, was an accomplishment of great magnitude. Octavian's victory in a civil conflict against one of Rome's favorite sons was not a political home run; subjugation of a foreign power, however, soared out of the ballpark.

The poets who gave literary life to Augustus's regime were perfectly amenable to using their lyrics to give rise to Cleopatra's legend. The famous shield scene in Virgil's *Aeneid* highlights Actium, Cleopatra's presence there, and her inevitable flight in the face of Octavian's omnipotence: "[The Queen,] pallid with death to come, then borne by waves and wind from the northwest, while the great length of mourning Nile awaited her with open bays, calling the conquered home."[4] And in one of Horace's odes, Cleopatra dies "nobly" and without fear.[5]

The shift of Cleopatra post mortem from harlot to noble queen, who in her newly found dignity underscored the majesty of an Octavian who was now Augustus, may explain in part Augustus's decision to keep her portrait on view in the temple in Caesar's forum and perhaps on the Athenian Acropolis as well. We don't know whether Augustus, with the Athenian portraits of Cleopatra and Mark Antony as Isis and Osiris in mind, was ever tempted to commission portraits of himself and Livia as gods in Rome. If so, the thought would have been immediately banished from his mind: the kind of ruler worship common in the East was unacceptable in Rome. Augustus's apparent resistance to being depicted in Rome with Livia in paired portraits as emperor and empress is surprising, however. Since Livia had sacrosanctity, had been granted the right of statuary, and was, as the consummate Roman matron, Augustus's secret weapon in his war against deteriorating morality, he would seem to have a lot to gain by being coupled publicly with the empress.

Augustus's perception of women and their place in Roman society appears to have been conflicted at best, as exemplified by the concept of the *univira*. On one hand, the *univira* who married once was exemplary; on the other, Augustus's legislation dictated swift remarriage for a woman who lost her husband. Even on the Ara Pacis, Livia is separated from Augustus, while the other imperial families are portrayed as intimate groups. Since Augustus and Livia seem not to have been presented as a couple in the capital, it is especially interesting that slaves and freedwomen in Rome embraced the paired portrait type with enthusiasm. Models were readily available elsewhere in the imperial circle, for example other couples with their children on the Ara Pacis (see Figs. 15.2 and 15.3). The portraits of these freedmen, the style in which their likenesses are carved, and the dress and hairstyles they wear are very informative: the men look like Caesar and the women resemble Cleopatra.

I am tempted to suggest that some of these non-elite patrons were from the East and, once in Rome, became fascinated with the myth of the infamous Cleopatra. She remained a vivid presence in Rome because of her gilded statue in the Temple of Venus Genetrix, which stood near portraits of Caesar and in one of Rome's busiest markets. The more likely explanation, however, is that these former slaves were mimicking portraits of aristocratic Romans. The prototypes would have been produced in the mid-40s B.C., in a late Republican style characterized by a wizened Caesarian verism and an ornate melon hairstyle resembling Cleopatra's. The hairstyle was taken up by Roman glitterati at the time of Cleopatra's Rome sojourn and adopted by contemporary working women with an eye for fashion.

A contemporary relief from a tomb on Rome's Via Statilia is an example of a group portrait of recently enfranchised slaves whose portrait artists looked to such models for inspiration (Fig. 19.3). Husband and wife stand side by side, with a marble slab behind them; their feet rest on a shared base. Both wear traditional Roman dress, he the tunic and toga and she the tunic and palla. The man's arm rests in a kind of sling formed by the upper edge of his garment, and she arranges her arms in the pose of a modest woman or *pudicitia,* with one arm across her waist and the other arm bent with the hand resting beneath her chin. Her pose and the veil over her head signal that she is a virtuous Roman woman. Even though, like most freed people, the couple had come to Rome from elsewhere, they look like Romans in their portraits. He is depicted in the veristic style, with deep facial creases and a receding hairline, and resembles Julius Caesar. She has the smooth oval face of other women of this period and looks considerably younger than her husband. What really stands out in an otherwise modest image is the woman's hairstyle. For a proper and decorously draped woman, it is quite elaborate. It is divided into sections, and there is a broad, flat segment of hair on the center top of her head. Corkscrew curls fall in front of her ears, and other tendrils of hair escape the elaborate hairdo. The woman closely resembles a Ptolemaic princess if not "the Queen" herself, even though she may have thought that her coiffure branded her as an aristocratic Roman. This example is not an aberration. Another freedwoman, Licinia Athena, probably of Greek extraction, also wears Cleopatra-like corkscrew curls and sectioned hair on a funerary relief from Rome.

19.3. These enfranchised slaves pose as if they were Mark Antony and Cleopatra; the woman is coiffed with the melon hairstyle of the Egyptian queen.

Cleopatra's presence in Rome in 46 and 44 B.C. had a galvanizing effect on the city's women. While the elite interacted with her at genteel social events at Caesar's villa or possibly in the private homes of Rome's high society, the non-elite undoubtedly clamored for the latest gossip, possibly transmitted through the slaves and freedwomen who held jobs in patrician residences where these soirées took place. Socialites and slave women alike were surely captivated by the queen's exotic makeup, imported silk garments, and especially her fabulous wigs and headdresses. What woman would have not been tempted to experiment with the Cleopatra style, especially when their husbands were openly marveling at Caesar's latest foreign conquest? Whether those at the lower end of Rome's social hierarchy thought they were imitating the Egyptian queen or their Roman owner who had already adopted the queen's look as her own is impossible to know.

Cleopatra clearly enjoyed being the center of attention and didn't shy away from being a trend setter. At the same time, her fashion instincts undoubtedly told her that "when in Rome, do as the Romans do." While she must have relished appearing in full Egyptian regalia with tripartite wig and triple *uraeus* in official settings, it is likely that she let her hair down at private social gatherings. Emulating the Romans meant selecting a more casual Hellenistic hairstyle, with wisps of hair escaping the top-knot. The melon hairstyle, popularized by earlier Ptolemic queens, was the perfect choice—elegantly contrived but at the same time spontaneously tousled. It was this Greek coiffure, worn by earlier Macedonian Cleopatras and Berenices, that Cleopatra probably wore around Rome, and it is the one selected by the many Roman matrons and girls who looked to Cleopatra as the ultimate role model. Women of all ages made this hairstyle their own in Caesarian Rome, and elite women were more likely to have been aware of its origins.

The young woman whose features are preserved in a marble portrait in the Palazzo Massimo alle Terme in Rome is one example of this trend (Fig. 19.4). Her finely carved face is framed by a an elegant upswept coiffure arranged in melon segments and secured in a chignon that is loose enough to allow corkscrew tendrils to escape on her neck and in front of her ears. Stray locks of hair also appear across the forehead. A slightly older woman, whose portrait was in Italy and is now in the British Mu-

19.4. Roman women, elite and non-elite alike, looked to Cleopatra as inspiration for their own hairstyles and dress, especially while the Queen was in Rome in the mid-40s B.C.

seum, is imaged as a near twin of "the Queen." The portraitist has accentuated the resemblance to such a degree that many scholars have mistaken the subject for Cleopatra. The woman is coiffed in the melon style, with corkscrew curls on the back of her neck and in front of her ears, but she does not wear the royal diadem—evidence that she was probably not Egypt's monarch. The holes in her ears indicate that she may even have taken to wearing pearl earrings like Cleopatra but also like elite Roman women of the day. Another Cleopatra look-alike is a Roman woman from Delos, whose portrait was discovered in the island's House of the Diadumenos. Like the London example, she has a Ptolemaic profile, a melon hairstyle, and corkscrew curls in front of her ears. Her lobes are also pierced to accommodate a pair of earrings.

Fashion statements like pearl earrings and sectioned hairstyles could be put on and taken off at will. It is also conceivable that Republican women in Rome commissioned Cleopatra-like portraits of themselves, even though they never would have dared to appear in the queen's guise in public. It is hard to imagine the freedwoman from the Via Statilia (Fig. 19.3) undertaking her daily chores as either a Ptolemaic princess or a Roman aristocrat.

Freed people in Augustan Rome also favored the reclining funerary portrait, and it is tempting to speculate about the reason for its unexpected ascendancy. All of a sudden, there was an interest in depicting deceased family members, especially children, lying on a bed, supported by a mattress and pillows. The Etruscans were especially fond of this kind of imagery as the lid for terracotta coffins, but these are freestanding monuments with the legs of the bed delineated. It has been conjectured that the earliest Roman examples were based on the Etruscan ones, and there are enough correspondences between Republican and Augustan funerary practices to support such a link. Yet it also seems plausible that Cleopatra may have inspired the introduction of the funerary bed portrait in Augustan Rome—not because of her own actions but because Augustus staged the unforgettable image for the Roman public. It would be fair to counter such a hypothesis with the argument that Augustus's victory at Actium was only one of several celebrated in his triple triumph, and that the parading of Cleopatra's effigy was only one small part of the occasion. Still, it is hard to imagine a more sensational tableau than the dead Queen lying on a couch "with an asp clinging to her," further dramatized by the accompaniment of two of her children by Antony. Octavian's after-death image of Cleopatra was carefully calculated. By portraying Cleopatra with the asp, Octavian was featuring the nobility of her death.

A surviving Roman scene that provides a close approximation of the pomp and circumstance surrounding the parading of Cleopatra's effigy is depicted on a relief from Amiternum (Fig. 19.5). It is not a triumph but a funerary procession, and the protagonists are freedmen rather than soldiers and foreign dignitaries. Nevertheless, the lifelike appearance of the deceased, the canopy with moon and stars, the bier with ornamental legs, the mournful children, and the festive musicians furnish an effective picture of what must have been a memorable scene.

The nobility of death and the potential for a person's reputation and accomplishments to endure was a winning message, especially for those freed people who saw their hopes for a better future disappear with the premature deaths of their children. The earliest surviving Roman recumbent portrait is that of a boy in the Palazzo Massimo alle Terme; with his handsome symmetrical features and his full head of hair with comma-shaped locks, he resembles Augustus and Gaius and Lucius Caesar. With their Roman blood, Caesarion, Alexander Helios, and Ptolemy Philadelphus might also have had a similar appearance. Even though this recumbent boy is a dead ringer for one of Augustus's grandsons, he was almost certainly the freeborn son of two former slaves who were motivated to display him for posterity as a true prince among boys.

The portraits of Ptolemaic princes were as interchangeable with one another and with those of their fathers and grandfathers as the portraits

19.5. This freedman funerary procession, with the deceased displayed on a bier, recalls Augustus's Alexandrian triumph where the effigy of Cleopatra was paraded.

of Gaius and Lucius Caesar were with Augustus. In fact, Augustus's image-makers were certainly studying Ptolemaic models. Careful examination of portraits of Livia and Tiberius reveals that mother and son are usually depicted with oversize eyes, which may have been a family trait but which may also reflect Ptolemaic models since that particular feature is common in Ptolemaic portraiture. It was from these same Ptolemaic prototypes that Augustus's court artists also learned to recast portraits of out-of-favor Romans into their more popular successors.

Cleopatra's impact may also be discernible in the appearance of children in Roman monuments. Ever since Cleopatra showed up in Rome with "Little Caesar" in tow, children were worthy of attention. The highly visible Ara Pacis provided all Romans with artistic models for family group portraits. Recently enfranchised slaves were motivated to commission such portraits for their tombs because the tumult of being forcibly removed from their hometowns and relatives was wrenching and caused them to value their new families even more highly. A few of these freedman family groups even predate the Ara Pacis and were in fact made right after the Battle of Actium. Of the dozen or so surviving examples, all depict parents with a single child. With one exception, all the children are boys (see Fig. 19.1). Many of the former slaves who commissioned these sepulchral stones came from the eastern part of the empire, and Greek names are prominent among their nicknames *(cognomina)*. While many of the women in these carved portraits have the *nodus* hairstyle of Octavia and Livia, others cling to the sectioned coiffure of Cleopatra, even well after her death. "The Queen" still cast a long fashion shadow in Rome, an impact probably perpetuated by her gilded statue in the Temple of Venus. For mothers of Greek extraction who proudly displayed themselves with their sons, there could be no better role model.

Some of Rome's freedwomen thus seem to have remained fascinated by Cleopatra's mystique, or a version of it adopted by elite Roman women. What elements they drew from their role models were, however, little more than queenly quotations. Augustus soon took excerpts from Cleopatra's pictorial vocabulary and melded them into his own art so that the queen's contributions became indistinguishable from the Augustan brand. This outcome brings us full circle because these citations grew out of the same episodes that featured Cleopatra's interaction with Rome—the unwrapping before Caesar, travel by barge, sojourn in Rome, meeting with Antony, and double suicide in Alexandria. Each of these archetypal incidents also exemplifies more generally part of the natural life cycle—birth from the enveloping womb of bed linens, voyage across the sea of life, death made heroic by self-infliction. Such human transitions may have also been in the minds of the authors who recorded these events.

Cleopatra's dealings with Rome involved interactions with several remarkable elite men and women and with an unknown number of relatives, politicians, intellectuals, artists, and staff, both Egyptian and Roman. Some maligned her; others praised her courage. Although the reasons for these divergent views of Cleopatra cannot be reconstructed with certainty, the historical, literary, and pictorial evidence is reassuringly consistent. Indeed, the story of Cleopatra and Rome can be encapsulated in one simple truism. To achieve her objectives for Egypt, Cleopatra linked her country with Rome, the superpower of the first century B.C., through a series of alliances with important Roman men. In turn, they sought her country's wealth and natural resources, both of which could help support Rome's imperialist goals. In short, she used them and they used her. It could be said that what separated this arrangement from the usual political partnerships is that Cleopatra had affairs with the same men with whom she was creating affiliations. Yet even that practice was routine in an Egypt and Rome where brothers married sisters and women were given in marriage to sanction treaties.

While some of Cleopatra's momentous interactions are confirmed in existing written sources, others will never be known. Still others are given material form only through surviving works of art. When episode and artifact are examined together, they give credence to my contention that one inimitable person can change the world. At the end of the first century B.C., Cleopatra was that person, serving on her own and in the able hands of the determined Augustus as a catalyst for the transition between a Hellenistic and a Roman society.

What seems certain is that Cleopatra made an enduring and memorable mark on Rome as a city and a civilization. Above all, she combined life and art in a unique way. She transformed everyday political meetings into matchless theatrical encounters among ersatz gods and goddesses dressed to the nines. Moreover, she preserved those events by creating an art to describe them. That art was sometimes commissioned by her alone and sometimes in concert with a variety of elite men from Egypt or Rome, and was crafted by the skilled non-elite architects and artists who were part of what must have been a nimble and efficient team of advisers, attendants, and designers. This art radiated from Alexandria to other major cities in the ancient world such as Antioch, Ephesus, and Athens, and it culminated at Rome, where Augustus embraced it. While the names of Caesar and Cleopatra and Antony and Cleopatra have long been associated, it was because of the initial clash and ultimate collaboration between the two true inimitables of the first century B.C., Cleopatra VII of Egypt and Octavian Augustus of Rome, that Cleopatra and Rome will forever be linked.

NOTES

BIBLIOGRAPHY

ILLUSTRATION CREDITS

ACKNOWLEDGMENTS

INDEX

NOTES

PROLOGUE

1. Plutarch, *Caesar* 48f.
2. Appian, *Civil Wars* 2.90; Suetonius, *Caesar* 52.
3. Plutarch, *Antony* 25.4–27.
4. Appian, *Civil Wars* 5.8.
5. Dio Cassius, *Roman History* 51.13.4; Plutarch, *Antony* 85.4; 86.1–3
6. Plutarch, *Antony* 86; Dio Cassius, *Roman History* 51.8.
7. Plutarch, *Caesar* 28.
8. Dio Cassius, *Roman History* 51.22.3.
9. Pliny, *Natural History* 9.121–122.

1. CLEOPATRA SUPERSTAR

1. Plutarch, *Antony* 27.3.4.

3. THE SUPPORTING CAST

1. Macrobius, *Saturnalia* 2.5.
2. Suetonius, *Tiberius* 23.

5. CLEOPATRA ARCHITECTA

1. Caesar, *The Alexandrian War* 33.
2. Lucan, *Civil War,* book 10.
3. Suetonius, *Caesar* 52.1.

6. ALEXANDRIA ON THE TIBER

1. Suetonius, *Caesar* 52.
2. Ibid., 46.
3. Ibid., 79.
4. Ibid., 44.
5. Pliny, *Natural History* 34.18; ibid., 8.64.154–155.
6. Suetonius, *Caesar* 61.1.
7. Dio Cassius, *Roman History* 45.7.1.
8. Suetonius, *Caesar* 84.1.

7. LIVING THE INIMITABLE LIFE

1. Plutarch, *Antony* 26.1–4.
2. Ibid., 28.2.
3. Ibid., 54.
4. Suetonius, *Augustus* 69.
5. Plutarch, *Antony* 58.
6. Dio Cassius, *Roman History* 50.15.2.
7. Ibid., 51.3–5.
8. Plutarch, *Antony* 85.

8. ERSATZ ALEXANDERS IN EGYPT AND ROME

1. Pliny, *Natural History* 34-35; Statius, *Silvae* 1.1.86.
2. Plutarch, *Pompey* 2.1.
3. Suetonius, *Caesar* 45.
4. Ibid., 79–80.
5. Statius, *Silvae* 1.1.86.
6. Plutarch, *Antony* 4.

9. "QUEEN OF KINGS"

1. Plutarch, *Antony* 27.2.
2. Appian, *Civil Wars* 2.102.
3. Dio Cassius, *Roman History* 51.22.3.

10. EVEN DEATH WON'T PART US NOW

1. Dio Cassius, *Roman History* 51.9.5–6.
2. Ibid., 51.15.1.

3. Ibid., 51.21.8.
4. Plutarch, *Antony* 86.3.
5. Ibid., 86.4.
6. Propertius, *Elegies* 3.11.39.
7. Plutarch, *Antony* 86.5.
8. Pliny, *Natural History* 58.119–122.
9. Dio Cassius, *Roman History* 51.17.4.

11. EGYPTOMANIA!

1. Pliny, *Natural History* 36.70–75.
2. Strabo, *Geographia* 5.3.8; Pliny, *Natural History* 36.69–74.
3. Dio Cassius, *Roman History* 53.2.4; Tacitus, *Annals* 2.85; Suetonius, *Tiberius* 36.1.
4. Propertius, *Elegies* 4.6.67.
5. Ibid., 2.31.3.

12. DIVINE ALTER EGOS

1. Plutarch, *Antony* 4.
2. Ibid., 24.
3. Suetonius, *Augustus* 70.
4. Ibid., 94.4; Dio Cassius, *Roman History* 45.2–3.
5. Suetonius, *Augustus* 50.
6. Pliny, *Natural History* 37.4.8–10.
7. Dio Cassius, *Roman History* 51.3.5–6.
8. Plutarch, *Antony and Demetrius* 3.3.

13. A ROMAN PHARAOH AND A ROMAN EMPEROR

1. Virgil, *Aeneid* 8.723–733.
2. Propertius, *Elegies* 3.11.39–41.

14. ROME ON THE TIBER

1. Dio Cassius, *Roman History* 47.18.
2. Suetonius, *Augustus* 95.
3. Dio Cassius, *Roman History* 51.19.2.
4. Suetonius, *Caesar* 83; Pliny, *Natural History* 2.93–94.
5. Augustus, *Res Gestae* 4.20.
6. Virgil, *Aeneid* 8.

7. Pliny, *Natural History* 36.189; 35.26; 34.62.
8. Dio Cassius, *Roman History* 53.27.1–3.
9. Josephus, *Antiquities of the Jews* 18.3.4.

15. DEATH, DYNASTY, AND A ROMAN DENDERA

1. Dio Cassius, *Roman History* 51.10.6–7.

16. COMPETING WITH CLEOPATRA ON COINS

1. Dio Cassius, *Roman History* 48.10.
2. Plutarch, *Antony* 10.5–6.

17. PRINCESSES AND POWER HAIR

1. Dio Cassius, *Roman History* 49.38.1.

19. FROM ASP TO ETERNITY

1. Plutarch, *Antony* 73.2, 74.2; Dio Cassius, *Roman History* 51.
2. Ovid, *Fasti* 5.157–158.
3. Dionysius of Halicarnassus, *Roman Antiquities* 8.55–56.
4. Virgil, *Aeneid* 8.709–713.
5. Horace, *Odes* 1.37.

BIBLIOGRAPHY

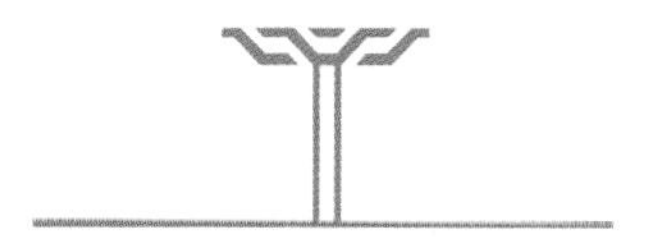

The bibliography gives the sources for the research that underlies this book. It is organized by chapter, with separate sections at the end on Cleopatra in fiction, Cleopatra in film, and Web sites containing information on Cleopatra and Rome. Most bibliographic citations are listed only once under the most relevant chapter; a few are repeated for the reader's convenience. Citations of ancient sources quoted in the text are given in the endnotes.

The text of this book was completed before I became aware of the publication by Susan Walker and Sally-Ann Ashton entitled *Cleopatra Reassessed: The British Museum Occasional Paper* 103 (London, 2003), and I was not able, therefore, to take its findings into consideration. The Walker and Ashton volume should be read by anyone interested in the finer points of scholarship on Cleopatra, but what is presented there does not change the thesis of my book.

PROLOGUE: FROM CARPET TO ASP

Primary Sources

Appian, *The Civil Wars,* Books II–V. A history of Rome from the Republic to Trajan, based on a variety of sources, including Livy.

Caesar, *The Civil War,* Books I–III. Julius Caesar's own account of the Civil Wars, mentioning his visit to Alexandria, but providing no details on his affair with Cleopatra.

Cicero, *Letters to Atticus.* Describes Cleopatra's sojourn in Rome in 44 B.C. and her impact at patrician dinner parties.

Dio Cassius, *Roman History.* A history of Rome from the Republic to the third century that depends on those of Livy and others and is an important source for the life of Cleopatra.

Horace, *Epodes; Odes.* Current events viewed through poetry, and Augustus as the bringer of a new Golden Age.

Josephus, *Antiquities of the Jews,* Books XIV–XV. Mentions Cleopatra's interactions with Herod the Great; written with a bias against the queen.

Livy, *History of Rome.* History of Rome from its founding through Augustus. The books dealing with the first century B.C. do not survive, but other ancient accounts are based on Livy's.

Lucan, *Civil War,* Book X. History of Rome's Civil War, written in the Neronian period; valuable evidence for Caesar and Cleopatra's affair in Alexandria.

Nicolaus of Damascus, *Autobiography.* A few surviving excerpts from the man who tutored Cleopatra's children and later those of Herod the Great.

Ovid, *Ars Amatoria* et al. Love poetry that entranced Julia and her circle but displeased Augustus and led to the Roman poet's exile.

Pliny the Elder, *Natural History.* Book IX of this first-century Latin encyclopedia notes Cleopatra's ostentation (the story of the pearl earrings) and uses it as an illustration of libertine life in Rome.

Plutarch, *Lives.* Essays on Caesar, Antony, and others, written in the second half of the first and early second century; they provide one of the most important and colorful sources for the lives of Cleopatra and her contemporaries. Especially valuable is Plutarch's version of Cleopatra's last days, based on the memoirs of Cleopatra's physician, Olympus.

Propertius, *Elegies,* Book III. Love poetry by a contemporary of Augustus, which includes a masterful denunciation of a nameless Egyptian.

Res Gestae Divi Augusti. A record of the accomplishments of Augustus, written by the emperor, inscribed on bronze pillars set up in front of Augustus's mausoleum in Rome.

Strabo, *Geographia.* Ancient topography produced shortly after the death of Cleopatra; provides extensive information on ancient Alexandria.

Suetonius, *The Twelve Caesars.* Sensational biographies—frequently based on gossip—written by the attorney, biographer, and secretary of the emperor Hadrian. These chronicle the public and private lives of Julius Caesar and the emperors through Domitian and offer a wealth of detail about Rome in the days of Caesar and Augustus.

Sulpicia, *Elegies.* Six elegies by a woman that have come down to us, featuring the unmarried poet's love affair with a man of comparable social status, and thus documenting the independence of elite Augustan women.

Tacitus, *The Annals of Imperial Rome.* History of Rome that covers the period from Augustus's death and Tiberius's accession to the principate of Nero.

Velleius Paterculus, *Roman History,* Book II. Contemporary events presented in the time of Tiberius; reverential view of Augustus but disapproval of Antony and Cleopatra.

Virgil, *Aeneid,* Book VIII. The saga of Aeneas by the renowned Augustan poet, with its evocation of the Battle of Actium and its intertwining of Aeneas and Dido with Augustus and Cleopatra. Virgil's *Eclogues* and *Georgics* also referenced current events such as land confiscations and the Battle of Actium.

CHAPTER 1. CLEOPATRA SUPERSTAR

Becher, Ilse, *Das Bild der Kleopatra in der griechischen und lateinischen Literatur* (Berlin, 1966). A study of Cleopatra in Greek and Latin literature; surveys such themes as leadership, luxury, love, amorality, and death.

Bernal, Martin, *Black Athena: The Afroasiatic Roots of Classical Civilization*, volume 1, *The Fabrication of Ancient Greece 1785–1985* (New Brunswick, N.J., 1987). The author contends that Greek civilization was highly dependent on that of Africa and Southeast Asia and suggests that a nineteenth-century European racism had obscured these origins. Even though Bernal does not mention Cleopatra, his theories led to speculation that Cleopatra may have been black, a contention that was widely reported in the media.

Bernal, Martin, *Black Athena Writes Back: Martin Bernal Responds to His Critics* (Durham and London, 2001). The author responds to critics of *Black Athena* and provides supplementary evidence for his theories.

Bowman, Alan K., *Egypt After the Pharaohs, 332 B.C.–A.D. 642, From Alexander to the Arab Conquest* (Berkeley and Los Angeles, 1986; second paperback printing, 1996).

Bradford, Ernle, *Cleopatra* (London, 1971).

Brenk, Frederick E., "Antony-Osiris, Cleopatra-Isis, The End of Plutarch's *Antony*," in P. A. Stadter, ed., *Plutarch and the Historical Tradition* (London and New York, 1992), pp. 159–182. Osiris and Isis as foils for Antony and Cleopatra.

Chauveau, Michel, *Egypt in the Age of Cleopatra* (Ithaca and London, 2000).

Chauveau, Michel, *Cleopatra Beyond the Myth* (Ithaca, 2002).

Clauss, Manfred, *Kleopatra* (Munich, 1995).

Desmond, Alice Curtis, *Cleopatra's Children* (New York, 1971).

Donato, Giuseppe, and Monique Seefried, *The Fragrant Past: Perfumes of Cleopatra and Julius Caesar* (Emory Museum of Art, 1989). Perfume in the first century and the recreation of Cleopatra's cosmetic workshop at En Boquet, by the Dead Sea.

Etman, Ahmed, "Cleopatra and Egypt in the Augustan Poetry," in *Roma e l'Egitto nell'antichita classica, Cairo 6–9, Febbraio 1989, Atti del I Congresso Internazionale Italo Egiziano* (Rome, 1992), pp. 161–175.

Flamarion, Edith, *Cleopatra: The Life and Death of a Pharaoh* (New York, 1997). Interweaves ancient literature, history, and monuments with later paintings and cinematic interpretations.

Flory, Marleen B., "*Abducta Neroni Uxor:* The Historiographical Tradition on the Marriage of Octavian and Livia," *Transactions and Proceedings of the American Philological Association* (1988), pp. 343–360. The author suggests that hostile accounts of Octavian's marriage to Livia were the result of Mark Antony's propaganda war against Octavian.

Foss, Michael, *Search for Cleopatra* (New York, 1997).

Grant, Michael, *Cleopatra* (London, 1972; paperback edition, 2002). This study remains the classic and most complete historical account of the life and times of Cleopatra.

Gruen, Erich, "Cleopatra in Rome: Facts and Fantasies," in David Braund and Christopher Gill, *Myth, History, and Culture in Republican Rome* (Exeter, 2003), pp. 258–274. The author attempts to dispel some deeply entrenched "myths" about Cleopatra.

Haley, Shelley P., "Black Feminist Thought and Classics: Re-membering, Reclaiming, Re-empowering," in Nancy Sorkin Rabinowitz and Amy Richlin, eds., *Feminist Theory and the Classics* (New York, 1993), pp. 23–43. One example of a body of literature on the ethnic heritage of Cleopatra that asserts that she was a black woman by birth or symbolically.

Hopkins, Keith, "Brother-Sister Marriage in Roman Egypt," *Comparative Studies in Society and History* 22 (1980), pp. 303–354.

Johnson, W. R., "A Queen, A Great Queen? Cleopatra and the Politics of Misrepresentation," *Arion* 6 (1967), pp. 387–402. The Augustan poets and the paradox of what they knew of Cleopatra and what they wrote about her.

Kraft, Konrad, "Zu Sueton, Divus Augustus 69.2: M. Anton und Kleopatra," *Hermes* 95 (1967), pp. 496–499. The author suggests that the "marriage" of Antony and Cleopatra may have occurred nine years earlier than traditionally thought.

Lampela, Anssi, *Rome and the Ptolemies of Egypt: The Development of Their Political Relations 273–80 B.C.* (Helsinki, 1998).

Lefkowitz, Mary R., and Guy MacLean Rogers, eds., *Black Athena Revisited* (Chapel Hill and London, 1996). Essays responding to the theories that Martin Bernal developed in *Black Athena* and that other scholars expanded, for example that Cleopatra was black.

Lefkowitz, Mary R., *Not Out of Africa* (New York, 1996; revised edition, 1997). Another contribution to the *Black Athena* controversy, in which the author makes a plea for the scientific study of history rather than the creation of self-promotional myth.

Lewis, Naphtali, *Life in Egypt under Roman Rule* (Atlanta, 1986; reprinted 1999).

Lindsay, Jack, *Cleopatra* (London, 1971).

Lovric, Michelle, *Cleopatra's Face: Fatal Beauty* (London and Chicago, 2001). A study of Cleopatra's physical features and the prose and poetry inspired by them to recreate her aura.

Maehler, Herwig, "Egypt under the Last Ptolemies," *Bulletin of the Institute of Classical Studies of the University of London* 30 (1983), pp. 1–16.

Maffii, Maffio, *Cleopatra Contro Roma* (Florence, 1939). The author focuses on Cleopatra's relationship with Rome through her personal interactions with Caesar, Antony, and Octavian.

Peek, Cecilia, "She, Like a Good King: A Reconstruction of the Career of Kleopatra VII," dissertation, Berkeley, 2000. The author explores the early career of Cleopatra.

Reinhold, Meyer, "The Declaration of War against Cleopatra," *Classical Journal* 77 (1981–1982), pp. 97–103. The author attempts to cull from an abundance of propaganda the legitimate charges against Cleopatra that prompted Octavian's declaration of war against her.

Rice, E. E., *Cleopatra* (Guernsey, 1999).

Ricketts, Linda M., "The Administration of Ptolemaic Egypt under Cleopatra VII," dissertation, University of Minnesota, 1980.

Rogers, J. A., *World's Great Men of Color*, volume 1 (New York, 1946), pp. 121–130. This author was probably the first to suggest that Cleopatra was black, basing his conclusion on Shakespeare's description of her as "tawny"

Samson, Julia, *Nefertiti and Cleopatra: Queen-Monarchs of Ancient Egypt* (reprint, London, 1997).

Samuel, A. E. "The Ptolemies and the Ideology of Kingship," in Peter Green, ed., *Hellenistic History and Culture* (Berkeley, 1993), pp. 168–210.

Stadelmann, Heinrich, *Cleopatra* (London, 1931).

Thompson, Dorothy, "Literacy and Power in Ptolemaic Egypt," in Alan K. Bowman and Greg Wolf, ed., *Literacy and Power in the Ancient World* (Cambridge, 1994), pp. 67–83.

Van Sertima, I., ed., *Black Women in Antiquity* (New Brunswick, N.J., 1984). The story of black queens and goddesses in antiquity, with a focus on Ethiopian and Egyptian women. Cleopatra is featured as non white and non-Greek

Volkmann, Hans, *Cleopatra: A Study in Politics and Propaganda* (New York, 1958).

Weigall, Arthur Edward Pearse Brome, *The Life and Times of Cleopatra, Queen of Egypt* (New York, revised edition, 1968).

Whitehouse, John, *Cleopatras* (New York, 1994). A study of the less famous predecessors to Cleopatra VII, who were also Macedonian and Ptolemaic queens.

Williams, J. H. C., "'Spoiling the Egyptians,' Octavian and Cleopatra," in Susan Walker and Peter Higgs, eds., *Cleopatra of Egypt: From History to Myth* (Princeton, 2001), pp. 190–199.

Wyke, Maria, "Augustan Cleopatras: Female Power and Poetic Authority," in

Anton Powell, ed., *Roman Poetry and Propaganda in the Age of Augustus* (London, 1992), pp. 98–140. Feminist rereading of poetry composed in the aftermath of the Battle of Actium; discusses literature's role in the social construction of gender and the use of Augustan poetry as a tool for securing and maintaining political power.

Zoffili, Ermanno, *Costume e cultura dell antico Egitto* (Milan, 1991). The author examines the dress, jewelry, cosmetics, and hairstyles of ancient Egypt and their situation in a cultural context.

CHAPTER 2. THE MAJOR PLAYERS

Abdullatif, A. Aly, "Cleopatra and Caesar at Alexandria and Rome," *Roma e l'Egitto nell'antichità classica, Cairo 6–9 febbraio 1989, Atti de I Congresso internazionale italo-egiziano* (Rome, 1992), pp. 47–61. The author reconsiders the chronological evidence for the relationship of Caesar and Cleopatra.

Balsdon, J. P. V. D., "The Ides of March," *Historia* 7 (1958), pp. 80–94. An account of the murder of Caesar based on an analysis of contemporary sources.

Barrett, Anthony A., *Livia, First Lady of Imperial Rome* (New Haven and London), 2002.

Bradford, Ernle, *Julius Caesar: The Pursuit of Power* (London, 1984).

Carter, John M., *The Battle of Actium: The Rise and Triumph of Augustus Caesar* (New York, 1970).

Ciccotti, Ettore, *Profilo di Augusto. Con un'appendice su le leggi matrimoniali di Augusto* (Turin, 1938). The author discusses Augustus's marriage and moral legislation.

Corbett, Percy Ellwood, *The Augustan Divorce* (Montreal, 1929).

Corbett, Percy Ellwood, *The Roman Law of Marriage* (reprint, Oxford, 1969).

Eck, Werner, *The Age of Augustus* (Oxford, 2003; translation of German book of 1998).

Flory, Marleen B., "Sic exemplar parantur: Livia's Shrine to Concordia and the Porticus Liviae," *Historia* (1984), pp. 309–330. Livia is presented as the patron of a portico that bore her name and also a shrine honoring Concord.

Flory, Marleen B., "Livia and the History of Public Honorific Statues for Women in Rome," *Transactions and Proceedings of the American Philological Association* 123 (1993), pp. 287–308. A history of the first public statues dedicated to women in early imperial Rome and the changing social context that allowed for such monuments.

Flory, Marleen B., "Dynastic Ideology, the Domus Augusta, and Imperial Women: A Lost Statuary Group in the Circus Flaminia," *Transactions of the American Philological Association* 126 (1996), pp. 287–306. The author argues that the statuary group of the *domus Augusta* underscored the familial nature of political power and Livia's role in transmitting that authority.

Gelzer, Matthias, *Caesar: Politician and Statesman* (Oxford, 1968). A classic political biography of Caesar; Cleopatra plays a very small part.

Grant, Michael, *Julius Caesar* (New York, 1992; reprint of 1969 edition).

Grether, G. E., "Livia and the Roman Imperial Cult," *American Journal of Philology* 67 (1946), pp. 222–252. Essay emphasizing Livia's participation in the imperial cult and her right to property and to being memorialized.

Gurval, Robert A., *Actium and Augustus* (Ann Arbor, 1988).

Heinen, Heinz, "Cäsar und Kaisarion," *Historia* 18 (1969), pp. 181–203.

Huntsman, Eric D., "The Family and Property of Livia Drusilla," dissertation, University of Pennsylvania, 1998. The author presents the familial wealth and status of Rome's first empress as both an exceptional case and a paradigm for other imperial women of means.

Huzar, Eleanor Goltz, *Mark Antony* (Minneapolis, 1978). A comprehensive biography of Mark Antony that analyzes the political rivalries and intrigue that marked his career, and his relationship with Cleopatra as it affected Roman foreign policy.

Huzar, Eleanor Goltz, "Augustus, Heir of the Ptolemies," *Aufstieg und Niedergang der römischen Welt* II.10 (1988), pp. 343–382. This essay argues that the policies Octavian initiated in Egypt after capturing Alexandria determined the present and future role of Egypt in the Roman Empire.

Kleiner, Fred S., "An Extraordinary Posthumous Honor for Livia," *Athenaeum* 78 (1990), pp. 508–514. Discussion of an arch honoring Livia that was never built by Tiberius, and imperial women on Augustan and Julio-Claudian arches as reference to the fecundity of Augustus's dynasty.

Linderski, Jerzy, "The Mother of Livia Augusta and the Aufidii Lurcones of the Republic," *Historia* 23 (1974), pp. 463–480. A reconciliation of antiquity's conflicting accounts of Livia's maternal ancestry.

Lindsay, Jack, *Marc Antony: His World and His Contemporaries* (London, 1936).

Marasco, Gabriele, "Marco Antonio 'Nuovo Dioniso' e il sua ebrietate," *Latomus* 51 (1992), pp. 538–548. Mark Antony as the new Dionysus and Augustus's use of Antony's Dionysiac love of wine as a way of discrediting his rival.

Meier, Christian, *Caesar* (New York, 1996). A comprehensive biography of Caesar in which there is only a brief discussion of Caesar's relationship with Cleopatra.

Parenti, Michael, *The Assassination of Julius Caesar: A People's History of Ancient Rome* (New York and London, 2003). A controversial interpretation of the events of 44 B.C., told from the perspective of those at the lowest end of the Roman social pyramid. The author suggests that Caesar's aristocratic murderers were motivated more by concern that Caesar would democratize Rome and strip them of their influence than by fear that his monarchical ambitions would grow.

Purcell, Nicholas, "Livia and the Womanhood of Rome," *Proceedings of the Cambridge Philological Association* 32 (1986), pp. 78–105. The author offers a detailed exploration of Livia's public life.
Raaflaub, Kurt A., and Mark Toher, *Between Republic and Empire: Interpretations of Augustus and His Principate* (Berkeley, Los Angeles, and Oxford, 1990).
Raubitschek, Antony E., "Octavia's Deification at Athens," *Transactions of the American Philological Association* 77 (1946), pp. 146–150. Essay on an inscription discovered in Athens and thought to make reference to the deification of Antony and Octavia and their celebration in Athens as Dionysus and Athena Polias.
Rehak, Paul, "Livia's Dedication in the Temple of Divus Augustus on the Palatine," *Latomus, Revue d'études latines* 49 (1990), pp. 117–125. Essay on an unusual dedication made by Livia Augusta in honor of her deified husband, and the empress's new role once her husband was a *divus.*
Weigall, Arthur, *The Life and Times of Mark Antony* (New York, 1931).
Yavetz, Zvi, "The Res Gestae and Augustus, Public Image," in Fergus Millar and Erich Segal, eds., *Caesar Augustus: Several Aspects* (Oxford, 1981), pp. 1–36. Augustus and the *Res Gestae* as self-representation.

CHAPTER 3. THE SUPPORTING CAST

Delia, Diana, "Fulvia Reconsidered," in Sarah B. Pomeroy, ed., *Women's History and Ancient History* (Chapel Hill and London, 1991), pp. 197–217.
Richlin, Amy, "Julia's Jokes, Galla Placidia, and the Roman Use of Women as Political Icons," in Barbara Garlick, Suzanne Dixon, and Pauline Allen, *Stereotypes of Women in Power* (Westport, Conn., 1992), pp. 65–91.

CHAPTER 4. THE PROFESSIONALS

Bradley, Keith R., *Slaves and Masters in the Roman Empire: A Study in Social Control* (New York and Oxford, 1987). Exploration of the Roman slave system under the Empire; special emphasis on adverse conditions for slaves.
Johnson, Janet H., ed., *Life in a Multi-Cultural Society: Egypt From Cambyses to Constantine and Beyond* (Chicago, 1992).
Treggiari, Susan, *Roman Freedmen during the Late Republic* (Oxford, 1969).
Treggiari, Susan, "Jobs in the Household of Livia," *Papers of the British School at Rome* 43 (1975), pp. 48–77.
Treggiari, Susan, "Family Life among the Staff of the Volusii," *Transactions of the American Philological Association* 105 (1975), pp. 393–401.
Treggiari, Susan, "Jobs for Women," *American Journal of Ancient History* 1 (1976), pp. 76–104.

CHAPTER 5. CLEOPATRA ARCHITECTA

Alexandria and Alexandrianism. Papers Delivered at a Symposium Organized by the J. Paul Getty Museum and the Getty Center for the History of Art, 1993 (Malibu, 1996). Includes essays on urban planning and art.

Arnold, Dieter, *Temples of the Last Pharaohs* (New York and Oxford, 1999). Includes discussions of the temples at Edfu and Dendera.

Casson, Lionel, *Libraries in the Ancient World* (New Haven and London, 2001).

Empereur, Jean-Yves, *Alexandria Rediscovered* (New York, 1998). Description of an underwater excavation at Alexandria in the 1990s, with finds that enhance our knowledge of this city before, during, and after the time of Cleopatra.

Empereur, Jean-Yves, *Alexandria Jewel of Egypt* (New York, 2001).

Fraser, Peter Marshall, *Ptolemaic Alexandria* (Oxford, 1972). Includes a discussion of Ptolemaic patronage of museums and libraries.

Goddio, Franck, *Alexandria: The Submerged Royal Quarters* (London, 1998). The exploration of Alexandria's eastern harbor and the way it conforms to the 25 B.C. eyewitness account of the geographer Strabo.

Grimal, N., et al., *La Gloire d'Alexandrie* (Paris, 1998). Catalogue for an exhibition on Alexandria.

Grimm, Günter, "Kleopatras Palast? Zu den jüngsten Untersuchungen im Hafenbecken von Alexandria," *Antike Welt* 27 (1996), pp. 509–512. Archaeological evidence found in the port of Alexandria that may shed light on the original appearance of Cleopatra's nearby palace.

Gruen, Erich, "Cleopatra in Rome: Facts and Fantasies," in David Braund and Christopher Gill, *Myth, History, and Culture in Republican Rome* (Exeter, 2003), pp. 258–274.

La Riche, William, *Alexandria: The Sunken City* (London, 1997). The author surveys the 1995 excavation of Alexandria.

MacLeod, Roy, ed., *The Library of Alexandria: Centre of Learning in the Ancient World* (London and New York, 2002).

Shafer, Byron E., ed., *Temples of Ancient Egypt* (Ithaca, 1997). Includes a scholarly essay on temples of the Ptolemaic and Roman periods.

CHAPTER 6. ALEXANDRIA ON THE TIBER

Anderson, James, *Historical Topography of the Imperial Fora* (Brussels, 1984).

Favro, Diane, *The Urban Image of Augustan Rome* (Cambridge, 1996).

Green, Peter, *Alexander to Actium* (Los Angeles, 1990). Sweeping overview of three hundred years of Hellenistic history.

Gruen, Erich, *Cultural and National Identity in Republican Rome* (Ithaca, 1992). A study of art in the service of Roman ideology even when the Romans displayed plundered Greek art or incorporated Hellenic features in their monuments.

Ulrich, Roger, "Julius Caesar and the Creation of the Forum Iulium," *American Journal of Archaeology* 97 (1993), pp. 49–80.

CHAPTER 7. LIVING THE INIMITABLE LIFE

Favro, Diane, *The Urban Image of Augustan Rome* (Cambridge, 1996).

Van de Walle, Baudoin, "La 'Cléopatre' de Mariemont," *Chronique d'Egypte* 24 (1949), pp. 19–32. The author suggests that a colossal Egyptian-style green granite head of Cleopatra was originally part of a full-length group portrait of Cleopatra and Antony as Isis and Osiris.

Van de Walle, Baudoin, "Un nouveau document concernant le prétendu groupe d'Antoine et Cléopatre," *Chronique d'Egypte* 25 (1950), pp. 31–55. The author reveals the contents of a letter that refers to fragments of black granite statues that may have represented Cleopatra and Antony.

CHAPTER 8. ERSATZ ALEXANDERS IN EGYPT AND ROME

Fishwick, Duncan, "The Statue of Julius Caesar in the Pantheon," *Latomus* 51 (2002), pp. 329–336. The author discusses the honorific statues of Julius Caesar and Augustus in Augustus's Pantheon in Rome as a possible response to Caesar's statues of Venus and Cleopatra in the Temple of Venus Genetrix.

Johansen, Flemming S., "The Portraits in Marble of Gaius Julius Caesar: A Review," *Ancient Portraits in the J. Paul Getty Museum* 1 (1987), pp. 17–40.

Kyrieleis, Helmut, *Bildnisse der Ptolemäer* (Berlin, 1975). A comprehensive study of Ptolemaic portraits, among them those of Auletes and Cleopatra.

Michel, Dorothea, *Alexander als Vorbild für Pompeius, Caesar und Marcus Antonius, Collection Latomus* 94 (1967). Study of the portraits of Alexander the Great as a model for those of Pompey, Caesar, and Antony.

Smith, R. R. R., *Hellenistic Royal Portraits* (Oxford, 1988), pp. 97–98, 132–134, 169.

Stanwick, Paul Edmund, *Portraits of the Ptolemies: Greek Kings as Egyptian Pharaohs* (Austin, 2002). 150 Ptolemaic portraits from Ptolemy I to Cleopatra and Caesarion are presented with a concentration on history, chronology, style, religion, literary evidence, and especially the coalescence of Egyptian and Greek elements into a unique image that encoded a distinctive Ptolemaic ideology.

Stewart, Andrew, *Faces of Power: Alexander's Image and Hellenistic Politics* (Berkeley, 1993).

Zanker, Paul, *The Power of Images in the Age of Augustus* (Ann Arbor, 1988). An influential book in which the author explores art in the service of ideology during the age of Augustus, ranging over the period's art, architecture, literature, religion, and society.

CHAPTER 9. "QUEEN OF KINGS": CLEOPATRA THEA NEOTERA

Antelme, Ruth Schumann, and Stéphane Rossini, *Sacred Sexuality in Ancient Egypt: The Erotic Secrets of the Forbidden Papyrus* (Rochester, Vt., 2001). Emphasis on the Egyptian goddess Hathor, and sexual philosophy and practice among the Egyptians.

Ashton, Sally-Ann, "Identifying the Egyptian-Style Ptolemaic Queens," in Susan Walker and Peter Higgs, eds., *Cleopatra of Egypt: History to Myth* (Princeton, 2001), pp. 148–155. Egyptian-style statues identified as Cleopatra.

Baldus, Hans Roland, "Ein neues Spätporträt der Kleopatra aus Orthosia," *Jahrbuch für Numismatik und Geldgeschichte* 23 (1973), pp. 19–43. Bronze coins with portraits of Cleopatra from Orthosia in northern Phoenicia.

Bianchi, Robert, ed., *Cleopatra's Egypt: The Age of the Ptolemies* (New York, 1988). Catalogue of an important exhibition on the age of Cleopatra at the Brooklyn Museum in New York.

Brett, Agnes Baldwin, "A New Cleopatra Tetradrachm of Ascalon," *American Journal of Archaeology* 41 (1937), pp. 452–463. The author surveys the chronology and significance of a coin from Ascalon depicting Cleopatra.

Brunelle, Edelgard, *Die Bildnisse der Ptolemäerinnen* (Frankfurt, 1976). Detailed study of the portraits of Ptolemaic queens that compares them to those of other royal women of the Hellenistic age.

Curtius, Ludwig, "Ikonographische Beitrage zum Porträt der römischen republik und der julisch-claudischen Familie IV Kleopatra VII Philopator," *Römische Mitteilungen* 48 (1933), pp. 182–192. Scholarly study of the numismatic and sculptured portraits of Cleopatra; the author places special emphasis on the statue in the Temple of Venus Genetrix.

Fittschen, Klaus, "Zwei Ptolemäerbildnisse in Cherchel," *Studi e materiali. Istituto di Archeologia Università di Palermo 4, Alessandria e il mondo ellenistico-romano. Studi in onore di Achille Adriani* (Rome, 1983), pp. 165–171. Two well-known heads in Cherchel are identified as Ptolemy Soter and Cleopatra.

Foreman, Laura, *Cleopatra's Palace: In Search of a Legend* (New York and Toronto, 1999). The Cleopatra legend with emphasis on archaeologist Franck Goddio's finds in the Alexandria harbor.

Goudchaux, Guy Weill, "Was Cleopatra Beautiful? The Conflicting Answers of Numismatics," in Susan Walker and Peter Higgs, eds., *Cleopatra of Egypt. From History to Myth* (Princeton, 2001), pp. 210–214.

Green, Lyn, "More Than a Fashion Statement: Clothing and Hairstyles as Indicators of Social Status in Ancient Egypt," *Bulletin of the Canadian Society for Mesopotamian Studies* 26 (1993), pp. 29–38.

Gruen, Erich, "Cleopatra in Rome: Facts and Fantasies," in David Braund and Christopher Gill, *Myth, History, and Culture in Republican Rome* (Exeter, 2003), pp. 258–274.

Hamer, Mary, *Signs of Cleopatra: History, Politics, Representation* (London and New York, 1993). Study on eroticism and power from antiquity to the present, as exemplified by Cleopatra and her representations over time.

Higgs, Peter, "Searching for Cleopatra's Image: Classical Portraits in Stone," in Susan Walker and Peter Higgs, eds., *Cleopatra of Egypt: From History to Myth* (Princeton, 2001), pp. 200–209. The author examines the ancient and post-antique portraits of Cleopatra.

Hughes-Hallett, Lucy, *Cleopatra: Histories, Dreams, and Distortions* (New York and London, 1990). The author surveys Cleopatra across the ages and discusses how Augustus and each succeeding era recreated her.

La Rocca, Eugenio, *L'età d'oro di Cleopatra. Indagine sulla Tazza Farnese* (Rome, 1984). The author suggests that a plate in Naples called the Tazza Farnese was manufactured in Alexandria and is an example of the opulent Ptolemaic lifestyle under Cleopatra.

Lesko, Barbara S., *The Great Goddesses of Egypt* (Norman, Okla., 1999). Study of all of Egypt's goddesses, among them the two most important for Cleopatra—Hathor and Isis.

Pollitt, Jerome J., *Art in the Hellenistic Age* (Cambridge, 1986). Includes a brief discussion of the portraiture of Cleopatra.

Pomeroy, Sarah B., *Women in Hellenistic Egypt from Alexander to Cleopatra* (New York, 1984).

Quaegebeur, Jan, "Cleopatra VII and the Cults of Ptolemaic Queens," in Robert Bianchi, ed., *Cleopatra's Egypt: The Age of the Ptolemies* (New York, 1988), pp. 41–54.

Robins, Gay, *Women in Ancient Egypt* (Cambridge, Mass., 1993).

Royster, Francesca T., *Becoming Cleopatra: The Shifting Image of an Icon* (New York, 2003). The author presents Cleopatra as an icon of popular culture and explores gender, race, and the interaction of a historical personage with a series of different eras and cultures, from antiquity to the present.

Sartain, John, *On the Antique Painting in Encaustic of Cleopatra Discovered in 1818* (Philadelphia, 1885). Study of an encaustic painting on wood of Cleopatra being bitten by an asp, which the author suggests was carried in Octavian's Actian triumph. Even if not antique, it may have been a copy of Octavian's version.

Smith, R. R. R., *Hellenistic Royal Portraits* (Oxford, 1988), pp. 97–98, 132–134, 169. Includes discussion of Cleopatra's portraits.

Stewart, Andrew, *Greek Sculpture: An Exploration* (New Haven and London, 1990), pp. 131–133. The author places the portraiture of Cleopatra in the context of Hellenistic art.

Traversari, Gustavo, "Nuovo ritratto di Cleopatra VII Philopator e rivistazione critica dell'iconografia dell'ultima regina dell'Egitto, *Rivista di Archeologia* 21 (1997), pp. 44–48. A portrait of Cleopatra on an engraved gem is added to the Queen's corpus.

Troy, Lana, *Patterns of Queenship in Ancient Egyptian Myth and History* (Uppsala, 1986).

Vierneisel, Klaus, "Die Berliner Kleopatra," *Jahrbuch der Berliner Museum* 22 (1980), 5–33. The author analyzes the Berlin portrait of Cleopatra and compares it to Cleopatra's marble head in the Vatican.

Walker, Susan, and Peter Higgs, eds., *Cleopatra of Egypt: From History to Myth* (Princeton, 2001). Catalogue from an exhibition on Cleopatra; includes essays on the Ptolemies, Alexandria, Cleopatra, and Octavian, and the impact of Egyptian art in Italy.

Walker, Susan, "Cleopatra's Images: Reflections of Reality," in Susan Walker and Peter Higgs, eds., *Cleopatra of Egypt: From History to Myth* (Princeton, 2001), pp. 142–147. The author concentrates on the portraits of Cleopatra in the so-called Greek Hellenistic style.

Watterson, Barbara, *Women in Ancient Egypt* (Gloucestershire, 1991).

CHAPTER 10. EVEN DEATH WON'T PART US NOW

Flory, Marleen B., "Pearls for Venus," *Historia* 37 (1988), pp. 498–504. Augustus presents Cleopatra's pearls to Venus in her temple in the Forum of Caesar.

Ullman, B. L., "Cleopatra's Pearls," *The Classical Journal* 52 (1957), pp. 193–201. Pliny the Elder's recounting of Cleopatra and her pearls, and whether or not the story has validity.

CHAPTER 11. EGYPTOMANIA!

Alfano, Carla, "Piramidi a Roma," *Geo-Archeologia* 1 (1993), pp. 33–81. Tombs in ancient Rome in the shape of Egyptian pyramids.

Alfano, Carla, "Egyptian Influences in Italy," in Susan Walker and Peter Higgs, eds., *Cleopatra of Egypt: From History to Myth* (Princeton, 2001), pp. 276–291.

Balensiefen, Lilian, "Überlegnungen zu Aufbau und Lage der Danaidenhalle auf dem Palatin," *Römischen Mitteilungen* 102 (1995), pp. 189–209. The author suggests that "antico nero" herms, found near the Temple of Apollo on the Palatine hill and representing women in a peplos, were part of the Danaid group decorating the portico.

Buchner, Edmund, *Die Sonnenuhr des Augustus* (Mainz am Rhein, 1982). Study of

the obelisk and sundial of a complex in Rome that also featured the Ara Pacis and the Mausoleum of Augustus.
Budge, Ernest Alfred Wallis, *Cleopatra's Needles and Other Egyptian Obelisks* (New York, 1990; reprint of 1926 volume).
Carettoni, Gianfilippo, *Das Haus des Augustus auf dem Palatin* (Mainz am Rhein, 1983). The paintings in the House of Augustus on Rome's Palatine hill are presented in this fundamental study.
D'Alton, Martina, *The New York Obelisk, or How Cleopatra's Needle Came to New York and What Happened When It Got Here*, reprinted from *The Metropolitan Museum of Art Bulletin*, Spring 1993.
De Vos, Mariette, *L'Egittomania in pitture e mosaici romano-campani della prima èta imperiale* (Leiden, 1980). The author catalogues Roman paintings and mosaics with Egyptian and Egyptianizing themes and motifs.
De Vos, Mariette, "Aegyptiaca Romana," *La parola del passato* 49 (1994), pp. 130–159. The author discusses the Temple of Isis and Serapis on the Oppian hill in Rome and the Egyptian cult in Italy.
L'Egitto fuori dell'Egitto (Bologna, 1991). Egyptian and Egyptianizing art in Italian collections.
Iacopi, Irene, *Le decorazione pittorica dell' aula isiaca* (Rome, 1997). Comprehensive study of the wall paintings in Rome's Aula Isiaca.
Kellum, Barbara, "Sculptural Programs and Propaganda in Augustan Rome: The Temple of Apollo on the Palatine," in R. Winkes, *The Age of Augustus* (Louvain and Providence, 1986), pp. 169–176; reprinted in Eve D'Ambra, *Roman Art in Context: An Anthology* (Englewood Cliffs, N.J., 1993), pp. 75–83.
Ling, Roger, *Roman Painting* (Cambridge, 1991).
Roullet, Anne M., *The Egyptian and Egyptianizing Monuments of Imperial Rome, Études Préliminaires aux Religions Orientales dans l'Empire Romain* 20 (Leiden, 1972).
Versluys, M. J., *Aegyptica Romana: Nilotic Scenes and the Roman Views of Egypt* (Leiden and Boston), 2002.

CHAPTER 12. DIVINE ALTER EGOS

Sutherland, C. H. V., *The Cistophori of Augustus* (London, 1970). Study of the cistophoric tetradrachms of Augustus struck in the eastern mints of the empire, including coins with the sphinx reverse.
Zanker, Paul, *The Power of Images in the Age of Augustus* (Ann Arbor, 1988).

CHAPTER 13. A ROMAN PHARAOH AND A ROMAN EMPEROR

Hallof, Gabriele, and Jochen Hallof, "Dendur: The Six Hundred Forty-Third Stone," *Metropolitan Museum Journal* 33 (1998), pp. 103–108. The author reveals the significance of a red sandstone block from Augustus's Temple at Dendur.

Porter, Bertha, *Topographical Bibliography of Ancient Egyptian Hieroglyphic Texts, Reliefs, and Paintings,* vol. II: *Theban Temples* (Oxford, 1929). Ptolemaic and Roman temples located at Karnak, Luxor, and various desert sites.

Porter, Bertha, *Topographical Bibliography of Ancient Egyptian Hieroglyphic Texts, Reliefs, and Paintings, vol. V: Upper Egypt* (Oxford, 1937). Ptolemaic and Roman temples situated at a wide variety of sites in Upper Egypt.

Porter, Bertha, *Topographical Bibliography of Ancient Egyptian Hieroglyphic Texts, Reliefs, and Paintings,* vol. VI: *Upper Egypt Chief Temples (Excluding Thebes)* (Oxford, 1939). Ptolemaic and Roman temples located at Abydos, Dendera, Esna, Edfu, Kôm Ombo, and Plilae.

CHAPTER 14. ROME ON THE TIBER

Bari, S. A., "Economic Interests of Augustan Rome in Egypt," *Roma e l'Egitto nell'antichità classica, Cairo 6–9 febbraio 1989, Atti de I Congresso internazionale italo-egiziano* (Rome, 1992), pp. 69–76.

Bartman, Elizabeth, "Sculptural Collecting and Display, in the Private Realm," in Elaine K. Gazda, *Roman Art in the Private Sphere: New Perspectives on the Architecture and Décor of the Domus, Villa, and Insula* (Ann Arbor, 1991), pp. 71–88.

Bauman, Richard A., *Women and Politics in Ancient Rome* (London and New York), 1992.

Dalby, Andrew, *Empire of Pleasures: Luxury and Indulgence in the Roman World* (London, 2000). An exploration of luxury and high living in Rome and the comparable life-style lived by those in such provinces as Egypt.

Eck, Werner, "Senatorial Self-Presentation: Developments in the Augustan Period," in Fergus Millar and Erich Segal, eds., *Caesar Augustus: Several Aspects* (Oxford, 1981), pp. 129–167.

Favro, Diane, *The Urban Image of Augustan Rome* (Cambridge, 1996). The author traces the development of Rome from an ad hoc jumble of buildings to a unified urban entity that reflected the political and social agenda of the emperor Augustus.

Kellum, Barbara, "The City Adorned: Programmatic Display at the *Aedes Concordiae Augustae,*" in K. A. Raaflaub and M. Toher, eds., *Between Republic and Empire* (Berkeley, Los Angeles, and Oxford, 1990), pp. 276–296. Augustus's deliberative and ideological redesign of Rome and the part played by architecture, sculpture, and painting.

Kleiner, Fred S., "The Arch in Honor of C. Octavius and the Fathers of Augustus," *Historia* 37 (1988), pp. 347–357. Study of the Lost Arch of Augustus on the Palatine hill in Rome that honored Augustus's human and divine fathers.

Leach, Eleanor Winsor, "The Politics of Self-Presentation: Pliny's *Letters* and Roman Portrait Sculpture," *Classical Antiquity* 9, no. 1 (1990), pp. 14–39.

Leen, Anne, "Cicero and the Rhetoric of Art," *American Journal of Philology* 112 (1991), pp. 229–245. How Cicero's art collection at his Tusculum villa reveals a carefully devised image of the owner and his political status and social ambitions.

Richardson, Lawrence, Jr., *A New Topographical Dictionary of Ancient Rome* (Baltimore and London, 1992).

Sherwin-White, Adrian Nicholas, *Roman Foreign Policy in the East, 168 B.C. to A.D. 1* (London, 1984).

Syme, Ronald, *The Roman Revolution* (Oxford, 1939). Highly influential book in which the author characterizes the age of Augustus and art in the service of ideology.

Wallace-Hadrill, Andrew, "Patronage in Roman Society: From Republic to Empire," in Andrew Wallace-Hadrill, ed., *Patronage in Ancient Society* (London and New York, 1989), pp. 63–87.

CHAPTER 15. DEATH, DYNASTY, AND A ROMAN DENDERA

Conlin, Diane Atnally, *The Artists of the Ara Pacis* (Chapel Hill and London, 1997). The author attempts to demonstrate that the artists who carved the Ara Pacis Augustae were not Greeks but sculptors trained in Italy.

Davies, Penelope J. E., *Death and the Emperor: Roman Imperial Funerary Monuments from Augustus to Marcus Aurelius* (Cambridge, 2000).

Fullerton, Mark D., "The *Domus Augusti* in Imperial Iconography of 13–12 B.C.," *American Journal of Archaeology* 89 (1985), pp. 473–483. The author discusses the theme of the glorification of the imperial family of Augustus on coins and in contemporary art and literature.

Galinsky, Karl, *Augustan Culture* (Princeton, 1996). The author examines politics, literature, and art in the age of Augustus and presents a post-Symian interpretation of the era, by replacing the concept of propaganda with that of *auctoritas* and effectively underscoring the polysemous nature of Augustan art.

Kaiser Augustus und die Verlorene Republik (Berlin, 1988). An exhibition in Berlin served as the basis for this important study of Roman art from the late Republic to the death of Augustus.

Kleiner, Diana E. E., "The Great Friezes of the Ara Pacis Augustae: Greek Sources, Roman Derivatives, and Augustan Social Policy," *Mélanges de l'Ecole Française de Rome,* 90.2 (1978), pp. 753–785, reprinted in Eve D'Ambra, *Roman Art in Context: An Anthology* (Englewood Cliffs, N.J., 1993), pp. 27–52. Exploration of the significance of women and children on the Ara Pacis in light of Augustus's dynastic and social policies, especially his marriage and moral legislation. The possible identities of the boys closest to Augustus in the south and north friezes are also discussed.

Kleiner, Diana E. E., *Roman Sculpture* (New York and London, 1992). The fundamental reference on the sculpture of Rome, which traces Roman public and private art from the Late Republic to the age of Constantine and examines that art in its political, social, and cultural context.

La Rocca, Eugenio, *Ara Pacis Augustae In Occasione del Restauro della Fronte Orientale* (Rome, 1983). Study of the altar's figural program and report on the restoration of the monument's eastern side.

Pollini, John, *The Portraiture of Gaius and Lucius Caesar* (New York, 1987).

Rose, Charles Bryan, "'Princes' and Barbarians on the Ara Pacis," *American Journal of Archaeology* 94 (1990), pp. 453–467, reprinted in Eve D'Ambra, *Roman Art in Context: An Anthology* (Englewood Cliffs, N.J., 1993), pp. 53–74. The two boys nearest Augustus on the south and north friezes are identified as barbarian children from the eastern (Bosporan royalty) and western (Gallic extraction) parts of the Roman Empire.

Schütz, Michael, "Zur Sonnenuhr des Augustus auf dem Marsfeld," *Gymnasium* 97 (1990), pp. 432–457. The author rethinks the orientation of the sundial to the Ara Pacis and the rest of the Augustan complex in the Campus Martius.

Simon, Erika, *Ara Pacis Augustae* (Greenwich, Conn., n.d.). Brief but useful overview of the monument.

Simon, Erika, *Augustus: Kunst und Leben in Rom um die Zeitenwende* (Munich, 1986). The author provides a comprehensive overview of art in the age of Augustus.

Varner, Eric, *From Caligula to Constantine. Tyranny and Transformation in Roman Portraiture* (Atlanta, 2000). Exhibition catalogue of the Roman use of *damnatio memoriae* to remake history, literature, and art; discusses the practical and political recasting of Ptolemaic portraiture as a precedent for the Roman practice.

Winkes, Rolf, ed., *The Age of Augustus* (Providence, 1982).

CHAPTER 16. COMPETING WITH CLEOPATRA ON COINS

Kent, J. P. C., *Roman Coins* (London, 1978).

Kleiner, Diana E. E., "Politics and Gender in the Pictorial Propaganda of Antony and Octavian," in *Echos du Monde Classique/Classical Views* 36, n.s. 11 (1992), pp. 357–367. Examination of the political clout of the women in Mark Antony's circle and how this was depicted on Antony's coinage.

Sutherland, C. H. V., *Roman Coins* (London, 1974).

CHAPTER 17. PRINCESSES AND POWER HAIR

Bartman, Elizabeth, *Portraits of Livia: Imaging the Imperial Woman in Augustan Rome* (Cambridge, 1999). The portraits of Julia are also discussed.

Corbier, Mireille, "Male Power and Legitimacy through Women: The *Domus Augusta* under the Julio-Claudians," in Richard Hawley and Barbara Levick, eds., *Women in Antiquity: New Assessments* (New York, 1995), pp. 178–193. The author underscores the important contribution of women to the complex web of alliances and political machinations.

Fantham, Elaine, Helene Foley, Natalie Kampen, Sarah Pomeroy, and H. Alan Shapiro, *Women in the Classical World: Image and Text* (New York and Oxford, 1994). An overview of women in the Greco-Roman world that analyzes texts and works of art and treats Cleopatra as one of many interesting classical women.

Fischler, Susan, "Social Stereotypes and Historical Analysis: The Case of the Imperial Women at Rome," in Léonie J. Archer, Susan Fischler, and Maria Wyke, eds., *Women in Ancient Societies: An Illusion of the Night* (New York, 1994), pp. 115–133.

Forbis, Elizabeth P., "Women's Public Image in Italian Honorary Inscriptions," *American Journal of Philology* 111 (1990), pp. 493–512. The author discusses inscriptions that honor Roman women as wealthy and generous public benefactors.

Hallett, Judith P., "Women as Same and Other in Classical Roman Elite," *Helios* 16 (1989), pp. 59–78. Drawing on the theories of Simone de Beauvoir, the author argues that male conceptions of elite Roman women were bipartite: women were both united with and separated from men.

Kampen, Natalie, "Between Public and Private: Women as Historical Subjects in Ancient Art," in Sarah B. Pomeroy, ed., *Women's History and Ancient History* (Chapel Hill and London, 1991), pp. 218–248. The author questions why women are depicted in or excluded from Roman state relief sculpture and offers possible explanations for that phenomenon.

Kleiner, Diana E. E., and Susan B. Matheson, eds., *I, Clavdia: Women in Ancient Rome* (New Haven, 1996). Exhibition catalogue in which the first comprehensive overview of the lives of Roman women as depicted in Roman art is presented.

Kleiner, Diana E. E., and Susan B. Matheson, eds., *I, Clavdia II: Woman in Roman Art and Society* (Austin, 2000). A sequel volume to the 1996 catalogue *I, Clavdia: Women in Ancient Rome,* with additional essays on Roman women and Roman society.

Kleiner, Diana E. E., "Semblance and Storytelling in Augustan Art," Chapter 8 in

Karl Galinsky, ed., *The Cambridge Companion to the Age of Augustus* (Cambridge, 2005).

Kunst, Christiane, and Ulrike Riemer, eds., *Grenzen der Macht. Zur Rolle der römischen Kaiserfrauen* (Stuttgart, 2000). Essays on women from the imperial circle; themes include elite woman in religion, politics, history, and art and cover the chronological period from the Republic through late antiquity.

Lefkowitz, Mary, "Influential Women," in Averil Cameron and Amélie Kuhrt, eds., *Images of Women in Antiquity* (London, 1993), pp. 49–64. Essay on the public life of ancient women, including Cleopatra.

Levine, Molly Meyerowitz, "The Gendered Grammar of Ancient Mediterranean Hair," in Howard Eilberg-Schwartz and Wendy Doniger, eds., *Off With Her Head: The Denial of Women's Identity in Myth, Religion, and Culture* (Berkeley, Los Angeles, and London, 1995), pp. 76–130. The evidence for hair and its meaning among the ancient Greeks, Romans, and Jews.

MacMullen, Ramsay, "Women in Public in the Roman Empire," *Historia* 29 (1980), pp. 208–218. Inscriptions and coins as evidence for the public life of Roman women.

MacMullen, Ramsay, "Women's Power in the Principate," *Klio* 68 (1986), pp. 434–443.

Richlin, Amy, "Making Up a Roman: The Face of Roman Gender," in Howard Eilberg-Schwartz and Wendy Doniger, eds., *Off With Her Head: The Denial of Women's Identity in Myth, Religion, and Culture* (Berkeley, Los Angeles, and London, 1995), pp. 185–213. Development of the idea that Roman thought presented women in antiquity as in need of cosmetics to cover their deficiencies.

Van Bremen, Riet, "Women and Wealth," in Averil Cameron and A. Kuhrt, eds., *Images of Women in Antiquity* (London, 1993).

Vanderpool, Catherine de Grazia, abstract, *American Journal of Archaeology* 90 (1994), p. 285. The portrait of a Roman woman from Corinth is identified as Augustus's daughter Julia.

Vanderpool, Catherine de Grazia, "Roman Portraiture: The Many Faces of Corinth," in Charles K. Williams and Nancy Bookidis, *Corinth, The Centenary, 1896–1996, Corinth 20* (Athens, 2003). The portrait of Julia from Corinth is discussed.

Winkes, Rolf, *Livia, Octavia, Julia. Porträts und Darstellungen* (Providence and Louvain-la-Neuve, 1995). The author examines the portraiture of Livia, Octavia, and Julia and provides line drawings of the women's coiffures that are an invaluable resource.

Wood, Susan, *Imperial Women: A Study in Public Images, 40 B.C.–A.D. 68* (Leiden, 1999). Presentation of imperial women as the models for portraiture of all

Roman women and their use as a vehicle for the proliferation of Augustan Rome's morality and behavioral codes for women.

Wyke, Maria, "Woman in the Mirror: The Rhetoric of Adornment in the Roman World," in Léonie J. Archer, Susan Fischler, and Maria Wyke, eds., *Women in Ancient Societies: An Illusion of the Night* (New York, 1994), pp. 134–151. The author treats Roman literary and visual images that present the female form as a reflection in a mirror, and discusses the implication of these images for gender identity.

CHAPTER 18. REGINA ROMANA

Anderson, Maxwell, "The Portrait Medallions of the Imperial Villa of Boscotrecase," *American Journal of Archaeology* 91 (1987), pp. 127–135. The author identifies the painted portraits in the villa's Cubiculum 15 as likenesses of Livia and Julia.

Bartman, Elizabeth, *Portraits of Livia: Imaging the Imperial Woman in Augustan Rome* (Cambridge, 1999).

Bernoulli, Johann, *Römische Ikonographie* II.1 (Berlin and Stuttgart, 1886). The first systematic listing of the portraits of Livia, Octavia, and Julia.

Gross, Walter Hatto, *Julia Augusta. Untersuchungen zur Grundlegung einer Livia Ikonographie* (Göttingen, 1962). Comprehensive study of the portraiture of Livia, with discussion of coins, relief sculpture, portrait types, and Livia's assumption of the role of *Diva Augusta.*

Rose, Charles Bryan, *Dynastic Commemoration and Imperial Portraiture in the Julio-Claudian Period* (Cambridge, 1997). Exploration of how statuary groups of Augustus and his family were used to disseminate dynastic policy.

Winkes, Rolf, *Livia, Octavia, Julia. Porträts und Darstellungen* (Providence and Louvain-la-Neuve, 1995).

CHAPTER 19. FROM ASP TO ETERNITY

Kampen, Natalie, *Image and Status: Roman Working Women in Ostia* (Berlin, 1981). Depictions of professional women at Ostia, the port of Rome, but with more general ramifications for Roman women at work.

Kleiner, Diana E. E., *Roman Group Portraiture: The Funerary Reliefs of the Late Republic and Early Empire* (New York, 1977). Comprehensive study of funerary reliefs commissioned from the Late Republic on. Their epitaphs and group portraits record the strength of family ties among a diverse group of slaves and former slaves.

Kleiner, Diana E. E., "Social Status, Marriage, and Male Heirs in the Age of Augustus: A Roman Funerary Relief," *North Carolina Museum of Art Bulletin* 14, 4 (1990), pp. 20–26. Study of an Augustan funerary relief, possibly from Rome, as an example of the respect for marriage and family among freedmen that emerged from their own family values and those espoused by Augustus and Livia.

Kleiner, Diana E. E., "Imperial Women as Patrons of the Arts in the Early Empire," in Diana E. E. Kleiner and Susan B. Matheson, eds., *I, Clavdia: Women in Ancient Rome* (New Haven, 1996), pp. 28–41. Octavia, and especially Livia, as the commissioners of such public buildings as porticoes, markets, museums, and temples.

Shipley, F. W., *Agrippa's Building Activities in Rome* (St. Louis, 1933).

CLEOPATRA'S STORY IN FICTION

Bradshaw, Gillian, *Cleopatra's Heir* (New York, 2002). The life of Caesarion, had he lived.

Butts, Mary, *Scenes from the Life of Cleopatra* (London, 1935; paperback reprint: Los Angeles, 1994).

Essex, Karen, *Kleopatra* (New York, 2001).

Essex, Karen, *Pharaoh* (New York, 2002). Sequel volume to *Kleopatra*, presenting part two of the story.

Falconer, Colin, *When We Were Gods, A Novel of Cleopatra* (New York, 2000).

Frain, Irène, *L'Inimitable* (Paris, 1998).

George, Margaret, *The Memoirs of Cleopatra* (New York, 1997). Fictional memoirs.

Haggard, H. Rider, *Cleopatra* (Berkeley Heights, N.J., 1999; reprint of a work originally published in 1889). The Cleopatra story told by a priest named Harmarchis.

Ludwig, Emil, *Cleopatra* (New York, 1971).

McCullough, Colleen, *The October Horse, A Novel of Caesar and Cleopatra* (New York, 2002).

STUDIES OF CLEOPATRA'S STORY IN FILM

Joshel, Sandra R., Margaret Malamud, and Donald T. McGuire, Jr., eds., *Imperial Projections: Ancient Rome in Modern Popular Culture* (Baltimore and London, 2001).

Lant, Antonia, "The Curse of the Pharaoh, or How Cinema Contracted Egyptomania," *Motion Picture News* 59 (1992), pp. 86–112.

Solomon, Jon, "In the Wake of Cleopatra: The Ancient World in the Cinema Since 1963," *The Classical Journal* 91.2 (1996), pp. 113–140.

Solomon, Jon, *The Ancient World in the Cinema* (New Haven and London, 2001; revised and expanded version of a 1978 book).
Winkler, Martin M., ed., *Classical Myth and Culture in the Cinema* (Oxford, 2001).
Wyke, Maria, *Projecting the Past, Ancient Rome, Cinema, and History* (New York and London, 1997).

CLEOPATRA FILMS

Cleopatra, directed by Charles L. Gaskill, with Helen Gardner; Helen Gardner Players, 1912, black-and-white. The first serious attempt to present the filmic version of Cleopatra's life and loves.

Marcantonio e Cleopatra, directed by Enrico Guazzoni, with Giovanna Terribili Gonzales and Antony Novelli; Cines, Rome, 1913, black-and-white. A silent film focusing on Cleopatra's life and loves, with several memorable scenes, peopled with the large crowds characteristic of this Italian production company.

Cleopatra, directed by J. Gordon Edwards; Fox Film Corporation, 1917, black-and-white. The film is now lost but is known through surviving still photographs. This was a silent film featuring Theda Bara at the height of her fame as Cleopatra, in a traditional rendition of the story with a lavishly costumed star and cast of thousands.

Cleopatra, directed by Cecil B. DeMille, with Claudette Colbert, Warren William, and Henry Wilcoxon; Paramount, 1934, black-and-white. The first sound movie of Cleopatra, in which she bewitches Julius Caesar and Mark Antony and leads them astray amid sumptuous sets and a barge scene worthy of Plutarch.

Caesar and Cleopatra, directed by Gabriel Pascal, written by George Bernard Shaw, with Vivien Leigh, Claude Rains, Stewart Granger, and Flora Robson; London: Rank Film Organization and Two Cities Film Ltd., 1945, Technicolor. This film focuses on the relationship between Cleopatra and Caesar: he is entranced with her intelligence and charm, and she expects that their relationship will benefit Egypt.

Due Notti con Cleopatra (Two Nights with Cleopatra), directed by Mario Mattoli, written by Ruggero Maccari and Ettore Scola, with Sophia Loren, Alberto Sordi and Ettore Manni; Italy: Minerva Film SpA, 1953 (1964 in the USA), color. A fictional caper in which a cold-blooded Cleopatra, having taken all her palace guards as lovers and then poisoned them, decides she wants to leave the palace to seduce Mark Antony, leaving a look-alike in her place.

Serpent of the Nile, directed by William Castle, with Raymond Burr and Rhonda Fleming; 1953, USA. Presents a strange twist on the well-known tale by asserting that Cleopatra preferred Antony's brother to him.

Le Legioni di Cleopatra (*Legions of Cleopatra,* also called *Legions of the Nile),* directed by Vittorio Cottafavi, with Linda Cristal, Ettore Manni, and Georges Marchal; 1959. Emphasizes action scenes, but the story line and characters are undeveloped.

Cleopatra, directed by Joseph L. Mankiewicz, with Elizabeth Taylor, Richard Burton, Rex Harrison, Roddy McDowall, Hume Cronyn; 20th Century Fox, 1963, color. The most famous Cleopatra film. It is a lavishly produced historical drama highlighting a Cleopatra who purportedly bolstered her power in Egypt by exploiting conflicts in the Roman Empire. This grand epic is best known for its expense, its ostentatious costumes and wigs, and the very public love affair of its stars. There are memorable scenes of Cleopatra unrolled from the carpet, entering Rome, and meeting Mark Antony at Tarsus. Nominated for nine Academy Awards, it won four, including best actor for Rex Harrison as Caesar.

Cleopatra, directed by Franc Roddam, with Leonor Varela, Billy Zane, and Timothy Dalton; USA, 1999, color. Made-for-television mini-series with conventional plot based on the novel by Margaret George.

The Royal Diaries: Cleopatra, Daughter of the Nile, with Elisa Moolecherry and Hrant Aliank; USA, 2000. Made for television as part of a series on exceptional young women in history, and based on a novel by Kristiana Gregory.

CLEOPATRA AND ROME ON THE INTERNET

Internet resources are growing, and those on Rome and Cleopatra are no exception. They vary in scope and quality but contribute in interesting ways to our understanding of the queen and her interaction with Rome. It is in the nature of this new medium that some will disappear, and even those that last will be transformed as technology is enhanced and greater sophistication is possible. A small selection is listed here, arranged under broad subject categories.

Egypt and the Ptolemies

Ashmawy, Alaa K., "Egypt WWW Index," *http://ce.eng.usf.edu/pharos/,* 2001.

Philippidis, Adam D., "The House of Ptolemy: Caesar, Cleopatra, and Marcus Antonius and the Transition to a Greco-Roman (Roman Imperial) Egypt," *http://www.houseofptolemy.org/housecle.htm,* 2001.

Cleopatra

Claudon, C. David. "The Cleopatra Costume on Stage and in Film," *http://www.davidclaudon.com/Cleo/Cleopatra1.html,* 2002.

"Cleopatra," *http://www.royalty.nu/Africa/Egypt/Cleopatra.html,* 2003.

"Cleopatra VII of Egypt," *http://en.wikipedia.org/wiki/Cleopatra_VII_of_Egypt.* Wikipedia, the Free Encyclopedia.

Spalding, Tim, "Cleopatra on the Web," *http://www.isidore-of-seville.com/cleopatra/,* 2000.

Roman History, Literature, the Emperors, and Art

Cristofori, Alessandro, ed., "Rassegna degli Strumenti Informatici per lo Studio dell'Antichità Classica (A Survey of Digital Resources on the Classical World)," *http://www.rassegna.unibo.it/indexeng.html,* 2003. Now in Italian (formerly *http://www.ukans.edu/history/index/europe/ancient_rome/E/Roman/home.html.*

Halsall, Paul, "Internet Ancient History Sourcebook," *http://www.fordham.edu/halsall/ancient/asbook09.html,* 1998.

Shipley, Graham, "Ancient History Internet Resources," *http://www.le.ac.uk/archaeology/intresources/anchis.html,* 1998.

Stevenson, Daniel C., "The Internet Classics Archive," *http://classics.mit.edu/index.html,* 2000.

Weigel, Richard D., "De Imperatoribus Romanis: An Online Encyclopedia of Roman Emperors," *http://www.roman-emperors.org,* 2003.

Julius Caesar

Bushnell, Thomas, ed., "Works by Julius Caesar," *http://classics.mit.edu/Browse/browse-Caesar.html,* 2000.

Cross, Suzanne. "Julius Caesar: The Last Dictator," *http://heraklia.fws1.com/,* 2003.

McManus, Barbara F., "Julius Caesar: Historical Background," *http://www.vroma.org/~bmcmanus/caesar.html,* 2001.

Augustus

Morford, Mark, "University of Virginia Electronic Text Center: Augustus—Images of Power," *http://etext.lib.virginia.edu/users/morford/augimage.html,* 2003.

Women in the Ancient World

Cross, Suzanne, "Feminae Romanae: The Women of Ancient Rome," *http://dominae.fws1.com/index.html,* 2002.

Fernalld, R. J., "Romanae Antiquae: An Informal Look at the Lives of Women in Ancient Rome," *http://www.realm-of-shade.com/RomanaeAntiquae/,* 1997. Includes "Lady Livia's Alcove."

Halsall, Paul, "Internet Women's History Sourcebook," *http://www.fordham.edu/halsall/women/womensbook.html,* 2001.

Scaife, Ross, and Suzanne Bonefas, "Diotima: Materials for the Study of Women and Gender in the Ancient World," *http://www.stoa.org/diotima/*, 2002. An interdisciplinary Web site for those interested in patterns of gender in the ancient Mediterranean world. There is extensive material relating to Cleopatra and Caesar in particular, including historical information, art, scholarly essays, and bibliographic resources.

Cleopatra in Film

The Internet Movie Database (IMDb), *http://www.imdb.com/*, 1990–2004. Internet movie resource with 60 matches for Cleopatra.

Van den Berg, Hans, "The Ancient Egypt Film Site," *http://www.wepwawet.nl/films/*, 2002.

ILLUSTRATION CREDITS

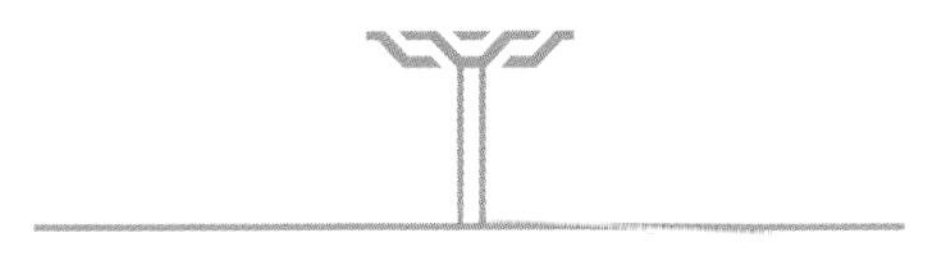

P.1. Jean André Rixens (1846–1924), *Death of Cleopatra.* Toulouse, Musée des Augustins, 1874. Erich Lessing/Art Resource, NY, ART 169936.

P.2. Cleopatra (Elizabeth Taylor) and Caesarion entering Rome; still from 1963 film. Bettmann/CORBIS BE 025413.

P.3. Louis Gauffier, *Cleopatra and Octavian.* Edinburgh, National Gallery of Scotland, 1787–1788. The Bridgeman Art Library, ID NGS 77127.

1.1. Head of a Ptolemaic queen, perhaps Cleopatra. Rome, Museo Capitolino, first century B.C. CORBIS VUO0433.

1.2. Head of Ptolemy XII Auletes. Paris, Musée du Louvre, 80–51 B.C. Réunion des Musées Nationaux/Art Resource, NY, ART 151975.

1.3. Giambattista Tiepolo (1696–1770), *Banquet of Cleopatra and Mark Antony at Tarsus,* Paris, Musée Cognacq-Jay, 1740s. Cameraphoto/Art Resource, NY, ART 163124.

2.1. Livia, detail of head, Ara Pacis Augustae, Rome, south frieze, 13–9 B.C. Forschungsarchiv für Antike Plastik Fitt80-43-12_0037889032.

2.2. Head of Octavia, from Velletri, Rome, Palazzo Massimo alle Terme, ca. 40 B.C. Photograph by Diana E. E. Kleiner, 2004.

2.3. Green basalt head, possibly of Mark Antony, Kingston Lacy, The National Trust, ca. 40–30 B.C. The National Trust Photo Library

2.4. Bust of Octavian, Rome, Museo Capitolino, ca. 30 B.C. Araldo de Luca/ CORBIS DE002385.

3.1. Head of Julia, Corinth, Corinth Museum, ca. 13 B.C. American School of Classical Studies and Corinth Excavations, photograph by I. Ioannidou and L. Bartziotou.

3.2. Head of Marcus Agrippa, Paris, Musée du Louvre, ca. 30–20 B.C. Erich Lessing/Art Resource, NY, ART 101877.

4.1. Altar with sculptor and woman client, Rome, Vatican Museums, early second century. Photograph by Diana E. E. and Fred S. Kleiner, 1973.

4.2. Relief with baking scene, Rome, Tomb of Eurysaces, late first century B.C. Photograph by Diana E. E. and Fred S. Kleiner, 1973.

4.3. Relief depicting a poultry vendor, from Ostia, Museo Ostiense, late second century A.D. Erich Lessing/Art Resource, NY, ART 41715.

4.4. Relief depicting a woman having her hair dressed, from the Elternpaarpfeiler, Neumagen, Trier, Landesmuseum, A.D. 235. Fototeca Unione 11016.

5.1. *Pharos of Alexandria,* engraving by Maerten van Heemskerck (1498–1574). Bettmann/CORBIS E2138.

5.2. Imaginary recreation of scholars in a hall of the Library at Alexandria, based on a Hungarian engraving, undated. Bettmann/CORBIS BE 063187.

5.3. Ptolemy XIII smiting enemies, pylon, Edfu, Temple of Horus, 40s B.C. Giraudon/Art Resource, NY, ART 94358.

5.4. Jean-Léon Gérôme, *Cleopatra Meeting with Caesar,* private collection, 1866. Bettmann/CORBIS SF14577.

5.5. Henri-Pierre Picou (1824–1895), *Cleopatra's Galley,* Musée Goupil, Bordeaux, 1875. Bettmann/CORBIS BEO83760.

5.6. Caesarion and Cleopatra as Osiris and Isis, making an offering to the goddess Hathor, south wall, Dendera, Temple of Hathor, 40s/30s B.C. Erich Lessing/Art Resource, NY, ART 80662.

6.1. Remains of Caesar's building projects, Rome, Roman Forum, ca. 42 B.C. Photograph by Diana E. E. Kleiner, 2004.

7.1. Giambattista Tiepolo (1696–1770), *The Meeting of Mark Antony and Cleopatra,* Venice, Palazzo Labia, 1746–1747. Erich Lessing/Art Resource, NY, ART 7173.

7.2. Bronze statue of a boy, possibly Alexander Helios as Prince of Armenia, ca. 34–30 B.C. Metropolitan Museum of Art, New York. Photo credit: The Metropolitan Museum of Art, Chapman Fund, 1949 (49.11.3); all rights reserved, The Metropolitan Museum of Art.

7.3. Terracotta plaque depicting the struggle of Apollo and Hercules for the Delphic tripod, from the Temple of Apollo Palatinus, Rome, Antiquario Palatino, ca. 28 B.C. Scala/Art Resource, NY, ART 123661.

7.4. Relief depicting warship with crocodile, from Palestrina, Temple of Fortuna Primigenia, Rome, Vatican Museums, Museo Gregoriano Profano, ca. 40–30 B.C. Scala/Art Resource, NY, ART 8233.

8.1. Head of Alexander the Great from Pella, Greece. Pella, Archaeological Museum, ca. 200–150 B.C. Art Resource, NY, ART 88862.

8.2. Silver tetradrachm with obverse head of Ptolemy I Soter, 305–285 B.C. Yale University Gallery, New Haven. Photo credit: Ruth Elizabeth White Fund.

8.3. Head of Pompey the Great from Rome, Via Salaria, Licinian Tomb, Claudian copy of a portrait of 50 B.C. Copenhagen, Ny Carlsberg Glyptotek. Photograph courtesy of the Ny Carlsberg Glyptotek, Copenhagen.

8.4. Denarius with obverse head of Julius Caesar, struck by Marcus Mettius, 44 B.C. American Numismatic Society, New York. Photo credit: American Numismatic Society 1937.158.290.

8.5. Green diabase head of Julius Caesar, ca. A.D. 1–50, Berlin, Staatliche Museen zu Berlin Antikensammlung. Sandro Vannini/CORBIS VU004397.

9.1. Stele with kilted sovereign, perhaps Cleopatra, dedicated by Onnophris. Paris, Musée du Louvre, 51 B.C.(?) Réunion des Musées Nationaux/Art Resource, NY, ART 185420.

9.2. Black basalt statue of Cleopatra with a triple *uraeus* headdress. St. Petersburg, Hermitage Museum, ca. 51–30 B.C. Courtesy of the State Hermitage Museum.

9.3. Tetradrachm with obverse head of Cleopatra with a necklace. New York, American Numismatic Society, 37–32 B.C. Photo credit: American Numismatic Society, 1977.158.621.

9.4. Denarius with obverse head of Mark Antony. London, British Museum, 32 B.C. Photo credit: Copyright © The British Museum.

9.5. Denarius of Mark Antony with reverse head of Cleopatra. London, British Museum, 32 B.C. Photo Credit: Copyright © The British Museum.

9.6. 80-drachm coin with obverse head of Cleopatra holding Caesarion, from the mint of Paphos, Cyprus, 46 B.C. New York, American Numismatic Society. Photo credit: American Numismatic Society, 1951.116.420.

9.7. Statue of a Ptolemaic prince, perhaps Caesarion. New York, Brooklyn Museum of Art, 54.117, first century B.C. Photo credit: Brooklyn Museum of Art, Charles Edwin Wilbour Fund.

9.8. Head of Cleopatra, found in Villa of the Quintilii, Rome, Vatican Museums, Museo Gregoriano Profano, ca. 50–30 B.C. Photo credit: Sandro Vannini/CORBIS VU004367.

9.9. Head of Cleopatra, found in Villa of the Quintilii, Rome, Vatican Museums, Museo Gregoriano Profano, ca. 50–30 B.C. Photo credit: Sandro Vannini/CORBIS VU004468.

9.10. Head of Cleopatra, Berlin, Antikensammlung, Staatliche Museen zu Berlin, 50-30 B.C. Bildarchiv Preussischer Kulturbesitz/Art Resource, NY, ART 177842.

11.1. Obelisk, Rome, Piazza di Montecitorio, sixth century B.C., but erected in Rome in 10 B.C. Photograph by Diana E. E. Kleiner, 2004.

11.2. Tomb of Gaius Cestius, Rome, 15 B.C. Photograph by Diana E. E. Kleiner, 2004.

11.3. Egyptianizing paintings, Rome, Palatine hill, Aula Isiaca, south wall. Photo credit: After Giovanni Rizzo, Le pitture dell'Aula Isiaca di Caligola, Rome, 1936.

12.1. Cistophorus of Augustus with Greek-style sphinx on reverse, London, British Museum, ca. 20 B.C. Photo credit: Copyright © The British Museum.

12.2. Statue of Augustus, from Livia's Villa at Primaporta, Rome, Vatican Museums, Tiberian copy of original of ca. 20 B.C. CORBIS DE004908.

12.3. Arretine clay mold, with Antony and Cleopatra as Hercules and Omphale in a chariot drawn by centaurs. New York, Metropolitan Museum of Art. Photo credit: The Metropolitan Museum of Art, Rogers Fund, 1919 (19.192.21), all rights reserved, The Metropolitan Museum of Art. (The Museum questions the authenticity of this piece.)

12.4. Arretine clay mold depicting Antony and Cleopatra as Hercules and Omphale, with Antony beneath a parasol looking back toward Cleopatra. New York, Metropolitan Museum of Art. Photo credit: The Metropolitan Museum of Art, Rogers Fund, 1919 (19.192.21), all rights reserved, The Metropolitan Museum of Art. (The Museum questions the authenticity of this piece.)

13.1. Augustus, as pharaoh, makes an offering to Thoth, Shu, and Tefnut, Temple of el-Dakka in Nubia. Photo credit: A. J. F. Champollion, *Monuments de l'Egypte et de la Nubie,* Vol. 1 (Paris, 1835), pl. LV bis.

13.2. Augustus, as pharaoh, makes an offering to Thoth and Sekhmet on the Temple of Augustus at Dendur. New York, Metropolitan Museum of Art, Augustan. Photo credit: Lee Snider/Photo Images/Corbis SN003481.

14.1. Remains of the Basilica Aemilia, Rome, Roman Forum, Augustan. Photograph by Diana E. E. Kleiner, 2004.

14.2. Curia and Rostra, Rome, Roman Forum, Augustan and later renovations. Photograph by Diana E. E. Kleiner, 2004.

14.3. Temple of Mars Ultor, Rome, Forum of Augustus, dedicated 2 B.C. Photograph by Diana E. E. Kleiner, 2004.

14.4. Relief depicting a statuary group of Mars, Venus, and Divus Julius, Algiers, National Museum of Antiquities, Augustan. Alinari/Art Resource, NY, ART 67016.

14.5. Baths of Agrippa: restored view from the west (after Hülsen). Fototeca Unione 2963.

15.1. Ara Pacis Augustae, Rome, view from northwest, 13–9 B.C. Scala/Art Resource, NY, ART 181978.

15.2. Ara Pacis Augustae, Rome, south frieze, detail with portraits of Marcus Agrippa, Livia, and Gaius Caesar, 13–9 B.C. Alinari/Art Resource, NY, ART 98322.

15.3. Ara Pacis Augustae, Rome, north frieze, detail with portraits of Julia and Lucius Caesar, 13–9 B.C. Alinari/Art Resource, NY, ART 27422.

15.4. Ara Pacis Augustae, Rome, southeast panel, seated woman with two babies, 13–9 B.C. Scala/Art Resource, NY, ART 14300.

16.1. Aureus with obverse head of a woman, possibly Fulvia, struck by C.

Numonius Vaala, London, British Museum, late 40s B.C. Photo credit: Copyright © The British Museum.

16.2. Aureus with obverse head of Mark Antony, eastern mint, London, British Museum, 38 B.C. Photo credit: Copyright © The British Museum.

16.3. Aureus with reverse head of Octavia, eastern mint, London, British Museum, 38 B.C. Photo credit: Copyright © The British Museum.

16.4. Denarius of Augustus with reverse heads of Julia and Gaius and Lucius Caesar, struck in Rome, ca. 13–12 B.C. New York, American Numismatic Society. Photo credit: American Numismatic Society, 1937.158.390.

18.1. Head of Livia, Rome, Palazzo Massimo alle Terme, Augustan. Photograph by Diana E. E. Kleiner, 2004.

18.2. Portrait of Livia from the Fayum, Copenhagen, Ny Carlsberg Glyptotek, after A.D. 4. Courtesy of the Ny Carlsberg Glyptotek, Copenhagen.

19.1. Funerary relief of Lucius Vibius, Vecilia Hila, and their son. Rome, Vatican Museums, 13 B.C.–A.D. 5. Scala/Art Resource, NY, ART 14671.

19.2. Temple of Roma and Augustus, Athens, Acropolis, after 27 B.C. Photograph by Diana E. E. Kleiner, 2004.

19.3. Funerary relief of man and wife, from the Via Statilia, Rome, 50–40 B.C. Rome, Museo del Palazzo dei Conservatori. Photo credit: Araldo de Luca/CORBIS DE004734.

19.4. Head of a woman, Rome, Palazzo Massimo alle Terme, 40s B.C. Photograph by Diana E. E. Kleiner, 2004.

19.5. Relief with funerary procession, from Amiternum, L'Aquila, Museo Nazionale, Augustan. Alinari/Art Resource, NY, ART 53785.

ACKNOWLEDGMENTS

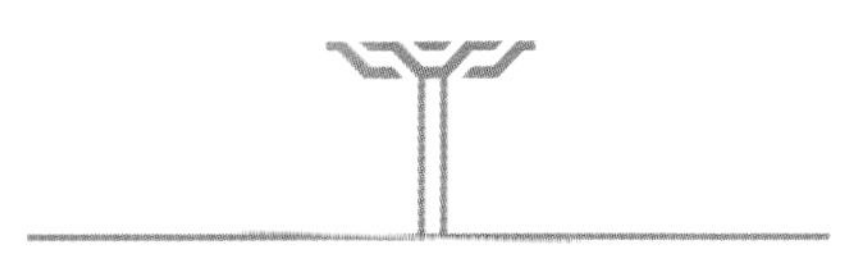

This book is dedicated to Alex the Great. Named for the peerless Macedonian leader, Alexander Mark Kleiner is, at nineteen, the same age as those who began their rise to greatness as teenagers. I hope that my belief that one inimitable person can change the world will always inspire my Alex to be his best self.

This book would not have been completed without the constant and unwavering support of Margaretta Fulton, General Editor for the Humanities at Harvard University Press. I am especially grateful to her for her flexibility in not only letting me go my own way but also urging me to do so.

Cleopatra and Rome was written while I was Yale's Deputy Provost for the Arts. It served as my academic oasis during eight years of administration, and I returned to it for intellectual sustenance over and over again. I am indebted to Yale University President Richard C. Levin and former Yale Provost Alison F. Richard for never trying to take the faculty member out of the administrator and for various kinds of support along the way. Provost Richard supplied special funds at one critical juncture so that I could hire Yale undergraduate Molly Worthen to help me do the annotated bibliography for this book. Molly was ever efficient and always cheerful, and I am grateful to her for the outstanding job she did.

Special gratitude is due my esteemed colleague and dear friend, Professor Karl Galinsky of the University of Texas at Austin. One of the staunchest supporters of this project, Karl heroically read the full manuscript of this book more than once, and his candid criticism and sound advice are greatly appreciated. Best of all, he is the kind of visionary who knows that there is no reward without risk, and his humorous way with e-mail has no peer.

I also appreciate more than words can say the contribution of Professor Erich Gruen of the University of California at Berkeley. Erich read this manuscript from beginning to end and helped me rethink and recast some of my contentions. Even though I don't think I have yet fully convinced him of my thesis, he has made this a better book.

Another cherished friend who made his mark on this study is Professor David D. Nolta of the Massachusetts College of Art. David, who took graduate courses with me when he was a doctoral student at Yale, came back into my life when I was writing this book and kindly read most of the manuscript, offering his insights not only as an art historian but also as a novelist.

I would also like to acknowledge the outside readers for Harvard University Press, who made further welcome and insightful contributions.

Mary Ellen Geer, Senior Editor at Harvard University Press, has been my constant editorial companion in the final stage of this project. Her vigilance caught last-minute infelicities, sparked me to rethink a critical section here and there, and was influential in helping me to temper (somewhat) my love affair with adjectives.

A book on visual culture, even among the fragmentary remains of antiquity, is nothing without illustrations. The Tarbell Fund of the Department of Classics at Yale University generously contributed toward the purchase of images, and I am grateful to Professor and Chair John Matthews for making that possible. Cleopatra's visual accomplishment and legacy could only be featured with the help of the curators and staff of a number of museum and photographic archives. It is a pleasure to acknowledge their support. I thank first and foremost Eileen Doyle, Jessica David, and Cherie Schnekenburger of Art Resource and Tiffany Miller of CORBIS for their help in locating most of the illustrations for this book. Additional photographs were provided by Edward Whitley for The Bridgeman Art Library, Lutgarde Vandeput for the Forschungsarchiv für Antike Plastik, Chris Lacey for The National Trust Photo Library, Ioulia

Tzonou-Herbst for the American School of Classical Studies and Corinth Excavations, Eileen Sullivan for the Metropolitan Museum of Art, William Metcalf, Susan Matheson, and Megan Doyon for the Yale University Art Gallery, Heidie Schjott for the Ny Carlsberg Glyptotek, Elena Stolyarik for the American Numismatic Society, Vladimir Matveyev and Anastasia Mikliaeva for the State Hermitage Museum, Ruth Janson for the Brooklyn Museum of Art, Alessandra Capodiferro for the Fototeca Unione, American Academy in Rome, and Janet Larkin and Kellie Leydon for the British Museum. Catherine de Grazia Vanderpool and Joan Mertens were also kind enough to answer questions on individual pieces.

INDEX